DEVILS & DEMONS

DEVILS & DEMONS

A Treasury of Fiendish Tales Old & New

Selected by
Marvin Kaye
with
Saralee Kaye

Doubleday & Company, Inc. Garden City, New York

Library of Congress Cataloging-in-Publication Data

Devils & demons.

Bibliography: p. 582
1. Horror tales. I. Kaye, Marvin. II. Kaye, Saralee.
PN6071.H727D4   1987   809.3'872   87-6772
ISBN 0-385-18563-4

ACKNOWLEDGMENTS

"The Queen of Sheba's Nightmare" copyright © 1954 by Bertrand Russell. Reprinted from *Nightmares of Eminent Persons* by Bertrand Russell by permission of the publisher, Allen & Unwin.

"The Brazen Locked Room" copyright © 1956 by Fantasy House, Inc. Reprinted by permission of the author.

"Tapestry" copyright © 1987 by C. H. Sherman. Printed by permission of the author.

"Seven Come Heaven?" copyright © 1987 by Diane Wnorowska. Printed by permission of the author.

"The Tenancy of Mr. Eex" copyright © 1987 by Paula Volsky. Printed by permission of the author.

"Just a Little Thing" copyright © 1987 by Joan Vander Putten. Printed by permission of the author.

"Rachaela" copyright © 1953 by Ziff-Davis Publications, Inc. Copyright renewed 1981 by Poul Anderson. Reprinted by permission of the author.

"Hell-Bent" copyright © 1951 by Mercury Press, Inc. Published by arrangement with Forrest J. Ackerman, 2495 Glendower Avenue, Hollywood, California 90027, Agent for the Estate of Ford McCormack.

"Damned Funny" copyright © 1975 by Eugene D. Goodwin (pseudonym for Marvin Kaye). All rights reserved. Reprinted from *Fiends and Creatures* (Popular Library, 1975).

"Me, Tree" copyright © 1987 by Morgan Llywelyn. Printed by permission of the author.

"Enoch" copyright © 1946 by *Weird Tales*. Reprinted by permission of Kirby McCauley, Ltd.

"Catmagic" copyright © 1987 by M. Lucie Chin. Printed by permission of the author.

"The Hound" by H. P. Lovecraft reprinted by permission of Arkham House Publishers, Inc., Sauk City, Wisconsin. All rights reserved.

"The Princess and Her Future" copyright © 1983 by Tanith Lee. Reprinted by permission of Donald A. Wollheim for Tanith Lee.

"The Celery Stalk in the Cellar" copyright © 1975 by Saralee Terry. Reprinted by permission of the author.

"The Vampire Cat of Nabeshima" from *Monsters Galore*, copyright © 1965 by Bernhardt J. Hurwood. Reprinted by permission of the author.

"Caliban's Revenge" copyright © 1978 by W. Paul Ganley. Reprinted from *Weirdbook 13* by permission of the author.

"The Trilling Princess" copyright © 1987 by Jessica Amanda Salmonson. Printed by permission of the author.

"The Graveyard Rats" copyright © 1936 by Henry Kuttner; renewed 1964 by Henry Kuttner. Reprinted by permission of Don Congdon Associates, Inc.

"Daddy" copyright © 1984 by Earl Godwin. Reprinted by permission of Parke Godwin for the estate of Earl Godwin.

"The Well-Meaning Mayor" by Leslie Charteris from *The Happy Highwayman*, copyright © 1935, 1936, 1937, 1938, 1939 by Leslie Charteris. Reprinted by permission of Doubleday & Company, Inc.

"A Madman," English adaptation copyright © 1987 by Marvin Kaye.

"High-Tech Insolence" copyright © 1986 by The New York Times Company. Reprinted by permission.

"Boogie Man" copyright © 1987 by Tappan King. Printed by permission of the author.

"The Maze and the Monster" copyright © 1963 by Health Knowledge, Inc. Reprinted by permission of the author.

"The Philosophy of Sebastian Trump or The Art of Outrage" copyright © 1975 by William E. Kotzwinkle and Robert Shiarella. Reprinted by permission of D. Robt. Shiarella.

"Don Juan's Final Night," English revision and adaptation copyright © 1987 by Marvin Kaye. All rights, including educational and charitable performances and/or readings, whether or not an admission fee is charged, are strictly reserved. Inquiries concerning performances of any sort must be addressed to The Open Book, 525 West End Avenue, #12E, New York City, New York 10024.

"A Friend in Need" copyright © 1925 by W. Somerset Maugham. Reprinted from *Cosmopolitans* by permission of Doubleday & Company, Inc.; reprinted from *The Collected Stories of W. Somerset Maugham* by permission of A. P. Watt, Ltd., on behalf of The Executors of W. Somerset Maugham and Wm. Heinemann Ltd.

"Armageddon" copyright © 1954 by Fredric Brown. Reprinted by permission of Roberta Pryor, Inc.

"Devil in the Drain" copyright © 1984 by Daniel Pinkwater. Reprinted by permission of the publisher, E. P. Dutton, a division of New American Library.

"I Am Returning" copyright © 1961 by Ray Russell. Reprinted from *Sardonicus and Other Stories* by permission of the author.

"The Shadow Watchers" copyright © 1975 by Dick Baldwin. Reprinted by permission of the author.

"The Demons" copyright © 1954 by Robert Sheckley. Reprinted from *Untouched by Human Hands* by permission of the author's agent, Kirby McCauley, Ltd.

"Lost Soul" copyright © 1987 by Jay Sheckley. Printed by permission of the author.

"The Last Demon" from *Short Friday*, copyright © 1961, 1962, 1963, 1964 by Isaac Bashevis Singer. Reprinted by permission of Farrar, Straus and Giroux, Inc.

"Influencing the Hell Out of Time and Teresa Golowitz" copyright © 1982 by Parke Godwin. Reprinted by permission of the author.

Thanks to C. H. Sherman for loaning me *The Encyclopedia of Witchcraft and Demonology* by R. H. Robbins and to Kit McDonald for lending me her scarce edition of Walter Scott's *Letters on Demonology and Witchcraft*. I am also grateful to the many friends who suggested various works for inclusion, including Donald Aamodt, Ellen Asher, Parke Godwin, Don Maass, Jessica Amanda Salmonson, Darrell Schweitzer, and whoever else I have forgotten that I hope won't be too irked at my devilishly poor memory.

Special thanks to my diligent, sunny-natured and endlessly patient editor, Mary Jatlow, to Pat LoBrutto for aid with the rubrics, and to Saralee Kaye for so ably administering the contracts and other paperwork involved in producing this mammoth volume.

Contents

HELLISH BUSINESS

INTRODUCTION

The Dialectic of the Devil

Lucifer, a ranking angel of light, challenged the status quo of Paradise and fell, figuratively and literally, into the pit of Hell where he was transformed into Satan, mankind's first and worst enemy. Disguised as the serpent in the Garden of Eden, the fiend tempted Adam and Eve to emulate his own nefarious example and fall from grace. That's what the Bible tells us, right?

Not exactly. Though both parts of the Bible refer to a satanic entity, the two do not equate directly with one another. In the Old Testament, the Hebrew word *satan* refers to an angel whose unpleasant duty, as in the Book of Job, is to bring misfortune that will test mankind's loyalty to the divine will. But *satanas* in the New Testament is a Greek word that introduces the notion of a heavenly, rather than earthly, opponent. Thus Satan—as he is popularly portrayed in Western fiction and drama—is a relatively youthful chap; the Jews did not link the angel's nature to the dire tasks he was required to perform and even the adversary of the New Testament was not officially acknowledged by the Roman Catholic Church until the Council of Toledo in A.D. 447.

By this we may observe that the Devil is a protean myth reshaped by each new age, nation and culture. In the Middle Ages, for instance, the Catholic church actively attempted to discourage the practice of Wicca, an ancient faith devoted to the revering of nature. The clergy rechristened its simple adherents *witches* and called their rites and symbols the appurtenances of diabolic worship. Wiccan shamans wore stags' antlers in anthropomorphic ceremonies that honored the beast by mimesis. In this fashion, the Devil acquired his horns and tail.

It is important to distinguish between Wiccan "circle worship" and the witches' sabbaths that sprang up during this same period. The medieval priest who preached a harsh code of behavior stirred the spirit of rebellion in persecuted Wiccans and renegade Christians alike. That diabolic ceremony conjured up by orthodoxy began to be practiced in earnest. Its form—a ring of congregants dancing about a horned figure in a forest clearing—came from Wicca, but its content was a dark parody of the Catholic mass. In this way, Satan became something of a folk hero, an outlaw who promised those pleasures forbidden by the church in return for (literally) undying allegiance.

As civilization and the human spirit both grew more complex, so, too, did the Devil as a literary institution. The hellish adversaries of Doctors Faust and Faustus are as far apart in character as the cultures and centuries that brought both into existence. As a result, the modern novelist, short story writer or dramatist has a rich myth to mine, from fundamentalist bogeyman devils like Satan to hubristic god-challengers like Lucifer.

You'll find examples of each in the selections of this book.

Devils and Demons?

Because the two titular nouns are so often used synonymously, in one sense the title of this anthology is as redundant as, say, *Dogs and Canines* or *Politicians and Liars*. But just as there are two "satans" in the Bible, there is a fine derivational distinction made between *devil* and *demon* in Webster's Dictionary of the English Language Unabridged (Encyclopedic edition). The former term stems from the Greek *diabolus,* denoting a slanderer and by extension, a heavenly foe and earthly tempter. Demon also has a Grecian root: *daemon*—a deity or spirit who serves as one's counseling spirit, whether for good or ill. The dictionary extends the meaning of this word to include a person or thing regarded as evil or cruel.

Taking these two broad definitions into account, I have included within the parameters of this collection—if one may excuse the term— a catholicity of fiends. Here you will meet Lucifer in his various guises as well as several of his diabolical crew, but you will encounter other hellish entities as well: queens and strumpets, vampires and lost souls, obsessed gamblers and possessed rodents, sentient vegetables, murderers, philanderers, rotters, landlords and other human devils. The literature in which this dubious company appears is representative of an unusually wide range of style, theme and mood: terror, comedy, pathos, melodrama, nightmare, nonsense, irony, tragedy, sheer horror and (perhaps most marvelous of all) compassion.

As in my earlier collections, *Ghosts* and *Masterpieces of Terror and the Supernatural,* I have limited each author to a single selection and have generally favored lesser-known works over overly familiar (albeit excellent) warhorses like Max Beerbohm's "Enoch Soames" or Stephen Vincent Benet's "The Devil and Daniel Webster." Though each selection is prefaced by a rubric, more extensive comments, when called for, have been reserved until Appendix I. Some more information on Lucifer and his wicked henchmen will be found in Appendix II and in the third appendix I have included suggestions for further hellish reading (and listening and film-viewing).

And now, if you are looking for one Hell of a time, it's time to don asbestos gloves, turn the pages and shake hands with the Devil.

—Marvin Kaye

Manhattan, 1986

DEVILS & DEMONS

Let's Make a Deal

Lucifer is a popular chap. Fabulists have been composing gossip about him for a long time and one mustn't forget that in the Middle Ages, the most popular part of the Miracle Plays was that moment in the performance when Hellmouth gaped and all the acrobats disguised as demons came tumbling out.

Probably the most common scenario in Luciferian literature is the so-called deal-with-the-Devil plot. Old Nick is well-known for entering into relatively straightforward contracts, such as the one he signed with Christopher Marlowe's Doctor Faustus. The terms are standard: Hell provides certain earthly benefits for a period of time, after which the Devil collects . . . and collects and collects his due. But Mr. Scratch, as he is called in New England, is also a gambler. (By his rules, he is entitled to cheat, and he does). In the tales that follow, executives of Hell write some unusual sporting clauses into their contracts, such as Ford McCormack's sin-as-you-go plan or Isaac Asimov's locked room poser, and once Satan is even willing to have a go at the old three-task game, in which a daring mortal risks his soul on the chance that he can propose at least one out of a possible trio of chores that the Devil cannot accomplish.

You may pick up a tantalizing tip or two in this section, but before you roll up your living room rug and chalk that pentagram on your floor, you'd better weigh the odds carefully. In the following fifteen selections, the Devil outwits his mortal opponents twice as often as he loses.

Philosopher, mathematician, scientist, essayist, iconoclast, 1950 winner of the Nobel Prize for Literature, BERTRAND RUSSELL (1872–1970) wrote scores of provocative and trenchantly witty works of nonfiction, but when he was eighty-one Lord Russell tried his accomplished hand at fiction, producing 2.5 books of fantasy and science fiction novellas and short stories: Satan in the Suburbs, Fact and Fiction (0.5) and Nightmares of Eminent Persons, from which the following sly tale is taken.

The Queen of Sheba's Nightmare

BY BERTRAND RUSSELL

PUT NOT THY TRUST IN PRINCES

The Queen of Sheba, returning from her visit to King Solomon, was riding through the desert on a white ass with her Grand Vizier beside her on an ass of more ordinary color. As they rode, she discoursed reminiscently about the wealth and wisdom of Solomon.

"I had always thought," she said, "that I do pretty well in the way of royal splendor, and I had hoped beforehand that I should be able to hold my own, but when I had seen his possessions I had no spirit left in me. But the treasures of his palace are as nothing to the treasures of his mind. Ah, my dear Vizier, what wisdom, what knowledge of life, what sagacity his conversation displays! If you had as much political sagacity in your whole body as that king has in his little finger, we should have none of these troubles in my kingdom. But it is not only in wealth and wisdom that he is matchless. He is also (though perhaps I am the only one privileged to know this) a supreme poet. He gave me as we parted a jeweled volume in his own inimitable handwriting, telling in language of exquisite beauty the joy that he had experienced in my company. There are passages celebrating some of my more intimate charms which I should blush to show you; but there are portions of this book which I may perhaps read to you to beguile the evenings of our journey through the desert. In this exquisite volume not only are his own words such as any lady would love to hear from amorous lips, but by a quintessence of imaginative sympathy he has attributed to me poetic words which I should be glad to have uttered. Never again, I am convinced, shall I find such perfect union, such entire harmony, and such penetration into the recesses of the soul. My public duties, alas, compel me to return to my kingdom, but I shall carry with me to my dying day the knowledge that there is on earth one man worthy of my love."

"Your Majesty," replied the Vizier, "it is not for me to instill doubts into the royal breast, but to all those who serve you, it is incredible that among men your equal should exist."

At this moment, emerging out of the sunset, a weary figure appeared on foot.

"Who may this be?" said the Queen.

"Some beggar, your Majesty," said the Grand Vizier. "I strongly advise you to steer clear of him."

But a certain dignity in the aspect of the approaching stranger seemed to her indicative of something more than a beggar. And in spite of the Grand Vizier's protests she turned her ass toward him. "And who may you be?" she said.

His answer dispelled at once the Grand Vizier's suspicions, for he spoke in the most polished idiom of the court of Sheba: "Your Majesty," he said, "my name is Beelzebub, but it is probably unknown to you, as I seldom travel far from the land of Canaan. Who you are, I know. And not only who you are, but whence you come, and what fancies inspire your sunset meditations. You have come, I know, from visiting that wise king who, though my humble guise might seem to belie my words, has been for many years my firm friend. I am convinced that he has told you concerning himself all that he wishes you to know. But if—though the hypothesis seems rash—there is anything that you wish to know concerning him beyond what he has seen fit to tell, you have but to ask me, for he has no secrets from me."

"You surprise me," said the Queen, "but I see that our conversation will be too long to be conducted conveniently while you walk and I ride. My Grand Vizier shall dismount and give his ass to you."

With an ill grace the Grand Vizier complied.

"I suppose," the Queen said, "that your conversations with Solomon were mainly concerned with statecraft and matters of deep wisdom. I, as a queen not unrenowned for wisdom, also conversed with him on these topics; but some of our conversation—so at least I flatter myself—revealed a side of him less intimately known, I should imagine, to you than to me. And some of the best of this he put into a book which he gave to me as we parted. This book contains many beauties, for example, a lovely description of the spring."

"Ah," said Beelzebub, "and does he in this description speak of the voice of the turtle?"

"Why, yes," said the Queen. "But how did you guess?"

"Oh, well," Beelzebub replied, "he was proud of having noticed the turtle talking in the spring and liked to bring it in when he could."

"Some of his compliments," the Queen resumed, "particularly pleased me. I had practiced Hebrew during the journey to Jerusalem, but was not sure whether I had mastered it adequately. I was therefore delighted when he said, 'Thy speech is comely.' "

"Very nice of him," said Beelzebub. "And did he at the same time remark that your Majesty's temples are like a piece of pomegranate?"

"Well, really," said the Queen, "this is getting uncanny! He did say so, and I thought it rather an odd remark. But how on earth did you guess?"

"Well," Beelzebub replied, "you know all great men have kinks, and one of his is a peculiar interest in pomegranates."

"It is true," said the Queen, "that some of his comparisons are a little odd. He said, for instance, that my eyes were like the fish pools of Heshbon."

"I have known him," said Beelzebub, "to make even stranger comparisons. Did he ever compare your Majesty's nose to the Tower of Lebanon?"

"Good gracious," said the Queen, "this is too much! He did make that comparison. But you are persuading me that you must have some more intimate source of knowledge than I had suspected."

"Your Majesty," Beelzebub replied, "I fear that what I have to say may cause you some pain. The fact is that some of his wives were friends of mine, and through them I got to know him well."

"Yes, but how about this love poem?"

"Well, you see, when he was young, while his father was still alive, he had to take more trouble. In those days he loved a farmer's virtuous daughter, and only overcame her scruples by his poetic gifts. Afterwards, he thought it a pity the gifts should be wasted, and he gave a copy to each of his ladies in turn. You see, he was essentially a collector, as you must have noticed when you went over his house. By long practice, he made each in turn think herself supreme in his affections; and you, dear lady, are his last and most signal triumph."

"Oh, the wretch!" she said. "Never again will I be deceived by the perfidy of man. Never again will I let flattery blind me. To think that I, who throughout my dominions am accounted the wisest of women, should have permitted myself to be so misled!"

"Nay, dear lady," said Beelzebub, "be not so cast down, for Solomon is not only the wisest man in his dominions, but the wisest of all men, and will be known as such through countless ages. To have been deceived by him is scarcely matter for shame."

"Perhaps you are right," she said, "but it will take time to heal the wound to my pride."

"Ah, sweet Queen," Beelzebub replied, "how happy could I be if I could hasten the healing work of Time! Far be it from me to imitate the wiles of that perfidious monarch. From me shall flow only simple words dictated by the spontaneous sentiments of the heart. To you, the Peerless, the Incomparable, the Matchless Jewel of the South, I would give—if you permit it—whatever balm a true appreciation of your worth can offer."

"Your words are soothing," she replied, "but can you match his splendors? Have you a palace that can compare with his? Have you such store of precious stones? Such robes, purveying the aroma of myrrh and frankincense? And, more important than any of these, have you a wisdom equal to his?"

"Lovely Sheba," he replied, "I can satisfy you on every point. I have a palace far grander than Solomon's. I have a far greater store of precious stones. My robes of state are as numerous as the stars in the sky. And as for wisdom, his is not a match for mine. Solomon is surprised that, although the rivers flow into the sea, yet the sea is not full. I know why this is, and will explain it to your Majesty on some long winter evening. To come to a more serious lapse, it was after he had seen you that he said 'there is no new thing under the sun.' Can you doubt that in his thoughts he was comparing you unfavorably with the farmer's daughter of his youth? And can any man be accounted wise who, having beheld you, does not at once perceive that here is a new wonder of beauty and majesty? No! In a competition of wisdom I have nothing to fear from him."

With a smile, half of resignation concerning the past, and half of dawning hope for a happier future, she turned her eyes upon Beelzebub and said: "Your words are beguiling. I made a long journey from my kingdom to Solomon's, and I thought I had seen what is most noteworthy on this earth. But, if you speak truth, your kingdom, your palace, and your wisdom, all surpass Solomon's. May I extend my journey by a visit to your dominion?"

He returned her smile with one in which the appearance of love barely concealed the reality of triumph. "I can imagine no greater delight," he said, "than that you should allow me this opportunity to place my poor riches at your feet. Let us go while yet the night is young. But the way is dark and difficult, and infested by fierce robbers. If you are to be safe, you must trust yourself completely to my guidance."

"I will," she said. "You have given me new hope."

At this moment they arrived at a measureless cavern in the mountainside. Holding aloft a flaming torch, Beelzebub led the way through long tunnels and tortuous passages. At last they emerged into a vast hall lit by innumerable lamps. The walls and roof glittered with precious stones whose scintillating facets flashed back the light of the lamps. In solemn state, three hundred silver thrones were ranged round the walls.

"This is indeed magnificent," said the Queen.

"Oh," said Beelzebub, "this is only my second-rate hall of audience. You shall now see the Presence Chamber."

Opening a hitherto invisible door, he led her into another hall, more than twice as large as the first, more than twice as brilliantly lit, and more than twice as richly jeweled. Round three walls of this hall were seven hundred golden thrones. On the fourth wall were two thrones, composed entirely of precious stones, diamonds, sapphires, rubies, huge pearls, bound together by some strange art which the Queen could not fathom.

"This," he said, "is my great hall, and of the two jeweled thrones, one is mine and the other shall be yours."

"But who," she said, "is to occupy the seven hundred golden thrones?"

"Ah well," he said, "you will know that in due course."

As he spoke, a queenly figure, only slightly less splendid than the Queen of Sheba, glided in and occupied the first of the golden thrones. With something of a shock, the Queen of Sheba recognized Solomon's chief consort.

"I had not expected to meet her here," she said with a slight tremor.

"Ah well," said Beelzebub, "you see I have magic powers. And while I have been wooing you, I have been telling this good lady also that Solomon is not all he seems. She listened to my words as you have listened, and she has come."

Scarcely had he finished speaking when another lady, whom also the Queen of Sheba recognized from her visit to Solomon's harem, entered and occupied the second golden throne. Then came a third, a fourth, a fifth, until it seemed as if the procession would never end. At last all the seven hundred golden thrones were occupied.

"You may be wondering," Beelzebub remarked in silken tones, "about the three hundred silver thrones. All these are by now occupied by Solomon's three hundred concubines. All the thousand in this hall and the other have heard from me words not unlike those that you have heard, all have been convinced by me, and all are here."

"Perfidious monster!" exclaimed the Queen. "How could I have had the simplicity to let myself be deceived a second time! Henceforth I will reign alone, and no male shall ever again be given a chance to deceive me. Good-by, foul fiend! If you ever venture into my dominions, you shall suffer the fate that your villainy has deserved."

"No, good lady," Beelzebub replied, "I am afraid you do not quite realize the position. I showed you the way in, but only I can find the way out. This is the abode of the dead, and you are here for all eternity —but not for all eternity on the diamond throne beside mine. That you will occupy only until you are superseded by an even more divine queen, the last Queen of Egypt."

These words produced in her such a tumult of rage and despair that she awoke.

"I fear," said the Grand Vizier, "that your Majesty has had troubled dreams."

The Brazen Locked Room

BY ISAAC ASIMOV

"Come, come," said Shapur quite politely, considering that he was a demon. "You are wasting my time. And your own, too, I might add, since you have only half an hour left." And his tail twitched.

"It's *not* dematerialization?" asked Isidore Wellby, thoughtfully.

"I have already said it is not," said Shapur.

For the hundredth time, Wellby looked at the unbroken bronze that surrounded him on all sides. The demon had taken unholy pleasure (what other kind indeed?) in pointing out that the floor, ceiling and four walls were featureless, two-foot-thick slabs of bronze, welded seamlessly together.

It was the ultimate locked room and Wellby had but another half hour to get out, while the demon watched with an expression of gathering anticipation.

It had been ten years previously (to the day, naturally) that Isidore Wellby had signed up.

"We pay you in advance," said Shapur, persuasively. "Ten years of anything you want, within reason, and then you're a demon. You're one of us, with a new name of demonic potency, and many privileges beside. You'll hardly know you're damned. And if you don't sign, you may end up in the fire, anyway, just in the ordinary course of things. You never know. . . . Here, look at me. I'm not doing too badly. I signed up, had my ten years, and here I am. Not bad."

"Why so anxious for me to sign then, if I might be damned anyway?" asked Wellby.

"It's not so easy to recruit hell's cadre," said the demon, with a frank shrug that made the faint odor of sulfur dioxide in the air a trifle stronger. "Everyone wishes to gamble on ending in heaven. It's a poor gamble, but there it is. I think *you're* too sensible for that. But meanwhile we have more damned souls than we know what to do with and a growing shortage at the administrative end."

Wellby, having just left the army and finding himself with nothing much to show for it but a limp and a farewell letter from a girl he somehow still loved, pricked his finger, and signed.

Of course, he read the small print first. A certain quantity of demonic powers would be deposited to his account upon signature in blood. He would not know in detail how one manipulated those powers, or even the nature of all of them, but he would nevertheless find his wishes fulfilled in such a way that they would seem to have come about through perfectly normal mechanisms.

Naturally, no wish might be fulfilled which would interfere with the higher aims and purposes of human history. Wellby had raised his eyebrows at that.

Shapur coughed. "A precaution imposed upon us by—uh—Above. You are reasonable. The limitation won't interfere with you."

Wellby said, "There seems to be a catch clause, too."

"A kind of one, yes. After all, we have to check your aptitude for the position. It states, as you see, that you will be required to perform a task for us at the conclusion of your ten years, one your demonic powers will make it quite possible for you to do. We can't tell you the nature of the task now, but you will have ten years to study the nature of your powers. Look upon the whole thing as an entrance qualification."

"And if I don't pass the test, what then?"

"In that case," said the demon, "you will be only an ordinary damned soul after all." And because he was a demon, his eyes glowed smokily at the thought and his clawed fingers twitched as though he felt them already deep in the other's vitals. But he added suavely, "Come, now, the test will be a simple one. We would rather have you as cadre than as just another chore on our hands."

Wellby, with sad thoughts of his unattainable loved one, cared little enough at that moment for what would happen after ten years and he signed.

Yet the ten years passed quickly enough. Isidore Wellby was always reasonable, as the demon had predicted, and things worked well.

Wellby accepted a position and because he was always at the right spot
at the right time and always said the right thing to the right man, he
was quickly promoted to a position of great authority.

Investments he made invariably paid off and, what was more grati-
fying still, his girl came back to him most sincerely repentant and
most satisfactorily adoring.

His marriage was a happy one and was blessed with four children,
two boys and two girls, all bright and reasonably well-behaved. At the
end of ten years, he was at the height of his authority, reputation and
wealth, while his wife, if anything, had grown more beautiful as she
had matured.

And ten years (to the day, naturally) after the making of the compact, he woke to find himself, not in his bedroom, but in a horrible
bronze chamber of the most appalling solidity, with no company other
than an eager demon.

"You have only to get out, and you will be one of us," said Shapur.
"It can be done fairly and logically by using your demonic powers,
provided you know exactly what it is you're doing. You should, by
now."

"My wife and children will be very disturbed at my disappearance,"
said Wellby, with the beginning of regrets.

"They will find your dead body," said the demon, consolingly. "You
will seem to have died of a heart attack and you will have a beautiful
funeral. The minister will consign you to heaven and we will not
disillusion him or those who listen to him. Now come, Wellby, you
have till noon."

Wellby, having unconsciously steeled himself for this moment for
ten years, was less panic-stricken than he might have been. He looked
about speculatively. "Is this room perfectly enclosed? No trick openings?"

"No openings anywhere in the walls, floor or ceiling," said the
demon, with a professional delight in his handiwork. "Or at the
boundaries of any of those surfaces, for that matter. Are you giving
up?"

"No, no. Just give me time."

Wellby thought very hard. There seemed no sign of closeness in the
room. There was even a feeling of moving air. The air might be entering the room by dematerializing across the walls. Perhaps the demon

had entered by dematerialization and perhaps Wellby himself might leave in that manner. He asked.

The demon grinned. "Dematerialization is not one of your powers. Nor did I myself use it in entering."

"You're sure now?"

"The room is my own creation," said the demon, smugly, "and especially constructed for you."

"And you entered from outside?"

"I did."

"With reasonable demonic powers which I possess, too?"

"Exactly. Come, let us be precise. You cannot move through matter but you can move in any dimension by a mere effort of will. You can move up, down, right, left, obliquely and so on, but you cannot move through matter in any way."

Wellby kept on thinking, and Shapur kept on pointing out the utter immovable solidity of the brazen walls, floor and ceiling, their unbroken ultimacy.

It seemed obvious to Wellby that Shapur, however much he might believe in the necessity for recruiting cadre, was barely restraining his demonic delight at possibly having an ordinary damned soul to amuse himself with.

"At least," said Wellby, with a sorrowful attempt at philosophy, "I'll have ten happy years to look back on. Surely that's a consolation, even for a damned soul in hell."

"Not at all," said the demon. "Hell would not be hell, if you were allowed consolations. Everything anyone gains on Earth by pacts with the devil, as in your case (or my own, for that matter), is exactly what one might have gained without such a pact if one had worked industriously and in full trust in—uh—Above. That is what makes all such bargains so truly demonic." And the demon laughed with a kind of cheerful howl.

Wellby said, indignantly. "You mean my wife would have returned to me even if I had never signed your contract?"

"She might have," said Shapur. "Whatever happens is the will of— uh—Above, you know. We ourselves can do nothing to alter that."

The chagrin of that moment must have sharpened Wellby's wits for it was then that he vanished, leaving the room empty, except for a surprised demon. And surprise turned to absolute fury, when the demon looked at the contract with Wellby which he had, until that moment, been holding in his hand for final action, one way or the other.

It was ten years (to the day, naturally) after Isidore Wellby had signed his pact with Shapur that the demon entered Wellby's office and said, most angrily, "Look here—"

Wellby looked up from his work, astonished. "Who are you?"

"You know very well who I am," said Shapur.

"Not at all," said Wellby.

The demon looked sharply at the man. "I see you are telling the truth, but I can't make out the details." He promptly flooded Wellby's mind with the events of the last ten years.

Wellby said, "Oh, yes. I can explain, of course, but are you sure we will not be interrupted?"

"We won't be," said the demon, grimly.

"I sat in that closed brazen room," said Wellby, "and—"

"Never mind that," said the demon, hastily. "I want to know—"

"Please. Let me tell this my way."

The demon clamped his jaws and fairly exuded sulfur dioxide till Wellby coughed and looked pained.

Wellby said, "If you'll move off a bit. Thank you. —Now I sat in that closed brazen room and remembered how you kept stressing the absolute unbrokenness of the four walls, the floor and the ceiling. I wondered: why did you specify? What else was there beside walls, floor and ceiling? You had defined a completely enclosed three-dimensional space.

"And that was it: *three*-dimensional. The room was not closed in the fourth dimension. It did not exist indefinitely in the past. You said you had created it for me. So if one traveled into the past one would find oneself at a point in time, eventually, when the room did not exist and then one would be out of the room.

"What's more, you *had* said I could move in any dimension, and time may certainly be viewed as a dimension. In any case, as soon as I decided to move toward the past, I found myself living backward at a tremendous rate and suddenly there was no bronze around me anywhere."

Shapur cried, in anguish, "I can guess all that. You couldn't have escaped any other way. It's this contract of yours that I'm concerned about. If you're not an ordinary damned soul, very well, it's part of the game. But you must be at least one of *us,* one of the cadre; it's what you were paid for, and if I don't deliver you down below, I will be in enormous trouble."

Wellby shrugged his shoulders. "I'm sorry for you, of course, but I can't help you. As an inexperienced time-traveler, I must have overaccelerated; for when I managed to brake my backward progress, I found myself just at the point in time at which I was making the bargain with you. There you were again; there I was, you were pushing the contract toward me, together with a stylus with which I might prick my finger. To be sure, as I had moved back in time, my memory of what was becoming the future faded out, but not, apparently, quite entirely. As you pushed the contract at me, I felt uneasy. I didn't quite remember the future, but I felt uneasy. So I didn't sign. I turned you down flat."

Shapur ground his teeth. "I might have known. If probability patterns affected demons, I would have shifted with you into this new *if-*world. As it is, all I can say is that you have lost the ten happy years we paid you with. That is one consolation. And we'll get you in the end. That is another."

"Well, now," said Wellby, "are there consolations in hell? Through the ten years I have now lived, I knew nothing of what I might have obtained. But now that you've put the memory of the ten-years-that-might-have-been into my mind, I recall that, in the bronze room, you told me that demonic agreements could give nothing that could not be obtained by industry and trust in Above. I have been industrious and I have trusted."

Wellby's eyes fell upon the photograph of his beautiful wife and four beautiful children, then traveled about the tasteful luxuriance of his office. "And I may even escape hell altogether. . . ."

And the demon, with a horrible shriek, vanished forever.

"Sir Dominick's Bargain" is the sort of story one hopes and expects to encounter in any respectable jaunt to the United Kingdom. Every castle and manor house ought to have at least one bloody legend, and the one that follows carries the ring of truth, thanks to the skilled ghostly storytelling craft of JOSEPH SHERI-DAN LEFANU *(1814–1873), Dublin-born author of such shivery classics as "Mr. Justice Harbottle" and "Carmilla." LeFanu's literary heritage is impressive; he was the grandnephew of the great eighteenth-century comedic dramatist Richard Brinsley Sheridan.*

Sir Dominick's Bargain
BY SHERIDAN LEFANU

In the early autumn of the year 1838, business called me to the south of Ireland. The weather was delightful, the scenery and people were new to me, and sending my luggage on by the mail-coach route in charge of a servant, I hired a serviceable nag at a posting-house, and, full of the curiosity of an explorer, I commenced a leisurely journey of five-and-twenty miles on horseback, by sequestered cross-roads, to my place of destination. By bog and hill, by plain and ruined castle, and many a winding stream, my picturesque road led me.

I had started late, and having made little more than half my journey, I was thinking of making a short halt at the next convenient place, and letting my horse have a rest and a feed, and making some provision also for the comforts of his rider.

It was about four o'clock when the road, ascending a gradual steep, found a passage through a rocky gorge between the abrupt termination of a range of mountain to my left and a rocky hill, that rose dark and sudden at my right. Below me lay a little thatched village, under a long line of gigantic beech-trees, through the boughs of which the lowly chimneys sent up their thin turf-smoke. To my left, stretched away for miles, ascending the mountain range I have mentioned, a wild park, through whose sward and ferns the rock broke, time-worn and lichen-stained. This park was studded with straggling wood, which thickened to something like a forest, behind and beyond the little village I was approaching, clothing the irregular ascent of the hillsides with beautiful, and in some places discoloured, foliage.

As you descend, the road winds slightly, with the grey parkwall, built of loose stone, and mantled here and there with ivy, at its left, and crosses a shallow ford; and as I approached the village, through breaks in the woodlands, I caught glimpses of the long front of an old ruined house, placed among the trees, about half-way up the picturesque mountainside.

The solitude and melancholy of this ruin piqued my curiosity, and when I had reached the rude thatched public-house, with the sign of St. Columbkill, with robes, mitre, and crozier displayed over its lintel, having seen to my horse and made a good meal myself on a rasher and eggs, I began to think again of the wooded park and the ruinous house, and resolved on a ramble of half an hour among its sylvan solitudes.

The name of the place, I found, was Dunoran; and beside the gate a stile admitted to the grounds, through which, with a pensive enjoyment, I began to saunter towards the dilapidated mansion.

A long grass-grown road, with many turns and windings, led up to the old house, under the shadow of the wood.

The road, as it approached the house, skirted the edge of a precipitous glen, clothed with hazel, dwarf-oak, and thorn, and the silent house stood with its wide-open hall-door facing this dark ravine, the further edge of which was crowned with towering forest; and great trees stood about the house and its deserted court-yard and stables.

I walked in and looked about me, through passages overgrown with nettles and weeds; from room to room with ceilings rotted, and here and there a great beam dark and worn, with tendrils of ivy trailing over it. The tall walls with rotten plaster were stained and mouldy, and in some rooms the remains of decayed wainscoting crazily swung to and fro. The almost sashless windows were darkened also with ivy, and about the tall chimneys the jackdaws were wheeling, while from the huge trees that overhung the glen in sombre masses at the other side, the rooks kept up a ceaseless cawing.

As I walked through these melancholy passages—peeping only into some of the rooms, for the flooring was quite gone in the middle, and bowed down toward the centre, and the house was very nearly unroofed, a state of things which made the exploration a little critical—I began to wonder why so grand a house, in the midst of scenery so picturesque, had been permitted to go to decay; I dreamed of the hospitalities of which it had long ago been the rallying place, and I thought what a scene of Redgauntlet revelries it might disclose at midnight.

The great staircase was of oak, which had stood the weather wonderfully, and I sat down upon its steps, musing vaguely on the transitoriness of all things under the sun.

Except for the hoarse and distant clamour of the rooks, hardly audible where I sat, no sound broke the profound stillness of the spot. Such a sense of solitude I have seldom experienced before. The air was stirless, there was not even the rustle of a withered leaf along the passage. It was oppressive. The tall trees that stood close about the building darkened it, and added something of awe to the melancholy of the scene.

In this mood I heard, with an unpleasant surprise, close to me, a voice that was drawling, and, I fancied, sneering, repeat the words: "Food for worms, dead and rotten; God over all."

There was a small window in the wall, here very thick, which had been built up, and in the dark recess of this, deep in the shadow, I now saw a sharp-featured man, sitting with his feet dangling. His keen eyes were fixed on me, and he was smiling cynically, and before I had well recovered my surprise, he repeated the distich:

" 'If death was a thing that money could buy,
    The rich they would live, and the poor they would die.'

"It was a grand house in its day, sir," he continued, "Dunoran House, and the Sarsfields. Sir Dominick Sarsfield was the last of the old stock. He lost his life not six foot away from where you are sitting."

As he thus spoke he let himself down, with a little jump, on to the ground.

He was a dark-faced, sharp-featured, little hunchback, and had a walking-stick in his hand, with the end of which he pointed to a rusty stain in the plaster of the wall.

"Do you mind that mark sir?" he asked.

"Yes," I said, standing up, and looking at it, with a curious anticipation of something worth hearing.

"That's about seven or eight feet from the ground, sir, and you'll not guess what it is."

"I dare say not," said I, "unless it is a stain from the weather."

" 'Tis nothing so lucky, sir," he answered, with the same cynical smile and a wag of his head, still pointing at the mark with his stick. "That's a splash of brains and blood. It's there this hundred years; and it will never leave it while the wall stands."

"He was murdered, then?"

"Worse than that, sir," he answered.

"He killed himself, perhaps?"

"Worse than that, itself, this cross between us and harm! I'm oulder than I look, sir; you wouldn't guess my years."

He became silent, and looked at me, evidently inviting a guess.

"Well, I should guess you to be about five-and-fifty."

He laughed and took a pinch of snuff, and said:

"I'm that, your honour, and something to the back of it. I was seventy last Candlemas. You would not 'a' thought that, to look at me."

"Upon my word I should not; I can hardly believe it even now. Still, you don't remember Sir Dominick Sarsfield's death?" I said, glancing up at the ominous stain on the wall.

"No, sir, that was a long while before I was born. But my grandfather was butler here long ago, and many a time I heard tell how Sir Dominick came by his death. There was no masther in the great house ever sinst that happened. But there was two sarvants in care of it, and my aunt was one o' them; and she kep' me here wid her till I was nine year old, and she was lavin' the place to go to Dublin; and from that time it was let to go down. The wind sthript the roof, and the rain rotted the timber, and little by little, in sixty years' time, it kem to what you see. But I have a likin' for it still, for the sake of ould times; and I never come this way but I take a look in. I don't think it's many more times I'll be turnin' to see the ould place, for I'll be undher the sod myself before long."

"You'll outlive younger people," I said.

And, quitting that trite subject, I ran on:

"I don't wonder that you like this old place; it is a beautiful spot, such noble trees."

"I wish ye seen the glin when the nuts is ripe; they're the sweetest nuts in all Ireland, I think," he rejoined, with a practical sense of the picturesque. "You'd fill your pockets while you'd be lookin' about you."

"These are very fine old woods," I remarked. "I have not seen any in Ireland I thought so beautiful."

"Eiah! your honour, the woods about here is nothing to what they wor. All the mountains along here was wood when my father was a gossoon, and Murroa Wood was the grandest of them all. All oak mostly, and all cut down as bare as the road. Not one left here that's fit to compare with them. Which way did your honour come hither— from Limerick?"

"No. Killaloe."

"Well, then, you passed the ground where Murroa Wood was in former times. You kem undher Lisnavourra, the steep knob of a hill about a mile above the village here. 'Twas near that Murroa Wood was, and 'twas there Sir Dominick Sarsfield first met the devil, the Lord between us and harm, and a bad meeting it was for him and his."

I had become interested in the adventure which had occurred in the very scenery which had so greatly attracted me, and my new acquaintance, the little hunchback, was easily entreated to tell me the story, and spoke thus, so soon as we had each returned his seat:

It was a fine estate when Sir Dominick came into it; and grand doings there was entirely, feasting and fiddling, free quarters for all the pipers in the counthry round, and a welcome for every one that liked to come. There was wine, by the hogshead, for the quality; and potteen enough to set a town a-fire, and beer and cidher enough to float a navy, for the boys and girls, and the likes of me. It was kep' up the best part of a month, till the weather broke, and the rain spoilt the sod for the moneen jigs, and the fair of Allybally Killudeen comin' on they wor obliged to give over their diversion, and attind to the pigs.

But Sir Dominick was only beginnin' when they wor lavin' off. There was no way of gettin' rid of his money and estates he did not try —what with drinkin', dicin', racin', cards, and all soarts, it was not many years before the estates wor in debt, and Sir Dominick a distressed man. He showed a bold front to the world as long as he could; and then he sould off his dogs, and most of his horses, and gev out he was going to thravel in France, and the like; and so off with him for awhile; and no one in these parts heard tale or tidings of him for two or three years. Till at last quite unexpected, one night there comes a rapping at the big kitchen window. It was past ten o'clock, and old Connor Hanlon, the butler, my grandfather, was sittin' by the fire alone, warming his shins over it. There was keen east wind blowing along the mountains that night, and whistling cowld enough through the tops of the trees, and soundin' lonesome through the long chimneys.

(And the story-teller glanced up at the nearest stack visible from his seat.)

So he wasn't quite sure of the knockin' at the window, and up he gets, and sees his master's face.

My grandfather was glad to see him safe, for it was a long time since there was any news of him; but he was sorry, too, for it was a changed place and only himself and old Juggy Broadrick in charge of the house, and a man in the stables, and it was a poor thing to see him comin' back to his own like that.

He shook Con by the hand, and says he:

"I came here to say a word to you. I left my horse with Dick in the stable; I may want him again before morning, or I may never want him."

And with that he turns into the big kitchen, and draws a stool, and sits down to take an air of the fire.

"Sit down, Connor, opposite me, and listen to what I tell you, and don't be afeard to say what you think."

He spoke all the time lookin' into the fire, with his hands stretched over it, and a tired man he looked.

"An' why should I be afeard, Masther Dominick?" says my grandfather. "Yourself was a good masther to me, and so was your father, rest his sould, before you, and I'll say the truth, and dar' the devil, and more than that, for any Sarsfield of Dunoran, much less yourself, and a good right I'd have."

"It's all over with me, Con," says Sir Dominick.

"Heaven forbid!" says my grandfather.

" 'Tis past praying for," says Sir Dominick. "The last guinea's gone; the ould place will follow it. It must be sold, and I'm come here, I don't know why, like a ghost to have a last look round me, and go off in the dark again."

And with that he tould him to be sure, in case he should hear of his death, to give the oak box, in the closet off his room, to his cousin, Pat Sarsfield, in Dublin, and the sword and pistols his grandfather carried in Aughrim, and two or three thriflin' things of the kind.

And says he, "Con, they say if the divil gives you money overnight, you'll find nothing but a bagful of pebbles, and chips, and nutshells, in the morning. If I thought he played fair, I'm in the humour to make a bargain with him to-night."

"Lord forbid!" says my grandfather, standing up with a start, and crossing himself.

"They say the country's full of men, listin' sogers for the King o' France. If I light on one o' them, I'll not refuse his offer. How contrary things goes! How long is it since me and Captain Waller fought the jewel at New Castle?"

"Six years, Masther Dominick, and ye broke his thigh with the bullet the first shot."

"I did, Con," says he, "and I wish, instead, he had shot me through the heart. Have you any whisky?"

My grandfather took it out of the buffet, and the masther pours out some into a bowl, and drank it off.

"I'll go out and have a look at my horse," says he, standing up. There was a sort of a stare in his eyes, as he pulled his riding-cloak about him, as if there was something bad in his thoughts.

"Sure, I won't be a minute running out myself to the stable, and looking after the horse for you myself," says my grandfather.

"I'm not goin' to the stable," says Sir Dominick; "I may as well tell you, for I see you found it out already—I'm goin' across the deer-park; if I come back you'll see me in an hour's time. But, anyhow, you'd better not follow me, for if you do I'll shoot you, and that'd be a bad ending to our friendship."

And with that he walks down this passage here, and turns the key in the side door at that end of it, and out wid him on the sod into the moonlight and the cowld wind; and my grandfather seen him walkin' hard towards the park-wall, and then he comes in and closes the door with a heavy heart.

Sir Dominick stopped to think when he got to the middle of the deer-park, for he had not made up his mind, when he left the house and the whisky did not clear his head, only it gev him courage.

He did not feel the cowld wind now, nor fear death, nor think much of anything, but the shame and fall of the old family.

And he made up his mind, if no better thought came to him between that and there, so soon as he came to Murroa Wood, he'd hang himself from one of the oak branches with his cravat.

It was a bright moonlight night, there was just a bit of a cloud driving across the moon now and then, but, only for that, as light a'most as day.

Down he goes, right for the wood of Murroa. It seemed to him every step he took was as long as three, and it was no time till he was among the big oak-trees with their roots spreading from one to another, and their branches stretching overhead like the timbers of a naked roof, and the moon shining down through them, and casting their shadows thick and twist abroad on the ground as black as my shoe.

He was sobering a bit by this time, and he slacked his pace, and he thought 'twould be better to list in the French king's army, and thry what that might do for him, for he knew a man might take his own life any time, but it would puzzle him to take it back again when he liked.

Just as he made up his mind not to make away with himself, what should he hear but a step clinkin' along the dry ground under the trees, and soon he sees a grand gentleman right before him comin' up to meet him.

He was a handsome young man like himself, and he wore a cocked-hat with gold-lace round it, such as officers wear on their coats, and he had on a dress the same as French officers wore in them times.

He stopped opposite Sir Dominick, and he cum to a standstill also.

The two gentlemen took off their hats to one another, and says the stranger:

"I am recruiting, sir," says he, "for my sovereign, and you'll find my money won't turn into pebbles, chips, and nutshells, by to-morrow."

At the same time he pulls out a big purse full of gold.

The minute he sets eyes on that gentleman, Sir Dominick had his own opinion of him; and at those words he felt the very hair standing up on his head.

"Don't be afraid," says he, "the money won't burn you. If it proves honest gold, and if it prospers with you, I'm willing to make a bargain. This is the last day of February," says he; "I'll serve you seven years, and at the end of that time you shall serve me, and I'll come for you when the seven years is over, when the clock turns the minute between February and March; and the first of March ye'll come away with me, or never. You'll not find me a bad master, any more than a bad servant. I love my own; and I command all the pleasures and the glory of the world. The bargain dates from this day, and the lease is out at midnight on the last day I told you; and in the year"—he told him the year, it was easy reckoned, but I forget it—"and if you'd rather wait," he says, "for eight months and twenty-eight days, before you sign the writin', you may, if you meet me here. But I can't do a great deal for you in the meantime; and if you don't sign then, all you get from me, up to that time, will vanish away, and you'll be just as you are to-night, and ready to hang yourself on the first tree you meet."

Well, the end of it was, Sir Dominick chose to wait, and he came back to the house with a big bag full of money, as round as your hat a'most.

My grandfather was glad enough, you may be sure, to see the master safe and sound again so soon. Into the kitchen he bangs again, and swings the bag o' money on the table; and he stands up straight, and heaves up his shoulders like a man that has just got shut of a load; and he looks at the bag, and my grandfather looks at him, and from him to it, and back again. Sir Dominick looked as white as a sheet, and says he:

"I don't know, Con, what's in it; it's the heaviest load I ever carried."

He seemed shy of openin' the bag; and he made my grandfather heap up a roaring fire of turf and wood, and then, at last, he opens it, and, sure enough, 'twas stuffed full o' golden guineas, bright and new, as if they were only that minute out o' the Mint.

Sir Dominick made my grandfather sit at his elbow while he counted every guinea in the bag.

When he was done countin', and it wasn't far from daylight when that time came, Sir Dominick made my grandfather swear not to tell a word about it. And a close secret it was for many a day after.

When the eight months and twenty-eight days were pretty near spent and ended, Sir Dominick returned to the house here with a troubled mind, in doubt what was best to be done, and no one alive but my grandfather knew anything about the matter, and he not half what had happened.

As the day drew near, towards the end of October, Sir Dominick grew only more and more troubled in mind.

One time he made up his mind to have no more to say to such things, nor to speak again with the like of them he met with in the wood of Murroa. Then, again, his heart failed him when he thought of his debts, and he not knowing where to turn. Then, only a week before the day, everything began to go wrong with him. One man wrote from London to say that Sir Dominick paid three thousand pounds to the wrong man, and must pay it over again; another demanded a debt he never heard of before; and another, in Dublin, denied the payment of a thundherin' big bill, and Sir Dominick could nowhere find the receipt, and so on, wid fifty other things as bad.

Well, by the time the night of the 28th of October came round, he was a'most ready to lose his senses with all the demands that was risin' up again him on all sides, and nothing to meet them but the help of the one dhreadful friend he had to depind on at night in the oak-wood down there below.

So there was nothing for it but to go through with the business that was begun already, and about the same hour as he went last, he takes off the little crucifix he wore round his neck, for he was a Catholic, and his gospel, and his bit o' the thrue cross that he had in a locket, for since he took the money from the Evil One he was growin' frightful in himself, and got all he could to guard him from the power of the devil. But to-night, for his life, he daren't take them with him. So he gives them into my grandfather's hands without a word, only he looked as white as a sheet o' paper; and he takes his hat and sword, and telling my grandfather to watch for him, away he goes, to try what would come of it.

It was a fine still night, and the moon—not so bright, though, now as the first time—was shinin' over heath and rock, and down on the lonesome oak-wood below him.

His heart beat thick as he drew near it. There was not a sound, not even the distant bark of a dog from the village behind him. There was not a lonesomer spot in the country round, and if it wasn't for his debts and losses that was drivin' him on half mad, in spite of his fears for his soul and his hopes of paradise, and all his good angel was whisperin' in his ear, he would 'a' turned back, and sent for his clargy, and made his confession and his penance, and changed his ways, and led a good life, for he was frightened enough to have done a great dale.

Softer and slower he stept as he got, once more, in undher the big branches of the oak-threes; and when he got in a bit, near where he met with the bad spirit before, he stopped and looked round him, and felt himself, every bit, turning cowld as a dead man, and you may be sure he did not feel much better when he seen the same man steppin' from behind the big tree that was touchin' his elbow a'most.

"You found the money good," says he, "but it was not enough. No matter, you shall have enough and to spare. I'll see after your luck, and I'll give you a hint whenever it can serve you; and any time you want to see me you have only to come down here, and call my face to mind, and wish me present. You shan't owe a shilling by the end of the year, and you shall never miss the right card, the best throw, and the winning horse. Are you willing?"

The young gentleman's voice almost stuck in his throat, and his hair was rising on his head, but he did get out a word or two to signify that he consented; and with that the Evil One handed him a needle, and bid him give him three drops of blood from his arm; and he took them in the cup of an acorn, and gave him a pen, and bid him write some words that he repeated, and that Sir Dominick did not understand, on two thin slips of parchment. He took one himself and the other he sunk in Sir Dominick's arm at the place where he drew the blood, and he closed the flesh over it. And that's as true as you're sittin' there!

Well, Sir Dominick went home. He was a frightened man, and well he might be. But in a little time he began to grow aisier in his mind. Anyhow, he got out of debt very quick, and money came tumbling in to make him richer, and everything he took in hand prospered, and he never made a wager, or played a game, but he won; and for all that, there was not a poor man on the estate that was not happier than Sir Dominick.

So he took again to his old ways; for, when the money came back, all came back, and there were hounds and horses, and wine galore, and no end of company, and grand doin's, and divarsion, up here at the great house. And some said Sir Dominick was thinkin' of gettin' married; and more said he wasn't. But, anyhow, there was somethin' troublin' him more than common, and so one night, unknownst to all, away he goes to the lonesome oak-wood. It was something, maybe, my grandfather thought was troublin' him about a beautiful young lady he was jealous of, and mad in love with her. But that was only guess.

Well, when Sir Dominick got into the wood this time, he grew more in dread than ever; and he was on the point of turnin' and lavin' the place, when who should he see, close beside him, but my gentleman, seated on a big stone undher one of the trees. In place of looking the fine young gentleman in goold lace and grand clothes he appeared before, he was now in rags, he looked twice the size he had been, and his face smutted with soot, and he had a murtherin' big steel hammer, as heavy as a half-hundhred, with a handle a yard long, across his knees. It was so dark under the tree, he did not see him quite clear for some time.

He stood up, and he looked awful tall entirely. And what passed between them in that discourse my grandfather never heered. But Sir Dominick was as black as night afterwards, and hadn't a laugh for anything nor a word a'most for any one, and he only grew worse and worse, and darker and darker. And now this thing, whatever it was, used to come to him of its own accord, whether he wanted it or no; sometimes in one shape, and sometimes in another, in lonesome places, and sometimes at his side by night when he'd be ridin' home alone, until at last he lost heart altogether and sent for the priest.

The priest was with him a long time, and when he heered the whole story, he rode off all the way for the bishop, and the bishop came here to the great house next day, and he gev Sir Dominick a good advice. He toult him he must give over dicin', and swearin', and drinkin', and all bad company, and live a vartuous steady life until the seven years' bargain was out, and if the divil didn't come for him the minute afther the stroke of twelve the first morning of the month of March, he was safe out of the bargain. There was not more than eight or ten months to run now before the seven years wor out, and he lived all the time according to the bishop's advice, as strict as if he was "in retreat."

Well, you may guess he felt quare enough when the mornin' of the 28th of February came.

The priest came up by appointment, and Sir Dominick and his raverence wor together in the room you see there, and kep' up their prayers together till the clock struck twelve, and a good hour after, and not a sign of a disturbance, nor nothing came near them, and the priest slep' that night in the house in the room next Sir Dominick's, and all went over as comfortable as could be, and they shook hands and kissed like two comrades after winning a battle.

So, now, Sir Dominick thought he might as well have a pleasant evening, after all his fastin' and praying; and he sent round to half a dozen of the neighbouring gentlemen to come and dine with him, and his raverence stayed and dined also, and a roarin' bowl o' punch they had, and no end o' wine, and the swearin' and dice, and cards and guineas changing hands, and songs and stories, that wouldn't do any one good to hear, and the priest slipped away, when he seen the turn things was takin', and it was not far from the stroke of twelve when Sir

Dominick, sitting at the head of his table, swears, "this is the best first of March I ever sat down with my friends."

"It ain't the first o' March," says Mr. Hiffernan of Ballyvoreen. He was a scholard, and always kep' an almanack.

"What is it, then?" says Sir Dominick, startin' up, and dhroppin' the ladle into the bowl, and starin' at him as if he had two heads.

" 'Tis the twenty-ninth of February, leap year," says he. And just as they were talkin', the clock strikes twelve; and my grandfather, who was half asleep in a chair by the fire in the hall, openin' his eyes, sees a short square fellow with a cloak on, and long black hair bushin' out from under his hat, standin' just there where you see the bit o' light shinin' again' the wall.

(My hunchback friend pointed with his stick to a little patch of red sunset light that relieved the deepening shadow of the passage.)

"Tell your master," says he, in an awful voice, like the growl of a baist, "that I'm here by appointment, and expect him downstairs this minute."

Up goes my grandfather, by these very steps you are sittin' on.

"Tell him I can't come down yet," says Sir Dominick, and he turns to the company in the room, and says he with a cold sweat shinin' on his face, "for God's sake, gentlemen, will any of you jump from the window and bring the priest here?" One looked at another and no one knew what to make of it, and in the meantime, up comes my grandfather again, and says he, tremblin', "He says, sir, unless you go down to him, he'll come up to you."

"I don't understand this, gentlemen, I'll see what it means," says Sir Dominick, trying to put a face on it, and walkin' out o' the room like a man through the press-room, with the hangman waitin' for him outside. Down the stairs he comes, and two or three of the gentlemen peeping over the banisters, to see. My grandfather was walking six or eight steps behind him, and he seen the stranger take a stride out to meet Sir Dominick, and catch him up in his arms, and whirl his head against the wall, and wi' that the hall-doore flies open, and out goes the candles, and the turf and wood-ashes flyin' with the wind out o' the hall-fire, ran in a drift o' sparks along the floore by his feet.

Down runs the gintlemen. Bang goes the hall-doore. Some comes runnin' up, and more runnin' down, with lights. It was all over with Sir Dominick. They lifted up the corpse, and put its shoulders again' the wall; but there was not a gasp left in him. He was cowld and stiffenin' already.

Pat Donovan was comin' up to the great house late that night and after he passed the little brook, that the carriage track up to the house crosses, and about fifty steps to this side of it, his dog, that was by his side, makes a sudden wheel, and springs over the wall, and sets up a yowlin' inside you'd hear a mile away; and that minute two men passed him by in silence, goin' down from the house, one of them short and square, and the other like Sir Dominick in shape, but there was little light under the trees where he was, and they looked only like shadows; and as they passed him by he could not hear the sound of their feet and he drew back to the wall frightened; and when he got up to the great house, he found all in confusion, and the master's body, with the head smashed to pieces, lying just on *that spot.*

The narrator stood up and indicated with the point of his stick the exact site of the body, and, as I looked, the shadow deepened, the red stain of sunlight vanished from the wall, and the sun had gone down behind the distant hill of New Castle, leaving the haunted scene in the deep grey of darkening twilight.

So I and the story-teller parted, not without good wishes on both sides, and a little "tip" which seemed not unwelcome, from me.

It was dusk and the moon up by the time I reached the village, remounted my nag, and looked my last on the scene of the terrible legend of Dunoran.

Even the Devil must adapt his methods to the electronic age, and he does just that in "Tapestry," a quiet little conte cruelle *by* C. H. SHERMAN, *whose career is divided between writing fantasy fiction and professional acting on daytime dramas, TV commercials and in the New York legitimate theater.*

Tapestry
BY C. H. SHERMAN

She crumpled the cellophane and placed it in the wastebasket. She removed the first cassette from its plastic bed and inserted it into the recorder. Relaxing comfortably in her tapestried Queen Anne wing chair rescued from the DePaul Society, Megan pushed the "play" button and closed her eyes.

"*The Mayor of Casterbridge* by Thomas Hardy. One evening of late summer, before the nineteenth century had reached one third of its span, a young man and woman, the latter carrying a child, were approaching the large village of Weydon-Priors, in Upper Wessex, on foot. They were plainly but not ill clad. . . .'"

Megan O'Rourke drifted along with the story, a classic she had long wanted to read. The taped version was a birthday gift from her younger sister Audrey. Her parents had given her the portable cassette player. Thanks to today's electronic revolution, the extravagance of personal tape decks was not too terribly unbearable, even for a family that battled to make the monthly rent payments.

Megan and Audrey shared a tiny studio apartment in Rego Park, a community of apartment complexes which housed more people in a four-mile radius than could be found in most cities in Idaho. Having grown up in Rego Park, with thousands and thousands of people so close and so noisy, Megan assumed this to be the way life was and therefore never questioned her environment. Just as she never questioned Audrey's nights out, which were becoming more and more frequent. Megan didn't mind the aloneness of it—Audrey was no great joy when she was around—but she did mind not knowing in advance so that she could make sure she had enough food and money.

Megan was blind and dependent upon Audrey.

"The wife mostly kept her eyes fixed ahead, though with little interest—the scene for that matter being one that might have been matched at almost any spot in any county in England at this time of the year. . . ."

The blindness was the result of an accident when Megan and Audrey were five and four respectively. Audrey shoved her sister off the playground slide and Megan fell ten feet to the hard ground, landing on her head and suffering damage to the left optic nerve. Sympathetic blindness claimed the sight of her other eye seven months later. It's a wonder she didn't break her neck, the girls' mother was fond of saying. Falling on her head sure didn't knock any sense into it was Audrey's standard follow-up. Guilt had never rubbed shoulders with Audrey, nor for that matter had compassion. Megan and her father never spoke about the accident or her blindness. Only one time when Megan was twelve and frightened by the onset of menstruation did she and her father finally speak of her disability. His words were encouraging and courageous but hiding beneath them Megan heard his dark disappointment. His perfect little lady was a cripple. Subtle blades of fury sliced her heart as her father warned her of the dangers awaiting her. The next ten years were full of fear and overprotection.

It took many months of pleading to finally convince their parents that the two girls would be safe in an apartment of their own. After all, they were in their twenties now. Audrey's motives were less for her blind sister's welfare than for her own freedom from her parents' tyranny. Megan didn't care what Audrey's motives were. She just wanted a chance to be an independent twenty-three-year-old woman who happened to have a handicap.

She was not a cripple.

The voice on the tape was pleasant and unhurried. It was masculine without being gruff, soothing without being sloppy. She imagined the person behind the voice to be tall and smiling, quick to laugh, quick to hug.

"But there was more in that tent than met the cursory glance; and the man, with the instinct of a perverse character, scented it quickly. After a mincing attack on his bowl—Hello Meganie—he watched the hag's proceedings from the corner of his eye, and saw. . . ."

Megan pushed the "stop" button.

"Dad? Did I leave the door unlocked? I thought I made sure the police lock was set. Dad?"

She crossed to the front door and, sure enough, the police lock was in place. She was alone.

Megan found her way back to her chair and groped for the cassette player which had fallen to the floor. She placed her four right-hand fingers on the controls, felt the "rewind" button and gave it a quick push.

". . . man, with the instinct of a perverse character, scented it quickly. After a mincing attack on his bowl, he watched the hag's proceedings from the corner of his eye, and saw the game she played. He winked. . . ."

Twice more she rewound the tape to see if she could find the words that sounded like "Hello Meganie." Meganie was the nickname her parents and grandparents called her.

A little concerned that her imagination was working overtime, Megan settled down to continue the tape.

"The child began to prattle impatiently, and the wife more than once said to her husband—Meganie, don't turn off the tape. This is a surprise birthday message just for you. Happy Birthday to You, Happy Birthday to You, Happy Birthday Dear Megan, Happy Birthday to You!"

Megan smiled. Audrey could be a pain in the ass sometimes but every once in a while she went out of her way to do something nice. Like this. But why didn't she record the message herself?

"Dear Meganie, this is a special birthday message just for you. For your birthday I have the power to give you the one thing you want most."

Where did Audrey find someone to record this? Obviously she had met an actor somewhere and promised him God knows what to go to all this trouble. She sure as hell didn't pay him. Audrey was tight with a buck.

"Just think, what is the one thing you want most? The one thing that would help you break free so you could have the kind of life you should be living. The one thing that would put you on an equal footing with Audrey. The one thing that would make sure you'd never have to lean on anyone ever again. The one thing that would show them you're not a cripple."

"My sight."

Megan spoke out loud without realizing she was answering the tape. She pushed the "stop" button.

What kind of joke was this?

She felt for the phone on the end table. Placing her fingers on the buttons, she pushed her parents' number. She let it ring at least fifteen times before she accepted the fact that they weren't home. The ringing sounded tinny and distant, as if the phone on the other end were in a foreign country.

Megan fumbled the phone back onto its cradle. Her hands found and clasped each other in her lap. Snorting a nervous laugh, she spoke aloud.

"Audrey, this isn't funny."

No, it wasn't funny at all. What the voice on the tape said hit home. But how did anybody know her frustration? Megan always kept her feelings to herself. No one was ever allowed to get close. Her blindness provided the distance she needed to keep the outrage in check.

Trembling, she pushed the "play" button.

"Happy Birthday once again, dear Meg. But this isn't a message from Audrey. This is a message from the one who has the power to grant that one special wish. Intrigued? Megan, you can answer. This is no ordinary tape, as I'm sure you've surmised. A great gift awaits you, if only you say the word. Just a short talk, hmm? I don't see the harm, do you?"

"Who are you?"

"I am Leviathan, brother to Satan, Lucifer and Mammon. No doubt you've heard of me and my colorful colleagues."

"You're the Devil?"

"Rather than go into complicated technicalities, suffice it to say yes."

Megan sat unmoving. Could she really be sitting in her own apartment carrying on a conversation with the Devil? And why wasn't she frightened?

"I'm here to give you an amazing opportunity. I'm here to restore your sight."

"How? The doctors said it's irreversible."

"Sweet Megan, nothing is irreversible. I have the power to help you. Or rather, you have the power to help yourself. I'm just here to offer you the means."

"What are the means?"

"Very, very simple. You order me to transmit your blindness to your sister Audrey."

Her lips tingled. Her breath tasted hot.

"Couldn't I just get my sight without taking it from someone else?"

"Not just someone else. Audrey."

Audrey. The one who had blinded her. Not intentionally, of course. Just a childish shove with a lifetime of consequences. How many times had Megan wished Audrey to suffer, to pay for the loss of all the trees and skies and faces and coloring books and puppies. Everything that had been stolen from her. Tasting and touching weren't enough. Only sound endured, but that wasn't enough either.

"You've missed a great deal. Now it's Audrey's turn."

Megan's fingertips traced her eyelids, sensing the dead orbs floating there, realizing she didn't remember their color. To see again, to really see, this time with the eyes of an adult.

"How would it happen?"

"Subtlety is important. We can't have anything that smacks of the miraculous."

She had stopped praying for a miracle a long time ago.

"A malfunctioning elevator that plummets, simultaneously restoring your sight as it robs hers. Nothing unsightly."

There was a self-appreciative chuckle from Leviathan.

"Why would you be willing to do this for me? I haven't asked for this."

"Oh, well, if you're content with your life, then back to Hardy's Henchard and his family."

"Wait! I just want to know why the hell. . . . You want my soul in return, right?"

"Your soul isn't mine to take, Megan. You have the freedom to choose. Responsibility and freedom of choice go hand in hand. Hell exists. You create it yourself. Think about it."

The clunk of the key in the lock woke her. Audrey was home. The three bolts rattled their distinctive sounds. The tape deck lay empty on the floor.

"What time is it?"

"Oh hi, Meg. It's almost nine."

"Is Robert with you?"

"No! The stupid fart is such a jerk. He wanted to hang out with his boss and his trashy wife. Real losers. You should see them. He's Fred Flintstone and she's Betty Boop. And I'm bored to tears."

"Why don't we get some pizza, Audrey? I'm starved."

"I'm beat, kid."

"Oh please, Audrey, we don't go out together any more. Come on. For my birthday."

"Have you listened to the tape yet?"

"Yes. It's just what I wanted." Megan's voice choked with emotion. "Thank you." A silent moment. "Please. Just one slice?"

"Okay, one slice. My treat."

The elevator door slid shut. Megan groped for the back rail. She felt Audrey's fingers drumming a syncopated beat on the wall. They were the only passengers.

Neither girl spoke as the elevator descended. The building was old, the trip slow and creaky.

The elevator jerked to a stop.

"Damn." Audrey punched the buttons on the control panel. "What the hell is wrong with this damned elevator? This building sucks."

Megan froze against the back wall as the car shot up suddenly. It bounced between floors, then plummeted abruptly. The girls collided with each other, Audrey's nose hitting Megan's chin. Audrey screamed in fear and pain. Megan grabbed her sister and held her close.

"No! I take it back! I don't want this! Leviathan! Don't do this!"

The elevator plunged.

"But her strong sense that neither she nor any human being deserved less than was given, did not blind her to the fact that there were others receiving less who had deserved much more. And in being forced to class herself among the fortunate she did not cease to wonder at the persistence of the unforeseen, when the one to whom such unbroken tranquility had been accorded in the adult stage was she whose youth had seemed to teach that happiness was but the occasional episode in a general drama of pain."

"The sausage seemed a little dry tonight but it was still good. Do you want another slice, Audrey?"

"No, one was enough."

"Okay, my turn to leave the tip."

Megan put two folded dollar bills on the table and crumpled her napkin into her empty cup. Mr. O'Rourke helped Audrey on with her coat.

Every Tuesday night was pizza night. The table in the back was reserved for the girls and their parents.

"Bundle up, it's getting cold, girls," cautioned Mrs. O'Rourke.

Megan felt her jaw tighten but she simply nodded and buttoned her coat.

The wind whipped around the buildings, making even the short walk to the corner a chilly one.

"Wait for the light, girls."

Megan and Audrey dutifully waited at the curb. The light changed and the two sisters held hands crossing the street, their white-tipped canes tapping the pavement in unison.

DIANE WNOROWSKA, *a former casino dealer whose work frequently appears in the trade publication* Gambling Times, *here deals us a glimpse into the curiously desperate world of the incurable bettor . . . and what better place than a gambling casino to catch a whiff of sulphur and brimstone?*

Seven Come Heaven?

BY DIANE WNOROWSKA

"Hey, baby, you're hot!"

"C'mon, little lady, do that again."

"Shit, she's fantastic!"

"Look, lady, this one's for you. One ten the hard way and we both can spend a week on the Riviera."

Artie could hear them from halfway across the casino. Ignoring all the glitter that Caesars had to offer, he quickened his pace and tried to shove in closer to the craps table, stepping on a few toes in the process. No one got mad, though; no one seemed to notice him.

"What's going on?" he asked one of the players. "What's all the excitement?"

"Get your money down on the table quick, buddy. This lady is one of the hottest rollers I've seen in a long time. Nine passes, hitting numbers all over the table, and still going strong. Look at this—I started with a hundred lousy bucks!"

Artie looked at the pile of chips in front of the man and turned white. He quickly counted more than $35,000.

He pulled out his last remaining $100. Before he could get the money down on the table, the woman rolled her point, a ten. The people at the table roared and picked up large stacks of chips.

Artie stole a glance at the woman. She appeared unmoved by all that was going on around her. She pulled $15,000 in winnings off the table, plus another $7,000—since she made her point the hard way, the man who bet for her sent her the winnings.

"Can you do it again, lady?"

"Hey, babe, can you keep this up?"

"Sure she can. I'm pressing the whole stack."

The dealer pushed the dice toward her and waited impatiently for her to throw them. She stared at him coolly and held the dice in her hands until all bets were down on the table.

Artie held his money in his hand. No one can keep this up, he told himself. She's gonna lose.

"Seven a winner," croaked the dealer. "Pay the pass line."

Artie blinked. If the guy next to him was right, this was the dame's tenth pass. Christ Almighty! This was every crapshooter's dream.

He threw his money to the dealer. "I want it all on the pass line."

Artie was in his mid-forties and was wearing a very expensive shirt and slacks, now quite worn. The markings on his wrist indicated that his inexpensive watch took the place of a far larger one. His fingers showed pale circles at their bases. His hair was thinning on top and his face had a kind of despairing frantic look.

The woman turned to look at him as he picked up his chip and placed it on the pass line. A slight smile curled up the corners of her lips.

She threw the dice, a slow, curving roll. Artie watched them as they spun and spun. His entire bankroll was tied to them. He watched as they traveled the length of the table, bounced off its end, landed and rolled. He watched one die stop at two. And when he looked at the other—a five!

The players went wild—and Artie with them. He knew he was a winner again. He left $100 on the line, picked up the $100 he had just won and waited for her come-out roll. He wanted her to make a point because that was how he'd get rich.

He watched the dice tumble and hit and bounce and roll—four! How lucky can I get? he wondered. Four is my number!

Artie threw the $100 he had just won to the dealer. "All of it on the hard four."

Again the woman took the dice and threw them in that same cool way, the barest smile on her lips.

"Oh, please, please, be there for me, please, be there, be there, be there for me—"

"The lady's a winner!" yelled the dealer. "Pay the hard four."

Vaguely aware of all the money being pushed around him, Artie could focus only on his own $1,000. It had been so long since he had won. He took his winnings, placed $500 on the pass line, held the rest and prayed for her to make a point.

"Six," the dealer called, "the lady's point is six."

Artie threw all of his chips to the dealer and told him to put them on six the hard way. He was so excited he paid no attention to the woman who was holding the dice. Neither did anyone else. No one saw her pull all her odds off the table. When she threw the dice, she had little money riding on them.

They all yelled and shouted as she threw the dice. They all screamed as the dice hit the end of the table, bounced and rolled. They all became silent as they came to rest.

"Seven, seven," the dealer called. "The lady sevens out."

All the players turned to her. But she was gone.

Artie walked away from the table with his hands in his pockets. He walked out of the casino, thinking about how he had nothing. He had less than nothing, really. When this losing streak began six months ago, he started borrowing from anyone he could. Artie now owed half a million—some of it to some very unpleasant people—and no one would give him another penny.

Artie lit a cigarette and walked past Caesars fountains and down the long drive toward the Strip. He smiled as he remembered what it was like to be a winner. For him it wasn't the money; he never really cared whether he wore silk or polyester, diamonds or rhinestones. But it was the people who came to him when he had money. All the gorgeous women who would normally not have given him a second glance. All the bigshot men who included him in their groups because he had bucks. All the headwaiters who knew him by name, all the hotels that welcomed him as a guest.

Artie remembered, too, how everyone smiled at him when he won. When he was in the money, everyone shared—dealers, cocktail waitresses, bellboys, doormen. When he had it, he spread it around.

But now, now when he needed the people, the smiles, no one would even look at him. As soon as they saw him coming, they turned away, as if they were afraid that his bad luck was contagious.

Artie watched the traffic on the Strip speed by. He wondered if maybe it wasn't time to cash in all his chips. He figured he couldn't lose if he threw himself under the wheels of a speeding car—what else was left?

"It wouldn't work," a voice next to him said. "You'd end up in a hospital, crippled, with medical bills added to everything else you owe."

He turned toward the sound of the voice and saw the woman from the casino. She sat behind the wheel of a fire-red Porsche.

"Get in," she said. "I'd like a drink."

He shook his head. "I couldn't afford a cup of coffee, honey."

"The name is Bel. And I want you for your company, not your nonexistent bankroll."

He looked at her skeptically. She was a real beauty—dark black hair, green eyes, a face that could have been copied from some statue. Her dress hadn't come from any rack and the jewels she wore weren't paste. He couldn't figure out what she wanted with him.

Then he laughed. Even if she did want something from him, she wouldn't get it: He was tap city.

"Sure," he said. "Why not?"

He climbed into the sweet little Porsche and was immediately aware of the woman's scent. It was musky and overpowering at first; soon, though, he grew used to it.

Bel pulled quickly out onto the Strip. As she drove, he watched the lights go by, each gaudy display carrying with it memories of a loss or a win.

She drove to the Peppermill Restaurant and led the way to the lounge. Artie was pleased with her choice; the Peppermill was a favorite place of his. In one corner of the room stood a large covered fireplace, the flame resting on top of a basin of bubbling water. The floor was covered in plush carpeting and the chairs were low and comfortable-looking, with full arms and backs. The tone throughout was subdued.

He followed Bel to a little table away from everyone else.

Bel gave her order to the waitress. "Stolichnaya on the rocks, please. Make it a double."

"I'll have a Charters and Seven," Artie told her.

Bel pulled out a gold cigarette case and handed him a gold lighter. He lit her cigarette.

"Having a bad streak?" she asked softly.

He was about to minimize his situation, to hand her the sort of line all losing gamblers hand other gamblers. Something stopped him.

He shrugged. "Yeah."

"How much are you in for?"

"What business is that of yours?"

Saying nothing, she watched him.

"I owe the casinos a quarter of a million, another two hundred thou to some buddies."

"How are you going to pay it back?"

He shrugged. "Don't know. Vegas is my only business. Been my business for years. Boy, I could tell you stories about—"

"You have no assets, no other sources of income?"

He looked at her, hurt because she wouldn't listen to his tales of the glorious past.

"No. None. I got . . ." Artie reached into his pocket and pulled out a handful of change. "I got this to my name. I got a tab running at some cheap motel on the Strip and some old clothes in the closet there. And that's it."

"I made twelve passes tonight," she said softly. "Six sevens, six points and six craps; but I never rolled craps on a come-out or when I had any money on the come line."

"We all get lucky," he said bitterly.

"No luck involved," she said. She reached into her purse and pulled out some bills. "Here." She put them on the table near his hand.

Artie stared at the bills, desperately wanting to grab them. Pride and wariness, though, kept him from doing so. "What do I have to do for this?"

"You come with me to the MGM. You bet the pass line, you take no more than four come bets and you stay away from all proposition bets. And, of course, you count. When I make twelve passes, you walk away from the table."

"That's all I do? You're giving me a thou—"

"Lending you, lending you. I don't give things away. You do what I say, you win, you pay me back."

"So what are you getting out of all this?"

"Belief." She called the waitress over, paid the bill and walked out. Artie followed.

They drove back along the Strip and walked into the MGM, with its big chandeliers and its book. They walked up to a craps table and watched someone seven out. Bel squeezed in just in time to get the dice.

Artie wasn't thrilled with the way she had told him to bet; it was too conservative for his style. But what the hell, he thought, it was her money. He put $200 on the pass line and figured he could make three come bets, take the odds and stay within his $1,000 bankroll.

Her point was nine and she rolled a four, five and ten next. She won all his come bets and he took new ones as the money came off the table. When she rolled her point, he had a couple of grand on the table and another couple of grand in his chip tray.

He put half his money down on the pass line and backed it up when she rolled a six. He started placing larger come bets on the table. When she made her point, he had five grand on the table and about seven in his tray.

He kept pressing. A couple of times he was going to take a proposition bet—four the hard way, a favorite of his—but he didn't know what Bel would do. And he didn't want to antagonize this lady.

She rolled the dice, he placed his bets and he counted. Four sevens, three points, two craps. The money built up on the table and in his chip tray. Everyone at the table was a winner because of Bel.

Five sevens, five points, four craps. Artie had a big stack of chips in his tray, a stack which he knew was going to get even bigger.

Six sevens, six points, six craps. Bel told the dealer she wanted her odds off, leaving only her basic bets at risk. Artie reluctantly did the same.

"Seven," the dealer called out. "Seven's a loser."

Artie grinned. Some loser. She had left about $15,000 on the table and walked away with more than $200,000. He was ahead $80,000. They walked up to the cashier and exchanged their chips for money. He handed her back her thousand.

"I don't suppose you could do that again?" he asked.

Bel smiled. "I could. And I will. But not now." She turned and began to walk away. Artie stood still, terrified at the prospect of losing her, not knowing what to do.

Suddenly Bel stopped and looked back at him. She beckoned him to follow her. She took him to her room and undressed him. Although the details of that night were blurred in a musky red haze, Artie knew the next morning that she had made love to him better than any woman had ever done before.

He spent the next month with her. They traveled to casinos all over the world: Paradise Island, Monte Carlo, Athens, Sun City. Everywhere she rolled six sevens, six craps and six points. He made enough money to pay off all his debts and to enable most people to live a lifetime of comfort.

The two of them continued to make wonderful love together and when she wasn't around there was always someone else for him. Now that he was in the chips again, beautiful women who wanted to share his winnings flocked around.

Artie never let himself think about his winning streak ending. Not until Bel forced him to.

"I have other commitments," she said one night. They were sitting in the lounge of the casino in Monte Carlo. Although adjoining the bustling game room, the old-world lounge itself was elegantly quiet.

"I'll be leaving you in a couple of days."

He stared at her, his mouth agape. "But, but . . . why . . . what—?"

"It has nothing to do with you. As I said, I have other commitments."

She watched him as he sat and saw his dreams fade away. She watched and said nothing.

"It's over," he finally said.

"It doesn't have to be."

"What do you mean?"

"You can do what I do."

He stared at her again, his expression going from hope to despair and back again.

"Hasn't it ever occurred to you," Bel asked, "that it's rather strange that I should be able to do this consistently? Have you thought that I was just an oddly lucky player on a streak? Haven't you ever wondered if I used some sort of method?"

"Well . . . you see . . . I . . . Umhh. I don't know how to tell you this."

She raised her eyebrows questioningly.

"Well," he interjected, "I always thought you cheated."

She laughed and shook her head. "If you would like to learn to do this, have another drink, give me about fifteen minutes and then come up to the room. But you'll be able to roll the dice like I do this one time only and you'll have to pay me ten percent of whatever you win. Fair?"

Artie nodded. Bel left the table. He had a drink. He went to the room to find it darkened. The bed was turned down.

He saw her and reached for her. "No, no," she admonished. "Business first."

She had him undress and rest comfortably on the bed. Picking up a large ruby pendant that Bel was fond of wearing, she moved it slowly over his head and he became lost in its facets.

Artie wakened with a start. The room was bright and on the pillow next to him was a note that read GO GET 'EM.

He rushed into his clothes and raced down to the casino. He knew —KNEW—that he could do it. He knew that he would roll exactly as she did.

And he made his twelve passes. And he walked away with $260,000. And he was surrounded by beautiful women and envious men. And the waitresses all smiled, as did the dealers. And the casino staff couldn't do enough for him.

Artie celebrated his victory and kept watching for Bel. But she never appeared. She didn't come back to the hotel either, not that night or the next.

When he went to the tables the following day, he sevened out immediately after making his point. He bet lightly on the other rollers, waiting for his turn to come again. He put a lot of money on the table and crapped out. He dropped $100,000, $200,000. He started to sweat mildly. As he dropped more and more money, he could see all the beautiful women moving away from him. Artie remembered what his life was before he met Bel.

"Why don't you buy me a drink?"

He turned and saw Bel standing next to him and almost cried in relief. "In a few minutes. Just take the dice, roll—"

She turned and walked away from him. He took one look at the table and followed her.

They sat down in the lounge. He ordered a double Stolichnaya for her, a straight bourbon for himself. He saw his hand shake as he picked up his glass.

"Do you have my money?" she asked.

"Not here. It's in the safety deposit box. I owe you—"

"$26,000," she concluded. "Do you know how much you just dropped?"

Artie shook his head.

"$337,600."

"I can afford it," he snapped.

"Thanks to me. But I'm leaving."

Artie buried his face in his hands. He wanted to argue with her but knew that she would be implacable.

He raised his eyes and stared at her. "Why just once?" he asked. "You do it every time. Why could I do it only once?"

"Because we only bargained for once. You'd like to be able to do it every time?"

Artie looked at her as if she had lost her mind. He wanted to reach across the table and slap her. Who wouldn't want to win every time? Softly, through clenched teeth, he whispered, "I would do anything for that. Anything."

She smiled. "Wonderful. I work for an organization that sells the very ability you would like to possess. I've taken the liberty of drawing up this contract."

She handed Artie a paper. He looked at it carefully. He would pay, during the next year, $1 million plus the $26,000 for the demonstration and—

"What is this? You want my soul? Who the hell are you? Satan?"

Bel laughed. "No. I'm just Bel. But my organization must be convinced of your desire for our product. People seem to attach a great deal of importance to their souls—even those who swear that they don't have one."

Artie went back to the contract. He also had to refer six people to her over the course of the next two years. Once this obligation was fulfilled, he would be possessor of the product for the rest of his life.

"Look, it'd be cheap at twice—five times the price. But I don't like this soul business."

"Fine. Why don't we go back to the hotel now, you can pay me the $26,000 and I'll be on my way."

She started to get up. He saw all his dreams walking out with her.

"Wait," he grabbed her hand. "Can't we—"

"I only represent my organization. I have no authority to negotiate. Except within the bounds they allow me. I was told that if you had any problems with this, I was to offer you the ability to make all your proposition bets."

Artie let go of her hand and seemed to collapse in his chair. "All of my proposition bets?" He thought of all those nine-to-one sixes, fifteen-to-one threes, thirty-to-one twelves. Then he thought of all the come-out-roll craps he'd roll and all those seven outs without her.

Bel said she wasn't Satan. She just worked for some sort of oddball organization. He was certain of that; he didn't really believe in Satan and souls. That was all bogeyman stories told to make little children behave.

"Give me that contract," he said.

So Artie signed and Bel gave him another of those sleep treatments. They said good-bye and she gave him a number to call whenever he had a prospect for her.

He returned to the casino the next day and won all of his money back—and then some. Following her instructions, he moved around and tried not to make himself too conspicuous.

In six months he sent her three recruits and paid the million.

Two months later he made another million and sent her another three recruits.

One month later he walked away from another winning table, surrounded by more beautiful women, once again fawned upon by the casino staff, and realized that he was overwhelmingly bored. Being unable to lose took all the fun out of the game for him. Sure, he could lose his money at the other tables, but nothing held the excitement for him of dice.

He put in a call to Bel. There was no answer at the number where he normally reached her, only static. He called the operator for help, but he was cut off when he tried to give her Bel's number. He walked from phone to phone and tried over and over to reach her.

Artie tried unsuccessfully for weeks. He traveled all around the world looking for her. She was nowhere and no one had seen her. It was as if she had dropped off the face of the earth.

Artie kept looking, though, financing his search with sessions with the dice. He spent all his time either winning at the craps tables or looking for Bel. He didn't eat or sleep. He spent no time with the tiresomely beautiful women. He paid no attention to any of the casino people who smiled at him with their phony pasted-on smiles.

He found himself back in Vegas. Despite all his wealth, he looked worse than he had when he first met Bel.

One night he finished playing at Caesars and tried again to call her. The results were as before.

He left the casino and walked past Caesars fountains and down the long drive toward the Strip.

Artie lit a cigarette and stood watching the traffic go by. He felt hopeless. The dice game had been his life, but Bel had taken that away from him. It was no longer a game; there could be no game if you couldn't lose. There could be no excitement, no thrill.

"I might just as well be dead," Artie said dejectedly. Without thinking, he started to walk onto the Strip.

As his foot touched the road, everything slowed and grew quiet. Artie walked directly into the path of an oncoming car. He turned and waited for it to strike him, praying to anyone who might be listening that he would win this one last time.

The car coming at him was a fire-red Porsche. Its license plate read BELIAL. Behind its wheel sat a creature more foul than anything Artie had ever seen in his worst nightmare. It raised its hand. Artie saw Bel's ruby pendant draped over the uncovered bones.

The creature grinned as the car hurtled closer. Artie screamed. Just before the car hit him, he realized that he was about to make the final payment on his contract. And he knew—KNEW—that he was going to spend eternity playing dice and winning.

H. G. WELLS *(1866–1946) is the renowned British author of many thrilling science-fantasy stories and novels, including* The Time Machine, The Invisible Man, The War of the Worlds *and (my personal favorite) the harrowing terror tale* The Island of Doctor Moreau. *He is generally associated with apocalyptic visions of doom, but he could also adopt a decidedly pawky tone, as in this amusing contest between Mephistopheles and a less-than-inspired painter.*

The Temptation of Harringay
BY H. G. WELLS

It is quite impossible to say whether this thing really happened. It depends entirely on the word of R. M. Harringay, who is an artist.

Following his version of the affair, the narrative deposes that Harringay went into his studio about ten o'clock to see what he could make of the head that he had been working at the day before. The head in question was that of an Italian organ-grinder, and Harringay thought—but was not quite sure—that the title would be the "Vigil." So far he is frank, and his narrative bears the stamp of truth. He had seen the man expectant for pennies, and with a promptness that suggested genius, had had him in at once.

"Kneel. Look up at that bracket," said Harringay. "As if you expected pennies."

"Don't *grin!*" said Harringay. "I don't want to paint your gums. Look as though you were unhappy."

Now, after a night's rest, the picture proved decidedly unsatisfactory. "It's good work," said Harringay. "That little bit in the neck . . . But."

He walked about the studio, and looked at the thing from this point and from that. Then he said a wicked word. In the original the word is given.

"Painting," he says he said. "Just a painting of an organ-grinder—a mere portrait. If it was a live organ-grinder I wouldn't mind. But somehow I never make things alive. I wonder if my imagination is wrong." This, too, has a truthful air. His imagination *is* wrong.

"That creative touch! To take canvas and pigment and make a man —as Adam was made of red ochre! But this thing! If you met it walking about the streets you would know it was only a studio production. The little boys would tell it to 'Garnome and git frimed.' Some little touch . . . Well—it won't do as it is."

He went to the blinds and began to pull them down. They were made of blue holland with the rollers at the bottom of the window, so that you pull them down to get more light. He gathered his palette, brushes, and mahl stick from his table. Then he turned to the picture and put a speck of brown in the corner of the mouth; and shifted his attention thence to the pupil of the eye. Then he decided that the chin was a trifle too impassive for a vigil.

Presently he put down his impedimenta, and lighting a pipe surveyed the progress of his work. "I'm hanged if the thing isn't sneering at me," said Harringay, and he still believes it sneered.

The animation of the figure had certainly increased, but scarcely in the direction he wished. There was no mistake about the sneer. "Vigil of the Unbeliever," said Harringay. "Rather subtle and clever that! But the left eyebrow isn't cynical enough."

He went and dabbed at the eyebrow, and added a little to the lobe of the ear to suggest materialism. Further consideration ensued. "Vigil's off, I'm afraid," said Harringay. "Why not Mephistopheles? But that's a bit *too* common. 'A Friend of the Doge'—not so seedy. The armour won't do, though. Too Camelot. How about a scarlet robe and call him 'One of the Sacred College'? Humour in that, and an appreciation of Middle Italian History."

"There's always Benvenuto Cellini," said Harringay; "with a clever suggestion of a gold cup in one corner. But that would scarcely suit the complexion."

He describes himself as babbling in this way in order to keep down an unaccountably unpleasant sensation of fear. The thing was certainly acquiring anything but a pleasing expression. Yet it was as certainly becoming far more of a living thing than it had been—if a sinister one—far more alive than anything he had ever painted before. "Call it 'Portrait of a Gentleman,' " Harringay; "A Certain Gentleman."

"Won't do," said Harringay, still keeping up his courage. "Kind of thing they call Bad Taste. That sneer will have to come out. That gone, and a little more fire in the eye—never noticed how warm his eye was before—and he might do for—? What price Passionate Pilgrim? But that devilish face won't do—*this* side of the Channel.

"Some little inaccuracy does it," he said; "eyebrows probably too oblique"—therewith pulling the blind lower to get a better light, and resuming palette and brushes.

The face on the canvas seemed animated by a spirit of its own. Where the expression of diablerie came in he found impossible to discover. Experiment was necessary. The eyebrows—it could scarcely be the eyebrows? But he altered them. No, that was no better; in fact, if anything, a trifle more satanic. The corner of the mouth? Pah! more than ever a leer—and now, retouched, it was ominously grim. The eye, then? Catastrophe! he had filled his brush with vermilion instead of brown, and yet he had felt sure it was brown! The eye seemed now to have rolled in its socket, and was glaring at him an eye of fire. In a flash of passion, possibly with something of the courage of panic, he struck the brush full of bright red athwart the picture; and then a very curious thing, a very strange thing indeed, occurred—if it *did* occur.

The diabolified Italian before him shut both his eyes, pursed his mouth, and wiped the colour off his face with his hands.

Then the *red eye* opened again, with a sound like the opening of lips, and the face smiled. "That was rather hasty of you," said the picture.

Harringay states that, now that the worst had happened, his self-possession returned. He had a saving persuasion that devils were reasonable creatures.

"Why do you keep moving about then," he said, "making faces and all that—sneering and squinting, while I am painting you?"

"I don't," said the picture.

"You *do*," said Harringay.

"It's yourself," said the picture.

"It's *not* myself," said Harringay.

"It *is* yourself," said the picture. "No! don't go hitting me with paint again, because it's true. You have been trying to fluke an expression on my face all the morning. Really, you haven't an idea what your picture ought to look like."

"I have," said Harringay.

"You have *not*," said the picture: "You *never* have with your pictures. You always start with the vaguest presentiment of what you are going to do; it is to be something beautiful—you are sure of that—and devout, perhaps, or tragic; but beyond that it is all experiment and chance. My dear fellow! you don't think you can paint a picture like that?"

Now it must be remembered that for what follows we have only Harringay's word.

"I shall paint a picture exactly as I like," said Harringay, calmly.

This seemed to disconcert the picture a little. "You can't paint a picture without an inspiration," it remarked.

"But I *had* an inspiration—for this."

"Inspiration!" sneered the sardonic figure; "a fancy that came from your seeing an organ-grinder looking up at a window! Vigil! Ha, ha! You just started painting on the chance of something coming—that's what you did. And when I saw you at it I came. I want a talk with you!"

"Art, with you," said the picture—"it's a poor business. You potter. I don't know how it is, but you don't seem able to throw your soul into it. You know too much. It hampers you. In the midst of your enthusiasms you ask yourself whether something like this has not been done before. And . . ."

"Look here," said Harringay, who had expected something better than criticism from the devil. "Are you going to talk studio to me?" He filled his number twelve hoghair with red paint.

"The true artist," said the picture, "is always an ignorant man. An artist who theorises about his work is no longer artist but critic. Wagner . . . I say!—What's that red paint for?"

"I'm going to paint you out," said Harringay. "I don't want to hear all that Tommy Rot. If you think just because I'm an artist by trade I'm going to talk studio to you, you make a precious mistake."

"One minute," said the picture, evidently alarmed. "I want to make you an offer—a genuine offer. It's right what I'm saying. You lack inspirations. Well. No doubt you've heard of the Cathedral of Cologne, and the Devil's Bridge, and—"

"Rubbish," said Harringay. "Do you think I want to go to perdition simply for the pleasure of painting a good picture, and getting it slated. Take that."

His blood was up. His danger only nerved him to action, so he says. So he planted a dab of vermilion in his creature's mouth. The Italian spluttered and tried to wipe it off—evidently horribly surprised. And then—according to Harringay—there began a very remarkable struggle, Harringay splashing away with the red paint, and the picture wriggling about and wiping it off as fast as he put it on. "*Two* masterpieces," said the demon. "Two indubitable masterpieces for a Chelsea artist's soul. It's a bargain?" Harringay replied with the paint brush.

For a few minutes nothing could be heard but the brush going and the spluttering and ejaculations of the Italian. A lot of the strokes he caught on his arm and hand, though Harringay got over his guard often enough. Presently the paint on the palette gave out and the two antagonists stood breathless, regarding each other. The picture was so smeared with red that it looked as if it had been rolling about a slaughterhouse, and it was painfully out of breath and very uncomfortable with the wet paint trickling down its neck. Still, the first round was in its favour on the whole. "Think," it said, sticking pluckily to its point, "two supreme masterpieces—in different styles. Each equivalent to the Cathedral . . ."

"*I* know," said Harringay, and rushed out of the studio and along the passage towards his wife's boudoir.

In another minute he was back with a large tin of enamel—Hedge Sparrow's Egg Tint, it was, and a brush. At the sight of that the artistic devil with the red eye began to scream. "*Three* masterpieces— culminating masterpieces."

Harringay delivered cut two across the demon, and followed with a thrust in the eye. There was an indistinct rumbling. "*Four* master-pieces," and a spitting sound.

But Harringay had the upper hand now and meant to keep it. With rapid, bold strokes he continued to paint over the writhing canvas, until at last it was a uniform field of shining Hedge Sparrow tint. Once the mouth reappeared and got as far as "Five master—" before he filled it with enamel; and near the end the red eye opened and glared at him indignantly. But at last nothing remained save a gleaming panel of drying enamel. For a little while a faint stirring beneath the surface puckered it slightly here and there, but presently even that died away and the thing was perfectly still.

Then Harringay—according to Harringay's account—lit his pipe and sat down and stared at the enamelled canvas, and tried to make out clearly what had happened. Then he walked round behind it, to see if the back of it was at all remarkable. Then it was he began to regret that he had not photographed the Devil before he painted him out.

This is Harringay's story—not mine. He supports it by a small canvas (24 by 20) enamelled a pale green, and by violent asseverations. It is also true that he never has produced a masterpiece, and in the opinion of his intimate friends probably never will.

*If you'll pardon the expression, this is one of the damnedest deal-with-the-Devil
stories I've ever run across, but then unconventional ideas are a hallmark of*
PAULA VOLSKY's *writing. Author of several sophisticated, refreshingly original
fantasy novels, including* Curse of the Witch Queen, The Sorcerer's Lady *and
the inimitable* The Luck of Relian Kru—*which is one of the most entertaining
fantasies I have ever read—Ms. Volsky is a resident of northern Virginia. She
assures us that the secret entrance to Luray Caverns that plays such an important part in "The Tenancy of Mr. Eex" really exists.*

The Tenancy of Mr. Eex
BY PAULA VOLSKY

I was sitting by myself in The Quorum after work, thinking of money
and men. Those two absorbing but ordinarily disparate subjects were
linked in my mind by the matter of child-support payments. Ben
hadn't sent a check in five months, and probably never would again.
There wasn't much I could do about it, either—he'd fled Washington,
D.C., and the last I'd heard was working with some accounting firm
out in California. If I managed to track him down, he'd most likely
cut and run again. Ben always was a bit of a weasel.

Strictly speaking, Jeanette and I didn't really need The Weasel's
contributions. As a GS-13 realty specialist at the Department of Hous-
ing and Urban Development, I earned a healthy salary of my own—
actually a little higher than Ben's. That slight but fatal inequality had
been a major factor in the demise of our marriage. Under the circumstances, Ben's reluctance to part with his money was understandable,
but not excusable. I don't need anything from him—I'm an adult,
thirty-three years old and capable of looking after myself—but Jeanette's another story. She's his daughter and he owes her support. He
also happens to owe her attention and affection, and he's sent her
exactly one letter in the past year—but there's no point in going into
all that. It's a very unpleasant topic, and I'm not as cool-headed about
the whole thing as I'd like to be.

The point is, we didn't need Ben's checks to live comfortably, but
without them I was feeling the pinch. I could handle the mortgage
payments on the Alexandria condo. Ditto the car payments, Jeanette's

ballet lessons, piano lessons and summer camp. But the taxes and maintenance on Stoneshadow Farm were beginning to break me.

Stoneshadow Farm is a beautiful white elephant of a place out in Luray, Virginia, about an hour and a half from D.C. There's a hundred acres of mostly unused land, a big old house whose central section dates back to the 1780s, an immense barn and several smaller outbuildings—springhouse, smokehouse, henhouse and so on. There's a muddy pond that exists as a kind of an overpopulated frog slum, and a sinkhole beside the barn that serves, according to local legend, as a gateway to the infernal regions. What the sinkhole really is, of course, is a back entrance to Luray Caverns. There's a lot more to those caverns than the paved and lighted chambers shown to hordes of tourists each year. The subterranean passageways extend for miles, and there's plenty of them that have never been mapped.

As for the hole beside the barn, it's devilishly attractive and more than a bit of a menace. Attraction notwithstanding, my own explorations therein ceased when I was around seven years old—Jeanette's present age. Naturally my parents had forbidden me to go down there by myself, and naturally I ignored their orders. Who could resist the lure of a place like that? One sunny day I sneaked down the hole, armed with a flashlight and a piece of chalk with which, as a gung-ho Brownie, I meant to mark my trail. I found myself wandering a wonderful maze of tunnels. Excitement! Adventure! Bliss! My delight died shortly thereafter when the flashlight went out and I found myself alone in total darkness. For a little while I stumbled around, blindly and vainly seeking an exit. I ended up bruised and confused. Then somehow I recalled my Girl Scout lore—remembered I'd marked my trail well with chalk, and realized that my best hope of rescue lay in remaining where I was. So I sat and waited in all that dank, chilly blackness. For hours. I'll never forget it to this day, and it still gives me a queasy feeling to think about it. But what was most peculiar about it all were the smells and noises that I remember noticing after I'd been there for—oh, I don't know, something approaching blind eternity. Perhaps I was hallucinating. I was a sightless and terrified little girl, and maybe fear acted on my imagination. In any event, after a time down there I began to notice a faint, peculiar odor. I recognized it years later in a college chemistry lab as a sulfur compound. Time passed and the odor grew stronger. Presently I began to think that I heard music—strange music—and moaning voices that didn't seem quite human. It didn't mean rescue, somehow I *knew* it didn't, and I froze into motionless, near-breathless silence, while the music grew louder and nearer and nearer. And then I thought I heard them wailing my name, and I wanted to run to them, but couldn't stir. So I remained in a state of hysterical paralysis until I heard my father's voice calling and saw the gleam of his lantern. Then I screamed my head off. It was only another couple of minutes before Dad reached me and carried me out of that place. I was in such a state of terror that he and Mom took pity, and I escaped punishment for disobedience. I didn't tell them or anyone else about the voices, for fear of being called a liar, a dreamer or both. And after a couple of hours in the sunlight, I began to suspect that I had indeed imagined some of it, particularly that music. I gave my solemn oath that I would keep away from the sinkhole, and it was a promise that I definitely intended to keep. Nevertheless, in order to forestall future misadventures, my parents got hold of an iron grating so heavy that it took the two of them to lift it, and laid it across the mouth of the hole—which should have solved the problem once and for all.

Except that the grating wouldn't stay put. Every couple of months or so, the thing was displaced and Dad would discover it lying in the mud, yards away from the hole. How it was moved, no one knew, and the mystery was never solved.

As recently as thirty-five years ago, Stoneshadow Farm was still a working farm—although never a particularly good one. The soil that appeared dark and rich never produced good crops, and the addition of assorted fertilizers did little to improve matters. The livestock survived, but never throve. The farm was able to sustain itself, but mysteriously failed to prosper. When Dad inherited the property, he wasn't minded to deal with the vagaries of neurotic cows and chickens. He worked for a D.C. law firm, and Stoneshadow Farm was used as a weekend retreat. When he and Mom retired to Florida eight years ago, they deeded the land to me—as a wedding gift, ironically enough. I say "ironically" because Ben never had any use at all for country living, and my love of the farm was yet another source of friction between the two of us. He was forever after me to sell it, and forever infuriated by my refusal. Did I not understand that the place was a financial liability? he'd reason with gritted teeth. Whipping out his calculator like a gunslinger pulling a Colt .45, he'd show me endless columns of figures on endless balance sheets. *Did I not UNDER-*

STAND? Oh, I understood well enough, but I didn't care. Stoneshadow Farm has been in my family since the eighteenth century. It's more of a real home than any twenty-year-old jerry-built condo in Alexandria could ever be, and I'm damned if I'll let it go.

But the bills this year have been crushing. The house and barn both needed new roofing. Most of the old wiring had to be replaced. There was some replastering, replacement of leaky pipes and fumigation of the farrowing house when termites were discovered there. Everything seemed to go wrong at once, and it couldn't have happened at a worse time. I wondered how I'd deal with it all. And while I was wondering, I decided to treat myself to a second glass of wine. Since Harriet Cohen was looking after Jeanette, I could afford the time and God knows I could use the consolation. I looked up to signal to one of those annoyingly pretty waitresses in which The Quorum specializes. It was then I became aware of the man watching me. He was leaning against the bar, and he brightened when he saw I'd noticed him.

There's nothing particularly unusual about that. Itinerant executives and conventioneers booked in at Loewe's L'Enfant Plaza Hotel frequently wander into The Quorum, and if I'm sitting alone they'll often try to strike up a conversation. I don't look much like a hooker. My briefcase and grey wool suit ought to signal low whoopee potential, but I suppose hope springs eternal in the male breast. I've perfected an expression of icy vacancy that usually stops them cold at twenty paces, and I used it now. Lifting my chin and allowing my lids to droop a little, I gazed off into infinity.

It didn't work. The stranger came straight to my table, paused and inquired in a limp, boneless sort of voice, "Meestress Gruber-Hadley?"

"Miss Hadley," I corrected. I don't use The Weasel's name anymore.

"The fair Lady of Stoneshadow Farm?"

I nodded, puzzled. He knew my name and he knew about the farm. He certainly wasn't a conventioneer. A colleague at HUD? Possible, but I didn't recall ever having seen him there. And if I'd ever seen this one, there's no way I'd have forgotten. He looked like Peter Lorre playing a child-molester. There was the same short, lumpish, pudgy form; the same soft lips of an infant in the face of an amphibian; and the same vast, goggling, unearthly eyes. And that accent! What was it

—Albanian? Turkish? Lebanese? I couldn't place it and I certainly couldn't place *him.*

"Ah. Ah." He cackled. "But thees ees delightful, most delightful. I have long awaited the pleasure." The stranger smiled, squirmed and fidgeted. The spectacle was downright riveting. "So charming! Leetle deed I dream. May we join?"

"I beg your pardon?"

"I sit. We talk. Yes?"

"Well, actually, I—"

"Thank you. You are most kind." He slid in beside me on the banquette. I caught a whiff of sulfurous after-shave. "Delightful! Meestress Hadley, I have proposition for you."

"Oh?" If he said what I was afraid he was going to say, then he was about to receive the remains of my nameless burgundy down the front of his white shirt.

"But first I eentroduce, for we shall do thees theeng friendly. That ees best, yes? Ah. Ah. I am—" It sounded as if he said something like "Goodman Eexenahfurulius," but I may have heard wrong. "You call me Goodman Eex."

"Do you work at HUD, Mr. Eex? Is that how you know me?"

"HUD? Delightful. Ah. Ah." The cackle soared to a high-pitched giggle that caught the attention of a couple of customers at the next table. They stared briefly. I knew I ought to chase this incredibly weird little creep away, but I couldn't bring myself to do it. He was so bizarre, I had to hear more. In any case, I had nothing to fear from him. If we'd both been standing, he'd have come about up to my chin. "No, Meestress Hadley," Mr. Eex continued, "I know of you seence long time, for I am your neighbor een Luray, Virgeenia! I own property—ah, ah—adjacent to your own."

"Do you?" He wasn't your classic Virginia country gentleman, but then, times they are a-changin'. "Are you the one who bought up the Delacroix land five years ago?"

"I have been there longer—longer!" He giggled again. "And now we meet at last, as good neighbors should, for I theenk we have need of one another. Yes?"

My answering smile was politely skeptical. I took a sip of wine and maintained silence.

"But Meestress Hadley must be all aflame with curiosity, so Goodman Eex explains. Ees simple. I am lord—proprietor, as you say—of what you call storage facility. Like beeg warehouse for—ah, ah—goods awaiting transfer to—other place. Here, there, deeferent places we store them, including Luray."

"Warehouses in Luray?" I'd never heard of any such thing.

"Aye, 'tees so. Not what you theenk a warehouse look like, but storage all the same. But now what happens? Warehouse full. No room left. Nowhere to relocate. Transfer of goods delayed. Delayed. Delayed again. Much confusion and deesmay, strife and grief. So what does Goodman Eex do?"

"Expand?" I suggested.

"So. He expand. And that ees why he comes to fair and so clever Meestress Hadley of Stoneshadow Farm, for permeession to use her land. The caverns below her land he bespeaks. Perchance the barn, if need arises. For thees favor, she ees reechly rewarded."

It sounded fishier than words can express. What was this little freak into? Drugs? Bulk storage of stolen merchandise? Whatever it was, I planned to stay out of it. "I'm sorry, Mr. Eex, but I have no intention of leasing any portion of my property at present."

"Ah. Ah. 'Tees a wise woman who places not her trust in strangers, although they be her good neighbors. I see. I see. She doubts. She fears. 'Tees meet that eet be so. But Goodman Eex weell set her teemorous heart to rest. Be at ease, Meestress. Here be no wrong-dealing. I deal not een stolen property, nor yet een matters forbidden. All ees honorable, moral, ethical and highly proper, as ordained to be seence forever. All thees I do swear to you."

He could swear till he was blue in the face and it wouldn't make a dent in me. I must admit, he looked almost tearfully sincere. Nonthe-less, it seemed risky. "The arrangement you suggest wouldn't really be convenient—"

"But yes! Yes! Most convenient, always convenient! Thees too do I swear." He sounded a little desperate. "You shall see! Quiet, no bother, no revels in the night! And reech reward! For first seex month —behold!" He reached into his breast pocket and withdrew a cashier's check.

A refusal expired upon my lips as I caught sight of the figure on that check. It was about ten times the amount I'd expected. There was the new roof for the farmhouse, rewiring and Jeanette's summer camp all paid for at one stroke.

"Ah. Ah." My silence appeared to gratify Mr. Eex no end. "Thees ees delightful. Now you sign contract, yes?"

"Contract? My attorney will—"

"No need! No need! We are neighbors, yes? We are friendly over thees. Here ees contract." The same pocket that produced the check now yielded a contract in duplicate, which he presented with a flourish.

It was a curious document, hand-lettered in reddish-brown on what appeared to be parchment. I read it carefully, while Mr. Eex peered over my shoulder with his praying mantis eyes. The contract was concise, clearly written and no doubt legal. I had no trouble at all in understanding it, particularly the paragraph specifying that princely rental payment, but there were a couple of clauses I didn't like. Removing a black Flair from my purse, I struck out the offending lines and printed in my revisions on both copies.

"What do you do? What do you do?" cried my mystery man.

"As it stands, this contract grants you rental rights in perpetuity."

"That ees the way eet must be."

"Sorry, that's entirely unacceptable. I'll give you six months on a trial basis, at the end of which we can renegotiate, provided the arrangement proves satisfactory."

"But no! No! Thees not right, thees not good!"

"That's my only offer. Take it or leave it."

It seemed to be a seller's market. Mr. Eex fidgeted violently. Sweat started out on his brow. He looked so uncomfortable, I almost felt sorry for him. Almost. At last he nodded. "Eef you weell have eet so."

"Good. And one more thing. By the terms of this contract, I forfeit all right of entry to the leased premises. That clause goes. As landlord, I insist upon access to my own property."

"No! You must believe, my dear lady, thees ees for your own protection—"

"Protection? From what? You're not intending to use my land for chemical dumping, are you?"

"No!"

"Radioactive waste?"

"No!"

"Are you planning to store explosives? You're working for the Libyans, aren't you? This deal is off."

"No! No! No! Very well, I agree to your condeetions! Unleemeeted access! Any time you like!"

"Well, then." My eyes jumped to the check that lay on the table before me. I scrawled my name across both copies of the contract. Mr. Eex did likewise. "Initial those changes, would you?" He complied with poor grace. "Thanks. And one more thing."

"More? There ees more?"

"Nothing much. I'd just like your phone number, please, in case I need to get in touch."

"Telephone number? Ah. Ah. Telephone? Delightful." He giggled shrilly, his good humor restored, and scribbled a nine-digit number on a cocktail napkin. "You call there."

"Odd, I don't recognize the exchange."

"Ah. Ah. But thees conclude our business, Meestress Hadley, and I must leave you now. I begeen transferring my goods forthweeth. I trust our association weel prove mutually rewardeeng, and I look forward to eets eternal prolongation. And so, adieu." So saying, Mr. Eex pocketed his copy of the contract, rose from the banquette, bowed deeply and scuttled out of The Quorum. I remained for that second glass of wine whose function, in view of my windfall, had switched from consolatory to self-congratulatory. I remember being somewhat stunned by the extraordinary brevity of the transaction.

My meeting with Mr. Eex took place on a Monday evening in February. During the remainder of the work week, concerns at the office and at home nearly wiped the incident from my mind. I was busy and preoccupied. Only once did I stop to consider the whole affair with the attention and curiosity that it actually deserved—when I was standing in line at the credit union, waiting to deposit that hefty cashier's check.

The week passed quickly. It's almost frightening how quickly they go. And then it was blessed Friday afternoon. I took a couple of hours of annual leave, as I often do on Friday to beat the rush hour traffic, and soon I was zipping over the Potomac, past the Jefferson Memorial, past the Pentagon and south on Shirley Highway toward Alexandria. The suitcases were already in the trunk. I didn't even need to stop off at the condo. I could drive straight to the school, pick up Jeanette and take off for Luray.

Jeanette was ready, willing and eager to go. She's a lovely child—bright, affectionate, with her father's even-featured blonde good looks and a sweet nature inherited from neither parent. She loves the farm almost as much as I do, and is more than delighted to spend her weekends there. Someday, probably soon, that's bound to change—she'll want to stay in town for parties and excursions with her friends—and when that happens, I'll have to take her feelings into account. But the problem hasn't arisen yet, and that afternoon, as we drove through the Virginia countryside together, my daughter was bubbling over with high spirits. I was feeling pretty good myself, with a weekend at the farm to look forward to, and for the first time in months—no money problems. I was therefore able to relax, enjoy my daughter's conversation and appreciate the scenery. It *is* beautiful out there, even in February. It's a fairly mild climate, and most of the time there's little snow on the ground, even in the dead of winter. The ground was completely clear that day, but still sodden. It had rained earlier, and drops of water hung by the million on the cross-hatching of bare charcoal branches that darkened the roadside. Mist lay thin on the hilltops and thick in the hollows, and colors were uniformly greyed. The mysterious veiling of the world's outlines reinforced the illusion I sometimes experience in that place of traveling back in time to another century.

We made a brief stop at the market to pick up supplies for the weekend, then drove the last five miles to Stoneshadow Farm. The days were getting longer—it was still light as we turned down the private dirt lane, navigated the curves and dips and crested the last hill to pull in near the old stone house. The place was silent and tranquil, as always. But somehow, as I switched off the ignition, the image of Mr. Eex's face popped into my mind and stayed there. Had he begun transferring his goods yet? Were the caverns beneath my land filling up with—whatever? Had I made a mistake in letting this soi-disant good neighbor onto my property, into my life and, more importantly, into my daughter's life? *Never mind,* I thought. *If there's trouble, I can handle it.*

Jeanette had her heart set on checking out the frog pond. I let her go, carried the groceries into the house, turned up the heat, went out and got the suitcases, then sat down with a book to relax for a few minutes before starting dinner.

I couldn't keep my mind on the book. I kept thinking of Mr. Eex.

Curiosity and uncertainty were getting the better of me. At last I stood up—I was still wearing my coat, since the house hadn't warmed up yet—ran outside and down to the barn. It was getting dark. The huge bulk of the old building loomed up in silhouette, stark black against a leaden sky and curiously ominous. Instinct drew me around to the west side, where the sinkhole lay. The first thing I saw was that the plug had been dislodged.

My parents never had any luck with that iron grating. Around the time that Jeanette was getting big enough to run around I'd had a concrete plug poured, and it had held for nearly five years. But now the sinkhole was open, and my first reaction was angry. It was Mr. Eex's doing, obviously. How dared he? Then reason came to the fore and I was forced to concede that my neighbor had his rights, which included easy access to the property he'd rented. Nevertheless, I was uncomfortable. I'd have to erect a chicken wire fence to keep Jeanette out of there. And in the meantime—

In the meantime I stood in the gathering darkness, my eyes fixed upon the sinkhole. I thought of my own sortie therein so many years ago, and remembered the odor and sounds I'd imagined back then. And it seemed that I could smell and hear them again. I inhaled deeply and breathed the scent of sulfur. It was *not* imagination. I listened. Stoneshadow Farm was extraordinarily silent in the dark February twilight. No noise from the road, of course; there never is. No insects at that time of year. No birdcalls. No sound from the neighbors—the nearest were a mile away. And in the midst of that profound silence, I caught the sound of voices, faint as the calling of ghosts, and dissonant music remembered from long ago. My hands clenched. I took a step nearer the hole and stooped to listen. I could hear it more clearly now—those lost, demented voices. I placed my hand on the ground at the edge of the hole and discovered that the soil there was warm. That did it. I'm not easily alarmed, but there are limits. Jumping to my feet, I ran for the house.

When I got there, I found that Jeanette had already come in. She'd tracked mud from the pond all over the kitchen floor, and ordinarilly I'd have objected, but that evening it just seemed wonderfully normal. "Listen, Blue Eyes," I told her. "I think you'd better keep away from the sinkhole this weekend."

She fixed me with that wide-eyed gaze that's earned her her nickname. "Why, Mummy?"

"You remember I told you about my agreement with our neighbor Mr. Eex? Well, I think he's busy down in that hole, and we'd better leave him alone. Let's just not bother him, O.K.?"

She nodded solemnly. "O.K. That sounds polite."

That was Friday evening. It took no time at all for things to get worse. Saturday passed uneventfully enough. There were no disturbances during the daylight hours—I was busy refinishing an old oak dresser, and Jeanette was busy harassing the squirrels—but I had a suspicion that it might change when darkness fell. Unfortunately, I was right.

All evening long, I tried to behave normally. I played Go Fish with Jeanette, parked in front of the television with her for a while and did my best to conceal my nervousness. I don't think she noticed anything. When her bedtime rolled around at nine o'clock, the incredibly sweet child retired without argument. I tucked her in, kissed her goodnight, left her room, grabbed a coat and flashlight and headed for the barn.

I was trying to move stealthily, but I might as well have spared myself the trouble. *They* made no effort at concealment. The moment I stepped outside, I could hear them—the crazed babble of human voices carried clearly on the night breeze. Crazed—that was certainly the word. I heard shrieks that expressed less of pain or fear than of pure lunacy—animal wailings of creatures with human lungs but no human reason. It was faint and far away as yet, but entirely audible; and underscoring it all was that relentless, urgent, dissonant music.

Flashlight in hand, I edged around the corner of the barn and stopped dead. The flashlight was quite unnecessary, for the sinkhole itself provided illumination. The hole was glowing—yes, glowing with a murky reddish light, like the cyclops' eye of a Hallowe'en jack-o'-lantern. By that light I could see the tendrils of heavy mist rising from the pit. The atmosphere was vile with the stench of sulfur. The voices and music were much louder here. For a moment I stood staring, then forced myself to approach. As I drew near, a furnace blast of heat hit me, and once again I paused. According to the terms of my contract, I had the right to enter that sinkhole any time, but was hesitant to exercise the privilege. Understandable, surely?

I confess I retreated. In fact, I threw dignity to the winds and raced for the house. Once inside I bolted the door, poured myself a stiff

Scotch and considered my alternatives. The Scotch helped restore my courage. Indignation helped too. This situation was clearly outrageous. The more I thought about it, the madder I got. Mr. Eex was going to learn—and soon—that he couldn't get away with this kind of thing. I would telephone him tomorrow, Sunday notwithstanding. He'd asked for it. And if he refused to cooperate? I'd signed a contract, after all. Well, I'd find a way to deal with him. "I can handle it," I said aloud.

My bitter ruminations were interrupted by the sound of Jeanette's voice calling me, and I went up to her bedroom at once. "What's wrong, Blue Eyes?"

"Nothing, Mummy. I was just wondering. Who's Mr. Eex got down in that hole?"

"You've heard them?"

"Yes. Who *are* they?"

"I don't know."

"I want to meet them."

This was starting to alarm me. "No, Jeanette. Don't even think it."

"Why?"

"Ummmmm—we haven't been invited, that's why."

"Wouldn't we be being good neighbors? What about last year when Mr. and Mrs. Stewart moved in and we brought them a pie? We weren't invited then, either."

"That was different!"

"Why?"

"Mr. and Mrs. Stewart do not live in a hole in the ground!"

"Didn't you tell me that it's snobby to hold it against people if they don't own nice houses?"

"Jeanette, you're being deliberately perverse. You know as well as I do there's something sticky about that hole."

"Well yes," she confessed. "And I want to find out *what*, Mummy. I can't stop wondering. I just can't stop."

Things were looking blacker all the time. Mr. Eex was going to hear from me.

The next morning I waited until Jeanette was out roaming the fields before dialing the nine-digit number scribbled on the cocktail napkin from The Quorum. I heard a faint, far-off ringing. The connection was a poor one, and there was tremendous static along the line. When Mr.

Eex answered, his voice was thin and tinny, as if it traveled an infinite distance. "Hello? Yes? Yes? Hello?"

"Is that you, Mr. Eex?"

"Fair Meestress Hadley! But how very delightful!"

"You may change your mind about that when you hear what I have to say to you."

"Ah. Ah. Speak louder, Meestress Hadley. I do not hear you."

I raised my voice. "I am calling to express my extreme dissatisfaction, Mr. Eex."

"There ees problem?"

"Indeed there is. I don't know what you're up to, and I don't know what's going on down in those caves of mine. What I do know is that the noise and the stench are intolerable."

"Alas, alas!"

"Something must be done at once, or I'll be forced to cancel our arrangement."

"I do not hear you. Alas!"

"I'LL CANCEL! Did you hear me that time?"

"You sign contract, Meestress, and eet bind you."

"Really? Try telling that to the local police when they're called in to investigate those caverns."

"You do not do that! Thees most unwise. You do not do that!"

"I won't have to. The neighbors will do it for me, once they figure out where that stink is coming from."

Static. Buzzes. Beeps. Static.

"Are you there, Mr. Eex?"

"Aye. Very well. Goodman Eex feex steenk."

"And I expect you to do something about the noise, as well. I won't tolerate it."

"We deescuss later."

"I require your assurance—"

"Alas, I do not hear you. We deescuss later, yes? I shall look forward. And now farewell, Meestress. Eet has been delightful. Ah. Ah. Telephone." His tiny, tinny giggle sounded as if it traveled half the universe.

Click.

"Damn!" He wasn't going to get off that easily. I dialed the number again and heard it ring. No one answered. I redialed periodically during the next several hours, without success. Mr. Eex was absent or else playing dead. Finally I gave up on it. I fixed lunch, put another coat of polyurethane on the dresser, cleaned up and then it was time to load the car for the drive back to Alexandria. As Jeanette and I chugged down the lane, I glanced back briefly at the dear, familiar old farmhouse and was reassured. Nothing had really been damaged. Certainly I had laid down the law to Mr. Eex, and if he valued his peace of mind, he'd comply with my demands. By the time I next returned, Stoneshadow Farm would be restored to normalcy. Of this I had little doubt.

As it happened, I didn't go back for weeks. Business and social obligations kept me in town for several Saturdays in a row, and the next time my daughter and I set eyes on Stoneshadow Farm, over a month had elapsed since our last visit. There was consolation for the delay, however—this time, our visit was to be an extended one. It was the end of March. Jeanette was on Easter vacation from school, I'd taken annual leave from work and we now had ten whole days to enjoy the country.

It started out normally enough. The sun was shining the afternoon we arrived. Green things were poking their heads out of the earth on all sides and the trees were loaded with buds. The breeze was damp and raw, but perceptibly vernal. It carried not the slightest hint of sulfur. All seemed bucolically tranquil. There was no hint at all of the outrages that lay in store.

The uproar began around nightfall. Jeanette and I were at the kitchen table finishing the last of the spaghetti when the music started up. We stared at each other. No mistaking that horrendous racket—that droning, desperate, hellish cacophony. Along with the music came the voices, the yammering, lunatic voices, clearly audible inside the house. Audible *inside* the house, with the doors and windows firmly shut. Mr. Eex was at it again, and things were worse than ever.

"That does it. *That just does it!*" Rising, I threw my napkin down like a gauntlet. "I told him! He's crazy if he thinks I'll sit still for this!"

"What are you going to do, Mummy?"

"I'm going out there and I'm going to put a stop to that noise."

My daughter appeared pleasantly excited. "Give 'em hell, Mummy!"

"Jeanette, watch your mouth!"

"May I come? *Please?!*"

"Get your coat."

The moment we stepped outdoors, the noise got louder—unbearably loud. If we'd had any neighbors nearby, there would have been complaints. As it was, Mr. Eex had little to fear on that score. However, he had plenty to fear from *me.* Hand in hand, Jeanette and I hurried down to the barn. The moment we got around to the west side, I was sorry I'd let her come. We stopped to gape.

The sinkhole had enlarged during my absence. It now yawned wide, easily ten feet in diameter. The aperture shone crimson, and its sanguinary glow illumined much of the surrounding barnyard. Wisps of thick yellowish mist waved about the opening like the tentacles of some huge anemone. Shrieks, groans, howls of mirth and madness tore their way out of the pit. The ground in the vicinity was so hot I could feel it through the soles of my shoes.

Jeanette's hand tightened in mine. "Mummy, are we going *in* there?"

"No."

"I'm not afraid. I'll go in."

"No you won't, kid."

"What'll we do, then?"

"We—or rather, I—will call Mr. Eex and tell him to do something about this fast. Or else."

"Or else what?" Jeanette inquired.

Good question.

"Don't worry, I'll think of something. I can handle it." We went back inside, and I jumped on the phone. I dialed Mr. Eex's number and listened to it ring, apparently a zillion miles away. Six rings—no answer. Twelve. Eighteen. No answer. I slammed the receiver down with a curse.

"Now what, Mummy?"

"I'll have to try again in a while. Don't worry, Blue Eyes—I'll get him. Wouldn't you like to go watch some television?"

She went obligingly enough, but television couldn't hold her attention. Every time I walked into the parlor I found her glued to the window, peering out through the darkness in the direction of the barn. It was hardly any wonder. The music, screams and hilarity from the sinkhole were increasingly objectionable and impossible to ignore. Finally I sent her to bed, with a pair of makeshift earplugs to block out the noise. As soon as she was gone, I flew to the phone.

I didn't succeed in reaching Mr. Eex with that call. Nor with the next. Nor the one after that. I phoned at half hour intervals throughout the night. Finally, at about three-thirty in the morning, I got through.

"Hello? Yes? Yes? Hello?"

"Eex, this is Liz Hadley. I've been trying to reach you all night. I'm calling to complain again about the noise in those caverns you've rented. I won't put up with this kind of thing. I want that racket stopped, or trust me, there'll be hell to pay."

"Ah. Ah. Goodman Eex feex steenk. Yes?"

"Yes, but that's not enough."

"Hello? Hello? I cannot hear you. Hello?"

How I was beginning to loathe that hypocritical little voice of his! "Oh, come off it. You hear me just fine. Now what are you going to do about it?"

"There ees deesturbance?"

"Yes, there's disturbance! It's enough to wake the dead, and it's been going on all night! I want it stopped!"

Static. Beep. Whoosh. Static. Maybe he really *couldn't* hear me.

"Remember the terms of our agreement, Eex? Remember your promises? 'Quiet, no bother, no revels in the night.' Your exact words."

"Thees not een our contract."

"We have a verbal contract as well as a written one. You made a promise, you swore to it and you are going to keep your word. Otherwise, I evict you and sue for damages."

"Sue? You sue me? Een court? Thees not friendly. No, you do not do thees."

"Try me."

Silence. Static. Silence.

"Eex, are you still there?"

"Aye. And Goodman Eex desolate to deescover noise deesturbeeng tranqueelity of fair Meestress Hadley. Meester Eex make amends. Thees he promise."

"Good. When?"

"Soon, dear lady. As soon as may be. You geeve Goodman Eex a day or two, and all ees well. Yes? Yes."

Click.

The receiver was dead in my hand. I considered calling him back, but gave it up. The two-faced little fruit probably wouldn't answer. Besides, I had extracted a promise, of sorts. Best to give him the time he'd asked for and hope he'd prove trustworthy, for once.

What a vain hope! Need I mention that Mr. Eex wasn't quite as good as his word? I gave him his two days. As a matter of fact, I gave him three. Eex didn't appear, and the situation degenerated. The noise —that dreadful noise—got louder, and soon we could hear it during the daylight hours. The dingy ochre haze remained anchored above the glowing pit beside the barn. And the band of hot, blackened, lifeless earth that surrounded the aperture widened day by day. All this was hard to bear, but worse lay in store. Monday night witnessed a new and ominous development.

We'd finished dinner hours earlier, and I'd only just gotten around to washing the dishes. Jeanette was in bed, again with the earplugs. All day long we'd endured a nerve-jangling aural assault. The din never stopped now. The unwholesome mists exuding from the sinkhole were starting to spread—the cloud now sprawled over half the barnyard—and Mr. Eex remained absent. I was in a vile mood. That mood did not improve as I glanced out the kitchen window to behold the barn glowing with weird red light. That is, light flickered from the windows and the chinks between the boards. There were voices there, and music. Evidently my tenant had chosen to expand his operations, without permission. He'd gone too far, way too far.

"I don't have to take this kind of garbage from anyone," I snarled and strode from the kitchen, girded for battle. But I didn't get far. The soil was warm beneath my feet, I noticed the moment I stepped out of the house. And I wasn't halfway to the barn before a rush of ferocious heat stopped me in my tracks. There was no way I could go in there. There was no way I could get anywhere near it. Even where I stood, the fierce dry heat clawed at my face and eyes. It was amazing that the old barn didn't burst into flame.

The red glow waxed and waned. By that uncertain light I could see dim figures inside the barn—insubstantial human shapes that whirled and writhed, capered and cavorted in a frenzied, joyless bacchanal. I don't know how many were in there. The horrid music drove them, drove them without rest.

"Since when did I grant you the right to sublet?" I addressed my absent tenant. "We'll see about this. We'll just see about it."

Whirling, I stamped back inside the house, slammed the door and snatched up the phone. I let it ring thirty times, but Mr. Eex did not answer. A slight sound behind me caused me to turn. Jeanette stood there, looking a little dazed.

"What are you doing out of bed, Blue Eyes? Aren't you feeling well?"

"I can't sleep. Mummy, who's out in the barn?"

"Friends of Mr. Eex's. And I don't plan to let them stay there."

"How do they know my name?"

"What?"

"I can hear them calling my name."

"No, darling. You must have been asleep and dreaming."

"No I *wasn't*, Mummy! I heard them. May I go say hello tomorrow?"

"No!" She gazed at me wide-eyed. "Listen, I think a glass of warm milk might help you sleep. And there'll be cookies to go with it. Would you like that?"

"Sure."

"And Jeanette—I want you to stay away from that barn. You promise?" She nodded dutifully, but I was not reassured. Jeanette is ordinarily a very truthful child, but now she had a faraway look that made me nervous. "Don't worry. I'll settle Mr. Eex's hash, and then things will be back to normal. I can handle it."

Jeanette's expression was uncharacteristically inscrutable. I gave her the cookies and milk, took her back to her bedroom and sat with her until she fell asleep. Then I raced downstairs to attack the phone. I got no answer on my first try, nor on my second or third. So I made myself a pot of coffee and settled in for a long siege. I was determined to get Mr. Eex if it took the rest of the night.

But it took longer than that. By the time I'd placed my twentieth unsuccessful call, dawn was breaking and so was I. Either Mr. Eex's willpower was superior to mine, or else he just wasn't there. I wasn't about to give up, but I needed some rest. I took to my bed, and despite the hellish uproar going on outside, fell asleep at once and slept until noon.

When I arose, I resumed my efforts. This time I dialed and got a busy signal. The signal was repeated a dozen times throughout the ensuing hours. Mr. Eex had obviously taken his phone off the hook. The diabolical little nerd!

That evening, they took over the smokehouse.

Late Wednesday afternoon, they moved into the henhouse.

I had spent a day or so sunk in a kind of fatalistic stupor, but now I rallied and tried once again to contact my tenant. I dialed, heard a click at the other end that filled me with hope; an empty pause, an electronic crackle and then a familiar voice.

"Hello? Thees a recordeeng. Goodman Eex not here now."

Mr. Eex had discovered technology.

"Eex, quit faking! I know you can hear me!"

"At sound of beep, you leave message, yes? Yes."

"I know you're there, Eex!" My voice had risen to a shout. "I know—"

Beeeeep.

"Eex, you know who this is. You can't hide forever. You may as well call me and get it over with."

A hiss, and the line went dead. Then I heard the dial tone again. Would he call? He had to talk to me sometime—didn't he?

As of Thursday night, red light glared from the springhouse and farrowing house. Wild, hopeless, translucent faces could be glimpsed at the windows. Wraithlike hands beat at the panes. A yellow haze shrouded all the outbuildings, and the entire barnyard was scorched and dead.

Mr. Eex did not return my call.

The temperature was up in the high nineties. The old stone house had no air-conditioning, ordinarily needed none. But now the vicious heat rising from the dead earth baked Jeanette and me like a couple of loaves in a stone oven. I dug some summer clothes out of the old maple chest, and the two of us ran around in March wearing shorts and halter tops. At least, I ran around. Jeanette wasn't very active. She'd lost interest in the television, her music, toys and even the frog pond. Which last was a good thing, because the frogs were dying by the hundreds, awakened from hibernation, then killed by the heat— practically boiled alive, poor little things. I tried to remove and dispose of the corpses when my daughter wasn't watching, but such discretion was quite superfluous. Jeanette just didn't care. From Thursday on, she spent most of her time sitting in the parlor staring out the window at the barn. She stayed like that for hours at a time.

Once when I came in to ask her if she'd like to play Chinese checkers, she told me to be quiet—an astonishing impertinence on the part of a normally polite child. I decided not to let her get away with it.

"Don't you talk to me that way, young lady, or you're going to find yourself in very serious trouble. I expect an apology."

She swiveled around to stare at me, astonished by my sharpness. It was the first time in hours her attention had been diverted from the barn. "I'm sorry, Mummy. I didn't mean to be rude. It's just that when you talk, I can't hear what they're saying."

"Are you talking about that caterwauling going on out there? They're not saying anything, Jeanette. It's senseless noise."

"Oh no. That's not true. They're talking."

"About what?"

"Oh—everything. *You* know. I can hear them, but I want to see them too."

"Jeanette, you keep *away* from those buildings. You understand?"

She shrugged and turned back to the window.

So why didn't I take her away from Stoneshadow Farm then and there? Obstinacy, for the most part. Rage, indignation and a determination not to let myself be run off my own land. Particularly not by a toad like Mr. Eex. If I must lose, let it be at least to someone I respect!

But I seemed to be fighting an increasingly uphill battle. On Saturday evening, the temperature in the house climbed to a hundred degrees. The vaporous air burned in our lungs. Our eyes stung and watered. I knew then that I'd have to retreat, else risk real damage to my daughter's health. I told Jeanette to go pack her clothes, and she obeyed with obvious reluctance. Her feet dragged as she left the parlor, and her eyes remained fixed on the window until the door closed behind her.

As soon as she was gone, I jumped on the phone for one last effort to reach Mr. Eex. I dialed, heard the distant ringing, heard the click as the receiver was lifted.

"Mr. Eex—"

And the telephone died. I don't mean that he hung up on me, although he may well have. An electronic squeal of anguish shrilled in my ear as the machine expired. There was no sound of voices along the line. No dial tone. No static. Nothing. I cursed, and as I stood there spluttering expletives, the electricity went off. Power failures sometimes occur during summer thunderstorms, but they're rare in

March. Now the lights blinked out. I stood alone in stifling darkness, still clutching the useless phone. My ears were filled with the discordant hum of inhuman voices. From the parlor I could see out to the barn, where the red light bled from the windows and the ghostly hands beat at the panes. The curses died on my lips. Somehow they seemed inadequate.

Fortunately, Stoneshadow Farm is equipped for emergencies. There are plenty of candles and matches around, flashlights and at least half a dozen kerosene lanterns in the house. I lit one of the candelabra, picked it up and went in search of Jeanette. My daughter was familiar enough with blackouts both in Luray and in Alexandria, but I suspected she'd feel safer if I were with her. As I mounted the stairs, I called her name. There was no reply.

Her bedroom door was closed. I rapped, got no answer and went in. The room was empty. Her clothes still hung in the wardrobe—she hadn't even begun to pack. Suppressing my annoyance, I went and looked in the bathroom. She wasn't there either. I searched the entire second floor, and there are a lot of rooms up there to look through. I found nothing. Periodically I called, and was answered only by demented howls and music from the barn, or possibly the henhouse. My irritation turned to worry, then to out-and-out fear.

Still armed with the candelabrum, I rushed downstairs to check the parlor—the hallway—the dining room—the sun-room—the kitchen—the pantry— All were dark, all empty. No sign of Jeanette. A subterranean scuffling caught my ear. I ran to the cellar door. The moment I opened it, a wave of superheated air rose to slap my face. I took an instinctive step backward, then poked my head through the doorway and called my daughter's name. No answer, but I thought I heard a faint murmuring down there, and it crossed my mind that she had fallen down the stairs in the dark and hurt herself. My heart started hammering. I clattered down the cellar stairs, and as I descended the temperature climbed. Before I was halfway to the bottom, I could see the flickering of red light.

The heat was infernal and the air almost unbreathable, but it didn't seem to bother Jeanette. There she sat, cross-legged on the floor, bathed in crimson light and apparently quite content. Four or five semitransparent, horrendous figures hovered about her, gibbering in her ear. My daughter, entirely at ease, gibbered right back at them.

It took a moment for this scene to register. Then a shriek of fear and fury escaped me and I hurled the candelabrum. It sailed straight over Jeanette's head and sent her companions floating in all directions. The candles died, but the alien red glow illuminated every corner of the cellar. I started for Jeanette, but the intruders, recovering quickly, drifted forward to block my path. They moved as gently and softly as dust settling, yet within the space of a heartbeat managed to cut me off from my child. They were all around me, more than I'd supposed at first, for I could see through them to Jeanette, and she too was surrounded. And I wanted so desperately to reach her, but my eyes swam, my legs went rubbery and the few feet that separated us stretched out like a hundred light-years. The monstrous figures *wouldn't* let me pass, no matter how I tried and when I beat at them it did no good—my fists passed right through their frigid insubstantiality. When they saw they had nothing to fear, they pressed in tight against me, chattering, gurgling, whispering, giggling in voices as shrill and maddening as locusts. And I felt their touch of fog upon me, and their voices went on and on. There was nowhere to turn—they were everywhere, and the voices were the voices I remembered from long ago. The music started up and that was familiar too, and all at once I was back again, back as a child in the sinkhole that serves, according to local legend, as a gateway to the infernal regions. And *they* who called to me that day had reached me at last after all these years, and now they were here and they were still calling. For I could hear them wailing my name, and whispering other things as well. Jeanette had been right, of course—they were speaking. It was intelligible to me now. The sounds of this world were receding, would soon be lost. I didn't care—the world meant nothing—all that mattered were these voices, which I dreaded and desired. I knew I could be with them, that I *would* be with them forever. It was happening *now,* and the inevitability of it paralyzed my mind and body, froze me into motionless, near-breathless silence, as the music grew louder and the voices more insistent, and I was filled at once with horror and inexpressible longing, as I had been as a child.

Only I was not a child. I was a grown woman with a daughter of my own, and through those clustering, gibbering, smothering forms I could still just barely see her, mouth squared, laughing hilariously—or was she crying? She extended her arms to her wraithlike companions —or was she reaching out to me? To this day I don't know, and it's really not important. Something suddenly gave way inside me. My limbs unfroze: I sprang for those open arms, passing straight through the surrounding phantoms. For one lost moment I was blind, deaf and icy cold in the midst of all that killing heat. The moment passed. My arms closed around Jeanette. I scooped her off the floor and ran up the cellar stairs as fast as I could go.

It was dark in the kitchen, but luckily I remembered where I'd left my purse, which contained the car keys. I found the bag, stumbled through the kitchen door and across the yard. The mist out there was fit for the Ripper's London, but the red glare from the barn and smaller outbuildings lighted the way to the Buick. Jeanette was silent and motionless, a dead weight in my arms. I wasn't altogether sure she was conscious.

We reached the car. I placed Jeanette in the front seat, circled around to the driver's side, got in, shut the door, turned the key in the ignition. Nothing happened. There wasn't a peep out of that motor, not the tiniest sign of life. The lights weren't working either. I had a full tank of gas and the battery was almost brand-new—that I was sure of, but the car was stone dead. I gave it a couple of tries, failed and sat there fuming. And while I sat, with the yellow haze nudging at the windshield, I saw the red light glow from the kitchen window of my farmhouse.

"Mummy?" A small voice beside me.

"Jeanette, how do you feel?"

"Fine."

"Do you think you can walk?"

"Sure." The question seemed to surprise her. "Walk where?"

"We're going to see Mr. and Mrs. Stewart." The Stewarts lived a mile away, but they were our closest neighbors.

Jeanette accepted this decree without comment.

It took an hour to walk the mile to the Stewarts' place. Ordinarily it's a fifteen-minute hop, but this time it was so dark and the mists were so thick and the noises coming out of the fog so distracting that I grew confused. Things got worse when we reached the creek and found that the bridge—heavily reinforced just this past autumn—had unaccountably collapsed. Worse yet when our feet sank in deep mud and we had to choose a new path. Worst of all when I thought I felt the touch of icy fingers upon my face—a shock that almost confounded my sense of direction. If I hadn't known the land so very well, we might never have found our way out that night. As it was, we advanced slowly and with difficulty. I judged we were approaching the boundaries of Stoneshadow Farm when the temperature started to drop. The ground was chill and dank as befitted the month of March. The air got colder and colder until Jeanette and I—both of us still clad in shorts and halters—were shivering miserably. The noise died away, the mists thinned, the moon appeared overhead and presently we hit the public roadway. A few hundred yards ahead, the Stewarts' porch lights shone like lucky stars. No power failure *here,* I noticed.

The elderly Stewarts are the best of good neighbors. They offered sympathy, hot soup, warm clothing and minimal inquisition. I told them that an emergency situation demanded my immediate return to Alexandria. My car had died and the phone was out of order. I don't know if they swallowed all that or not, but they certainly believed the bit about the phone. Mrs. Stewart remarked that she had called me a dozen times during the week, and never got anything but buzzes and whistling at my number. Mr. Stewart, bless him, volunteered to drive Jeanette and me all the way back to Alexandria, but I wasn't about to put him through that. I accepted a lift as far as the drugstore in Luray that serves as the local bus terminal. There was plenty of cash in the purse I still carried. I bought two tickets and we caught the next bus aimed at D.C.

Jeanette was unusually quiet during the long ride to Washington. She was tired, clearly bewildered and perhaps frightened. She spoke very little, but did frame one question. "Mummy, are we ever going back to the farm?"

"Oh yes, Blue Eyes. We're going back, all right," I promised grimly. "I absolutely guarantee we're going back."

"With them in the house?"

"Mummy's going to kick them out. Mummy is not about to be run off her property by freaks and creeps. Nobody messes with Mummy."

We got back to the condo in the middle of the night. Both of us were exhausted. We hit our respective beds and slept deeply until noon of the following day—Sunday, it was. Jeanette woke up bright-eyed, refreshed, in good spirits, with apparently no recollection of the incident in the cellar of Stoneshadow Farm. I was not nearly as cheerful as my daughter, and not as healthy, either. Rage—sheer teeth-grinding, rug-chewing rage—was tying my nerves into knots. I couldn't eat, read a book or write a letter. All I could do was pace the floor, back and forth for hours on end, while considering the various strategies whereby I might deal with the unspeakable Eex. I made my decision at last, but all that feverish concentration wore me out. Despite my emotional turmoil, I slept soundly that night.

I was back at HUD the next morning. You're not supposed to use the federal WATS line for personal calls, but this time I made an exception. If Mr. Eex refused to answer my call, then I'd go ahead with my plan of tracing his telephone number. Fortunately, such measures proved unnecessary. He answered on the first ring.

"Hello? Yes? Yes? Hello?"

"Mr. Eex, this is Liz Hadley." My voice was perfectly even and neutral. I'd rehearsed it a dozen times. "I want to talk to you face to face at five-thirty this afternoon in The Quorum. If you wish to avoid immediate termination of your tenancy at Stoneshadow Farm, you'll be there." I replaced the handset in its cradle. Such cavalier tactics, so impressive on the screen, are rarely effective in real life. Mr. Eex, however, struck me as a gentleman with whom firm measures were appropriate. The accuracy of my judgment was confirmed by his presence in the bar at the specified hour.

I saw him as soon as I walked in. He was scrunched up in the corner, looking furtive. As I joined him, the hunted expression was replaced by an effusive smile, the effect of which was somewhat spoiled by pointed canines that I hadn't noticed the first time around.

"Meestress Hadley—but how delightful. How very delight—"

"Mr. Eex, after having given the matter a great deal of thought, I've concluded that it may be possible to avoid prosecution—provided, of course, that I receive your full cooperation."

"Prosecution? Een court? Ah. Ah." The extraterrestrial eyes bugged out at me. "Dear lady, you astound me."

"That is probably true. You never expected to have to face me, did you? You never thought that Jeanette and I would get away from that farm."

"Thees unfair! Thees untrue! These words wound the heart of Goodman Eex, who means no harm to Meestress Hadley and her so charming daughter! All ees done friendly here!"

"Friendly? You call it friendly when those cockamamie spooks of yours break into my house and terrorize my child?"

"Ah? Ah?" He shrugged. "A small meesunderstandeeng. I speak to them."

"I expect you to do more than speak to them. I want them out of the house. Also out of the barn and all the other outbuildings, which will henceforth be regarded as off-limits. Your activities are to be confined to the caverns, as specified in our original contract. I want the sinkhole filled in and kept plugged."

"Alas, alas—thees not posseeble."

"It better be possible. And that's not all. I want an end to the noise and heat, or our agreement is off. I also want my telephone, my electrical system and my car restored to working order, and I want them to stay that way. Oh yes—and you'll repair the bridge—

"—We do nothing to breedge!"

"—And anything else you may have tampered with."

"Tampered? Tampered? Meestress, you wrong Goodman Eex—"

"You'll agree to these conditions and stick to them, or our agreement is terminated and I'll throw you off my land tomorrow."

"Lady get nasty, eh? She does not weesh to do thees friendly? Ah. Ah. Very foolish. Now we are no longer nice." His expression changed. The conciliatory smile vanished, and he looked like Peter Lorre about to commit an ax murder. "Now you leesten, Shrew-Lady. You sign contract. Not so easy to break contract weeth Goodman Eex. Many try, few succeed. You theenk you reep up contract, just like that? You try, and maybe you are surprised. Maybe your daughter surprised. A delightful child. Ah. Ah." He cackled.

"Maybe you'll be surprised too, Mr. Eex." I think my equanimity disappointed him. "Surprised when I call in the Page County Sheriff to examine the premises. And my lawyer. And the Landlord/Tenant Relations Office. Not to mention the Board of Health, the Better Business Bureau and the Immigration Service. I have a hunch that some of your associates might just qualify as illegal aliens. What do you think?"

"Your proof? Your proof? Hah! Thees weell not help you!"

"It won't help you much either. But that's just for starters. How would you like to face the media, Mr. Eex? The newspaper and magazine reporters, the radio and television coverage? I think the contents of that sinkhole might generate a lot of interest. Are you fond of publicity? If so, I can issue a blanket invitation to every psychic investigator, parapsychologist and ghost-groupie in the world. They'll descend on Stoneshadow Farm by the truckload. I'll tell them to bring asbestos suits. A week from now, they'll be breaking down the doors of that barn."

"They weell not be admeeted!"

"Sure they will. Our contract grants me unlimited access to the leased premises. Remember? I can bring in anyone I want. And I will."

"Goodman Eex scorn such rabble!"

"Does he? What about the Church, then? Have you ever undergone an exorcism, Mr. Eex? Have you ever been—how shall I put it—cast out?"

"I do not know what you mean!"

"I mean bell, book and candle. The works, Mr. Eex."

"Nay, you are a pagan, Meestress. Thees I know."

"I'll convert. If Paris is well worth a Mass, so's Stoneshadow Farm." Silence, while he glowered at me. "I've always admired the Jesuits," I added conversationally. "It's my opinion they will eat you alive and spit out the seeds."

"You do not do thees thing! You do not!"

"I'll do all of it and more. I mean business, Mr. Eex."

I stared at him steadily and watched him wilt beneath my gaze. At last he muttered reluctantly, "We talk. New deal."

I knew the little wimp would crack under pressure.

It didn't take much more argument to win Mr. Eex's consent. He accepted my terms, and he's kept his word. These days the house and all outbuildings at Stoneshadow Farm are clear of spectral trespassers. No red light glares from the windows in the night. The sinkhole beside the barn is firmly plugged, the air is clear and cool. Lights, appliances and car work perfectly. The bridge has been repaired. Silent tranquility reigns over all. True, the barnyard grass remains scorched and dead, but it will grow back. If I put my ear to the ground above the sinkhole, I can still hear the faintest moan of ghastly music, but that's all right—I'm willing to be reasonable.

Mr. Eex is reasonable too, and apparently bears no grudge. I encounter him from time to time in D.C. or Luray and he, all slimy amiability, extols the "renewed cordialeety" of our relationship.

Cordiality? That's what he thinks. He's about to learn differently.

I haven't brought Jeanette back to the farm yet, of course. I won't until I'm sure it's safe. But it won't be long now. Mr. Eex's six-month lease lapses in three weeks. He doesn't know it yet, but I don't plan to renew.

In Gottfried August Bürger's famous German poem "Lenore" (included in my earlier collection Masterpieces of Terror and the Supernatural), *a grief-stricken woman met a dreadful fate when she rode away with a phantom she took to be her longlost lover. A similar fate awaits the heroine of "The Demon Lover," but in her case, at least, it is her selfish streak that damns her.*

The Demon Lover
ANONYMOUS

"Oh, where have you been, my long, long love,
    This long seven years and more?"
"Oh, I've come to seek my former vows
    Ye granted me before."

"Oh, do not speak of your former vows,
    For they will breed sad strife;
Oh, do not speak of your former vows,
    For I have become a wife."

He turned him right and round about,
    And the tear blinded his ee:
"I would never have trodden on this ground
    If it had not been for thee."

"If I was to leave my husband dear,
    And my two babes also,
Oh, what have you to take me to,
    If with you I should go?"

"I have seven ships upon the sea—
    The eighth brought me to land—
With four-and-twenty bold mariners,
    And music on every hand."

She has taken up her two little babes,
    Kissed them on cheek and chin
"Oh, fare ye well, my own two babes,
    For I'll never see you again."

She set her foot upon the ship—
    No mariners could she behold;
But the sails were of the taffeta,
    And the masts of the beaten gold.

She had not sailed a league, a league,
    A league but barely three,
When dismal grew his countenance,
    And drumly grew his ee.

They had not sailed a league, a league,
    A league but barely three,
Until she espied his cloven foot,
    And she wept right bitterly.

"Oh, hold your tongue of your weeping," said he,
    "Of your weeping now let me be;
I will show you how the lilies grow
    On the banks of Italy."

"Oh, what hills are yon, yon pleasant hills,
    That the sun shines sweetly on?"
"Oh, yon are the hills of Heaven," he said,
    "Where you will never win."

"Oh, whaten a mountain is yon," she said,
    "So dreary with frost and snow?"
"Oh, yon is the mountain of Hell," he cried,
    "Where you and I will go."

He struck the top-mast with his hand,
    The fore-mast with his knee;
And he broke that gallant ship in twain,
    And sank her in the sea.

The hero of "The Imitation Demon" evidently believes in the old adage: "If you can't lick 'em, join 'em." Unfortunately, there is a nasty double meaning in that sentiment. This clever tale appeared in the last issue of the original run of Weird Tales *magazine. Researchers have been trying to uncover information on its author, but so far the only fact is a negative one:* ROBERT KUTTNER *is not related to Henry Kuttner, whose story, "The Graveyard Rats" appears elsewhere in this volume.*

The Imitation Demon

BY ROBERT KUTTNER

James Tibbets had no need for the services of a demon. He had everything an educated young man of good family could desire: a beautiful fiancee, a promising career in advertising, a fine game of tennis, some fame as an amateur yachtsman and a rich uncle. At the last count, however, he was short the rich uncle. Old Eric Tibbets yielded one morning to a tired heart and sought his rest in another sphere. James, as favorite nephew, received at once the benefits that are inherent in all rich but sickly relatives. The bank attended to those details too worldly to engage the attention of a grieving nephew. James himself made the sacrifice of spending one evening away from his usual haunts to go through the personal effects of a man who had lived eighty years and had spent most of that time collecting personal effects.

Tibbets Manor presented a weedy appearance to the motorists who passed it on their way along the Hudson. It had been built when millionaires still indulged the whimsies of classic minded architects. The natural beauty of the region had proved too strong a rival for the manor and the building soon took on a dark, sulking atmosphere that grew in intensity through the years.

To Tibbets' eyes, the interior of the building offered no improvement over the brooding exterior. Nevertheless, in common with the motion-picture trained public, he accepted as a truism that wealthy eccentrics always lived in tomb-like houses on rundown estates.

The long drive up from the city had been very tiring. Tibbets found the liquor closet and poured himself a refresher several times the volume old Uncle Eric would have approved of. A glance about the halls convinced him that it would take more than one night to examine all the treasures accumulated by the old man. Tibbets had sense enough not to disturb the gun collection or to open the many glass gem cases. The woodcuts and paintings also escaped his touch. He had been in enough museums to suspect that such things had value. Drink in hand, he wandered into the library. First editions and rare books were somewhat beyond his ken. A pile grew at his feet as he swept several shelves free of their contents.

He had no particular need for money but on impulse wished to see if perhaps the books weren't masking a wall safe. Library safes, he knew, were common enough. Handling the dusty volumes reminded Tibbets of his thirst. He found his way back to the sitting room. One thing he would never sell was the rare brandies and old wines that filled the cellars and service cabinets. No connoisseur could appreciate the contents as well as he could. He smiled to himself as he filled his glass.

After more dreary work in the library and more trips to the liquor closet, Tibbets sat down and surveyed the ruin. Faded, torn books were scattered on the floor, empty shelves leered at him—and still no wall safe. He was mildly disappointed. At his elbow on an antique table lay several heavy tomes. Piqued at his failure, he hurled the books at their companions on the floor. One volume, however, stayed in his hand. The touch of it under his fingers had filled him with a sudden, cold revulsion. It was as if he had touched a living, squirming thing. The texture of the cover was soft and fleshy. He drew the book close to his face and felt sick again. The faded yellow binding was like parched human skin. Looking closely he could make out a few coarse black hairs that seemed to be growing from the cover.

Then he laughed weakly. What was there to be alarmed about? Dead protoplasm was simply so much inert chemical. Protein matter, if he remembered his college biology correctly. Didn't they make his shoes from tanned cowhide? Tibbets laughed more strongly—pleased with his control over himself. He had reasoned away blind panic like an educated man. Now he examined the book with interest. Faint blue lettering traced out a pattern on the cover that seemed at first to be the aimless wanderings of subcutaneous veins. Then he found the tracings formed a word—he recognized one or two letters from the Greek alphabet. Tibbets cursed. This mysterious book was written in Greek —a language he had never mastered in school. Then looking again, he saw the title in English—in conventional newsprint capitals! "The Conjuration of Demons." He chuckled. A most obliging book. If you couldn't read it, it translated itself. The blue vein-like letters pulsed faintly on the page. Tibbets had the positive conviction that if he scratched the book deeply it would bleed an appalling amount of blood.

Some instinct of survival sent a hesitant shiver through his body. There was no more question in his mind that he was handling a supernatural object. For a few seconds he paused, then swiftly drained his glass and opened the book. The brandy had extinguished what little prudence he had. It came as a slight relief to find that the inside lettering was something other than living capillaries and that a fairly ordinary grade of parchment constituted the rest of the volume.

The technique for conjuring demons, as disclosed in the book, presented no unusual difficulties as far as methodology went. A few of the necessary magical ingredients were admittedly hardly obtainable in ordinary society but still not so rare as to deter a curious person. Near the end of the book he found a series of very life-like portraits which all bore signatures written in blood. The first pictures showed men with classic features, not a few of them wearing olive wreath crowns and appearing to be early Greek philosophers. Then came faces unmistakably Arab, then some Romans, one even with legion helmet and the look of an emperor; cowled monks followed, then kingly portraits, crowned and bearded, and finally faces that resembled modern makers of history—soldiers, writers, princes, scientists, bankers. On the very last page was the well-remembered features of Uncle Tibbets with his name spelled out neatly in caked blood. Tibbets roared with laughter and stumbled out to refill his glass.

"So that's how the old boy got so filthy rich! I'll be damned if he didn't get damned in the process!" Then he laughed some more and returned to the book.

The last hundred or so pages were all illustrated. "A catalogue of satisfied users! What an advertisment—what a promotion scheme! Got to hand it to those devils. I'm ready to try a little magic myself." Tibbets shook with keen enjoyment over the situation. "That old demon is sure some salesman. If I had a little corpse fat I'd call him up and tell him so myself."

As he slammed the book shut a slip of paper flew out. It was a bookmark he hadn't noticed before. He picked it up and saw that it contained the neat handwriting of his uncle. The paper bore a list of substances and a reference to certain cabinets in the study. Tibbets sat up straight. This was a supernatural challenge! The ingredients were the ones needed to generate the most potent spell in the book. Already his shrewd mind was weighing the advantages of summoning a demon. He had not the slightest doubt about the effectiveness of the conjuration book. There were the many proofs presented in the book itself—in portrait form!

Tibbets raced into the study and began to search for the ritual materials. Some of the substances were obviously supplied by chemical houses, certain others could only have been procured by criminal means. From a lead cannister he poured a glowing powder onto the bare floor in the outline of a crude pentagram.

"Radioactive," muttered Tibbets drunkenly. "This is one modern demon! Real 20th century stuff."

His other preparations took three hours. The study had been fitted out partly as a laboratory and this allowed the rapid completion of many steps that would have occupied a medieval wizard many long days. Shortly before midnight he cast aside the last vestige of skepticism and began the incantation that climaxed the ceremony.

The response was almost instantaneous. A copper-hued individual of average size stood within the glowing pentacle. Tibbets had seen certain stained glass windows in European churches which professed to illustrate scenes from Hell. He had a new respect for those anonymous artists. What he had taken to be caricatures he now knew were mosaics modeled from life—exact down to the last goat-like detail. A few wisps of smoke carried across to Tibbets' nostrils the smell of burnt flesh. This was no olfactory illusion since the demon had a very charred appearance. Tiny coals sparked on the creature's body and no amount of restless slapping could ever quite smother them all.

"It must be hot where you come from," said Tibbets in a flippant tone.

"Not at all," answered the demon blandly, turning to face Tibbets and giving up on a very persistent ember. "One can't burn up time answering a call without getting burned oneself. Friction, you know. That was a very urgent spell you used. I came as fast as possible."

"Are you—ah—in shape to do business?" asked Tibbets.

"Do not be concerned about me," said the demon. "What is it you wish for yourself?"

"First, tell me what are the conditions of any agreement we may draw up?"

"The same simple ones that are ascribed by legend and tradition to all supernatural pacts. For services rendered, we require the unconditional assignment to us of the one commodity humans possess that can be transferred to our continuum. The ego, soul, spirit—call it what you will. The natural resources of our own realm are too skimpy in this substance. We are forced to a blackmarket trade with humans for this material and as you can see, the journey to this world entails no little hardship for us. I am roundly singed. I wouldn't be surprised if seeing me in this condition has led many traders, possibly even you, to visualize my habitat as one having an unfavorable climate. Nothing could be further from the truth."

Tibbets was not so drunk as to believe this propaganda. But he was still ready to bargain. "What must I do?" he asked.

"Sign your name to the last page of the book and you shall have whatever you wish."

"You must have forgotten," smiled Tibbets. "The last page bears a facsimile of my late, lamented uncle."

"Look again," commanded the fiend.

Tibbets opened the book. Another page had appeared after his uncle's picture. He also noticed that a tiny thorn in the book had pierced one of his fingers. This was to supply the appropriate ink. Tibbets signed with his blood.

"It is done. Now, what do you wish?"

"I wish the powers of a demon! I command you to give me the supernatural attributes of a demon! I want power greater than yours!"

"I can give you power only equal to mine. There are laws of economy even in my universe."

"Then give me such power!" demanded Tibbets. "I will be a god among men!"

"With our power comes certain weaknesses. Churches, for instance, will be barred to you. Many who trade with us like the consolations of religion—especially when they near their end. This will be denied you. I knew a bishop who told me that were it not for his prayers, he would have lost his mind long before I came for him. Then there are other hazards—."

"Never mind! Power satisfies all wants. That is my choice. I have signed the book, you must give me what I ask. Power equal to yours!" "It is yours," spoke the demon.

Tibbets experienced no physical change. Doubt entered his mind. He pointed to a large desk. "Burn!" he commanded. To his incredulous eyes, every atom of wood and paint was instantly oxidized to ash. He gave a silent word of command and the ashes turned to gold.

The demon spoke. "Some things you cannot do, like creating life. Some things you dare not do, like taking life. Remember, this is a protected preserve. If you try to destroy it, powers greater than yours will dispose of you in a manner that even I find unpleasant to think of. And where I come from, unpleasantness is the ordinary run of things."

"Demon, you needn't worry," answered Tibbets elatedly. "I'll live like a benevolent god. Then, when you come for me, you'll see a power equal to your own ready to resist you. I'm immortal, as you are, and strong enough to keep you from being too persistent a caller."

With these words, Tibbets launched a lightening bolt at the demon who side stepped adroitly and began to disappear. All that remained was a persistent laughter that followed the dissolving fiend's parting words: "I'll see you—soon!"

It took a minute for Tibbets to realize that the laughter was supernatural. He stopped it by preventing the air molecules from vibrating in the old house. This small triumph greatly encouraged him. In a vague sort of way, he realized that he drew energy from another sphere, where apparently it was more abundant, and that he could transmit it in any form to any place he could see, could remember, or could imagine. This energy also permitted considerable manipulation of matter—gross and molecular. He could transmute elements, levitate objects and even make solids condense into ether. The scope of his powers amazed him. He realized he still had a whole lifetime to experiment and further perfect his talents. This gave him confidence to believe he could survive the inevitable return of the demon.

"As a fledgling demon, it's only right that I go out and celebrate," Tibbets said to himself. "But first to remove the evidences of my little session in sorcery."

Tibbets stepped up to the chalked pentagram and tried to erase it with his heel. He was very surprised to find his feet would not penetrate the mystic diagram. Then he understood. No demon could pass the magic chalk—in either direction. He shrugged. A small matter. It merely proved he really was a demon. The second small disappointment came when he saw the conjuration book was missing. The demon had recovered his property before vanishing. Fair enough, Tibbets granted. Demonic power for a useless signature. He laughed some more as he restored the study to order. Then he drove back to the city at a speed greater than the manufacturer of his car would have believed possible.

New York City, as Tibbets rightly knew, contained places where even the damned were welcome And if you weren't damned when you went in, you were by the time you left. He parked his car on the sidewalk, made it transparent, and walked into a very questionable den. He leaned on the bar and watched the dancers through the smoky haze. The small band itself was almost invisible in the dimly lit room. Sipping drinks which the bar man never realized he was pouring, Tibbets finally settled his gaze on the girl with the lowest-cut evening gown. She had green eyes, blonde hair and a form designed from blueprints hijacked from heaven. Her companion, suddenly hearing a large number of whiskey glasses tinkling in his stomach, rushed from the room and fainted. At the emergency hospital he was considered a prodigy by the operating room staff.

The girl eventually found herself at the only vacant space at the bar —next to Tibbets. A bottle appeared at her elbow and poured automatically into a glass.

"Soda or ginger?" asked Tibbets politely.

The girl gulped the drink quickly. "Did you see that?" she asked.

"Yes," said Tibbets calmly as the bottle poured another drink.

The girl gripped the edge of the bar tightly. "Am I drunk or are you a magician?"

"The latter," admitted Tibbets.

"Hypnotism! You should be on the stage."

"The stage? Oh, no! I think I'll become president first. Or maybe king of New York—with a harem, of course. How would you like to be the first queen?"

"You're drunk."

"Let's dance."

"No. Let's wait for that new Cuban rhythm. The Ghumba. They'll play it next."

"The Ghumba? Never heard of it," said Tibbets. "How do you dance it?"

"You'll see," answered the girl. "They're getting ready to play it now."

"This Latin-American music never made much sense to me. Can't make head or tail out of it."

"It's really very simple. Most of the music is really African. So is the rhythm. The slaves brought it with them. It sort of fermented in Haiti and Cuba for a while. Some of it has changed but a lot of it is still played like it was in Africa. Listen, don't those drums sound like tom-toms?"

"Yeah, thanks for the information. Let's try the step."

The girl shook his arm off. "Wait! Listen first. Isn't it fascinating? Can't you just see natives in some tribal clearing doing this dance? Maybe they're celebrating a wedding. Or bringing rain. Maybe it's evil music. Voodoo music! That band leader, he's real sinister looking, just like a witchdoctor! I bet it's a dance to ward off evil spirits—to drive devils away from the village feast."

"Say, do you always get like this when you hear drums and a couple of rattles?" said Tibbets very disappointedly. He had seen education do this to a lot of nice-looking girls.

"Don't you see things when you hear music?" asked the girl.

"Are you sick?"

"No, Mr. Tibbets, are you sick?"

"No, say, how did you know my name?"

"I've been waiting for you all evening. And you should be feeling sick—or at least very dizzy. The band has been playing a very potent demonicidal composition for almost two minutes. That Voodoo chant is one of the strongest things against our kind this side of the Atlantic. A genuine Bantu purification rite—almost unchanged from the original. I'm used to exorcisms, of course, but I don't pretend to like them. Sort of wilts one, don't you think?"

Tibbets was now hanging from the bar. His knees had experienced a sudden weakness and every nerve tingled and burned. The demon, as usual, was lying because he didn't feel dizzy or sick. Just weak. He materialized a stream of silver bullets which he projected at the grinning fiend, now no longer camouflaged as a female. The bullets melted and silver-plated the demon's body. This armor protected the creature when Tibbets launched a shower of sharpened hickory stakes at the heart region of the fiend. Tibbets slipped closer to the floor and extravagantly sent the rest of his silver bullets, ordinary lead would have done as well, in the direction of the still chanting musicians. These also failed to reach their targets. By now the club was empty—the fleeing patrons confirmed teetotalers before they reached the door. One completely intoxicated customer stumbled into Tibbets' transparent automobile, drove it off by sheer reflex and later sold it to a circus.

The demon was bending over the half conscious Tibbets. "When the strain is too great, you will slip from this continuum into a region more suitable for an imitation demon. There you will be my sole concern for a very long time." The demon laughed cruelly in a way best described as demonic and vanished after Tibbets.

JOAN VANDER PUTTEN *writes of herself: "I am married and the mother of five children. I left a full-time career in banking so that I could give my lifelong dream of being a writer a chance to bloom. I'm working on a horror novel set in Mexico centered around Aztec human sacrifices and reincarnation." "Just a Little Thing" is not nearly so dire; in it you will meet one of Hell's blue-collar workers, an imp who, though by nature annoying, sounds like he'd be more at home with Doc, Sneezy, Grumpy and those other huggable dwarfs.*

Just a Little Thing

BY JOAN VANDER PUTTEN

"Millie, why'd you take my watch?" Ted roared from the bedroom upstairs. Millie hustled the children out the kitchen door to the school bus, then turned, raising her voice over the radio's blare. "I didn't take your watch!"

Millie knew Ted's thundering footsteps on the stairs were calculated to strike terror into her heart, but she was learning not to be so intimidated by Ted's anger, thanks to the assertiveness course she was taking. She thrust out her chin and waited for the onslaught.

"Damn it, Millie, my watch was right there on the bedroom dresser, where I *always* put it, before I went into the bathroom. I came back and it was gone. What kind of bullshit are you trying to pull lately by hiding my stuff?"

"You're getting paranoid, Ted. Why, in God's name, would I want to hide your things? Your watch is probably right where you left it."

Ted glared at Millie. She glared back with a courage she didn't completely feel. Ted raised his fist. Millie flinched in surprise. With an evil grin of conquest, Ted snatched his briefcase and stomped through the kitchen. He tripped over a laundry basket. "Damn it, you're the lousiest housekeeper I've ever seen!" The door slammed behind him.

Angrily, Millie threw her son's half-eaten piece of toast on the floor; then, trembling, she slumped into the chair. Ted had never raised his hand to her before, but then, she'd never stood up to him before, either. Being assertive after the years of Ted's verbal abuse was one thing—but if it led to physical abuse, Millie questioned its wisdom.

She tossed a Cheerio across the table. Cheerio—the British term for good-bye. That's what she should tell Ted. Her marriage was a sham and she knew it. She stayed for the kids, she stayed for security—both bad reasons, Millie knew. After what he'd just done, Ted had only one redeeming quality left, Millie realized. He was faithful. Big deal. Still, it was better than nothing, and more than could be said for her friends' husbands. Ted knew fidelity was Millie's bottom line, the one he must not cross. He never had. *Be thankful for small favors,* she rationalized, then chuckled at the double entendre. Sighing, she rose to start her day.

Millie scooped up the clumps of toys and clothes littering the stairs as she headed to her bedroom to dress. She dumped the collection on the accumulated pile on the upstairs landing. No matter how much she cleaned, the kids undid her work in a matter of minutes. And, she guiltily admitted, looking around her bedroom at the mess, she was pretty careless about where she tossed her belongings as well.

It was strange about Ted's watch disappearing, though. Ted always knew exactly where his things were and he exploded if Millie dared touch something of his. Except his dirty laundry, of course. Thinking again of the watch, Millie frowned. What could've happened to it? Maybe Ted was starting to lose his memory.

To be fair to Ted, Millie admitted a lot of things around the house *had* been getting lost lately. Her hairbrush, which she'd only put down for a second to answer the phone, and Kim's doll, left in her cradle before dinner and missing afterward, were only two things that immediately came to mind.

Pondering the whereabouts of the missing items, Millie reached for the bra she'd flung over the chair next to the bed last night. It was gone. How could that *be?* It had been there, just a second ago. Suddenly she spied the lacy whiteness sliding across the floor, disappearing behind the chair. Without thinking about who . . . or *what* might be pulling it, Millie followed.

I'm losing my mind! Millie thought when she saw what was crouching against the gold velvet fabric. Staring up at her with Ted's watch clutched in one small hand and the bra in the other was the tiniest man she'd ever seen. Not more than nine inches tall, he was clad in green, spanking new overalls. The morning sun glinted off the bald spot on his head and his bushy black brows arched in surprise.

"Who are you? *What* are you?"

The little man bowed with a stately flourish. "Allow me to introduce myself. My name is Annoyance, and what I am is one of life's small frustrations."

Millie saw Ted's watch trembling in the imp's hand and noticed the worried wrinkle creasing his brow. "I must be going crazy," she whispered, rubbing her temples.

"I wish I were allowed to make you think you are, but that's a job for the *big* boys—Trials and Tribulations," he said respectfully.

"What are you talking about?" She took a threatening step toward him.

He cowered, flinging the hand holding her bra in front of his face. He lost his grip on the satin and one cup landed squarely on his head, making him look like an oversized, green-stemmed mushroom. His obvious fear halted Millie, and the sight of the imp's predicament made her smile.

Peeking up from under the scalloped edge, he hastened to explain, whisking the bra off his head and holding it before him like a top hat. "I didn't mean to anger you, ma'am. Anger would be *furious* if he thought I was trying to steal his job. I'm only supposed to annoy. I've been assigned to your house by *the man downstairs.*" His finger jabbed at the floor with a quick, exaggerated motion.

"Ted?"

"No, no!" The Old Man himself—the D-E-V-I-L! My job, ma'am, is to take little things, just before you're ready to use them. That causes annoyance, doesn't it?" he asked hopefully.

"Well, yes—sure it does." Millie knew that this conversation—*and* this man—were totally ludicrous, but she found his very proper demeanor amusing.

"Good." He sighed, relieved. "Then I'm doing my job right for a change. Although I'm sure I'd catch HE . . . HECK if the boss knew I'd been discovered. You won't tell him, will you?"

Millie hadn't the vaguest notion how she could do that, but decided to use his fear. "Well, not if you return my husband's watch and my bra and promise never to take anything again."

"Oh my, no. That simply won't do. You see, ma'am, this job is my last chance. I'm on final notice and I've got a quota to meet by the end of the month. If I don't produce a certain number of items by then . . ." Annoyance gulped, terror in his voice. "I'll get friared."

Millie chuckled at his mispronunciation. "Don't you mean fired?"

"Friared is worse than fired. I'll be sent where all the holy men who didn't make heaven wind up—and believe me, that's the hottest, nasti-est place down there," Annoyance said, shivering.

Millie felt sympathy for him, was amazed that she actually *believed* him. Suddenly an idea slipped into her mind. It was sneaky, devious and *altogether* enjoyable. "I'll make a deal with you," she said. "If you leave everything alone that belongs to me and the children and take only my husband's things, I won't tell your boss."

"Agreed!" Annoyance leapt almost an inch off the floor with joy. He held out her bra and Millie took it. Then he waved good-bye and disappeared, watch and all.

Over the next week Millie saw Annoyance from time to time as he went about his business. They never talked but always waved, two happy conspirators. Ted's things began to disappear at an alarming rate; just little things—a comb, a tie, a nail clipper. And everything always vanished just before Ted needed it. But because Millie now clucked sympathetically and helped him look for the missing items, Ted never got really angry—just annoyed. Millie thought her small friend's boss must be proud of him. Annoyance kept his part of the bargain and Millie savored her small revenge.

Saturday night Millie put the finishing touches on the canapés just before the crowd from Ted's office arrived. The party was a yearly ritual she hated, but one Ted loved. He insisted she arrange it, and to keep peace she always had. The group was large and, because she saw most of them only once a year, Millie felt like a stranger in her own house. Ted rarely even bothered to introduce her to most of the guests.

As Millie passed food around all night, Ted kept the liquor flowing. Before long his liberal tilt of the bottles had everyone, including him-self, loud and garrulous.

Millie avoided him as much as possible, knowing he was a nasty drunk. But he finally grabbed her arm as she passed and dragged her into the group he was entertaining with ribald jokes.

"Meet my wife Millie. She's the hostess with the leastess." Millie winced at his insult.

"Oh Ted, stop teasing," a woman in the group giggled. She turned to Millie. "Everything's lovely, and your home's just gorgeous."

Millie was about to thank her, but Ted sneered. "You should've seen what a pigpen this place was until this morning, Betty. Millie's a real little slob, aren't you, hon?" His mouth smiled, but his eyes challenged her to defy him in public.

Millie refused the bait. Breaking from his grip, she backed away. "Excuse me, folks, I've got something cooking." She needed a drink. She moved to the bar and poured herself a glass of wine, then squeezed down into the remaining seat on the couch.

"Hi, my name's Judy," a voice next to her said.

Millie turned and saw an overly made-up blonde in a tight red dress. The dress wasn't the only thing tight. Her unfocused eyes played drunkenly across Millie's face.

Before Millie could introduce herself, Judy continued. "You here alone too? Well, I'm not *really* alone—but my sweetie's married, and his li'l wifey doesn't know about us. She's here, so I hafta *make b'lieve* I'm alone, if ya know what I mean."

Indeed Millie did. She was face-to-face with one of the creatures out of her friends' nightmares, "The Other Woman." "Who's your sweetie?" she asked.

Judy frowned, forcing her eyes to focus. "There he is." She dimpled, spotting him.

Millie looked in the direction indicated by the red nail.

"There's my Teddy Bear—but I don't know who his wife is," Judy pouted. "He wouldn't introduce me. But he told me we'd sneak away from her tonight. Said it'd be easy to do with all these people around." Giggling, Judy nudged Millie conspiratorially. "He wants to have a quickie in their bed—said the idea turns him on. All I hafta do is watch for his signal, then follow him upstairs."

Millie's heart dropped to her stomach and died. Ted had crossed her bottom line. Nothing left. An icy, numbing anger gripped her, *pulled* her—to the darkest corner of her soul and there she found her answer. Calmly she stood and told Judy, "Have fun." Then she went upstairs.

As the evening wore on, Millie relaxed and actually enjoyed her own party. From time to time she'd dart a look at Ted, then at Judy. Whenever she did, she smiled.

She saw Ted sneak up the stairs, shooting a furtive look in her direction. Millie pretended to be deeply engrossed in arranging a plate of canapés. After he'd left, Millie saw Judy weave across the living room and stumble up after her "Teddy Bear."

Five minutes later, Ted and Judy screamed simultaneously. Millie, positioned at the foot of the staircase in anticipation, hurried upstairs, her lips curling into a smile. As she entered the bedroom, out of the corner of her eye Millie saw Annoyance scooting under the dresser.

Millie clucked sympathetically at Ted. "Oh, did you lose something again, dear?"

WILLIAM MAKEPEACE THACKERAY *(1811–1863) was born in Calcutta and studied at Cambridge. He began his career as an artist, but soon showed greater interest in writing and eventually became lionized by British society for such popular novels of manners as* Vanity Fair *and* Henry Esmond *and essays like the texts of his lectures on* The Four Georges *"The Devil's Wager" is early Thackeray (1836), but it already contains that wicked sense of humor that one associates with the compositions of his maturer days.*

The Devil's Wager

BY WILLIAM MAKEPEACE THACKERAY

It was the hour of the night when there be none stirring save church-yard ghosts—when all doors are closed except the gates of graves, and all eyes shut but the eyes of wicked men.

When there is no sound on the earth except the ticking of the grass-hopper, or the croaking of obscene frogs in the pool.

And no light except that of the blinking stars, and the wicked and devilish wills-o'-the-wisp, as they gambol among the marshes, and lead good men astray.

When there is nothing moving in heaven except the owl, as he flappeth along lazily; or the magician, as he rideth on his infernal broomstick, whistling through the air like the arrows of a Yorkshire archer.

It was at this hour (namely, at twelve o'clock of the night,) that two things went winging through the black clouds, and holding converse with each other.

Now the first was Mercurius, the messenger, not of gods (as the heathens feigned), but of demons; and the second, with whom he held company, was the soul of Sir Roger de Rollo, the brave knight. Sir Roger was Court of Chauchigny, in Champagne; Seigneur of Santerre, Villacerf and autres lieux. But the great die as well as the humble; and nothing remained of brave Roger now, but his coffin and his deathless soul.

And Mercurius, in order to keep fast the soul, his companion, had bound him round the neck with his tail; which, when the soul was stubborn, he would draw so tight as to strangle him wellnigh, sticking into him the barbed point thereof; whereat the poor soul, Sir Rollo, would groan and roar lustily.

Now they two had come together from the gates of purgatory, being bound to those regions of fire and flame where poor sinners fry and roast *in saecula saeculorum.*

"It is hard," said the poor Sir Rollo, as they went gliding through the clouds, "that I should thus be condemned for ever, and all for want of a single ave."

"How, Sir Soul?" said the demon. "You were on earth so wicked, that not one, or a million of aves, could suffice to keep from hell-flame a creature like thee; but cheer up and be merry; thou wilt be but a subject of our lord the Devil, as am I; and, perhaps, thou wilt be advanced to posts of honour, as am I also:" and to show his authority, he lashed with his tail the ribs of the wretched Rollo.

"Nevertheless, sinner as I am, one more ave would have saved me; for my sister, who was Abbess of St. Mary of Chauchigny, did so prevail, by her prayer and good works for my lost and wretched soul, that every day I felt the pains of purgatory decrease; the pitchforks which, on my first entry, had never ceased to vex and torment my poor carcass, were now not applied above once a week; the roasting had ceased, the boiling had discontinued; only a certain warmth was kept up, to remind me of my situation."

"A gentle stew," said the demon.

"Yea, truly, I was but in a stew, and all from the effects of the prayers of my blessed sister. But yesterday, he who watched me in purgatory told me, that yet another prayer from my sister and my bonds should be unloosed, and I, who am now a devil, should have been a blessed angel."

"And the other ave?" said the demon.

"She died, sir—my sister died—death choked her in the middle of the prayer." And hereat the wretched spirit began to weep and whine piteously; his salt tears falling over his beard, and scalding the tail of Mercurius the devil.

"It is, in truth, a hard case," said the demon; "but I know of no remedy save patience, and for that you will have an excellent opportunity in your lodgings below."

"But I have relations," said the Earl; "my kinsman Randal, who has inherited my lands, will he not say a prayer for his uncle?"

"Thou didst hate and oppress him when living."

"It is true; but an ave is not much; his sister, my niece, Matilda—"

"You shut her in a convent, and hanged her lover."

"Had I not reason? besides, has she not others?"

"A dozen, without a doubt."

"And my brother, the prior?"

"A liege subject of my lord the Devil: he never opens his mouth, except to utter an oath, or to swallow a cup of wine."

"And yet, if but one of these would but say an ave for me, I should be saved."

"Aves with them are *rarae* aves," replied Mercurius, wagging his tail waggishly; "and, what is more, I will lay thee any wager that no one of these will say a prayer to save thee."

"I would wager willingly," responded he of Chauchigny; "but what has a poor soul like me to stake?"

"Every evening, after the day's roasting, my lord Satan giveth a cup of cold water to his servants; I will bet thee thy water for a year, that none of the three will pray for thee."

"Done!" said Rollo.

"Done!" said the demon; "and here, if I mistake not, is thy castle of Chauchigny."

Indeed, it was true. The soul, on looking down, perceived the tall towers, the courts, the stables and the fair gardens of the castle. Although it was past midnight there was a blaze of light in the banqueting-hall, and a lamp burning in the open window of the Lady Matilda.

"With whom shall we begin?" said the demon: "with the baron or the lady?"

"With the lady, if you will."

"Be it so; her window is open, let us enter."

So they descended, and entered silently into Matilda's chamber.

The young lady's eyes were fixed so intently on a little clock, that it was no wonder that she did not perceive the entrance of her two visitors. Her fair cheek rested in her white arm, and her white arm on the cushion of a great chair in which she sat, pleasantly supported by sweet thoughts and swan's down; a lute was at her side, and a book of prayers lay under the table (for piety is always modest). Like the amorous Alexander, she sighed and looked (at the clock)—and sighed for ten minutes or more, when she softly breathed the word "Edward!"

At this the soul of the Baron was wroth. "The jade is at her old pranks," said he to the devil; and then addressing Matilda: "I pray thee, sweet niece, turn thy thoughts for a moment from that villainous page, Edward, and give them to thine affectionate uncle."

When she heard the voice, and saw the awful apparition of her uncle (for a year's sojourn in purgatory had not increased the comeliness of his appearance), she started, screamed, and of course fainted.

But the devil Mercurius soon restored her to herself. "What's o'clock?" said she, as soon as she had recovered from her fit: "is he come?"

"Not thy lover, Maude, but thine uncle—that is, his soul. For the love of heaven, listen to me: I have been frying in purgatory for a year past, and should have been in heaven but for the want of a single ave."

"I will say it for thee tomorrow, uncle."

"Tonight, or never."

"Well, tonight be it:" and she requested the devil Mercurius to give her the prayer-book, from under the table; but he had no sooner touched the holy book than he dropped it with a shriek and a yell. "It was hotter," he said, "than his master Sir Lucifer's own particular pitchfork." And the lady was forced to begin her ave without the aid of her missal.

At the commencement of her devotions the demon retired, and carried with him the anxious soul of poor Sir Roger de Rollo.

The lady knelt down—she sighed deeply; she looked again at the clock, and began—

"Ave Maria."

When a lute was heard under the window, and a sweet voice singing—

"Hark!" said Matilda.

> "Now the toils of day are over.
> And the sun hath sunk to rest,
> Seeking, like a fiery lover,
> The bosom of the blushing west—
>
> "The faithful night keeps watch and ward,
> Raising the moon, her silver shield,
> And summoning the stars to guard
> The slumbers of my fair Mathilde!"

"For mercy's sake!" said Sir Rollo, "the ave first, and next the song."

So Matilda again dutifully betook her to her devotions, and began—"Ave Maria gratia plena!" but the music began again, and the prayer ceased of course.

"The faithful night! Now all things lie
Hid by her mantle dark and dim,
In pious hope I hither hie,
And humbly chant mine ev'ning hymn.

"Thou art my prayer, my saint, my shrine!
(For never holy pilgrim knee'd,
Or wept at feet more pure than mine),
My virgin love, my sweet Mathilde!"

"Virgin love!" said the Baron. "Upon my soul, this is too bad!" and he thought of the lady's lover whom he had caused to be hanged.

But *she* only thought of him who stood singing at her window.

"Niece Matilda!" cried Sir Roger, agonizedly, "wilt thou listen to the lies of an impudent page, whilst thine uncle is waiting but a dozen words to make him happy?"

At this Matilda grew angry: "Edward is neither impudent nor a liar, Sir Uncle, and I will listen to the end of the song."

"Come away," said Mercurius; "he hath yet got wield, field, sealed, congealed, and a dozen other rhymes beside; and after the song will come the supper."

So the poor soul was obliged to go; while the lady listened and the page sung away till morning.

"My virtues have been my ruin," said poor Sir Rollo, as he and Mercurius slunk silently out of the window. "Had I hanged that knave Edward, as I did the page his predecessor, my niece would have sung mine ave, and I should have been by this time an angel in heaven."

"He is reserved for wiser purposes," responded the devil: "he will assassinate your successor, the lady Mathilda's brother; and, in consequence, will be hanged. In the love of the lady he will be succeeded by a gardener, who will be replaced by a monk, who will give way to an ostler, who will be deposed by a Jew pedlar, who shall, finally yield to a noble earl, the future husband of the fair Mathilde. So that you see, instead of having one poor soul a-frying we may now look forward to a goodly harvest for our lord the Devil."

The soul of the Baron began to think that his companion knew too much for one who would make fair bets; but there was no help for it; he would not, and he could not cry off: and he prayed inwardly that the brother might be found more pious than the sister.

But there seemed little chance of this. As they crossed the court, lackeys, with smoking dishes and full jugs, passed and repassed continually, although it was long past midnight. On entering the hall, they found Sir Randal at the head of a vast table surrounded by a fiercer and more motley collection of individuals than had congregated there even in the time of Sir Rollo. The lord of the castle had signified that "it was his royal pleasure to be drunk," and the gentlemen of his train had obsequiously followed their master. Mercurius was delighted with the scene, and relaxed his usually rigid countenance into a bland and benevolent smile, which became him wonderfully.

The entrance of Sir Roger, who had been dead about a year, and a person with hoofs, horns, and a tail rather disturbed the hilarity of the company. Sir Randal dropped his cup of wine; and Father Peter, the confessor, incontinently paused in the midst of a profane song, with which he was amusing the society.

"Holy Mother!" cried he, "it is Sir Roger."

"Alive!" screamed Sir Randal.

"No, my lord," Mercurius said; "Sir Roger is dead, but cometh on a matter of business; and I have the honour to act as his counsellor and attendant."

"Nephew," said Sir Roger, "the demon saith justly; I am come on a trifling affair, in which thy service is essential."

"I will do anything, uncle, in my power."

"Thou canst give me life, if thou wilt?" But Sir Randal looked very blank at this proposition. "I mean life spiritual, Randal," said Sir Roger; and thereupon he explained to him the nature of the wager.

Whilst he was telling his story, his companion Mercurius was playing all sorts of antics in the hall; and, by his wit and fun, became so popular with this godless crew, that they lost all the fear which his first appearance had given them. The friar was wonderfully taken with him, and used his utmost eloquence and endeavours to convert the devil; the knights stopped drinking to listen to the argument; the men-at-arms forebore brawling; and the wicked little pages crowded round the two strange disputants, to hear their edifying discourse. The ghostly man, however, had little chance in the controversy, and certainly little learning to carry it on. Sir Randal interrupted him. "Father Peter," said he, "our kinsman is condemned for ever, for want of a single ave: wilt thou say it for him?" "Willingly, my lord," said the monk "with my book," and accordingly he produced his missal to read, without which aid it appeared that the holy father could not manage the desired prayer. But the crafty Mercurius had, by his devilish art, inserted a song in the place of the ave, so that Father Peter, instead of chanting a hymn, sang the following irreverent ditty:

> "Some love the matin-chimes, which tell
> 　The hour of prayer to sinner:
> But better far's the mid-day bell,
> 　Which speaks the hour of dinner;
> For when I see a smoking fish,
> 　Or capon drowned in gravy,
> Or noble haunch on silver dish,
> 　Full glad I sing mine ave.
>
> "My pulpit is an ale-house bench,
> 　Whereon I sit so jolly;
> A smiling rosy country wench
> 　My saint and patron holy.
> I kiss her cheek so red and sleek,
> 　I press her ringlets wavy.
> And in her willing ear I speak
> 　A most religious ave.
>
> "And if I'm blind, yet heaven is kind,
> 　And holy saints forgiving;
> For sure he leads a right good life
> 　Who thus admires good living.
> Above they say, our flesh is air,
> 　Our blood celestial ichor:
> Oh, grant! mid all the changes there,
> 　They may not change our liquor!"

And with this pious wish the holy confessor tumbled under the table in an agony of devout drunkenness; whilst the knights, the men-at-arms, and the wicked little pages, rang out the last verse with a most melodious and emphatic glee. "I am sorry, fair uncle," hiccupped Sir Randal, "that, in the matter of the ave, we could not oblige thee in a more orthodox manner; but the holy father has failed, and there is not another man in the hall who hath an idea of a prayer."

"It is my own fault," said Sir Rollo; "for I hanged the last confessor." And he wished his nephew a surly good night, as he prepared to quit the room.

"Au revoir, gentlemen," said the devil Mercurius; and once more fixed his tail round the neck of his disappointed companion.

The spirit of poor Rollo was sadly cast down; the devil, on the contrary, was in high good humour. He wagged his tail with the most satisfied air in the world, and cut a hundred jokes at the expense of his poor associate. On they sped, cleaving swiftly through the cold night winds, frightening the birds that were roosting in the woods, and the owls that were watching in the towers.

In the twinkling of an eye, as it is known, devils can fly hundreds of miles: so that almost the same beat of the clock which left these two in Champagne found them hovering over Paris. They dropped into the court of the Lazarist Convent, and winded their way, through passage and cloister, until they reached the door of the prior's cell.

Now the prior, Rollo's brother, was a wicked and malignant sorcerer; his time was spent in conjuring devils and doing wicked deeds, instead of fasting, scourging, and singing holy psalms: this Mercurius knew; and he, therefore, was fully at ease as to the final result of his wager with poor Sir Roger.

"You seem to be well acquainted with the road," said the knight.

"I have reason," answered Mercurius, "having for a long period had the acquaintance of his reverence, your brother; but you have little chance with him."

"And why?" said Sir Rollo.

"He is under a bond to my master, never to say a prayer, or else his soul and his body are forfeited at once."

"Why, thou false and traitorous devil!" said the enraged knight; "and thou knewest this when we made our wager?"

"Undoubtedly: do you suppose I would have done so had there been any chance of losing?"

And with this they arrived at Father Ignatius's door.

"Thy cursed presence threw a spell on my niece, and stopped the tongue of my nephew's chaplain; I do believe that had I seen either of them alone, my wager had been won."

"Certainly; therefore, I took good care to go with thee; however, thou mayest see the prior alone, if thou wilt; and lo! his door is open. I will stand without for five minutes when it will be time to commence our journey."

It was the poor Baron's last chance: and he entered his brother's room more for the five minutes' respite than from any hope of success.

Father Ignatius, the prior, was absorbed in magic calculations: he stood in the middle of a circle of skulls, with no garment except his long white beard, which reached to his knees; he was waving a silver rod, and muttering imprecations in some horrible tongue.

But Sir Rollo came forward and interrupted his incantation. "I am," said he, "the shade of thy brother Roger de Rollo; and have come, from pure brotherly love, to warn thee of thy fate."

"Whence camest thou?"

"From the abode of the blessed in Paradise," replied Sir Roger, who was inspired with a sudden thought; "it was but five minutes ago that that Patron Saint of thy church told me of thy danger, and of thy wicked compact with the fiend. 'Go,' said he, 'to thy miserable brother, and tell him there is but one way by which he may escape from paying the awful forfeit of his bond.' "

"And how may that be?" said the prior; "the false fiend hath deceived me; I have given him my soul, but have received no worldly benefit in return. Brother! dear brother! how may I escape?"

"I will tell thee. As soon as I heard the voice of blessed St. Mary Lazarus"—the worthy Earl had, at a pinch, coined the name of a saint —"I left the clouds, where, with other angels, I was seated, and sped hither to save thee. 'Thy brother,' said the Saint, 'hath but one day more to live, when he will become for all eternity the subject of Satan; if he would escape, he must boldly break his bond, by saying an ave.' "

"It is the express condition of the agreement," said the unhappy monk, "I must say no prayer, or that instant I become Satan's, body and soul."

"It is the express condition of the Saint," answered Roger, fiercely; "pray, brother, pray, or thou art lost for ever."

So the foolish monk knelt down, and devoutly sung out an ave. "Amen!" said Sir Roger, devoutly.

"Amen!" said Mercurius, as, suddenly, coming behind, he seized

Ignatius by his long beard, and flew up with him to the top of the church-steeple.

The monk roared, and screamed, and swore against his brother; but it was of no avail: Sir Roger smiled kindly on him, and said, "Do not fret, brother; it must have come to this in a year or two."

And he flew alongside of Mercurius to the steeple-top; *but this time the devil had not his tail round his neck.* "I will let thee off thy bet," said he to the demon; for he could afford, now, to be generous.

"I believe, my lord," said the demon, politely, "that our ways separate here." Sir Roger sailed gaily upwards: while Mercurius having bound the miserable monk faster than ever, he sunk downwards to earth, and perhaps lower. Ignatius was heard roaring and screaming as the devil dashed him against the iron spikes and buttresses of the church.

POUL ANDERSON *is the popular author of many superb science-fantasy novels and stories, notable among which are* Three Hearts and Three Lions *and* The High Crusade. *Born in 1926 of Scandinavian parents, Poul studied physics at the University of Minnesota. He resides in the San Francisco Bay area with his writer wife, Karen, with whom he is currently collaborating on a novel,* The King of Ys. *"Rachaela", one of Mr. Anderson's less familiar works, is a poignant tale that haunts the memory long after it has been read.*

Rachaela

BY POUL ANDERSON

If you think writing is an easy and glamorous profession, you have another think coming. Physically, of course, it doesn't involve much, though several straight hours of key-punching can leave you pretty bushed; but then, lack of exercise is hard on the body too. And your brain sweats for you. It isn't built for monotonous work—if it were, you wouldn't be a writer—but that's what the job all too often becomes. Only in the rare moments of being "hot" can the average writer turn out page after page of really good stuff without a pause or a sense of effort; and his creditors don't wait for his inspirations. Anyway, editors usually bounce his proudest masterpieces right back at him, or if they do get published the readers' columns present a similar lack of judgment. "It stinks! Why can't he write more like *Three To Make Ready?* There was a *story!" Three To Make Ready,* our author recalls wearily, was a piece of machine-tooled hack written by the simple process of fitting jig-saw plot elements together and then grimly pecking away till it was done, and all solely for the purpose of meeting his bills.

Everybody's out of step but Willy.

As for the glamour, you can have it and welcome. The profession is about as glamorous as bricklaying.

Carsten leaned back, gave his room a bitter glance, and lit another cigarette. Smoke hazed the cluttered drabness around him, the rumpled bed, the untidy heap of books, the stuffed and bulging wastebasket, the coffeepot sitting on the hotplate and thinking its own dark thoughts. *If I stay here much longer,* he thought, *I'll go stark, staring*

mad and begin turning out nothing but schizophrenic clinical material.
Maybe it'd be an improvement at that. Look what Joyce got by with in
Ulysses.

His moody eyes turned back to the tumbled heap of manuscript
before him. He slipped the first page from the bottom and read the
beginning with a dislike approaching nausea.

THE LADY IS A STRANGER
by William Carsten

She was tall, almost as tall as I, and she moved with a flow of
strength and grace, like a young lioness. That was what she xxxxxxx
xxxx made me think of, the first time I saw her, a great tawny cat, hair
like dull gold tumbling to her wide golden shoulders and xxx shining
ever so softly in the muted light. Her face was strange, high wide cheek-
bones sloping down lovely planes to the xxxxx full strong mouth—red,
red as new-spilled blood, that mouth, and I didn't think it was cosmetic.
In spite of the perfection of her figure, it was her eyes eyes that held me
most stongly.

"Bah," said Carsten aloud. "You may quote me." Automatically, he
penciled out the excess "eyes" and slipped an "r" into "stongly." It
wasn't very clean copy. Or a very clean story. Or a very good one.

In fact, the whole thing stank.

He sighed and ruffled his hair. What was the matter with him? He
wasn't any genius, no Tolstoy or de Maupassant, and he knew it. But
he'd done better than this. His adventure stories had been well received. They weren't the *Iliad,* but they showed the influence. So when
he wanted to write something more quiet and arty, why wouldn't it
jell?

He walked over to the bed and flopped down on it with his hands
behind his head. It was a good plot he had. Nothing extraordinary,
but a good sound idea which in the hands of a real master could have
been a minor classic. But then, everything the masters wrote, regardless of plot, was that way, wherefore they were the masters.

Boy meets girl. Picks her up in a bar, in a nice sort of way. She's
what he's always been looking for, beautiful and wise and generally
desirable, and quickly wraps him around her little finger. Only this is
wartime Portugal, overrun with Allied and Axis agents, and our hero
works for the O.S.S. He thinks she's Swedish, and in the course of

events lets slip certain important information. Then he learns she's working for the Italians, less because she wants to than because the Fascists hold her father on a trumped-up charge, and he's their hostage for her good behavior. He can't bring himself to turn her in—it'd be hard to do, anyway—but he keeps her prisoner till too late for her knowledge to do them any good. He wants her to break with the enemy, but in spite of being in love with him too she won't, and in the end he lets her go, wondering if he's played the traitor or not and if he'll ever see her again. Gentle sob. The end. Six thousand words.

So why does it come out to be overwritten sickly purple crud that no editor would touch even with the famous eleven-foot-four-and-three-quarter-inch pole? It couldn't be the fact that his exchequer was getting low. He'd written fairly good stuff before, under worse pressure—in fact, his bank balance was still safely plus.

Maybe he just wasn't cut out to write anything but bang-bang sizz-boom up-and-at-'em. After all, he knew a little something about that. He'd never seen actual combat, but he was a fair man with a gun, a horse, or a fencing saber, he'd crossed oceans and cruised a bit in sailboats, and he went down to the Y once a month or so for a little boxing . . . Well, what of it? He knew as much about women as any normal bachelor with a ready flow of words, he should be able to do a fairly convincing heroine.

Still, his exotically named Rachaela was no ordinary woman. Insofar as he had modeled her after anyone, she was a combination of a blonde he'd known, a woman as beautiful and about as warm and friendly as an iceberg, and a small dark nymphomaniac he'd once had the pleasure of meeting. Only of meeting—she'd been living with someone else at the time—but he'd liked her wry sense of humor. She had looked on the world with what must have been a rather horribly clear vision. He wondered where she was now.

The mixture didn't mix, though. No sane human could have two such diverse components. And yet, damn it, he *knew* what a strange and complex being he wanted to describe. The trouble lay in getting her into words.

Of course, even if he had character trouble, that was no excuse for bad writing. And his prose this time was just plain rotten.

"Hell!" Carsten flung himself to his feet as the cigarette burned too close to his lips. "The Devil take her! Let's go out and get some personal experience of alcohol. Authors have to gather atmosphere, don't they?"

It was five o'clock and he hadn't had a drink all day. What he needed was relaxation, escape from the circumscribed shabbiness of his room and himself. Let's see—he counted the money in his wallet. Enough for a few nips in a really decent place. That ought to snap him out of his doldrums.

His favorite bar was only a few blocks from his shabby apartment house. Study in contrasts—you walked down a dingy street, turned a corner, and were out on a thoroughfare of shining store fronts, exclusive night clubs, and the elite of Manhattan. He liked the lounge in the Hotel Margrave. It was quiet and well-upholstered and discreetly lit, and the bartender knew how to fix a Martini. Let's go!

By the time he had cleaned up, changed clothes, and gotten down there, it was close to six, and the violet dusk of early autumn was closing in. Lights were winking through, one-eyed glow of street lamps, flash and flicker of neon. The rush hour crowd had thinned, people moved more leisurely, a dim cloak of peacefulness was dripping over the city. *L'heure bleu*—what a genius for expression the French had!

He strolled up to the long mahogany gleam of the bar. "Hi, Joe," he said. "The usual."

"You bet," said the bartender. He wrought a Martini around a pickled onion, set it on the bar, and collected for it. Carsten draped himself over a stool, lit a cigarette, and felt the tension sieving out of his muscles. Idly, he looked around.

There weren't many people in as yet. Residents lingering over a cocktail before supper, a few middle-aged businessmen having a quick one before going home, a couple of anomalous transients like himself. And—and—hold on!

What a woman! *What a woman!*

He took her in slowly, savoring her with an appreciation as much esthetic as sexual. Gods in heaven, she was tall and built like a more slender Aphrodite of Milos, her skin was white with the faintest hint of gold as if the liquid metal flowed in her veins, she moved with a grace he had not thought possible to human beings. Soft blonde hair fell low over her broad forehead and then tumbled to her bare shoulders, and he'd always been a sucker for that particular bob. The face

was strange, not fitting into any race he knew of—Russian? A suggestion of Mongoloid in the high cheekbones and oblique eyes, but the
nose was straight and thin, the mouth like a red flower.

After a minute or two, he grew aware of her outfit. She seemed to be
as expensive as one would guess, a long evening dress of deep shimmering green hugged her, a barbarically massive gold bracelet coiled
around one slim wrist and a huge fire ruby glittered in the necklace at
her throat. But he noticed that her ring finger was bare, and she sat
alone in the corner, half in shadow.

Her eyes swung toward him and met his stare with a cool green
appraisal. Almost automatically, Carsten picked up his drink and
went over to her table.

"Why, hello, there," he said. "Haven't seen you for a long time.
How are things? How's Barbara?"

"Barbara?" She smiled, ever so faintly. Her voice was low and
sweet, just the way it should be.

"Sure, your sister—oh, I beg your pardon, miss. The light's bad
here. I mistook you for someone else." It came to him with a dim
wonder that somehow she really did look familiar. "But you do look a
lot like her. Any relation? Helen Andrews, her name is."

"No," she said. "No relation."

"Well, please excuse my rudeness, then." Carsten smiled. "May I
expiate it by buying you a drink?"

"Is this a pickup?" She didn't sound angry, only mildly amused.

"If the Fates permit, though I doubt they're so kind." Carsten sat
down across the little table from her. "If you want to tell me to go
chase myself, I'll do so. If you're expecting someone, I'll scram. But if
you can and will share half an hour with me, I'll be most grateful."

She smiled, a slow curve ending in a flash of white. "No, I'm not
waiting for anyone. Stay if you like."

"Then introductions are in order," he said, wondering how in the
name of Hell his ancient and whiskery approach had worked on a
goddess. He'd tried more out of a sense of duty to himself than in any
real hope. "I'm William Carsten, though my friends call me Hey,
You."

Her eyes regarded him steadily from between incredible lashes.
They were gold-flecked green, he saw—or was it gray, or a strange
shade of blue? "Not the writer?" She didn't sound awed, only coolly

interested. She nodded. "I've read some of your stories. They're good."

"Thank you, fair lady." Carsten signaled the waiter. "For that, I'll make you the heroine of my next."

"What's her name?" she asked.

"Why—uh—Rachaela," he blurted.

"Good," she smiled. "Let that be my *nom de guerre,* then."

This, thought Carsten, *is entirely too good to be true. I walk into a bar, effortlessly strike up an acquaintance with the most gorgeous wench I've ever seen or heard of, and now she plays the game on, won't tell me her name—E. Phillips Oppenheim, here I come!*

The waiter materialized beside them. "Cognac," said Rachaela.

"You don't live here, do you?" asked Carsten. "I'd've seen you before if you did."

"No, I'm from out of town," she said noncommittally. Her eyes went over him and left small shivers in their wake. "So you're the swashbuckling William Carsten. I'm disappointed not to see you wearing a cutlass."

"I left it at home," he grinned. "Always trip over the damn thing." He extended his cigarettes. "Smoke?"

"No, thanks. I stick to my own brand." She waved one long slim hand. "Tell me, Mr. Carsten—"

"Will."

"Will, or Hey, You. Tell me, how does it feel to be a successful writer?"

The conventional question. He returned a somewhat franker answer than usual. "Who said I was successful? Oh, sure, I make a living at it, and the living gets better all the time as I sell more and move into higher-paying markets. But somehow I never write what I'd like to."

"The Great American Novel?"

"It's been written. *Moby Dick.* And Homer sewed up the epic and Shakespeare the drama and Kipling the ballad and other people everything else so thoroughly that there's nothing left for us to do now. Just as all Western philosophy has been described as a series of footnotes to Plato, so we cannot hope to beat the masters at their own game. They were in green pastures; at best, we can only be worthy followers. All our great moderns are saying and doing nothing which wasn't said and done years or centuries ago. You can't be *original* any more . . .

As for me, well, at my best I'm competent, and I know damn well I'll never exceed that. So—" He shrugged.

She nodded, slowly. "But aren't you giving up without a struggle? You're a young man, you still have to learn—"

"Oh, I'll improve, but never that much. I won't take any Nobel Prizes, and I won't deserve any, even in my own conceited estimation. It's quite clear to me, from studying my own works, including things I've tried to make really 'great.' Those are invariably the most miserable botches of all." Carsten grinned crookedly and paid for her drink as it arrived. "Sorry. I didn't mean to go off that way. Tell me about yourself."

"Oh, come now, Will, you can give me the thrill of playing mysterious *femme fatale* just for this evening, can't you?"

This evening— A rush of excitement was overlaid by a worried mental counting of his assets. Joe would cash a check for him, but it would mean staving off his rent payments and going hungry till he made his next sale . . . Devil take it! A chance like this comes once in several thousand lifetimes.

"In that case," he said, "you'll have to live up to your role, you know. Move over."

The plush seats were easily wide enough for two. He sat down beside her with a dazed feeling that all this was entirely too good to last. Unless—unless he was somehow being taken for a ride—

No, hardly. He didn't have enough money to be worth robbing, and his various indiscretions had and would continue to be such that he wouldn't give a damn about a blackmailer's threats to publish them, and he had access to no secret information. No, no, this—Rachaela— must just be out for a good time. Maybe her boy friend had stood her up—though he'd hardly have been human then—or maybe she was an adventuress looking for amusement, or maybe—

Once in a long-drawn crap game he'd had a fantastic run of luck. He'd known that he simply couldn't lose, there had been no doubt about it, and he'd walked away at last with several hundred dollars in his pocket. It was like that again tonight. Things wouldn't go wrong, no matter what he did, because it wasn't in their nature to do so. He was "hot."

They talked for a while; he wasn't sure what they talked about or of anything except that she was wise and witty and utterly charming and captivating. Nor was he doing so badly himself.

"Tell me, Will," she asked finally, "this story you are writing now, of which I am the heroine—what is it like?"

"It—uh—" He hesitated, shrugged, and plunged ahead. She wouldn't be offended, not on this enchanted night. "Well, you made an unfortunate choice, Rachaela. It's about an Axis spy of that name."

"Well," she smiled, "you may not be too far off the mark."

He discovered with a pleased surprise that they were holding hands, and squeezed hers. She squeezed back. "Don't tell me you're a Russian agent. Sorry, I'm not a nuclear physicist."

"Oh, no. I'm a demon, Will, and all I want is your soul. We need writers down below." As he blinked at her in surprise, she said merely, "But go on. Tell me about this story."

For a moment he hesitated, wondering why on earth she had said it. A hell of an obscure game, and somehow it didn't sound like an affectation. But she was near and beautiful and he had the usual male desire to talk about himself and his work to a woman. She shrugged again. "Well, O Best Beloved, it's told in the first person, which is sheer wishful thinking on my part—" He related the plot in detail.

"It's not like your ordinary writing," she said.

"No. For once, it's a notion I really think is good. Only—it won't write. Comes out disgusting, like a sophomore's first discovery that he can Create Art."

"Why?" she asked. "I don't think it's that you're only fit to write adventure, Will. I've admired a lot in your work. The purely descriptive passages especially, sunrise over the sea, storms, snowfall, the creak and pitch of ships. And even your human characters come alive at times. You've talent enough to write this story too."

He was only vaguely offended; like most modest people, he liked to be told how excellent he really was. His conscious mind admitted that she was quite right, and that it was good of her to be so honest with him. The way you'd want your wife to be honest—

"I don't know why it won't go. It just won't. Maybe it's a jinx, or a subconscious block of some kind. Or maybe it's the trouble with characterization. It's hard to show the mixed-up mess of good and evil that we all are. Nobody, even the worst villain, is all black—or white. Unless I allow your claim, I've never met or known of a real fiend. Not even a literal devil."

"How do you know?" she bantered him. "After all, no competent demon today would go around in horns and hoofs. He'd be laughed out of town. Oh, no, Will, the modern Devil is an ultrarespectable businessman, punctual as clockwork, a member of all the best clubs, with a silent partnership in an influential newspaper and a controlling vote in a key corporation; or he is a demagogue of a union leader, setting his dupes against their own ultimate interests; or a politician hounding honest men out of public office with baseless slanders; or the power behind a dictator; or the leader of a racist group too cowardly to show its viciousness except behind masks; or—oh, any one of the million cancers in this dying civilization. You've met the agents of Hell, you meet them every day of your life."

"Speaking of course, figuratively," he said, a little uneasily. Her smile had faded and she talked so seriously, all at once.

"Not in the least." Her voice was grave, her eyes huge and luminous. "Hell has had many names, and the Devil has taken many forms; those I speak of are simply the most suitable today. In earlier days he was known as Setesh and Nergal and the Furies and Loki and Lucifer and Mara and—you reel them off. The primitive folk of Earth live closer to reality than you do, Will, and most of them recognize the truth, that this world is closer to Hell than it is to Heaven. So their gods are all demons, to be appeased rather than worshipped. Your new mythology is beginning to recognize that fact, under still another switch of names. They talk of the second law of thermodynamics, now, you know, and of the subconscious mind; and wave mechanics suggests at least one other universe may co-exist with ours—Oh, yes, whatever you choose to call it, Hell is a fact."

"First girl I ever heard talk that way. What are you, a mystic?"

"No. Goodness, no!" She laughed, a low and lovely sound. "I'm just a lady demon out after your soul, Will."

"You've got it already, I'm afraid," he grinned, glad to be back in the more comfortable realm of persiflage. She was a strange, contradictory sort. "But I still have an inner man. What say to a spot of supper?"

"I say yes." Her smile left him weak in the knees. "If you'll excuse me while I go powder my nose, as the euphemism has it—"

He watched her move away. She was like a panther, a hovering falcon, a flowing stream, like music and laughter and unforgotten springtimes. Shaking his head, dazedly, he went over to the bar.

"Cash a large-ish check, Joe?" he asked.

"I guess so. My tires need a retread." Joe clicked his tongue admiringly. "Man, oh, man, you sure pick 'em. Who is she?"

"Old friend." They didn't approve of pickups in the Margrave. "But isn't she staying here?" If she was, he could get her name and address from the desk.

"Nope. Never saw her before in my life, worse luck. She came in just a minute or two before you did." Joe gave Carsten a sharp glance, but shrugged leniently and cashed his check. A hundred and fifty bucks—that should see him through tonight, whatever they did, and if he couldn't get an advance out of his agent or a loan from a friend he could live on spaghetti and memories for a while.

Rachaela came back and he helped her into her coat. It looked as costly as the rest of her get-up, a sleek and shining thing of a dark fur he couldn't identify.

"What animal gave up the ghost for this?" he asked.

"Scythian gryphon," she said, and took his arm. Since she was obviously determined to have her game, he let it go at that, saying only:

"It died in a good cause. I would suggest the Tzigani. Nice and small sort of place, Hungarian, and the chef loves his work."

"Sounds like fun." She leaned against him in a way that wrapped a curtain of intimacy about them, even on the street.

He kissed her in the taxi. She hung back a moment, then responded as he'd never been responded to before. After quite a few centuries the bells stopped ringing and the birds sang more quietly and all the sunbeams danced to a halt and glowed inside him. She sighed happily and relaxed against his shoulder.

"Psychologists," said Carsten dizzily, "tell us that love at first sight is childish. Don't just sit there, honey—change me!"

She laughed again, soft and low, and the little bells woke up once more.

"Rachaela," he whispered. His lips brushed her hair, the sweet wild smell of it hung in his nostrils with a whisper of springtime that he would never forget. Ever afterward, he knew, he would be haunted by the fragrance of her hair.

"Rachaela, who are you? Where are you from? How do I rate this?"

"You're a nice guy, Will." She kissed him again. When he woke up, the taxi was pulling to a halt.

They entered a dim anteroom and checked their coats. The head-waiter scuttled up, a lean dark man with something feline in his gait, and bowed. "Good efening, sir. Villkom."

"Small and secluded," said Carsten.

"Yes, sir." The man stiffened. His eyes fastened on Rachaela and widened. For an instant, there was something ugly in his face. Fear, crawling out of the dark cellars of his brain, fear and an old inherited hate and—

Rachaela gave him a cool green stare. He dropped his eyes, bowed again, and led the way inside but it was with the walk of a badly rattled man.

"Now what in—" Carsten paused. What had it been? A fleeting shift of expression, a shaken demeanor—he was suddenly angry, angry and puzzled both. He took a long step, as if to whirl the man around and poke him one for looking at *her* that way. Rachaela's hand stopped him.

"Will, don't," she murmured.

"What was the matter? Do you know him?" Carsten whispered the words.

"No. I must look like someone he does know." She grinned at him. "I seem to look like quite a few other people tonight."

"That was a dodge, and you know it," he answered, shoving the darkness back down into the bottom of his mind where it belonged. Not tonight, not tonight. "But I still don't see why—"

"I told you. I'm a demon out to buy your soul, and he, being a Romany, could sense what I am. Obviously that's the answer. For he's either right or insane. But an insane man could not be a headwaiter, he wouldn't be able to snub the patrons. Therefore he's correct as to my nature. *Quod erat demonstrandum.*"

"Shucks, you spoiled one of my quotations for me. I know three and only three Latin phrases, which I roll out sonorously on appropriate occasions, thus giving the impression of being highly educated. That was one of them."

"And the others—?"

"De gustibus non disputandum est. Anguis in herba. There, now I've said 'em, so we can relax and be lowbrows for the rest of the evening."

"But you're not a lowbrow," she said when they were seated. It was small and dark here, a niche in which they sat looking out over the dimly lit room. The other diners seemed very far away, the strolling gypsy players very near. "You're quite an intelligent and well-read man, Will. You could do great things if you cared to. Why are you by your own admission a second-rate writer when you could be a first-rater in any of a dozen other fields?"

"Such as what? No, honey, I held down several jobs before discovering I could write saleable fiction. Farmhand, lumberjack, grocery clerk, on up to fairly exotic things like deckhand on a sponge boat and janitor in an observatory. I have a B.A. degree in chemistry, too, and my professor wanted me to go on for a Ph.D. It's not that I haven't tried a lot of things."

"And been good at them. If you'd stayed with one—"

"Ah, there's the trouble, macushla. Specializing. So I could have been a chemist of some note. So I could have stayed in the grocery business and been a millionaire at fifty. Maybe so. But damn it, there are other things in life than the synthesis of parachlorothiazeostrichide or the current wholesale price of grapefruit. I'm not one of these first-rate geniuses who can be great names in science, learn a dozen languages and their literatures, travel round the world, have a significant voice in national policy, and write a book on a new philosophy they've worked out in odd moments—beside a score of other things. I haven't got what it takes to be a universalist, and won't submit to the jail of being a specialist. So I'm a dilettante."

"You write salable fiction and unsalable poetry," she nodded. "You paint and sculp a little, not at all badly. You read books on every conceivable subject and argue with specialist friends of yours on their own grounds, which leaves you on the defensive but also learning from them. You travel as much as you can afford. You feel at home in waterfront dives and the Diamond Horseshoe, with truck drivers and college professors. You are pretty much of a hedonist, but you'd like to be more."

"You do understand, don't you?" he murmured. "Yeah, that's about it, Rachaela. And writing is the closest a person of my limitations can come to universalism. It touches every field; in a shadowy sort of fashion, you live in all space and time. And you're pretty much your own boss, choose your own working hours and working pace, knock off for months at a time and take a leisurely jaunt somewhere whenever you've accumulated the money. If at times it seems rather futile, playing with toys you should have put away long ago, well, that's part of the price."

He sipped his cocktail moodily. *"Carpe diem,* too. It seems useless and wasteful to plan very far ahead these days. Any thinking man can see the world is going to smash. Why sacrifice and save and look to a high goal ten years off, when you know that before those ten years are up there'll be war again, and ruin, and you yanked into service or some damned dreary war job—and economic and social chaos to follow, when it'll be all that anyone can do to keep himself and his dependents above water? I'm just living from day to day, Rachaela, enjoying myself while I can, because there's really nothing else that's possible for me." He smiled wearily. "Maybe you're right. Maybe Hell is very close to us today."

"It is," she said soberly. "Very near."

"Well, tell me, then, most charming of devils—" He forced a lightness into his tone, seeking to recover their gaiety. "Give me the inside dope. What's it like? What is Hell, really? It's been variously described as bitter cold and white-hot, the home of all merry gentlemen and an eternity of boredom, aristocratic and bourgeois, everything and nothing. Come on, now, let's have the truth!"

Suddenly she shuddered, and leaned over against him. Her hand sought his, as if for comfort, and it was cold. Her eyes were wide, staring at him from a shining blankness, and her voice dropped to a shaky whisper.

"It is terrible," she said slowly. "It is all and none, flame and ice, howling chaos and frozen stasis, and it screams with the horror of being eternal— Oh, no, darling, don't ask me again!"

She gulped her drink and he watched her with a narrowed gaze, wondering if she might be insane and knowing that if she were, if she suddenly mouthed meaningless slaver at him and grinned from empty eyes, he would be damned to his own private hell for the rest of his life.

She laughed at him, a sudden warm pulse of mirth and sweetness. It was as if he saw winter ending, ice breaking on a river and buds on a willow and a steel-gray sky cloven by sunlight. He joined in, a bit too loudly in his relief.

"Oh, Will," she said. "Oh, my poor hardheaded scientifically trained agnostic! You know, I think you actually believed that!"

"Heh! Next time, don't be quite so good an actress, honey. Ah, here comes the soup."

Twice in the course of the meal he asked her to marry him. She laughed and stroked his cheek and did not answer, and the evening had wings. The fiddlers came over to their table and played for them, a lilting old air which set her feet to tapping out the rhythm and her voice to humming the melody. When they had gone she went on humming, a strange little tune which found its way into Carsten's head and made itself at home and started telling him of things he had forgotten. He remembered sunset over a quiet lake, a trembling bridge of moonlight on a tropic sea, the touch of his mother's hands. The corner was suddenly full of ghosts.

"Who wrote that?" he asked.

"That? Oh—you mean that song? I don't know. It's very old. They say that Hecuba sang her children to sleep with it, long ago in windy Troy. But this night is young."

"Is that a hint? How about going somewhere that we can dance, after we finish here?"

She was like another part of him—no, more, they were both part of the same, they swayed through a blue twilight where white water poured down a cliff of sounding crystal, they were one with the fireflies glimmering in cool dusk and the slow wheeling of stars and the sobbing, crying music. She could dance!

Then there was another place, noisy and smoky, full of beer smell and boisterous laboring men, and her laughter was a red flame pulsing through the racket and she kissed him till his head spun and the soft hair tumbled past her flushed cheeks.

They were in the shadowy interior of a car, going somewhere else, light flickering over her face as they went past vague buildings, darkness slipping back when they crossed quieter streets and deserted sections.

"Who are you, Rachaela? Who are you?"

"I've told you time and again, I am a demon assigned to get your soul. What price are you asking, sir?"

"Will you marry me?"

"You don't want to marry a career girl, do you? Especially one with my career . . . Will, my dress . . . oh, well . . . mmm . . ."

Somehow, it didn't seem strange that they should walk through a great flowering garden where huge white blooms nodded overhead and filled the night with perfume. They were swimming then, plunging into a cool lake, laughing and playing tag, crawling out on a mossy bank to let the warm moonlit air dry them.

"Sure it's not a case of mistaken identity? You look more like an angel to me."

"Oh, no, just a hard-working white-collar devil."

"But what would—he—want with human souls, anyway? As if we mattered to the Principle of Universal Evil."

"We do. Believe me, not the smallest thing is without meaning."

"And what becomes of—the damned?"

She shuddered, and he laid an arm about her shoulders. "All right, Rachaela, I'm sorry, I won't ask again. Only I assure you Hell would be Paradise enow, if you are there too."

"You don't know what you're talking about!" Her voice grew thin and shrill. He kissed her fear and his own away.

Later, quite prosaically, they were down in a tavern in the Village, surrounded by several of Carsten's madder friends, consuming beer and settling the problems of the universe.

"Theogamy," said Charleston. "Theogamy, that's the only solution."

"Poor etymology," clucked the Professor.

"Etymology," said Maryanne, "is the study of insects. Buy me a beer, insect."

"Where did you find this goddess, W. C.?" asked young Jones. He was sitting at Rachaela's feet, worshipping her.

"I told you," grinned Carsten. "I'm gathering material for a story on demoniac possession. She's my demon."

"It just goes to prove the basic injustice of a mad society," declared Swenson. "You, my dear W. C., sit on your fat can four hours a day, four days a week, forty weeks a year, and grind out pure, unadulterated garbage, pandering to the tasteless millions, and you wallow in money, simply wallow in it, sleep on mattresses stuffed with it, I say, have gorgeous women at your beck and call, bathe in champagne, whereas I, who have not only the first original thing to say since Gautama, but have invented a whole new system of expression to say it in, starve for my art. Can I borrow ten bucks?"

"No," said Carsten. It was a ritual between them.

"Oh, well, there's always beer," said Swenson. He buried his nose in foam, came up for air, and sang mournfully:

"Jag tippar att jag supar maj ihjel en dag till slut,
nar Fanden takar sjalan min och kroppan kastas ut—"

Carsten joined in, and they went on to *Cathusalem, The Jolly Tinker,* and *Les Trois Orfèvres.*

"And now for some sophistication," he said later, and they found themselves after a rather wonderful while in the newest and most fashionable nightclub the cab driver could locate.

"Who was seen where on what evening with which ex-wife of guess who?" he smiled. His head was whirling, he was a little drunk, but it was more with her than with alcohol. "Let's be different, Rachaela. Let's get married and come here again as man and wife. If they don't throw us out for it."

"You're very sweet, Will," she murmured, and her answering smile was soft.

"You want to buy my soul?" he asked a bit wildly. "Sure, it's for sale. Price, one marriage. To you. For permanent."

"You could get more than that, Will."

"What more would I want?"

"Oh—money, power, intelligence, energy, everything in life. You could become great in all fields of human work if you wanted to. You could write the finest piece of literature Earth will ever see."

"Hm. I'll consider it. Smoke?"

"No, thanks, I told you I preferred my own. They're rather strong. Here—" She fished a case out of her big, medieval-looking purse and handed it to him. He slid one out for her and took another himself, experimentally. Before he could light them, a dragon flew out of her purse—a very small dragon, scarcely four inches long, exquisite and golden. It hovered in the air, lit their cigarettes with a puff of flame, and popped back into its nest. He had to admit it was a good stunt.

The tobacco was too strong for him. He gasped, wiped the tears from his eyes, and stubbed it out. Rachaela smiled lazily and blew an acrid cloud at him.

"I told you I was a demon," she said, too casually.

"Now I believe it," he answered, more than half truthfully but not feeling surprised. After all, this was an enchanted evening.

"Hullo, Carsten, where'd you get this delicious piece of flesh?"

Carsten looked up, scowling. He had always disliked Tommy Delmarr, though he had to put up with the pest once in a while. "Beat it," he said.

"When so sharmin' a damsel is right to hand? No, no, no." Tommy sat down and leered vacantly at Rachaela. "Name, addressh, phone number?"

"Tommy," said Carsten, "I give you just one second to get away from here. Then I'm going to throw a punch at you."

"Ah, shaddap." Tommy leaned over, reaching for Rachaela's hand.

"I really mean it."

"Look, beautiful, how 'bout leavin' this character an' comin' over t' our table—"

Carsten stood up. With a savage glee quite foreign to his usually mild nature, he hauled Tommy erect, belted him once in the stomach, and followed with a right to the jaw that sent him across the adjoining table. And somehow that was the last touch needed to make the evening perfect.

What happened afterward, he wasn't very sure, but presently he and Rachaela were standing on the roof of the Empire State Building. How it had been done, he didn't know either, but it was nice to be alone again.

The moon was high and nearly full, riding through a deep-blue sky of stars and ghostly clouds. The city winked and blazed below them, mile after mile of it, fire and fury and the arrogance of man, and they stood above it all, looking down.

His gaze traveled to Rachaela. In the streaming moonlight her proud and lovely face was white, remote and mysterious, softened to a wistful beauty that seemed at the verge of tears. A line from Rupert Brooke crossed his mind: *"The lordliest lass of earth"*—and he nodded, slowly.

"Darling, darling!" He kissed her, laid his cheek to hers and buried his face in the tumbled waves of her hair. Her cheek was soft and smooth and cold in the keen fall night. "Oh darling, I love you so much—"

"Will—" She pulled herself against him, close, huddling to him like a child. "Will, Will—" Her breath sobbed in her throat.

"You will marry me, won't you? I'll not sell my soul for anything less."

"I really am damned, you know. I'm a demon from Hell."

"Sure, I know." He saw that her eyes shone with their own green light, up here in the dark and the thin whimpering wind. Gently, he ruffled the heavy hair back from her forehead and kissed the small horns. "What of it? I love you."

She laughed, shakily, and tears dimmed the cold fire of her eyes. Breaking away from him, but clinging to one hand, she said in an unsteady voice: "But this isn't according to the rules at all. I'm supposed to take you up on a high place and show you all the riches of the world and offer you what you will of them."

She gestured at the sea of flame below. "It can be yours, Will, yours to rule for a hundred years. Make what you want of it. Make a world of peace and sanity, where a man can think beyond the next day. They'll bless your name forever, and *he* won't mind, because time is long and the agents of Hell are many. You can sound out the world's deepest knowledge, Will, you can play on its heart as if on a harp, you can drink every cup of Earth to its bottom and there will be no dregs in your wine. Your shadow can fall over all of human history, man to the end of his existence will remember you and bear the stamp you chose to put on him, you, the happy god of Earth." She laughed, and the sound was wild and brittle. "Take it!"

"I only want you," he said, watching the moonlight play its frosty fingers over her hair. The wind whined and nuzzled under his coat, he shivered and stamped his feet and heard the noise ring loud under the moon. "I only want you, Rachaela."

"You can have that too," she whispered, so softly he could barely hear it. She was looking down at the floor, her face was in shadow. "But why not take the rest as well?"

"Oh, all right. For a hundred years, my darling." He tilted her chin up and saw the tears glimmering in the cold colorless moonlight.

"It's a high price to pay then." Her voice was almost a croak. She wouldn't meet his eyes.

"Then isn't now. Bring on your parchment, Rachaela, and don't forget a needle for my blood." He laughed, and there was only joy in him, his heart was laughing too, so softly, so softly.

"Come on, then!" She grabbed his hand and whirled around.

There was an instant of darkness, and they were in his room. His room, his old disordered shabby lodging, but now a haze of red and gold drifted through it, the fragrance of flowers and her hair, someone was singing in a high lovely voice and bells were crying their mirth to all the world.

"Oh, darling, darling, darling!" He grabbed her close and kissed her, again and again, as if he could never have enough. And he never would, not ever in his hundred years.

"I love you," he said.

"And I—love you too, Will." Her lips brushed his, soft as the touch of sunlight, sweet as the first springtime in Eden. "I love you too."

"Bring on the contract," he said. "Come on, let's get that part of it over with so I can have you all the sooner."

"Will—wait—" He saw the tears again, shining on her cheeks. "You ought to know what it means. You'll be damned forever."

"I've made my choice, haven't I? It's worth it. Well worth it."

"But *forever*—Will, you have no concept of Hell. You cannot imagine what it is. Your worst nightmares, the foulest thoughts that ever welled from a diseased brain, flame that burns you alive, hopelessness and misery—Will, none of them touch what *he* does!" Rachaela shook, as if it were suddenly cold amid the swirling golden mists. "Will, Hell is Hell, and it *never* ends—"

He read the panic crawling behind her eyes. His voice harshened. "Why are you afraid? What did they do to you there?"

"I'm a demon." Her teeth rattled together, and she crept into his arms and hid her face against his breast. "We're a p-privileged class, yes, b-b-but we're with the damned too, and the punishments for failure—" She sucked her breath in, fighting for control.

"You're not going to fail, Rachaela." He strained her to him. "Give me that contract."

"But Will—Will—you'll be among the damned then, you'll be in Hell forever and forever, worlds will crumble and the sun fall to ash before they've well begun with you, and it will last for all eternity—"

She shook her head, slowly, and freed herself. For a moment she stood with her head bowed, the long shining hair sweeping down past her face, and he saw that she was crying.

"I can't do it," she gasped.

"Rachaela—" He took a step forward, and the sudden knowledge was a desolation within him.

"No, Will, I won't do it, I won't, they can do what they want to me but I won't—I love you, Will. Always and forever, I love you." Her mouth trembled into a pathetic smile. "They think that'll be part of my punishment, but they're wrong. It will be the one thing I have through all those centuries till—till—" She shivered, and finished dully: "Till they decide I've had enough, and send me back to work."

"Rachaela," he whispered.

"No, no, I can't stay now. The quicker, the better, Will." She came back into his arms. "Goodbye—"

He held her close, held her for a very long time, knowing that she would go and not wasting his time in begging her to stay. His heart did that for him. And then she was gone, and he stood alone in his room. It smelt of stale cigarette smoke, and an unshaded bulb glared from the ceiling.

He wished he could cry, but he seemed empty of tears, empty and hollow as if they really had ripped the soul out of him. Tomorrow he might start thinking and feeling again, but it wasn't in him now.

He looked at the manuscript on his desk. *Rachaela,* he thought drearily. He took the sheets up one by one and crumpled them and threw them in the wastebasket. Then he went over to his dresser and took out a bottle.

About half a fifth, he estimated dimly. It should last him till the bars opened again.

When I read FORD MCCORMACK*'s "Hell-Bent" in the mid-1950s, it made such an impact on me that thirty years later it was one of the first stories that came to mind when I began devising the contents of this book. A subsequent perusal reveals it has lost none of its morbid power. (See Appendix I, page 573, for further comment.)*

Hell-Bent
BY FORD McCORMACK

"I do believe," said Satan, "that you are about the youngest scoundrel I have ever had the pleasure of calling upon."

I remember staring at him in speechless fascination. I was sprawled on my bed, where I had been making a half-hearted attempt to study the lessons I had neglected for weeks. And there he was, sitting at ease in my Morris chair.

Beyond any doubt, I knew who it was. Yet, try as I will, I cannot resurrect any clear image of his appearance on that occasion, for he looks quite different to me now. And the explanation is simple: I myself have changed.

When you look upon the Lord of Darkness—as perhaps you will—you behold all that is evil in yourself. Try to imagine, not a creature with horns and cloven hoofs, but a being both glamorous and revolting, whose shape and countenance, whose clothing or the lack of it, whose every gesture and expression, suggest precisely what your inmost mind conceives to be unholy.

That, or its equivalent, was what confronted me in my room on that remote afternoon.

"But it's mainly a business call," Satan went on abruptly. "I've come to make a bargain with you."

A bargain—a pact with the Devil! I had read of such a thing, but I hadn't really thought—I certainly hadn't expected—

"Why not?" Satan challenged my thoughts. "It isn't so much your experience of evil that counts—it's your aptitude for it. At sixteen, you show more downright talent for wickedness than most hardened criminals."

I recall feeling a little giddy at such eminent recognition. But Satan made a casual gesture.

"You needn't feel quite so flattered. I'm not referring to the hare-brained car-stealing episode that all but landed you in the reformatory. A criminal record can be a serious handicap.

"No, I have in mind a number of activities which you have wisely never revealed to anyone. I know, for instance, what really happened to your cousin Preston on that hike along the river. Ah, yes, and that little matter involving Mrs. Bonniwell's cat." Satan smiled. "Truly fiendish! . . . Well—need I say more?"

I shook my head, a little breathless. Somehow, I managed to find my voice:

"But—a pact—that means I give you my soul in exchange for—a charmed life, or something—doesn't it?"

Satan snorted, "Medieval nonsense! What's your idea of a charmed life—or did you ever stop to think?"

"Why—it's when nothing can hurt you, no matter what you do, or what danger you're in—"

"For how long?"

"Well, all your life, I suppose—that is, until—well . . ."

"Until you die of old age? You'd be surprised what effect that kind of deadline has on even the worst humans. I've tried it. They invariably turn holy and try to squirm out of it. Of course, they never succeed, and I get my price—so what? Nine chances out of ten, I'd have got the soul in question anyhow, and in the meantime I've tied up several of my best operators for years, during which they could have been undoing a lot of good. Instead, they have to stay on the alert constantly, in order to stymie some of the most elaborate and ingenious efforts at self-destruction ever devised.

"Besides," Satan went on, "there's no shortage of souls, these days —I get far more than I can give personal attention to, anyway. But there is one type I've never managed to get quite enough of—can you guess what it is?"

I shook my head.

"Operators," was the answer. "Or demons, as they were once popularly called. The boys that carry on the bad work. Eligible material isn't keeping up with the population increase."

"Why?"

" 'Rule Seventeen: Regarding any candidate for appointment as malevolent agent, it must be established that at the time of mundane demise, no trait of character could be ascribed to him which, in the judgment of his fellow men, would be deemed a virtue.' " Satan made a wry face. "Now, you'd be surprised how few arrivals can qualify, these days—at a time, strangely enough, when the quota is at an all-time high.

"Some of that few," he went on bitterly, "I lose on a mere technicality. Take the case of a recent consignee I had set great store by. He was a thorough-going blackguard who had just completed, on the gallows, a career of distinguished corruption. But it turned out that he had been kind to his children.

"Now, it wasn't that he really liked children as such; he merely saw his own as reflections of himself, which was true, to a certain extent— I shall probably get them all, eventually. But to his typically shallow-minded neighbors, being kind to anybody is a virtue, whatever the reason. And there was no deceptive intent on his part; if there had been, nobody else's opinion would have counted. As it was, one vestige of his soul remained white, and he was disqualified. I tell you, that quibbling decision burned me up—almost as much as it did him!"

I was beginning to grasp the general idea, I thought. But the prospect was so magnificent that I hardly dared allow my mind to dwell upon it, nor phrase the question I longed to ask.

Nor did I need to. I had forgotten—or had not fully realized—that the Lord of Darkness can read the minds of mortals.

He nodded slowly. "That is my offer. If you can qualify, you will become a full-fledged operator, after your earthly death. In that capacity, you will find plenty of opportunity for the sport you love best— making trouble. Subject, of course, to my orders. What do you say?"

Excitement constricted my throat, and I had to swallow to free it. "Yes! Oh, yes sir! That would be swell!"

"Mind you," said Satan sharply, "you can't afford to make any mistakes. You're still mortal and can die at any time, accidentally or otherwise. If that happens, and there's a single white mark against you —well, there'll be the Devil to pay."

I felt supremely confident. My apprenticeship would be successful, all right. And after that I would be endowed with superhuman powers —black magic and such!

"Yes," I said firmly. "It's a deal! Do you want my signature, in—uh —blood?"

"Get those old-fashioned notions out of your head!" said Satan without rancor. "I've told you it's not what you do, it's your intentions that count. Incidentally, I expect you to get busy on your schoolwork. I can't abide ignorant assistants! I'll leave you now, but you may summon me at any time merely by wishing it—just don't abuse the privilege, as I am very busy these days. Any questions? . . . No? . . . Then, au revoir!"

The next instant, bright sunlight dazzled my eyes. While we had been talking, the sun had changed position, and now shone through the window full in my face.

But why had I not noticed it before?

The Morris chair was empty.

Satan's sound advice notwithstanding, I accomplished very little on my schoolwork that day. During the next week or so, however, I was able to catch up on all my lessons. As the means to an infinitely desirable end, they no longer seemed onerous.

But in other respects, I was a little slow in launching my chosen career—or rather in furthering it, since I had already been officially credited with a fair start. While my "pact"—as I liked to think of it— had given me a thrilling objective in my earthly life, it had also introduced a new and serious consideration: risk.

Gradually, I learned to distinguish between truly evil impulses and merely reckless ones, and found that the former could, with cunning, usually be acted upon in such a way as not to jeopardize life or freedom. An episode which occurred not long before my graduation from high school resolved the last of my confusion, and pointed clearly to a *modus operandi* that was nearly foolproof.

The affair concerned the class president, a boy of noble character, who had been waylaid in a dark place, knocked semi-conscious with a club, and badly beaten. He had caught only a glimpse of his assailant, by the light of a distant streetlamp, and had somehow acquired the notion that it was me.

In the principal's office the next day, he gradually changed his mind. After all, as the principal pointed out, the two of us were barely acquainted—neither friends nor enemies.

"Can you imagine," the principal concluded his argument, "what earthly reason Robert could have had for doing such a thing?"

The class president was obliged to admit that he couldn't. And they were both right.

It wasn't an earthly reason.

Thinking the matter over that evening at home, I realized that I had made an important discovery. Although I would have phrased it differently then, the essence of it was this:

Just as the most irresistible form of benefaction is altruism, or that which seeks no reward, so does evil-doing achieve its greatest potency when it takes no thought of revenge or material gain. For demonstrable motivation is the cornerstone of criminology.

And with that thought came the realization of what my profession —the preliminary, or earthly, one—would be. I would become a criminal lawyer. As such, I could kill two birds with one stone: get rich helping guilty people escape punishment. I toyed delightedly with the idea for a while, then turned with renewed purpose to my studies. I was pretty well up on them, but final exams were just around the corner.

At that moment I became aware that I was not alone.

I was a little startled at beholding Satan again. It was not, I recall, that there had been any major alteration in his appearance, but rather a number of minor ones, as if some modeler in clay had shifted the emphasis by a few deft pats and pinches, sharpening a feature or an expressive line of the countenance here and there, and subtly distorting the bodily contours. The result was a masterly—and somewhat disturbing—image of what my soul had now become.

And then he smiled, indescribably, but in such a way as to send a tingle along my nerves.

"Yes," he nodded, "I have changed, and, by the same token, so have you. The picture in your mind shows that you have made definite progress. And the fundamental principle you discovered this evening should be very useful to you."

I frowned. "If you knew that, why didn't you tell me about it before?"

"Because, like many principles, it has more significance when you are able to figure it out for yourself. Incidentally, I like your tentative choice of a profession. But it will be several years before you can engage in it. In the meantime, there is the problem of your parents. That is what I came to warn you about."

"Warn me?"

"Yes. Although you have been successfully eradicating other virtues, your esteem for your mother and father, while less than devotion, is holding fairly steady. And you seem almost unaware of the possible consequences. Frankly, I had not anticipated any such difficulty—particularly since they are only foster-parents, and have by their own standards done a miserable job of raising you."

I was stung. "There's a reason for that! As you probably know, my father has been in poor health for years, and my mother spends most of her time taking care of him. Outside of that, they've always treated me as if I were—" I broke off in some confusion, aware that Satan was regarding me with sardonic surprise.

"Spoken like any member of the Opposition!" he said, after a moment. "The matter is more serious than I had thought. I am quite aware, thank you, that ingratitude is a sin. And believe me, I have known for a long time that charity begins at home. It follows that if charity is to be nipped in the bud, home is the place to do it. But I have no time to argue with you. If you're going to let such trifling and temporal considerations as filial piety stand in the way of *permanent* objectives, the choice is yours."

Satan finished soberly: "Think it over, my boy. I don't need to tell you that you're already in pretty deep, and—well, I'd rather be your boss than your keeper. But now, I have business elsewhere, so—"

"Wait!" My voice was so loud that I jumped, suddenly aware that my parents downstairs thought I was alone.

"Don't worry," said Satan. "Even the stupidest of my operators knows the simple spell necessary to soundproof a room. With me, it's automatic."

Despite his reassurance, I went on in hushed tones: "What would I have to do—kill them?"

"I'm making no recommendations," Satan returned casually. "You're supposed to be winning your own spurs, remember. Murder would, of course, eclipse any pre-existing kind feelings—even if, as in your case, they were pretty strong. Ordinarily, complete indifference to the fate of one's parents would be sinful enough."

"But—but how could I be sure I really didn't care what happened to them?"

Satan shrugged. "How, indeed? That, I must emphasize, is your problem. If you'll excuse me, I shall be off. There has been a severe earthquake in Chile, and I must get up a crew to delay the arrival of the relief busybodies."

Again, I accomplished very little in the way of studying that evening, after Satan had left, but this time it was for a quite different reason.

My parents did not attend the graduation exercises, since my father was in one of his low periods of health, and my mother disliked to leave him. On that day, I began to see that there was some truth—which even the Devil can speak—in the accusations he had leveled against them. They could at least have hired a nurse to stay with my father while my mother attended the exercises. In fact, they were sufficiently well off to have afforded one during the several years of my father's illness, if my mother had been much concerned with her duties to a mere foster-child.

Two or three days later I was coming home from the drugstore, after replenishing my father's supply of a long-standing prescription, when a sudden thought stopped me in my tracks. Retiring to the privacy of some nearby shrubs, I unwrapped the vial carefully and shook some of the tablets into my hand. Yes, they looked for all the world like ordinary aspirin!

I had no idea what they really were, beyond hearing my father say semi-jokingly that they were all that kept him alive. But I knew they could be nothing like aspirin, which my father reacted to strongly and had been specifically warned against.

After about an hour of aimless walking, I stopped by a different drugstore before going home . . .

My father succumbed so readily, I was somewhat shocked to discover how delicate his health had actually been. Plainly, I had had a narrow escape. He could easily have died at almost any time, leaving me with a dangerous amount of affection for him.

Although the doctor was not particularly surprised at his patient's sudden turn for the worse, he methodically had the prescription analyzed. But I had anticipated him there, and the bottle was found to contain the right kind and number of tablets. My father had taken his last aspirin almost twenty-four hours before his death, so that even an autopsy, had one been ordered, would probably have revealed nothing.

My mother was quite literally inconsolable: her grief remained undiminished even after a long time. In view of my father's fragile health when living, this was an unrealistic attitude, which inevitably began to affect her mental stability. It also showed clearly how secondary had been my own status in her esteem.

She became totally insane about the time I graduated from law school, and my first legal case was to have her declared incompetent to administer what was left of my father's estate after the considerable expense of my education. I then had her committed to a suitable institution. There was no doubt in anyone's mind that she belonged there.

For I had taken the precaution of telling her what really happened to my father.

In another year I had a going law practice, complete with useful political connections, and was maintaining a fair batting average of acquittals. Privately, of course, I regarded as favorable decisions those which convicted innocent clients. I took such cases only where they appeared sufficiently hopeless to be lost without obvious bungling on my part, which would have been injurious to my reputation.

It was about this time that I began to have difficulties with my mistress. Martha Torrance was no ordinary kept woman, but a girl of reputable family whom I had met while attending law school. I had reduced her to the present status by a long process of attrition, including the promise of marriage. Now that I had graduated and established a practice, it had become hard to find excuses for further delay of the nuptials.

There came the day of her ultimatum, and I was inclined to believe she meant it. Quite simply, she gave me the choice of setting a definite date for the wedding or walking out of her life.

The latter alternative was out of the question. In the first place, there was little doubt that I was somewhat fond of her, which for me was an inadvisably wholesome way to wind up the affair. Then, too, I was not at all sure I had corrupted her sufficiently that she would continue an immoral existence. I was obliged to set a date, as far ahead as possible, and to hope that in the meantime some dishonorable solution would suggest itself.

A few days later, in a flash of inspiration, one did. It would necessitate going through with the marriage and remaining in that status for some time, but as a culminating act of villainy, it would be well worth the trouble.

My plan called for a male third party, and at once I culled the list of my acquaintances for a man to suit the role. I selected a personable bachelor named Douglas Wakefield, and began to cultivate him. He became a close enough friend, during the next few months, to officiate as best man at my wedding. By this time, I was confident that I could not have made a better choice. Doug Wakefield was attractive to women, but seemed to have a fairly strict code of ethics regarding them. And Martha liked him.

I let several months go by before I considered that the time was ripe, and shortly thereafter the perfect opportunity presented itself. I found myself one morning with little to do for the rest of the day, the result of an uncontrived lull in my business affairs. Then, as I sat in my private office, mentally reviewing the steps of my infamous plan, it suddenly dawned on me that I was actually reluctant to go through with the thing!

After the first shock of surprise at my own weakness, I thought I understood the basis of my feeling. It was simply the recognition that the deed I contemplated would amount to a final commitment, placing me far beyond any conceivable hope of redemption. Not, of course, that there was much hope anyway.

The possibility that Satan, who was reputed to have tricked many mortals, might be tricking me was ruled out by due consideration. It made sense that he needed help, that the mushrooming population of earth called for an expansion of his staff. It did not make sense that he would waste his chicanery on what could be termed a cinch deal: the mere acquisition of my soul. No, here was my chance to complete my qualification for an eternal job of mischief-making, and I had delayed overly long already.

I flipped the toggle-switch on the interoffice communicator and called my secretary for dictation. My secretary, incidentally, was an attractive but not very capable young lady of rather high morals. I was paying her so handsomely that for the first time she was able to take adequate care of her widowed mother. Jobs were getting scarce, and I expected to have a new mistress soon.

As she sat waiting, her pretty face showing the usual strain of un-limbering her incompetent shorthand, I said casually:

"By the way, I feel a little sluggish today—I've been thinking an afternoon of golf might help. Get Mr. Wakefield on the phone and I'll ask him to join me."

Fortunately, Doug had not yet gone to lunch, and a minute later I was receiving his courteous refusal:

"Gosh, I'd like to, Bob, but I've got a dozen calls to make today. I thought you knew my busiest time is in the afternoon—on weekdays, at least. How about Saturday?"

We made it tentative for Saturday and said goodbye. So far so good: I now had a witness to the fact that Douglas Wakefield thought I was going to the country club that afternoon. I had known, of course, that he wouldn't accept. He was district sales manager for a chain of stores and did a lot of field work, mostly in the afternoons.

After dictating a short letter, I sent my secretary to lunch. When she had gone, I phone Martha and told her I was a little indisposed—nothing serious—and would be home before long. I was fairly sure she had not planned to go out; now it was certain she would be there.

Twenty minutes later, I called the café where Douglas Wakefield was accustomed to eat lunch. Keeping my voice just light enough so the waitress could not later swear whether it was that of a man or woman, I asked for Mr. Wakefield. He was there.

"Doug," I said. "I just got home, and—something has happened. I don't want to talk about it over the phone, but can you come right over? And don't mention it to anybody, please."

I had known that I could probably count on him to answer such a mystifying summons without insisting on further information, but his response was even better than I expected.

"I'll be right there," he said after a short pause, and hung up.

It would not have mattered too much if my secretary had not returned promptly from lunch, but she did. I contrived a slightly haggard expression.

"I've changed my mind about golf," I told her. "I'm not feeling so well. I believe I'll just go home and take it easy."

She looked concerned. "Do you think you ought to drive? I'll be glad to—"

"Oh, no! It'll be all right. I haven't even called my wife—it'll be soon enough for her to start worrying when I get there."

Driving homeward in my car, I chuckled over the ambiguity of that last remark, which had set the stage completely. Yes, my simple little plan was ticking off nicely. Any jury in the world would unquestionably agree that Martha and Doug were guiltier than I, would secretly scoff at the purely negative evidence to the contrary. Even I, as my own lawyer, could get myself off with a few years' imprisonment, at most—and I intended to be better represented than that.

While waiting for a traffic signal, I took out the revolver I had kept in the glove compartment for a long time—and for which I had a permit—checked it to reassure myself it was fully loaded, and slipped it in my coat pocket.

I approached my home slowly from a side street off the direct route from town. Although Doug had started perhaps ten minutes earlier, he had had farther to come than I, and might not have arrived yet.

Then I saw his car. It was parked—rather brazenly, people would say—in front of my house. I pulled up two doors away and hurried in, lest I should be seen by the "paramours" and confronted in an unclandestine way on my own front porch.

Doug and Martha were standing in the living room as I entered. He was still holding his hat in his hand. They really made a handsome, if surprised, couple. Of course, the police would find them in a more disheveled—and compromising—pose.

Just now, their faces showed mixed feelings, in which bafflement seemed to predominate. I had to admit that for them it would be a puzzling situation. But I had no intention of wasting time with explanations based on mere braggadocio, and taking the risk of spoiling a perfect set-up. I simply drew my revolver, aimed carefully at Douglas Wakefield and fired, I then turned my attention to Martha, who stood transfixed, evidently trying to scream.

It was then that the unexpected happened. By a sort of acquired instinct, I had shot Doug in the stomach, so that he would die not instantly but in great pain. That was where I made my mistake. As I shot Martha through the heart, to avoid any suspicious repetition, I saw Doug straighten from his convulsion of agony, and pull something shiny from the belt of his trousers. I had no time to stop him, nor in fact to do anything but wonder vaguely why he, too, should have been carrying a gun. There was a burst of pain within me—I was not even sure just where—and I blacked out.

My next conscious awareness was of standing naked in an immense cavern before the Throne of Hell.

Sitting upon it was a creature so appalling in its hideousness that for a moment I failed to identify it. And then, as my eyes became accustomed to the reddish light which suffused the great chamber, every lineament of the gargoyle-like figure began to convey subtle meaning.

The modeler, the Master Caricaturist—and I was beginning to suspect who that might be—had outdone himself. Here was no bestial symbology, such as confuses mere animalism with true depravity; every detail of this foul simulacrum was intensely human. And, in its idiomatic way, acutely familiar.

Yet the very frightfulness of what I saw was, in a sense, reassuring. After all, I *was* a candidate. Surely, there could be no question—

"None whatever!" Satan's voice boomed hollowly in the cavern. I found myself impaled by those insanely staring eyes, and below them the bloated, grinning lips moved again: "I am delighted to report that you passed the test with a single flying color—black!"

He was toying with what seemed to be two small and slimy animals on his lap. They growled continually. Other than that the silence became lengthy. I grew a little impatient.

"Well," I said brusquely, but my voice sounded thin in the vast room, "what do I do now?"

Satan smiled crookedly. "There are no formalities. Consider yourself on duty. I'll even give you your first assignment here and now. It is to remove these playthings from my lap and dispose of them. They no longer amuse me."

I was puzzled. "What are they—imps?"

"No." The leer on that ghastly countenance grew broader. "Come closer."

Hesitantly, I walked toward him. And—strangely—I seemed to get no nearer at first. Then, with a shock, I realized the truth. The throne was at least a hundred feet away, and Satan was—huge!

I had assumed, on the basis of our earlier meetings, that his present size was no greater than my own, and the odd glow of this place had preserved the illusion. The monster confronting me, if erect, would have stood twelve or fourteen feet high.

Sitting, he was imposing enough, but I strode on to the very base of the rough-carved platform under him. Mere size, I told myself, was of no importance.

Yet the burning gaze of those mad eyes was hard to take, point-blank. I looked at the two squirming things on his great thighs. They also appeared proportionately larger, and not quite so shapeless. I could see now why they had looked so slimy. They were, to all appearances, masses of entrails, very much like those of humans. I had the sudden impression that here were two living human beings turned wrong side out! What I had interpreted from a distance as growling was now recognizable as muffled screams issuing from their involuted throats.

"Amazing!" I gasped. "I wouldn't have thought it could be done!"

"As a matter of fact, it's anatomically impossible," said Satan, "but that's no limitation here." He plunged his misshapen hands into the two slithering masses, felt around briefly, and gave a sharp jerk. Instantly, two complete human beings sat on his knees like a pair of ventriloquists' dummies, and the combined volume of their shrieking became ear-splitting. I noticed with a start that one of them was a woman, and then, despite their contorted faces and wide-open mouths, I recognized them both—Martha and Douglas!

As I stood there stupefied, Satan rocked and drooled with harsh laughter, raising a bedlam of echoes. And when he subsided, there was silence. Although Martha and Douglas were obviously still screaming at the top of their lungs, the sound of it had in some fashion been suppressed. I was glad of that much, at least.

"Does this mean—" I faltered.

Satan nodded. "They had been having an affair for months. But the infinitely amusing part of it is that they were going to tell you about it, and ask for a divorce. Douglas was afraid you had found out, when you made your mysterious request, which was the reason he brought a gun for protection, just in case. But if you had delayed the shooting as much as a minute, they would have confessed everything. And that—" Satan gave vent to a bubbling chuckle—"that would have tied your hands! Do you see the supreme irony of it? That would have told you there was a modicum of justice in what you intended to do, and you wouldn't have dared to do it!"

After another interval of more restrained but equally derisive mirth, he sobered somewhat. "Of course," he said, "I wouldn't really have preferred it to happen that way. As it works out, you have increased my inventory by two souls who, if left among the living, might have turned penitent and escaped me. Not to mention the advantage of having your services available at this time, when I need you—as it were—badly."

I had begun to collect my scattered wits. "And that's why you didn't tell me about the affair! I presume you were aware of it all along?"

Satan bowed sardonically. "I contrive to keep posted on most such matters."

Oddly, at that moment I felt less resentment toward Satan than I did toward my guilty wife and supposed friend. The Devil had at least behaved true to form. But they—

"What did you mean," I asked, "when you said you wanted those two disposed of?"

"Oh—the usual thing. Fling them into the Fiery Pit."

"Fling them? I'm fairly husky, but—"

"You now," Satan pointed out, "have the strength of a demon. Here, catch!" And with an easy motion, he sent the writhing body of Douglas Wakefield flying through the air toward me. I stepped aside but caught an arm as he went past. Surprisingly, I was able to stop him with ease, and he felt light as a kitten. It was child's play to put an end to his struggles by pinioning all four limbs against his torso, and to tuck him under my arm.

Martha came next, and I gathered her up in similar fashion. This was going to be fun.

"Now, where in Hell," I inquired almost cheerfully, "might the Fiery Pit be?"

"In Hell," was the immediate rejoinder, "things are arranged—and rearranged—to suit my convenience. Just now, the Pit is right behind you."

As he finished speaking, I became aware of an intense wave of heat at my back, and the smell of burning sulphur stung my nostrils. At the same time, the low roaring of a mighty holocaust filled the air. I turned and all but fell over the edge of an enormous chasm. Its walls were hundred-foot precipices, perhaps a quarter of a mile apart and of unguessable length. Its floor was a glowing, changing mass of coals, seen through flickering tongues of blue and orange flame. The effect was that of a wide underground river of fire.

Faintly audible in the steady muttering of the flames, there was an incessant chorus of human wailing. Looking closely, I saw a moving figure on the bed of coals below. And another—and several more. Then, as my eyes became more accustomed to the fierce glare, I could distinguish them everywhere, most of them creeping slowly, and I realized it had been partly the random motion of these hundreds of creatures which had lent a seething aspect to the entire surface.

They were all human—or had been—and as I watched, it became clear that their continual crawling, which had seemed aimless, was not without purpose, after all. The general motivation was quite simple: to get to a cooler spot. Here and there, places could be seen where the coals merely smouldered or were black. The nearest dozen humans would inch their way to one of these thermal islands, all reaching it at about the same time, when it would promptly flare into searing brightness. With anguished shrieks, the cluster of souls would begin the frantic but feeble dispersal toward other points only slightly less unendurable.

There was a sort of dynamic simplicity about the set-up that I had to admire. And, I thought grimly, it was just the place for Douglas and Martha.

At that moment, my gloating was interrupted by what could only have been a huge foot planted between my shoulder blades, for I felt its toes against the back of my head. Hampered as I was, I had no chance to save myself, and the next instant a powerful thrust sent me headlong over the brink.

Plummeting toward the fiery depths, I relinquished my human burdens, and they went their separate ways, limbs flailing. It was the last glimpse I ever had of Douglas and Martha. And then I struck the bed of coals, with a wrenching impact that would have knocked out or killed any living mortal instantly.

But in Hell, there is no unconsciousness, nor any other means of alleviating pain—and, obviously, there is no death. The shifting coals broke my fall sufficiently so that of all my bones only two ribs cracked. But I was not even aware of that minor injury at the time. For over my entire body, the skin was blistering and peeling away, and I was engulfed in a tidal wave of agony.

Convulsively, I scrambled to my feet and staggered toward the wall a few feet away, falling twice before reaching it. But its glazed and scorching surface was nearly unbroken, offering no real hand-holds whatever. Along it on both sides of me, other humans were stretching up their arms to clutch at every tiny crevice, but none had managed to lift himself clear of the flames, which seemed to leap more furiously here than elsewhere.

And—half-blinded though I was—I must have noticed a certain odd fact at that moment, since I remembered it later: While my own skin and part of my flesh was charring and smoking acridly, the others seemed to have no worse than a mild first-degree burn all over. Yet their gasping screams indicated their anguish could not be much less than mine.

My groping fingers found a small crack in the wall over my head and I found to my amazement that I was able to raise myself a little. Frantically, with fingers and toes, I searched for other holes, and presently I had climbed precariously out of reach of the flames. But it had taken the full measure of my newly-acquired, demoniac strength, plus the utmost desperation, to accomplish it. I was seemingly beyond exhaustion; my body felt as if it were bathed in lye. And the mere act of clinging there was taking a further toll.

It was not will-power alone that sustained me through the rest of that climb. Only the tenacity born of consuming hatred could have done it. Hatred toward all the beings of Heaven, Hell and between— but, toweringly, hatred toward the sardonic Prince of Fiends who had done this to me!

By any standard, it must have taken me a long time to reach the top. And when I finally pulled myself over the rim and lay prone, still fully conscious but unaware of anything other than the pain and weariness which permeated me, it seemed that I had used up a great slice of eternity.

But I was not to be left alone for long. After an all-too-brief interval, I felt a mashing weight on my back. It moved irresistibly, rolling me over twice, then lifted. In sudden panic, I raised myself on all fours and looked around, sickened by the fresh agony of the effort. But I was no longer near the Pit—in fact, it was nowhere to be seen. The object that had rolled me over had apparently been Satan's gargantuan foot; it was stretching out toward me again, threateningly.

"Get up!" was his rasping command, and he went on ironically: "Perhaps that little lesson will teach you to carry out my orders more promptly."

A surge of anger brought me, swaying, to my feet.

"Promptly!" I croaked. "But you—you—" I broke off, incoherent with rage. I had been about to point out that he himself had engaged freely in the conversation after giving those orders, that there had been no intimation of any penalty for delay, and that—

Then I saw that Satan was reading my thoughts, for he was nodding his head and grinning horrendously. He spoke with slow emphasis: "Unfair, isn't it?"

The simple remark was like a physical blow, because of its tremendous implications. It was then that I truly felt the cold, tightening grip of ultimate despair.

"And yet," Satan said complacently, "it is amazing how little downright falsehood it was necessary to use on you. You were fairly gullible —and of course if I can make the partial truth serve my ends, it always enhances the deception. At no time did I guarantee that you would *like* the job, when you got it, or that you would not suffer. The presumption that you could come here with your soul completely black and escape punishment required a minimum of suggestion on my part, and a maximum of wishful thinking on yours. Actually, the tortures in store for you are considerably more intense and diversified than those of the run-of-the-mill damnees in the Pit, who, as you noticed, are conditioned for permanent residence therein. You will forever undertake to do my bidding, and my bidding will invariably be more than you can do. And the woe which shall betide you when you fail to do it does not compare with that which shall follow when you fail to try."

Satan paused, and the great foot advanced significantly again, for I had slumped to my knees in pain and utter dejection. With excruciating effort, I managed to get my seared and swollen feet under me again.

"And now," Satan went on, "it is time you met some of your colleagues. They are all very busy, but I have called in several of them anyhow. Since they are aware that this will mean extra punishment for neglecting their various assignments, they should be delighted to make your acquaintance."

As he spoke, there were stirrings in the dim, red shadows of the cavern; now vague shapes began to emerge. They drew nearer, becoming more distinct, and in spite of my preoccupation with the undiminished torment of my flesh, I shuddered. For any one of them was the horrid equal of Satan, and there were at least a dozen.

No two of them were alike. Each was the cunning caricature of an unspeakably vile human soul; a few made the guise of Satan look almost ingenuous. But there was one striking difference: none of them was smiling. Instead, despair and suffering were written indelibly on each visage, though without altering its essential evil. This eloquent expression, as much as their combined repulsiveness, made the sight of them unbearable, and I closed my aching eyes.

As if it were a signal, they all rushed me at once; I was caught completely off guard. The next instant I was down, crushed by the onslaught of a group of which each member was, for the time being, stronger than myself. And—I quickly discovered—much more vicious. They clutched and gouged at every part of my already excoriated body, yet with uncanny precision seemed to seek out the most sensitive spots. And the small part of my mind that was not exploding with pain was paralyzed with horror, not so much at the likelihood of being torn apart, but at not being able to die when it happened.

Suddenly, incredibly, the attack ceased, and within seconds I was left lying there alone. But the agony lingered, and in fact had hardly lessened when Satan's inexorable foot rolled me over again. This time, he was obliged to plague me at length before I could so much as raise my head.

"I had to send them away," he observed casually. "They were beginning to enjoy themselves. Such pleasures as tearing people to bits I reserve for myself—unless some of the boys take a notion to gang up on you behind my back, as sometimes happens to rookies. In that case, your punishment would be double, both for providing them with amusement and for giving me the trouble of putting you back together. Your only insurance is never to close your eyes, not even for sleep—which, of course, you will crave with increasing desperation.

"Nonetheless, I think you will contrive to keep them open, somehow, in spite of the fact that the aspect of your co-workers will grow ever more loathsome to your sight. For in all creation, you could not find so despicable a crew of backbiting stool-pigeons as that which you have joined. Each of them, incidentally, sees me as a replica of himself, except for size. Henceforth, the same will apply to you. When at long last your flesh has healed recognizably, you will look exactly as you see me now. And since the sight of yourself will be most revolting of all, you will avoid reflecting surfaces everywhere—but you cannot avoid me.

"By that time, you will have been introduced to other and more deadly forms of mental suffering. And you will find that, just as you cannot die to end physical pain, so also the escape of insanity is denied you . . ."

There was more—more that Satan said on that occasion, and much more that I have learned since. But time is running short. Fortunately the full meaning of the phrase "behind my back," with its implication that Satan does not perpetually concern himself about the doings of each and every henchman, did not occur to me until an hour ago. Since then, his attention has remained elsewhere, otherwise this story could not reach you, the reader. There is still the chance that it may not.

I am relating this account into the wire-recorder of a hack writer who has fallen asleep at his work. He will know how to go about getting it published, and since he apparently has a tendency to live beyond his means, he will undoubtedly be anxious to do so. He will, of course, take full credit for its authorship, and may even leave these concluding comments as they stand, if he thinks they will make him appear more clever. But that is of no importance to me. I shall be satisfied if, somewhere, a single candidate reads my story. For he will understand, and take warning.

And if you are that one, let there be no mistake. I am utterly, irrevocably evil, and I detest all human beings, including you. It is only the thought of frustrating my dread Master, whom I hate far more, that makes me tremble with eagerness to betray him in this fashion.

I shall now backwind this spool of wire to the point where Satan's deception is revealed, start it playing forward, and turn the volume up loud. That should wake the writer, and once a mortal has heard my tale, Satan will be helpless to suppress it. But he will, of course, strain his ingenuity to reward me suitably.

Whatever he does, one thing is ironically certain: I won't lose my job.

In the introduction to this section, I promised you a three-task deal and here it is—the second short story I ever wrote. Since an anthologist who includes his own work commits an act of hubris, I shall not offend the reader by offering any defense. Instead, I will swiftly sneak offstage and let the spotlight play upon Tiny Tom, Hell's answer to Lou Costello. (For additional comment, see Appendix I, page 573.)

Damned Funny

BY MARVIN KAYE

Hell was very much on Drake's mind—and the way he imagined it was like a Medieval woodcut. This image was partly dictated by his rigorous religious upbringing but mostly by the paucity of his creative faculties. His mind was so preoccupied with visions of willowy women in intimate states of disarray that he had little energy left over to summon up inventive pictures of the Pit.

So when he thought about Hell, he envisioned a fundamentalist nightmare peopled with lean, sinewy demons, fiends who raked long, encrusted claws along the tortured, pustulant loins of the damned.

Yet in spite of this sharply-etched cerebral phantasma, Drake could not put aside the notion of betting with the Devil. His compulsive daydreams—in which he wallowed in forests of distaff flesh—had gained the upper hand, especially since their fulfillment fled further from his grasp with the waning years. So, at length, he determined to test his wits against the foul fiend and his infernal minions, bargaining for those carnal pleasures which had long been denied him by the God he feared was nothing more than myth.

He studied the problem for a long time, researching the traps and pitfalls which had damned other hapless contestants in battles with the dark powers. At length, Drake evolved a strategy that promised to be virtually failsafe, and one midnight, set about to test it. With considerable trepidation, he etched a pentagram upon the bare floor of his chilly walkup studio apartment. As he chanted the fateful words, he trembled at the prospect of the hideous entity who soon would materialize in the middle of the five-sided figure.

So when a short, pot-bellied devil in a red-flannel union suit plopped in a heap in the center of the pentagram, Drake was understandably nonplussed.

Whistling, the diabolic visitor sat for a moment trying to catch his breath. "Damn," he complained, "that was one powerful telegram you sent!" He adjusted a stubby spade-tip tail through the emergency flap of his underwear, then, mustering up what dignity he could, addressed his host in a gravelly voice. "Yeah, boy, what the hell do you want?"

Drake couldn't find his voice.

"Come on, come on," the fiend rasped, extracting a black stogey and lighting it with a snap of his talons, "I ain't got the whole damned night!"

"Are . . . are you," Drake stammered, "the . . . uh, honest-to-God devil?"

The other scowled. "Look, watch your language, will you? And, anyway, I'm not the Big Boss, who the hell do you think you are?"

"But you are—*a* demon?"

"What's the matter, you blind? Don't I look like the devil?"

Studying the tubby creature trapped within the chalk walls of the pentagram, Drake smirkingly conceded the point. The dumpy fiend reminded him of Lou Costello. Lumpy, short and rotund, the imp—who said his name was Tiny Tom—had two plastic horns pasted to his head, a threadbare cape too short to hide the scraggly protuberance that was an excuse of a tail, and a rubber pitchfork clutched in a smudgy, unmanicured paw.

Tiny Tom belched. "Okay, kiddo, what's the deal? You wanna sell your you-know-what for my what-do-you-want?"

Drake shook his head. "None of that kind of contract. I want to pose three tasks. If you can't do any of them, I do not forfeit my soul."

"A threesie, a threesie!" the demon whooped, "I ain't had one of them for years!" With that, the devil ignored his host's protests and launched into an enumeration of three-task contract rules in the tireless manner of a daytime TV game show emcee.

When the tirade was over, Drake removed the crushed remnant of a cigarette pack from his pocket and fished out the charred stub of a butt.

"I have one modification in mind," he told Tiny Tom. "I want a wish for any task you can't accomplish."

"A snap," said the other. "That's Contract 34 B. What do you want me to give you?"

"Riches, irresistibility to women, and immortality," the mortal replied, puffing nervously on the weed.

Tiny Tom looked crestfallen. "Boy, are those typical!" he moaned. "I thought I had a live wire for a minute. Okay," he continued over Drake's protests, "the loot and the broads is okay, but the immortality is out."

It was Drake's turn to look crestfallen. "Why? I thought you could do just about anything."

"Not immortality, buster."

"Why not?"

"Not our department." He held up a paw in a gesture of reassurance. "Tell you what, though, I *might* be able to give you an extended life."

"How extended?"

"Hold on a minute, I have to check it out." Reaching inside the moth-eaten cape, Tiny Tom extracted a sheaf of papers, referred to them, then began to work out a complicated series of calculations. He looked like a seedy insurance agent working on his actuarial tables. After a few minutes, the fiend looked up from his jottings.

"As of this minute, boy," he said, "your probability span runs up to five hundred years."

"Probability span?" Drake asked. "What's that?"

"It's sorta complicated. You have to compute capacities for good and evil, divide them into the inertia factor of probable harmlessness, and come up with the optimum time you can be *tolerated* on earth." Tom shrugged, and put the papers away. "So, anyway, your probability span is five centuries. That okay?"

"I guess it'll have to do," Drake sighed. "Shall we get on with it?"

The devil nodded.

"All right," the mortal warned, "now I don't want any misunderstandings. I'll give you three tasks to perform, one for each wish. You can't back out of the sequence once it's begun. If you can't perform *any single task* out of the three, I forfeit nothing. You must perform *all three* in order to take my soul, understand?"

"Yeah, yeah, I'm not a dummy," said Tom, "I've been in this business a long time. When I *can't* do something, you get that particular wish."

"Now—do I sign anything?"

"Nope," the demon demurred. "Not till it looks like I've got a chance to collect." Drake looked suspicious, but the fiend waved a deprecating paw. "Look, it's not a trick, it just makes for less book-keeping!"

"All right," the other said. "Now one more thing—no tricks about my wishes, see? No 'witches money' that vanishes by dawn. If I win unlimited wealth, I want it in contemporary legal American currency—"

"Don't worry already!" Tiny Tom said, exasperated. "Such shyster tricks I wouldn't pull! *Enough* with the technicalities—what's the first task?"

"You are to appear inside a certain building which I will describe." Drake took a piece of paper out of his pocket and referred to it. Tiny Tom, scowling, held up an admonitory talon.

"Now look here, you don't gimme no churches! That's absolutely forbid in Contract 34B!"

"It's not a church," Drake replied, annoyed. "Give me *some* credit. You are to appear inside this building at two a.m. on Christmas Eve. You will walk to the front door, open it and step outside."

"That's all?" Tiny Tom inquired, amazed.

"Uh-huh. The building is on the Virginia side of the Potomac River on a site once called—(appropriately enough)—Hell's Bottom. The precise situation is seventy-seven degrees, two minutes west by——"

It was December 25.

At 2:05 a.m., Drake stood ankle-deep in snow, shivering and cursing. Tiny Tom, standing by his side, looked insufferably smug.

"Like to see me do it again?" he asked.

"No!" the other snapped, his teeth chattering. "But how did you manage? The barrier was unbroken! I'd swear it!"

"Only it wasn't a barrier," the pudgy imp conceded. "Not that you didn't have a clever idea, getting me to materialize inside what you figured would be The Pentagon after working hours in mid-winter on a holiday."

"I figured," said Drake, "that the night staff would be minimal and it would be cold enough so all the doors and windows would be shut, making the building into a perfect pentagram, which you can't cross."

"Only I did!" the demon taunted.

"How?! Did somebody leave a window or a door open?"

"Nope."

"Well, are you going to tell me, or do I have to guess?" the mortal asked somewhat testily.

"I'm surprised at you," Tom grinned, spitting between two blades of grass. A tiny column of steam rose hissing from the snow. "You were too hung up on technicalities," he continued, scratching his back with the rubber prongs of his pitchfork. "You gave me exact latitude and longitude, but didn't restrict my movements in other dimensions."

Drake stared at him with a blank expression.

"Look," Tom said impatiently, "I had to use time travel just to get to Christmas Eve . . ." He shuddered as he said the words.

"Time travel? What good would *that* do you? I said 2 a.m.—"

"Of what year?"

"What difference would that make?"

"Because you only told me the proper parallels and meridians, but you never said the building had to be The Pentagon. So I materialized one hundred and ninety-five years into the future."

Drake whirled. "You mean this is—?"

"2,167 A.D., you should pardon the expression."

"And *that?*" he asked, pointing a frostbitten finger at the large building. "It *looks* like The Pentagon. They didn't tear it down."

"Nope," said the devil, "just the opposite—they added on to it. You're looking at The Hexagon!"

Striking his forehead with a chilly palm, Drake laughed heartily, in spite of himself.

"I'll be with you in a minute, Tom," he said, "I want a drink."

They were back in the dingy living-room. Drake pulled on a sweater, still icy from the nocturnal visit to Washington, then poured three fingers of Bushmills and drank it down neat.

Tom settled back in the armchair his host had placed, upon request, within the pentagram and urged Drake to take his time. He cleaned his long nails with the tip of his tail, which had somehow stretched to many times its original length. He leered at the mortal.

"Irresistibility, huh?" Tom chuckled. "Good choice. So you don't get lots of money, so what? You get just what a man *really* needs, right?" Winking obscenely, he pulled a rolled parchment from the folds of his cape.

"What's that?" asked Drake.

"Our contract," said Tiny Tom, scratching his ear. "This time we have to get it on paper." He tossed the scroll across the room. Drake caught it, read it carefully, weighing each word and syllable. At last, he nodded and as soon as he did, a twinge shot through his arm and the contract flew back through the air to the devil—who held it open long enough to verify Drake's scarlet signature on the dotted line.

"It's automatic," Tom explained proudly. "New model."

"All right," the other replied, rubbing his arm, "now the second task depends on the truth of your answer to my very first question earlier this evening—whether you are, in fact, a fully accredited demon, authorized to act on behalf of your Boss."

"Yeah, yeah, I *said* I am. Go ahead."

"But understand, Tom—my task, by logical extension, must be binding on any and all existing demons dwelling within the boundaries of the space-time continuum in which I—"

"Damn it!" Tom swore impatiently. "Are you a lawyer?"

"The action you are to perform must be irrevocable and eternal."

"Technicalities! *All right,* but what am I supposed to *do* already?!"

"Destroy Hell," Drake replied.

Ten minutes later, Tiny Tom's jaw was still flapping, though no coherent sound had yet emerged. Smiling superciliously, Drake helped himself to another slug of Irish.

"Well, Tom," he asked at last, "what's the matter? You stuck?"

The demon shook his head, blew out his cheeks and puffed in disgust. "No, boy, I'm not stuck. But you listen to me and ditch this dumb idea!"

"Why should I?" Drake retorted cockily. "It's obvious I've stumped you!"

"Like Hell you have! I can do what you're asking, if that's what you *really* want . . ."

The mortal stopped grinning. "Only what? Is there a catch somewhere?"

"You bet there is! You asked me to 'Destroy Hell,' a physical locality, but you didn't say nothing about devils."

"Which means?" Drake asked, suddenly worried.

"Which means you're going to kick a whole bunch of fiends out of their homes—including the Boss. They'll be plenty sore, and they'll be waiting for you, just you, every single one of them."

"Waiting for what?" Drake turned pale.

"To get even."

The mortal paced nervously, trapped in a predicament of his own making. If he insisted on the task, he would find himself the object of concerted diabolic wrath. On the other hand, if he withdrew it, it would make him one task short in the sequence of three. It had taken him months to come up with his original trio of demonic stultifiers, none of which seemed to stop Tiny Tom at all.

"Hold on a minute!" he exclaimed suddenly. "If I withdraw this task, Tom, *and* if you give me nothing in return, then our original bargain is automatically invalidated."

"It is not! You gotta give me a new second task!"

"Uh-uh," Drake objected, "the terms specify three wishes and three tasks. But you're letting me take back the second one, an option which I am taking. So now I could either go on to task number three or else bow out entirely, but there's nothing that says I have to come up with a fourth stunt for you."

"You signed the contract!"

"I received no material commodity, so I doubt that you can make it stick. Coming up with a fourth task would violate the symmetry of the three-wish formula. Now, if I can just find that prayer book around here someplace—"

Tiny Tom hopped up and down in mingled fear and anger. "Wait a minute, wait a minute!" he howled frantically, dropping his pitchfork on the armchair and stepping to the very edge of the pentagram. "Tell you what—show you what a nice guy I am! I'll make you a special offer. Go on with the third task and I'll forget about the second one."

Drake looked dubious.

"That's not all, either!" he wheedled. "If you stump me and win the extended life-span, I'll even throw in the unlimited wealth bit for nothing. That way the irresistibility will practically be assured!"

Drake turned his back on Tom to hide the triumphant smile on his lips. The sight of the ridiculous little demon prancing up and down on both hooves was genuine low comedy. The fact that his decision meant so much to Tom richly satisfied the normally ineffectual mortal.

"I don't know," Drake drawled, "maybe . . . *maybe* if I had the money right now—"

"You've got it!" Tiny Tom yelped. Gleefully, Drake agreed to the new arrangement, and the devil, uttering a sigh of relief, plopped back down into the armchair.

Unfortunately, the pitchfork was still on the seat.

Drake rolled on the floor with uncontrolled laughter. Tiny Tom, who leapt about four feet into the air, rubbed his ample bottom and glowered at his ungracious host.

"Haw-haw!" he grumbled. "How'd you like it if it was sticking in *you???*"

"Sorry, Tom," the mortal gasped, "but it *was* funny! Lucky your pitchfork is only rubber!"

"*I'll* say," the demon mumbled sullenly. Then, yawning without covering his mouth, he declared that the night's exertions had worn him out. "Call me again tomorrow night. Make it at midnight, and we'll wrap up the final task."

Before his host could raise any objections, Tiny Tom dematerialized with a near-terminal burp.

Drake immediately consulted the bank book which his ex-girlfriend, Ethel Gassner, had so recently depleted. The balance staggered him; it was in seven figures. He replaced it in the upper left-hand corner of his battered desk and as he did, he noticed an unfamiliar sheaf of papers and folders. Examining them, he found his name was on all of them; they were composed of various title deeds to valuable real estate and a generous sprinkling of bluechip securities.

He was impressed by the promptness and dependability of the pudgy imp. Yet his enthusiasm was somewhat tempered by the fact that the following day was Sunday, making it impossible to do anything meaningful with his new-found pelf.

Drake slept for several hours. He woke from a night of unpleasant dreams. His sudden affluence was more than offset by a growing uneasiness. As he reconsidered the idea of an extended life-span, the less certain Drake was that he really wanted it. In spite of Tiny Tom's cynical reassurance, the unwilling celibate was only too keenly aware of his usual worth in feminine eyes. Did he really crave five hundred years of frustration, with an occasional respite in the form of another Ethel Gassner?

As Sunday slowly, inexorably passed, he grew increasingly nervous about his bet with the devil. Though his plans had seemed foolproof at first, the preposterous fiend had bested him twice, and he was still in jeopardy. Though he was positive the third task could not possibly bring him any grief, Drake was still anxious about it. His confidence had been severely shaken.

As the shadows lengthened, so did his fears. By nine o'clock, he had bitten his nails to the tips of his fingers. At ten, he started to feel queasy and thought he was being watched.

By eleven p.m., Drake hit upon a new third wish, one born of desperation. The wording, he decided, was positively brilliant.

But Tiny Tom did not agree.

"Don't ask me to accept that wish," he warned, shaking his head so hard that one of his plastic horns swung loose and dangled above his right eye.

"Why shouldn't I?" Drake challenged. "It really has you beat this time, *doesn't it?*" He was pretending an arrogance he did not feel.

"Look, boy, it's about time you realized these brilliant ideas of yours have a habit of backfiring."

"The wording stands," said Drake. "I wish that the contract between us be considered null and void *if* you perform my third task."

It seemed perfect. If Tiny Tom figured out a way to perform the third task and still threaten the mortal, the new wish would neatly get him off the hook. And then he would still have all that wealth—

But Tiny Tom shook his head, and the horn fell off and dropped in his lap. "I'm warning you, boy, you're leaving a bad chink in your defences."

"Such as?"

"Such as a sloppy implied meaning—and the law is rough on them. What happens if Hell loses?"

"Huh?"

"Look, you're asking to scrap the contract if I perform the third task. *What if I can't?*"

Drake swallowed hard.

"Your third wish implies that if I *couldn't* perform the final task, then I *could* take your soul. See the trap?"

Drake nodded miserably. "But why are you telling me this?"

"Because," Tom said, pawing the floor with a hoof in the attitude of a naughty schoolboy, "I like your style. You're my first threesie in years, and I don't want you to screw up on a technicality. You're giving the Boss a great run for his money."

"Well, then," Drake murmured gamely, "I guess I'll risk it after all. Put me down for the women."

"Attaboy!" Tiny Tom crowed, delighted. "That's *my* kinda wish!" He rubbed his paws together enthusiastically, which made the talons click. He pulled a cigar out of his pocket, lit it and waved it grandly at the mortal, inviting him to name the final task.

Drake cleared his throat.

"Tell his Infernal Majesty that he—that is, Satan, Lucifer, Dis, Beelzebub, Ahrimanes, Old Scratch, or whatever other diabolic nomenclature—"

"All right, all right, I *know* who you mean."

"Tell him he must offer up unqualified contrition for his boundless catalog of nefarious misdeeds and commend his soul to eternal reconciliation.

"In other words," Drake ordered, a triumphant grin spreading over his face, "I want your Boss to reform and apologize to God!"

Tiny Tom said nothing for a long while. Then he rose slowly, withdrew the contract from his cape and tore the scroll to bits; then he tossed a phial full of green liquid to Drake.

"Drink it," he said. "It will make you irresistible." Without another word, Tiny Tom disappeared.

Dazed by his sudden success, Drake swallowed the bitter liquor and immediately picked up the phone and called Ethel Gassner. To his surprise and delight, she promised to come right over. He hung up and began to devise sexual punishments for the anguish she had caused him. Then, slumping onto his thread-bare sofa, he began to imagine carnal junkets to Hollywood, the Riviera, possibly Monaco . . .

"I'll make a list," he told himself. Then, with a satisfied smirk on his face, he fell asleep.

He awoke facedown, naked, on a jagged rocky floor. His body was covered with sweat and he lay near a noxious pool of filth. When he tried to raise his head, a tidal wash of agony engulfed him. He moaned.

Painfully, Drake rolled slowly onto his back and opened his eyes. A dazzling crimson light blinded him, then he saw polished stone walls arched high above him and nearby, a lean hideous figure which strode forward and straddled him, one leg on either side of his body.

It was Tiny Tom—and yet it was not. Taller, thinner, more sinewy, the creature had a hairy body matted with perspiration and ordure.

The comical scarlet tights and cape were missing, and in place of the rubber pitchfork was an axe clutched in one taloned claw. The haft and blade bore sinister stains.

The creature spoke.

"Welcome, *boy,*" said the fiend. "Welcome to Hell."

Drake screamed. "What am I doing here? I was asleep!"

"That's true, but you died while you slept," the demon explained. "Unfortunately, when you signed my contract, you rather drastically altered your probability span."

"But my wishes—"

"Are immaterial. You were *so* concerned with technicalities that you missed a transparent danger, one so apparent that I capered and postured and played the clown to keep your attention diverted."

"What are you talking about?" Drake shuddered, as he saw thousands of vermin running over the fiend's scabrous body.

"My friend," the other answered, "there are many roads to Hell, and you have chosen one of them. Bargaining with me is a dangerous practice. It is a grave affront to beneficent forces: by choosing to gamble with me, you automatically put yourself in jeopardy!"

"But I won!"

"Yes," the Devil sardonically replied, "and *what* did you win? Vast wealth? That might not have mattered, no more than a preternaturally extended life would have—not if you had put them to good use. But *you* selected irresistibility—much to my intense delight! It is a wish that depends for its fulfillment on the subversion of free spirits. One doesn't get into Hell by accident: one earns it!"

"No!" Drake protested, trying to rise, but the Devil pushed him down with a cloven hoof. "This is *not* fair! Our contract—"

"Is null and void. When you make deals with me, betting and bargaining for the opportunity to warp other flesh to your will, it makes no difference whether you best me in three bets or three thousand. By common law, as it were, you have sold your soul to Hell!"

Drake groaned and tried to escape. But the Devil lifted him upon his back and bore him to the brink of the abyss. Satan hurled the mortal into the gaping chasm, and as he fell, Drake scanned the awful panorama of the Pit.

It resembled a Medieval woodcut.

MORGAN LLYWELYN, *the international best-selling creator of such acclaimed historical novels as* The Wind from Hastings, Lion of Ireland, The Horse Goddess *and* Bard *was born in New York City and raised in Dallas where she became "horse-crazy." Her busy career rarely permits her the leisure to write short fiction, so it is a great pleasure to introduce this unique devil tale especially written for this anthology. Its bizarre premise might have failed in the hands of a lesser author, but thanks to Ms. Llywelyn's intensely moving artistry, "Me, Tree" possesses a strange and potent magic.*

Me, Tree

BY MORGAN LLYWELYN

Sentience is something you don't think about very much. You have it or you do not. People have it, trees do not.

But I am (how curious that I can even consider the concept "I am!") I am a tree, and I feel. I perceive, I am aware.

As a tree standing on damp earth, with my roots ever seeking more water, more nourishment, I became aware that if the water dried up I could not go somewhere else to find more. Animals and birds constantly moved around me, seeking the things they needed to keep them alive, but I had to stand in one place and wait. And hope. That, I realized, was not an enviable situation. I did not enjoy it.

What? Oh, yes, I am capable of enjoyment. That is how I first learned I was aware. All my life I had responded with pleasure to the sun as it summoned my sap to rise and triggered the photosynthesis making my existence possible. Light reacted upon me in ways I enjoyed without thinking, for thought did not seem necessary.

Then a new pleasure came to me. A human female began sitting beneath me almost every day when the sun was highest. Often she leaned against my trunk and read poetry; sometimes aloud. I cannot say when I discovered I was actually listening to her and trying to make sense of the patterns of sound she made. But I looked forward to her arrival each day. Something about the vibrations of her voice sank through my bark and set up answering vibrations within my core. In time I understood her language.

From things she said, I perceived she was unhappy because she was lonely. The nature of humans, it seems, is to want to be in pairs, and this human female did not have another of her own kind to pair with.

Neither did I, I realized. So I must have been lonely—until the human female came to me, like sun or rain, and began providing something I had needed without knowing it.

In time she talked to me as her kind talk to one another. She spoke of what she called her troubles. She was not pretty, she said. She was only clever, and young males copied her papers in class but took other girls to dances. I did not understand what pretty and clever meant, or what classes and dances were, but by listening I learned. I learned that I stood upon a college campus, at the far end of an athletic field, and the female who came to me every day at her lunch hour was studying science.

How she perceived I was interested I cannot tell, but she began reading aloud from her textbooks. Perhaps she only did it to clarify her thought processes, but in this way I learned about sentience, and photosynthesis, and a galaxy of concepts I had never concerned myself with before.

The school year passed. I lost my leaves and should have slept, but as long as the weather was not too cold my human female still came to me, so I forced myself to stay at least partially awake, listening to her. Her presence rescued me from the loneliness I had not known I was suffering. She became very precious to me, like sun and rain.

How could I communicate with her and tell her these things? My whole existence was changed by her, yet she did not know.

She began a new class, one on something called theosophy, and I listened to her muse aloud on the questions of divinity, seeking spiritual insight rather than empirical knowledge. She spoke of souls, and destiny, and heaven, and hell, and I stretched myself like a young sapling in an effort to keep up with her leaping thoughts.

Then her mood turned darker. In her class was a young man more passionate about spirituality than she, and from her words I learned he was a devotee of an organized religion. His was a sect obsessed with sin and his zealotry was beginning to have an influence on her. She began to worry aloud about the condition of her own soul.

I was forced to consider the question, then, of whether a tree could have a soul. Was sentience proof of the possession of one? Then I remembered some poetry she had once read, a phrase about the soul being love's vessel.

I loved, surely. I loved her, as I loved sun and rain and for the same reasons; she had become necessary to me. She had expanded my existence and without her I would shrink back into a darkness I had not recognized as darkness. I loved; I had a soul.

That human male, he was dragging her into a darkness. I could sense it, I could feel the flagging of her bright spirit. With his talk of sins and hellfire he was crushing her. Was he telling her the truth?

If there were souls, they must have been created; the girl and I agreed on that point. So there was a constructive principle in the universe—and there must be a destructive principle as well, dark for light. The Devil, Prince of Hell. He surely had power, I saw evidence of evil every day in the way human beings treated each other. So the Devil had power over physical actions.

The human male made my girl cry. I stood helplessly over her and suffered with her, this girl who read poetry and studied the sciences and searched for answers.

I raised my branches and tried praying with all my might to our Creator, begging that I might be allowed to help her.

Nothing happened. Her eyes were frequently red-rimmed and she was growing thinner as the periods of daylight lengthened again. She had, in her loneliness, tried to pair with the human male in her class, the one who was obsessed by the notion of sin. Her desires for procreation, which seemed perfectly natural to any tree, had been rejected by him as sinful. He had rejected her.

I hated him. Hatred was another new feeling for me.

I knew him by sight for I had seen them together. I had seen her go up to him, talk to him, and I had watched immobile as he seized her mind but never her body. He was convincing her that her own nature was evil. He was making my girl hate herself.

The Creator, having given me life, did not seem disposed to give me something more. But perhaps his opposite would. If I understood correctly, the Devil would bargain for souls. And surely I had a soul to offer him, for I had learned to love and hate.

When I lifted my branches next in prayer, it was not to the Creator. And the thing of fire and ice that came to me in the night was not a constructive force, but it listened to me. It bared its fangs and licked its lips and listened. Then it vanished in a flash of lightning, leaving the bark on one side of me scorched.

Next day I saw her walking on the campus, and the human male was with her, at her elbow, yammering at her. I could tell from the way her shoulders slumped that he was making her miserable with his fanaticism. She moved closer to him as if to warm his cold heart with her own young warmth, but he pulled away from her.

He pulled away from a creature as pliant as a willow tree, with skin as white as the underbark of a sycamore. I would not have pulled away from her.

I felt myself yearning toward her, yearning to comfort her . . . and my roots tore free from the earth. They moved beneath me, shaping themselves into clawed feet capable of carrying me. At first I was too shocked to move, but then I realized my offer had been accepted and the bargain was sealed. And I was glad. Glad!

I set off across the campus toward my girl and the human male. My weight crushed the grass and gouged the earth and I swayed unsteadily, for such movement was strange to me. But I was not thinking of myself. I thought only of the girl, of getting to her and comforting her. I thought of stopping the human male from hurting her any more.

He saw me first, over her shoulder. His face contorted and he took a step backward, but I was gaining better control of myself by then. I got to him while he was too astonished to run and I slammed him across the throat with one of my branches, being careful not to let it hit her. I am an oak tree. It took little effort to smash his neck, for humans are flimsy things. He fell in a heap onto the earth, his body already surrendering its heat, ready to furnish nutrients to the waiting soil.

The girl screamed. I had not expected her to be frightened of me, for we were friends. We were more than friends. I leaned toward her, trying to reassure her, and I heard myself making sounds. The sounds I made surprised, then horrified me. Unfortunately I did not have a human voice, any more than my roots were human feet. I had an oak tree's voice, huge and deep and echoing with an oak tree's approximation of human words.

The girl's eyes dilated with terror. She ran from me, faster than I with all my weight could follow. The other humans within sight of me were running too, racing toward the nearest building. Doors slammed. Then some men came out of that building, shouting and gesturing in my direction. One of them dragged a metal canister with a hose and a valve. When he touched the valve, a tongue of flame licked the air.

Without a glance backward, my girl fled from me and hid herself in

the manmade caverns of brick and stone. She rejected me and everything I was, as the human male had rejected what she was.

Too late, I understood heaven. Heaven was sun and rain and the
lazy tenderness of new leaves unfolding in the spring.

With no reason to try to save myself, I stood on the damp earth and
watched the men come cautiously toward me with their canister of
bottled flame. They would turn me into a pillar of fire. If she watched
from a window, the girl would see it; she would be able to hear my
roar of agony.

I stood on the damp earth and waited for hell.

Hellspawn

Monsters, imps, vampires, felines, canines and rodents, all of them invested with hideous purpose, abound in the eleven selections included under this heading.

Some of these nasty critters, such as Robert Bloch's Enoch or Henry Kuttner's graveyard rats, are directly affiliated with the fiery pit, while those of a more mysterious nature—Lucie Chin's sorcerous cats, for instance—have been clept "hellspawn" in a broad generic sense. But whichever category these creatures fit, it is best to approach them with extreme caution. Most of them are unrepentantly nasty.

ROBERT BLOCH *is one of America's most popular horror writers and is assuredly best known for his* Psycho *novels, although he has written many other gory tales and novels, including the frequently anthologized "Yours Truly, Jack the Ripper." "Enoch" is a grisly tale that opens with a weird question which I fervently hope the reader is able to answer in the negative.*

Enoch

BY ROBERT BLOCH

It always starts the same way.

First, there's the *feeling*.

Have you ever felt the tread of little feet walking across the top of your skull? Footsteps on your skull, back and forth, back and forth?

It starts like that.

You can't see who does the walking. After all, it's on top of your head. If you're clever, you wait for a chance and suddenly brush the hand through your hair. But you can't catch the walker that way. He *knows*. Even if you clamp both hands to your head, he manages to wriggle through, somehow. Or maybe he jumps.

Terribly swift, he is. And you can't ignore him. If you don't pay any attention to the footsteps, he tries the next step. He wriggles down the back of your neck and whispers in your ear.

You can feel his body, so tiny and cold, pressed tightly against the base of your brain. There is something numbing in his claws because they don't hurt—although later you'll find little scratches on your neck that bleed and bleed. But at the time, all you know is that something tiny and cold is pressing there. Pressing, and whispering.

That's when you try to fight him. You try not to hear what he says. Because when you listen, you're lost. You have to obey him, then.

Oh, he's wicked and wise!

He knows how to frighten and threaten, if you dare to resist.

But I seldom try, anymore. It's better for me if I listen, and then obey.

As long as I'm willing to listen, things don't seem so bad. Because he can be soothing and persuasive, too. Tempting. The things he has promised me in that little silken whisper!

He keeps his promises, too.

Folks think I'm poor because I never have any money and live in that old shack on the edge of the swamp. But he has given me riches.

After I do what he wants, he takes me away—out of myself—for days. There are other places besides this world, you know; places where I am king.

People laugh at me and say I have no friends; the girls in town used to call me "scarecrow." Yet sometimes—after I've done his bidding—he brings the riches of the world to me.

Just dreams? I don't think so. It's the other life that's a dream, the life in the shack at the edge of the swamp. That doesn't seem real anymore.

Not even the killing . . .

Yes, I kill people.

That's what Enoch wants, you know. That's what he whispers about. He asks me to kill people, for him.

I don't like that. I used to fight against it—I told you that before, didn't I? But I can't anymore.

He wants me to kill people for him. Enoch. The thing that lives on the top of my head.

I can't see him. I can't catch him. I can only feel him, and hear him, and obey him.

Sometimes he leaves me alone for days. Then, suddenly, I'll feel him there, scratching away at the roof of my brain. I'll hear his whisper ever so plainly, and he'll be telling me about someone who is coming through the swamp.

I don't know how he knows about them. He couldn't have seen them, yet he describes them perfectly.

"There's a tramp walking down the Aylesworthy Road. A short, fat man, with bald head. That makes it easier."

Then he'll laugh for a minute, and go on.

"His name is Mike. He's wearing a brown sweater and blue overalls. He's going to turn into the swamp in about 10 minutes, when the sun goes down. He'll stop under the big tree next to the dump.

"Better hide behind that tree. Wait until he starts to look for firewood. Then you know what to do. Get the hatchet, now. Hurry."

Sometimes I ask Enoch what he will give me. Usually, I just trust him. I know I'm going to have to do it anyway. So I might as well go ahead at once. Enoch is never wrong about things, and he keeps me out of trouble.

That is, he always did—until the last time.

One night, I was sitting in the shack eating supper when he told me about this girl.

"She's coming to visit you," he whispered. "A beautiful girl, all in black. She has a wonderful quality to her head—fine bones. Fine."

At first I thought he was telling me about one of my *rewards*. But Enoch was talking about a real person.

"She will come to the door and ask you to help her. To fix her car. She has taken the side road, planning to go into town by a shorter route. Now the car is well into the swamp, and one of the tires needs changing."

It sounded funny, hearing Enoch talk about things like automobile tires. But he knows about them. Enoch knows *everything*.

"You will go out to help her when she asks you. Don't take anything. She has a wrench in the car. Use that."

This time I tried to fight him. I kept whimpering, "I won't do it, I won't do it."

He just laughed. And then he told me what he'd do if I refused. He told me over and over again.

"Better that I do it to her and not to you," Enoch reminded me. "Or would you rather I—"

"No!" I said. "No. I'll do it."

"After all," Enoch whispered, "I can't help it. I must be served ever so often. To keep me alive. To keep me strong. So I can serve you. So I can give you things. That is why you have to obey me. If not, I'll just stay right here and—"

"No," I said. "I'll do it."

And I did it.

She knocked on my door just a few minutes later, and it was just as Enoch whispered it. She was a pretty girl—with blonde hair. I like blonde hair. I was glad, when I went out into the swamp with her, that I didn't have to harm her hair. I hit her behind the neck with the wrench.

Enoch told me what to do, step by step.

After I used the hatchet, I put the body in the quicksand. Enoch was with me, and he cautioned me about heel-marks. I got rid of them.

I was worried about the car, but he showed me how to use the end of a rotten log and pitch it over. I wasn't sure it would sink, too, but it did. And much faster than I would have believed.

It was a relief to see the car go. I threw the wrench in after it. Then Enoch told me to go home, and I did, and at once I felt the dreamy feeling stealing over me.

Enoch had promised me something extra special for this, and I sank down into sleep right away. I could barely feel the pressure leave my head as Enoch left me, scampering off back into the swamp for *his* reward . . .

I don't know how long I slept. It must have been a long time. All I remember is that I finally started to wake up, knowing somehow that Enoch was back with me again, and feeling that something was wrong.

Then I woke up all the way, because I heard the banging on my door.

I waited a moment. I waited for Enoch to whisper to me, tell me what I should do.

But Enoch was asleep now. He always sleeps afterwards. Nothing wakes him for days on end; and during that time I am free. Usually I enjoy such freedom, but not now. I needed his help.

The sounding on my door grew louder, and I couldn't wait any longer.

I got up and answered.

Old Sheriff Shelby came through the doorway.

"Come on, Seth," he said. "I'm taking you up to the jail."

I didn't say anything. His beady little black eyes were peeping everywhere inside my shack. When he looked at me, I wanted to hide, I felt so scared.

He couldn't see Enoch, of course. Nobody can. But Enoch was there; I felt him resting very lightly on top of my skull, burrowed down under a blanket of hair, clinging to my curls and sleeping as peacefully as a baby.

"Emily Robbins' folks said she was planning on cutting through the swamp," the Sheriff told me. "We followed the tire tracks up to the old quicksand."

Enoch had forgotten about the tracks. So what could I say? Besides.

"Anything you say can be used against you," said Sheriff Shelby. "Come on, Seth."

I went with him. There was nothing else for me to do. I went with him into town, and all the loafers were out trying to rush the car. There were women in the crowd too. They kept yelling for the men to "get" me.

But Sheriff Shelby held them off, and at last I was tucked away safe and sound in back of the jailhouse. He locked me up in the middle cell. The two cells on each side of mine were vacant, so I was all alone. All alone except for Enoch, and he slept through everything.

It was still pretty early in the morning, and Sheriff Shelby went out again with some other men. I guess he was going to try and get the body out of the quicksand, if he could. He didn't try to ask any questions, and I wondered about that.

Charley Potter, now, he was different. He wanted to know *everything.* Sheriff Shelby had left him in charge of the jail while he was away. He brought me my breakfast after a while, and hung around asking questions.

I just kept still. I know better than to talk to a fool like Charley Potter. He thought I was crazy. Just like the mob outside. Most people in that town thought I was crazy—because of my mother, I suppose, and because of the way I lived all alone out in the swamp.

What could I say to Charley Potter? If I told him about Enoch he'd never believe me anyway.

So I didn't talk.

I listened.

Then Charley Potter told *me* about the search for Emily Robbins, and about how Sheriff Shelby got to wondering over some other disappearances a while back. He said that there would be a big trial, and the District Attorney was coming down from the County Seat. And he'd heard they were sending out a doctor to see me right away.

Sure enough, just as I finished breakfast, the doctor came. Charley Potter saw him drive up and let him in. He had to work fast to keep some of the oafs from breaking in on with him. They wanted to lynch me, I suppose. But the doctor came in all right—a little man with one of those funny beards on his chin—and he made Charley Potter go up front into the office while he sat down outside the cell and talked to me.

His name was Dr. Silversmith.

Now, up to this time, I wasn't really *feeling* anything. It had all happened so fast I didn't get a chance to think.

It was like part of a dream; the sheriff and the mob and all this talk about a trial and a lynching and the body in the swamp.

But somehow the sight of this Dr. Silversmith changed things.

He was real, all right. You could tell he was a doctor by the quiet way he talked; he sounded like the doctor who wanted to send me to the institution after they found my mother.

That was one of the first things Dr. Silversmith asked me—what happened to my mother?

He seemed to know quite a lot about me, and that made it easier for me to talk.

Pretty soon I found myself telling him all sorts of things. How my mother and I lived in the shack. How she made the philtres and sold them. About the big pot and the way we gathered herbs at night. About the nights when she went off alone and I would hear the queer noises from far away.

I didn't want to say much more, but he knew, anyway. He knew they had called her a witch. He even knew the way she died—when Santo Dinorelli came to our door that evening and stabbed her because she had made the potion for his daughter who ran away with that trapper. He knew about me living in the swamp alone after that, too.

But he didn't know about Enoch.

Enoch, up on top of my head all the time, still sleeping, not knowing or caring what was happening to me . . .

Somehow, I was talking to Dr. Silversmith about Enoch. I wanted to explain that it wasn't really I who had killed this girl. So I had to mention Enoch, and how my mother had made the bargain in the woods. She hadn't let me come with her—I was only twelve—but she took some of my blood, pricking me with a needle and dropping it into a little bottle.

I don't know exactly what she did, but when she came back in the morning, Enoch was with her. I couldn't see him, of course, but she told me about him—and I could feel him when he perched on my head.

He was to be mine forever, she said, and look after me and help me in all ways.

I told this very carefully and explained why it was I had to obey Enoch, ever since my mother was killed. Enoch protected me, just as my mother had planned, because she knew I couldn't get along alone.

I admitted this to Dr. Silversmith because I thought he was a wise man and would understand.

That was wrong.

I knew it at once. Because while Dr. Silversmith leaned forward and stroked his little beard and said, "Yes, yes," over and over again, I could feel his eyes watching me.

He had the same kind of eyes as Sheriff Shelby. Beady eyes. Mean eyes. Eyes that don't trust you when they see you. Prying, peeping eyes.

Then he began to ask me all sorts of funny questions. You'd think he'd ask me about Enoch, since *he* was the explanation of everything. But instead, Dr. Silversmith asked me if I ever heard any *other* voices. If I ever saw things that I knew weren't there.

He asked me how I felt when I killed Emily Robbins and whether I —but I won't repeat that question! Why, he talked to me as if I was some kind of—crazy person!

I just laughed at him then, and shut up tighter than a clam.

After awhile he gave up and went away, shaking his head. I laughed after him because I knew he hadn't found out what he wanted to find out. He wanted to know all my mother's secrets, and my secrets, and Enoch's secrets too.

But he didn't, and I laughed. And then I went to sleep. I slept almost all afternoon.

When I woke up, there was a new man standing in front of my cell. He had a big, fat smiling face, and nice eyes.

"Hello, Seth," he said, very friendly. "Having a little snooze?"

I reached up to the top of my head. I couldn't feel Enoch, but I knew he was there, and still asleep. He moves fast, even when he's sleeping.

"Don't be alarmed," said the man. "I won't hurt you."

"Did that doctor send you?" I asked.

The man laughed. "Of course not," he told me. "My name's Cassidy. Edwin Cassidy. I'm the District Attorney, and I'm in charge here. Can I come in and sit down, do you suppose?"

"I'm locked in," I said.

"I've got the keys from the sheriff," said Mr. Cassidy. He took them out and opened my cell; walked right in and sat down next to me on the bench.

"Aren't you afraid?" I asked him. "You know, I'm supposed to be a murderer."

"Why Seth," Mr. Cassidy laughed, "I'm not afraid of you. I know you didn't mean to kill anybody."

He put his hand on my shoulder, and I didn't draw away. It was a nice, fat, soft hand. He had a big diamond ring on his finger that twinkled in the sunshine.

"How's Enoch?" he said.

I jumped.

"Oh, that's all right. That fool doctor told me when I met him down the street. He doesn't understand about Enoch, does he, Seth? But you and I do."

"That doctor thinks I'm crazy," I whispered.

"Well, just between us, Seth, it did sound a little hard to believe, at first. But I've just come from the swamp. Sheriff Shelby and some of his men are still working down there. Digging, you know.

"They found Emily Robbins' body just a little while ago. And other bodies, too. A fat man's body, and a small boy, and some Indian. The quicksand preserves them, you know."

I watched his eyes, and they were still smiling, so I knew I could trust this man.

"They'll find other bodies, too, if they keep on, won't they, Seth?"

I nodded.

"But I didn't wait any longer. I saw enough to understand that you were telling the truth. Enoch must have made you do these things, didn't he?"

I nodded again.

"Fine," said Mr. Cassidy, pressing my shoulder. "You see, we do understand each other now. So I won't blame you for anything you tell me."

"What do you want to know?" I asked.

"Oh, lots of things. I'm interested in Enoch, you see. Just how many people did he ask you to kill—altogether, that is?"

"Nine," I said.

"And they're all buried in the quicksand?"

"Yes."

"Do you know their names?"

"Only a few."

I told him the names of the ones I knew. "Sometimes Enoch just describes them for me and I go out to meet them," I explained.

Mr. Cassidy sort of chuckled and took out a cigar. I frowned.

"Don't want me to smoke, eh?"

"Please—I don't like it. My mother didn't believe in smoking; she never let me."

Mr. Cassidy laughed out loud now, but he put the cigar away and leaned forward.

"You can be a big help to me, Seth," he whispered. "I suppose you know what a District Attorney must do."

"He's a sort of a lawyer, isn't he—at trials and things?"

"That's right. I'm going to be at your trial, Seth. Now you don't want to have to get up in front of all those people and tell them about —what happened. Right?"

"No, I don't, Mr. Cassidy. Not those mean people here in town. They hate me."

"Then here's what you do. You tell me all about it, and I'll talk for you. That's friendly enough, isn't it?"

I wished Enoch was there to help me, but he was asleep. I looked at Mr. Cassidy and made up my own mind.

"Yes," I said. "I can tell you."

So I told him everything I knew.

After a while he stopped chuckling, but he was just getting so interested he couldn't bother to laugh or do anything but listen.

"One thing more," he said. "We found some bodies in the swamp. Emily Robbins' body we can identify, and several of the others. But it would be easier if we knew something else. You can tell me this, Seth. Where are the heads?"

I stood up and turned away. "I won't tell you that," I said, "because I don't know."

"Don't know?"

"I give them to Enoch," I explained. "Don't you understand— that's why I must kill people for him. Because he wants their heads."

Mr. Cassidy looked puzzled.

"He always makes me cut the heads off and leave them," I went on. "I put the bodies in the quicksand, and then go home. He puts me to sleep and rewards me. After that he goes away—back to the heads. That's what he wants."

"Why does he want them, Seth?"

I told him. "You see, it wouldn't do you any good if you could find them. Because you probably wouldn't recognize anything anyway."

Mr. Cassidy sat up and sighed. "But why do you let Enoch do such things?"

"I must. Or else he'd do it to me. That's what he always threatens. He has to have it. So I obey him."

Mr. Cassidy watched me while I walked the floor, but he didn't say a word. He seemed to be very nervous all of a sudden, and when I came close, he sort of leaned away.

"You'll explain all that in the trial, of course?" I said. "About Enoch, and everything?"

He shook his head.

"I'm not going to tell about Enoch at the trial, and neither are you," Mr. Cassidy said. "Nobody is even going to know that Enoch exists."

"Why?"

"I'm trying to help you, Seth. Don't you know what the people will say if you mention Enoch to them? They'll say you're crazy! And you don't want that to happen."

"No. But what can you do? How can you help me?"

Mr. Cassidy smiled at me.

"You're afraid of Enoch, aren't you? Well, I was just thinking out loud. Suppose you gave Enoch to me?"

I gulped.

"Yes. Suppose you gave Enoch to me, right now? Let me take care of him for you during the trial. Then he wouldn't be yours, and you wouldn't have to say anything about him. He probably doesn't want people to know what he does, anyway."

"That's right," I said. "Enoch would be very angry. He's a secret, you know. But I hate to give him to you without asking—and he's asleep now."

"Asleep?"

"Yes. On top of my skull. Only you can't see him, of course."

Mr. Cassidy gazed at my head and then he chuckled again.

"Oh, I can explain everything when he wakes up," he told me. "When he knows it's all for the best, I'm sure he'll be happy."

"Well—I guess it's all right, then," I sighed. "But you must promise to take good care of him."

"Sure," said Mr. Cassidy.

"And you'll give him what he wants? What he needs?"

"Of course."

"And you won't tell a soul?"

"Not a soul."

"Of course you know what will happen to you if you refuse to give Enoch what he wants," I warned Mr. Cassidy. "He will take it—from you—by force."

"Don't you worry, Seth."

I stood still for a minute. Because all at once I could feel something move. Enoch was waking up!

"He's awake," I whispered. "Now I can tell him."

Yes, Enoch was awake. I could feel him crawling over my scalp, moving towards my ear.

"Enoch," I whispered. "Can you hear me?"

He heard.

Then I explained everything to him. How I was giving him to Mr. Cassidy.

Enoch didn't say a word.

Mr. Cassidy didn't say a word. He just sat there and grinned. I suppose it must have looked a little strange to see me talking to—nothing.

"Go to Mr. Cassidy," I whispered. "Go to him now."

And Enoch went.

I felt the weight lift from my head. That was all, but I knew he was gone.

"Can you feel him, Mr. Cassidy?" I asked.

"What—oh, sure!" he said, and stood up.

"Take good care of Enoch," I told him.

"The best."

"Don't put your hat on," I warned. "Enoch doesn't like hats."

"Sorry, I forgot. Well, Seth, I'll say goodbye now. You've been a mighty great help to me—and from now on we can just forget about Enoch, as far as telling anybody else is concerned.

"I'll come back again and talk about the trial. That Dr. Silversmith, he's going to try and tell the folks you're crazy. Maybe it would be best if you just denied everything you told him—now that I have Enoch."

That sounded like a fine idea, but then I knew Mr. Cassidy was a smart man.

"Whatever you say, Mr. Cassidy. Just be good to Enoch, and he'll be good to you."

Mr. Cassidy shook my hand and then he and Enoch went away. I felt tired again. Maybe it was the strain, and maybe it was just that I felt a little queer, knowing that Enoch was gone. Anyway, I went back to sleep for a long time.

It was night time when I woke up. Old Charley Potter was banging on the cell door, bringing me my supper.

He jumped when I said hello to him, and backed away.

"Murderer!" he yelled. "They got nine bodies out 'n the swamp. You crazy fiend!"

"Why, Charley," I said. "I always thought you were a friend of mine."

"Loony! I'm gonna get out of here right now—leave you locked up for the night. Sheriff'll see that nobuddy breaks in to lynch you—if you ask me, he's wasting his time."

Then Charley turned out all the lights and went away. I heard him go out the front door and put the padlock on, and I was all alone in the jailhouse.

All alone! It was strange to be all alone for the first time in years—all alone, without Enoch.

I ran my fingers across the top of my head. It felt bare and queer.

The moon was shining through the window and I stood there looking out at the empty street. Enoch always loved the moon. It made him lively. It made him restless and greedy. I wondered how he felt now, with Mr. Cassidy.

I must have stood there for a long time. My legs were numb when I turned around and listened to the fumbling at the door.

The lock clicked open, and then Mr. Cassidy came running in. He was all out of breath, and he was clawing at his head.

"Take him off me!" he yelled. "Take him away!"

"What's the matter?" I asked.

"Enoch—that thing of yours—I thought you were crazy—maybe I'm the crazy one—but take him off!"

"Why, Mr. Cassidy! I told you what Enoch was like."

"He's crawling around up there now. I can feel him. I can *hear* him. The things he whispers!"

"But I explained all that, Mr. Cassidy. Enoch wants something, doesn't he? You know what it is. You'll have to give it to him. You promised."

"I can't. I won't kill for him—he can't make me—"

"He can. And he will."

Mr. Cassidy gripped the bars on the cell door. "Seth, you must help me. Call Enoch. Take him back. Make him go back to you. Hurry."

"All right, Mr. Cassidy," I said.

I called Enoch. He didn't answer. I called again. Silence.

"It's no use," I sighed. "He won't come back. He likes you."

Mr. Cassidy started to cry. It shocked me, and then I felt kind of sorry for him. He just didn't understand, after all. I know what Enoch can do to you when he whispers that way. First he coaxes you, and then he pleads, and then he threatens—

"You'd better obey him," I told Mr. Cassidy. "Has he told you who to kill?"

Mr. Cassidy didn't pay any attention to me. He just cried. And then he took out the jail keys and opened up the cell next to mine. He went in and locked the door.

"I won't," he sobbed. "I won't, I won't!"

"You won't what?" I asked.

"I won't kill Dr. Silversmith at the hotel and give Enoch his head. I'll stay here, in the cell, where I'm safe! Oh, you fiend, you devil—"

He slumped down sideways and I could see him through the bars dividing our cell, sitting all hunched over while his hands tore at his hair.

"You'd better," I called out. "Or else Enoch will do something. Please, Mr. Cassidy—oh, hurry—"

Then Mr. Cassidy gave a little moan and I guess he fainted, because he didn't say anything more and he stopped clawing. I called to him once but he wouldn't answer.

So what could I do? I sat down in the dark corner of my cell and watched the moonlight. Moonlight always makes Enoch wild.

Then Mr. Cassidy started to scream. Not loud, but deep down in his throat. He didn't move at all, just screamed.

I knew it was Enoch, taking what he wanted—from him.

What was the use of looking? You can't stop him, and I had warned Mr. Cassidy.

I just sat there and held my hands to my ears until it was all over.

When I turned around again, Mr. Cassidy still sat slumped up against the bars. There wasn't a sound to be heard.

Oh yes, there was! A purring. A soft, faraway purring. The purring of Enoch after he has eaten. Then I heard a scratching. The scratching of Enoch's claws, when he frisks because he's been fed.

The purring and the scratching came from inside Mr. Cassidy's head.

That would be Enoch, all right, and he was happy now.

I was happy, too.

I reached my hands through the bars and pulled the jail keys from Mr. Cassidy's pocket. I opened my cell door and I was free again.

There was no need for me to stay now, with Mr. Cassidy gone. And Enoch wouldn't be staying, either. I called to him.

"Here, Enoch!"

That was as close as I've ever come to really *seeing* Enoch—a sort of white streak that came flashing out of a big red hole he had eaten in the back of Mr. Cassidy's skull.

Then I felt the soft, cold, flabby weight landing on my own head once more, and I knew Enoch had come home.

I walked through the corridor and opened the outer door of the jail. Enoch's tiny feet began to patter on the roof of my brain.

Together we walked out into the night. The moon was shining, everything was still, and I could hear, ever so softly, Enoch's happy chuckling in my ear.

M. LUCIE CHIN *recently completed a novel for Ace Books,* The Fairy of Ku-She, *and is the author of several highly regarded fantasy tales, including "Lan Lung," which appeared in my earlier collection* Masterpieces of Terror and the Supernatural. *In the suspenseful "Catmagic," we meet some decidedly unpettable felines. Cats have long been associated with witches and other practitioners of black magic, so it may be logical to assume that they may be proficient in the necromantic arts as well.*

Catmagic

BY M. LUCIE CHIN

The cat could walk through walls whenever it pleased him, and it pleased him often.

He was black, or could be as he chose. He ran the spectrum at whim but generally his shade drifted with his mood, and his mood was black a great deal of the time. At the moment his eyes were also nearly black, making him virtually impossible to see. He was a shadow in the shadows, a rustle of motion by a wall, a fleeting moment of darkness across the stars, a hiss of steam by the pipes in the corner near the bureau.

The cat was a magician. To be sure. The magician was not a cat. That had always been wrong. One did not shape-change and assume the form of cat. Cat would not permit it. And cat was a powerful magic.

He ran now along the alleyways, behind crates and trash, and over sleeping, besotted, or mindwarped bodies. His guard hairs and whiskers caught the subtle shift of air currents at his right side, where he skimmed along inches from a wall. But alleyways and rooftops could not take him where he needed to go, and occasionally his path must cross one of the wide man-lit avenues. At such times, if he was not in a great hurry, he might assume a more congenial form and scamper across the street unnoticed or even approved. But it was very late with few to see, and he did not have time for sauntering, and he did not much care.

His nose told him things his eyes could not, though they gathered every candle flicker of light the night gave up. Ahead there was a rat.

His myopic vision registered a large, slow-moving, grey-brown blur in the angle of a crate and the wall, but his nose proclaimed Rat. It was not important. He had eaten earlier. Efficiently, with no foreplay, a clean snap to the back of the neck, he had eaten half and left the rest, a perverse gift, upon the kitchen steps of a tavern in another alley.

The rat knew him too. Though her tiny eyes saw even less well than the cat's, her nose was accurate. She sensed her doom and the cat smelled that too. It tickled the portion of his mind which held that which is as close to humor as cat can come, and he headed straight for her, ghosting into the air, no more than a scent on the nightwind. He flew upward to the crate tops and on higher still to the next and next, then to the gutter and rooftop, leaving the rat shrieking below, her voice keening upward beyond what even the cat could hear. There were more rats in the alley, the cat knew, but he would see none of them now, even if he had stayed below.

He was not at all concerned.

He sped along the spines of the roofs, seeking as he went. Habit and experience dictated his path. His nose told him where to deviate and where he must pause and what he would find there.

In the shadow of a chimney a cinnamon tabby surprised in mid-snack upon sparrow; barely a moment spent and they were both gone their different ways, the bird forgotten. A battered yellow tom with mutilated ears and a bad temper, a longer delay but a delay only, and the black cat continued. On a fencetop a wooing abandoned. At a window a housecat; the magic invoked and walls became insubstantial. A hiss, a low moan, a rumble deep in the throat.

> "Put aside your quarrels and pleasures,
> Find and bring along your mate.
> Meet me on The Hill at midnight,
> I have news I must relate.
> I have news that can not wait."

In the deepest moment of the night, the cats converged upon the granary hill, where the rats ran thick around the millstones of a dozen grinding houses, where fish massed at spawning time, swimming against the swift current and the falls that drove the mills. It was an area of great luck and long ago the cats had chosen it as their meeting ground and a place of ritual magic.

Word had spread through the town and beyond into the farmland.

There were few who did not hear and few who heard who did not respond to the summons; some with kittens too young to leave, a few too feeble or old or ill, fewer still so satisfied with hearth and pleasure that they had forgotten what they were.

The black cat had climbed the dead tree traditionally used by the teller of the night's news. He sat upon a bent and naked branch high above his silent listeners. The moon hung behind him. The night was clear and crowded with stars and he, blacker than ever now, was a blot upon the brightness. Sometimes he paced the limb, but mainly he sat, erect, tail curled tightly over his forepaws, and spoke to them of cat and the ultimate evil of their kind, an evil trying earnestly to happen and already too close to success for safety.

The multitude clustered tightly together on the hillside began to bristle and murmur deep in their throats. No questions were asked. The black cat had said all that needed saying. Every cat in the world, no matter how the traditions of magic might differ with the customs of the land, knew the basic answer to the question of that ultimate evil.

No sooner had the black cat finished than the purring began. Softly at first, perfectly in unison, till every cat on The Hill had joined in. Later, when the work would be done, they would not all be needed. The black cat would take only those he required; the older and wiser (though none had ever faced *this* event before), the younger but stronger, the undisputed masters of their art; two dozen at most. But for now *all* were needed for the ritual. Together they would sing, lending their power to the gathering of the Greater Magic.

Slowly the gentle rumble grew and pulsed until the black cat could feel it trembling ever so slightly within the limb of the tree. Then the oldest cats began to stutter and broke rhythm, setting up a counter-purr which became more and more complex as other cats joined in and broke away. Louder and louder. A yowl, a hiss, and a screech. The purring thundered on beneath the growing din of *catcalls*. Not a hair was lifted, not a fang displayed. The black cat paced his limb, seeking those below upon whom the magic was gathering most strongly, and one by one he called them into the tree.

Still deep in the night and very far from dawn the rats finally crept from the shelter of the night-quiet millstones, noses working hysterically, but there was no sign of cat any longer. And the rats, their memories short and their noses filled with the smell of meal, scuttered about the millhouses of the granary hill without a thought or a question or a care, now that cat had gone.

Peter sat high atop a bookcase at the very back of the shop, his long, soft, white fur slightly soiled at the belly where he crouched on the dusty shelf, green eyes intently watching a mouse scurrying back and forth below. Its naked pink tail left a faint trail behind it in the dirt on the floor. The old man hadn't cleaned back here in years; not floors, not shelves, not books. Even the lamp chimney was so filthy one could barely read by its light. Pete watched the mouse sneaking in and out of dull shadows into the dim light, watched its tiny pink ears twitch and swivel, saw its fragile whiskers bristle as its little nose tested the air. The smell was heavy with dust and age, old paper, rotten leather, musty, crumbling pasteboard; filth and decay to be sure, but there was a power to it.

Pete had not the slightest doubt that the mouse could not smell him up there. And as long as he stayed perfectly still, its constantly moving ears would not discover him either. Not till he was ready. If he ever was. He still had not decided if he wanted to try for a mouse yet. He watched it disappearing in and out of shadows for a bit longer and decided, all things considered, hanging about was getting boring. A good chase would be much more fun. Not that he had any desire to eat the thing. Cornering it, however, and torturing it till it died of shock appealed to him a great deal at the moment. Maybe he would leave it on the old man's desk with its head torn off, just for the fun of it.

Pete disliked the old man. He was a fool, and Pete despised him for it. He sold books instead of filling himself with the power they contained. Particular books most especially.

His gaze shifted to a compact volume bound in rotting green leather lying open on the desk below, its yellow pages so badly spotted with brown that some of the words were barely legible. If the old man only knew what power he harbored in the filth at the back of the shop . . .

Pete thought to smile and was rather annoyed that he could not. Then, suddenly, he noticed the mouse scurrying across the floor at the foot of the desk, getting away. Poised on the top of the bookcase, muscles tensed, Pete hesitated. It was a long way down. But the leap from floor to desk to shelf had been nearly effortless. So he launched himself, hit the floor with a thud, gathered his bearings in time to see the mouse vanish into the shadow beneath a bookcase, and dashed after it. But it was gone. He groped in the dark space with his right paw a moment, thought of the traps the old man left lying about, and quickly withdrew. His lovely white paw was filthy, and somewhere in the back of his mind was the tickling notion that he should lick it clean, but the front of his mind disliked that notion almost as much as it had not cared for the idea of eating a warm, raw mouse. He crouched closer to the floor and peered under the bookcase. It was dark under there and nothing moved that he could see. He tried moving his ears to catch the sound of tiny feet, but he was not sure which angle was right for that kind of thing. He sniffed, but all he could smell was dust so strong it made him sneeze.

That was it. He gave up on the rotten mouse. It was only a diversion. Besides, exterminating lousy little rodents was not what this was all about. The cat guise was only a step along the way to bigger and better things, though of the four forms he had successfully achieved thus far the cat was the most potentially useful. There was hardly any end to the places a cat of fair appearance could gain entry, nor the things a man in such a form might hear and find use for later. And there was much still to learn. A shape-shifter with a dozen forms at his instant command would be nearly invincible.

He had found the little book quite by accident. For all he knew there might well be other, stronger magics hidden away here, but for now he would content himself with what he could learn from the green book while he searched the shop as unobtrusively as he could.

In fact, he could not claim to understand the greatest part of what that one book held. But Pete was young and, if his patience was not always great, at least he had time to absorb all the book contained and still make himself rich before he was twenty-five. There was *serious* work to do, though actually leaving the job in his uncle's shop before he had searched through all the books seemed unwise.

Pete left off watching for the mouse and strolled back to the desk, making the leap from the floor with a smug, silent grace he felt suited him perfectly. He wrapped his tail about his paws and began scanning the faded brown handwriting on the page before him, but oddly it seemed to be growing less legible as he read. Concentration did not help. The letters were becoming fuzzy and the lamplight was flaring.

He sat erect and shut his eyes a moment. Fatigue, he thought. In fact, he felt a little odd all over. He had been in this form since shortly after supper, longer than he had been in any form before, and it was well after midnight now. When it came down to actual use, he doubted he would have reason to remain bound to any form so long.

This was more than a little upsetting, though. As he watched, the bookcase across from the desk became increasingly unfocused, until he could barely make out the individual books. At the same time the room was growing amazingly bright.

Then a chilling realization settled on Pete, and he stopped what he was doing. He looked down at a clean, damp paw poised directly beneath his nose. He had been licking it as he sat thinking. Somehow that tickling little thought which had been at the back of his mind a moment ago had made its way to the part of his mind more immediately present in reality than his ruminations. And at the same time he understood that some part of his altered self had been *enjoying* it.

Enough of this! It's definitely time to unbind.

Pete turned to the book beside him and panic struck. It lay there on the desk, a pale shape on a dark surface, absolutely unreadable. Not a word, not a line could his eye discern.

Calm, he told himself. *Calm. You have done this three times now. The spells for unbinding are all basically the same. Think. The variation is not complicated. You can remember it if you think.*

He sat beside the useless book, tense as a spring, and tried to concentrate, but the growing brightness was distracting. The shadows were gone, reduced to areas less dim than the lamplight had been. The scrabbling sound of tiny feet tickled the edges of his hearing and his ears swiveled about to sharpen the sounds without his will or desire for them to do so. He was feeling *very* odd now, but, blessedly, the variation came to mind without effort and he closed his eyes in relief.

Slowly and carefully, meticulously pronouncing each of the words in his mind, Pete recited the twelve lines of the charm and opened his eyes to a bright blur not noticeably different from the one upon which he had closed them.

Shit. He reviewed the words quickly but could not decide where he had gone wrong. So once more he closed his eyes and concentrated totally upon the lines, giving them the most careful mental articulation, feeling the formation of unvoiced sounds in his throat, visualizing the shape of the mouth about each syllable, trying to remember the feel of the change as the charm worked its release.

There seemed to be a slight tingle in his nervous system. His skin felt hypersensitive, almost on the threshold of perceiving the touch of the motionless air around him. It did not give him a great sense of confidence, and he was reluctant to open his eyes, but he had no choice.

Only a moment was required to confirm his fears, and he shut them tight again at once.

Don't panic. Think, damn it, think. Stay calm.

His body felt very strange indeed now. Every hair of his coat seemed directly connected to a nerve ending. His ears twitched and cocked to the slightest sound, and the rich, musty aroma of the back room had broken down into a myriad of distinct and powerful scents which his nose could distinguish as easily as his eye had once differentiated colors. His body housed a great cacophony of unfamiliar information, from every source except the clarity of sight he desperately needed. Concentration was nearly impossible.

THINK!

Instead he found himself in silent supplication to a nameless god.

Please, just let me get out of this. I swear I will never touch that book again. Oh please.

The cacophony still raged, but there seemed to be new elements within it now. As indefinable as everything else, but definitely present.

Cautiously Pete opened his eyes. The focus was as bad as ever, but his other senses helped draw a clearer picture of what confronted him. A black cat sat in the middle of the aisle between the bookshelves.

Black. That was the human part of his brain still seeking something familiar to hang onto. While his mind was thinking black, however, all the hairs on his spine were standing on end and his nerves were bristling. He felt his throat catch hold of a round, low note rather like a moan, and with a pure act of will he managed to stifle the sound and calm the prickling in his skin till the fur lay flat again.

That was stupid. He had far more important things to do than pop off at the sight of another cat. He could not allow himself to descend into the realms of feline body instinct.

The cat was still as a statue. Still as only a cat can be.

Where the hell did you come from?

He felt his hackles rising again and tried to shake off the creepy, itching feeling.

His ears and nose twitched, and he found his attention drawn to the right. The second cat was a light-colored smudge, "yellow" his mind said, only a few feet from the desk.

His mouth opened and Pete felt a hiss gathering at the back of his palate. His diaphragm contracted before he fully understood what he was doing and a long, liquid whisper was carried out upon his breath. There was an answering hiss from somewhere above Pete's head. Another cat crouched on the top shelf of a bookcase.

That was when he became aware of the purring. It was a very soft unison, perfectly in rhythm, but as the purring increased in volume it also increased in voices. More and more cats sauntered into his view. He felt every one of them before he saw them. They walked along the bookshelves with barely enough freeboard between book spines and edge for narrow paws to fit, sure-footed and seemingly careless. They glided through the dusty aisles. There was the subtle rustle of fur as cats sat, as cats rubbed cheeks and shoulders along the bindings of books and the corners of cases; invading *his* territory, marking *his* landmarks upon which he had never left his own scent.

As the cats gathered, the dimensions of the room began to shift. Heights did not seem as great, yet lateral distances seemed greater. The narrow path along the bookshelf looked like a highway. The whole room was warping into strange and terrifying spatial relations. But worse, the cacophony was becoming well ordered and quieter even as his surroundings became more alien.

The purring continued and he looked around carefully. Twelve, he counted twelve. He could still count, then. Well, that was something.

Twelve. He wondered. Could it have any relation to the spell? Twelve lines to get in. Twelve lines to get out. Twelve cats to lock him away from release? He was certain now that it was not an accident, no lapse of memory or fault of judgment and no simple paranoia. They were *doing* this to him.

He began to know things: who they were, what they were; and he knew that they hated him. Not a hair was raised or a fang bared. They sat prim and perfect as house pets and sang their spell, pulling him deeper into their world, their reality, their sorcery, and their hate.

And it was working.

Pete knew they would not just toy with him, terrify him, and let him go. The magic was too great for such trivia. They would play him like a mouse, remorselessly, carelessly, till he died of them, for despite all he knew and felt, he was still a man, still human. That would not change, and for that reason they would not suffer him to live.

He was frantic. The room continued to evolve and time had vanished from his awareness. He wanted to scream, and the body answered the need by hurling a ragged, throat-rasping screech from his mouth.

The cats bristled and tensed, but did not rise and did not break the rhythm of their purr.

Pete's ears flattened and his whisker pads twitched, exposing long fangs. He danced a sidling little step or two toward the edge of the desk, growling low in his chest. His mind's eye could see the image he presented. Despite his fear, the posture of aggression in the face of danger felt right. His nerves tingled again as the fur rose, and it was a stimulating sensation. He puffed himself and his eyes grew large. He felt dangerous and it pleased him, even as the human within knew this was a worthless and insane action.

All of them were crouching now. All but the black cat. He was moving toward the table, back arched, eyes fierce. The rest continued to purr, but it was beginning to change, to break and stutter and find counter-purrs. The black cat was no longer purring, however. He growled a low and nasty note to match Pete's own.

In that distant little part of his brain from whence the paw-licking had come there was another urge growing: attack. The provocation was clear. He knew it was wanted. He knew he wanted it too and fought the compulsion frantically. His ears twitched and he broke eye contact with the black cat long enough to cast a fuzzy glance around him. All the cats were on their feet, moving in a slow prowl toward the desk, hemming him in.

THINK, damn it. Use your head, it's the only weapon you have. What do they expect you to do?

The black cat, though not actually the closest, was clearly the leader, the focus of the magic, the spell binder. He suspected that, logically, he should go for the nearest, most immediate threat. But reason was on his side and reason said he should go for the power. So.

Pete seized the moment and sprang directly at the black cat, a howl in his throat and a curse in his mind.

But the cat was not there.

He had vanished like smoke in a breeze. With tall bookcases on either side, Pete had been sure there was no place for him to go but into battle or into retreat. But he was gone.

He spun about instantly, hoping to regain his position of small advantage upon the desk, but the cats were all behind him now. They had shifted position as instantly as the black cat had vanished.

A grave error in judgment there, he realized. He had no idea of the strategies of an actual catfight, but this had obviously not surprised them as much as he had intended.

Stop trying to outthink the cats and think like a man.

Never having faced any real danger before in his young life, however, Pete found his mind a terrifying blank. But as the cats advanced slowly, one idea did come blazingly to mind, and Pete acted upon it instantly.

With a speed that astonished only him, he turned and fled toward the front of the shop, only to come up short at the end of the first row against a large, scruffy yellow tom with tattered ears who dropped into his path from a high shelf. Pete swerved to the right, claws scrabbling frantically for traction on the wooden floor, and bolted into the shadows between shelves. But there were cats there already. Waiting. One of them threw its back up and spit noisily into his face while the other leaped forward and raked him across the nose with claws which looked, to Pete's altered perceptions, like carving knives.

Pete's reflexes were not thoroughly under his command yet, and he collided with the two cats amid screeches and slashing claws. Once free, he bolted down the nearest aisle only to find more cats blocking his way at every turn. They fell on him and seemed to appear out of thin air. He ran and ran. The aisles between bookcases seemed endless corridors. The twelve cats seemed like twelve hundred. They chased him, slashed him with claws, tore his ears with sharp teeth, always ahead of him, always behind him. He could not evade them or outrun them, or outwit them. He felt as though he had run for miles. Half blind, his cat-altered perceptions showed him a place he could barely recognize, and finally he found himself running foolishly into blind corners from which he escaped only by leaping onto nearby shelves.

They were playing with him, deliberately confusing him, wearing him out. Then somehow he found himself back on the desk. Not a perfectly defensible position, but the best one he had been in since his stupid attack. He was tired and scared and ultimately trapped; at the mercy of those *without* mercy.

Pete and the black cat watched each other closely. There were no words, but Pete understood. That he would have been ruthless and merciless with the power he had only begun to play with was of no concern to them. This was not retribution; and yet it was. He was being punished, but not for his planned abuses to his fellow man. This was cat. He had trespassed upon forbidden ground and cat would not permit it. Not ever. Not in innocence, nor ignorance, nor curiosity, nor any of the motives known to Pete. Cat would *never* permit it, and cat was a powerful magic indeed.

He knew too that *they* understood *him* and they did not care.

He had no hope any longer of escape or of breaking their concentration long enough to work the charm.

I'm a man, damn it! It is stupid to have to die like this. There MUST be a way out.

But there was not. He knew without being told how the cats had gotten in. The catmagic was strong enough for that too, but *he* did not know how to use it. He was only as much cat as they forced him to be, which was not truly cat at all, and his own little smattering of magic, poorly known, barely practiced, was no use against them.

Or was it?

Pete's mind settled upon an earlier moment of clear vision when he had crouched atop the bookcase and watched a mouse scurry to safety just inches from the tip of the black cat's tail. Surely the night could not last forever. The old man would come in the morning and the cats would have to go. All he had to do was hide till then. Staying out of a mousetrap was a minor matter compared to the threat facing him now.

But would the charm work? He had never gone directly from one form to another without unbinding first. Shape-shifting was different from unbinding, and if all they could control was cat then at least he had a chance.

He did not have a mouse among his forms, but he did have a rat. It would do.

To Pete's vast amazement it worked. It was also a shock. The room suddenly expanded around him to stunning proportions. The light level dropped abruptly and sights, sounds, and smells changed. It sent him reeling, and the disorientation was so overwhelming he could not be sure if things were back to what he would once have called normal. All he knew was that this choice of form had been a mistake. Every cat in the room suddenly underwent a radical and vicious transformation. Fighting stance was abandoned for hunting stance. Eyes were bright and intense, fangs bared, whiskers bristled, and several of the cats began a chattering in the back of their throats. Quick as he realized his error, Pete also recognized that there was no time to do anything about it.

In an instant they moved on him and he fled. Leaping onto the nearest bookshelf, he dashed along just ahead of the black cat on the floor below. He had hoped to make it to the end of the shelf with enough of a lead to drop to the floor and duck under the bottom shelf of the bookcase, but as he looked down at his intended goal he saw that the rat was too large to fit where the mouse had gone easily.

Damn!

He turned, seeking other sources of refuge, and discovered the yellow tom with the battered ears on the shelf at the other end. It stalked him slowly with an evil joy in its eyes while the rest waited in a row below. He was cornered again, but this time he felt less desperate. It had worked once, it would work again.

He recited the twelve lines of the second charm, and where the rat had crouched a moment before stood a fat grey pigeon. The cats were still in hunting form, but they could not catch him in the air.

It took him a while to understand, but the bird too was not a way out. They stalked him relentlessly, and all the windows and doors were locked tight.

If he had been a real bird, he might have been able to stay in the air all night without tiring, but somehow he doubted that. The cats kept him in flight constantly. There was no place he could perch for more than a moment before a cat was within reach of him. Trying for cover under a bookcase was out of the question. He doubted he would fit, in any event, but on the ground he would be slow and clumsy, the nearest cat would have him in an instant. In the air he was not terribly graceful either. He had not yet mastered the mechanics of flight to more than a functional degree, and after what seemed like an unmercifully long time in the air he felt himself tiring badly. If he kept this up, they would have him before too long anyway. But the time in the air had given him a new outlook on things. He was no longer as frightened. His anger had begun to rise and he felt a growing hatred of his own.

Escape had been his primary motive, but something else was in his mind. Panic aside, he realized that his last form should have been his first choice, but he did not stop to berate himself. He was ready to do battle on his own now.

You want me? Then here I am. Come for me if you dare.

He flew from his last perch, aiming to land on the floor directly in front of the black cat, and as he descended he began to recite the lines of the charm.

What landed on the floor with a solid thud was no longer a bird, but a large dog.

Pete felt the power of his anger surge through him and he sprang to attack. The cats scattered before him like leaves on a strong wind, and he raced after them, jaws snapping at tails, snarling and frantic in his hate-lust. The chase was on in earnest and the tables were turned. It was *he* who pursued through the dusty aisles of the shop, certain death in the snap of his jaws, merciless in his vengeance.

The black cat was his special target, and his mind's eye saw it crushed in his jaws. He knew how glorious it would be to kill them, but tonight he would settle for just driving them from the shop. Once they were gone he could unbind without worry. He would never use cat again, but there were other forms and some might be useful for cat hunting. They had declared war, and if they thought he would forget they were miserably wrong.

Yet they evaded him. He leaped at them where they crouched on shelves, scattered them from the top of the desk, relentlessly kept them from refuge.

They were everywhere. At each turn another cat fled before him and another and another; for their very lives, and yet they did not *leave.* There were every bit as many as before. And Pete was growing exhausted. They had tired first the cat and then the bird. Though the dog was bigger and stronger, his rage had levied an even greater tax upon his strength.

He stopped in the middle of the aisle and tried to catch his breath, concealing his fatigue behind a show of snarls. It was then that Pete once more became aware of the purring.

Purring, purring, constantly purring. Did *nothing* daunt them? He looked about. Seven cats sat on shelves on either side of him, just barely within snapping range if he jumped well. They could have gone higher and been absolutely safe, but they had not. Four of them sat, tails curled, ears swiveling, fur unruffled, fangs unseen. Two stood rubbing against the spines of old books. One crouched on the narrow freeboard, belly and hip partially unsupported, forepaws neatly tucked, tail dangling. Purring, purring. Watching him.

Pete snarled louder, lunged and snapped at the nearest cat. He missed, but not much. The cat never moved.

They were baiting him. Still.

They could not get him as he was, but he could not get them. So why did they not just *leave?* It could not be much longer till dawn. The old man would be coming soon to open the shop. He would shoo the cats away, and Pete too most likely, but he would be free to find a safe, quiet hiding place to unbind. There was nothing left they could do.

The black cat sat in the wide spot at the intersection of two aisles, side-lit in a vaguely eerie way by the lamp on the desk, the last four cats behind him just into the shadows.

Pete, furious, lunged again. But when he landed the black cat had vanished. The other four had not moved, not so much as blinked.

He spun about and found himself ringed with cats. And the black one was behind him now.

He sprang at them again, and again there was nothing in his jaws, yet they still ringed him. Purring, purring, breaking into the funny counter-rhythms for a moment, then not, then again, and for the second time that night the room began to warp and his senses altered. His vision became keener, his hearing more acute, though not as sensitive as cat. Smells became complex once more, but there were different odor priorities.

No! Not again! They can't do this. I'm not a cat now. THEY CAN'T DO THIS IF I'M NOT A CAT!

But they could and Pete knew that they could. They could do anything they wanted to do. They could have killed him without a single pawswipe if they had wished. But they had not wished. They could have kept him from changing forms as easily as they had kept him from unbinding. But they had not wished. It has amused them to play with him. It amused them now. And as surely as Pete had once known that they eventually intended to kill him, he now knew that his doom was at hand, but it was not death any longer. To shape-shift to dog had been the gravest error of all, and they had seized upon it with glee.

Slowly and carefully they worked their magic, consigning him to the worst hell cat could imagine. Purring, purring, the black cat advanced. It amused them, and in that portion of the mind which is as close to humor as cat can come, this night's work would amuse them for the rest of Pete's life.

The old man put down the hammer and fitted the last of the new shelves in place. It had taken weeks to clean and air and refit the shelving in the back room of the bookshop, and even now he could still smell the odor of smoke and burned books.

He was not angry. He had felt great and consuming horror at first when the neighbors pulled him out of bed at dawn to tell him his shop was burning. He had felt panic and terror when his sister told him Pete had not been home since dinner. But there was no body, charred and reeking, among the corpses of the books. In fact, the back room was not badly damaged at all, really. Only the books. The old books. The dearest things he possessed, bought in strange and obscure places all over the world. The old ones he cherished and hoarded and did not even *think* of selling. There had been magic in them; old stories, ancient lore, fallacious facts, curious turns of logic. Not real magic, perhaps, but the magic of men's mind turned to odd and often naïvely inventive paths. He grieved for them, and for the fact that he was old and settled in the shop and the town and would never find their like again. He felt very tired and very lonely as he stood in the back room with the new bookshelves all about and nothing to put on them but a dozen volumes that had not been fatally damaged.

He *had* been angry, when all the speculation began to fly about and he could piece together what had happened. He was blazingly furious at Pete, for it had clearly been the boy's fault. But that had not lasted. When Pete did not come home, he felt as devastated for his sister's loss as he did for his own. She and the boy were his only family now and if Pete had run off from the shame of his guilt . . . well, that could have been forgiven in time. It had been meant as a joke. The boy did not aim to burn the store. He was a strange kid, and locking the dog in the shop as a prank . . . well, Pete would *do* something like that. He couldn't know the dog would knock over the lamp. He shouldn't have left it burning, but he couldn't have expected a thing like that. It wasn't worth losing half a man's family over.

A ferocious barking began behind the shop and the old man got up and trudged to a new cabinet he had built in one of the cases by the back door. He took out a bowl and filled it with dry meal and bits of stale meat from a bag he had brought with him from home. In the water closet he drew a deep bowl of water and set it on the floor beside the dish of food. Then he went outside into the evening dusk to bring in the dog. He was an unruly critter, snappish and ill-tempered, but he had a huge and vicious bark and no one with any sense came near him. That bark had saved the rest of the shop, after all, and he was a fine watchdog for all that he gave the old man a great deal of trouble handling him.

And oh, how he hated cats!

The old man stood on the stoop at the back door and watched the dog straining at his chain, howling with rage at the sleek black tom sitting quietly on the fence post. It was becoming a regular ritual. In fact, it seemed as though every cat in the neighborhood had taken a fancy to tormenting that dog. Sometimes they even sat on the roof of his little house, just out of reach. Just to drive him crazy, it seemed.

Enough ruckus for one night, he thought. Picking up the stick he kept by the back door, he reached a bit farther and gathered a couple of small stones, which he lobbed at the cat.

"Off with you, cat," he called as it vanished from the post.

"Come on now, Petey," he said to the dog, advancing on it with the stick in his hand. "It's into the shop for you and no more of this snapping at me or you'll get another whacking." The dog snarled and dodged the old man's prodding stick while the chain was unfastened. When he balked at being taken inside, he received a stinging smack across the ribs. The old man did not *like* beating the dog, but it had not responded in the slightest to attempts at kindness and in the end the old man had decided it was a better watchdog as it was.

With a quick swat to the tail, he sent the dog inside, locked the back door, walked through the alley to the street and checked the front. Satisfied all was secure, he turned toward the street again and saw the black cat sitting in the alley by the shop.

"Good night, cat," he said, "good hunting to you."

Then the old man turned away and walked home.

Probably the author most often affiliated with the late great Weird Tales *magazine was* H. P. LOVECRAFT *(1890–1937). Lovecraft haunted the streets of Providence, Rhode Island and there penned some extremely powerful tales of terror, including "The Rats in the Walls," "The Dunwich Horror," "The Outsider" and the following story, one of his earlier gruesome efforts.*

The Hound
BY H. P. LOVECRAFT

In my tortured ears there sounds unceasingly a nightmare whirring and flapping, and a faint distant baying as of some gigantic hound. It is not dream—it is not, I fear, even madness—for too much has already happened to give me these merciful doubts.

St. John is a mangled corpse; I alone know why, and such is my knowledge that I am about to blow out my brains for fear I shall be mangled in the same way. Down unlit and illimitable corridors of eldritch phantasy sweeps the black, shapeless Nemesis that drives me to self-annihilation.

May heaven forgive the folly and morbidity which led us both to so monstrous a fate! Wearied with the commonplaces of a prosaic world; where even the joys of romance and adventure soon grow stale, St. John and I had followed enthusiastically every aesthetic and intellectual movement which promised respite from our devastating ennui. The enigmas of the symbolists and the ecstasies of the pre-Raphaelites all were ours in their time, but each new mood was drained too soon of its diverting novelty and appeal.

Only the sombre philosophy of the decadents could help us, and this we found potent only by increasing gradually the depth and diabolism of our penetrations. Baudelaire and Huysmans were soon exhausted of thrills, till finally there remained for us only the more direct stimuli of unnatural personal experiences and adventures. It was this frightful emotional need which led us eventually to that detestable course which even in my present fear I mention with shame and timidity—that hideous extremity of human outrage, the abhorred practice of grave-robbing.

I cannot reveal the details of our shocking expeditions, or catalogue

even partly the worst of the trophies adorning the nameless museum
we prepared in the great stone house where we jointly dwelt, alone and
servantless. Our museum was a blasphemous, unthinkable place,
where with the satanic taste of neurotic virtuosi we had assembled an
universe of terror and decay to excite our jaded sensibilities. It was a
secret room, far, far, underground; where huge winged daemons
carven of basalt and onyx vomited from wide grinning mouths weird
green and orange light, and hidden pneumatic pipes ruffled into kalei-
doscopic dances of death the lines of red charnel things hand in hand
woven in voluminous black hangings. Through these pipes came at
will the odors our moods most craved; sometimes the scent of pale
funeral lilies; sometimes the narcotic incense of imagined Eastern
shrines of the kingly dead, and sometimes—how I shudder to recall it!
—the frightful, soul-upheaving stenches of the uncovered grave.

Around the walls of this repellent chamber were cases of antique
mummies alternating with comely, lifelike bodies perfectly stuffed and
cured by the taxidermist's art, and with headstones snatched from the
oldest churchyards of the world. Niches here and there contained
skulls of all shapes, and heads preserved in various stages of dissolu-
tion. There one might find the rotting, bald pates of famous noblemen,
and the fresh and radiantly golden heads of new-buried children.

Statues and paintings there were, all of fiendish subjects and some
executed by St. John and myself. A locked portfolio, bound in tanned
human skin, held certain unknown and unnameable drawings which it
was rumored Goya had perpetrated but dared not acknowledge. There
were nauseous musical instruments, stringed, brass, and wood-wind,
on which St. John and I sometimes produced dissonances of exquisite
morbidity and cacodaemoniacal ghastliness; whilst in a multitude of
inlaid ebony cabinets reposed the most incredible and unimaginable
variety of tomb-loot ever assembled by human madness and perver-
sity. It is of this loot in particular that I must not speak—thank God I
had the courage to destroy it long before I thought of destroying
myself!

The predatory excursions on which we collected our unmentionable
treasures were always artistically memorable events. We were no vulgar ghouls, but worked only under certain conditions of mood, landscape, environment, weather, season, and moonlight. These pastimes
were to us the most exquisite form of aesthetic expression, and we
gave their details a fastidious technical care. An inappropriate hour, a

jarring lighting effect, or a clumsy manipulation of the damp sod, would almost totally destroy for us that ecstatic titillation which followed the exhumation of some ominous, grinning secret of the earth. Our quest for novel scenes and piquant conditions was feverish and insatiate—St. John was always the leader, and he it was who led the way at last to that mocking, accursed spot which brought us our hideous and inevitable doom.

By what malign fatality were we lured to that terrible Holland churchyard? I think it was the dark rumor and legendry, the tales of one buried for five centuries, who had himself been a ghoul in his time and had stolen a potent thing from a mighty sepulchre. I can recall the scene in these final moments—the pale autumnal moon over the graves, casting long horrible shadows; the grotesque trees, drooping sullenly to meet the neglected grass and the crumbling slabs; the vast legions of strangely colossal bats that flew against the moon; the antique ivied church pointing a huge spectral finger at the livid sky; the phosphorescent insects that danced like death-fires under the yews in a distant corner; the odors of mould, vegetation, and less explicable things that mingled feebly with the night-wind from over far swamps and seas; and, worst of all, the faint deep-toned baying of some gigantic hound which we could neither see nor definitely place. As we heard this suggestion of baying we shuddered, remembering the tales of the peasantry; for he whom we sought had centuries before been found in this selfsame spot, torn and mangled by the claws and teeth of some unspeakable beast.

I remember how we delved in the ghoul's grave with our spades, and how we thrilled at the picture of ourselves, the grave, the pale watching moon, the horrible shadows, the grotesque trees, the titanic bats, the antique church, the dancing death-fires, the sickening odors, the gently moaning night-wind, and the strange, half-heard directionless baying of whose objective existence we could scarcely be sure.

Then we struck a substance harder than the damp mould, and beheld a rotting oblong box crusted with mineral deposits from the long undisturbed ground. It was incredibly tough and thick, but so old that we finally pried it open and feasted our eyes on what it held.

Much—amazingly much—was left of the object despite the lapse of five hundred years. The skeleton, though crushed in places by the jaws of the thing that had killed it, held together with surprising firmness, and we gloated over the clean white skull and its long, firm teeth and its eyeless sockets that once had glowed with a charnel fever like our own. In the coffin lay an amulet of curious and exotic design, which had apparently been worn around the sleeper's neck. It was the oddly conventionalized figure of a crouching winged hound, or sphinx with a semicanine face, and was exquisitely carved in antique Oriental fashion from a small piece of green jade. The expression of its features was repellent in the extreme, savoring at once of death, bestiality, and malevolence. Around the base was an inscription in characters which neither St. John nor I could identify; and on the bottom, like a maker's seal, was graven a grotesque and formidable skull.

Immediately upon beholding this amulet we knew that we must possess it; that this treasure alone was our logical pelf from the centuried grave. Even had its outlines been unfamiliar we would have desired it, but as we looked more closely we saw that it was not wholly unfamiliar. Alien it indeed was to all art and literature which sane and balanced readers know, but we recognized it as the thing hinted of in the forbidden *Necronomicon* of the mad Arab Abdul Alhazred; the ghastly soul-symbol of the corpse-eating cult of inaccessible Leng, in Central Asia. All too well did we trace the sinister lineaments described by the old Arab daemonologist; lineaments, he wrote, drawn from some obscure supernatural manifestation of the souls of those who vexed and gnawed at the dead.

Seizing the green jade object, we gave a last glance at the bleached and cavern-eyed face of its owner and closed up the grave as we found it. As we hastened from the abhorrent spot, the stolen amulet in St. John's pocket, we thought we saw the bats descend in a body to the earth we had so lately rifled, as if seeking for some cursed and unholy nourishment. But the autumn moon shone weak and pale, and we could not be sure.

So, too, as we sailed the next day away from Holland to our home, we thought we heard the faint distant baying of some gigantic hound in the background. But the autumn wind moaned sad and wan, and we could not be sure.

Less than a week after our return to England, strange things began to happen. We lived as recluses; devoid of friends, alone, and without servants in a few rooms of an ancient manor-house on a bleak and unfrequented moor; so that our doors were seldom disturbed by the knock of the visitor.

Now, however, we were troubled by what seemed to be a frequent fumbling in the night, not only around the doors but around the windows also, upper as well as lower. Once we fancied that a large, opaque body darkened the library window when the moon was shining against it, and another time we thought we heard a whirring or flapping sound not far off. On each occasion investigation revealed nothing, and we began to ascribe the occurrences to imagination which still prolonged in our ears the faint far baying we thought we had heard in the Holland churchyard. The jade amulet now reposed in a niche in our museum, and sometimes we burned a strangely scented candle before it. We read much in Alhazred's *Necronomicon* about its properties, and about the relation of ghosts' souls to the objects it symbolized; and were disturbed by what we read.

Then terror came.

On the night of September 24, 19__, I heard a knock at my chamber door. Fancying it St. John's, I bade the knocker enter, but was answered only by a shrill laugh. There was no one in the corridor. When I aroused St. John from his sleep, he professed entire ignorance of the event, and became as worried as I. It was the night that the faint, distant baying over the moor became to us a certain and dreaded reality.

Four days later, whilst we were both in the hidden museum, there came a low, cautious scratching at the single door which led to the secret library staircase. Our alarm was now divided, for, besides our fear of the unknown, we had always entertained a dread that our grisly collection might be discovered. Extinguishing all lights, we proceeded to the door and threw it suddenly open; whereupon we felt an unaccountable rush of air, and heard, as if receding far away, a queer combination of rusting, tittering, and articulate chatter. Whether we were mad, dreaming, or in our senses, we did not try to determine. We only realized, with the blackest of apprehensions, that the apparently disembodied chatter was beyond a doubt *in the Dutch language*.

After that we lived in growing horror and fascination. Mostly we held to the theory that we were jointly going mad from our life of unnatural excitements, but sometimes it pleased us more to dramatize ourselves as the victims of some creeping and appalling doom. Bizarre manifestations were now too frequent to count. Our lonely house was seemingly alive with the presence of some malign being whose nature we could not guess, and every night that daemoniac baying rolled over the wind-swept moor, always louder and louder. On October 29 we found in the soft earth underneath the library window a series of footprints utterly impossible to describe. They were as baffling as the hordes of great bats which haunted the old manor-house in unprecedented and increasing numbers.

The horror reached a culmination on November 18, when St. John, walking home after dark from the dismal railway station, was seized by some frightful carnivorous thing and torn to ribbons. His screams had reached the house, and I had hastened to the terrible scene in time to hear a whir of wings and see a vague black cloudy thing silhouetted against the rising moon.

My friend was dying when I spoke to him, and he could not answer coherently. All he could do was to whisper, "The amulet—that damned thing—"

Then he collapsed, an inert mass of mangled flesh.

I buried him the next midnight in one of our neglected gardens, and mumbled over his body one of the devilish rituals he had loved in life. And as I pronounced the last daemoniac sentence I heard afar on the moor the faint baying of some gigantic hound. The moon was up, but I dared not look at it. And when I saw on the dim-lighted moor a wide nebulous shadow sweeping from mound to mound, I shut my eyes and threw myself face down upon the ground. When I arose, trembling, I know not how much later, I staggered into the house and made shocking obeisance before the enshrined amulet of green jade.

Being now afraid to live alone in the ancient house on the moor, I departed on the following day for London, taking with me the amulet after destroying by fire and burial the rest of the impious collection in the museum. But after three nights I heard the baying again, and before a week was over felt strange eyes upon me whenever it was dark. One evening as I strolled on Victoria Embankment for some needed air, I saw a black shape obscure one of the reflections of the lamps in the water. A wind, stronger than the night-wind, rushed by, and I knew that what had befallen St. John must soon befall me.

The next day I carefully wrapped the green jade amulet and sailed for Holland. What mercy I might gain by returning the thing to its silent, sleeping owner I knew not; but I felt that I must try any step conceivably logical. What the hound was, and why it had pursued me, were questions still vague; but I had first heard the baying in that ancient churchyard, and every subsequent event including St. John's dying whisper had served to connect the curse with the stealing of the amulet. Accordingly I sank into the nethermost abysses of despair when, at an inn in Rotterdam, I discovered that thieves had despoiled me of this sole means of salvation.

The baying was loud that evening, and in the morning I read of a nameless deed in the vilest quarter of the city. The rabble were in terror, for upon an evil tenement had fallen a red death beyond the foulest previous crime of the neighborhood. In a squalid thieves' den an entire family had been torn to shreds by an unknown thing which left no trace, and those around had heard all night a faint, deep, insistent note as of a gigantic hound.

So at last I stood again in the unwholesome churchyard where a pale winter moon cast hideous shadows, and leafless trees drooped sullenly to meet the withered, frosty grass and cracking slabs, and the ivied church pointed a jeering finger at the unfriendly sky, and the night-wind howled maniacally from over frozen swamps and frigid seas. The baying was very faint now, and it ceased altogether as I approached the ancient grave I had once violated, and frightened away an abnormally large horde of bats which had been hovering curiously around it.

I know not why I went thither unless to pray, or gibber out insane pleas and apologies to the calm white thing that lay within; but, whatever my reason, I attacked the half-frozen sod with a desperation partly mine and partly that of a dominating will outside myself. Excavation was much easier than I expected, though at one point I encountered a queer interruption; when a lean vulture darted down out of the cold sky and pecked frantically at the grave-earth until I killed him with a blow of my spade. Finally I reached the rotting oblong box and removed the damp nitrous cover. This is the last rational act I ever performed.

For crouched within that centuried coffin, embraced by a closepacked nightmare retinue of huge, sinewy, sleeping bats, was the bony thing my friend and I had robbed; not clean and placid as we had seen it then, but covered with caked blood and shreds of alien flesh and hair, and leering sentiently at me with phosphorescent sockets and sharp ensanguined fangs yawning twistedly in mockery of my inevitable doom. And when it gave from those grinning jaws a deep, sardonic bay as of some gigantic hound, and I saw that it held in its gory filthy claw the lost and fateful amulet of green jade, I merely screamed and ran away idiotically, my screams soon dissolving into peals of hysterical laughter.

Madness rides the star-wind . . . claws and teeth sharpened on centuries of corpses . . . dripping death astride a bacchanale of bats from night-black ruins of buried temples of Belial . . . Now, as the baying of that dead fleshless monstrosity grows louder and louder, and the stealthy whirring and flapping of those accursed web-wings circles closer and closer, I shall seek with my revolver the oblivion which is my only refuge from the unnamed and unnameable.

"The Princess and Her Future" is a neat antidote to those fairy tales that end happily ever after. Its author, TANITH LEE, *is a British writer whose children's books and such adult fantasies as* The Birthgrave, Death's Master *and* Red as Blood *have won the two most prestigious awards in the genre, both the British and the World Fantasy Awards.*

The Princess and Her Future
BY TANITH LEE

Down in the deep darkness of the green water of the cistern, where no reflection and no sunlight ever come, Hiranu waits. Not with patience, for patience is not a virtue to such as he. Nor with resignation, nor with despair. Hiranu knows, as he has always known, known from the actual instant of his binding, that at last his waiting must come to an end. Some hundreds of years have passed, in the emerald mud of the cistern's bottom. Above, far above, the temple has been crumbling to pink powder, and the great trees of the jungle-forest have woven a parasol against the sky. None of this is of any consequence to Hiranu, neither does it dismay him. He is immortal. He is incorrigibly optimistic. He understands that on one burning day or on one star-watered night—both of which have no meaning in the cistern—he will hear a step on the marble paving, loud as thunder, soft as a leaf. And that step will be for him. That step will be the release of Hiranu.

So he waits. And he waits.

The palace of the Ruler poised at the summit of a downpouring of gardens. The palace was modest, for the Kingdom was small; however, the gardens were very beautiful, the product of great devotion on the part of the Ruler's slaves. At their farther end was a high wall, and in the wall a little door that gave on an overgrown pathway. The path led into the jungle-forest, and so to the clearing where an ancient temple stood. Creepers bound the pillars of the temple and flowers grew among its myriad carvings. Portions of the roof had collapsed. Harmless jewel-like snakes lived in the courts. Long ago, the rulers in the palace would leave the gardens by the little door, take the private pathway, seek the temple and worship there. But no longer. Somehow, the temple had fallen from its good repute.

The Ruler's daughter, Jarasmi, discovered the unused door as a child, and learned where it led. She was also told by her nurse that a demon haunted the temple, one of the *Rakshasas,* which could take any form it chose: lovely, to entice; fearsome—to terrify.

When Jarasmi was sixteen, she was attended by two maids. Her nurse was dead, and Jarasmi no longer believed the tale.

Jarasmi knew that in half a year's time she was to be married, and she thought a great deal of this, sometimes with pleasure, and sometimes with doubt. One day, as she passed through the marketplace in her litter, a man prostrated himself before it, begging that he might show the princess his wares. Jarasmi's maids spoke haughtily, but Jarasmi, looking out, caught a hint of gold and heard protestations of magic.

"Bring him to me at once," cried Jarasmi.

So he was brought.

He was a strange person, and she did not like him. He wore rags, and humbled himself, yet he had the bearing of one of importance. His eyes, which he kept mostly lowered, were very odd. Rather than dark, they were yellow, and the pupils were not round, but slotted, like a serpent's. Surely, he was not quite human. He spoke.

"Some while before," he said, "I served a mighty prince, but I have come down in the world. Now I am a seller of sorcerous toys. Nevertheless, I dare approach the Ruler's daughter. Not that I may sell my goods, but that I may bring her a gift."

Jarasmi drew back, for she was uncertain now. But the man of the serpent's eyes held out to her a ball of golden glass, so clear the sun passed through it in a bolt of light.

"See," he said. "It is a thing of prophecy. If the princess wishes to know her future, she has only to cast the ball upon the ground with sufficient force to break it. What is to be found within will tell her all she desires."

Next instant, he had placed the glass ball in Jarasmi's hand. Uncannily, he slipped aside into the crowd and was immediately invisible.

Jarasmi's maids fluttered about her, all curiosity, but Jarasmi ordered her attendants to conduct her home to the palace. There, she sat alone in her chamber, and brooded upon the magical gift.

It was surely true, she wished to find out the secrets of her future, what her husband might be, and if she should love him and if he should love her, and whether she would bear him sons, and if her sons might become heroes. Such things she had pondered often. At first, she was almost afraid to try the golden ball in case it failed her, showing nothing. Then she grew more afraid, supposing it would show everything.

At length, her need for enlightenment outweighed her alarm. She raised her hand to throw the ball upon the floor—and checked. She had thought so long on the matter it seemed to her the whole palace might guess her intent. The moment any heard the splintering of glass, they would realize what she had done. Jarasmi became nervous and abashed at such a notion. She did not want her Father, the Ruler, to discover what she was about.

Finally, she stole out into the gardens. Here, she again prepared to throw the ball of golden glass. But glancing up, she saw a bird floating in the sky, watching her. She hid herself under a cinnamon tree, but the noon breeze ruffled its branches, and played with her hair—she was not alone.

Bronze fish stared from the pools. Shadows stirred. The flowers whispered as if someone were walking between them.

After some time, Jarasmi found herself beside the high wall of the gardens, and before her was the unguarded little door, which led a short distance through the forest to the old and unfrequented temple.

Jarasmi hesitated for the duration of ten heartbeats. Then she unbarred the door, and stepped out into the deep green shade of the jungle.

Down in the dark of the cistern, where it is neither night nor day, Hiranu stirs. He senses his bonds, which are incorporeal and therefore not to be felt—and yet which he feels with great intensity—shiver, like strings that have been brushed by fingernails.

Then the step falls upon the paving. It is soft as a leaf.

The princess found herself uneasy at being in the temple. The hollow intensity of a deserted building hung about it. The bright snakes glinted from the walls. Here and there a spear of sunlight clove the dark, but mostly there was no light at all. And yet she had somehow found her way into a sunken court where there was a large cistern, still full of water, let into the marble pavement. Not a glimpse of sun entered this place, nor into the well, for the temple roofs leaned close and the trees bound up the sky in their veils.

Jarasmi knew a sudden fear, remembering her nurse's tale of the *Rakshasa*. But such an idea was foolish.

"Come," she said to herself, aloud but very low, wary of echoes, "throw the golden ball and learn the secret, if there is one to be learned. Then hurry home."

So, without further compunction, she cast the ball of glass down against the paving.

But it seemed her temerity had marred her aim. Rather than strike the marble and shatter, the ball skimmed over the cistern's rim, and fell into the water.

With a sharp cry of distress, that strangely roused not a single echo, Jarasmi ran to the cistern, and gazed into it. The ball was gone for sure. Not one bright trace could she see of it. Nor any other thing beneath the surface.

For a moment, her princess's vexation outweighed her nervousness, and Jarasmi smote the water with her ringed fist. "Give it me," she whispered foolishly to the cistern. "Am I never to know my future? Give back the glass ball."

And then she turned to fly, for a peculiar surge ran through the pool, another and another. Yet, reaching the doorway of the court, some extraordinary shrinking inquisitiveness made her hesitate, and look over her shoulder.

Something lay now on the skin of the water, round and glittering— the golden ball. It had been returned as she demanded.

Jarasmi hurried near, and stretched out her hand to retrieve the ball. But no sooner did she touch the glass than it broke into a thousand fragments, small as grains of dust, which showered in a sparkling pollen all across the water. Jarasmi screamed—and screamed a second time, for now her outstretched hand was caught fast in the grip of something cold and glutinous that had trapped it just beneath the surface. She could not see what held her so; her hand had vanished at the wrist in green water, as if severed, and struggle as she would, she could not pull away.

And then, as abruptly as it had taken her prisoner, the unseen creature let her go.

Half blind with horror, and stunned by a curious weakness, Jarasmi stumbled from the court and away through the ruined temple.

There seemed now a thunderous silence hung there, and in the forest beyond the outer doorway a silence like deafness. But the Ruler's daughter did not heed it as she fled. Nor did she note the jewelery serpents hid, as it seemed, from her. While the monkeys, which had scrambled amid the boughs above the path, were gone. At last she reached the door in the high wall and dashed through it, shutting and barring it behind her.

As she knelt by a fountain, rinsing her hands over and over, the bronze fish quivered, and darted under stones. But her two maids ran toward her laughing. The sun was low, and soon she must dine beside her Father, the Ruler, in his palace.

The red light on the hills beyond the forest came through the windows and splashed the fine plates, the goblets.

The musicians, mindful of Jarasmi's wedding half a year away, played music that had to do with bridal processions.

The Ruler was in a good humor. He urged his daughter to eat. "See," he said, "how tenderly the meats have been cooked to please you, and how cunningly the spices have been prepared. And how the gold flashes on your fingers as you move them. While, only too soon, I shall lose you to a fine and wealthy lord, who will carry you away to his own palace and make you mistress of it. What can have stolen your appetite with so much of joy and success about you?"

"Pardon me, my Father," said Jarasmi, "I do not know."

But she did.

The sun on the western hills changed from clear red to dark red. Servants came, drawing down the ornate lamps to light them.

The musicians played a bridal dance.

The sun sank.

The hills, the jungle-forest, and finally all the long windows turned black as ebony.

There came a strange sound, audible even above the music, though plainly it was far away.

"Now, what can that be?" inquired the Ruler, growing testy, for the evening was not as carefree as he had envisaged—his grateful daughter sullen and uneasy, his musicians faltering, and weird rappings echoing up from his garden like stony blows at the bottom of a cistern.

Just then a servant entered, and prostrated himself.

"Master-of-the-Palace, someone knocks for admittance—not at the great gate, but at the little door in the high wall of your garden."

The Ruler plucked at his robe, examined a ruby ring.

"It will be some beggar."

"No, Master-of-my-life, no beggar. For when one of your guard questioned who knocked, a voice answered from the darkness: 'The Princess summoned me.' "

"What is this?" demanded the Ruler angrily.

"I do not know," said Jarasmi.

But she did.

And now the dire rapping sounded again, hollow, far away, filling up the night.

"Tell them," said the Ruler, "they must not open the door."

But it was too late. One of the young guard had opened it, and stepping out on the jungle path, had challenged the depths of the silent forest and the tall pillars of the trees. No one was there.

"The noise has stopped now," said the Ruler. "All is quiet."

Indeed it was. A river of quiet was in the gardens, rolling toward the lighted palace. And as it came, the leaves grew still on the bushes, and the night-flying insects lay heavy as drops of moisture in the bowls of flowers. The fountains fell spent and did not rise again.

Quite suddenly, the birds in the cages about the room stopped twittering. The musicians' hands slid from their instruments.

Something smote upon the palace door. Again, and again and again. Cold the blows were, as if smitten under water, where sunlight had never once penetrated.

"This is too much," said the Ruler.

Rising, he drew his rich robe about him. He walked into the glittering vestibule, his servants round him, his slaves throwing themselves respectfully down, his guards massed, threatening with their leaf-headed spears.

All confronted the door, which rang and shook.

"Who dares to knock?" cried the Ruler.

From the soundless gardens beyond the door came a voice:

"The Princess summoned me."

"You lie," said the Ruler. "Be gone, and I shall act leniently. Knock once more, and I will set my guard upon you."

The knock came. The palace vibrated at it.

"Open the door," thundered the Ruler, "and kill whatever is out there."

"No!" cried Jarasmi. "Do not open the door."

"Why do you say this?"

"I do not know," said Jarasmi.

But she did.

Next minute, the palace door stood wide, and the guard burst out upon the terrace. Only the black of night was waiting to be let in, and the motionless shrubs that did not stir in the windless air. The wind had crept instead into the palace. It blew upon the lamps and they flickered. It shook the draperies.

"Who is there?" shouted the Ruler.

But no one answered.

Then, returning to the table, one of the servant-women exclaimed. Jarasmi's untouched plate had been emptied. Her untouched cup was drained.

The Princess went to her apartment, and her steps were slow. She sat on a little stool while her maids brushed and anointed her hair, took from her her finger-rings and earrings, and clad her in a loose robe for sleep.

Below, two sorcerers were busy in the palace, and smokes rose. A priest discussed the nature of demons reassuringly with the Ruler. The young guard, who had opened the garden door, had been savagely beaten, and hung from a post, groaning.

"How strangely cold the chamber is," said one of Jarasmi's maids.

"It must be the season," said the other.

Unlike the Princess, they had hurried, and now hurried to leave, the anklets clinking on their dainty feet. Bowing low, they were gone.

Jarasmi sat motionless as a figurine upon the stool.

Jarasmi waited.

But it was not long before the voice spoke to her, from behind her left shoulder.

"You know that I am here, Princess."

"Yes," murmured Jarasmi, "I do."

And she did.

"Why not turn about, then, and see what you called from the cistern in the temple."

Jarasmi wept. She felt a dreadful, drawing weakness.

The voice, however, laughed gently.

"But what could I be that is so fearsome, if a small cistern can have held me?"

"Oh, you are something monstrous," cried Jarasmi wildly. "A beast like a fish, or a frog, thick-scaled and dripping slime, with talons and the teeth of a tiger, and the bulging eyes of a lizard."

The voice laughed again.

"So much? Oh, Jarasmi—a fish? A frog? A tiger? Turn and see."

Then her fear became so vast she was powerless to deny any command of her tormentor's, and she did turn and she did see. And so she beheld Hiranu.

There in the lamplight was a young and handsome Prince, clothed in beautiful garments, and burning jewels, his dark eyes burning more fiercely than any of them.

"I," said Hiranu, "was bound by the spell of an enemy, to abide in the mud of the well until an innocent girl might free me by some inadvertent deed, such as desiring a favor of me. How unlikely this seemed. But never once did I lose my faith that one turn of the wheel should bring reprieve."

Then the handsome prince came to her, and took Jarasmi's hand. His touch was delightful, and all her strength seemed to flow away.

"And now, exquisite Princess, I wish only that you will come with me to my Kingdom, and rule with me. And I will love you all your life."

At which, he kissed her, and every lamp in the chamber died.

In the pale azure hour before sunrise, the Ruler gave his only daughter to a foreign prince, to be his wife.

Presently, a wonderful carriage was driven into the court before the great gate of the palace. It was hung with scarlet, and fringed with gold, while silver discs made rippling music from each drape and fold. The window-spaces were filled by screens of carved ivory, and their eyelets closed with precious gems, so none might look in—or out. Reddish horses pulled the carriage, and the moment they stopped, their driver leapt down and ran to Hiranu, kneeling at his feet.

"This is my loyal servant," said Hiranu, "who all these years has patiently awaited my return."

And he embraced the man, and sent him to kneel also to Jarasmi.

This the servant did, placing in her hands a white flower. When he rose, she saw his eyes were bright yellow as a snake's.

Jarasmi entered the carriage with her bridegroom, and the carriage was closed.

The Ruler stood before the palace door and watched the carriage rush away. He caressed the huge emerald the young Prince had given him, which was larger than a pigeon's egg, and the diamond that was even larger. The Ruler's face was sallow and his hands trembled so that soon he dropped both jewels. His slaves scrambled to retrieve them, as, from the halls of the Palace, there lifted the notes of a dreadful lamentation.

In the darkened carriage, Hiranu is almost done, now, with waiting.

Beyond the scarlet, gold and ivory, the day begins to blossom, but he will not see it; day and night are all one within the dark. He can, of course, see his bride perfectly well. And if she sees him less perfectly in the blackness, she may at last be glad of it.

How swiftly they travel through the jungle-forest. Perhaps, by moonrise, he will have reached his home. His bride, unfortunately will not. But it was true, he will love her all her life.

Hiranu turns to her, the means of his deliverance. She is finding it hard to smile at him; her smiles resemble, more often than not, winces of terror. Yet, garnished by her flower, she attends. She is here, and no one can come to her aid at all.

Hiranu ceases to wait. He assumes, very quickly, and with a degree of simple pleasure, his other form.

The sealed carriage does not reveal it. While Jarasmi's frenzied shrieks are muffled, and in any case, do not continue long.

ARTHUR MACHEN *(1863–1947) is one of Great Britain's acknowledged masters of macabre fiction. Born Arthur Llewellyn Jones in Caerleon-on-Usk, Wales, a town associated in myth with another Arthur and a Round Table, Machen began his writing career in London composing childrens' verse, working as a journalist and translating, most notably* The Memoirs of Casanova. *His most popular fantasies include "The Bowmen," "Novel of the Black Seal" and the loathsome history of the white powder, a self-contained episode from Machen's loosely constructed novel* The Three Imposters. *(For additional remarks, consult Appendix I, page 574.)*

Novel of the White Powder
BY ARTHUR MACHEN

My name is Leicester; my father, Major-General Wyn Leicester, a distinguished officer of artillery, succumbed five years ago to a complicated liver complaint acquired in the deadly climate of India. A year later my only brother, Francis, came home after a exceptionally brilliant career at the University, and settled down with the resolution of a hermit to master what has been well called the great legend of the law. He was a man who seemed to live in utter indifference to everything that is called pleasure; and though he was handsomer than most men, and could talk as merrily and wittily as if he were a mere vagabond, he avoided society, and shut himself up in a large room at the top of the house to make himself a lawyer. Ten hours a day of hard reading was at first his allotted portion; from the first light in the east to the late afternoon he remained shut up with his books, taking a hasty half-hour's lunch with me as if he grudged the wasting of the moments, and going out for a short walk when it began to grow dusk. I thought that such relentless application must be injurious, and tried to cajole him from the crabbed textbooks, but his ardour seemed to grow rather than diminish, and his daily tale of hours increased. I spoke to him seriously, suggesting some occasional relaxation, if it were but an idle afternoon with a harmless novel; but he laughed, and said that he read about feudal tenures when he felt in need of amusement, and scoffed at the notions of theatres, or a month's fresh air. I confessed that he looked well, and seemed not to suffer from his labours, but I knew that such unnatural toil would take revenge at last, and I was not mistaken. A look of anxiety began to lurk about his eyes, and he seemed languid, and at last he avowed that he was no longer in perfect health; he was troubled, he said, with a sensation of dizziness, and awoke now and then of nights from fearful dreams, terrified and cold with icy sweats. "I am taking care of myself," he said, "so you must not trouble; I passed the whole of yesterday afternoon in idleness, leaning back in that comfortable chair you gave me, and scribbling nonsense on a sheet of paper. No, no; I will not overdo my work; I shall be well enough in a week or two, depend upon it."

Yet in spite of his assurances I could see that he grew no better, but rather worse; he would enter the drawing-room with a face all miserably wrinkled and despondent, and endeavour to look gaily when my eyes fell on him, and I thought such symptoms of evil omen, and was frightened sometimes at the nervous irritation of his movements, and at glances which I could not decipher. Much against his will, I prevailed on him to have medical advice, and with an ill grace he called in our old doctor.

Dr. Haberden cheered me after examination of his patient.

"There is nothing really much amiss," he said to me. "No doubt he reads too hard and eats hastily, and then goes back again to his books in too great a hurry, and the natural sequence is some digestive trouble and a little mischief in the nervous system. But I think—I do indeed, Miss Leicester—that we shall be able to set this all right. I have written him a prescription which ought to do great things. So you have no cause for anxiety."

My brother insisted on having the prescription made up by a chemist in the neighbourhood. It was an odd, oldfashioned shop, devoid of the studied coquetry and calculated glitter that make so gay a show on the counters and shelves of the modern apothecary; but Francis liked the old chemist, and believed in the scrupulous purity of his drugs. The medicine was sent in due course, and I saw that my brother took it regularly after lunch and dinner. It was an innocent-looking white powder, of which a little was dissolved in a glass of cold water; I stirred it in, and it seemed to disappear, leaving the water clear and colorless. At first Francis seemed to benefit greatly; the weariness vanished from his face, and he became more cheerful than he had ever been since the time when he left school; he talked gaily of reforming himself, and avowed to me that he had wasted his time.

"I have given too many hours to law," he said, laughing; "I think you have saved me in the nick of time. Come, I shall be Lord Chancellor yet, but I must not forget life. You and I will have a holiday together before long; we will go to Paris and enjoy ourselves, and keep away from the Bibliothèque Nationale."

I confessed myself delighted with the prospect.

"When shall we go?" I said. "I can start the day after to-morrow if you like."

"Ah! that is perhaps a little too soon; after all, I do not know London yet, and I suppose a man ought to give the pleasures of his own country the first choice. But we will go off together in a week or two, so try and furbish up your French. I only know law French myself, and I am afraid that wouldn't do."

We were just finishing dinner, and he quaffed off his medicine with a parade of carousal as if it had been wine from some choicest bin.

"Has it any particular taste?" I said.

"No; I should not know I was not drinking water," and he got up from his chair and began to pace up and down the room as if he were undecided as to what he should do next.

"Shall we have coffee in the drawing-room?" I said; "or would you like to smoke?"

"No, I think I will take a turn; it seems a pleasant evening. Look at the afterglow; why, it is as if a great city were burning in flames, and down there between the dark houses it is raining blood fast. Yes, I will go out; I may be in soon, but I shall take my key; so good-night, dear, if I don't see you again."

The door slammed behind him, and I saw him walk lightly down the street, swinging his malacca cane, and I felt grateful to Dr. Haberden for such an improvement.

I believe my brother came home very late that night, but he was in a merry mood the next morning.

"I walked on without thinking where I was going," he said, "enjoying the freshness of the air, and livened by the crowds as I reached more frequented quarters. And then I met an old college friend, Orford, in the press of the pavement, and then—well, we enjoyed ourselves, I have felt what it is to be young and a man; I find I have blood in my veins, as other men have. I made an appointment with Orford for to-night; there will be a little party of us at the restaurant.

Yes; I shall enjoy myself for a week or two, and hear the chimes at midnight, and then we will go for our little trip together."

Such was the transmutation of my brother's character that in a few days he became a lover of pleasure, a careless and merry idler of western pavements, a hunter out of snug restaurants, and a fine critic of fantastic dancing; he grew fat before my eyes, and said no more of Paris, for he had clearly found his paradise in London. I rejoiced, and yet wondered a little; for there was, I thought, something in his gaiety that indefinitely displeased me, though I could not have defined my feeling. But by degrees there came a change; he returned still in the cold hours of the morning, but I heard no more about his pleasures, and one morning as we sat at breakfast together I looked suddenly into his eyes and saw a stranger before me.

"Oh, Francis!" I cried. "Oh, Francis, Francis, what have you done?" and rending sobs cut the words short. I went weeping out of the room; for though I knew nothing, yet I knew all, and by some odd play of thought I remembered the evening when he first went abroad, and the picture of the sunset sky glowed before me; the clouds like a city in burning flames, and the rain of blood. Yet I did battle with such thoughts, resolving that perhaps, after all, no great harm had been done, and in the evening at dinner I resolved to press him to fix a day for our holiday in Paris. We had talked easily enough, and my brother had just taken his medicine, which he continued all the while. I was about to begin my topic when the words forming in my mind vanished, and I wondered for a second what icy and intolerable weight oppressed my heart and suffocated me as with the unutterable horror of the coffin-lid nailed down on the living.

We had dined without candles; the room had slowly grown from twilight to gloom, and the walls and corners were indistinct in the shadow. But from where I sat I looked out into the street; and as I thought of what I would say to Francis, the sky began to flush and shine, as it had done on a well-remembered evening, and in the gap between two dark masses that were houses an awful pageantry of flame appeared—lurid whorls of writhed cloud, and utter depths burning, grey masses like the fume blown from a smoking city, and an evil glory blazing far above shot with tongues of more ardent fire, and below as if there were a deep pool of blood. I looked down to where my brother sat facing me, and the words were shaped on my lips, when I saw his hand resting on the table. Between the thumb and forefinger of the closed hand there was a mark, a small patch about the size of a six-pence, and somewhat of the colour of a bad bruise. Yet, by some sense I cannot define, I knew that what I saw was no bruise at all; oh! if human flesh could burn with flame, and if flame could be black as pitch, such was that before me. Without thought or fashioning of words grey horror shaped within me at the sight, and in an inner cell it was known to be a brand. For the moment the stained sky became dark as midnight, and when the light returned to me I was alone in the silent room, and soon after I heard my brother go out.

Late as it was, I put on my hat and went to Dr. Haberden, and in his great consulting room, ill lighted by a candle which the doctor brought in with him, with stammering lips, and a voice that would break in spite of my resolve, I told him all, from the day on which my brother began to take the medicine down to the dreadful thing I had seen scarcely half an hour before.

When I had done, the doctor looked at me for a minute with an expression of great pity on his face.

"My dear Miss Leicester," he said, "you have evidently been anxious about your brother; you have been worrying over him, I am sure. Come, now, is it not so?"

"I have certainly been anxious," I said. "For the last week or two I have not felt at ease."

"Quite so; you know, of course, what a queer thing the brain is?"

"I understand what you mean; but I was not deceived. I saw what I have told you with my own eyes."

"Yes, yes of course. But your eyes had been staring at that very curious sunset we had tonight. That is the only explanation. You will see it in the proper light to-morrow, I am sure. But, remember, I am always ready to give any help that is in my power; do not scruple to come to me, or to send for me if you are in any distress."

I went away but little comforted, all confusion and terror and sorrow, not knowing where to turn. When my brother and I met the next day, I looked quickly at him, and noticed, with a sickening at heart, that the right hand, the hand on which I had clearly seen the patch as of a black fire, was wrapped up with a handkerchief.

"What is the matter with your hand, Francis?" I said in a steady voice.

"Nothing of consequence. I cut a finger last night, and it bled rather awkwardly. So I did it up roughly to the best of my ability."

"I will do it neatly for you, if you like."

"No, thank you, dear; this will answer very well. Suppose we have breakfast; I am quite hungry."

We sat down and I watched him. He scarcely ate or drank at all, but tossed his meat to the dog when he thought my eyes were turned away; there was a look in his eyes that I had never yet seen, and the thought flashed across my mind that it was a look that was scarcely human. I was firmly convinced that awful and incredible as was the thing I had seen the night before, yet it was no illusion, no glamour of bewildered sense, and in the course of the evening I went again to the doctor's house.

He shook his head with an air puzzled and incredulous, and seemed to reflect for a few minutes.

"And you say he still keeps up the medicine? But why? As I understand, all the symptoms he complained of have disappeared long ago; why should he go on taking the stuff when he is quite well? And by the by, where did he get it made up? At Sayce's? I never send any one there; the old man is getting careless. Suppose you come with me to the chemist's; I should like to have some talk with him."

We walked together to the shop; old Sayce knew Dr. Haberden, and was quite ready to give any information.

"You have been sending that in to Mr. Leicester for some weeks, I think, on my prescription," said the doctor, giving the old man a pencilled scrap of paper.

The chemist put on his great spectacles with trembling uncertainty, and held up the paper with a shaking hand

"Oh, yes," he said, "I have very little of it left; it is rather an uncommon drug, and I have had it in stock some time. I must get in some more, if Mr. Leicester goes on with it."

"Kindly let me have a look at the stuff," said Haberden, and the chemist gave him a glass bottle. He took out the stopper and smelt the contents, and looked strangely at the old man.

"Where did you get this?" he said, "and what is it? For one thing, Mr. Sayce, it is not what I prescribed. Yes, yes, I see the label is right enough, but I tell you this is not the drug."

"I have had it a long time," said the old man in feeble terror; "I got it from Burbage's in the usual way. It is not prescribed often, and I have had it on the shelf for some years. You see there is very little left."

"You had better give it to me," said Haberden. "I am afraid something wrong has happened."

We went out of the shop in silence, the doctor carrying the bottle neatly wrapped in paper under his arm.

"Dr. Haberden," I said, when we had walked a little way—"Dr. Haberden."

"Yes," he said, looking at me gloomily enough.

"I should like you to tell me what my brother has been taking twice a day for the last month or so."

"Frankly, Miss Leicester, I don't know. We will speak of this when we get to my house."

We walked on quickly without another word till we reached Dr. Haberden's. He asked me to sit down, and began pacing up and down the room, his face clouded over, as I could see, with no common fears.

"Well," he said at length, "this is all very strange; it is only natural that you should feel alarmed, and I must confess that my mind is far from easy. We will put aside, if you please, what you told me last night and this morning, but the fact remains that for the last few weeks Mr. Leicester has been impregnating his system with a drug which is completely unknown to me. I tell you, it is not what I ordered; and what the stuff in the bottle really is remains to be seen."

He undid the wrapper, and cautiously tilted a few grains of the white powder on to a piece of paper, and peered curiously at it.

"Yes," he said, "it is like the sulphate of quinine, as you say; it is flaky. But smell it."

He held the bottle to me, and I bent over it. It was a strange, sickly smell, vaporous and overpowering, like some strong anaesthetic.

"I shall have it analysed," said Haberden; "I have a friend who has devoted his whole life to chemistry as a science. Then we shall have something to go upon. No, no; say no more about that other matter; I cannot listen to that; and take my advice and think no more about it yourself."

That evening my brother did not go out as usual after dinner.

"I have had my fling," he said with a queer laugh, "and I must go back to my old ways. A little law will be quite a relaxation after so sharp a dose of pleasure," and he grinned to himself, and soon after went up to his room. His hand was still all bandaged.

Dr. Haberden called a few days later.

"I have no special news to give you," he said. "Chambers is out of town, so I know no more about that stuff than you do. But I should like to see Mr. Leicester, if he is in."

"He is in his room," I said; "I will tell him you are here."

"No, no, I will go up to him; we will have a little quiet talk together. I dare say that we have made a good deal of fuss about a very little; for, after all, whatever the powder may be, it seems to have done him good."

The doctor went upstairs, and standing in the hall I heard his knock, and the opening and shutting of the door; and then I waited in the silent house for an hour, and the stillness grew more and more intense as the hands of the clock crept round. Then there sounded from above the noise of a door shut sharply, and the doctor was coming down the stairs. His footsteps crossed the hall, and there was a pause at the door; I drew a long, sick breath with difficulty, and saw my face white in a little mirror, and he came in and stood at the door. There was an unutterable horror shining in his eyes; he steadied himself by holding the back of a chair with one hand, his lower lip trembled like a horse's, and he gulped and stammered unintelligible sounds before he spoke.

"I have seen that man," he began in a dry whisper. "I have been sitting in his presence for the last hour. My God! And I am alive and in my senses! I, who have dealt with death all my life, and have dabbled with the melting ruins of the earthly tabernacle. But not this, oh! not this," and he covered his face with his hands as if to shut out the sight of something before him.

"Do not send for me again, Miss Leicester," he said with more composure. "I can do nothing in this house. Good-bye."

As I watched him totter down the steps; and along the pavement towards his house, it seemed to me that he had aged by ten years since the morning.

My brother remained in his room. He called out to me in a voice I hardly recognized that he was very busy, and would like his meals brought to his door and left there, and I gave the order to the servants. From that day it seemed as if the arbitrary conception we call time had been annihilated for me; I lived in an ever-present sense of horror, going through the routine of the house mechanically, and only speaking a few necessary words to the servants. Now and then I went out and paced the streets for an hour or two and came home again; but whether I were without or within, my spirit delayed before the closed door of the upper room, and, shuddering, waited for it to open. I have said that I scarcely reckoned time; but I suppose it must have been a fortnight after Dr. Haberden's visit that I came home from my stroll a little refreshed and lightened. The air was sweet and pleasant, and the hazy form of green leaves, floating cloud-like in the square, and the smell of blossoms, had charmed my senses, and I felt happier and walked more briskly. As I delayed a moment at the verge of the pavement, waiting for a van to pass by before crossing over to the house, I happened to look up at the windows, and instantly there was the rush and swirl of deep cold waters in my ears, my heart leapt up and fell down, down as into a deep hollow, and I was amazed with a dread and terror without form or shape. I streched out a hand blindly through the folds of thick darkness, from the black and shadowy valley, and held myself from falling, while the stones beneath my feet rocked and swayed and tilted, and the sense of solid things seemed to sink away from under me. I had glanced up at the window of my brother's study, and at that moment the blind was drawn aside, and something that had life stared out into the world. Nay, I cannot say I saw a face or any human likeness; a living thing, two eyes of burning flame glared at me, and they were in the midst of something as formless as my fear, the symbol and presence of all evil and all hideous corruption. I stood shuddering and quaking as with the grip of ague, sick with unspeakable agonies of fear and loathing, and for five minutes I could not summon force or motion to my limbs. When I was within the door, I ran up the stairs to my brother's room and knocked.

"Francis, Francis," I cried, "for Heaven's sake, answer me. What is the horrible thing in your room? Cast it out, Francis; cast it from you."

I heard a noise as of feet shuffling slowly and awkwardly, and a choking, gurgling sound, as if some one was struggling to find utterance, and then the noise of a voice, broken and stifled, and words that I could scarcely understand.

"There is nothing here," the voice said. "Pray do not disturb me. I am not very well to-day."

I turned away, horrified, and yet helpless. I could do nothing, and I wondered why Francis had lied to me, for I had seen the appearance beyond the glass too plainly to be deceived, though it was but the sight of a moment. And I sat still, conscious that there had been something else, something I had seen in the first flash of terror, before those burning eyes had looked at me. Suddenly I remembered; as I lifted my face the blind was being drawn back, and I had had an instant's glance of the thing that was moving it, and in my recollection I knew that a hideous image was engraved forever on my brain. It was not a hand; there were no fingers that held the blind, but a black stump pushed it aside, the mouldering outline and the clumsy movement as of a beast's paw had glowed into my senses before the darkling waves of terror had overwhelmed me as I went down quick into the pit. My mind was aghast at the thought of this, and of the awful presence that dwelt with my brother in his room; I went to his door and cried to him again, but no answer came. That night one of the servants came up to me and told me in a whisper that for three days food had been regularly placed at the door and left untouched; the maid had knocked but had received no answer; she had heard the noise of shuffling feet that I had noticed. Day after day went by, and still my brother's meals were brought to his door and left untouched; and though I knocked and called again and again, I could get no answer. The servants began to talk to me; it appeared they were as alarmed as I; the cook said that when my brother first shut himself up in his room she used to hear him come out at night and go about the house; and once, she said, the hall door had opened and closed again, but for several nights she had heard no sound. The climax came at last; it was in the dusk of the evening, and I was sitting in the darkening dreary room when a terrible shriek jarred and rang harshly out of the silence, and I heard a frightened scurry of feet dashing down the stairs. I waited, and the servant-maid staggered into the room and faced me, white and trembling.

"Oh, Miss Helen!" she whispered; "oh! for the Lord's sake, Miss Helen, what has happened? Look at my hand, miss; look at that hand!"

I drew her to the window, and saw there was a black wet stain upon her hand.

"I do not understand you," I said. "Will you explain to me?"

"I was doing your room just now," she began. "I was turning down the bed-clothes, and all of a sudden there was something fell upon my hand, wet, and I looked up, and the ceiling was black and dripping on me."

I looked hard at her and bit my lip.

"Come with me," I said. "Bring your candle with you."

The room I slept in was beneath my brother's, and as I went in I felt I was trembling. I looked up at the ceiling, and saw a patch, all black and wet, and a dew of black drops upon it, and a pool of horrible liquor soaking into the white bed-clothes.

I ran upstairs and knocked loudly.

"Oh, Francis, Francis, my dear brother," I cried, "what has happened to you?"

And I listened. There was a sound of choking, and a noise like water bubbling and regurgitating, but nothing else, and I called louder, but no answer came.

In spite of what Dr. Haberden had said, I went to him; with tears streaming down my cheeks I told him all that had happened, and he listened to me with a face set hard and grim.

"For your father's sake," he said at last, "I will go with you, though I can do nothing."

We went out together; the streets were dark and silent, and heavy with heat and a drought of many weeks. I saw the doctor's face white under the gas-lamps, and when we reached the house his hand was shaking.

We did not hesitate, but went upstairs directly. I held the lamp, and he called out in a loud, determined voice—

"Mr. Leicester, do you hear me? I insist on seeing you. Answer me at once."

There was no answer, but we both heard that choking noise I have mentioned.

"Mr. Leicester, I am waiting for you. Open the door this instant, or I shall break it down." And he called a third time in a voice that rang and echoed from the walls—

"Mr. Leicester! For the last time I order you to open the door."

"Ah!" he said, after a pause of heavy silence, "we are wasting time here. Will you be so kind as to get me a poker, or something of the kind?"

I ran into a little room at the back where odd articles were kept, and found a heavy adze-like tool that I thought might serve the doctor's purpose.

"Very good," he said, "that will do, I dare say. I give you notice, Mr. Leicester," he cried loudly at the keyhole, "that I am now about to break into your room."

Then I heard the wrench of the adze, and the woodwork split and cracked under it; with a loud crash the door suddenly burst open, and for a moment we started back aghast at a fearful screaming cry, no human voice, but as the roar of a monster, that burst forth inarticulate and struck at us out of the darkness.

"Hold the lamp," said the doctor, and we went in and glanced quickly round the room.

"There it is," said Dr. Haberden, drawing a quick breath; "look, in that corner."

I looked, and a pang of horror seized my heart as with a white-hot iron. There upon the floor was a dark and putrid mass, seething with corruption and hideous rottenness, neither liquid nor solid, but melting and changing before our eyes, and bubbling with unctuous oily bubbles like boiling pitch. And out of the midst of it shone two burning points like eyes, and I saw a writhing and stirring as of limbs, and something moved and lifted up what might have been an arm. The doctor took a step forward, raised the iron bar and struck at the burning points; he drove in the weapon, and struck again and again in the fury of loathing.

A week or two later, when I had recovered to some extent from the terrible shock, Dr. Haberden came to see me.

"I have sold my practice," he began, "and tomorrow I am sailing on a long voyage. I do not know whether I shall ever return to England; in all probability I shall buy a little land in California, and settle there for the remainder of my life. I have brought you this packet, which you may open and read when you feel able to do so. It contains the report of Dr. Chambers on what I submitted to him. Good-bye, Miss Leicester, good-bye."

When he was gone I opened the envelope; I could not wait, and proceeded to read the papers within. Here is the manuscript, and if you will allow me, I will read you the astounding story it contains.

"My dear Haberden," the letter began, "I have delayed inexcusably in answering your questions as to the white substance you sent me. To tell you the truth, I have hesitated for some time as to what course I should adopt, for there is a bigotry and orthodox standard in physical science as in theology, and I knew that if I told you the truth I should offend rooted prejudices which I once held dear myself. However, I have determined to be plain with you, and first I must enter into a short personal explanation.

"You have known me, Haberden, for many years as a scientific man; you and I have often talked of our profession together, and discussed the hopeless gulf that opens before the feet of those who think to attain to truth by any means whatsoever except the beaten way of experiment and observation in the sphere of material things. I remember the scorn with which you have spoken to me of men of science who have dabbled a little in the unseen, and have timidly hinted that perhaps the senses are not, after all, the eternal, impenetrable bounds of all knowledge, the everlasting walls beyond which no human being has ever passed. We have laughed together heartily, and I think justly, at the 'occult' follies of the day, disguised under various names—the mesmerisms, spiritualisms, materializations, theosophies, all the rabble rout of imposture, with their machinery of poor tricks and feeble conjuring, the true back-parlour of shabby London streets. Yet, in spite of what I have said, I must confess to you that I am no materialist, taking the word of course in its usual signification. It is now many years since I have convinced myself—convinced myself, a sceptic, remember—that the old ironbound theory is utterly and entirely false. Perhaps this confession will not wound you so sharply as it would have done twenty years ago; for I think you cannot have failed to notice that for some time hypotheses have been advanced by men of pure science which are nothing less than transcendental, and I suspect that most modern chemists and biologists of repute would not hesitate to subscribe the *dictum* of the old Schoolman, *Omnia exeunt in mysterium,* which means, I take it, that every branch of human knowledge if traced up to its source and final principles vanishes into mystery. I need not trouble you now with a detailed account of the painful steps which led me to my conclusions; a few simple experiments suggested a doubt as to my then standpoint, and a train of thought that rose from circumstances comparatively trifling brought me far; my old conception of the universe has been swept away, and I stand in a world that seems as strange and awful to me as the endless waves of the ocean seen for the first time, shining, from a peak in Darien. Now I know that the walls of sense that seemed so impenetrable, that seemed to loom up above the heavens and to be founded below the depths, and to shut us in for evermore, are no such everlasting impassable barriers as we fancied, but thinnest and most airy veils that melt away before the seeker, and dissolve as the early mist of the morning about the brooks. I know that you never adopted the extreme materialistic position; you did not go about trying to prove a universal negative, for your logical sense withheld you from that crowning absurdity; but I am sure that you will find all that I am saying strange and repellent to your habits of thought. Yet, Haberden, what I tell you is the truth, nay, to adopt our common language, the sole and scientific truth, verified by experience; and the universe is verily more splendid and more awful than we used to dream. The whole universe, my friend, is a tremendous sacrament; a mystic, ineffable force and energy, veiled by an outward form of matter; and man, and the sun and the other stars, and the flower of the grass, and the crystal in the test-tube, are each and every one as spiritual, as material, and subject to an inner working.

"You will perhaps wonder, Haberden, whence all this tends; but I think a little thought will make it clear. You will understand that from such a standpoint the whole view of things is changed, and what we thought incredible and absurd may be possible enough. In short, we must look at legend and belief with other eyes, and be prepared to accept tales that had become mere fables. Indeed this is no such great demand. After all, modern science will concede as much, in a hypocritical manner; you must not, it is true, believe in witchcraft, but you may credit hypnotism; ghosts are out of date, but there is a good deal to be said for the theory of telepathy. Give superstition a Greek name, and believe in it, should almost be a proverb.

"So much for my personal explanation. You sent me, Haberden, a phial, stoppered and sealed, containing a small quantity of flaky white powder, obtained from a chemist who has been dispensing it to one of your patients. I am not surprised to hear that this powder refused to yield any results to your analysis. It is a substance which was known to a few many hundred years ago, but which I never expected to have submitted to me from the shop of a modern apothecary. There seems no reason to doubt the truth of the man's tale; he no doubt got, as he says, the rather uncommon salt you prescribed from the wholesale chemist's, and it has probably remained on his shelf for twenty years, or perhaps longer. Here what we call chance and coincidence begin to work; during all these years the salt in the bottle was exposed to certain recurring variations of temperature, variations probably ranging from 40° to 80°. And, as it happens, such changes, recurring year after year at irregular intervals, and with varying degrees of intensity and duration, have constituted a process, and a process so complicated and so delicate, that I question whether modern scientific apparatus directed with the utmost precision could produce the same result. The white powder you sent me is something very different from the drug you prescribed; it is the powder from which the wine of the Sabbath, the *Vinum Sabbati,* was prepared. No doubt you have read of the Witches' Sabbath, and have laughed at the tales which terrified our ancestors; the black cats, and the broomsticks, and dooms pronounced against some old woman's cow. Since I have known the truth I have often reflected that it is on the whole a happy thing that such burlesque as this is believed, for it serves to conceal much that it is better should not be known generally. However, if you care to read the appendix to Payne Knight's monograph, you will find that the true Sabbath was something very different, though the writer has very nicely refrained from printing all he knew. The secrets of the true Sabbath were the secrets of remote times surviving into the Middle Ages, secrets of an evil science which existed long before Aryan man entered Europe. Men and women, seduced from their homes on specious pretences, were met by beings well qualified to assume, as they did assume, the part of devils, and taken by their guides to some desolate and lonely place, known to the initiate by long tradition, and unknown to all else. Perhaps it was a cave in some bare and windswept hill, perhaps some inmost recess of a great forest, and there the Sabbath was held. There, in the blackest hour of night, the *Vinum Sabbati* was prepared, and this evil gruel was poured forth and offered to the neophytes, and they partook of an infernal sacrament; *sumentes calicem principis inferorum,* as an old author well expresses it. And suddenly, each one that had drunk found himself attended by a companion, a share of glamour and unearthly allurement, beckoning him apart, to share in joys more exquisite, more piercing than the thrill of any dream, to the consummation of the marriage of the Sabbath. It is hard to write of such things as these, and chiefly because that shape that allured with loveliness was no hallucination, but, awful as it is to express, the man himself. By the power of that Sabbath wine, a few grains of white powder thrown into a glass of water, the house of life was riven asunder and the human trinity dissolved, and the worm which never dies, that which lies sleeping within us all, was made tangible and an external thing, and clothed with a garment of flesh. And then, in the hour of midnight, the primal fall was repeated and re-presented, and the awful thing veiled in the mythos of the Tree in the Garden was done anew. Such was the *nuptioe Sabbati.*

"I prefer to say no more; you, Haberden, know as well as I do that the most trivial laws of life are not to be broken with impunity; and for so terrible an act as this, in which the very inmost place of the temple was broken open and defiled, a terrible vengeance followed. What began with corruption ended also with corruption."

Underneath is the following in Dr. Haberden's writing:—

"The whole of the above is unfortunately strictly and entirely true. Your brother confessed all to me on that morning when I saw him in his room. My attention was first attracted to the bandaged hand, and I forced him to show it to me. What I saw made me, a medical man of many years' standing, grow sick with loathing, and the story I was forced to listen to was infinitely more frightful than I could have believed possible. It has tempted me to doubt the Eternal Goodness which can permit nature to offer such hideous possibilities; and if you had not with your own eyes seen the end, I should have said to you— disbelieve it all. I have not, I think, many more weeks to live, but you are young, and may forget all this.

JOSEPH HABERDEN, M.D.

In the course of two or three months I heard that Dr. Haberden had died at sea shortly after the ship left England.

"The Celery Stalk in the Cellar" first terrorized the neighborhood in a scarce 1975 Pinnacle Books anthology, Brother Theodore's Chamber of Horrors. SARALEE TERRY *is the pseudonym of an obscure novelist who writes humorous verse on napkins.*

The Celery Stalk in the Cellar

BY SARALEE TERRY

The celery stalk in the cellar
Gets bigger and bigger each day;
'Twas grown by an aged bank-teller
And it feeds on tobacco and hay.

It grows and it grows in the night-time;
Its flowers are pieces of chalk;
Its fruit-yield is three quarts of quicklime—
Oh, Lord! Now it's starting to walk!

Oh, help! It devoured the plumber!
(The garbageman ran up a tree)
It's gotten the landlady's number
And now it's advancing on *me!!!*

*   *   *   *   *

Oh, goody, 'twas only a nightmare!
(I wake up and heave a big sigh)
Ere bedtime I solemnly now swear
No more to eat celery pie.

But hark! I hear noise on the stairways!
(My heart is beginning to balk)
AARGH! AT THE DOOR! FEEL MY HAIR RAISE!
It's a ten-foot-high celery stalk!

BERNHARDT J. HURWOOD *died while* Devils & Demons *was in preparation. He was a prolific Manhattan author beloved by a legion of friends, including many authors helped along in their careers by "Bernie." His huge output includes fiction, essays, anthologies and collections of allegedly true weird anecdotes derived from folklore, popular literature and word-of-mouth. Under the pseudonym of Mallory T. Knight, he wrote the amusing "mod" vampire novel* Dracutwig *and also penned (as Ted Mark) an outrageously funny send-up of James Bondish sex-and-espionage adventures, the "Man from O. R. G. Y." series. The following bloody tale was adapted by the late Mr. Hurwood from the Japanese; it first appeared in his anthology* Monsters Galore.

The Vampire Cat of Nabeshima

BY BERNHARDT J. HURWOOD

Adapted from the Japanese

It is written that long ago one of the Nabeshima princes was plagued by the foul spell of a demoniac, vampire cat. There lived in this prince's household a ravishing beauty named Otoyo, whose charm and wit made her the favorite royal concubine. One afternoon His Highness chose to enjoy Otoyo's favors in the garden, amidst the fragrance of the blossoms. Forgetting about the passage of time, the amorous couple dallied until after the sun had set. Thus, amongst the creeping shadows of dusk, they failed to notice the silent tread of a huge cat that followed them stealthily back to the palace.

After bidding her lord a tender farewell Otoyo went to her apartment and retired for the night. But restful sleep did not come to her. After many hours of fearful dreams the girl awoke suddenly at midnight, her heart pounding heavily within her dainty breast. Struck dumb with terror she saw two hideous red eyes gleaming like embers in the darkness. As they grew larger she could make out the dreadful shape of a monstrous cat approaching her like the figure of doom. Frozen with fear she watched the creature helplessly as it prepared to spring. Only as it leaped did she find her voice and cry out, but it was too late. Burying its powerful fangs in her pale throat, the beast held Otoyo fast until her spirit had fled to the abode of her ancestors. After accomplishing its cruel and wicked deed, the unnatural cat dug a grave beneath Otoyo's window into which it dragged her torn and bleeding corpse. Then, transforming itself into the identical likeness of the dead girl, it began casting its evil spell upon the prince.

The prince, of course, knew nothing about the dreadful event which had taken place. He continued, therefore, to sport daily in the scented arms of his beautiful mistress. Lost as he was in the delicious transports of passion, the prince never suspected that he was in the clutches of a fiendish vampire that desired only to suck out his blood and life.

As time passed the prince began to grow weak. His complexion became sallow and leaden, and it became apparent that he was the victim of some strange and awful malady. With growing alarm his wife and ministers sent for physicians to heal their lord. But it was in vain, for despite the medicines which were prescribed, the prince's condition became more grave. The most baffling part of the illness was his nocturnal distress. Each night after sleep had overtaken him he was plagued by ghastly nightmares. In an attempt to overcome their liege's troubled sleep, the ministers ordered a guard of one hundred men to sit with the prince and maintain a close watch over him. But no matter how hard they tried, each night at about ten, a mysterious drowsiness overcame the guards, and soon they were in a deep and dreamless slumber. It was then that the demon, in the shape of the unfortunate Otoyo, would come creeping to the prince's bedside and take its terrible toll of his life's blood.

After such a lack of success, several of the prince's ministers determined to stay with him themselves in hopes of fathoming the mystery. But unfortunately, when the hour of ten arrived, their eyes too were closed by the overpowering fingers of the mysterious sleep. Thus, on the following day, they gathered in solemn session, and Isahaya Buzen, the prime minister, spoke, "It is very strange indeed that a hundred guards should be overtaken by sleep each night at the same hour. Most assuredly an evil spirit is upon our prince and his servants. Since our efforts avail us nothing, let us call upon Ruiten, the chief priest of the Miyo Temple. We shall then ask him to make prayers and offerings for our lord's recovery."

Wholeheartedly approving of Isahaya Buzen's proposal, the ministers carried it out at once, and called upon the holy offices of the priest. That night Ruiten the priest began his special prayers for the prince. After several nights had passed, the priest, after finishing his ceremonial duties, prepared to go to sleep. Just as he was about to lie down he heard an unfamiliar sound coming from the grounds outside. Looking down from his window, he observed a young soldier washing himself near the well. After finishing his ablutions he stood reverently before the image of Buddha and began praying for the prince's recovery. When he had completed his prayer the soldier rose to depart, but he was stopped by the priest, who called to him, "Wait, honored warrior, I would have some words with you."

Looking up the soldier answered, "I am at your service, revered sir. What is your pleasure?"

"Be so kind as to come up here, that we may talk together."

"At once," said the young man, hurrying to obey the priest.

When the soldier had entered the temple Ruiten said to him, "It is very pleasing for me to see a young man with such a loyal heart. I am the chief priest of this temple and even now I am offering prayers for the recovery of our prince. Tell me, who are you?"

The soldier answered, "My name, reverend sir, is Ito Soda, and I am a humble foot soldier in the Nabeshima army. Ever since my prince began suffering from his dread sickness, I have wished with all my heart to aid in caring for him. But alas, I am of so low a rank it would be improper for me to appear before him. Therefore I can do nothing but pray to Buddha for the recovery of my lord."

Ruiten wept upon hearing such a declaration of loyalty. With that he related to Ito Soda the story of their prince's terrible nightmares, and of the strange sleep that descended nightly upon the royal guards. After listening to the priest's tale, a knowing look came over the face of Ito Soda.

"This must be the work of an evil spirit," he said. "If only I might be permitted to watch over the prince for one night I would try to fight off the spell and learn the nature of the demon."

Ruiten paused for a moment, then said, "I am on terms of friendship with the prime minister, Isahaya Buzen. Perhaps if I speak with him your desire to help the prince may be fulfilled."

With heartfelt expressions of gratitude, Ito Soda promised to await the answer of the prime minister; so after the proper formalities the two men parted.

The next night Ruiten took Ito Soda to the house of Isahaya Buzen and spoke on the young man's behalf. Although the soldier was of a very humble rank, it was finally decided that he might be allowed to watch over the prince in the company of the other hundred men.

The prince's bedroom was quite large. Sleeping in the very center he was thus able to surround himself with the loyal men who sought to guard him through the night. Ito Soda observed that as the others conversed among themselves to pass away the time they began to fall asleep one by one. As the hour of ten approached, he too, began to feel an overpowering drowsiness beginning to spread through his limbs. Trying every device imaginable to keep himself awake, Ito Soda realized he would have to take extreme steps. Fighting the somnolence that threatened to deprive him of his senses, he spread a piece of oiled paper upon the floor beneath the spot upon which he sat. Then he reached beneath his robe, drew out a small, sharp dagger and plunged it into his thigh. The pain was excruciating, but it enabled him to stay the crushing hand of sleep. But since it was a sleep induced by sorcery, it nevertheless began to get the better of him. Seizing the hilt of his dagger, Ito Soda twisted it sharply. The pain became so strong that all drowsiness left him, and he watched the prince so intently that he hardly noticed his own blood stream from the wound and onto the oiled paper.

Before long Ito Soda's alertness bore him fruit. He stiffened as he heard the doors to the prince's chamber slide softly open. Looking in the direction of the doors he observed a muffled figure that tiptoed gently into the room. It approached the sleeping figure of the prince. Ito Soda strained in the darkness to see and when he was able to distinguish the details of the intruder's form he gasped. It was the most beautiful maiden he had ever seen. She glanced about the chamber and smiled at the sight of the sleeping men. Then, just as she was about to approach the prince, she noticed Ito Soda staring at her.

"Who are you?" she asked with surprise.

"I am Ito Soda and this is my first night here."

"How is it that you are not asleep like the others?"

"I am here to stand guard, not to sleep."

Observing the dark red stain on Ito Soda's thigh, the masquerading demon pointed and asked,

"I see blood on your thigh. How were you wounded?"

"I felt so drowsy that I had to stab my thigh to keep awake."

"Such fidelity," said the demon, inwardly burning with hatred.

Ito Soda shrugged. "The soldier who is not willing to die for his lord is delinquent in his duty."

The false Otoyo then bent over the recumbent prince and asked, "How does my lord feel this night?"

But as he was weak to the point of utter debilitation he said nothing. Watching suspiciously, Ito Soda determined to kill the girl on the spot should she attempt to make any untoward movements in the prince's direction. She was unable to do anything, however, for she could feel the eyes of Ito Soda virtually burning holes in her back. Under the circumstances she left the prince alone and withdrew from his chamber.

At daybreak when the hundred others awoke and discovered that Ito Soda had stabbed himself to remain awake, they were covered with shame and departed with downcast spirits. The ministers of the prince, however, were overjoyed at the young soldier's bravery and enjoined him to stand watch again that night. Surely enough, at the usual hour all the men fell asleep except Ito Soda. As before, the demon entered and approached its sleeping victim only to be thwarted by the faithful soldier who had remained awake.

After many nights, the false Otoyo, seeing that her nocturnal attempts upon the prince were doomed to failure, came no more. The prince began to sleep again untroubled by nightly horrors, and he recovered his health quite rapidly. Honors and rank were bestowed upon Ito Soda and he was granted a fine estate.

Several weeks later Ito Soda noticed something very interesting. The hundred guards no longer fell asleep each night at the stroke of ten. It seemed odd to him that this sudden change should correspond with the cessation of Otoyo's midnight visits. It became clear to him that the beautiful concubine was actually a vampire, and he revealed his suspicion to Isahaya Buzen, the prime minister.

After listening to Ito Soda, Isahaya Buzen asked, "How do you propose to rid us of this monster dwelling in our midst?"

"I will go directly to her apartment and endeavor to kill her. If, however, she attempts to escape, I pray that you place eight armed men outside to destroy her lest I fail."

Accordingly, Ito Soda waited until nightfall. Then he knocked at the demon's door, pretending to have a message for her from her lord. Upon opening the door to her chamber she asked, "What is the message you bring me?"

"Look at this," replied Ito Soda.

Then, reaching under his cloak, he drew forth not a letter but a long, gleaming dagger. He sprang, but the demon was too agile. Seizing a battle axe, she glared ferociously and shrieked in a voice like the winds, "How dare you assault me thus?" and she struck fiercely at him with the weapon. Again and again she lunged at him, but each time Ito Soda managed to parry her thrusts. Unable to match his warlike skill, she cast away the battle axe and changed before his eyes into a great shaggy cat. Then, leaping to the window she sprang to the roof and disappeared.

Isahaya Buzen and the eight armed men were taken completely by surprise. Although they shot arrows at the creature, it eluded them and escaped to the mountains. There it wreaked much havoc among the hill folk until at last Prince Nabeshima organized a great hunt. It was thus the monster was finally tracked down and killed.

Born in New Jersey in 1952, the indefatigable DARRELL SCHWEITZER *is a novelist, essayist, editor, literary agent and short story writer whose novels include* The Shattered Goddess *and* We Are All Legends *and whose shorter fiction has appeared in* Twilight Zone, Fantastic, Weirdbook, *and other periodicals. In the following mordant story, Mr. Schweitzer speculates on what may have happened to the characters of Shakespeare's* The Tempest *after the curtain fell on Act V. Caliban, offspring of the witch Sycorax and the Devil, vows revenge upon his late master, Prospero, but does not reckon with the possibility that there may be greater monsters in the world than he.* (NOTE: *Though it is not absolutely necessary to be familiar with* The Tempest *to appreciate "Caliban's Revenge," some knowledge of Shakespeare's plot line may be helpful. Therefore, a brief précis of the play may be found in Appendix I, page 574.)*

Caliban's Revenge
BY DARRELL SCHWEITZER

They said they were my friends. Their names were Trinculo and Stephano, and they said they would help me get rid of Him. I sang for them. I made myself foolish. I showed them all the secrets of the Isle, but still they betrayed me in the end. When we had Him in our grasp, when we could have killed Him, they quarrelled over gaudy robes! All was lost because of their greed, and finally, when we were in the swamp and the dogs and ghosts were after us, those two did nothing to save me. I was slower than them, and when the spirits swarmed over me to pinch and bite, and I bellowed with rage and pain, what did my comrades do? One of them tugged the other and said, "Come on! While they're after him we can get away!"

Base treachery!

Afterwards, when I am sure that He has gone, I come out of my hiding place and climb a tree to scan the horizon. Far away, a white speck against the blue flesh of the sea, their ship. They are all gone, all of them; He is gone, and with Him He has taken the kings, the sailors, Miranda, my two wicked friends, and the rest, every one glad to be spared the sight of me. I curse, I rage at this new betrayal, but I am not surprised by it.

Alone, I climb down and search the cave He called His cell, and it is empty. I call out to the spirits of the air, commanding them, and I am obeyed. Ariel, that accursed brat of a sprite, has vanished back into the winds that birthed him, but the others are still roaming about, and they answer me. Like childish bullies long protected by an indulgent father and at last left to fend for themselves, they are afraid of me, and they do what I tell them. *Fetch his book! Fetch the book that he has drowned!*

They run, they slither, they scamper to do my bidding. Golden butterflies with wings a yard across and bodies like naked boys glide over the island and the sea. An hour or so later a wallowing thing like a huge fish with the arms and hands of a man beaches itself at my feet and hands the dripping volume to me. I hold it at once ecstatically to my breast, and I leap into a little dance of joy and triumph. Now I, I, Caliban, at last and for the first time since my slavery began, am more powerful than my master. The old fool has broken his staff and drowned his book, and I can't repair the staff, but I have the book. Warped and waterstained as it is I have it and with it I shall overthrow him. He thinks to maroon me here forever, does he? He said once that I was beyond improvement, "a devil, a born devil, on whose nature nurture can never stick"— I will show him a thing or two when my wisdom in magic exceeds his own! *Ha, Prospero, coward and dog! I never dared to speak your name before but now I do, and I spit on it! Your monster calls out your name and laughs. Prospero!*

I spend the next few days repairing the wet book. I carefully soak the water from the pages with cloth, then leave it open in the bright sun, exposing each page for perhaps a quarter of an hour until it is dry and I can turn to the next one. And in that time I read each one. Never do I get up from where I sit by the shore, from where I first got the book—the fish thing is gone now, swallowed back by the surf— and I labor over the meanings of the words. Spirits fetch food and drink for me. All my time goes into my studies.

He who once said I was hopeless but never sincerely tried to teach me, He who never showed mercy or compassion when He had nothing to gain from it— He probably never realised that I knew letters. I do, a little, for my mother Sycorax taught me to read the words of power she inscribed on bones, and as I ponder over the blurry print and running ink of the book, slowly my skill improves. Little windows of language flash open for me if only for an instant, affording glimpses of the treasure hoards locked behind.

I don't know why He never thought me capable of anything more than rude grunts and the simplest guttural snortings. After all, I am the son of One whose eloquence has never been questioned.

One of my first exercises is an attempt to raise a storm. I have seen Him do it many times. He never knew how I spied on Him. I would hide myself in the bushes by His cave and watch Him as He came out. I'd follow Him stealthily like a stalking fox as He walked up the path to the top of the island's only hill, to the highest point, and as He went He was often in a fit of abstraction, muttering noble words in Greek or Latin. After that He would be occupied with His spells and His spirits, and I'd be left alone. The spirits only plagued me when He told them to.

So I go to the same spot myself, and this time I do not hide, but stand out in the open, the book in hand, and I read the words He once read for raising a storm. But nothing happens. Then, memorizing the words, I put the book aside and say them again, raising both my hands as He raised His. This time a little wind whirls around my feet, stirring the dust. Still something is wrong.

A wand. He always used a wand, or the staff now broken, but I have neither, so I shall have to make do with a stick. I repeat the words once more, raising my arms in His manner, and with my stick I point in the four directions, shouting:

"Come from the four winds, O storm!"

Something comes—from the north, bitterly cold air, and snow piles down over me. From the south, fire. The snow melts into slush. The east brings a wet wind, and the west a dry one. I leap aside, and in my place the four winds meet and contend in the form of a small cyclone of water and fire and snow, sometimes spewing hailstones, sometimes ashes. Tiny bolts of lightning flash within the writhing column, and the birds in the trees and the spirits in the underbrush chatter with terror and flee. I go after them, and from a safe distance look back at my creation, ecstatic in my newfound power. My art is rude and unpolished yet, but I know that someday soon I shall be as great and learned in the dark lore as He ever was.

My storm rages for three days on the hilltop, and on the fourth, when all is still, I return to the spot and find every tree there levelled, every bush torn up by the root, and the ground itself turned into glass, as if blasted by the breath of a dragon.

For the first time, after many long months of trial and error experiments, when I am confident enough to work magic upon myself, I practise the art of changing. My mastery of all things is much greater, my resolve still firm, and my plan is forming like a newly opened blossom in my mind. I attempt to take what was denied me at birth, the shape of a man. I read words from the book and do a little dance, the steps of which are contrary to the Earth's movement, so I can undo the mischief of Time. A new image must be formed in my mind as I do these things, and I choose something simple at the outset, the simple form of a simple, drunken, oafish man, but a man nevertheless. I steal the face and body of Stephano, the butler to the King of Naples. When the magic has taken its effect, at the end of the dance, I whirl dizzily about and for an instant the island, the sky, and the sea are hidden from my eyes by a mist. Then all is clear again and I right myself, stand firm, and realise what I have done. Unable to control my excitement I run to a secret place I know, a hidden glade deep in the innermost recesses of the island, and there in a pool I behold my image, my ridiculous image. I have become him! When I stand there for a minute I am aware that I even smell like him, rank with piss and old sack. I should puke but I don't. I am too busy laughing with happiness and hatred and glorious victory.

I am coming, Master, coming!

Then I do a thing even I have long doubted I would ever dare. I make myself look like Prospero, just for a little while, to relish my mastery over all things that were once His. I gaze at myself in this guise in the pool. I prance around, doing ridiculous things to wound His dignity. Then, lest I cast myself from a cliff out of hatred for the face I wear, I change again, rationally this time, considering what I need and what I intend. I remove the grey from my hair and beard, then turn both the color of flax, quite unlike His. I become several inches taller, broader at the shoulder and more thickly muscled in the arms, and I make my skin more sun-touched, like that of the sailors I have seen. The sum of all this is something new, a man no other has yet seen, a stranger to all the world.

There remains only for me to reach that world, and this I do with a signal fire, lighted every day and tended until well into the night. My wait is long and during it I read more of the book, but at last I catch the attention of a passing ship and am picked up. The men aboard speak a tongue unknown to me, but in time I come to understand a few of their words, and surely they understand what appears to be my predicament. I am a shipwrecked scholar whose book is his only, his dearest, possession. They smirk a little when I will let none of them take it from me, but they find me plausible.

Since I cannot converse with them I cannot ask them where they are bound. I hope they will take me to Italy, where my work awaits me, but alas, no. After an almost endless voyage we come to Cadiz, in Spain. This, it turns out, is for the better. The Inquisition I escape narrowly, the wars I witness, the religious slaughters in France, all are my education, my immersion into the ways of mankind. The Alps with their robbers are my university. When I come down out of them, after two and a half years of wandering, at last I am prepared for what I must do.

Considerations of geography: Coming down the peninsula of Italy from the north, Milan obviously lies in my path, but I turn aside from it and keep on going. My sense of rightness demands this. I want to work my way up to my greatest deeds, starting with those of lesser importance. It will entail some extra miles, but I am willing. I have come so far already.

In my travels, whenever I can, I stop at monasteries. Invariably the monks are good to me, and when they have vast libraries I ask to be allowed to read some of their books, to increase my understanding of human wisdom. Always I am given permission, my lineage and nature never suspected. Inwardly I smile at the quaint ways of the monks, but I respect them.

Naples. Trinculo the jester is the first to fall. I find him with ease, for he has cut a swath through the women of the town like Hannibal's elephants through a field of wheat. I come upon him at last in a crowded inn-yard, where a bawdy comedy is being performed. I see him opposite me, on the far side of the yard, laughing like a jackass, swilling wine, and fondling two wenches he has with him. I work my way slowly, patiently through the howling audience, and when I stand just behind him I draw from beneath my cloak a long thin knife and thrust it deep into his back, shouting, "Die! Traitor!"

And someone tugs at me, saying, "Hush! That's not in the play."

Making myself by my art as thin as smoke, I pass out of the yard. There is no disturbance even though a few people look at me strangely, not sure if they are seeing anything as I go smoothly by. For them what they see is impossible—ghosts do not walk in the daytime —therefore they see nothing.

Once I have safely accomplished my task and am away, and have reflected upon the meaning of what I have done, I don't feel as I had imagined I would. I feel strange, numb . . . as if there is nothing inside me, as if I am an automaton.

Stephano running in a back street, knowing or at least sensing that he is pursued. Finally when my shadow overtakes his, and I trap him against a wall—

"Who—who are you? What do you want? I have no money . . ."

My knife gleams in the moonlight.

"Do you not recognize me?"

"No—no! You are a stranger!"

"But surely—" I make a face and begin to sing for him, *"Ban ban Caliban, got a new master, got a new man . . ."*

And he stares wide-eyed, and the memory registers, and he *knows.*

"You, *ape?* How wondrously you are transformed. How did it happen?"

"The world is full of miracles, master."

"Aye, that it is! You call me master still—yes, we can be friends— there are many things you, I mean we, can do now, together, my good monster, in your new—"

"You call me monster still," I say as I stab him. He squeals like a struck pig, falls and writhes on the cobblestones like some obscene, animate hunk of lard.

Again, inexplicably, the wild bloody joy I had expected is not there. I watch Stephano die dispassionately. His blood runs out like spilled wine.

But hark! Sounds from far off. Shouts of alarm. Running feet.

I sheathe my blade and hurry to the end of the street, round a corner, and confront the mob, pointing back the way I have come.

"A monster!" I yell. "Did you hear what he said? An ape, a monster, has slain him. I saw it climbing over the rooftops. It was a thing out of Hell surely!"

The people surge forward to have a look, and soon the whole town is awake and alarmed. Troops of guardsmen bearing torches run through the streets, their swords and armor clattering. They are looking for the monster everyone seems to have seen. I talk to frightened beggars huddled in doorsteps. They have glimpsed this creature. It is at least twenty feet high, with shaggy fur, flaming red eyes, and tusks like swords. It can swallow a man in a single gulp. There is a stench of sulfur about it and some say it breathes fire. Others tell how it knocks down houses with its tail.

In any case, since I don't fit any of those descriptions even remotely, I am able to leave the city unmolested.

Another long walk and the seasons turn and my story comes to a head. Milan and the climax.

I watch His palace for days, in many guises. I can change freely now, without the book if I want to. The Art Magical is as familiar to me as breathing. But still I keep the book with me. It is too precious a treasure to leave with anyone.

I come to the gate as an old woman selling sweet cakes to the guards. They let me inside. Then, as soon as I am out of sight for an instant, words are chanted and the little dance done, and I am a dirty, barefoot brat carrying a rough cloth satchel (containing the book). I run across the open, sun-drenched courtyard and am taken, no doubt, for the child of one of the poorer servants. Then I am one of the guards, in armor and bearing a pike. Very businesslike, assured of where I am going, I mount several flights of stairs and pass through doors. In truth I am not sure of my destination, but from the talk of the others I learn much. I become a messenger from a distant city with a letter for the Duke. Where is he? Laughter. No one sees the Duke, I am told. I might as well deliver my message to a bird in a cage.

What is this? I go in the direction I am told, to the office of some noble person whose name is meaningless to me, but once around a corner I am transformed once more, into a washerwoman. Pail in hand, the satchel with the book under my apron, I scrub my way past several sets of guards, some highborn ladies who kick me aside and laugh (I can only cower, remembering my station), several young princelings whose royal pleasure it is to bounce a ball off me, until at last I am outside a massive golden door, which strangely is left unguarded.

But it is locked, and I change again, this time into a mist, and I pass through the keyhole. The book will not come with me. It drops to the floor outside with a thud, and I must rematerialize inside the room, open the door, and recover it. When I do the door lock clicks and a shaft of light breaks into the gloomy chamber.

A weak voice calls, "Who is it? Who has come for me at last?"

The room has many windows, but the curtains of them are drawn. The south facing ones faintly catch the orange glow of the setting sun. It has taken me that long. It is nearly dusk.

At the far end of the room there is a large bed covered over by a canopy. The voice comes from within the hangings.

Steadily, inexorably, I approach, my pent-up fury building inside me. This is what I have worked for all these months and years. I am a volcano beyond restraint, about to explode. I, who in his eyes could accomplish nothing, have accomplished everything. I assume my composite shape, which more than a little resembles his own. I stand near the bed, my right hand tight on the hilt of my dagger.

"Who is it?" he calls again in little more than a dry croak.

"*It is I.* Do you not know me?"

I tear aside the hangings and confront him, and he blinks back at me. At a glance I can tell he is nearly blind. As I behold him my anger vanishes, like one of his spirits in the old days, up and away on invisible wings.

He has aged terribly. His hair is now entirely white, his face sunken. He lies in a sea of pillows, almost smothering in them. Both his feet are swollen, bandaged, and hanging from slings which are suspended from the ceiling. He has gout severely.

Still his mind seems quick. He shows no alarm, but is startled.

"Who are you? You imply that I should know you, but I don't. But then you are only a blur to me. I have growths in both my eyes, you see. Yes—very funny it is—you see and I don't that I don't see. A slip. Pardon me. My doctors tell me I'll be in total darkness soon—one way or the other."

I can find nothing to say. I feel like a child, a child who for some trivial reason decides it hates its mother, or father, and plots dire revenge, and seething with rage goes to carry out this vengeance, only to find when face-to-face with the parent that all such intent has gone away and there is nothing left to do except shuffle, stare down at one's feet, and look ridiculous.

What can I say to Prospero?

What?

The truth: "I am your monster, Caliban. It is I."

"Caliban? How did you—no. It's impossible!"

"It is quite possible, my Lord. I am here and I have the book you dropped into the sea." I take the volume from my satchel and hand it to him. He can see little and certainly read nothing in the dim light with his infirm eyes, but when he touches it and runs his hands over the covers and binding he must have held a thousand times, he knows it is indeed his book. He sighs, and a smile spreads over his face.

"I had feared a terrible thing, my good Caliban. I had feared that you did not exist, that the whole episode on the island was a pleasant fancy, something out of a poet's imagination, or a dream sent to me by a merciful spirit to relieve briefly the agonies of the world. But now I know that it was all real, and truly it was the happiest time of my life. How foolishly I ended it by bringing Alonso's ship to my shore! If I could go on forever as I was, with Miranda always a child, and inno-cent—Oh what would I not give for such a thing?"

"What would you give?"

"There is nothing in the whole world one can use to buy back a piece of time which is past. This is indeed the pearl beyond price. You, Caliban, have read my book and you must be aware of this. There are many trifles between its covers, but the essence of all, the art of retain-ing happiness, is not there." He hands the volume back to me. I am too startled to react. "Here, take it. Read more, as you must. In the end I am sure that you too will cast it away as I did."

At last, when I could speak, I say, "But my Lord, how did this happen? I thought all . . . would be well—I—"

"How did it come about? The way all things do, born out of greed, lust, hatred, petty jealousy—and grand jealousy too. To covet a king-dom is not a petty thing. My friends remained my friends only until it was politic to become my enemies. Those I had forgiven sent spies into my court. Fortune spun her wheel against me and war came. Thou-sands of young men died who never knew a thing about the quarrels of one or two of the nobly born. But they died for us all the same. Again there were traitors in my own household, and they could not bring themselves to slay me outright. So they walled me up in this tomb while I yet lived, and my own body conspired with them to set me apart from all the things I love. I cannot move from where I lie. The sweet birds sing outside my window, but I cannot rise to draw the curtains and look at them. My servants—nay, not mine, but the hirelings of the ones who rule in my name—torment me and will not fulfill so small a request."

Dumbly, like a puppet directed by another, I walk to the nearest window and pull open the drapes. Orange light floods the room and the bones of my master's face seem even more starkly prominent. He turns his head slowly toward me and says, "Thank you." Then he sees the dagger I have for so long held in my hand, but my whole arm is suddenly numb and I cannot drop it or put it away.

"I understand," he says. "Even though you have come to murder me, Caliban, I think you remain innocent. You have not lived in the world as long as I have. You don't know how it can crush you, grind you down, until all potential for joy has been stamped out. Your rage at me is simple, not the foul, festering malice of a courtier, who must smile to the last at the man he intends to overthrow."

I look at my delicate knife, my stiletto, curiously, as if it were a new thing. I am disoriented. What is he talking about? What am I doing? I have planned this scene so many times, acted it out in my imagination. It should be different. I should not feel like this at all.

"Your daughter? What of her? She worshipped you. I know. I saw. On the island. How long ago?"

At this, Prospero sighs as if he is letting his life out and with it his soul, to fly free and skyward.

"My daughter. I have not heard from her in years. She has drifted away from me on the tide of alliances. Alonso is dead—slashed with a venomed razor—and Ferdinand is King of Naples now. Our two cities . . . do not . . . get along."

He can bring himself to say no more. He glances once more at the weapon I hold, a weapon specially made and named in these cities, and then he sinks deep into his pillows, closes his eyes, and puts his chin up, his head back.

I understand. I do what I must. My hands act for me as if of their own volition. He makes no sound as I slowly cut his throat from ear to ear.

Afterwards, outside in the streets of the city, I ask myself over and over why I did such a thing. Was it to tie up the loose ends in a tale written by another, over which I have no control? Was it even I who performed the deed, or some ghost in a dream? I am not myself.

Another walks in my flesh and I only dimly follow what he does and thinks.

For the first time after one of these killings my heart is awake and I know genuine emotion. I weep.

Anti-climax. Back in Naples, outside a door, invisible now, I over-hear a dialogue between a steely-voiced King and a sobbing Queen:

"Sweet Ferdinand, can that be you? Where is the beloved man I met that day, in that dream in a far place—how long ago was it? I don't know. It seems as long as since the Fall. Before that—"

"Dearest Miranda, you babble."

"Do not call me dearest, husband. You are not the same. He was tender and kind. *You*—you are an imposter! You are possessed by a devil! I hate you!"

"The other man that I was, the weepy, naive, silly, poetical ass, is gone and I say good riddance. I have matured. I have learned much since I ascended the throne."

"You have lost your soul!"

"That is one of the things a king must learn to do without. You still have yours, I trust, and so does your lover, though it may not still linger in his body—"

A shriek of purest terror.

"My babies! What have you done to my babies?"

"Your bastards? Your rivals to the throne you hoped would one day unseat me? Strangled, all of them, and buried secretly in little boxes. Your lover, too, I have buried, in my dungeon, only he is not blue yet, and last I visited him he still whimpered beneath the torturer's iron."

"Monster! You monster!"

That word again, only with an entirely different meaning, I think. I must leave. I cannot listen to any more of this. Once I had harbored some fantastic scheme in which I would come upon Miranda in her bedchamber and in a moment of exquisite vengeance against the one who sired her, have her as my own.

But no, I cannot. Another Caliban thought these thoughts. It was not I. Once more I stand impotent, and the stranger within me guides my steps away from the palace. I am not sure what I should feel, but in the confusion my mind and my heart are dead.

The world has raped her already.

Lastly now, a walk to the sea and then I shall leave the world I have come to know. He was wrong. I am not innocent. I have drunk deep of the black wine of living, but now I spit it out. I will not be a part to this. I, who was called a monster for my shape, find that I cannot bear to live among those monsters whose shapes are within them. They are far, far more grotesque than I, the stranger, alone, the outsider always.

My externals shall change again, for a last time. I still have the book and its spells are lodged in my mind. I can become—anything. I shall melt myself down, let the evil humors flow from me, and then take on a new, different visage as I pass into the breast of the ocean. I shall become a giant fish, as large as a galleon, as large as an island, and I shall glide through the murky and silent depths, apart from land-hugging men and their cities forever, hidden, a brother to the whales.

—*with sincerest apologies to that Most Estimable Gentleman, Mr. W. S.*

The Trilling Princess

BY JESSICA AMANDA SALMONSON

It was a very uncomfortable parlor and Hershfield and I looked at each other in a nervous way, waiting for the princess to receive us.

"Is this a good idea?" I asked.

"Oh, certainly," he replied, managing to sound cheerful, though the room was by no means conducive to cheer or even the simplest of comforts. It was bare and stark and there were no windows. The chairs were heavy wooden things tucked up close to the walls, placed far apart so that no position could be found from which seated gentlemen such as ourselves might easily or privately converse. One wished to pull the chairs to the middle of the carpetless room, but they were too thickly designed to lift, and dragging them across the walnut floor would be both noisy and damaging. So we sat in these monstrosities, like the fading spectres of long-dead kings shrunk upon their sombre thrones; and we continued to smile across the way to each other in a strained manner.

Hershfield had led me through the nighted streets of the city to this place, promising something curious. What possessed me to succumb to a whim of his, I cannot say. The route took us through neighborhoods of old, once-fine houses that were irreparably ruined, inhabited by the blighted poor and by rats. The streets were narrow and littered; the sidewalks severely cracked and pushed upward by the roots of decrepit, dying trees. Televisions flickered colored lights from otherwise dark windows. Ill-kept automobiles lined every inch of curb and were often parked upon the sidewalks as well. "Isn't it dangerous here?" I asked, and Hershfield replied, "Why, no." It was a crooked route as well; and I wondered if I should be able to find my way back to the office if left to my own device. I wondered that so vile a neighborhood was in walking distance of modern shops, and theatres, and office towers . . . so near to vastly more wholesome neighborhoods. I followed the man whose coat lent him a faintly Victorian dignity in the twilight, and I felt lost in time. "Have you forgotten the way?" I asked, for he had twice assured me it wasn't much farther on, though farther we went. His reply was, "I don't think I have." I was relieved when a particular crumbling mansion before us proved to be the one; although once established in its parlor, by an arthritic butler who soon vanished down a long dark hall, I had rather felt it best if Hershfield had lost the way and decided to call our visit off.

There was scant furniture or decoration in the parlor. On the wainscoting hung a few very large and terrible wood-engravings with hints of color-tint that only served to make the foxed and faded prints the more gloomy and grey-seeming. The wide, baroque frames were in supremely poor taste to begin with, besides being chipped and darkened with age and lack of proper cleaning. The artists and engravers were alike unknown to me, but their subject matter conjured the same moods as Goya's grim portraits of war and terror and mad gods, or Munch's silent screamer. One of these menacing engravings hung directly at my back and above my head, causing me to look over my shoulder from time to time to be certain the bleary faces were not grimacing in some new way, or the evilly suggestive events progressing by some uncanny method.

There was no electricity, but only candelabra of chunky design, placed on the third-rate gothic end-tables by the chairs, and on the mantel of a shallow fireplace. The fireplace was an artificial affair incapable of burning logs. I even fancied it might disguise a secret entry, and kept a subtle eye upon it.

There was a table in the center of the room, a lonesome thing and ridiculously little compared to the chairs and the huge engravings; a frail table with five legs (though it scarcely needed four) with a ragged bit of lace hanging over it on two sides. Upon it sat another candelabrum, blunt candles dripping wax on the lace.

"This is a queer place, Harry," I said, meaning to confess the whole place made me nervous.

"Isn't it," he agreed, but with an insufferably pleasant tone I could by no means return. He was a decent chap but I could never feel close to him. We weren't actually good friends, but something of rivals at the firm. But, as he was always so innocently congenial, and seemed genuinely to like me more than not, I tried always to reflect his attitude of camaraderie. In the nerve-wracking room, however, his complacently generous nature struck me as an annoyance and a falsehood.

I might be forgiven my vile and startled mood. In our modern age, a candlelit room can only seem alien, and dim, and strange. Perhaps it was the same in any age; but the eeriness is accentuated by so great an unfamiliarity. One wished to stand up from one's uncomfortable chair and exclaim, "Good Lord, where's the light switch!" And one felt as though the world were nothing but a stateroom of a sunken luxury liner, two luckless men alone within, mere wraiths with no awareness that the ship would never reach any destination.

"Time has passed this place by," said Hershfield, breaking the dreadful silence with a needed bit of understatement.

"And the princess as well, eh?" I forced a smile.

"As you will see, old man," he promised. "She's really very kind, poor soul. But it is in the nature of these lingering traces of the royal class to not want to appear too easily at our beck and call. She's old, and long in exile—though I dare guess she could return to her country after all this time, it wouldn't be at all the same place, so she might as well stay here. She's aware of herself as an anachronism, I do believe. She's been denied a lot; but we cannot deny her a sense of dignity in what, for her, is so greatly ruined a world."

"There's not much dignity in *this* spare, dark room!" I protested.

He raised his hand and said, "Quietly, please," with an unexpected edge in his voice, for he was obviously protective of the mysterious princess. Then, reverting to his congenial attitude, he said, "So much has been sold over the years, you know; that's why the place is a bit empty. As for the lights—well, even today, some of those little East European states haven't much electricity. She certainly never had it in her heyday; and she refuses to have it now. It's rather romantic if you let it be. One doesn't have to see the poverty."

"About as romantic as a brown-out in New Jersey, I should say! And it isn't poverty I sense here; it's . . ." I sought the precise word. "It's decay!"

"Do be . . . ah, Princess!" Hershfield rose from his seat and started across the floor toward the old woman who appeared in the entry from the dim hall. Hershfield's steps echoed in the hollow of the expansive parlor, and his voice sounded deeper and more masculine than was actually the case.

I doubted the elderly princess had heard my last rude commentary, for surely I had smelled the moment of her arrival! She positively reeked of powder and paint and perfume—expensive stuff for all I could tell, but a dreadful stink nonetheless. A whore in a tavern couldn't have smelled more extreme.

For a moment, as Hershfield approached her, I had the sense of being in a laughable, low-budget period movie with a few cheap props and worn-out costumes: Hershfield in his antiquated, high collar affecting such odd manners for the sake of the doddering princess, and she decked out like a wax figure in a museum's depiction of King Louis' court.

I stood before my hard chair, glad to rest my aching buttocks, my hands locked behind my back, striving to project the proper "character" for this piteous scrap of bad cinema. My eyes roved over the huge, black, antique engravings, finding them no more or less suspicious than a moment before. Hershfield was urging me near, and it had taken me a moment to realize it, my mind was so preoccupied with vagaries. In a moment I lurched into attentiveness and strode to meet the princess near the undersized table, where candlelight made us all look sickly and crazed.

"This is my good friend John Hemmings," said he, "a partner like myself in the firm that oversees your estate, Princess. I hope you will forgive my wishing to introduce him to you; but how dare I boast of my acquaintance with actual royalty, unless circumventing the potential snobbery by sharing my social fortunes? And so! I present to you Mr. Hemmings—with my total assurance that he does indeed represent the best of our city's fine young gentlemen . . . (in spite of his rude origins)." Hershfield whispered this last bit, play-acting that I might not hear, then winked at me on the sly. Then to me: "John, I give you the Princess Carmia di Potecske."

I took her proffered hand and bowed toward it. The long red nails gave me the sensation of kissing a dry, crinkly spider whose feet were dripping blood. A single ring with too large a garnet reflected the slender flame of a guttering candle, blinking like the eye of a sinister cat.

With few other words, and after Hershfield led the Princess di Potecske to a large seat near the artificial fireplace, he and I retired to our respective chairs near the walls . . . and we stared at one another. The princess had a gargoyle's expression of leering joy at our presence, but was much too senile to make the idlest of conversation. Hershfield cleared his throat a few times, looking decent enough in his old-fashioned manner, but lacking any semblance of talent when it came to filling so great a void. I whispered to him once, "What do we do now?" but the whisper echoed horribly and I dared not speak again.

"You will see," he said, and was somewhat smug about the whole affair, though I could not imagine how it was he was having a good time. The room was positively chilly, yet I was sweating from embarrassment and discomfiture.

Then of a sudden, Princess di Potecske leaped to her feet, surprisingly dainty and only slightly short of graceful, and began exclaiming in a whining affectation that I supposed to approximate a coy girlishness: "Do monsieurs Hershfield and Hemmings, my fine cavaliers, wish to hear me sing?"

"Ah, yes!" said Hershfield, clapping hands to knees and grinning through his bushy mustache at the horrid princess, whose motions in the stark room sent wafts of syrupy putrescence everywhere.

"As you know," she said in my direction, though I knew nothing of the matter, "I was once famed throughout Europe, East and West, as 'the trilling princess,' and oh!, it was daring of me to go upon the stage. Yes, it is true! You do know what they thought of actors in those days. Hated and admired! But as you see, I am liberal in all things, then as now . . . and so the more confused that things went badly for me in my country's revolution. But, oh, I refuse to bring gloom upon our happy party by remembering that! Instead, I will sing for you the aria that was called for in all the great theatres as my traditional encore."

And snapping open a feather fan she had held close to her bosom, and which looked, opened, like a molting parakeet's lice-ridden corpse smashed into the general dimensions of a fan, she began to sing.

How can I describe it? It was hideous. It was opera, I suppose; I am ignorant of the subject. Yet I cannot believe that it was merely my untrained ear that could not appreciate her odious mewlings. Her voice broke into scratchy falsetto, then fell several octaves so that she sounded something like an aged, hard-smoking wino growling with delirium tremens. She could hold something of a tune for brief passages, in what language I could not fathom, though it was like a jumble of Slavic and Italian spun together randomly, with occasional utterances of guttural German poking out of the arrangement like porcupine quills. Hideous, did I say? It was worse! It was dreadful! It grated so horribly that I thought I might actually fall from that straight-backed flat-bottomed wooden chair and regurgitate then and there upon the floor. You think I exaggerate? I do not. I felt like a man at sea in a storm, the wind wailing around me, the world tipping left then right. I was positively ill.

And the dreadful tune grew louder around me, more insistent, the trilling princess more insinuating. Lace and fluttering silk came at me, a monster drifting through a tomb, its darkly painted lips stretched into the shape of an enormous lima bean, shrieking the whole while, as the fan fanned an overpowering odor in my face. Stench permeated my clothing, my nostrils. Puffs of power came loose from her hair and drifted at me like a fog. The dried-up, red-toed spider that was her free hand waggled in the air—an obscene gesture I suppose was intended as theatric, but it positively undid me. I stood suddenly and began shouting at the top of my lungs. I fled the parlor in abject horror, out into the glaring streetlights of the city.

I had not run far when I realized what a fool I'd played. I stopped, whirled around, and saw Hershfield coming at me. The mercury vapor lamps made him seem like four or five men in the night, his images following after himself, as when one passes one's hand before a television screen and grows many fingers as the result. He drew up to me in a pant, his expression jubilant. "Well, old man!" he said. "Was it worth it?"

"Worth it!" I retorted, fully annoyed. *"Worth* it? Good God, man! How could you put me in that situation without a hint of warning? And that pathetic old witch! You could at least have remained long enough to apologize for me. She's *your* repulsive friend, after all."

"Oh, there was no need to stay," he said, and clamped his cold fingers around my wrist, anchoring himself to me. "She's coming this way, old man! You can apologize yourself!"

HENRY KUTTNER *(1915–1958) began his career at a literary agency but turned to full-time freelance writing after he sold his first story, a hideous nightmare called "The Graveyard Rats." It appeared in the March 1936 issue of* Weird Tales *. . . surely one of the most memorable débuts in the annals of horror fiction.*

The Graveyard Rats

BY HENRY KUTTNER

Old Masson, the caretaker of one of Salem's oldest and most neglected cemeteries, had a feud with the rats. Generations ago they had come up from the wharves and settled in the graveyard, a colony of abnormally large rats, and when Masson had taken charge after the inexplicable disappearance of the former caretaker, he decided that they must go. At first he set traps for them and put poisoned food by their burrows, and later he tried to shoot them, but it did no good. The rats stayed, multiplying and overrunning the graveyard with their ravenous hordes.

They were large, even for the *mus decumanus,* which sometimes measures fifteen inches in length, exclusive of the naked pink and gray tail. Masson had caught glimpses of some as large as good-sized cats, and when, once or twice, the grave-diggers had uncovered their burrows, the malodorous tunnels were large enough to enable a man to crawl into them on his hands and knees. The ships that had come generations ago from distant ports to the rotting Salem wharves had brought strange cargoes.

Masson wondered sometimes at the extraordinary size of these burrows. He recalled certain vaguely disturbing legends he had heard since coming to ancient, witch-haunted Salem—tales of a moribund, inhuman life that was said to exist in forgotten burrows in the earth. The old days, when Cotton Mather had hunted down the evil cults that worshipped Hecate and the dark Magna Mater in frightful orgies, had passed; but dark gabled houses still leaned perilously toward each other over narrow cobbled streets, and blasphemous secrets and mysteries were said to be hidden in subterranean cellars and caverns, where forgotten pagan rites were still celebrated in defiance of law and sanity. Wagging their gray heads wisely, the elders declared that there were worse things than rats and maggots crawling in the unhallowed earth of the ancient Salem cemeteries.

And then, too, there was this curious dread of the rats. Masson disliked and respected the ferocious little rodents, for he knew the danger that lurked in their flashing, needle-sharp fangs; but he could not understand the inexplicable horror which the oldsters held for deserted, rat-infested houses. He had heard vague rumors of ghoulish beings that dwelt far underground, and that had the power of commanding the rats, marshaling them like horrible armies. The rats, the old men whispered, were messengers between this world and the grim and ancient caverns far below Salem. Bodies had been stolen from graves for nocturnal subterranean feasts, they said. The myth of the Pied Piper is a fable that hides a blasphemous horror, and the black pits of Avernus have brought forth hell-spawned monstrosities that never venture into the light of day.

Masson paid little attention to these tales. He did not fraternize with his neighbors, and, in fact, did all he could to hide the existence of the rats from intruders. Investigation, he realized, would undoubtedly mean the opening of many graves. And while some of the gnawed, empty coffins could be attributed to the activities of the rats, Masson might find it difficult to explain the mutilated bodies that lay in some of the coffins.

The purest gold is used in filling teeth, and this gold is not removed when a man is buried. Clothing, of course, is another matter; for usually the undertaker provides a plain broadcloth suit that is cheap and easily recognizable. But gold is another matter; and sometimes, too, there were medical students and less reputable doctors who were in need of cadavers, and not overscrupulous as to where these were obtained.

So far Masson had successfully managed to discourage investigation. He had fiercely denied the existence of the rats, even though they sometimes robbed him of his prey. Masson did not care what happened to the bodies after he had performed his gruesome thefts, but the rats inevitably dragged away the whole cadaver through the hole they gnawed in the coffin.

The size of these burrows occasionally worried Masson. Then, too, there was the curious circumstance of the coffins always being gnawed open at the end, never at the side or top. It was almost as though the rats were working under the direction of some impossibly intelligent leader.

Now he stood in an open grave and threw a last sprinkling of wet earth on the heap beside the pit. It was raining, a slow, cold drizzle that for weeks had been descending from soggy black clouds. The graveyard was a slough of yellow, sucking mud, from which the rain-washed tombstones stood up in irregular battalions. The rats had retreated to their furrows, and Masson had not seen one for days. But his gaunt, unshaved face was set in frowning lines; the coffin on which he was standing was a wooden one.

The body had been buried several days earlier, but Masson had not dared to disinter it before. A relative of the dead man had been coming to the grave at intervals, even in the drenching rain. But he would hardly come at this late hour, no matter how much grief he might be suffering, Masson thought, grinning wryly. He straightened and laid the shovel aside.

From the hill on which the ancient graveyard lay he could see the lights of Salem flickering dimly through the downpour. He drew a flashlight from his pocket. He would need light now. Taking up the spade, he bent and examined the fastenings of the coffin.

Abruptly he stiffened. Beneath his feet he sensed an unquiet stirring and scratching, as though something was moving within the coffin. For a moment a pang of superstitious fear shot through Masson, and then rage replaced it as he realized the significance of the sound. The rats had forestalled him again!

In a paroxysm of anger Masson wrenched at the fastenings of the coffin. He got the sharp edge of the shovel under the lid and pried it up until he could finish the job with his hands. Then he sent the flashlight's cold beam darting down into the coffin.

Rain spattered against the white satin lining; the coffin was empty. Masson saw a flicker of movement at the head of the case, and darted the light in that direction.

The end of the sarcophagus had been gnawed through, and a gaping hole led into darkness. A black shoe, limp and dragging, was disappearing as Masson watched, and abruptly he realized that the rats had forestalled him by only a few minutes. He fell on his hands and knees and made a hasty clutch at the shoe, and the flashlight incontinently fell into the coffin and went out. The shoe was tugged from his grasp, he heard a sharp, excited squealing, and then he had the flashlight again and was darting its light into the burrow.

It was a large one. It had to be, or the corpse could not have been dragged along it. Masson wondered at the size of the rats that could carry away a man's body, but the thought of the loaded revolver in his pocket fortified him. Probably if the corpse had been an ordinary one Masson would have left the rats with their spoils rather than venture into the narrow burrow, but he remembered an especially fine set of cuff-links he had observed, as well as a stickpin that was undoubtedly a genuine pearl. With scarcely a pause he clipped the flashlight to his belt and crept into the burrow.

It was a tight fit, but he managed to squeeze himself along. Ahead of him in the flashlight's glow he could see the shoes dragging along the wet earth of the bottom of the tunnel. He crept along the burrow as rapidly as he could, occasionally barely able to squeeze his lean body through the narrow walls.

The air was overpowering with its musty stench of carrion. If he could not reach the corpse in a minute, Masson decided, he would turn back. Belated fears were beginning to crawl, maggot-like, within his mind, but greed urged him on. He crawled forward, several times passing the mouths of adjoining tunnels. The walls of the burrow were damp and slimy, and twice lumps of dirt dropped behind him. The second time he paused and screwed his head around to look back. He could see nothing, of course, until he had unhooked the flashlight from his belt and reversed it.

Several clods lay on the ground behind him, and the danger of his position suddenly became real and terrifying. With thoughts of a cave-in making his pulse race, he decided to abandon the pursuit, even though he had now almost overtaken the corpse and the invisible things that pulled it. But he had overlooked one thing: the burrow was too narrow to allow him to turn.

Panic touched him briefly, but he remembered a side tunnel he had just passed, and backed awkwardly along the tunnel until he came to it. He thrust his legs into it, backing until he found himself able to turn. Then he hurriedly began to retrace his way, although his knees were bruised and painful.

Agonizing pain shot through his leg. He felt sharp teeth sink into his flesh, and kicked out frantically. There was a shrill squealing and the scurry of many feet. Flashing the light behind him, Masson caught his breath in a sob of fear as he saw a dozen great rats watching him intently, their slitted eyes glittering in the light. They were great misshapen things, as large as cats, and behind them he caught a glimpse of a dark shape that stirred and moved swiftly aside into the shadow; and he shuddered at the unbelievable size of the thing.

The light had held them for a moment, but they were edging closer, their teeth dull orange in the pale light. Masson tugged at his pistol, managed to extricate it from his pocket, and aimed carefully. It was an awkward position, and he tried to press his feet into the soggy sides of the burrow so that he should not inadvertently send a bullet into one of them.

The rolling thunder of the shot deafened him, for a time, and the clouds of smoke set him coughing. When he could hear again and the smoke had cleared, he saw that the rats were gone. He put the pistol back and began to creep swiftly along the tunnel, and then with a scurry and a rush they were upon him again.

They swarmed over his legs, biting and squealing insanely, and Masson shrieked horribly as he snatched for his gun. He fired without aiming, and only luck saved him from blowing a foot off. This time the rats did not retreat so far, but Masson was crawling as swiftly as he could along the burrow, ready to fire again at the first sound of another attack.

There was a patter of feet and he sent the light stabbing back of him. A great gray rat paused and watched him. Its long ragged whiskers twitched, and its scabrous, naked tail was moving slowly from side to side. Masson shouted and the rat retreated.

He crawled on, pausing briefly, the black gap of a side tunnel at his elbow, as he made out a shapeless huddle on the damp clay a few yards ahead. For a second he thought it was a mass of earth that had been dislodged from the roof, and then he recognized it as a human body.

It was a brown and shriveled mummy, and with a dreadful unbelieving shock Masson realized that it was moving.

It was crawling toward him, and in the pale glow of the flashlight the man saw a frightful gargoyle face thrust into his own. It was the passionless, death's-head skull of a long-dead corpse, instinct with hellish life; and the glazed eyes swollen and bulbous betrayed the thing's blindness. It made a faint groaning sound as it crawled toward

Masson, stretching its ragged and granulated lips in a grin of dreadful hunger. And Masson was frozen with abysmal fear and loathing.

Just before the Horror touched him, Masson flung himself frantically into the burrow at his side. He heard a scrambling noise at his heels, and the thing groaned dully as it came after him. Masson, glancing over his shoulder, screamed and propelled himself desperately through the narrow burrow. He crawled along awkwardly, sharp stones cutting his hands and knees. Dirt showered into his eyes, but he dared not pause even for a moment. He scrambled on, gasping, cursing, and praying hysterically.

Squealing triumphantly, the rats came at him, horrible hunger in their eyes. Masson almost succumbed to their vicious teeth before he succeeded in beating them off. The passage was narrowing, and in a frenzy of terror he kicked and screamed and fired until the hammer clicked on an empty shell. But he had driven them off.

He found himself crawling under a great stone, embedded in the roof, that dug cruelly into his back. It moved a little as his weight struck it, and an idea flashed into Masson's fright-crazed mind. If he could bring down the stone so that it blocked the tunnel!

The earth was wet and soggy from the rains, and he hunched himself half upright and dug away at the dirt around the stone. The rats were coming closer. He saw their eyes glowing in the reflection of the flashlight's beam. Still he clawed frantically at the earth. The stone was giving. He tugged at it and it rocked in its foundation.

A rat was approaching—the monster he had already glimpsed. Gray and leprous and hideous it crept forward with its orange teeth bared, and in its wake came the blind dead thing, groaning as it crawled. Masson gave a last frantic tug at the stone. He felt it slide downward, and then he went scrambling along the tunnel.

Behind him the stone crashed down, and he heard a sudden frightful shriek of agony. Clods showered upon his legs. A heavy weight fell on his feet and he dragged them free with difficulty. The entire tunnel was collapsing!

Gasping with fear, Masson threw himself forward as the soggy earth collapsed at his heels. The tunnel narrowed until he could barely use his hands and legs to propel himself; he wriggled forward like an eel and suddenly felt satin tearing beneath his clawing fingers, and then his head crashed against some thing that barred his path. He moved his legs, discovering that they were not pinned under the collapsed earth. He was lying flat on his stomach, and when he tried to raise himself he found that the roof was only a few inches from his back. Panic shot through him.

When the blind horror had blocked his path, he had flung himself into a side tunnel, a tunnel that had no outlet. He was *in a coffin,* an empty coffin into which he had crept through the hole the rats had gnawed in its end!

He tried to turn on his back and found that he could not. The lid of the coffin pinned him down inexorably. Then he braced himself and strained at the coffin lid. It was immovable, and even if he could escape from the sarcophagus, how could he claw his way up through five feet of hard-packed earth?

He found himself gasping. It was dreadfully fetid, unbearably hot. In a paroxysm of terror he ripped and clawed at the satin until it was shredded. He made a futile attempt to dig with his feet at the earth from the collapsed burrow that blocked his retreat. If he were only able to reverse his position he might be able to claw his way through to air . . . air . . .

White-hot agony lanced through his breast, throbbed in his eyeballs. His head seemed to be swelling, growing larger and larger; and suddenly he heard the exultant squealing of the rats. He began to scream insanely but could not drown them out. For a moment he thrashed about hysterically within his narrow prison, and then he was quiet, gasping for air. His eyelids closed, his blackened tongue protruded, and he sank down into the blackness of death with the mad squealing of the rats dinning in his ears.

"Daddy," a masterful blend of horror and pathos, is the only short story published during the tragically brief life of EARL GODWIN *(1933–1986). Earl was a resident of Brownsville, Texas, and brother of Parke Godwin, whose Devil story "Influencing the Hell Out of Time and Teresa Golowitz" appears elsewhere in this volume. Parke writes: "Earl was a sharp critic of his own work and destroyed most of his manuscripts. However, he left two other completed short stories with me and I hope to present them to the public in the not-too-distant future."*

Daddy
BY EARL GODWIN

I stay away from singles bars. I never was good at clever small talk, and I'm at my fumbling worst when the whole idea is to strike up a relationship with a woman. That's why I choose neighborhood haunts where the serious drinkers gather to pass the evening in comfortable ambience. However, the thought is always tucked away in the back of my mind that I just might meet a special lady who could laugh aside my clumsy, inarticulate style and find charming the rather eccentric limitations of my bachelor life.

I met her in spades.

It had been raining and there was a chill in the air, so I sat in the back of the crowded bar in my raincoat nursing a straight bourbon. There were a lot of women in the place, some very attractive, but not that special one with whom I'd consider dancing through a night's fantasy. In life I've settled for some very ordinary women. In my dreams I always go first-class.

She came in with a man, and they threaded their way back through the crowd until a waitress seated them in a booth right next to my table. The man hung up their raincoats and she stood next to me, shaking the water from her dark, shoulder-length hair. A drop landed on my upper lip; I slowly licked it off, staring at her.

They weren't happy: this I could see right away. Worry traced its path across her darkly beautiful features. This was a queen, not just worthy of my idle fantasy but one for whom I could work my whole life to wash the torment from that exquisite face and replace it with happiness. I don't say that easily, because I consider myself an accredited critic of beauty. I'm a photographer, and even if my sexual successes have been among the mediocre, I have a sharp eye for real beauty, and this creature with her eyes that leaped out and grabbed you would steal the heart out of a polar bear. The man? Who knows? I wouldn't remember him if he fell on me.

I tried not to stare. Her eyes flicked over me for a preoccupied instant and then away. I listened to the soft, tense tone of their conversation. He was saying things like, "Tired of it . . . had enough . . . impossible." I couldn't make out much. Most of it was in whispers and I don't hear well. They raised their voices slightly. The conversation was becoming more intense. The man leaned over the table, his face strained and angry, hers desperate and afraid. She hissed something that sounded like an ultimatum. He jumped up and shouldered his way through the crowd to the front door. I looked quickly at the woman. Her expression was one of weary defeat. It seemed to add years to her face.

Alone and nervous, she fumbled her way through several matches until she managed to light her cigarette. I caught her eye and raised my shot glass in a sympathetic toast. She started to raise hers, but the glass was empty. "I seem to be abandoned and the gentleman had all the money." She flashed a vulnerable smile.

I signaled the waitress. "May I join you?"

"By all means." Her confidence had returned, but there was still that air of vulnerability about her that excited me. I prayed I wouldn't overplay my hand.

I have a book at home called *How to Pick Up Women.* There are hundreds of opening lines for starting a conversation; I couldn't remember a single one of them. We looked at each other for an awkwardly long time until I blurted, "Was that your husband?"

"No."

"He sure ran off and left you like a lone duck."

"No, just a friend. It's not important now. Do you have the time? I have to go soon."

I felt my hopes plummet. "It's nine o'clock. Please—don't go. I love talking to pretty ladies."

She looked at me sharply, an appraising glance. "Aren't you the charmer." Then she fumbled with another match. I leaned over to steady her hand.

"Eres muy caballero."

"You're Spanish?"

"I've been a lot of things. Do you live around here?"

I hadn't expected that. My pulse started to hammer faster. "Yeah. I've got a studio apartment a couple of blocks from here. I'm a photographer," I added for no good reason.

"Oh?" Her fingers drummed lightly on the table.

"Yeah. Uh . . . I'd like to take some pictures of you." Oh Jesus! I winced inwardly to hear that tired old line come out of my mouth.

"I'll bet you would." She ground out her cigarette in the ashtray, stood up, and reached for her raincoat. My heart sank; she was leaving. She put her coat on and fluffed that wonderful hair out around her shoulders. I sat staring up, hypnotized by her. She was older than I thought at first, pushing forty but still an incredibly beautiful woman. I would have said younger when she first came in, perhaps a trick of the light. But now she was leaving, the kind of woman ministers leave home for, and I'd never see her again. Jesus.

She smiled at me. "Your place?"

I couldn't believe it.

I was all thumbs and stupid remarks as I tried to appear suave while attacking the suddenly impossible task of putting on my raincoat. She leaned against the booth with a tired patience and glanced up at the clock. She finally helped me with the coat before someone had to cut me out of the damned thing. We walked out of the bar with her in the lead, and I gave a few friends a debonair wave, as if leaving with the finest fox in the house was old stuff for me. Taking her hand, I couldn't help thinking how I'd almost let her get away from me.

My studio apartment was quite naturally a mess. I turned on a light and watched her as she picked her way through a maze of lightstands and reflectors. My furnishings were rather sparse, but I did have a studio couch and a couple of easy chairs. The kitchen area was in the rear corner of the big room, away from the window. The sink was full of vintage dishes and maybe some new life forms.

She moved around and studied the pictures on the walls as I fixed a couple of drinks and turned on the stereo. "Very pretty women. How many have you slept with?"

"All" would have been a great answer, "half" would have been half true. "None of them," I muttered.

"I love honesty," she laughed. Then in a husky whisper as she came to me: "It makes me feel so warm toward a man."

We were standing in the middle of my front-room studio with the stereo low and the dim light struggling against the chilled gloom of the big room. She took my hand and guided me to the bedroom in the back of the apartment.

I kissed her full lips. They felt soft and full of promise, parting under mine, searching with her tongue, bringing me to quick readiness. I didn't rush. I'd been waiting a lifetime for this and I was going to enjoy the hell out of it. We undressed each other, pausing to caress favorite parts. Her large breasts were straining to be touched. She stroked and teased me and I pushed her gently back onto the bed—not in a hurry. Hell, I could have foreplayed with her until the cows came home. She was the one in a rush. She cried out then, a sound of relief and hope and something like fear, wrapping her legs around me as we rocked together in abandon. She held me like a vise with her arms and legs, squeezing me tight.

"No, honey, stay. I want it all."

I came and felt a surge of relief flood through me. For her that was it: show's over. She rolled me off her and stood up. "Thank you."

Odd thing to say after an interlude like that. I rolled over and found myself staring up into the wickedest gun barrel I'd ever seen.

"I don't get it. We were having a good time. What gives?"

She stood naked before me, unsmiling, with the pistol leveled at my head. She looked stricken. "Please. I haven't much time and I'm going to need your help. Don't ask questions, I don't have the answers. You have to deliver my baby."

I must have looked classically stupid with my jaw down around my ankles. "You're not pregnant."

"I am now and you're the father."

I managed a laugh like a choking gargle. "Aren't we a little premature? I mean like this stuff usually takes nine months." I laughed again, feeling ridiculous, sitting on the edge of the bed naked as a baseball. But there was nothing funny about her rage or the fear it came out of.

"Stop laughing, goddamnit! I—" She gasped in pain. The pistol dropped from her hand and she fell face forward, curling into a fetal position, holding her stomach. I picked the gun up and dropped it into a drawer. Rolling her over onto her back, I couldn't help notice that she looked even older than I thought the last time. I couldn't explain any of it, the whole thing was beyond me, but I had the feeling that what was happening here was as unique as it was awful.

I showered and dressed. She was moaning and rubbing her stomach when I got back to her. I stood by the bed looking down at her. There was a grotesque aspect to the situation now. I watched in helpless horror as the woman's belly began to swell—a little at first, then faster, as if someone were blowing her up with an air pump. And all the while her hair was graying like flickers of light in the dark mass of it. Sagging, wrinkled skin and brittle bones, long past the ability to stretch against the obvious labor pains, punished themselves to do what they were made for. She looked—she *was* now—sixty years old, the sound of her breathing like a saw in wood.

"Help me, please! Oh God, it's almost too late!"

She gave a low animal growl and drew her knees up against her breasts, her hands clamped on the headboard. The gasps were coming every couple of seconds—and then I could see the first sign of a small head.

She'd asked me to help. Me? In a normal birth I would have been useless as pants on a bird. Here I was a blithering idiot. I could only stand frozen and helpless as the nightmare unfolded in front of me. The baby's head and shoulders protruded now; the woman writhed like a trapped fish. Unintelligible gibberish escaped from her withering lips. Then, somehow shaking out of the trance, I grasped the slippery little shoulders and began tugging, pulling life out of death. The woman was actually shrinking now, falling in on herself, seventy-five, eighty years old. She'd stopped moving by now, gone stiff, gone beyond that, *way* beyond it, and the smell emanating from the decaying mess of her was almost too much to bear. I had the baby almost all the way out. Only the feet were inside. By the time I cleared them, the thing on the bed had been dead a very long time. The smell was sickening. I fought the need to vomit, stumbling into the bathroom for a fresh razor blade to cut the umbilical cord binding the baby to something that didn't quite make it out of the body.

It was a girl. Remembering old movies, I held her up by the little feet and gave the tiny buttocks a sharp smack. Her gasp and yowl started her breathing.

My daughter.

I carried her into the bathroom and washed her down with lukewarm water. Then, messed with blood and other matter I'd rather not think about, I stared at my reflection in the mirror. He looked like I felt, every bit of it. And he was a father.

I wrapped the baby in a blanket and the now unrecognizable remains of my date in the sheets. What to do with the gruesome bundle was a problem. I couldn't take it to the police . . . Sure, they'd believe me. Sure they would . . .

The baby was crying. It was hungry. I collapsed by the picture window in the front-room studio with her in my arms as she nursed at the makeshift bottle I scrounged from my photo equipment, some milk from the icebox and—hell, why not?—an unused condom from a pack in the dresser.

What the hell was I going to do? The shock was wearing off, replaced by exhaustion. I wearily placed the bundle on the floor next to my chair, adjusted the bottle for her to work at it, and sat back with a very deep sigh. I'd had a hard night.

I watched the rain sifting past the streetlights as the drops splashed on the pavement. Cars plowed through puddles and sent sheets of dirty water up on the deserted sidewalks. The clock across the street said midnight. I yawned and looked down at the baby. She was happily pulling away on her bottle, watching me with clear blue eyes. A little while ago they were barely open and still milky, unfocused. God help me—she'd grown.

I fell asleep in the chair, lulled by the soft drumming of the rain against the window. I must have slept for over three hours when I snapped awake suddenly, more out of a sense of guard duty than from any particular noise. The rain had stopped but the streets were shining wet, and I caught the reflection of the stoplight on the corner in the damp sheen of the sidewalk. I remembered and sat up.

The blanket was empty and the bottle lay next to it. Behind me I heard faintly the soft tread of tiny feet. Turning, I could just make out the small form coming toward me out of the dark. My hair rose; I jumped up, knocking over the chair. She approached with careful child-precision. She was wrapped in a sheet that trailed behind her, and her dark hair was tousled down around her bare shoulders, and she pulled at my pants leg, urgent and trusting.

"I'm hungry, Daddy."

I went into the bedroom, picked up the bundle of bedding, and carried it down to the dumpster in the back alley. And I disposed of the remains of that thing I had made love to. The mother of that thing in my apartment. I wasn't thinking; clear-cut thought was impossible. I walked back into the apartment. The little girl was standing by the window, peering out.

"Where'd you go, Daddy?"

"I just threw your mother in the garbage. From what I knew of her, she ought to feel right at home."

Her eyes weren't that young anymore. She pulled her curls away from her shoulders and shook her head. A beautiful child. She didn't look anything like me. I made her a sandwich and a glass of milk, watching her as she ate—six or seven years old, only I knew better. She wasn't that many hours old. I retreated to my chair by the window and stared hopelessly out into the wet streets. Then she was at my side.

"What was my mother like?"

"I don't know. We didn't spend much time cultivating a relationship."

She giggled, pressing my hand in her two small ones. "I love you, Daddy. You talk funny."

She leaned over and kissed me with a little hug. I felt myself go soft but I couldn't let her know it. We held onto each other as a fresh sheet of rain beat against the windows and made little wet rainbows out of the blurry neon signs across the street. We talked together about nothing much until finally, just before daylight, we both drifted off to sleep.

The roar of a bus outside the front window woke me with a start. I yawned and stretched; a glance at the clock across the street said it was a little after 8 A.M.

"You want something to eat, Dad?"

A pretty adolescent girl carried a plate of eggs into the dining area. "C'mon, Dad. I know you're hungry. The one without the sausage is mine. I hate sausage."

I wasn't in shock anymore but still not ready to accept this thing as it was. She sat down and scraped eggs off into her plate from the skillet.

"What are you staring at, Dad? You act like you've never seen me before. C'mon—eat up before it gets cold."

While I ate, I studied her: seventeen or eighteen now, well formed, rapidly becoming the woman I had been with the night before. She devoured her food hungrily and downed a glass of milk in one pull, leaving a white mustache on her upper lip. I leaned over and wiped it off.

"Thanks, I'm always so messy. Okay if I do the dishes later? *All Quiet on the Western Front* is on TV, and I've never seen it. It's a classic."

Whoever, whatever, from wherever, these things were born with some memories. I waved my hand helplessly. She could do whatever she wanted as far as I was concerned. The only thing she couldn't do was leave this apartment. I'd have to see to that. Until whatever was going to happen . . . happened . . . I'd just sit tight.

The morning passed in front of the television as we watched Lew Ayres in a dated but vivid story of a doomed German infantryman in World War I. She sat with her eyes glued to the screen. I couldn't help admire the beauty budding, blooming in front of me. She was full-bodied now, the woman I'd loved and watched give birth to her about sixteen hours before. The same woman.

The movie ended. She stood up and stretched, her breasts straining against the sheet that fit her a lot better now. She caught my glance. "Like what you see?"

I felt the surge of heat. I must have blushed. "Sorry. You're very beautiful. But I shouldn't have been staring."

"Were you in the war?"

"I was in Korea," I mumbled, glad for the change of subject.

She sat down again, drawing the sheet up around her. "Men don't have much to look forward to, going off to war all the time. I'm glad I'm a woman."

I thought, *Honey, they've got a lot more to look forward to than you do, any way you slice it.*

In a moment she went over to the stereo, sifting through the records, smiling over her shoulder at me. "Got an idea." She put on a record and came to me, holding out her hands in invitation. "Let's dance, Daddy."

I moved with her to the music, feeling the same power begin to sap at me as the night before. She pressed against me and hummed in my ear. I wrapped my fingers in that lush head of hair and pressed my face to hers, completely lost to the moment. She tilted her head back and looked up dreamily through seductive half slits of eyes. Her lovely mouth was so close to mine.

"I love you, Daddy," she whispered.

Her mouth came up and I mashed mine down on it. That one second none of the sick, bizarre truth of this thing was going to rob me of the one moment a guy like me remembers all his life. Then, as she writhed her body against me, I felt something else, something cold. As if I were detached, across the room watching, I saw myself pressing back against her urgently thrusting body, sucking at her mouth, the mouth I remembered. A flash of her mother darted through my mind, the woman, the old woman, decaying before she was even dead. The same woman kissing me now. I saw the whole monstrous thing for what it was and pushed away from her so hard that she fell backward onto the floor, frightened.

"Get off of me!" I screamed. "Don't touch me. What are you? I don't think there's a *word* for you."

Tears of fear and rejection welled up in her eyes, a last piece of the fast-fading little girl in her. "I'm sorry," I said at last. "I shouldn't have done that. But . . . do you know what in hell you are?"

She sighed resignedly and got up, adjusting the sheet around her, slipped over to my liquor cabinet and fixed us both a drink. She handed me the glass, holding me with those eyes, the total woman now, cycle complete. "Yes. I know what I am. Does it matter? I know you want me."

"You're my own daughter."

She sipped at her drink. "I've been a lot of men's daughter. Does it bother you?"

"Damn right it bothers me. You can't possibly think I can treat this like your everyday affair."

I saw the lost look in her then, the same as the night before, only now I knew what it was: the sense of too little time already running out. "You'll just let me die."

"I don't know what I'm going to do."

I collapsed in the easy chair by the window. She moved to it and looked out at the rain. It was still blowing against the glass. The watery reflection did sad things to her face. She already looked much older. I felt I had to say something.

"How long has this been going on? How could it ever start?"

"Does it matter?"

"You've got to admit it's an awful lot for a man to accept."

"I don't remember how it started. A long time ago, hundreds of years. You wouldn't believe it." I heard the despair, saw it in her maturing face. She knew this was going to be her last night. I wasn't going to let her out of the apartment.

With a set of handcuffs sometimes used as a prop, I cuffed her to the radiator in the bedroom and made sure she was comfortable. She didn't fight it; maybe she figured it was time. I wasn't actually killing her, only allowing her to die. I guessed about six more hours would do it.

I'll say one thing for her, she never begged. While I cuffed her to the radiator, she just watched me with a weary resignation. When I started to leave the apartment, she was crying—softly, trying to hide it from me. Somehow I couldn't just close a door on her.

"Look . . . I'm sorry."

"I love you, Daddy."

"Don't say that."

"Why not? That's part of it. Can't there be that much beauty to it, and can't you believe that much?"

I closed the door between us.

Mostly, I just walked in the drizzling rain, stopping now and then for a drink in one of the bars I knew. I wanted to get drunk and blot out the whole impossible thing. I ended up in the bar where I'd picked her up the night before. I realized now that it wasn't a different woman at all; she was always the same. I sat nursing my drink, glancing at my watch now and then. Two hours . . . a long time yet. I couldn't even feel the drinks.

Just going to let her die, aren't you?

A friend came over to my booth. We talked for a while, how's business, that sort of thing.

How does it feel to be God?

I played the juke. All the songs sounded the same, but who listened? The hallway to the men's room was crowded with drunks. I fumbled my way through. Clear the way for The Lord Who Giveth and Taketh Away.

The mirror in the john was the sort that really tells you what you look like. I never should have looked. *Hey, you've seen it all before, a guy doing all the impossible things to keep a beautiful woman.*

I love you, Daddy.

What kind of guy would deliver a baby and dispose of a corpse every night for the rest of his life?

I love you. That's part of it. Can't there be that much beauty?

I walked out of the bar and headed up the street toward my apartment. It was raining harder now, and I pulled the collar of my raincoat up around my neck as I turned down my street, knowing when I got up in the morning I'd have to raise a little girl to womanhood. I climbed the stairs and walked down the hall to my door.

And then at night, make love to your own daughter so she can live one day to do it all over again. The full cycle of life a man goes through once, three hundred and sixty-five times a year. But the guys I knew, those guys back in the bar, how many of them ever found a woman like this?

You tell yourself: nobody is God. They can call it what they want—incest, Dracula's daughter, whatever. Me? I was going for it. I opened the door to my apartment and shed my raincoat, dropping it on the floor, and walked over to the stereo to put on something soft and dreamy. I walked into the bedroom; there she was, still wrapped in the sheet, the most beautiful woman in the world at the late end of her prime, still . . . the impossible best. Her head came up when I entered the room. She looked at me uncertainly a moment, reading me surely, reading me right, then a slow smile curled that seductive mouth. Hell, I'd need a decent nursing bottle and baby food.

"Hurry, Daddy, or we'll be too late."

The Possessed and the Damned

Tales of possession and infernal intervention herein share the spotlight with vivid accounts of novel punishments devised by Satan for such unusually promising damned souls as Edward Page Mitchell's diabolic rodent or Edmond Rostand's Freudian variation on that illustrious rascal Don Juan.

In an earlier section of this book, "Let's Make a Deal," Lucifer was chiefly concerned with the snaring of new souls to keep up the population of the Underworld, but in most of the following "unlucky thirteen" selections, the Devil shows an equally keen interest in "making it hot" for sinners while they are still alive. Sometimes he is able to do it on his own; on other occasions he uses the tool at hand. In the following tales, you will encounter such thoroughly mundane rotters as Bram Stoker's rapacious crew of pauper-cutthroats, Leslie Charteris' all-too-plausible small-town politico-fiend and Somerset Maugham's amiable businessman-cum-murderer.

Long before James Bond was issued his license to kill or Charles Bronson went into the vigilante business, there was Simon Templar, the Saint, who took his commission to persecute criminals from no higher authority than his own conscience. In most cases, the Saint displays a twisted genius for invention that invests his Robin Hood-ish adventures with a ghoulish sense of humor . . . but there are times when a nasty adversary forces Simon to get back to basics, such as in the case of "The Well-Meaning Mayor." LESLIE CHARTERIS, *born in Singapore in 1907, now lives in semiretirement in England, but still rides herd on other authors whom he licenses to continue writing new Saintly exploits.*

The Well-Meaning Mayor
BY LESLIE CHARTERIS

Sam Purdell never quite knew how he became mayor. He was a small and portly man with a round blank face and a round blank mind who had built up a moderately profitable furniture business over the last thirty-five years and acquired in the process a round pudding-faced wife and a couple of suet dumplings of daughters; but the inexhaustible zeal for improving the circumstances and morals of the community, that fierce drive of ambition and the twitching of the ears for the ecstatic screams of *"Heil"* whenever he went abroad, that indomitable urge to be a leader of his people from which Hitlers and Mussolinis are born, was not naturally in him.

It is true that at the local reform club, of which he was a prominent member, he had often been stimulated by an appreciative audience and a large highball to lay down his views on the way in which he thought everything on earth ought to be run, from Japanese immigration to the permissible percentage of sulphur dioxide in dried apricots; but there was nothing outstandingly indicative of a political future in that. This is a disease which is liable to attack even the most honest and respectable citizens in such circumstances. But the idea that he himself should ever occupy the position in which he might be called upon to put all those beautiful ideas into practice had never entered Sam Purdell's head in those simple early days; and if it had not been for the drive supplied by Al Eisenfeld, it might never have materialized. "You ought to be in politics, Sam," Al had insisted at the close of one of these perorations several years before.

Sam Purdell considered the suggestion. "No, I wouldn't be clever enough," he said modestly. To tell the truth, he had heard the suggestion before, had repudiated it before and had always wanted to hear it contradicted. Al Eisenfeld obliged him. It was the first time anybody had been so obliging.

This was three years before the columnist of the *Elmford News* was moved to inquire: "How long does our mayor think he can kid reporters and deputations with his celebrated pose of injured innocence? We always thought it was a good act while it lasted; but isn't it time we had a new show?"

It was not the first time that it had been suggested in print that the naive and childlike simplicity which was Sam Purdell's greatest charm was one of the shrewdest fronts for ingenious corruption which any politician had ever tried to put over on a batch of sane electors, but this was the nearest that any commentator had ever dared to come to saying that Sam Purdell was a crook. It was a suggestion which left Sam a pained and puzzled man. He couldn't understand it. These adopted children of his, these citizens whose weal occupied his mind for twenty-four hours a day, were turning round to bite the hand that fed them. And the unkindest cut of all, the blow which struck at the roots of his faith in human gratitude, was that he had only tried to do his best for the city which had been delivered into his care.

For instance, there was a time when, dragged forth by the energy of one of his rotund daughters, he had climbed laboriously one Sunday afternoon to the top of the range of hills which shelter Elmford on the north. When he had got his wind and started looking round, he realized that from that vantage point there was a view which might have rejoiced the heart of any artist. Sam Purdell was no artist, but he blinked with simple pleasure at the panorama of rolling hills and wooded groves with the river winding between them like the track of a great silver snail; and when he came home again he had a beautiful idea.

"You know, we got one of the finest views in the state up there on those hills! I never saw it before, and I bet you didn't either. And why? Because there ain't no road goes up there; and when you get to my age it ain't so easy to go scrambling up through those trees and brush."

"So what?" asked Al Eisenfeld, who was even less artistic and certainly more practical.

"So I tell you what we do," said Sam, glowing with the ardour of his enthusiasm almost as much as with the aftereffects of his unaccustomed exercise. "We build a highway up there so they can drive out in their automobiles week ends and look around comfortably. It makes work for a lot of men, and it don't cost too much; and everybody in Elmford can get a lot of free pleasure out of it. Why, we might even get folks coming from all over the country to look at our view."

He elaborated this inspiration with spluttering eagerness, and before he had been talking for more than a quarter of an hour he had a convert.

"Sure, this is a great idea, Sam," agreed Mr. Eisenfeld warmly. "You leave it to me. Why, I know—we'll call it the Purdell Highway . . ."

The Purdell Highway duly came into being at a cost of four million dollars. Al Eisenfeld saw to it. In the process of pushing Sam Purdell up the political tree he had engineered himself into the strategic post of chairman of the board of aldermen, a position which gave him an interfering interest in practically all the activities of the city. The fact that the cost was about twice as much as the original estimate was due to the unforeseen obstinacy of the owner of the land involved, who held out for about four times the price which it was worth. There were rumors that someone in the administration had acquired the territory under another name shortly before the deal was proposed, and had sold it to the city at his own price—rumors which shocked Sam Purdell to the core of his sensitive soul. "Do you hear what they say, Al?" he complained, as soon as these slanderous stories reached his ears. "They say I made one hundred thousand dollars graft out of the Purdell Highway! Now, why the hell should they say that?"

"You don't have to worry about what a few rats are saying, Sam," replied Mr. Eisenfeld soothingly. "They're only jealous because you're so popular with the city. Hell, there are political wranglers who'd tell stories about the Archangel Gabriel himself if he was mayor, just to try and discredit the administration so they could shove their own crooked party in. I'll look into it."

Mr. Eisenfeld's looking into it did not stop the same rumours circulating about the Purdell Bridge, which spanned the river from the southern end of the town and linked it with the State Highway, eliminating a detour of about twenty miles. What project, Sam Purdell asked, could he possibly have put forward that was more obviously designed for the convenience and prosperity of Elmford? But there were whispers that the Bennsville Steel Company, which had obtained the contract for the bridge, had paid somebody fifty thousand dollars to see that their bid was accepted. A bid which was exactly fifty percent higher than the one put in by their rivals. "Do you know anything about somebody taking fifty thousand dollars to put this bid through?" demanded Sam Purdell wrathfully, when he heard about it; and Mr. Eisenfeld was shocked.

"That's a wicked idea, Sam," he protested. "Everyone knows this is the straightest administration Elmford ever had. Why, if I thought anybody was taking graft, I'd throw him out of the City Hall with my own hands."

There were similar cases, each of which brought Sam a little nearer to the brink of bitter disillusion. Sometimes he said that it was only the unshaken loyalty of his family which stopped him from resigning his thankless labours and leaving Elmford to wallow in its own ungrateful slime. But most of all it was the loyalty and encouragement of Mr. Eisenfeld. Mr. Eisenfeld was a suave sleek man with none of Sam Purdell's rubicund and open-faced geniality, but he had a cheerful courage in such trying moments which was always ready to renew Sam Purdell's faith in human nature. This cheerful courage shone with its old unfailing luminosity when Sam Purdell thrust the offending copy of the *Elmford News* which we have already referred to under Mr. Eisenfeld's aggrieved and incredulous eyes.

"I'll show you what you do about that sort of writing, Sam," said Mr. Eisenfeld magnificently. "You just take it like this—" He was going on to say that you tore it up, scattering the libellous fragments disdainfully to the four winds; but as he started to perform this heroic gesture his eye was arrested by the next paragraph in the same column, and he hesitated.

"Well, how do you take it?" asked the mayor peevishly.

Mr. Eisenfeld said nothing for a second and the mayor looked over his shoulder to see what he was reading. "Oh, that!" he said irritably. "I don't know what that means. Do you know what it means, Al?"

"That" was a postscript about which Mr. Purdell had some excuse to be puzzled. "We hear that the Saint is back in this country. People who remember what he did in New York a couple of years ago might feel like inviting him to take a trip out here. We can promise he would find plenty of material on which to exercise his talents."

"What Saint are they talkin' about?" asked the mayor. "I thought all the Saints was dead."

"This one isn't," said Mr. Eisenfeld; but for the moment the significance of the name continued to elude him. He had an idea that he had heard it before and that it should have meant something definite to him. "I think he was a crook who had a great run in New York a while back. No, I remember it now. Wasn't he a sort of free-lance reformer who had some crazy idea he could clean up the city and put everything to rights . . . ?"

He began to recall further details; and then as his memory improved he closed the subject abruptly. There were incidents among the stories that came filtering back into his recollection which gave him a vague discomfort in the pit of his stomach. It was ridiculous, of course—a cheap journalistic glorification of a common gangster; and yet, for some reason, certain stories which he remembered having read in the newspapers at the time made him feel that he would be happier if the Saint's visit to Elmford remained a theoretical proposition. "We got lots of other more important things to think about, Sam," he said abruptly, pushing the newspaper into the wastebasket. "Look here— about this monument of yours on the Elmford Riviera . . ."

The Elmford Riviera was the latest and most ambitious public work which the administration had undertaken up to that date. It was to be the crowning achievement in Sam Purdell's long list of benevolences towards his beloved citizens. A whole two miles of the riverbank had been acquired by the city and converted into a pleasure park which the sponsors of the scheme claimed would rival anything of its kind ever attempted in the state. At one end of it a beautiful casino had been erected where the citizens of Elmford might gorge themselves with food, deafen themselves with three orchestras and dance in tightly wedged ecstasy till feet gave way. At the other end was to be provided a children's playground, staffed with trained attendants, where the infants of Elmford might be left to bawl their heads off under the most expert and scientific supervision while their elders stopped to enjoy the adult amenities of the place. Behind the riverside drive, a concession had been arranged for an amusement park in which the populace could be shaken to pieces on roller coasters, whirled off revolving discs, thrown about in barrels, skittered over the falls and generally enjoy all the other elaborate forms of discomfort which help to make the modern seeker after relaxation so contemptuous of the unimaginative makeshift tortures which less enlightened souls had to get along with in medieval days. On the bank of the river itself, thousands of tons of sand had been imported to create an artificial beach where droves of holiday-makers could be herded together to blister and steam themselves into blissful imitations of the well-boiled prawn. It was, in fact, to be a place where Elmford might suffer all the horrors of Coney Island without the added torture of getting there. And in the centre of this Elysian esplanade there was to be a monument to the man whose unquenchable devotion to the community had presented it with this last and most delightful blessing.

Sam Purdell had been modestly diffident about the monument, but Mr. Eisenfeld had insisted on it. "You gotta have a monument, Sam," he had said. "The town owes it to you. Why, here you've been working for them all these years; and if you passed on tomorrow," said Mr. Eisenfeld, with his voice quivering at the mere thought of such a calamity, "what would there be to show for all you've done?"

"There's the Purdell Highway," said Sam deprecatingly, "the Purdell Suspension Bridge, the Purdell—"

"That's nothing," said Mr. Eisenfeld largely. "Those are just names. Why, in ten years after you die they won't mean any more than Grant or—or Pocahontas. What you oughta have is a monument of your own. Something with an inscription on it. I'll get the architect to design one."

The monument had duly been designed—a sort of square, tapering tower eighty feet high, crowned by an eagle with outspread wings, on the base of which was to be a great marble plaque on which the beneficence and public-spiritedness of Samuel Purdell would be recorded for all time. It was about the details of the construction of this monument that Mr. Eisenfeld had come to confer with the mayor. "The thing is, Sam," he explained, "if this monument is gonna last, we gotta make it solid. They got the outside all built up now; but they say if we're gonna do the job properly, we got to fill it up with cement."

"That'll take an awful lot of cement, Al," Sam objected dubiously, casting an eye over the plans; but Mr. Eisenfeld's generosity was not to be balked.

"Well, what if it does? If the job's worth doin' at all, it's worth doin' properly. If you won't think of yourself, think of the city. Why, if we let this thing stay hollow and after a year or two it began to fall down, think what people from out of town would say."

"What would they say?" asked Mr. Purdell obtusely.

His adviser shuddered. "They'd say this was such a cheap place we couldn't even afford to put up a decent monument for our mayor. You wouldn't like people to say a thing like that about us, would you, Sam?"

The mayor thought it over. "Okay, Al," he said at length. "Okay. But I don't deserve it, really I don't."

Simon Templar would have agreed that the mayor had done nothing to deserve any more elaborate monument than a neat tombstone in some quiet worm cafeteria. But at that moment his knowledge of Elmford's politics was not so complete as it was very shortly to become.

When he saw Molly Provost slip the little automatic out of her bag he thought that the bullet was destined for the mayor; and in theory he approved. He had an engaging callousness about the value of political lives which, if universally shared, would make democracy an enchantingly simple business. But there were two policemen on motorcycles waiting to escort the mayoral car into the city, and the life of a good-looking girl struck him as being a matter for more serious consideration. He felt that if she were really determined to solve all of Elmford's political problems by shooting the mayor in the duodenum, she should at least be persuaded to do it on some other occasion when she would have a better chance of getting away with it. Wherefore the Saint moved very quickly, so that his lean brown hand closed over hers just at the moment when she touched the trigger and turned the bullet down into the ground.

Neither Sam Purdell nor Al Eisenfeld, who were climbing into the car at that moment, even so much as looked around; and the motorcycle escort mercifully joined with them in instinctively attributing the detonation to the backfire of a passing truck.

It was such a small gun that the Saint's hand easily covered it; and he held the gun and her hand together in a viselike grip, smiling as if he were just greeting an old acquaintance, until the wail of the sirens died away. "Have you got a license to shoot mayors?" he inquired severely.

She had a small pale face which under a skillfully applied layer of cosmetics might have taken on a bright doll-like prettiness; but it was not like that yet. But he had a sudden illuminating vision of her face as it might have been, painted and powdered, with shaved eyebrows and blackened eyelashes, subtly hardened. It was a type which he had seen often enough before, which he could recognize at once. Some of them he had seen happily married, bringing up adoring families; others . . . For some reason the Saint thought that this girl ought not to be one of those others. Then he felt her arm go limp, and took the gun out of her unresisting hand. He put it away in his pocket. "Come for a walk," he said.

She shrugged dully. "All right."

He took her arm and led her down the block. Around the corner, out of sight of the mayor's house, he opened the door of the first of a line of parked cars. She got in resignedly. As he let in the clutch and the car slipped away under the pull of a smoothly whispering engine, she buried her face in her hands and sobbed silently.

The Saint let her have it out. He drove on thoughtfully, with a cigarette clipped between his lips, until the taller buildings of the business section rose up around them. In a quiet turning off one of the main streets of the town, he stopped the car outside a small restaurant and opened the door on her side to let her out. She dabbed her eyes and straightened her hat mechanically. As she looked around and realized where they were, she stopped with one foot on the running board. "What have you brought me here for?" she asked stupidly.

"For lunch," said the Saint calmly. "If you feel like eating. For a drink, if you don't. For a chat, anyhow."

She looked at him with fear and puzzlement still in her eyes. "You needn't do that," she said steadily. "You can take me straight to the police station. We might as well get it over with."

He shook his head. "Do you really want to go to a police station?" he drawled. "I'm not so fond of them myself, and usually they aren't very fond of me. Wouldn't you rather have a drink?"

Suddenly she realized that the smile with which he was looking down at her wasn't a bit like the grimly triumphant smile which a detective should have worn. Nor, when she looked more closely, was there anything else about him that quite matched her idea of what a detective would be like. It grieves the chronicler to record that her first impression was that he was too good-looking. But that was how she saw him. His tanned face was cut in a mould of rather reckless humour which didn't seem to fit in at all with the stodgy and prosaic backgrounds of the law. He was tall, and he looked strong—her right hand still ached from the steel grip of his fingers—but it was a supple kind of strength that had no connection with mere bulk. Also he wore his clothes with a gay and careless kind of elegance which no sober police chief could have approved. The twinkle in his eyes was wholly friendly. "Do you mean you didn't arrest me just now?" she asked uncertainly.

"I never arrested anybody in my life," said the Saint cheerfully. "In fact, when they shoot politicians I usually give them medals. Come on in and let's talk."

Over a couple of martinis he explained himself further. "My dear, I think it was an excellent scheme, on general principles. But the execution wasn't so good. When you've had as much experience in bumping people off as I have, you'll realize that it's no time to do it when a couple of cops are parked at the curb a few yards away. I suppose you realize that they would have got you just about ten seconds after you created a vacancy for a new mayor?"

She was still staring at him rather blankly. "I wasn't trying to do anything to the mayor," she said. "It was Al Eisenfeld I was going to shoot, and I wouldn't have cared if they did get me afterwards."

The Saint frowned. "You mean the seedy gigolo sort of bird who was with the mayor?"

She nodded. "He's the real boss of the town. The mayor is just a figurehead."

"Other people don't seem to think he's as dumb as he looks," Simon remarked.

"They don't know. There's nothing wrong with Purdell, but Eisenfeld—"

"Maybe you have inside information," said the Saint.

She looked at him over her clenched fists, dry-eyed and defiant. "If there were any justice in the world Al Eisenfeld would be executed."

The Saint raised his eyebrows and she read the thought in his mind and met it with cynical denial. "Oh no—not in that way. There's no murder charge that anyone could bring against him. You couldn't bring any legal evidence in any court of law that he'd ever done any physical harm to anyone that I ever heard of. But I know that he is a murderer. He murdered my father."

And the Saint waited without interruption. The story came tumbling out in a tangle of words that bit into his brain with a burden of meaning that was one of the most profound and illuminating surprises that he had known for some considerable time. It was so easy to talk to him that before long he knew nearly as much as she did herself. He was such an easy and understanding listener that somehow it never seemed strange to her until afterwards that she had been pouring out so much to a man she had known for less than an hour. Perhaps it was not such an extraordinary story as such stories go—perhaps many people would have shrugged it away as one of the commonplace trage-dies of a hard-boiled world. "This fellow Schmidt was a pal of Eisenfeld's. So they tried to make Dad lay off him. Dad wouldn't listen to them. He was police commissioner before this administration came in and he'd never listened to any politicians in his life. He always said that he went into the force as an honest man, and he was going to stay that way. So when they found they couldn't keep him quiet, they framed him. They made out that he was behind practically every racket in the town. They did it cleverly enough. Dad knew they'd got him. He knew the game too well to be able to kid himself. He was booked to be thrown out of the force in disgrace—probably sent to jail as well. How could he hope to clear himself? The evidence which he had collected against Schmidt was in the district attorney's office, but when Dad tried to bring that up they said that the safe had been burgled and it was gone. They even turned it around to make it look as if Dad had got rid of the evidence himself—the very thing he had told them he would never agree to do, so—I suppose he took the only way out that he could see. I suppose you'd say he was a coward to do it, but how could you ever know what he must have been suffering?"

"When was this?" asked the Saint quietly.

"Last night. He—shot himself. With his police gun. The shot woke me up. I—found him. I suppose I must have gone mad too. I haven't slept since then—how could I? This morning I made up my mind. I came out to do the only thing that was left. I didn't care what hap-pened to myself after that." She broke off helplessly. "Oh, I must have been crazy! But I couldn't think of anything else. Why should he be able to get away with it? Why should he?" she sobbed.

"Don't worry," said the Saint quietly. "He won't." He spoke with a quiet and matter-of-fact certainty which was more than a mere con-ventional encouragement. It made her look at him with a perplexity which she had been able to forget while he made her talk to him reawakening in her gaze. For the first time since they had sat down, it seemed, she was able to remember that she still knew nothing about him; that he was no more than a sympathetic stranger who had loomed up unheralded and unintroduced out of the fog which had still not completely cleared from her mind.

"Of course you aren't a detective," she said childishly. "I'd have recognized you if you were; but if you aren't, what are you?"

He smiled. "I'm the guy who gives all the detectives something to work for," he said. "I'm the source of more aches in the heads of the ungodly than I should like to boast about. I am Trouble, Incorporated —President Simon Templar, at your service. They call me the Saint."

"What does that mean?" she asked helplessly.

In the ordinary way Simon Templar, who had no spontaneous modesty bred into his composition, would have felt a slight twinge of disappointment that his reputation had not preceded him even to that out-of-the-way corner of the American continent; but he realized that there was no legitimate reason why she should have reacted more dramatically to the revelation of his identity, and for once he was not excessively discontented to remain unrecognized. There were practical disadvantages to the indulgence of this human weakness for publicity which, at that particular moment and in that particular town, he was prepared to do without. He shook his head with the same lazy grin that was so extraordinarily comforting and clear-sighted. "Nothing that you need worry about," he said. "Just write me down as a bloke who never could mind his own business, and give me some more of the inside dope about Al."

"There isn't a lot more to tell you," she said. "I think I've already given you almost everything I know."

"Doesn't anyone else in the town know it?"

"Hardly anybody. There are one or two people who guess how things really are, but if they tried to argue about it they'd only get laughed at. He's clever enough to have everybody believing that he's just Sam Purdell's mouthpiece; but it's the other way around. Sam Purdell really is dumb. He doesn't know what it's all about. He thinks of nothing but his highways and parks and bridges, and he honestly believes that he's only doing the best he can for the city. He doesn't get any graft out of it. Al gets all that; and he's clever enough to work it so that everybody thinks he's innocent and Sam Purdell is the really smart guy who's getting all the money out of it—even the board of aldermen think so. Dad used to talk to me about all his cases and he found out a lot about Eisenfeld while he was investigating this man Schmidt. He'd have gone after Eisenfeld himself next—if he'd been able to keep going. Perhaps Eisenfeld knew it and that made him more vicious."

"He didn't have any evidence against Eisenfeld?"

"Only a little. Hardly anything if you're talking about legal evidence, but he knew plenty of things he might have proven if he had been given time. That's how it is, anyway."

The Saint lighted a cigarette and gazed at her thoughtfully through a stream of smoke. "You understood a lot more than I did, Molly," he murmured. "But it's a great idea . . . And the more I think of it, the more I think you must be right."

He let his mind play around with the situation for a moment. Maybe he was too subtle himself, but there was something about that fundamental master stroke of Mr. Eisenfeld's cunning that appealed to his incorrigible sense of the artistry of corruption. To be the power behind the scenes while some lifelike figurehead stood up to receive the rotten eggs was just ordinary astuteness. But to choose for that figurehead a man who was so honest and stupid that it would take an earthquake to make him realize what was going on, and whose honest stupidity might appear to less simple-minded inquirers as an impudent disguise for double-dyed villainy—that indicated a quality of guile to which Simon Templar raised an appreciative hat. But his admiration of Mr. Eisenfeld's ingenuity was purely theoretical.

He made a note of the girl's address. "I'll keep the gun," he said before they parted. "You won't be needing it, and I shouldn't like you to lose your head again when I wasn't around to interfere." His blue eyes held her for a moment with quite confidence. "Al Eisenfeld is going to be dealt with—I promise you that."

It was one of his many mysteries that the fantastic promise failed to rouse her to utter incredulity. Afterwards she would be incredulous, after he had fulfilled the promise even more so; but while she listened at that moment there was a spell about him which made all miracles seem possible. "What can you do?" she asked, in the blind but indescribably inspiring belief that there must be some magic which he could achieve.

"I have my methods" said the Saint. "I stopped off here anyhow because I was interested in the stories I'd heard about this town, and we'll just call it lucky that I happened to be out trying to take a look at the mayor when you had your brainstorm. Just do one thing for me. Whatever happens, don't tell a living soul about this lunch. Forget that you ever met me or heard of me. Let me do the remembering."

Mr. Eisenfeld's memory was less retentive. When he came home a few nights later, he had completely forgotten the fleeting squirm of uneasiness which the reference to the Saint in the *Elmford News* had given him. He had almost as completely forgotten his late police commissioner; although when he did remember him, it was with a feeling of pleasant satisfaction that he had been so easily got rid of. Already he had selected another occupant for that conveniently vacated office, who he was assured would prove more amenable to reason. And that night he was expecting another visitor whose mission would give him an almost equal satisfaction.

The visitor arrived punctually, and was hospitably received with a highball and a cigar. After a brief exchange of cordial commonplaces, the visitor produced a bulging wallet and slid it casually across the table. In the same casual manner Mr. Eisenfeld picked it up, inspected the contents and slipped it into his pocket. After which the two men refilled their glasses and smoked for a while in companionable silence. "We got the last of that cement delivered yesterday," remarked the visitor, in the same way that he might have bridged a conversational hiatus with some bromidic comment on the weather.

Mr. Eisenfeld nodded. "Yeah, I saw it. They got the monument about one quarter full already—I was by there this afternoon."

Mr. Schmidt gazed vacantly at the ceiling. "Any time you've got any other job like that, we'll still be making good cement," he said, with the same studied casualness. "You know we always like to look after anyone who can put a bit of business our way."

"Sure, I'll remember it," said Mr. Eisenfeld amiably.

Mr. Schmidt fingered his chin. "Too bad about Provost, wasn't it?" he remarked.

"Yeah," agreed Mr. Eisenfeld, "too bad."

Half an hour later he escorted his guest out to his car. The light over the porch had gone out when he returned to the house, and without giving it any serious thought he attributed the failure to a blown fuse or a faulty bulb. He was in too good a humour to be annoyed by it; and he was actually humming complacently to himself as he groped his way up the dark steps. The light in the hall had gone out as well, and he frowned faintly over the idle deduction that it must have been a fuse. He pushed through the door and turned to close it; and then a hand clamped over his mouth, and something hard and uncongenial pressed into the small of his back. A gentle voice spoke chillingly in his ear. "Just one word"—it whispered invitingly—"just one word out of you, Al, and your life is going to be even shorter than I expected."

Mr. Eisenfeld stood still, with his muscles rigid. He was not a physical coward but the grip which held his head pressed back against the chest of the unknown man behind him had a firm competence which announced that there were adequate sinews behind it to back up its persuasion in any hand-to-hand struggle. Also, the object which prodded into the middle of his spine constituted an argument in itself which he was wise enough to understand. The clasp on his mouth relaxed tentatively and slid down to rest lightly on his throat. The same gentle voice breathed again on his right eardrum. "Let us go out into the great open spaces and look at the night," said the Saint.

Mr. Eisenfeld allowed himself to be conducted back down the walk over which he had just returned. He had very little choice in the matter. The gun of the uninvited guest remained glued to his backbone as if it intended to take root there, and he knew that the fingers which rested so caressingly on his windpipe would have detected the first shout he tried to utter before it could reach his vocal cords. A few yards down the road a car waited with its lights burning. They stopped beside it. "Open the door and get in."

Mr. Eisenfeld obeyed. The gun slipped round from his back to his left side as his escort followed him into the seat behind the wheel. Simon started the engine and reached over to slip the gear lever into first. The headlights were switched on as they moved away from the curb; and Mr. Eisenfeld found his first opportunity of giving vent to the emotions that were chasing themselves through his system. "What the hell's the idea of this?" he demanded violently.

"We're going for a little drive, dear old bird," answered the Saint. "But I promise you won't have to walk home. My intentions are more honourable than anyone like you could easily imagine."

"If you're trying to kidnap me," Eisenfeld blustered, "I'm telling you you can't get away with it. I'll see that you get what's coming to you! Why, you . . ."

Simon let him make his speech without interruption. The lights of the residential section twinkled steadily past them, and presently even

Eisenfeld's flood of outraged eloquence dwindled away before that impenetrable calm. They drove on over the practically deserted roads —it was after midnight, and there were very few attractions in that area to induce the pious citizens of Elmford to lose their beauty sleep —and presently Mr. Eisenfeld realized that their route would take them past the site of the almost completed Elmford Riviera on the bank of the river above the town.

He was right in his deduction, except for the word "past." As a matter of fact, the car jolted off the main highway onto the unfinished road which led down to Elmford's playground; and exactly in the middle of the two-mile esplanade, under the very shadow of the central monument which Sam Purdell had been so modestly unwilling to accept, it stopped. "This is as far as we go," said the Saint, and motioned politely to the door.

Mr. Eisenfeld got out. He was sweating a little with perfectly natural fear, and above that there was a growing cloud of mystification through which he was trying to discover some coherent design in the extraordinary series of events which had enveloped him in those last few minutes. He seemed to be caught up in the machinery of some hideous nightmare, in which the horror was intensified by the fact that he could find no reason in the way it moved. If he was indeed the victim of an attempt at kidnapping, he couldn't understand why he should have been brought to a place like that; but just then there was no other explanation that he could see.

The spidery lines of scaffolding on the monument rose up in a futuristic filigree over his head, and at the top of it the shadowy outlines of the chute where the cement was mixed and poured into the hollow mould of stone roosted like a grotesque and angular prehistoric bird. "Now we'll climb up and look at the view," said the Saint.

Still wondering, Mr. Eisenfeld felt himself steered towards a ladder which ran up one side of the scaffolding. He climbed mechanically, as he was ordered, while a stream of unanswerable questions drummed bewilderingly through his brain. Once the wild idea came to him to kick downwards at the head of the man who followed him; but when he looked down he saw that the head was several rungs below his feet, keeping a safely measured distance, and when he stopped climbing, the man behind him stopped also. Eisenfeld went on, up through the dark. He could have shouted then, but he knew that he was a mile or more from the nearest person who might have heard him.

They came out on the plank staging which ran around the top of the monument. A moment later, as he looked back, he saw the silhouette of his unaccountable kidnapper rising up against the dimly luminous background of stars and reaching the platform to lean lazily against one of the ragged ends of scaffold pole which rose above the narrow catwalk. Behind him, the hollow shaft of the monument was a square void of deeper blackness in the surrounding dark. "This is the end of your journey, Al," said the stranger softly. "But before you go, there are just one or two things I'd like to remind you about. Also, we haven't been properly introduced, which is probably making things rather difficult for you. You had better know me . . . I am the Saint."

Eisenfeld started and almost overbalanced. Where had he heard that name before? Suddenly he remembered, and an uncanny chill crawled over his flesh.

"There are various reasons why it doesn't seem necessary for you to go on living," went on that very gentle and dispassionate voice, "and your ugly face is only one of them. This is a pretty cockeyed world when you take it all round, but people like you don't improve it. Also, I have heard a story from a girl called Molly Provost—her father was police commissioner until Tuesday night, I believe."

"She's a liar," gasped Eisenfeld hoarsely. "You're crazy! Listen—"

He would have sworn that the stranger had never touched him except with his gun since they got into the car, but suddenly an electric flashlight spilled a tiny strip of luminance over the boards between them, and in the bright centre of the beam he saw the other's hand running through the contents of a wallet which looked somehow familiar. All at once Eisenfeld recognized it and clutched unbelievingly at his pocket. The wallet which his guest had given him an hour ago was gone; and Eisenfeld's heart almost stopped beating. "What are you doing with that?" he croaked.

"Just seeing how much this installment of graft is worth," answered the Saint calmly. "And it looks exactly like thirty thousand dollars to me. Well, it might have been more, but I suppose it will have to do. I promised Molly that I'd see she was looked after, but I don't see why it shouldn't be at your expense. Part of this is your commission for getting this cenotaph filled with cement, isn't it? . . . It seems very appropriate."

Eisenfeld's throat constricted, and the blood began to pound in his temples. "I'll get you for this," he snarled. "You lousy crook."

"Maybe I am a crook," said the Saint, in a voice that was no more than a breath of sound in the still night. "But in between times I'm something more. In my simple way I am a kind of justice . . . do you know any good reason why you should wait any longer for what you deserve?"

There is a time in every man's life when he knows beyond doubt or common fear that the threads of destiny are running out. It had happened to Al Eisenfeld too suddenly for him to understand—he had no time to look back and count the incredible minutes in which his world had been turned upside down. Perhaps he himself had no clear idea what he was doing, but he knew that he was hearing death in the quiet voice that spoke out of the darkness in front of him. His muscles carried him away without any conscious command from his brain, and he was unaware of the queer growling cry that rattled in his throat. There was a crash of sound in front of him as he sprang blindly forward, and a tongue of reddish-orange flame spat out of the darkness almost in his face . . .

Simon Templar steadied himself on one of the scaffold poles and stared down into the square black mould of the monument; but there was nothing that he could see, and the silence was unbroken. After a while his fingers let go the gun, and a couple of seconds later the thud of its burying itself in the wet cement at the bottom of the shaft echoed hollowly back to him. Presently he climbed up to the chute from which the monument was being filled. He found a great mound of sacks of cement stacked beside it ready for use, and, after a little more search, a hose conveniently arranged to provide water. He was busy for three hours before he decided that he had done enough.

"And knowing that these thoughts are beating in all our hearts," boomed the voice of the Distinguished Personage through eight loudspeakers, "it will always be my proudest memory that I was deemed worthy of the honour of unveiling this eternal testimonial to the man who has devoted his life to the task of making the people of Elmford proud and happy in their great city—the mayor whom you all know and love so well, Sam Purdell!"

The flag which covered the carved inscription on the base of the Purdell memorial fluttered down. A burst of well-organized cheering volleyed from five thousand throats. The cameramen dashed forward with clicking shutters. The bandmaster raised his baton. The brass and woodwinds inflated their lungs. A small urchin close to the platform swallowed a piece of chewing gum, choked, and began to cry . . . the strains of "The Star-Spangled Banner" blasted throbbingly through the afternoon air.

Then, to the accompaniment of a fresh howl of cheering, Sam Purdell stepped to the microphone. He wiped his eyes and swallowed once or twice before he spoke. "My friends," he said, "this is not a time when I would ask you to listen to a speech. There ain't—isn't anything I can think of worthy of this honour you have done me. I can only repeat the promise which you have all heard me make before— that while I am mayor of this city there will be only one principle in everything over which I have control: Honesty and a square deal for every man, woman and child in Elmford."

The cheers followed his car as he drove away accompanied by his round perspiring wife and his round perspiring daughters. Mrs. Purdell clutched his hand in a warm moist grip. "That was such a beautiful speech you made, Sam," she said a little tearfully.

Sam Purdell shook his head. He had one secret sorrow. "I wish Al could have been there," he said.

"A Madman" is a neat little exercise in morbid psychology by MAURICE LEVEL *(1875–1928), author of many memorable* contes cruelles. *For more than fifty years, the few biographical facts about this masterful and unjustly obscure writer have been drawn from the introduction to the rare English collection of his short stories,* Tales of Mystery and Horror, *published in 1920 by Robert M. McBride and Co. According to it, Level was a sportsman, surgeon, and a patriot who was made a Chevalier of the Legion of Honour for his services in the First World War. But recently, while I was in Washington, D.C., I found a surprising entry in the Library of Congress Card Catalog that unequivocally stated that "Maurice Level" was the pseudonym of one Jeanne Mareteux-Level. Was this great French horror writer actually a woman? (For further comment, see Appendix I, page 575.)*

A Madman

BY MAURICE LEVEL

He was neither wicked nor cruel, but he hungered for the unexpected. The theatre did not interest him, yet he attended often, hoping for the outbreak of a fire. He went to the fair at Neuilly to see if perhaps one of the menagerie animals might go wild and mangle its trainer. Once he even visited the bullring, but its calculated bloodshed was mundane, too controlled. Meaningless suffering revolted him; he craved the thrill of sudden catastrophe.

Then, after ten years of waiting, fire indeed ravaged the Opera Comique one night when he was there. He escaped uninjured, but soon afterwards he saw the celebrated lion-tamer Frederick torn to pieces by his cats. The madman was only a few feet away from the cage when it happened. He lost interest in wild beast shows and the theatre and fell into a deep depression.

But then one morning he saw a garish poster, one of many that covered the walls of Paris. Against a blue background, a peculiar slanted track descended, curled itself into a circular loop and then plummeted straight down. The top of the billboard depicted a tiny cyclist about to dare the dangerous route.

The newspapers ran a story explaining that the cyclist intended to ride down just such a track. "When I reach the loop," he told report-

ers, "you'll actually see me round it *upside down!*" The press was
invited to inspect the track and the bicycle. "I use no mechanical
trickery," the daredevil bragged, "nothing but precise scientific calcu-
lation. That—and my ability to keep up my nerve."

When the madman read the article, his good spirits returned. He
immediately went to buy a ticket. He did not want his attention distracted when the rider looped the loop, so he purchased an entire box
of seats opposite the track and sat alone on opening night. After a
suspenseful wait, the cyclist appeared high above the audience at the
top of the ribbon of road. A moment of tense anticipation, then down
he sped. As promised, he circled the loop with head underneath and
feet in the air—and then it was all over.

The performance certainly thrilled the madman, but as he exited
with the crowd, he knew he might experience the same intense sensation once or twice more and then, as always, the novelty would die.
Still . . . bicycles break, road surfaces wear out . . . and no man's
nerve holds out forever. Sooner or later, there must be an accident.

The cyclist was scheduled to perform for three months in Paris and
then tour the provinces. The madman decided to go to every single
performance, even if he had to follow the show on its travels. He
bought the same box for the entire Parisian run and sat in the same
seat night after night.

One evening two months later, the performance had just ended and
the madman was on his way out when he noticed the performer standing in one of the corridors of the auditorium. He walked up to him,
but before he could utter a word, the cyclist greeted him affably.

"I know you. You come to my show every night."

"That's true. Your remarkable feat fascinates me. But who told you
I'm always here?"

"No one," the rider smiled. "I see you myself."

"But how can you, so high up? At such a moment, are you actually
able to study the audience?"

The cyclist laughed. "Hardly. It'd be dangerous for me to look at a
crowd shifting around and prattling. But confidentially, there's a little
trick involved in what I do."

"A trick?" The madman was surprised and dismayed.

"No, no, I don't mean a hoax. But there's something I do which the
public is unaware of." The cyclist winked. "This'll be our little secret,
yes? When I mount my bicycle and grasp the handlebars, I never

worry about my own strength and coordination, but the total concentration the ride demands concerns me. It's almost impossible for me to empty my mind of all but one idea. My greatest danger is that my eyes may stray. But here's my trick—I find one spot in the auditorium and focus all my attention on it. The first time I rode in this hall, I spied you in your box and chose you as my spot. The next evening, there you were again . . ."

The madman sat in his customary seat. The usual excited buzz filled the hall. A hush fell when the rider made his entrance, a black speck far overhead. Two men held his bicycle. The cyclist gripped the handlebars, stared out over the heads of the crowd and shouted the signal. The men gave the machine a shove.

At that instant, the madman rose and walked to the opposite side of his box. The audience screamed as cycle and rider shot off the track and plunged into the midst of the crowd.

The madman donned his coat, smoothed his hat against one sleeve and departed.

—*English adaptation by Marvin Kaye*

One of America's earliest science-fiction writers was EDWARD PAGE MITCHELL *(1852–1927), an American journalist who from 1903 until the year of his death edited the New York* Sun, *an illustrious newspaper founded by Alexander Hamilton that later became the New York* Post. *Mitchell's imaginative fiction included an occasional foray into fantasy, such as this parodistic but still unsettling example originally published anonymously in the January 27, 1878, issue of the newspaper he was later to run.*

The Devilish Rat
BY EDWARD PAGE MITCHELL

You know that when a man lives in a deserted castle on the top of a great mountain by the side of the river Rhine, he is liable to misrepresentation. Half the good people of the village of Schwinkenschwank, including the burgomaster and the burgomaster's nephew, believed that I was a fugitive from American justice.

The other half were just as firmly convinced that I was crazy, and this theory had the support of the notary's profound knowledge of human character and acute logic.

The two halves to the interesting controversy were so equally matched that they spent all their time in confronting each other's arguments, and I was left, happily, pretty much to myself.

As everybody with the slightest pretension to cosmopolitan knowledge is already aware, the old Schloss Schwinkenschwank is haunted by the ghosts of twenty-nine mediaeval barons and baronesses. The behavior of these ancient spectres was very considerate. They annoyed me, on the whole, far less than the rats, which swarmed in great numbers in every part of the castle.

When I first took possession of my quarters, I was obliged to keep a lantern burning all night, and continually to beat about me with a wooden club in order to escape the fate of Bishop Hatto. Afterward I sent to Frankfort and had made for me a wire cage in which I was able to sleep with comfort and safety as soon as I became accustomed to the sharp gritting of the rats' teeth as they gnawed the iron in their impotent attempts to get in and eat me.

Barring the spectres and the rats, and now and then a transient bat or owl, I was the first tenant of the Schloss Schwinkenschwank for three or four centuries.

After leaving Bonn, where I had greatly profited by the learned and ingenious lectures of the famous Calcarius, Herr Professor of Metaphysical Science in that admirable university, I had selected this ruin as the best possible place for the trial of a certain experiment in psychology.

The Hereditary Landgraf, von Toplitz, who owned Schloss Schwinkenschwank, showed no signs of surprise when I went to him and offered six thalers a month for the privilege of lodging in his ramshackle castle. The clerk of a hotel could not have taken my application more coolly or my money in a more business-like spirit.

"It will be necessary to pay the first month's rent in advance," said he.

"That I am fortunately prepared to do, my well-born Hereditary Landgraf," I replied, counting out six thalers. He pocketed them, and gave me a receipt for the same. I wondered whether he ever tried to collect rent from his ghosts.

The most inhabitable room in the castle was that in the northwest tower, but it was already occupied by the Lady Adelaide Maria, eldest daughter of the Baron von Schotten, who was starved to death in the thirteenth century by her affectionate papa for refusing to wed a one-legged freebooter from over the river.

As I could not think of intruding upon a lady, I took up my quarters at the head of the south turret stairway, where there was nobody in possession except a sentimental monk, who was out a good deal nights and gave me no trouble at any time.

In such calm seclusion as I enjoyed in the Schloss it is possible to reduce physical and mental activity to the lowest degree consistent with life. Saint Pedro of Alcantara, who passed forty years in a convent cell, schooled himself to sleep only an hour and a half a day, and to take food but once in three days.

While diminishing the functions of his body to such an extent, he must also, I firmly believe, have reduced his soul almost to the negative character of an unconscious infant's. It is exercise, thought, friction, activity, that brings out the individuality of a man's nature. Prof. Calcarius's pregnant words remained burned into my memory:

"What is the mysterious link that binds soul to the living body? Why am I Calcarius, or rather why does the soul called Calcarius inhabit this particular organism? (Here the learned professor slapped his enormous thigh with his pudgy hand.) Might not I as easily be another, and might not another be I? Loosen the individualized Ego from the fleshy surroundings to which it coheres by force of habit and by reason of long contact, and who shall say that it may not be expelled by an act of volition, leaving the living body receptive, to be occupied by some non-individualized Ego, worthier and better than the old?"

This profound suggestion made a lasting impression upon my mind. While perfectly satisfied with my body, which is sound, healthy, and reasonably beautiful, I had long been discontented with my soul, and constant contemplation of its weakness, its grossness, its inadequacy, had intensified discontentment to disgust.

Could I but escape myself, could I but tear this paste diamond from its fine casket and replace it with a genuine jewel, what sacrifices would I not consent to, and how fervently would I bless Calcarius and the hour that took me to Bonn!

It was to try this untried experiment that I shut myself up in the Schloss Schwinkenschwank.

Excepting little Hans, the innkeeper's son, who climbed the mountain three times a week from the village to bring me bread and cheese and white wine, and afterward Hans' sister, my only visitor during the period of my retirement was Professor Calcarius. He came over from Bonn twice to cheer and encourage me.

On the occasion of his first visit night fell while we were still talking of Pythagoras and metempsychosis. The profound metaphysicist was a corpulent man and very short-sighted.

"I can never get down the hill alive," he cried, wringing his hands anxiously. "I should stumble, and, Gott im Himmel, precipitate myself peradventure upon some jagged rock."

"You must stay all night, Professor," said I, "and sleep with me in my wire cage. I should like you to meet my room mate, the monk."

"Subjective entirely, my dear young friend," he said. "Your apparition is a creature of the optic nerve and I shall contemplate it without alarm, as becomes a philosopher."

I put my Herr Professor to bed in the wire cage and with extreme difficulty crowded myself in by his side. At his especial request I left the lantern burning. "Not that I have any apprehension of your subjective spectres," he explained. "Mere figments of the brain they are. But in the dark I might roll over and crush you."

"How progresses the self-suppression?" he asked at length—"the subordination of the individual soul? Eh! What was that?"

"A rat, trying to get in at us," I replied. "Be calm: you are in no peril. My experiment proceeds satisfactorily. I have quite eliminated all interest in the outside world. Love, gratitude, friendship, care for my own welfare and the welfare of my friends have nearly disappeared. Soon, I hope, memory will also fade away, and with my memory my individual past."

"You are doing splendidly!" he exclaimed with enthusiasm, "and rendering to psychologic science an inestimable service. Soon your psychic nature will be a blank, a vacuum, ready to receive—God preserve me! What was that?"

"Only the screech of an owl," said I, reassuringly, as the great grey bird with which I had become familiar fluttered noisily down through an aperture in the roof and lit upon the top of our wire cage.

Calcarius regarded the owl with interest, and the owl blinked gravely at Calcarius.

"Who knows," said the Herr Professor, "but what that owl is animated by the soul of some great dead philosopher? Perhaps Pythagoras, perhaps Plotinus, perhaps the spirit of Socrates himself, abides temporarily beneath those feathers."

I confessed that some such idea had already occurred to me.

"And in that case," continued the Professor, "you have only to negate your own nature, to nullify your own individuality, in order to receive into your body this great soul, which, as my intuitions tell me, is that of Socrates, and is hovering around your physical organization, hoping to effect an entrance. Persist, my worthy young student, in your most laudable experiment, and metaphysical science—Merciful Heaven! Is that the devil?"

It was the huge gray rat, my nightly visitor. This hideous creature had grown in his life, perhaps of a century, to the size of a small terrier. His whiskers were perfectly white and very thick. His immense tusks had become so long that they curved over till the points almost impaled his skull. His eyes were big and blood red. The corners of his upper lip were so shrivelled and drawn up that his countenance wore an expression of diabolical malignity, rarely seen except in some human faces.

He was too old and knowing to gnaw at the wires; but he sat outside on his haunches, and gazed in at us with an indescribable look of hatred. My companion shivered. After a while the rat turned away, rattled his callous tail across the wire netting, and disappeared in the darkness. Professor Calcarius breathed a deep sigh of relief, and soon was snoring so profoundly that neither owls, rats, nor spectres ventured near us till morning.

I had so far succeeded in merging my intellectual and moral qualities in the routine of mere animal existence that when it was time for Calcarius to come again, as he had promised, I felt little interest in his approaching visit. Hansel, who constituted my commissariat, had been taken sick of the measles, and I was dependent for my food and wine upon the coming of his pretty sister Emma, a flaxen-haired maiden of eighteen, who climbed the steep path with the grace and agility of a gazelle.

She was an artless little thing, and told me of her own accord the story of her simple love. Fritz was a soldier in the Emperor Wilhelm's army. He was now in garrison at Cologne. They hoped that he would soon get a lieutenancy, for he was brave and faithful, and then he would come home and marry her.

She had saved up her dairy money till it amounted to quite a little purse, which she had sent him that it might help purchase his commission. Had I ever seen Fritz? No? He was handsome and good, and she loved him more than she could tell.

I listened to this prattle with the same amount of romantic interest that a proposition in Euclid would excite, and congratulated myself that my old soul had so nearly disappeared.

Every night the gray owl perched above me. I knew that Socrates was waiting to take possession of my body, and I yearned to open my bosom and receive that grand soul.

Every night the detestable rat came and peered through the wires. His cool, contemptuous malice exasperated me strangely. I longed to reach out from beneath my cage and seize and throttle him, but I was afraid of the venom of his bite.

My own soul had by this time nearly wasted away through disciplined disuse. The owl looked down lovingly at me with his great placid eyes. A noble spirit seemed to shine through them and to say, "I will come when you are ready." And I would look back into their lustrous depths and exclaim with infinite yearning, "Come soon O Socrates, for I am almost ready!"

Then I would turn and meet the devilish gaze of the monstrous rat, whose sneering malevolence dragged me back to earth and to earth's concerns.

My detestation of the abominable beast was the sole lingering trace of the old nature. When he was not by, my soul seemed to hover around and above my body, ready to take wing and leave it free forever. At his appearance, an unconquerable disgust and loathing undid in a second all that had been accomplished, and I was still myself. To succeed in my experiment I felt that the hateful creature whose presence barred out the grand old philosopher's soul must be dispatched at any cost of sacrifice or danger.

"I will kill you, you loathsome animal!" I shouted to the rat, "and then to my emancipated body will come the soul of Socrates which awaits me yonder."

The rat turned on me his leering eyes and grinned more sardonically than ever. His scorn was more than I could bear. I threw up the side of the wire cage and clutched desperately at my enemy.

I caught him by the tail. I drew him close to me. I crunched the bones of his slimy legs, felt blindly for his head, and when I got both hands to his neck, fastened upon his life with a terrible grip.

With all the strength at my command, and with all the recklessness of a desperate purpose, I tore and twisted the flesh of my loathsome victim. He gasped, uttered a horrible cry of wild pain, and at last lay limp and quiet in my clutch. Hate was satisfied, my last passion was at an end, and I was free to welcome Socrates.

When I awoke from a long and dreamless sleep, the events of the night before and, indeed, of my whole previous life were as the dimly remembered incidents in a story read years ago.

The owl was gone but the mangled corpse of the rat lay by my side. Even in death his face wore its horrible grin. It now looked like a Satanic smile of triumph.

I arose and shook off my drowsiness. A new life seemed to tingle in my veins. I was no longer indifferent and negative. I took a lively interest in my surroundings and wanted to be out in the world among men, to plunge into affairs and exult in action.

Pretty Emma came up the hill bringing her basket. "I am going to leave you," said I. "I shall seek better quarters than the Schloss Schwinkenschwank."

"And shall you go to Cologne," she eagerly asked; "to the garrison where the emperor's soldiers are?"

"Perhaps so—on my way to the world."

"And will you go for me to Fritz?" she continued, blushing. "I have good news to send him. His uncle, the mean old notary, died last night. Fritz now has a small fortune and he must come home to me at once."

"The notary," said I slowly, "died last night?"

"Yes sir; and they say he is black in the face this morning. But it is good news for Fritz and me."

"Perhaps," continued I, still more slowly—"perhaps Fritz would not believe me. I am a stranger, and men who know the world, like your young soldier, are given to suspicion."

"Carry this ring," she quickly replied, taking from her finger a worthless trinket. "Fritz gave it to me and he will know by it that I trust you."

My next visitor was the learned Calcarius. He was quite out of breath when he reached the apartment I was preparing to leave.

"How goes our metempsychosis, my worthy pupil?" he asked. "I arrived last evening from Bonn, but rather than spend another night with your horrible rodents, I submitted my purse to the extortion of the village innkeeper. The rogue swindled me," he continued taking out his purse and counting over a small treasure of silver. "He charged me forty groschen for a bed and breakfast."

The sight of the silver, and the sweet clink of the pieces as they came in contact in Professor Calcarius's palm, thrilled my new soul with an emotion it had not yet experienced.

Silver seemed the brightest thing in the world to me at that moment, and the acquisition of silver, by whatever means, the noblest exercise of human energy. With a sudden impulse that I was unable to resist, I sprang upon my friend and instructor and wrenched the purse from his hands. He uttered a cry of surprise and dismay.

"Cry away!" I shouted; "it will do no good. Your miserly screams will be heard only by rats and owls and ghosts. The money is mine."

"What's this?" he exclaimed. "You rob your guest, your friend, your guide and mentor in the sublime walks of metaphysical science? What perfidy has taken possession of your soul?"

I seized the Herr Professor by the legs and threw him violently to the floor. He struggled as the grey rat had struggled. I tore pieces of wire from my cage, and bound him hand and foot so tightly that the wire cut deep into his fat flesh.

"Ho! Ho!" said I, standing over him; "what a feast for the rats your corpulent carcass will make," and I turned to go.

"Good Gott!" he cried. "You do not intend to leave me: no one ever comes here."

"All the better," I replied, gritting my teeth and shaking my fist in his face; "the rats will have uninterrupted opportunity to relieve you of your superfluous flesh. Oh, they are very hungry, I assure you, Herr Metaphysician, and they will speedily help you to sever the mysterious link that binds soul to living body. They will know how to loosen the individualized Ego from the fleshly surroundings. I congratulate you on the prospect of a rare experiment."

The cries of Professor Calcarius grew fainter and fainter as I made my way down the hill. Once out of hearing I stopped to count my gains. Over and over again, with extraordinary joy, I told the thalers in his purse, and always with the same result. There were just thirty pieces of silver.

My way into the world of barter and profit led me through Cologne. At the barracks I sought out Fritz Schneider of Schwinkenschwank.

"My friend," said I, putting my hand upon his shoulder, "I am going to do you the greatest service which one man may do another. You love little Emma the inkeeper's daughter?"

"I do indeed," he said. "You bring news of her?"

"I have just now torn myself away from her too ardent embrace."

"It is a lie!" he shouted. "The little girl is as true as gold."

"She is as false as the metal in this trinket," said I with composure, tossing him Emma's ring. "She gave it to me yesterday when we parted."

He looked at the ring, and then put both hands to his forehead. "It is true," he groaned. "Our bethrothal ring!" I watched his anguish with philosophical interest.

"See here," he continued, taking a neatly knitted purse from his bosom. "Here is the money she sent to help me buy promotion. Perhaps that belongs to you?"

"Quite likely," I replied, very coolly. "The pieces have a strangely familiar look."

Without another word the soldier flung the purse at my feet and turned away. I heard him sobbing, and the sound was music. Then I picked up the purse and hastened to the nearest cafe to count the silver.

There were just thirty pieces again.

To acquire silver, that is the chief joy possible to my new nature. It is a glorious pleasure, is it not? How fortunate that the soul, which took possession of my body in the Schloss, was not Socrates's, which would have made me, at best, a dismal ruminator like Calcarius; but the soul that had dwelt in the grey rat till I strangled him.

At one time I thought that my new soul came to me from the dead notary in the village. I know, now, that I inherited it from the rat, and I believe it to be the soul that once animated Judas Iscariot, that prince of men of action.

Rokuro-Kubi

BY LAFCADIO HEARN

Nearly five hundred years ago there was a samurai, named Isogai Héïdazaëmon Takétsura, in the service of the Lord Kikuji, of Kyūshū. This Isogai had inherited, from many warlike ancestors, a natural aptitude for military exercises, and extraordinary strength. While yet a boy he had surpassed his teachers in the art of swordsmanship, in archery, and in the use of the spear, and had displayed all the capacities of a daring and skillful soldier. Afterwards, in the time of the Eikyō[1] war, he so distinguished himself that high honors were bestowed upon him. But when the house of Kikuji came to ruin, Isogai found himself without a master. He might then easily have obtained service under another daimyō; but as he had never sought distinction for his own sake alone, and as his heart remained true to his former lord, he preferred to give up the world. So he cut off his hair, and became a traveling priest, taking the Buddhist name of Kwairyō.

But always, under the *koromo*[2] of the priest, Kwairyō kept warm within him the heart of the samurai. As in other years he had laughed at peril, so now also he scorned danger; and in all weathers and all seasons he journeyed to preach the good Law in places where no other priest would have dared to go. For that age was an age of violence and disorder; and upon the highways there was no security for the solitary traveler, even if he happened to be a priest.

In the course of his first long journey, Kwairyō had occasion to visit the province of Kai. One evening, as he was traveling through the

1. The period of Eikyō lasted from 1429 to 1441.
2. The upper robe of a Buddhist priest is thus called.

mountains of that province, darkness overtook him in a very lonesome district, leagues away from any village. So he resigned himself to pass the night under the stars; and having found a suitable grassy spot by the roadside, he lay down there, and prepared to sleep. He had always welcomed discomfort; and even a bare rock was for him a good bed, when nothing better could be found, and the root of a pine-tree an excellent pillow. His body was iron; and he never troubled himself about dews or rain or frost or snow.

Scarcely had he lain down when a man came along the road, carrying an axe and a great bundle of chopped wood. This woodcutter halted on seeing Kwairyō lying down, and, after a moment of silent observation, said to him in a tone of great surprise:

"What kind of a man can you be, good Sir, that you dare to lie down alone in such a place as this? . . . there are haunters about here, many of them. Are you not afraid of Hairy Things?"

"My friend," cheerfully answered Kwairyō, "I am only a wandering priest, a 'Cloud-and-Water-Guest,' as folks call it: *Un-sui-no-ryokaku.* And I am not in the least afraid of Hairy Things, if you mean goblin-foxes, or goblin-badgers, or any creatures of that kind. As for lonesome places, I like them: they are suitable for meditation. I am accustomed to sleeping in the open air: and I have learned never to be anxious about my life."

"You must be indeed a brave man, Sir Priest," the peasant responded, "to lie down here! This place has a bad name—a very bad name. But, as the proverb has it, *Kunshi ayayuki ni chikayorazu* ['The superior man does not needlessly expose himself to peril']; and I must assure you, Sir, that it is very dangerous to sleep here. Therefore, although my house is only a wretched thatched hut, let me beg of you to come home with me at once. In the way of food, I have nothing to offer you; but there is a roof at least, and you can sleep under it without risk."

He spoke earnestly; and Kwairyō, liking the kindly tone of the man, accepted this modest offer. The woodcutter guided him along a narrow path, leading up from the main road through mountain-forest. It was a rough and dangerous path—sometimes skirting precipices—sometimes offering nothing but a network of slippery roots for the foot to rest upon—sometimes winding over or between masses of jagged rock. But at last Kwairyō found himself upon a cleared space at the top of a hill, with a full moon shining overhead; and he saw before him a small thatched cottage, cheerfully lighted from within. The wood-cutter led him to a shed at the back of the house, whither water had been conducted, through bamboo-pipes, from some neighboring stream; and the two men washed their feet. Beyond the shed was a vegetable garden, and a grove of cedars and bamboos; and beyond the trees appeared the glimmer of a cascade, pouring from some loftier height, and swaying in the moonshine like a long white robe.

As Kwairyō entered the cottage with his guide, he perceived four persons—men and women—warming their hands at a little fire kindled in the *ro*[3] of the principal apartment. They bowed low to the priest, and greeted him in the most respectful manner. Kwairyō wondered that persons so poor, and dwelling in such a solitude, should be aware of the polite forms of greeting. "These are good people," he thought to himself; "and they must have been taught by some one well acquainted with the rules of propriety." Then turning to his host—the *aruji,* or house-master, as the others called him—Kwairyō said:

"From the kindness of your speech, and from the very polite welcome given me by your household, I imagine that you have not always been a woodcutter. Perhaps you formerly belonged to one of the upper classes?"

Smiling, the woodcutter answered:

"Sir, you are not mistaken. Though now living as you find me, I was once a person of some distinction. My story is the story of a ruined life —ruined by my own fault. I used to be in the service of a daimyō; and my rank in that service was not inconsiderable. But I loved women and wine too well; and under the influence of passion I acted wickedly. My selfishness brought about the ruin of our house, and caused the death of many persons. Retribution followed me; and I long remained a fugitive in the land. Now I often pray that I may be able to make some atonement for the evil which I did, and to reëstablish the ancestral home. But I fear that I shall never find any way of so doing. Nevertheless, I try to overcome the karma of my errors by sincere repentance, and by helping, as far as I can, those who are unfortunate."

3. A sort of little fireplace, contrived in the floor of a room, is thus described. The *ro* is usually a square shallow cavity, lined with metal and half-filled with ashes, in which charcoal is lighted.

Kwairyō was pleased by this announcement of good resolve; and he said to the *aruji*:

"My friend, I have had occasion to observe that men, prone to folly in their youth, may in after years become very earnest in right living. In the holy sûtras it is written that those strongest in wrong-doing can become, by power of good resolve, the strongest in right-doing. I do not doubt that you have a good heart; and I hope that better fortune will come to you. To-night I shall recite the sûtras for your sake, and pray that you may obtain the force to overcome the karma of any past errors."

With these assurances, Kwairyō bade the *aruji* good-night; and his host showed him to a very small side-room, where a bed had been made ready. Then all went to sleep except the priest, who began to read the sûtras by the light of a paper lantern. Until a late hour he continued to read and pray: then he opened a window in his little sleeping-room, to take a last look at the landscape before lying down. The night was beautiful: there was no cloud in the sky; there was no wind; and the strong moonlight threw down sharp black shadows of foliage, and glittered on the dews of the garden. Shrillings of crickets and bell-insects made a musical tumult; and the sound of the neighboring cascade deepened with the night. Kwairyō felt thirsty as he listened to the noise of the water; and, remembering the bamboo aqueduct at the rear of the house, he thought that he could go there and get a drink without disturbing the sleeping household. Very gently he pushed apart the sliding-screens that separated his room from the main apartment; and he saw, by the light of the lantern, five recumbent bodies—without heads!

For one instant he stood bewildered, imagining a crime. But in another moment he perceived that there was no blood, and that the headless necks did not look as if they had been cut. Then he thought to himself: "Either this is an illusion made by goblins, or I have been lured into the dwelling of a Rokuro-Kubi. . . . in the book *Sōshinki* it is written that if one find the body of a Rokuro-Kubi without its head, and remove the body to another place, the head will never be able to join itself again to the neck. And the book further says that when the head comes back and finds that its body has been moved, it will strike itself upon the floor three times—bounding like a ball—and will pant as in great fear, and presently die. Now, if these be Rokuro-

Kubi, they mean me no good; so I shall be justified in following the instructions of the book" . . .

He seized the body of the aruji by the feet, pulled it to the window, and pushed it out. Then he went to the back-door, which he found barred; and he surmised that the heads had made their exit through the smoke-hole in the roof, which had been left open. Gently unbarring the door, he made his way to the garden, and proceeded with all possible caution to the grove beyond it. He heard voices talking in the grove; and he went in the direction of the voices, stealing from shadow to shadow, until he reached a good hiding-place. Then, from behind a trunk, he caught sight of the heads—all five of them—flitting about, and chatting as they flitted. They were eating worms and insects which they found on the ground or among the trees. Presently the head of the aruji stopped eating and said:

"Ah, that traveling priest who came to-night! how fat all his body is! When we shall have eaten him, our bellies will be well filled . . . I was foolish to talk to him as I did; it only set him to reciting the sûtras on behalf of my soul! To go near him while he is reciting would be difficult; and we cannot touch him so long as he is praying. But as it is now nearly morning, perhaps he has gone to sleep . . . some one of you go to the house and see what the fellow is doing."

Another head—the head of a young woman—immediately rose up and flitted to the house, lightly as a bat. After a few minutes it came back, and cried out huskily, in a tone of great alarm:

"That traveling priest is not in the house; he is gone! But that is not the worst of the matter. He has taken the body of our aruji; and I do not know where he has put it."

At this announcement the head of the aruji—distinctly visible in the moonlight—assumed a frightful aspect: its eyes opened monstrously; its hair stood up bristling; and its teeth gnashed. Then a cry burst from its lips; and—weeping tears of rage—it exclaimed:

"Since my body has been moved, to rejoin it is not possible! Then I must die! . . . and all through the work of that priest! Before I die I will get at that priest! I will tear him! I will devour him! . . . *and there he is*—behind that tree—hiding behind that tree! See him! the fat coward!" . . .

In the same moment the head of the aruji, followed by the other four heads, sprang at Kwairyō. But the strong priest had already armed himself by plucking up a young tree; and with that tree he struck the heads as they came, knocking them from him with tremendous blows. Four of them fled away. But the head of the aruji, though battered again and again, desperately continued to bound at the priest, and at last caught him by the left sleeve of his robe. Kwairyō, however, as quickly gripped the head by its topknot, and repeatedly struck it. It did not release its hold; but it uttered a long moan, and thereafter ceased to struggle. It was dead. But its teeth still held the sleeve; and, for all his great strength, Kwairyō could not force open the jaws.

With the head still hanging to his sleeve he went back to the house, and there caught sight of the other four Rokuro-Kubi squatting together, with their bruised and bleeding heads reunited to their bodies. But when they perceived him at the back-door all screamed, "The priest! the priest!" and fled, through the other doorway, out into the woods.

Eastward the sky was brightening; day was about to dawn; and Kwairyō knew that the power of the goblins was limited to the hours of darkness. He looked at the head clinging to his sleeve, its face all fouled with blood and foam and clay; and he laughed aloud as he thought to himself: "What a *miyagé!*⁴—the head of a goblin!" After which he gathered together his few belongings, and leisurely descended the mountain to continue his journey.

Right on he journeyed, until he came to Suwa in Shinano; and into the main street of Suwa he solemnly strode, with the head dangling at his elbow. Then women fainted, and children screamed and ran away; and there was a great crowding and clamoring until the *torité* (as the police of those days were called) seized the priest, and took him to jail. For they supposed the head to be the head of a murdered man who, in the moment of being killed, had caught the murderer's sleeve in his teeth. As for Kwairyó, he only smiled and said nothing when they questioned him. So, after having passed a night in prison, he was brought before the magistrates of the district. Then he was ordered to explain how he, a priest, had been found with the head of a man fastened to his sleeve, and why he had dared thus shamelessly to parade his crime in the sight of the people.

Kwairyō laughed long and loudly at these questions; and then he said:

---

4. A present made to friends or to the household on returning from a journey is thus called. Ordinarily, of course, the *miyagé* consists of something produced in the locality to which the journey has been made: this is the point of Kwairyō's jest.

"Sirs, I did not fasten the head to my sleeve: it fastened itself there
—much against my will. And I have not committed any crime. For
this is not the head of a man; it is the head of a goblin; and, if I caused
the death of the goblin, I did not do so by any shedding of blood, but
simply by taking the precautions necessary to assure my own safety"
. . . and he proceeded to relate the whole of the adventure, bursting
into another hearty laugh as he told of his encounter with the five
heads.

But the magistrates did not laugh. They judged him to be a hardened criminal, and his story an insult to their intelligence. Therefore,
without further questioning, they decided to order his immediate execution—all of them except one, a very old man. This aged officer had
made no remark during the trial; but, after having heard the opinion
of his colleagues, he rose up, and said:

"Let us first examine the head carefully; for this, I think, has not yet
been done. If the priest has spoken truth, the head itself should bear
witness for him . . . bring the head here!"

So the head, still holding in its teeth the *koromo* that had been
stripped from Kwairyō's shoulders, was put before the judges. The old
man turned it round and round, carefully examined it, and discovered,
on the nape of its neck, several strange red characters. He called the
attention of his colleagues to these, and also bade them observe that
the edges of the neck nowhere presented the appearance of having
been cut by any weapon. On the contrary, the line of severance was
smooth as the line at which a falling leaf detaches itself from the stem
. . . then said the elder:

"I am quite sure that the priest told us nothing but the truth. This is
the head of a Rokuro-Kubi. In the book *Nan-hō-ï-butsu-shi* it is written that certain red characters can always be found upon the nape of
the neck of a real Rokuro-Kubi. There are the characters: you can see
for yourselves that they have not been painted. Moreover, it is well
known that such goblins have been dwelling in the mountains of the
province of Kai from very ancient time . . . but you, Sir," he exclaimed, turning to Kwairyō, "what sort of sturdy priest may you be?
Certainly you have given proof of a courage that few priests possess;
and you have the air of a soldier rather than of a priest. Perhaps you
once belonged to the samurai-class?"

"You have guessed rightly, Sir," Kwairyō responded. "Before becoming a priest, I long followed the profession of arms; and in those

days I never feared man or devil. My name then was Isogai Héïdazaëmon Takétsura, of Kyūshū: there may be some among you who remember it."

At the utterance of that name, a murmur of admiration filled the court-room; for there were many present who remembered it. And Kwairyō immediately found himself among friends instead of judges —friends anxious to prove their admiration by fraternal kindness. With honor they escorted him to the residence of the daimyō, who welcomed him, and feasted him, and made him a handsome present before allowing him to depart. When Kwairyō left Suwa, he was as happy as any priest is permitted to be in this transitory world. As for the head, he took it with him, jocosely insisting that he intended it for a *miyagé.*

And now it only remains to tell what became of the head.

A day or two after leaving Suwa, Kwairyō met with a robber, who stopped him in a lonesome place, and bade him strip. Kwairyō at once removed his *koromo,* and offered it to the robber, who then first perceived what was hanging to the sleeve. Though brave, the highwayman was startled: he dropped the garment, and sprang back. Then he cried out: "You! what kind of a priest are you? Why, you are a worse man than I am! It is true that I have killed people; but I never walked about with anybody's head fastened to my sleeve . . . well, Sir priest, I suppose we are of the same calling; and I must say that I admire you! . . . now that head would be of use to me: I could frighten people with it. Will you sell it? You can have my robe in exchange for your *koromo;* and I will give you five ryō for the head."

Kwairyō answered:

"I shall let you have the head and the robe if you insist; but I must tell you that this is not the head of a man. It is a goblin's head. So, if you buy it, and have any trouble in consequence, please to remember that you were not deceived by me."

"What a nice priest you are!" exclaimed the robber. "You kill men, and jest about it! . . . but I am really in earnest. Here is my robe; and here is the money; and let me have the head . . . what is the use of joking?"

"Take the thing," said Kwairyō. "I was not joking. The only joke— if there be any joke at all—is that you are fool enough to pay good

money for a goblin's head." And Kwairyō, loudly laughing, went
upon his way.

Thus the robber got the head and the *koromo;* and for some time he
played goblin-priest upon the highways. But, reaching the neighborhood of Suwa, he there learned the real history of the head; and he
then became afraid that the spirit of the Rokuro-Kubi might give him
trouble. So he made up his mind to take back the head to the place
from which it had come, and to bury it with its body. He found his
way to the lonely cottage in the mountains of Kai; but nobody was
there, and he could not discover the body. Therefore he buried the
head by itself, in the grove behind the cottage; and he had a tombstone
set up over the grave; and he caused a Ségaki-service to be performed
on behalf of the spirit of the Rokuro-Kubi. And that tombstone—
known as the Tombstone of the Rokuro-Kubi—may be seen (at least
so the Japanese story-teller declares) even unto this day.

Most readers are familiar with BRAM STOKER *(1847–1912), the Irish author of* Dracula, *the most famous vampire novel of all time, but Stoker's other novels and shorter fiction are not nearly so well known. "The Burial of the Rats," one of his more obscure stories, starts out in a leisurely manner not uncommon in Victorian fiction, but builds with subtly inexorable gruesomeness to one of the most harrowing chase sequences I ever white-knuckled my way through.*

The Burial of the Rats
BY BRAM STOKER

Leaving Paris by the Orleans road, cross the Enceinte, and, turning to the right, you find yourself in a somewhat wild and not at all savoury district. Right and left, before and behind, on every side rise great heaps of dust and waste accumulated by the process of time.

Paris has its night as well as its day life, and the sojourner who enters his hotel in the Rue de Rivoli or the Rue St. Honore late at night or leaves it early in the morning, can guess, in coming near Montrouge—if he has not done so already—the purpose of those great waggons that look like boilers on wheels which he finds halting everywhere as he passes.

Every city has its peculiar institutions created out of its own needs; and one of the most notable institutions of Paris is its rag-picking population. In the early morning—and Parisian life commences at an early hour—may be seen in most streets standing on the pathway opposite every court and alley and between every few houses, as still in some American cities, even in parts of New York, large wooden boxes into which the domestics or tenement-holders empty the accumulated dust of the past day. Round these boxes gather and pass on, when the work is done, to fresh fields of labour and pastures new, squalid, hungry-looking men and women, the implements of whose craft consist of a coarse bag or basket slung over the shoulder and a little rake with which they turn over and probe and examine in the minutest manner the dustbins. They pick up and deposit in their baskets, by aid of their rakes, whatever they may find, with the same facility as a Chinaman uses his chopsticks.

Paris is a city of centralisation—and centralisation and classification are closely allied. In the early times, when centralisation is becoming a fact, its forerunner is classification. All things which are similar or analogous become grouped together, and from the grouping of groups rises one whole or central point. We see radiating many long arms with innumerable tentaculae, and in the centre rises a gigantic head with a comprehensive brain and keen eyes to look on every side and ears sensitive to hear—and a voracious mouth to swallow.

Other cities resemble all the birds and beasts and fishes whose appetites and digestions are normal. Paris alone is the analogical apotheosis of the octopus. Product of centralisation carried to an *ad absurdum,* it fairly represents the devil fish; and in no respects is the resemblance more curious than in the similarity of the digestive apparatus.

Those intelligent tourists who, having surrendered their individuality into the hands of Messrs. Cook or Gaze, "do" Paris in three days, are often puzzled to know how it is that the dinner which in London would cost about six shillings, can be had for three francs in a café in the Palais Royal. They need have no more wonder if they will but consider the classification which is a theoretic speciality of Parisian life, and adopt all round the fact from which the chiffonier has his genesis.

The Paris of 1850 was not like the Paris of to-day, and those who see the Paris of Napoleon and Baron Hausseman can hardly realise the existence of the state of things forty-five years ago.

Amongst other things, however, which have not changed are those districts where the waste is gathered. Dust is dust all the world over, in every age, and the family likeness of dust-heaps is perfect. The traveller, therefore, who visits the environs of Montrouge can go back in fancy without difficulty to the year 1850.

In this year I was making a prolonged stay in Paris. I was very much in love with a young lady who, though she returned my passion, so far yielded to the wishes of her parents that she had promised not to see me or to correspond with me for a year. I, too, had been compelled to accede to these conditions under a vague hope of parental approval. During the term of probation I had promised to remain out of the country and not to write to my dear one until the expiration of the year.

Naturally the time went heavily with me. There was no one of my own family or circle who could tell me of Alice, and none of her own folk had, I am sorry to say, sufficient generosity to send me even an occasional word of comfort regarding her health and well-being. I spent six months wandering about Europe, but as I could find no satisfactory distraction in travel, I determined to come to Paris, where, at least, I would be within easy hail of London in case any good fortune should call me thither before the appointed time. That "hope deferred maketh the heart sick" was never better exemplified than in my case, for in addition to the perpetual longing to see the face I loved there was always with me a harrowing anxiety lest some accident should prevent me showing Alice in due time that I had, throughout the long period of probation, been faithful to her trust and my own love. Thus, every adventure which I undertook had a fierce pleasure of its own, for it was fraught with possible consequences greater than it would have ordinarily borne.

Like all travellers I exhausted the places of most interest in the first month of my stay, and was driven in the second month to look for amusement whithersoever I might. Having made sundry journeys to the better-known suburbs, I began to see that there was a *terra incognita,* in so far as the guide book was concerned, in the social wilderness lying between these attractive points. Accordingly I began to systematise my researches, and each day took up the thread of my exploration at the place where I had on the previous day dropped it.

In process of time my wanderings led me near Montrouge, and I saw that hereabouts lay the Ultima Thule of social exploration—a country as little known as that round the source of the White Nile. And so I determined to investigate philosophically the chiffonier—his habitat, his life, and his means of life.

The job was an unsavoury one, difficult of accomplishment, and with little hope of adequate reward. However, despite reason, obstinacy prevailed, and I entered into my new investigation with a keener energy than I could have summoned to aid me in any investigation leading to any end, valuable or worthy.

One day, late in a fine afternoon, toward the end of September, I entered the holy of holies of the city of dust. The place was evidently the recognised abode of a number of chiffoniers, for some sort of arrangement was manifested in the formation of the dust heaps near the road. I passed amongst these heaps, which stood like orderly sentries, determined to penetrate further and trace dust to its ultimate location.

As I passed along I saw behind the dust heaps a few forms that flitted to and fro, evidently watching with interest the advent of any stranger to such a place. The district was like a small Switzerland, and as I went forward my tortuous course shut out the path behind me. Presently I got into what seemed a small city or community of chiffoniers. There were a number of shanties or huts, such as may be met with in the remote parts of the Bog of Allan—rude places with wattled walls, plastered with mud and roofs of rude thatch made from stable refuse—such places as one would not like to enter for any consideration, and which even in water-colour could only look picturesque if judiciously treated. In the midst of these huts was one of the strangest adaptations—I cannot say habitations—I had ever seen. An immense old wardrobe, the colossal remnant of some boudoir of Charles VII, or Henry II, had been converted into a dwelling-house. The double doors lay open, so that the entire menage was open to public view. In the open half of the wardrobe was a common sitting-room of some four feet by six, in which sat, smoking their pipes round a charcoal brazier, no fewer than six old soldiers of the First Republic, with their uniforms torn and worn threadbare. Evidently they were of the *mauvais sujet* class; their blear eyes and limp jaws told plainly of a common love of absinthe; and their eyes had that haggard, worn look which stamps the drunkard at his worst, and that look of slumbering ferocity which follows hard in the wake of drink. The other side stood as of old, with its shelves intact, save that they were cut to half their depth, and in each shelf of which there were six, was a bed made with rags and straw. The half-dozen of worthies who inhabited this structure looked at me curiously as I passed; and when I looked back after going a little way I saw their heads together in a whispered conference. I did not like the look of this at all, for the place was very lonely, and the men looked very, very villainous. However, I did not see any cause for fear, and went on my way, penetrating further and further into the Sahara. The way was tortuous to a degree, and from going round in a series of semi-circles, as one goes in skating with the Dutch roll, I got rather confused with regard to the points of the compass.

When I had penetrated a little way I saw, as I turned the corner of a half-made heap, sitting on a heap of straw an old soldier with threadbare coat.

"Hallo!" said I to myself; "the First Republic is well represented here in its soldiery."

As I passed him the old man never even looked up at me, but gazed on the ground with stolid persistency. Again I remarked to myself: "See what a life of rude warfare can do! This old man's curiosity is a thing of the past."

When I had gone a few steps, however, I looked back suddenly, and saw that curiosity was not dead, for the veteran had raised his head and was regarding me with a very queer expression. He seemed to me to look very like one of the six worthies in the press. When he saw me looking he dropped his head; and without thinking further of him I went on my way, satisfied that there was a strange likeness between these old warriors.

Presently I met another old soldier in a similar manner. He, too, did not notice me whilst I was passing.

By this time it was getting late in the afternoon, and I began to think of retracing my steps. Accordingly I turned to go back, but could see a number of tracks leading between different mounds and could not ascertain which of them I should take. In my perplexity I wanted to see someone of whom to ask the way, but could see no one. I determined to go on a few mounds further and so try to see someone —not a veteran.

I gained my object, for after going a couple of hundred yards I saw before me a single shanty such as I had seen before—with, however, the difference that this was not one for living in, but merely a roof with three walls open in front. From the evidences which the neighbour-hood exhibited I took it to be a place for sorting. Within it was an old woman wrinkled and bent with age; I approached her to ask the way.

She rose as I came close and I asked her my way. She immediately commenced a conversation; and it occurred to me that here in the very centre of the Kingdom of Dust was the place to gather details of the history of Parisian rag-picking—particularly as I could do so from the lips of one who looked like the oldest inhabitant.

I began my inquiries, and the old woman gave me most interesting answers—she had been one of the ceteuces who sat daily before the guillotine and had taken an active part among the women who signal-ised themselves by their violence in the revolution. While we were talking she said suddenly: "But m'sieur must be tired standing," and dusted a rickety old stool for me to sit down. I hardly liked to do so for many reasons; but the poor old woman was so civil that I did not like to run the risk of hurting her by refusing, and moreover the conversation of one who had been at the taking of the Bastille was so interesting that I sat down and so our conversation went on.

While we were talking an old man—older and more bent and wrinkled even than the woman—appeared from behind the shanty. "Here is Pierre," said she. "M'sieur can hear stories now if he wishes, for Pierre was in everything, from the Bastille to Waterloo." The old man took another stool at my request and we plunged into a sea of revolutionary reminiscences. This old man, albeit clothed like a scarecrow, was like any one of the six veterans.

I was now sitting in the centre of the low hut with the woman on my left hand and the man on my right, each of them being somewhat in front of me. The place was full of all sorts of curious objects of lumber, and of many things that I wished far away. In one corner was a heap of rags which seemed to move from the number of vermin it contained, and in the other a heap of bones whose odour was something shocking. Every now and then, glancing at the heaps, I could see the gleaming eyes of some of the rats which infested the place. These loathsome objects were bad enough, but what looked even more dreadful was an old butcher's axe with an iron handle stained with clots of blood leaning up against the wall on the right hand side. Still these things did not give me much concern. The talk of the two old people was so fascinating that I stayed on and on, till the evening came and the dust heaps threw dark shadows over the vales between them.

After a time I began to grow uneasy, I could not tell how or why, but somehow I did not feel satisfied. Uneasiness is an instinct and means warning. The psychic faculties are often the sentries of the intellect; and when they sound alarm the reason begins to act, although perhaps not consciously.

This was so with me. I began to bethink me where I was and by what surrounded, and to wonder how I should fare in case I should be attacked; and then the thought suddenly burst upon me, although without any overt cause, that I was in danger. Prudence whispered: "Be still and make no sign," and so I was still and made no sign, for I knew that four cunning eyes were on me. "Four eyes—if not more." My God, what a horrible thought! The whole shanty might be surrounded on three sides with villains! I might be in the midst of a band of such desperadoes as only half a century of periodic revolution can produce.

With a sense of danger my intellect and observation quickened, and I grew more watchful than was my wont. I noticed that the old woman's eyes were constantly wandering toward my hands. I looked at them too, and saw the cause—my rings. On my left little finger I had a large signet and on the right a good diamond.

I thought that if there was any danger my first care was to avert suspicion. Accordingly I began to work the conversation round to rag-picking—to the drains—of the things found there; and so by easy stages to jewels. Then, seizing a favourable opportunity, I asked the old woman if she knew anything of such things. She answered that she did, a little. I held out my right hand, and, showing her the diamond, asked her what she thought of that. She answered that her eyes were bad, and stooped over my hand. I said as nonchalantly as I could: "Pardon me! You will see better thus!" and taking it off handed it to her. An unholy light came into her withered old face, as she touched it. She stole one glance at me swift and keen as a flash of lightning.

She bent over the ring for a moment, her face quite concealed as though examining it. The old man looked straight out of the front of the shanty before him, at the same time fumbling in his pockets and producing a screw of tobacco in a paper and a pipe, which he proceeded to fill. I took advantage of the pause and the momentary rest from the searching eyes on my face to look carefully round the place, now dim and shadowy in the gloaming. There still lay all the heaps of varied reeking foulness; there the terrible blood-stained axe leaning against the wall in the right hand corner, and everywhere, despite the gloom, the baleful glitter of the eyes of the rats. I could see them even through some of the chinks of the boards at the back low down close to the ground. But stay! these latter eyes seemed more than usually large and bright and baleful!

For an instant my heart stood still, and I felt in that whirling condition of mind in which one feels a sort of spiritual drunkenness, and as though the body is only maintained erect in that there is no time for it to fall before recovery. Then, in another second, I was calm—coldly calm, with all my energies in full vigour, with a self-control which I felt to be perfect and with all my feeling and instincts alert.

Now I knew the full extent of my danger: I was watched and surrounded by desperate people! I could not even guess at how many of them were lying there on the ground behind the shanty, waiting for the moment to strike. I knew that I was big and strong, and they knew it, too. They knew also, as I did, that I was an Englishman and would make a fight for it; and so we waited. I had, I felt, gained an advantage in the last few seconds, for I knew my danger and understood the situation. Now, I thought, is the test of my courage—the enduring test: the fighting test may come later!

The old woman raised her head and said to me in a satisfied kind of way:

"A very fine ring, indeed—a beautiful ring! Oh, me! I once had such rings, plenty of them, and bracelets and earrings! Oh! for in those fine days I led the town a dance! But they've forgotten me now! They've forgotten me! They? Why, they never heard of me! Perhaps their grandfathers remember me, some of them!" and she laughed a harsh, croaking laugh. And then I am bound to say that she astonished me, for she handed me back the ring with a certain suggestion of old-fashioned grace which was not without its pathos.

The old man eyed her with a sort of sudden ferocity, half rising from his stool, and said to me suddenly and hoarsely:

"Let me see!"

I was about to hand the ring when the old woman said:

"No! no, do not give it to Pierre! Pierre is eccentric. He loses things; and such a pretty ring!"

"Cat!" said the old man, savagely. Suddenly the old woman said, rather more loudly than was necessary:

"Wait! I shall tell you something about a ring." There was something in the sound of her voice that jarred upon me. Perhaps it was my hyper-sensitiveness, wrought up as I was to such a pitch of nervous excitement, but I seemed to think that she was not addressing me. As I stole a glance round the place I saw the eyes of the rats in the bone heaps, but missed the eyes along the back. But even as I looked I saw them again appear. The old woman's "Wait!" had given me a respite from attack, and the men had sunk back to their reclining posture.

"I once lost a ring—a beautiful diamond hoop that had belonged to a queen, and which was given to me by a farmer of the taxes, who afterwards cut his throat because I sent him away. I thought it must have been stolen, and taxed my people; but I could get no trace. The police came and suggested that it had found its way to the drain. We descended—I in my fine clothes, for I would not trust them with my beautiful ring! I know more of the drains since then, and of rats, too! but I shall never forget the horror of that place—alive with blazing eyes, a wall of them just outside the light of our torches. Well, we got beneath my house. We searched the outlet of the drain, and there in the filth found my ring, and we came out.

"But we found something else also before we came! As we were coming toward the opening a lot of sewer rats—human ones this time —came toward us. They told the police that one of their number had gone into the drain, but had not returned. He had gone in only shortly before we had, and, if lost, could hardly be far off. They asked help to seek him, so we turned back. They tried to prevent me going, but I insisted. It was a new excitement, and had I not recovered my ring? Not far did we go till we came on something. There was but little water, and the bottom of the drain was raised with brick, rubbish, and much matter of the kind. He had made a fight for it, even when his torch had gone out. But they were too many for him! They had not been long about it! The bones were still warm; but they were picked clean. They had even eaten their own dead ones and there were bones of rats as well as of the man. They took it cool enough those other— the human ones—and joked of their comrade when they found him dead, though they would have helped him living. Bah! what matters it —life or death?"

"And had you no fear?" I asked her.

"Fear!" she said with a laugh. "Me have fear? Ask Pierre! But I was younger then, and, as I came through that horrible drain with its wall of greedy eyes, always moving with the circle of the light from the torches, I did not feel easy. I kept on before the men, though! It is a way I have! I never let the men get it before me. All I want is a chance and a means! And they ate him up—took every trace away except the bones; and no one knew it, nor no sound of him was ever heard!" Here she broke into a chuckling fit of the ghastliest merriment which it was ever my lot to hear and see. A great poetess describes her heroine singing: "Oh! to see or hear her singing! Scarce I know which is the divinest."

And I can apply the same idea to the old crone—in all save the divinity, for I scarce could tell which was the most hellish—the harsh, malicious, satisfied, cruel laugh, or the leering grin, and the horrible square opening of the mouth like a tragic mask, and the yellow gleam of the few discoloured teeth in the shapeless gums. In that laugh and with that grin and the chuckling satisfaction I knew as well as if it had been spoken to me in words of thunder that my murder was settled, and the murderers only bided the proper time for its accomplishment. I could read between the lines of her gruesome story the commands to her accomplices. "Wait," she seemed to say, "bide your time. I shall strike the first blow. Find the weapon for me, and I shall make the opportunity! He shall not escape! Keep him quiet, and then no one will be wiser. There will be no outcry, and the rats will do their work!"

It was growing darker and darker; the night was coming. I stole a glance round the shanty, still all the same! The bloody axe in the corner, the heaps of filth, and the eyes on the bone heaps and in the crannies of the floor.

Pierre had been still ostensibly filling his pipe; he now struck a light and began to puff away at it. The old woman said:

"Dear heart, how dark it is! Pierre, like a good lad, light the lamp!"

Pierre got up and with the lighted match in his hand touched the wick of a lamp which hung at one side of the entrance to the shanty, and which had a reflector that threw the light all over the place. It was evidently that which was used for their sorting at night.

"Not that, stupid! Not that! The lantern!" she called out to him.

He immediately blew it out, saying: "All right, mother, I'll find it," and he hustled about the left corner of the room—the old woman saying through the darkness:

"The lantern! the lantern! Oh! That is the light that is most useful to us poor folks. The lantern was the friend of the revolution! It is the friend of the chiffonier! It helps us when all else fails."

Hardly had she said the word when there was a kind of creaking of the whole place, and something was steadily dragged over the roof.

Again I seemed to read between the lines of her words. I knew the lesson of the lantern.

"One of you get on the roof with a noose and strangle him as he passes out if we fail within."

As I looked out of the opening I saw the loop of a rope outlined black against the lurid sky. I was now, indeed, beset!

Pierre was not long in finding the lantern. I kept my eyes fixed through the darkness on the old woman. Pierre struck his light, and by its flash I saw the old woman raise from the ground beside her where it had mysteriously appeared, and then hide in the folds of her gown, a long sharp knife or dagger. It seemed to be like a butcher's sharpening iron fined to a keen point.

The lantern was lit.

"Bring it here, Pierre," she said. "Place it in the doorway where we can see it. See how nice it is! It shuts out the darkness from us; it is just right!"

Just right for her and her purposes! It threw all its light on my face, leaving in gloom the faces of both Pierre and the woman, who sat outside of me on each side.

I felt that the time of action was approaching; but I knew now that the first signal and movement would come from the woman, and so watched her.

I was all unarmed, but I had made up my mind what to do. At the first movement I would seize the butcher's axe in the right-hand corner and fight my way out. At least, I would die hard. I stole a glance round to fix its exact locality so that I could not fail to seize it at the first effort, for then, if ever, time and accuracy would be precious.

Good God! It was gone! All the horror of the situation burst upon me; but the bitterest thought of all was that if the issue of the terrible position should be against me Alice would infallibly suffer. Either she would believe me false—and any lover, or any one who has ever been one, can imagine the bitterness of the thought—or else she would go on loving long after I had been lost to her and to the world, so that her life would be broken and embittered, shattered with disappointment and despair. The very magnitude of the pain braced me up and nerved me to bear the dread scrutiny of the plotters.

I think I did not betray myself. The old woman was watching me as a cat does a mouse; she had her right hand hidden in the folds of her gown, clutching, I knew, that long, cruel-looking dagger. Had she seen any disappointment in my face she would, I felt, have known that the moment had come, and would have sprung on me like a tigress, certain of taking me unprepared.

I looked out into the night, and there I saw new cause for danger. Before and around the hut were at a little distance some shadowy forms; they were quite still, but I knew that they were all alert and on guard. Small chance for me now in that direction.

Again I stole a glance round the place. In moments of great excitement and of great danger, which is excitement, the mind works very quickly, and the keenness of the faculties which depend on the mind grows in proportion. I now felt this. In an instant I took in the whole situation. I saw that the axe had been taken through a small hole made in one of the rotten boards. How rotten they must be to allow of such a thing being done without a particle of noise.

The hut was a regular murder-trap, and was guarded all around. A garroter lay on the roof ready to entangle me with his noose if I should escape the dagger of the old hag. In front the way was guarded by I know not how many watchers. And at the back was a row of desperate men—I had seen their eyes still through the crack in the boards of the floor, when last I looked—as they lay prone waiting for the signal to start erect. If it was to be ever, now for it!

As nonchalantly as I could I turned slightly on my stool so as to get my right leg well under me. Then with a sudden jump, turning my head, and guarding it with my hands, and with the fighting instinct of the knights of old, I breathed my lady's name, and hurled myself against the back wall of the hut.

Watchful as they were, the suddenness of my movement surprised both Pierre and the old woman. As I crashed through the rotten timbers I saw the old woman rise with a leap like a tiger and heard her low gasp of baffled rage. My feet lit on something that moved, and as I jumped away I knew that I had stepped on the back of one of the row of men lying on their faces outside the hut. I was torn with nails and splinters, but otherwise unhurt. Breathless I rushed up the mound in front of me, hearing as I went the dull crash of the shanty as it collapsed into a mass.

It was a nightmare climb. The mound, though but low, was awfully steep, and with each step I took the mass of dust and cinders tore down with me and gave way under my feet. The dust rose and choked me; it was sickening, foetid, awful; but my climb was, I felt, for life or death, and I struggled on. The seconds seemed hours; but the few moments I had in starting, combined with my youth and strength, gave me a great advantage, and, though several forms struggled after me in deadly silence which was more dreadful than any sound, I easily reached the top. Since then I have climbed the cone of Vesuvius, and as I struggled up that dreary steep amid the sulphurous fumes the memory of that awful night at Montrouge came back to me so vividly that I almost grew faint.

The mound was one of the tallest in the region of dust, and as I struggled to the top, panting for breath and with my heart beating like a sledge-hammer, I saw away to my left the dull red gleam of the sky, and nearer still the flashing of lights. Thank God! I knew where I was now and where lay the road to Paris!

For two or three seconds I paused and looked back. My pursuers were still well behind me, but struggling up resolutely, and in deadly silence. Beyond, the shanty was a wreck—a mass of timber and moving forms. I could see it well, for flames were already bursting out; the rags and straw had evidently caught fire from the lantern. Still silence there! Not a sound! These old wretches could die game, anyhow.

I had no time for more than a passing glance, for as I cast an eye round the mound preparatory to making my descent I saw several dark forms rushing round on either side to cut me off on my way. It was now a race for life. They were trying to head me on my way to Paris, and with the instinct of the moment I dashed down to the right-hand side. I was just in time, for, though I came as it seemed to me down the steep in a few steps, the wary old men who were watching me turned back, and one, as I rushed by into the opening between the two mounds in front, almost struck me a blow with that terrible butcher's axe. There could surely not be two such weapons about!

Then began a really horrible chase. I easily ran ahead of the old men, and even when some younger ones and a few women joined in the hunt I easily distanced them. But I did not know the way, and I could not even guide myself by the light in the sky, for I was running away from it. I had heard that, unless of conscious purpose, hunted men turn always to the left, and so I found it now; and so, I suppose, knew also my pursuers, who were more animals than men, and with cunning or instinct had found out such secrets for themselves: for on finishing a quick spurt, after which I intended to take a moment's breathing space, I suddenly saw ahead of me two or three forms swiftly passing behind a mound to the right.

I was in the spider's web now indeed! But with the thought of this new danger came the resource of the hunted, and so I darted down the next turning to the right. I continued in this direction for some hundred yards, and then, making a turn to the left again, felt certain that I had, at any rate, avoided the danger of being surrounded.

But not of pursuit, for on came the rabble after me, steady, dogged, relentless, and still in grim silence.

In the greater darkness the mounds seemed now to be somewhat smaller than before, although—for the night was closing—they looked bigger in proportion. I was now well ahead of my pursuers, so I made a dart up the mound in front.

Oh joy of joys! I was close to the edge of this inferno of dustheaps. Away behind me the red light of Paris in the sky, and towering up behind rose the heights of Montmartre—a dim light, with here and there brilliant points like stars.

Restored to vigour in a moment, I ran over the few remaining mounds of decreasing size, and found myself on the level land beyond. Even then, however, the prospect was not inviting. All before me was dark and dismal, and I had evidently come on one of those dank, low-lying waste places which are found here and there in the neighbour-hood of great cities. Places of waste and desolation, where the space is required for the ultimate agglomeration of all that is noxious, and the ground is so poor as to create no desire of occupancy even in the lowest squatter. With eyes accustomed to the gloom of the evening, and away now from the shadows of those dreadful dustheaps, I could see much more easily than I could a little while ago. It might have been, of course, that the glare in the sky of the lights of Paris, though the city was some miles away, was reflected here. Howsoever it was, I saw well enough to take bearings for certainly some little distance around me.

In front was a bleak, flat waste that seemed almost dead level, with here and there the dark shimmering of stagnant pools. Seemingly far off on the right, amid a small cluster of scattered lights, rose a dark mass of Fort Montrouge, and away to the left in the dim distance, pointed with stray gleams from cottage windows, the lights in the sky showed the locality of Bicêtre. A moment's thought decided me to take to the right and try to reach Montrouge. There at least would be some sort of safety, and I might possibly long before come on some of the cross roads which I knew. Somewhere, not far off, must lie the strategic road made to connect the outlying chain of forts circling the city.

Then I looked back. Coming over the mounds, and outlined black against the glare of the Parisian horizon, I saw several moving figures, and still a way to the right several more deploying out between me and my destination. They evidently meant to cut me off in this direction, and so my choice became constricted; it lay now between going straight ahead or turning to the left. Stooping to the ground, so as to get the advantage of the horizon as a line of sight, I looked carefully in this direction, but could detect no sign of my enemies. I argued that as they had not guarded or were not trying to guard that point, there was evidently danger to me there already. So I made up my mind to go straight on before me.

It was not an inviting prospect, and as I went on the reality grew worse. The ground became soft and oozy, and now and again gave way beneath me in a sickening kind of way. I seemed somehow to be going down, for I saw round me places seemingly more elevated than where I was, and this in a place which from a little way back seemed dead level. I looked around, but could see none of my pursuers. This was strange, for all along these birds of the night had followed me through the darkness as well as though it was broad daylight. How I blamed myself for coming out in my light-coloured tourist suit of tweed. The silence, and my not being able to see my enemies, whilst I felt that they were watching me, grew appalling, and in the hope of some one not of this ghastly crew hearing me I raised my voice and shouted several times. There was not the slightest response; not even an echo rewarded my efforts. For a while I stood stock still and kept my eyes in one direction. On one of the rising places around me I saw something dark move along, then another, and another. This was to my left, and seemingly moving to head me off.

I thought that again I might with my skill as a runner elude my enemies at this game, and so with all my speed darted forward.

Splash!

My feet had given way in a mass of slimy rubbish, and I had fallen headlong into a reeking, stagnant pool. The water and the mud in which my arms sank up to the elbows was filthy and nauseous beyond description, and in the suddenness of my fall I had actually swallowed some of the filthy stuff, which nearly choked me, and made me gasp for breath. Never shall I forget the moments during which I stood trying to recover myself almost fainting from the foetid odour of the filthy pool, whose white mist rose ghostlike around. Worst of all, with the acute despair of the hunted animal when he sees the pursuing pack closing on him, I saw before my eyes whilst I stood helpless the dark forms of my pursuers moving swiftly to surround me.

It is curious how our minds work on odd matters even when the energies of thought are seemingly concentrated on some terrible and pressing need. I was in momentary peril of my life: my safety depended on my action, and my choice of alternatives coming now with almost every step I took, and yet I could not but think of the strange dogged persistency of these old men. Their silent resolution, their steadfast, grim persistency even in such a cause commanded, as well as fear, even a measure of respect. What must they have been in the vigour of their youth. I could understand now that whirlwind rush on the bridge of Arcola, that scornful exclamation of the Old Guard at Waterloo! Unconscious cerebration has its own pleasures, even at such moments; but fortunately it does not in any way clash with the thought from which action springs.

I realised at a glance that so far I was defeated in my object, my enemies as yet had won. They had succeeded in surrounding me on three sides, and were bent on driving me off to the left-hand, where there was already some danger for me, for they had left no guard. I accepted the alternative—it was a case of Hobson's choice and run. I had to keep the lower ground, for my pursuers were on the higher places. However, though the ooze and broken ground impeded me my youth and training made me able to hold my ground, and by keeping a diagonal line I not only kept them from gaining on me but even began to distance them. This gave me new heart and strength, and by this time habitual training was beginning to tell and my second wind had come. Before me the ground rose slightly. I rushed up the slope and found before me a waste of watery slime, with a low dyke or bank looking black and grim beyond. I felt that if I could but reach that dyke in safety I could there, with solid ground under my feet and some kind of path to guide me, find with comparative ease a way out of my troubles. After a glance right and left and seeing no one near, I kept my eyes for a few minutes to their rightful work of aiding my feet whilst I crossed the swamp. It was rough, hard work, but there was little danger, merely toil; and a short time took me to the dyke. I rushed up the slope exciting; but here again I met a new shock. On either side of me rose a number of crouching figures. From right and left they rushed at me. Each body held a rope.

The cordon was nearly complete. I could pass on neither side, and the end was near.

There was only one chance, and I took it. I hurled myself across the dyke, and escaping out of the very clutches of my foes threw myself into the stream.

At any other time I should have thought that water foul and filthy, but now it was as welcome as the most crystal stream to the parched traveller. It was a highway of safety!

My pursuers rushed after me. Had only one of them held the rope it would have been all up with me, for he could have entangled me before I had time to swim a stroke; but the many hands holding it embarrassed and delayed them, and when the rope struck the water I heard the splash well behind me. A few minutes' hard swimming took me across the stream. Refreshed with the immersion and encouraged by the escape, I climbed the dyke in comparative gaiety of spirits.

From the top I looked back. Through the darkness I saw my assailants scattering up and down along the dyke. The pursuit was evidently not ended, and again I had to choose my course. Beyond the dyke where I stood was a wild, swampy space very similar to that which I had crossed. I determined to shun such a place, and thought for a moment whether I would take up or down the dyke. I thought I heard a sound—the muffled sound of oars, so I listened, and then shouted.

No response; but the sound ceased. My enemies had evidently got a boat of some kind. As they were on the up side of me I took the down path and began to run. As I passed to the left of where I had entered the water I heard several splashes, soft and stealthy, like the sound a rat makes as he plunges into the stream, but vastly greater; and as I looked I saw the dark sheen of the water broken by the ripples of several advancing heads. Some of my enemies were swimming the stream also.

And now behind me, up the stream, the silence was broken by the quick rattle and creak of oars; my enemies were in hot pursuit. I put my best leg foremost and ran on. After a break of a couple of minutes I looked back, and by a gleam of light through the ragged clouds I saw several dark forms climbing the bank behind me. The wind had now begun to rise, and the water beside me was ruffled and beginning to break in tiny waves on the bank. I had to keep my eyes pretty well on the ground before me, lest I should stumble, for I knew that to stumble was death. After a few minutes I looked back behind me. On the dyke were only a few dark figures, but crossing the waste, swampy ground were many more. What new danger this portended I did not know—could only guess. Then as I ran it seemed to me that my track kept ever sloping away to the right. I looked up ahead and saw that the river was much wider than before, and that the dyke on which I stood fell quite away, and beyond it was another stream on whose near bank I saw some of the dark forms now across the marsh. I was on an island of some kind.

My situation was now indeed terrible, for my enemies had hemmed me in on every side. Behind came the quickening roll of the oars, as though my pursuers knew that the end was close. Around me on every side was desolation; there was not a roof or light, as far as I could see. Far off to the right rose some dark mass, but what it was I knew not. For a moment I paused to think what I should do, not for more, for my pursuers were drawing closer. Then my mind was made up. I slipped down the bank and took to the water. I struck out straight ahead, so as to gain the current by clearing the backwater of the island for such I presume it was, when I had passed into the stream. I waited till a cloud came driving across the moon and leaving all in darkness. Then I took off my hat and laid it softly on the water floating with the stream, and a second after dived to the right and struck out under water with all my might. I was, I suppose half a minute under water, and when I rose came up as softly as I could, and turning, looked back. There went my light brown hat floating merrily away. Close behind it came a rickety old boat, driven furiously by a pair of oars. The moon was still partly obscured by the drifting clouds, but in the partial light I could see a man in the bows holding aloft ready to strike what appeared to me to be that same dreadful pole-axe which I had before escaped. As I looked the boat drew closer, closer, and the man struck savagely. The hat disappeared. The man fell forward, almost out of the boat. His comrades dragged him in but without the axe, and then as I turned with all my energies bent on reaching the further bank, I heard the fierce whirr of the muttered "Sacre!" which marked the anger of my baffled pursuers.

That was the first sound I had heard from human lips during all this dreadful chase, and full as it was of menace and danger to me it was a welcome sound for it broke that awful silence which shrouded and appalled me. It was as though an overt sign that my opponents were men and not ghosts, and that with them I had, at least, the chance of a man, though but one against many.

But now that the spell of silence was broken the sounds came thick and fast. From boat to shore and back from shore to boat came quick question and answer, all in the fiercest whispers. I looked back—a fatal thing to do—for in the instant someone caught sight of my face, which showed white on the dark water, and shouted. Hands pointed to me, and in a moment or two the boat was under weigh, and following hard after me. I had but a little way to go, but quicker and quicker came the boat after me. A few more strokes and I would be on the shore, but I felt the oncoming of the boat, and expected each second to feel the crash of an oar or other weapon on my head. Had I not seen that dreadful axe disappear in the water I do not think that I could have won the shore. I heard the muttered curses of those not rowing and the laboured breath of the rowers. With one supreme effort for life or liberty I touched the bank and sprang up it. There was not a single second to spare, for hard behind me the boat grounded and several dark forms sprang after me. I gained the top of the dyke, and keeping to the left ran on again. The boat put off and followed down the stream. Seeing this I feared danger in this direction, and quickly turning, ran down the dyke on the other side, and after passing a short stretch of marshy ground gained a wild, open flat country and sped on.

Still behind me came on my relentless pursuers. Far away, below me, I saw the same dark mass as before, but now grown closer and greater. My heart gave a great thrill of delight, for I knew that it must be the fortress of Bicêtre, and with new courage I ran on. I had heard that between each and all of the protecting forts of Paris there are strategic ways, deep sunk roads, where soldiers marching should be sheltered from an enemy. I knew that if I could gain this road I would be safe, but in the darkness I could not see any sign of it, so, in blind hope of striking it, I ran on.

Presently I came to the edge of a deep cut, and found that down below me ran a road guarded on each side by a ditch of water fenced on either side by a straight, high wall.

Getting fainter and dizzier, I ran on; the ground got more broken—more and more still, till I staggered and fell, and rose again, and ran on in the blind anguish of the hunted. Again the thought of Alice nerved me. I would not be lost and wreck her life: I would fight and struggle for life to the bitter end. With a great effort I caught the top of the wall. As, scrambling like a catamount, I drew myself up, I actually felt a hand touch the sole of my foot. I was now on a sort of causeway, and before me I saw a dim light. Blind and dizzy, I ran on, staggered, and fell, rising, covered with dust and blood.

"Halt la!"

The words sounded like a voice from heaven. A blaze of light seemed to enwrap me, and I shouted with joy.

"Qui va la?" The rattle of musketry, the flash of steel before my eyes. Instinctively I stopped, though close behind me came a rush of my pursuers.

Another word or two, and out from a gateway poured, as it seemed to me, a tide of red and blue, as the guard turned out. All around seemed blazing with light, and the flash of steel, the clink and rattle of arms, and the loud, harsh voices of command. As I fell forward, utterly exhausted, a soldier caught me. I looked back in dreadful expectation, and saw the mass of dark forms disappearing into the night. Then I must have fainted. When I recovered my senses I was in the guard room. They gave me brandy, and after a while I was able to tell them something of what had passed. Then a commissary of police appeared, apparently out of the empty air, as is the way of the Parisian police officer. He listened attentively, and then had a moment's consultation with the officer in command. Apparently they were agreed, for they asked me if I were ready now to come with them.

"Where to?" I asked, rising to go.

"Back to the dust heaps. We shall, perhaps, catch them yet!"

"I shall try!" said I.

He eyed me for a moment keenly, and said suddenly:

"Would you like to wait a while or till tomorrow, young Englishman?" This touched me to the quick, as, perhaps, he intended, and I jumped to my feet.

"Come now!" I said; "now! now! An Englishman is always ready for his duty!"

The commissary was a good fellow, as well as a shrewd one; he slapped my shoulder kindly. "Brave garçon!" he said. "Forgive me, but I knew what would do you most good. The guard is ready. Come!"

And so, passing right through the guard room, and through a long vaulted passage, we were out into the night. A few of the men in front had powerful lanterns. Through courtyards and down a sloping way we passed out through a low archway to a sunken road, the same that I had seen in my flight. The order was given to get at the double, and with a quick, springing stride, half run, half walk, the soldiers went swiftly along. I felt my strength renewed again—such is the difference between hunter and hunted. A very short distance took us to a low-lying pontoon bridge across the stream, and evidently very little higher up than I had struck it. Some effort had evidently been made to damage it, for the ropes had all been cut, and one of the chains had been broken. I heard the officer say to the commissary:

"We are just in time! A few more minutes, and they would have destroyed the bridge. Forward, quicker still!" and on we went. Again we reached a pontoon on the winding stream; as we came up we heard the hollow boom of the metal drums as the efforts to destroy the bridge was again renewed. A word of command was given, and several men raised their rifles.

"Fire!" A volley rang out. There was a muffled cry, and the dark forms dispersed. But the evil was done, and we saw the far end of the pontoon swing into the stream. This was a serious delay, and it was nearly an hour before we had renewed ropes and restored the bridge sufficiently to allow us to cross.

We renewed the chase. Quicker, quicker we went towards the dust heaps.

After a time we came to a place that I knew. There were the re-mains of a fire—a few smouldering wood ashes still cast a red glow, but the bulk of the ashes were cold. I knew the site of the hut and the hill behind it up which I had rushed, and in the flickering glow the eyes of the rats still shone with a sort of phosphorescence. The commissary spoke a word to the officer, and he cried:

"Halt!"

The soldiers were ordered to spread around and watch, and then we commenced to examine the ruins. The commissary himself began to lift away the charred boards and rubbish. These the soldiers took and piled together. Presently he started back, then bent down and rising beckoned me.

"See!" he said.

It was a gruesome sight. There lay a skeleton face downwards, a woman by the lines—an old woman by the coarse fibre of the bone. Between the ribs rose a long spike-like dagger made from a butcher's sharpening knife, its keen point buried in the spine.

"You will observe," said the commissary to the officer and to me as he took out his note book, "that the woman must have fallen on her dagger. The rats are many here—see their eyes glistening among that heap of bones—and you will also notice"—I shuddered as he placed his hand on the skeleton—"that but little time was lost by them, for the bones are scarcely cold!"

There was no other sign of any one near, living or dead; and so deploying again into line the soldiers passed on. Presently we came to the hut made of the old wardrobe. We approached. In five of the six compartments was an old man sleeping—sleeping so soundly that even the glare of the lanterns did not wake them. Old and grim and grizzled they looked, with their gaunt, wrinkled, bronzed faces and their white moustaches.

The officer called out harshly and loudly a word of command, and in an instant each one of them was on his feet before us and standing at "attention!"

"What do you here?"

"We sleep," was the answer.

"Where are the other chiffoniers?" asked the commissary.

"Gone to work."

"And you?"

"We are on guard!"

"Peste!" laughed the officer grimly, as he looked at the old men one after the other in the face and added with cool deliberate cruelty, "Asleep on duty! Is this the manner of the Old Guard? No wonder, then, a Waterloo!"

By the gleam of the lantern I saw the grim old faces grow deadly pale, and almost shuddered at the look in the eyes of the old men as the laugh of the soldiers echoed the grim pleasantry of the officer.

I felt in that moment that I was in some measure avenged.

For a moment they looked as if they would throw themselves on the taunter, but years of their life had schooled them and they remained still.

"You are but five," said the commissary; "where is the sixth?" The answer came with a grim chuckle.

"He is there!" and the speaker pointed to the bottom of the wardrobe. "He died last night. You won't find much of him. The burial of the rats is quick!"

The commissary stooped and looked in. Then he turned to the officer and said calmly:

"We may as well go back. No trace here now; nothing to prove that man was the one wounded by your soldiers' bullets! Probably they murdered him to cover up the trace. See!" again he stooped and placed his hands on the skeleton. "The rats work quickly and they are many. These bones are warm!"

I shuddered, and so did many more of those around me.

"Form!" said the officer, and so in marching order, with the lanterns swinging in front and the manacled veterans in the midst, with steady tramp we took ourselves out of the dust-heaps and turned backward to the fortress of Bicêtre.

My year of probation has long since ended, and Alice is my wife. But when I look back upon that trying twelvemonth one of the most vivid incidents that memory recalls is that associated with my visit to the City of Dust.

One of the things that New York Times *readers regularly look forward to is the witty sardonicism of* RUSSELL BAKER's *thrice-weekly "Observer" column. Mr. Baker, who spent his youth in Virginia, won the Pulitzer Prize for commentary in 1979 and in 1983 for his autobiographical book* Growing Up. *He currently resides in the vicinity of Washington, D.C. "High-Tech Insolence," the "Observer" column for the May 18, 1986, edition of the* Times Sunday Magazine, *superficially seems to be a typical Bakerian exercise in sustained irony, but what if Mr. Baker and Stephen King (who described a possessed car in his novel* Christine) *and the producers of the old TV sitcom "My Mother the Car" actually have touched upon a dark infernal truth? I've long suspected all inanimate objects are devilishly opposed to the human race. It is a much more plausible theory than the alternative my friends propose: that I am a world-class klutz.*

High-Tech Insolence
BY RUSSELL BAKER

I suspect my new talking car is a psychopathic killer. At first I thought it was merely having a nervous breakdown. That was when it first started saying, "Thank you. Thank you" every morning as soon as I opened the door to get behind the wheel.

It was amusing at first, but after awhile it seemed silly. I finally said so one morning after opening the door and hearing, "Thank you. Thank you."

"It's stupid to thank me before I do anything for you," I said, "and thanking me twice seems like groveling."

This exchange led to what at first seemed like an outburst of insolence. Arriving at a friend's house, I opened the door and heard:

"Your oil pressure is low and requires immediate attention. Your headlights are on. Please fasten your seat belt. Your windshield-washer fluid is low. Your parking brake is on. A door is ajar. Your gasoline tank is almost empty. . . ."

My friend was so amused by the car's garrulity that after I closed the door he opened it again to see if the car would keep talking.

"Your oil pressure is low and requires immediate attention," the car said. "Your headlights are on. Please fasten your seat belt. Your windshield-washer fluid is low. Your parking brake is on. A door is ajar. Your gasoline. . . ."

I slammed the door to silence it, but my friend's wife, emerging from the house, said, "Did I hear a blabbermouth car out here?" and opened the door.

"Your oil pressure is low and requires immediate attention," said the car. "Your headlights are on. Please fasten your seat belt. Your windshield-washer fluid is. . . ."

I had boasted about having a car I could talk to, but this demonstration that it could not discuss modern art, existentialism or the death of the novel had exposed both of us as a pair of intellectual lightweights.

As we drove away, I said, "You probably thought you owed me that little humiliation for the way I spoke to you about saying, 'Thank you. Thank you.' "

"Please fasten your seat belt," the car replied.

I did.

"Thank you," said the car. Just once. O.K., I figured, we're back to normal.

Next day I rise, go to the car, open the door. It does not say, "Thank you. Thank you." Great. We have reached an understanding. I start the car, start to drive away, but the car does not want to move. Then I realize I've forgotten to release the parking brake.

Wait a minute! This is when the car is supposed to say "Your parking brake is on," but it didn't say it. Come to think of it, it didn't say "Please fasten your seat belt" either, though I have forgotten to fasten mine.

The car had apparently decided during the night never to speak to me again. What's more, the radio had also taken the vow of silence, because it refused to come across with any of the 150 rock stations with which it had blasted my brains in the past.

Well, I wasn't going to put up with mutiny. When I buy a car to talk to me I don't intend to be cheated. I telephoned the dealer and made an appointment for four days later. For three days, I suffered the car's surly silences.

Bound for the shop on the fourth day, I pulled from the curb and heard a familiar voice. "Please fasten your seat belt," it said.

I did so. "Thank you," it said.

I opened the door slightly. "A door is ajar," said the car. The radio gave me a stupefying blast of rock music.

We went to the shop anyhow. The mechanic looked at me in that funny way. "So you haven't been hearing things?" he said. "That's a switcheroo."

After we left the shop, "Are you deliberately plotting to humiliate me?" I asked. I didn't expect to hear a sinister little "Heh, heh, heh," but I listened for it. Oh yes, I listened.

Days passed. I left the car at an airport, recovered it three days later on a cold rainy night, got in, drove away, turned on the heater and drove 20 minutes with the world getting colder and colder.

Did the car say, "By turning on your heater you have mysteriously activated your air conditioner and will require immediate attention to avoid becoming covered with frost"?

No, the car did not say that. It had become murderous. Only by opening the windows to let the freezing air out and the cold rainy air in did I frustrate its nasty little scheme.

Naturally, I made an appointment four days later at the shop. And with good reason. Even with the heater off, the air-conditioner ran full blast.

Until the morning of the fourth day, of course. Then, as we pulled from the curb, torrents of hot air poured through the car's interior.

The mechanic was amused. A car trying to destroy me? He suggested I "go easy on those Stephen King thrillers."

If anything should happen to me, this note is to be turned over to the Traffic Police, Homicide Division.

When one employs the terms "possessed" or "damned", EDGAR ALLAN POE
*(1809–1849) readily comes to mind. Author of such macabre classics as "The
Black Cat," "The Cask of Amontillado," "The Masque of the Red Death,"
"The Tell-Tale Heart" and perhaps America's greatest Gothic horror story,
"The Fall of the House of Usher," Poe lived a short, tragic life. The death of his
young wife Virginia is a recurrent theme in his writings. Some regard "The
Raven" as Poe's ultimate expression of husbandly grief, but it was published
almost two years to the day before Virginia's demise on January 30, 1847,
whereas "Ulalume" first appeared in* American Review *in December 1847. Its
feverishly subjective pedanticism may be an artistic flaw, but as a document of
unbearable human grief, "Ulalume" far surpasses "The Raven" in emotive
power. The version below includes the almost forgotten tenth and concluding
stanza that Poe (perhaps wisely) later excised. (For further comment, see Appendix I, page 576.)*

Ulalume
(unabridged)

BY EDGAR ALLAN POE

The skies they were ashen and sober;
　　The leaves they were crispèd and sere—
　　The leaves they were withering and sere;
It was night in the lonesome October
　　Of my most immemorial year;
It was hard by the dim lake of Auber,
　　In the misty mid region of Weir—
It was down by the dank tarn of Auber,
　　In the ghoul-haunted woodland of Weir.

Here once, through an alley Titanic,
　　Of cypress, I roamed with my Soul—
　　Of cypress, with Psyche, my Soul.

These were days when my heart was volcanic
     As the scoriac rivers that roll—
     As the lavas that restlessly roll
Their sulphurous currents down Yaanek
     In the ultimate climes of the pole—
That groan as they roll down Mount Yaanek
     In the realms of the boreal pole.

Our talk had been serious and sober,
     But our thoughts they were palsied and sere—
     Our memories were treacherous and sere—
For we knew not the month was October,
     And we marked not the night of the year—
     (Ah, night of all nights in the year!)
We noted not the dim lake of Auber—
     (Though once we had journeyed down here)—
We remembered not the dank tarn of Auber,
     Nor the ghoul-haunted woodland of Weir.

And now, as the night was senescent
     And star-dials pointed to morn—
     As the star-dials hinted of morn—
At the end of our path a liquescent
     And nebulous lustre was born,
Out of which a miraculous crescent
     Arose with a duplicate horn—
Astarte's bediamonded crescent
     Distinct with its duplicate horn.

And I said—"She is warmer than Dian:
     She rolls through an ether of sighs—
     She revels in a region of sighs:
She has seen that the tears are not dry on
     These cheeks, where the worm never dies
And has come past the stars of the Lion
     To point us the path to the skies—
     To the Lethean peace of the skies—
Come up, in despite of the Lion,
     To shine on us with her bright eyes—

Come up through the lair of the Lion,
    With love in her luminous eyes."

But Psyche, uplifting her finger,
    Said—"Sadly this star I mistrust—
    Her pallor I strangely mistrust:—
Oh, hasten!—oh, let us not linger!
    Oh, fly!—let us fly!—for we must."
In terror she spoke, letting sink her
    Wings until they trailed in the dust—
In agony sobbed, letting sink her
    Plumes till they trailed in the dust—
    Till they sorrowfully trailed in the dust.

I replied—"This is nothing but dreaming:
    Let us on by this tremulous light!
    Let us bathe in this crystalline light!
Its Sibyllic splendor is beaming
    With Hope and in Beauty to-night:—
    See!—it flickers up the sky through the night!
Ah, we safely may trust to its gleaming,
    And be sure it will lead us aright—
We safely may trust to a gleaming
    That cannot but guide us aright,
    Since it flickers up to Heaven through the night."

Thus I pacified Psyche and kissed her,
    And tempted her out of her gloom—
    And conquered her scruples and gloom;
And we passed to the end of the vista,
    But were stopped by the door of a tomb—
    By the door of a legended tomb;
And I said—"What is written, sweet sister,
    On the door of this legended tomb?"
    She replied—"Ulalume—Ulalume—
    'Tis the vault of thy lost Ulalume!"

Then my heart it grew ashen and sober
    As the leaves that were crispèd and sere—

As the leaves that were withering and sere,
And I cried—"It was surely October
On *this* very night of last year
That I journeyed—I journeyed down here—
That I brought a dread burden down here—
On this night of all nights in the year,
Ah, what demon has tempted me here?
Well I know, now, this dim lake of Auber—
This misty mid region of Weir—
Well I know, now, this dank tarn of Auber,
This ghoul-haunted woodland of Weir."

Said we then,—the two, then: "Ah, can it
Have been that the woodlandish ghouls—
The pitiful, the merciful ghouls—
To bar up our way and to ban it
From the secret that lies in these wolds
From the thing that lies hidden in these wolds—
Have drawn up the spectre of a planet
From the limbo of lunary souls—
This sinfully scintillant planet
From the Hell of the planetary souls?"

A few years ago, Richard Monaco, novelist, literary agent, and scholar, edited a high-quality new periodical, Imago, *but unfortunately the project never quite materialized. However, the first issue got as far as the layout stage and I had the privilege of reading the page proofs. The contents included excellent fiction by Piers Anthony, Alan Dean Foster and "Boogie Man," a funky horror story by* TAPPAN KING, *who specially revised it for this anthology. Formerly a consulting editor at Bantam Books, where he helped establish the Spectra science-fantasy imprint, Tappan is the author of short stories, essays and two novels, most recently* Down Town, *a collaboration with Viido Polikarpus. Tappan is editor-in-chief of* Twilight Zone *magazine.*

Boogie Man

BY TAPPAN KING

The nights are the worst, after the show is over, the instruments and equipment stashed, and I'm all alone in my hotel room. Most of the time I can't sleep. When I can, the dreams come, and I replay the whole goddamn thing over again like a busted '45.

We were cutting the second album, *Judd Cain,* in a tight little studio just outside of Memphis. No sidemen, just the band: Judd, me on drums, Casey on bass, Nick the harp player. We'd laid down a half dozen good tracks, but it was all B-side, the kind of stuff an FM DJ will play on a rainy Saturday. We needed a single, and it wouldn't come.

That's when Judd started to come apart. No sooner would we start cooking with some powerful riff than he'd shut it down, complaining about fingering or giving Nick hell for coming in too late.

We'd cranked it up again, and everything was going fine, with Judd cutting loose on a cover of "Mannish Boy" that did Mud proud. He was slamming that guitar like he was trying to kill it. Then a string broke.

I heard a howl like a wounded animal, and saw Judd heft that guitar over his head and chuck it through the window. The glass smashed into shards and the guitar busted into a million pieces against the far wall, damn near decapitating Charlie, the board man.

When I looked around, Judd was gone and Charlie was blotting the blood from a gash in his cheek with an old bandanna.

"You okay?" I asked.

"I guess so, Hap," said Charlie. "What the fuck's got into Judd, anyway?"

I shook my head. "Session's over, boys," I said. "Let's try it again tomorrow."

I was still standing there in the wreckage when Len Devore came barreling in. Bad news travels fast.

"Where did he go, Hap?"

I jerked my head to the door. Devore took a couple of steps, and turned around, stopping me dead with a glance. Now I'm over six foot, and weigh about two-forty, and Devore is this dinky little guy with starched hankies and three-piece suits who only comes up to about here on me. But if you've heard that Len Devore is the meanest son of a bitch record producer ever lived, you only heard half of it. One look in those eyes, and I was in no mood to mess.

He stuck his hands on his hips, and cut me dead with that sarcastic English drawl of his:

"Nice work, Hap. You were *supposed* to keep him straight. I'm not paying you for your looks, you know."

That riled me. "He *is* straight, Len. Has been all week. Shit, he won't even blow weed anymore, says it 'fucks up his energies,' whatever the hell that means."

"Those 'energies' are paying your salary, in case you've forgotten. Look, Hap, we had an agreement, you and I. You were brought on here for two reasons. First, you're supposed to be the best goddamned drummer in the States—he damn near killed the last one. And second, you're supposed to keep the dealers and dopers away, and the freaks and starfuckers off his back. Now if that's too difficult for you—"

"I swear, Len, he hasn't come *near* the stuff."

"Well, *something's* bothering him," he said. "And it's getting worse. I want you to find out what it is."

"Just what the hell do you expect me to do, exactly?"

"I don't know, Hap," he said, softening up a little. "I've known Judd longer than anybody, and I'll be damned if I know how to help him." Then he gives me his little-boy-lost look. "Listen, I'm sorry I've been riding you, Hap. Go *talk* to him, will you? I don't care how you do it, or what it costs. We've *got* to get this album finished before the tour starts."

"I'll do my damndest, Len."

"That's all I'm asking."

I took a couple of minutes to suck up a Coors and cool out, then went looking for Judd. I found him in his trailer. The door was open, but the room was dark, and it took my eyes a little while to get used to it. The only light came from the green glow of the tuner and the red coal of Judd's cigarette.

He was sitting half-naked on the bed, arms kind of wrapped around his knees, that long cornsilk hair of his just hanging down over his bare shoulders to his feet. I guess he must have heard me come in, because his head came up. But he looked right through me.

"Judd?"

No answer.

"Judd. I want to talk with you for a minute."

"Go ahead."

"Mind if I sit down?"

He didn't answer. I took a seat opposite the bed.

"What's got into you, Judd?"

He finally seemed to respond. He unfolded himself slowly and dropped his legs over the edge of the bed, pressing his palms together between his knees. He looked totally wasted, and there was this terrible distance in his eyes, and in his voice.

"How do you think the session went today, Hap?"

"You mean, before you trashed that Fender? Fine. Just fine. I think it was your best work yet, Judd."

He shook his head. "No, Hap. It was garbage. Worthless garbage."

"How do you mean?"

He stood up. "I'll show you." He opened the safe, took out an old half-sized 78-rpm sleeve, and drew the disc from it like it was something sacred. He settled it on the turntable, lowering the tonearm real gently.

The speakers crackled as the old disc spun. The recording was poor, the fidelity lousy, but the sound that came out of those speakers hooked me in the gut with the first bar. A mean blues guitar laid down a bass line so basic, so funky, it felt like my heart slowed down to meet it. My foot began tapping against my will.

The voice was unearthly. It sang in a thick, wolflike growl:

> I'm the Boogie Man,
> That's who I am.
> I said I'm the Boogie Man,
> Everybody knows that's who I am.
> Baby I'm the Boogie Man,
> I'll get you if I can.

Judd bobbed to the beat like a puppet. His lips formed the words silently. Then it was over, and I went all hollow inside. I felt an almost unbearable urge to start the record up again. I shook my head to clear it of the music's hold on me.

"Who the hell *was* that, Judd?"

He got this weird smile on his face. "His name is *Blind Joe Death.*"

"You're kidding."

"No. That's the name. What do you think?"

"Incredible. He's the best goddamned blues player I've ever heard."

"That's the point, Hap. He's *too* damn good."

"*Too* good?" I said. "I don't get you. That song sounds like just what we've been after for the single. Why don't we give a try at cutting it tomorrow?"

"I can't."

"What do you mean, you can't?"

"I've tried to do what he does on that cut, and I can't. He's doing things with his hands and his voice that just can't be done, Hap."

"Hell, nobody's *that* good, Judd. I mean, you've played with Muddy Waters, Bo Diddley, the Hook, all of them. You're as good as any blues player alive."

Judd's eyes suddenly came to life. What I saw in them scared the shit out of me.

"Don't you understand, Hap?" he said, getting real intense. "This guy's tapping into something that's way beyond all of us. He makes everybody's work sound like pure, unadulterated horseshit. He's the fucking *source,* man. I'd give *anything* to play like he does. I've been trying to get even part of this down for six months now, and I can't come near it. Don't you see? It's no use. I'm not going to cut that song —or *any* song—until I can do it just like he does."

Judd was getting into dangerous ground. If I didn't get him back in the studio, I could kiss my ass good-bye.

"Now hold on, Judd. If he's so damn good, how come nobody's ever heard of this guy before? Whatever happened to him?"

"Nobody knows. One or two of the old guys know the name, but they won't talk about him. One of Len's people turned this up in a record shop in Paris. It cost him a hell of a lot. The dealer said he was last heard from in the late fifties, on the South Side of Chicago. That's all I've been able to find out."

"Probably dead by now," I said, and found Judd's hands locked in my T-shirt.

"Don't say that!" he hissed. "He *can't* be dead."

"Whoa!" I said, breaking his grip. This was getting weird. "Easy, brother. Why not?"

"Because I've got to find him. Watch him. Listen to him. Play with him."

"You got an album to finish, Judd."

"Fuck the album. *This* is what matters!"

"Now you listen to me, Judd," I said. "I don't care if you go bugshit over some old blues hand—that's your privilege. But Devore says if I don't get you back in the studio tomorrow, he's gonna personally hand me my balls on a platter."

I must have reached him, because it was like he suddenly saw me again. But he still didn't say anything. I stood there, watching that old 78 go round, and something turned, somewhere deep inside me.

"I'll make a deal with you," I found myself saying. "You do your damndest in the studio tomorrow and get this album finished, and I'll track down this Blind Joe Death character for you. How about it? What do you say?"

Judd's eyes widened.

"You will?" he said. "You'll help me find him?"

"I swear it, Judd," I said, wondering what the hell I was getting myself in for. "If he's anywhere to be found, I'll find him for you. Now look, why don't you just put all this out of your head for one night? There's a sweet little thing been hanging around all day trying to get next to you. I'll send her over. There's nothin' wrong with you a little R 'n' R won't cure. Okay, Judd?"

"Whatever you say, Hap."

By some miracle, the album got finished. Judd came bounding into the studio the next morning like a new man. The single, "Oh, Yeah!," mastered in one white-hot take, broke the charts at number five. The next week the album hit the charts at ten, and kept climbing.

Judd seemed to be keeping his side of the bargain. He didn't make any more trouble, stayed clean, devoted himself to the tour. So I kept to mine. I put it out on the grapevine that Judd Cain would pay good money for information concerning a certain blues player. It turned out that Judd's obsession with old Blind Joe didn't hurt his reputation one bit. If anything, it improved his pedigree as number one student of the blues. Devore said I'd worked a minor miracle, and doubled my retainer. I didn't argue.

Of course I had to deal with every flake and fruitcake and con artist who thought he could hustle me for a quick buck. I heard a lot of outrageous stories—guesses, rumors, tall tales. One old dude even whispered that Blind Joe had sold his soul to the Devil himself to get to play the blues like that. I turned the losers away, paid the rest. What the hell. It wasn't my money.

But as the weeks went by, and nothing more substantial turned up, I began to get a little edgy. I would have given a small fortune for one solid lead. By the time we reached the end of the tour Judd was wound up like a cheap E-string ready to break. If something didn't turn up damn quick, there'd be hell to pay.

It happened in Chicago, at a party the night before the big show. Judd Cain's twenty-second birthday party—a blowout to end all blowouts. Judd was up, way up. I was worried. First I figured he was speeding. When I finally figured out what was causing it, I really started to get scared.

Chicago. The town where Blind Joe Death was supposed to have played his last gig. The town where all our leads gave out. Judd was expecting to find the man here. When he didn't show up, I didn't want to be around.

And then there was this guy at the door.

He was black, short, almost a dwarf, wearing a shabby, greasy black suit. His face was seamed and scarred and his nose looked like a squashed strawberry.

"You Judd Cain?" he asked. His voice was a faint, hoarse whisper, barely audible over the blaring music.

"What?" I said, not quite all there.

"You Judd Cain?" he asked again, louder this time.

"No," I said. "He's upstairs. Anything you've got to tell him you can tell me first."

His eyes got desperate and his mouth worked a little. Then he reached under his coat and pulled out a flat package, lowering it gently to the glass tabletop. I peeled away the oily newspaper.

It looked like Judd's 78 of "Boogie Man." The blue label was the same, but in the center were the words:

"Devil Child"
Blind Joe Death

A moment later, I was on my feet. "I'll go get Judd."

"Wait!" His whisper stopped me at the door. His hands were clenched and beads of sweat stood out on his brow. He seemed to be fighting some inner battle.

"I got to tell you something."

"Shoot," I said.

"You ain't gonna believe me."

"Let me be the judge of that," I said.

"All right," he said, wiping his mouth. "You heard those stories about Joe and the Devil?"

I nodded.

"They're true," he whispered. "Joe—he—he ain't human. I mean, he *used* to be human, but now there's this—this *thing* inside him where his heart and soul used to be." His voice faltered. "A bad thing. An evil thing that lives off people's souls, that drains the life out of them."

He looked at me like he was daring me to laugh. I just shrugged. I'd heard weirder shit before.

Before I could say anything, the door of the suite flew open. Judd was standing at the door.

"There you are. I wondered where—" He stopped when he spotted the record on the table. "Where in hell did you get that?"

I looked at the little man, and something passed between us. No matter how I tried, I couldn't say a word about what I'd just heard. Instead, I found myself saying:

"This man can take you to Blind Joe Death, Judd—that is, if you want to go."

"Hell, yes, I want to go. What are we waiting for? C'mon, Hap!"

"No," I said. "You go ahead. Just make it back in time for the show, okay?"

"Sure, Hap."

They were almost out the door when the little guy turned to me and whispered: "Just one more thing. I had to tell you the story, man. I knew you wouldn't believe it, but I had to tell you all the same."

He was right. I didn't believe him then. Just like you don't believe me now.

When Judd missed the afternoon run-through, I began to get spooked. Nick and Casey asked me if I'd seen him. I couldn't say a damned thing.

At seven o'clock, when the opening act went on, Judd was still missing. Devore swore he'd take me apart if Judd missed the show. I was more scared for Judd than for me.

By eight, the audience was getting restless. The kids were standing up in their seats, waving lighters and matches and clapping their hands above their heads. Ten minutes later, they began to whistle and stomp and shout.

About eight-thirty, I called the guys together, said we should stall with a jam. I just was getting settled behind my drums, when I heard a low roar from the crowd, and Judd was suddenly on stage. He held up two fingers, and we swung into "Who Do You Love?" Judd was white lightning. I was caught up in the fever, laying down some of the best drumming ever. When the song stopped and the lights dimmed, the kids were in pandemonium.

Judd nodded to the wings. A white guitar was brought on and placed next to a chair set in the middle of the stage. A white hat was perched rakishly on one of the posts.

"It is my pleasure," said Judd Cain, "to present one of the living legends of the blues. Will you welcome, please—*Blind Joe Death!*" As the lights went dark, I felt a cold surge of fear in my gut.

Silence. In the tight spot on that empty chair a red glow moved. A cigarette in a jet-black hand. The white hat tilted. The bone-white guitar lifted itself slowly. There was a man seated in the chair. An old man all in black. A man with eyes as black as death.

I watched, paralyzed, as the spindly figure moved without aid to the microphone, calling out in a voice halfway between a laugh and a howl:

"Everybody ready to *boogie?*"

"Yeah!" the kids screamed.

"I can't hear you. Do you wanna *boogie,* children?"

"Yeah!" the kids screamed louder.

"Well, *all right!* Gonna give you a *Devil Child!*"

Blind Joe Death began to play, with a beat that was wild, evil, older than the blues. My hands leapt to the drums against my will, moving to that ancient rhythm.

Blind Joe Death began to sing:

> Oh Devil, Oh Devil
> I'm so wild,
> People call me
> A Devil Child!

As he hammered that white axe, the kids went wild, surging up out of their seats and boogeying in the aisle. Then he turned to Judd, who took the next verse:

> Oh Devil, Oh Devil
> Tell me true,
> Ain't I a Devil
> Child like you?

The two cut loose on intertwining riffs that wove an unholy spell. They sang the next verse together:

> Get on up!
> Watch me fly.
> Gonna be a Devil Child
> By and by!

The two moved to opposite sides of the stage and sang out as one voice:

> Get up!
> Get on up!
> Get up!
> Get on up!

Blind Joe Death pointed to the audience, singing out *"Get up! Get on up!"* in that wolfgrowl of his. Where he pointed, the kids were pulled to their feet like somebody was yanking on their strings. He moved his long fingers across the hall, and they bobbed to the music.

Judd Cain raised his pale hand and pointed it at the audience. *"Get up! Get on up!"* They were pulled to their feet. *"Get up! Get on up!"* All of them were up now, cheering, screaming. My arms were pounding out the beat, and there was nothing I could do to stop them.

Blind Joe Death swept his hand back slowly. The bodies began to fall like reaped wheat. A wave of panic swept those still standing as the others fell around them.

You probably heard about it on the news. They called it an accident. Some kind of mass hysteria. But I was there. I watched in helpless horror as hundreds of kids tried to run from the savage force loosed among them. I listened as the shouting and cheering turned to shrieks of pain and moans of terror. I saw the pale fire that leaped from those dying bodies.

And I saw Judd Cain standing alone at center stage, his eyes wells of dark fire, as he picked up that hat and that old guitar and sang that old song in a wolfgrowl, with every note, every intonation precisely right:

> I'm the Boogie Man,
> That's who I am.
> I said I'm the Boogie Man,
> Everybody knows that's who I am.
> Baby I'm the Boogie Man,
> I'll get you if I can.

One of the great puzzles in modern genre literature is how EDWARD D. HOCH *can be so stunningly prolific and yet always turn in a first-rate performance. Past president of the Mystery Writers of America, he is the author of more than seven hundred short stories, which, in addition to the Rand espionage series and the wonderful Nick Velvet puzzles, include the adventures of Simon Ark, an immortal priest who battles Satan through the centuries. Some of Ed's more obscure efforts are the horror stories he wrote for Robert A. Lowndes'* excellent Magazine of Horror. *"The Maze and the Monster" appeared in volume I, number 1, of that late lamented periodical.*

The Maze and the Monster
BY EDWARD D. HOCH

The tangled chain of half-forgotten events which had carried William Nellis from a comfortable existence on London's West End to the wild waters off the Atlantic Coast of North Africa were such that even he would have been hard pressed to explain his presence that bleak December day in the middle of a sandy beach so far from home. The ship he'd come on had floundered in a storm the day before, and now he alone of all the crew seemed to have safely reached the shelter of this island. The ship itself was no longer on the horizon. Perhaps it had been carried to the bottom; more likely, the crew had regained control after the storm passed and sailed on without him.

In any event, he was not to be alone on the beach for long. Two men wearing a sort of greenish uniform unfamiliar to him appeared from the underbrush, leveling rifles of a type he'd imagined were obsolete fifty years ago. They spoke in Spanish, a language he hardly knew, but their commands were obvious. He was a prisoner, captured on the beach of an island he hardly knew existed, by men who spoke a different language. And within an hour he found himself cast into the darkness of a cell in the far interior of the island, without food or water or any clothing but the tattered remains of his seagoing garments.

He remained in the dungeon—for it was nothing more than that—for more than a day, until his thirst was such that he'd taken to licking water from the walls where it trickled down in the darkness from some dampness unseen above. Then, without warning, the guards came for him again. This time he was taken down a long passageway that seemed to connect the prison with a sort of palace, a vast glistening sparkle of a place that reminded him of those old pictures of Versailles in the days of Saint-Simon. The guards led him into a high-ceilinged chamber at the end of which sat an elderly man who gave every evidence of being strong and active despite his years. His face was deeply tanned, almost brown, and the whiteness of his wrinkled hair gave to the whole head an air of motion, of matter arrested but momentarily. The man might have been a conqueror or a prime minister. He was most certainly a ruler.

"Good evening," he said quietly, speaking in English with just a trace of Spanish accent. "Welcome to the Island of Snails."

"My ship lost me," Nellis started to explain. "The storm . . ."

"No need for explanations." The other held up his hand. "We are always anxious to have visitors here."

"This is your island?"

"Quite correct. I am Captain Cortez, direct descendant of the Spanish conqueror. My island, my people. I own everything you can see."

"I'd be very pleased if you could arrange transportation for me back to the mainland," Nellis said, with a growing tension in the pit of his stomach. There was something about this place and this man which struck fear into him, a fear he had not even felt during his day in the dungeon.

"Well," the white-haired man answered slowly, "that would be a bit difficult at this time. I think you'd better plan to remain with us here."

Nellis took a step forward and immediately the guards were upon him. "What in hell is this? Am I a prisoner?"

The Spaniard's eyes sparkled like the jeweled chandelier overhead. "Yes, you are a prisoner! You are a prisoner because you dared to set foot on my island!" Then, to the guards, "Take him away! Talk is of no use with scum like this. Prepare the maze for him!"

Nellis struggled in the grip of the guards. "You're a madman. I'm not staying here any longer." But then there was a thudding blow to his temple, and he was falling, into a blackness of unknowing, into a dream of madness that was not a dream . . .

And when he awakened, with a splatter of icy water across his face, he found himself in a place far below the ground, where the air was chilled by a dampness that clutched at his bones. The guards were there, and the man named Cortez, and ahead of them was only a long passageway, lit by torches such as one might find in the tunnels of the pyramids or the catacombs of Rome.

"Have they removed the last one?" Cortez asked.

"They are in there now, getting him."

"Very good." He turned to look down at Nellis. "This is a maze," he explained carefully, "built for me at great expense out of the earth and solid rock in spots. It has about two miles of passageways. You will enter through here, and the door will be sealed behind you. Thereafter, you will come upon one of two possible exits to the maze. At one exit you will find a paradise of pleasure beyond your wildest dreams. At the other, a . . . what shall I say? . . . a monster."

As if on cue, two uniformed guards emerged from the passageway, carrying between them a stretcher heavy with the weight of what had once been a man. The body, stripped of clothing, was torn and ripped as if by a tiger or other great beast. There was hardly a square inch of skin area unmarked by the violence of the assault. The man had died, horribly, back there in the maze.

"You're insane," Nellis told the Spaniard.

"Perhaps. Actually, the idea for this was suggested by a countryman of yours named Stockton—is that the name? Yes, Stockton. He wrote a story called *The Lady or the Tiger?* which has fascinated me ever since my youth."

"Stockton was an American," Nellis corrected, though at the moment it seemed to make very little difference. "And you're still crazy."

"Enough talk. I wish you good luck and a safe return—a safe journey to paradise or a quick death in the monster's claws. I advise you to keep moving. It is cold in the maze, and I know you are hungry. We would not want you to die of starvation."

"Don't I even get a weapon to defend myself?"

"Your weapons are your hands, though they will be quite useless if you should come upon our monster. Now, into the maze with you!"

The guards tore away what remained of his shredded clothing and cast him a few feet into the passageway. Almost immediately, a door of thin steel slid quietly into place, blocking out the sight of the smiling Captain Cortez. But though the passage was dim, there seemed to be a flicker of light from somewhere up ahead. Nellis hurried toward it, knowing full well that neither monster nor paradise could lurk that close to the beginning. What he found was a torch burning in the wall, and he pried it free of its metal bracket. It was some weapon at least, against the monster, and it also gave him light.

He went on, quite openly at first, holding the torch high and carefully avoiding the occasional pebbles that might threaten the bareness of his feet. After walking some fifty feet farther on he came to a branching of the maze and his first decision. He decided on the right-hand passageway, and carefully made an X on the floor of the passageway with the butt of his torch, so he would know if he passed this way again while going in circles. Then he moved on, slower this time, holding the torch high above his head.

The walls here were of smooth stone, but the ground underneath seemed mostly of dirt. He imagined Cortez laboring on the maze for so many months or years, pouring a fortune into the construction of the thing, and anticipating the coming torments of the men who might be his prisoners. Nellis remembered the horribly torn body they'd carried out of the maze, and wondered if there really was a safe way out. Wouldn't it be more in keeping with the madness of Cortez to have every passageway lead to the monster?

A low roaring sound suddenly filled the tunnel, and he froze every muscle. An animal—the monster? Or perhaps only the rushing of water somewhere? After a moment he continued walking, but more slowly still. Maybe he should simply sit down against the wall, wait for starvation to overtake him. But what if the monster came prowling, found him in a weakened condition with no chance to defend himself? No, it was better to go on, while some slight hope remained.

He came to another branching of the maze, this time with three narrower passages leading off the main one. Again he chose the one on the far right and made his X on the ground. He'd remembered reading somewhere that one method of solving a maze—at least on paper— was always to follow one wall of it. Though it might not be the shortest path, sooner or later you would find the exit. Of course such magazine-made mazes did not include a monster that might lurk around any turning.

He seemed so far away from London then, so far away that memory itself was difficult for him. This might have been another world, another lifetime, an existence cut off from all reality except the reality of the pebbles beneath his feet and the chill dampness of the passage.

Suddenly, without warning, a gust of cold air filled the tunnel, blowing out the flame of his torch like a puff of some giant mouth. He cursed silently and then went on. The deadened torch could still serve as a club, at least, though he would have to travel much slower now, feeling his way along the cool stone wall of the maze. He decided he would stick with the right-hand wall, and hope for the best.

Aware, too aware, of the sweat forming even on his icy flesh, he wandered the maze for what seemed like hours. Once he hit out at something that might have been a rat, scurrying across his left foot. And again once he heard the howling cry of the beast, or the wind, reverberating through the maze, almost seeming to seek him out. The seconds, minutes, hours went by; the hunger grew within him like a physical presence; and still he kept moving along the right wall, aware now and then of other dark tunnels branching off, aware too of occasional hints of movement close at hand. Rats, perhaps again, or something stalking him like a tiger in the doubt-filled dark. If only he knew the nature of the monster, then at least the fear that welled within him might be lessened.

Then, ahead, he thought he saw a flicker of light. Was it possible? Had he reached one of the maze's two exits, or would he find only another torch flaming on the wall. He went forward more slowly than ever, careful lest his bare toes might hit some pebble and send out a click of warning. Slowly, slowly . . .

He rounded the last corner and found himself in a high-ceilinged room lit by a score of torches. There were vivid red couches here, and ferns and drapes that made the whole thing seem like a great room overlooking the sea. And, standing in the very center of the chamber, a woman of such beauty that she left him breathless. A woman tall and sleek and raven-haired, wearing a garment of gold that fell loosely from one lovely shoulder. She held out her arms to him, and he dropped his stump of expired torch and ran forward, the hunger of his stomach forgotten now.

"Thank God," he mumbled, flinging himself into her arms. "I never thought I'd find the way out. I never thought . . ."

"You're with me now," she said, and her voice was as smooth as honey.

"I've fooled him," he gasped out. "I've defeated Cortez and his maze. I've found his paradise . . ."

He stopped because her fingers had pressed against a nerve and he could neither move nor speak, nor close his eyes. Her face was only inches from him as she answered, "Oh, no! You don't seem to understand. You found the monster."

He had only time to see the madness deep within her eyes before her blood-red fingernails ripped across his eyeballs. Then there was nothing. Nothing but endless pain . . .

Edward White Benson, once the Archbishop of Canterbury, had four brilliant children: Arthur Christopher, poet and essayist; Edward Frederick, author of "The Room in the Tower," "How Fear Departed from the Long Gallery" and other classic tales of terror; Margaret; and ROBERT HUGH BENSON *(1871–1914), a Monsignor in the Catholic Arch-Diocese of Westminster who wrote two apocalyptic science-fantasy novels,* The Necromancers *and* The Dawn of All. *He also wrote enough ghost stories to fill two rare volumes,* The Light Invisible *and* A Mirror of Shalott, *from which the following powerful tale of demonic possession is taken.*

Father Meuron's Tale

BY ROBERT HUGH BENSON

Father Meuron was very voluble at supper on the Saturday. He exclaimed; he threw out his hands; his bright black eyes shone above his rosy cheeks, and his hair appeared to stand more on end than I had ever known it.

He sat at the further side of the horse-shoe table from myself, and I was able to remark on his gaiety to the English priest who sat beside me without fear of being overheard.

Father Brent smiled.

"He is drunk with *la gloire,*" he said. "He is to tell the story tonight."

This explained everything.

I did not look forward, however, to his recital. I was confident that it would be full of tinsel and swooning maidens who ended their days in convents under Father Meuron's spiritual direction; and when we came upstairs I found a shadowy corner, a little back from the semicircle, where I could fall asleep if I wished without provoking remark.

In fact, I was totally unprepared for the character of his narrative.

When we had all taken our places, and Monsignor's pipe was properly alight, and himself at full length in his deck chair, the Frenchman began. He told his story in his own language; but I am venturing to render it in English as nearly as I am able.

"My contribution to the histories," he began, seated in his upright arm-chair in the centre of the circle, a little turned away from me— "my contribution to the histories which these good priests are to recite is an affair of exorcism. That is a matter with which we who live in Europe are not familiar in these days. It would seem, I suppose, that grace has a certain power, accumulating through the centuries, of saturating even physical objects with its force. However men may rebel, yet the sacrifices offered and the prayers poured out have a faculty of holding Satan in check and preventing his more formidable manifestations. Even in my own poor country at this hour, in spite of widespread apostasy, in spite even of the deliberate worship of Satan, yet grace is in the air; and it is seldom indeed that a priest has to deal with a case of possession. In your respectable England, too, it is the same; the simple piety of Protestants has kept alive to some extent the force of the Gospel. Here in this country of Italy it is somewhat different. The old powers have survived the Christian assault, and while they cannot live in Holy Rome, there are corners where they do so."

From my place I saw Padre Bianchi turn a furtive eye upon the speaker, and I thought I read in it an unwilling assent.

"However," went on the Frenchman with a superb dismissory gesture, "my recital does not concern this continent, but the little island of La Souffrière. These circumstances are other than here. It was a stronghold of darkness when I was there in 1891. Grace, while laying hold of men's hearts, had not yet penetrated the lower creation. Do you understand me? There were many holy persons whom I knew, who frequented the Sacraments and lived devoutly, but there were many of another manner. The ancient rites survived secretly among the negroes, and darkness—how shall I say it?—dimness made itself visible.

"However, to our history."

The priest resettled himself in his chair and laid his fingers together like precious instruments. He was enjoying himself vastly, and I could see that he was preparing himself for a revelation.

"It was in 1891," he repeated, "that I went there with another of our Fathers to the mission-house. I will not trouble you, gentlemen, with recounting the tale of our arrival, nor of the months that followed it, except perhaps to tell you that I was astonished by much that I saw. Never until that time had I seen the power of the Sacraments so evident. In civilized lands, as I have suggested to you, the air is charged with grace. Each is no more than a wave in the deep sea. He who is without God's favor is not without His grace at each breath he draws. There are churches, religions, pious persons about him; there are centuries of prayers behind him. The very buildings he enters, as M. Huysmans has explained to us, are browned by prayer. Though a wicked child, he is yet in his father's house: and the return from death to life is not such a crossing of the abyss, after all. But there in La Souffrière all is either divine or Satanic, black or white, Christian or devilish. One stands, as it were, on the seashore to watch the breakers of grace, and each is a miracle. I tell you I have seen holy Catechumens foam at the mouth and roll their eyes in pain, as the saving water fell on them, and that which was within went out. As the Gospel relates, *'Spiritus conturbavit illum: et elisus in terram, volutabatur spumans.' "*

Father Meuron paused again.

I was interested to hear this corroboration of evidence that had come before me on other occasions. More than one missionary had told me the same thing; and I had found in their tales a parallel to those related by the first preachers of the Christian religion in the early days of the Church.

"I was incredulous at first," continued the priest, "until I saw these things for myself. An old father of our mission rebuked me for it. 'You are an ignorant fellow,' he said; 'your airs are still of the seminary.' And what he said was just, my friends.

"On one Monday morning as we met for our council I could see that this old priest had somewhat to say. M. Lasserre was his name. He kept very silent until the little businesses had been accomplished, and then he turned to the Father Rector.

" 'Monseigneur has written,' he said, 'and given me the necessary permission for the matter you know, my father. And he bids me take another priest with me. I ask that Father Meuron may accompany me. He needs a lesson, this zealous young missionary.'

"The Father Rector smiled at me as I sat astonished, and nodded at Father Lasserre to give permission.

" 'Father Lasserre will explain all to you,' he said as he stood up for the prayer.

"The good priest explained all to me as the Father Rector had directed."

It appeared that there was a matter of exorcism on hand. A woman who lived with her mother and husband had been affected by the devil, Father Lasserre said. She was a Catechumen, and had been devout for several months, and all seemed well until this—this assault had been made on her soul. Father Lasserre had visited the woman and examined her, and had made his report to the Bishop, asking permission to exorcise the creature, and it was this permission that had been sent on that morning.

"I did not venture to tell the priest that he was mistaken and that the affair was one of epilepsy. I had studied a little in books for my medical training, and all that I heard now seemed to confirm me in the diagnosis. There were the symptoms, easy to read. What would you have?"—the priest again made his little gesture—"I knew more in my youth than all the Fathers of the Church. Their affairs of devils were nothing but an affection of the brain—dreams and fancies! And if the exorcisms had appeared to be of direct service, it was from the effect of the solemnity upon the mind. It was no more."

He laughed with a fierce irony.

"You know it all, gentlemen!"

I had lost all desire to sleep now. The French priest was more interesting than I had thought. His elaborateness seemed dissipated; his voice trembled a little as he arraigned his own conceit, and I began to wonder how his change of mind had been wrought.

"We set out that afternoon," he continued. "The woman lived on the further side of the island, perhaps a couple of hours' travel, for it was rough going; and as we went up over the path Father Lasserre told me more.

"It seemed that the woman blasphemed. (The subconscious self, said I to myself, as M. Charcot has explained. It is her old habit reasserting itself.)

"She foamed and rolled her eyes. (An affection of the brain, said I.)

"She feared holy water; they dared not throw it on her, her struggles were so fierce. (Because she has been taught to fear it, said I.)

"And so the good father talked, eyeing me now and again, and I smiled in my heart, knowing that he was a simple old fellow who had not studied the new books.

"She was quieter after sunset, he told me, and would take a little food then. Her fits came on her for the most part at midday. And I smiled again at that. Why it should be so I knew. The heat affected her. She would be quieter, science would tell us, when evening fell. If it were the power of Satan that held her she would surely rage more in the darkness than in the light. The Scriptures tell us so.

"I said something of this to Father Lasserre, as if it were a question, and he looked at me.

" 'Perhaps, brother,' he said, 'she is more at ease in the darkness and fears the light, and that she is quieter therefore when the sun sets.'

"Again I smiled to myself. What piety, said I, and what foolishness!

"The house where the three lived stood apart from any others. It was an old shed into which they had moved a week before, for the neighbors could no longer bear the woman's screaming. And we came to it towards a sunset.

"It was a heavy evening, dull and thick, and as we pushed down the path I saw the smoking mountain high on the left hand between the tangled trees. There was a great silence round us, and no wind, and every leaf against the rosy sky was as if cut of steel.

"We saw the roof below us presently, and a little smoke escaped from a hole, for there was no chimney.

" 'We will sit here a little, brother,' said my friend. 'We will not enter till sunset.'

"And he took out his office book and began to say his Matins and Lauds, sitting on a fallen tree-trunk by the side of the path.

"All was very silent about us. I suffered terrible distractions, for I was a young man and excited; and though I knew it was no more than epilepsy that I was to see, yet epilepsy is not a good sight to regard. But I was finishing the first Nocturn when I saw that Father Lasserre was looking off his book.

"We were sitting thirty yards from the roof of the hut, which was built in a scoop of the ground, so that the roof was level with the ground on which we sat. Below it was a little open space, flat, perhaps twenty yards across, and below that yet further was the wood again, and far over that was the smoke of the village against the sea. There was the mouth of a well with a bucket beside it; and by this was standing a man, a negro, very upright, with a vessel in his hand.

"This fellow turned as I looked, and saw us there, and he dropped the vessel, and I could see his white teeth. Father Lasserre stood up and laid his finger on his lips, nodded once or twice, pointed to the west, where the sun was just above the horizon, and the fellow nodded to us again and stooped for his vessel.

"He filled it from the bucket and went back into the house.

"I looked at Father Lasserre and he looked at me.

" 'In five minutes,' he said; 'that is the husband. Did you not see his wounds?'

"I had seen no more than his teeth, I said, and my friend nodded again and proceeded to finish his Nocturn."

Again Father Meuron paused dramatically. His ruddy face seemed a little pale in the candle-light, and yet he had told us nothing yet that could account for his apparent horror. Plainly, something was coming soon.

The Rector leaned back to me and whispered behind his hand in reference to what the Frenchman had related a few minutes before, that no priest was allowed to use exorcism without the special leave of the Bishop. I nodded and thanked him.

Father Meuron flashed his eyes dreadfully round the circle, clasped his hands and continued:

"When the sun showed only a red rim above the sea we went down to the house. The path ran on high ground to the roof and then dipped down the edge of the cutting past the window to the front of the shed.

"I looked through this window sideways as I went after Father Lasserre, who was carrying his bag with the book and the holy water, but I could see nothing but the light of the fire. And there was no sound. That was terrible to me!

"The door was closed as we came to it, and as Father Lasserre lifted his hand to knock there was a howl of a beast from within.

"He knocked and looked at me.

" 'It is but epilepsy!' he said, and his lips wrinkled as he said it."

The priest stopped again, and smiled ironically at us all. Then he clasped his hands beneath his chin like a man in terror.

"I will not tell you all that I saw," he went on, "when the candle was lighted and set on the table, but only a little. You would not dream well, my friends—as I did not that night.

"But the woman sat in a corner by the fireplace, bound with cords by her arms to the back of the chair and her feet to the legs of it.

"Gentlemen, she was like no woman at all. . . . The howl of a wolf came from her lips, but there were words in the howl. At first I could not understand till she began in French, and then I understood. My God!

"The foam dripped from her mouth like water, and her eyes—but there! I began to shake when I saw them until the holy water was spilled on the floor, and I set it down on the table by the candle. There was a plate of meat on the table, roasted mutton, I think, and a loaf of bread beside it. Remember that, gentlemen—that mutton and bread! And as I stood there I told myself, like making acts of faith, that it was but epilepsy, or at the most madness.

"My friends, it is probable that few of you know the form of exorcism. It is neither in the Ritual or the Pontifical, and I cannot remember it all myself. But it began thus:"

The Frenchman sprang up and stood with his back to the fire, with his face in the shadow.

"Father Lasserre was here where I stand, in his cotta and stole, and I beside him. There where my chair stands was the square table, as near as that, with the bread and meat and the holy water and the candle. Beyond the table was the woman; her husband stood beside her on the left hand, and the old mother was there"—he flung out a hand to the right, "on the floor telling her beads and weeping—but weeping.

"When the Father was ready and had said a word to the others, he signed to me to lift the holy water again—she was quiet at the moment —and then he sprinkled her.

"As he lifted his hand she raised her eyes, and there was a look in them of terror, as if at a blow, and as the drops fell she leaped forward in the chair, and the chair leaped with her. Her husband was at her and dragged the chair back. But my God! it was terrible to see him; his teeth shone as if he smiled, but the tears ran down his face.

"Then she moaned like a child in pain. It was as if the holy water burned her; she lifted her face to her man as if she begged him to wipe off the drops.

"And all the while I still told myself that it was the terror of her mind only at the holy water—that it could not be that she was possessed by Satan—it was but madness—madness and epilepsy!

"Father Lasserre went on with the prayers, and I said Amen, and there was a psalm—*Deus in nomine tuo salvum me fac*—and then came the first bidding to the unclean spirit to go out, in the name of the Mysteries of the Incarnation and Passion.

"Gentlemen, I swear to you that something happened then, but I do not know what. A confusion fell on me and a kind of darkness. I saw nothing—it was as if I were dead."

The priest lifted a shaking hand to wipe off the sweat from his forehead. There was a profound silence in the room. I looked once at Monsignor, and he was holding his pipe an inch off his mouth, and his lips were slack and open as he stared.

"Then when I knew where I was, Father Lasserre was reading out of the Gospels; how Our Lord gave authority to his Church to cast out unclean spirits, and all this while his voice never trembled."

"And the woman?" said a voice hoarsely from Father Brent's chair.

"Ah! the woman! My God! I do not know. I did not look at her. I stared at the plate on the table; but at least she was not crying out now.

"When the Scripture was finished Father Lasserre gave me the book.

" 'Bah, Father!' he said; 'it is but epilepsy, is it not?'

"Then he beckoned me, and I went with him, holding the book till we were within a yard of the woman. But I could not hold the book still, it shook, it shook——"

Father Meuron thrust out his hand. "It shook like that, gentlemen.

"He took the book from me, sharply and angrily. 'Go back, sir,' he said, and he thrust the book into the husband's hand.

" 'There,' he said.

"I went back behind the table and leaned on it.

"Then Father Lasserre—my God! the courage of this man!—he set his hands on the woman's head. She writhed up her teeth to bite, but he was too strong for her, and then he cried out from the book the second bidding to the unclean spirit.

" '*Ecce crucem Domini!* Behold the Cross of the Lord! Flee ye adverse hosts! The lion of the tribe of Judah hath prevailed!'

"Gentlemen"—the Frenchman flung out his hands—"I who stand here tell you that something happened. God knows what. I only know this, that as the woman cried out and scrambled with her feet on the floor, the flame of the candle became smoke-coloured for one instant. I told myself it was the dust of her struggling and her foul breath . . . Yes, gentlemen, as you tell yourselves now. . . . Bah! it is but epilepsy, is it not so, sir?"

The old Rector leaned forward with a deprecating hand, but the Frenchman glared and gesticulated; there was a murmur from the room, and the old priest leaned back again and propped his head on his hand.

"Then there was a prayer. I heard *Oremus,* but I did not dare to look at the woman. I fixed my eyes so on the bread and meat; it was the one clean thing in that terrible room. I whispered to myself, 'Bread and mutton, bread and mutton.' I thought of the refectory at home— anything. You understand me, gentlemen—anything familiar to quiet myself.

"Then there was the third exorcism . . ."

I saw the Frenchman's hands rise and fall, clenched, and his teeth close on his lip to stay its trembling. He swallowed in his throat once or twice. Then he went on in a very low, hissing voice.

"Gentlemen, I swear to you by God Almighty that this was what I saw. I kept my eyes on the bread and meat. It lay there beneath my eyes, and yet I saw, too, the good Father Lasserre lean forward to the woman again, and heard him begin, '*Exorcizo te . . .*'

"And then this happened—this happened . . .

"The bread and the meat corrupted themselves to worms before my eyes . . ."

Father Meuron dashed forward, turned round and dropped into his chair as the two English priests on either side sprang to their feet.

In a few minutes he was able to tell us that all had ended well; that the woman had been presently found in her right mind, after an incident or two that I will take leave to omit; and that the apparent paroxysm of nature that had accompanied the words of the third exorcism had passed away as suddenly as it had come.

Then we went to night-prayers and fortified ourselves against the dark.

WILLIAM E. KOTZWINKLE *is the prolific author of short stories and several critically acclaimed novels, including* The Fan Man, Fata Morgana *and* Doctor Rat, *which won the World Fantasy Award for Best Novel of 1976.* ROBERT SHIARELLA *has written articles and humor for* Argosy *and other magazines, as well as a brilliantly satiric cult novel,* Your Sparkle Cavalcade of Death, *which began as a Kotzwinkle-Shiarella novella. Now meet their Melmothian madman, Sebastian Trump, who gleefully espouses the dark side of the farce. Would you believe that a major men's magazine once reluctantly rejected this humorous piece as too shocking? O tempora! O mores! (For additional comment, see Appendix I, page 577.)*

The Philosophy of Sebastian Trump or The Art of Outrage

BY WILLIAM E. KOTZWINKLE AND ROBERT SHIARELLA

Stepping from his townhouse, he paused to adjust the fit of his calfskin gloves. It was early evening; it was time. Flipping one end of his cape over his shoulder, he stepped lithely to the sidewalk. He walked—slim, delicate and dangerous—humming an obscure passage from Dargomijsky, tapping his cane lightly upon the cobblestones. His face carried no expression, save a crooked, lemon-twist smile.

A handsome woman approached through the semidarkness, clasping the delicate hand of her angelic blue-eyed little girl. He ignored the woman, but paused briefly to bow to the child. Her azure eyes bulged like agates as she watched a hideous obscenity form on his sensitive mouth. The woman gasped.

He smiled and spake. "The first lesson of history, madam, is that evil is good. I quote from Emerson." So saying, he bowed and walked on. He heard the woman hiss through trembling lips:

". . . outrageous, loathsome man!"

A delicious tingle cascaded through his body. Outrageous. With a hiss of exaltation, he struck out with his cane, but the hummingbird he aimed for had already backed out of the flower and flown away. No matter. The flower, the last from a widow's garden, was soon impaled upon the tiny steel point of his cane. He plucked it off and inserted it in his button-hole.

Though it was evening for the world, Sebastian Trump had just begun his day. With his accustomed Style. Grace. Wit. With any kind of luck, he might be able to defile a nanny before the rising of the moon.

Does this brief passage stir your soul? Does it nibble on the dog-ends of your imagination? Does it ring an elusive chord in the darkest corners of your bowels, as if struck somehow by the blackest muse of Hell?

Of course it does.

Every man carries the dry seeds of bestiality within him. Each of us, however splendid our virtue, dreams once of being a splendid bastard, a sniggering swine, an *outrageous* ruin of time. It is an ancient memory of our race, cherished by all men, nourished by few.

Come. Let me water your Child's Garden of Contempt. Let me throw the Obscenities Ball, where the couples shall whirl, dream-like and delicate. The music will build, caress, climb to incredible crescendos. And then—You shall appear. The crowd will draw back. And beneath your goat's mask, you shall commit the many Outrages which have too long been festering within you.

Let me, Sebastian Trump, draw examples from my own life and show you how!

It is difficult to be truly Outrageous before the age of eighteen, which is to say, before one enters college, although occasionally one runs across the grammar school child (such as myself) who exposes himself at Mother's Tea, or tortures a little playmate, or, perhaps, ignites a beggar. Such occurrences have been recorded, but usually they are nipped in the first splendid bud and all pride and inventiveness are quickly stripped from the promising youngster by civilization's watchdogs. Therefore, work in this area being so rare, we shall commence our little lecture with the conquering of the universities—known alternately as The College Outrage, or The Academic Atrocity.

ARRIVAL—PHASE ONE

"I begin to smell a rat." *Cervantes, Don Quixote.*

The *way* one arrives at college is of the utmost importance. Remember, this is to be your very first Outrage. You must choose your rhymes carefully. You are a freshman and you are, therefore, dirt. It is tradition. You, however, shall break tradition and emulate Sebastian Trump, arriving at college dressed as the Archbishop of Canterbury.

ARRIVAL—PHASE TWO

"Tom's no more, and so, no more of Tom." *Lord Byron.*

Very well. You have created a minor stir on the first day and people are uneasy in your presence. There are still barriers to surmount. The first of them is, of course, the life of your roommate. As a freshman, you will undoubtedly be assigned to a dormitory and you will have a roommate. This is clumsy, but is easily turned to good use. Remember —*you are building a legend.* Therefore, the first thing you must do upon entering college is to drive your roommate to suicide. Nothing could be more impressive, nothing could be easier. Observe:

"You had quite a dream last night, roomie."

"I did?"

"Yes, frightfully amusing. Kept calling me 'Mommy' and tried to crawl in bed with me. I suspect you'll get over it in time. I've written to your parents and your pastor for advice."

After your roommate has committed suicide, you, of course, embellish the event. Make it known that he took his life because of an unnatural love for you.

By now, you must begin wearing a black cloak and start collecting dark rocks. Take your meals in your room and rarely be seen in daylight. Carry a single shred of paper with you and read it over and over until it finally comes apart in your hands.

Then disappear for three days. When you return, discontinue the above, burn your bedsheets in the open air, act as if nothing has happened, and never mention your roommate's name again.

This should do nicely as a beginning at college.

THE SCANDAL SYNDROME

"Get thee to a nunnery, go." *Shakespeare, Hamlet, Act III, Scene 1, line 142.*

Now you have truly begun. People are starting to avoid you. Stories have been circulated that you cast no shadow, or that cloven hoof-prints were discovered in the snow beneath your window. You, of course, are the one who has initiated these stories. (If, however, when you pass, young women make the sign of the cross, you have overdone things a bit.)

You must surround yourself with scandal. This can be nothing so ordinary as getting some silly coed pregnant, although, of course, a few of these thrown in each semester can do no harm. No, you must strive for the Higher Scandal, that which sets teeth on edge, and makes lesser men shout out with rage and fear in the night.

For instance, at some student-faculty function, you might walk up to the Dean of the Philosophy Department and ask him to dance, remarking something about "You and I being the only ones to truly appreciate the Greek culture." Before he has a chance to answer, sweep him into your arms and begin to reminisce tenderly about your father: "Yes, papa has existed for the last forty years on checks from the government. Interesting story, really. Happened in the Argonne Forest during World War One. He was shot in the gluteus maximus while bolting in the face of the enemy. Of course, father kept *that* fact to himself by shooting the only Allied witness to his unfortunate re-treat, one Toby Whistler, a young British officer. My father carries with him to this day the last words of Toby Whistler, which were, I believe, 'A bit thick, Yank.' Well, I've got to run now. It's been de-lightful. Thanks for asking me." Whereupon you quickly fling yourself away from the Dean declaring in a loud voice that you wish to be released immediately. Retreat from the room backwards, fixing him with a frosty eye.

Major Outrages such as the above may be lent perspective if aug-mented by minor atrocities, such as sending your soiled laundry to an Oriental exchange student. With any sort of luck, you might create an international incident. ("The king has sent me some of his dirty linen to wash." *Voltaire. Reply to General Manstein.)*

Also, you might care to attempt the interesting little pastime of dressing up as a Cardinal and excommunicating yourself in chapel on the Sunday of Homecoming Week.

While we are speaking of it, let us pass on to the crucially important subject of how to dress Outrageously.

THE OUTRAGEOUS UNIFORM

"How then was the devil dressed?" *Robert Southey, A Devil's Walk, A Ballad, Stanza 3.*

The way you attire yourself must be both remarkable *and* thoroughly outlandish. You must always appear to be on the way to a duel, immaculate, contemptuous of custom, and ready to die. Vienna, at the turn of the century, is always suitable. Grey top hat, ruffled sleeves and collar, grey gloves and spats, the entire ensemble graced by an ebony cane, would do nicely. I found such an habit admirable, and was adjudged both mad and dangerous. To one constructing a legend of Outrage, nothing better suits one's purposes.

THE OPPOSITE SEX

"I think this piece will help boil thy pot." *Wolcot, The Bard Complimenteth Mr. West (c. 1790).*

Now we must concentrate upon the handling of women, in this case college coeds, and thus sub-designated The Cardigan Conquest. Needless to say, your behavior shall be loathsome, but the finer points must be discussed. Dialogue is of the utmost importance.
Example:
SHE: What do you plan to do when you leave college, Sebastian?
I: I'm thinking of becoming a professional rapist.
Example:
SHE: Do you mind my asking what your religion is, Sebastian?
I: Not at all. I am a Druid, my dear. Sacrificing virgins, that sort of thing. A dying practice.
Example:
SHE: Have you ever been in love, Sebastian?
I: Not since Mother died.

It is a well-known fact that women secretly dream of being Outraged, but the average man withdraws from the use of this knowledge. You, however, will feel quite free to heap endless humiliations and perversities upon them. For this bestial behavior, you shall be adored. In spite of themselves, they will dance the goat's dance with you, flinging themselves willingly, yea, desperately upon your Altar of Outrage.

SHE: Hello, Sebastian.

I: Let me touch it.

For dates, you will generally have women calling at your room for you. Always receive them in bed. A suitable remark might be, "Oh. You're early. You probably passed the Dean of Women on the staircase. Interesting lady. Wanted me to dress up as a chicken."

If you should call on your date, always arrive at least an hour late, giving some excuse such as ". . . couldn't tear myself away from the splendid sunset."

Next, you must take her where she has never been before and most certainly would never care to go.

Example:

"Some farmer boys I know are having a cock fight. I know you'll love it."

Throughout the evening, intimate that you are actually a woman. (NOTE: An excellent variation on this I once employed was to lead a young woman to believe that I had been castrated while serving with the Peace Corps in Casablanca. She was consumed with curiosity, pathos, and desire.)

At this point, all that remains for you to do is to desert her in the middle of the evening.

Example:

If walking down the street together, wait until you come to an alley. Then, without a word, tear yourself from her arm and dart down the alleyway, an imprecation on your lips. Disappear into the shadows, your shoes tapping a faint but sinister progress through the bowels of the night. Utter a single maniacal laugh, but cut it off at its peak.

The next time you see her, you will, of course, act as if nothing has happened. Your name will soon be on every lip in every girls' dormitory in the school. We have only to observe the conversation which undoubtedly must take place when your date returns to her room that first night:

SHE: Well, first of all he took me to a cock fight . . .

OTHERS: *(gasping) A what?*

SHE: . . . and then he told me how he's actually a woman, but then some crazy doctor in Casablanca cut off . . . I mean . . . well, you know, *cas*trated him, and . . .

OTHERS: Do you know for sure?!

SHE: . . . well, no . . . you see, he was too busy applauding the sunset, and then he hit a little girl with his cane . . . and then . . . well, he disappeared.

OTHERS: He *what?*

SHE: *(embarrassed and confused)* He . . . disappeared down an alley.

OTHERS: Oh, God, I hope he asks *me* out!

Touché!

An interesting little added touch in the handling of women (actually a confusion tactic) that I found most amusing was to go steady with a dwarf for a period of time, letting it be known that I was only dating her for her body.

DEPARTURE

"Nothing in life is so exhilarating as to be shot at without result."
Winston Spencer Churchill, The Malakand Field Force (1898).

Thus does one pass one's days at college. At the conclusion of one's academic career, one reflects how splendid a time it has been. One has trampled and ravaged. One has eaten all the flowers. There is, of course, but one stroke yet to be delivered—the last.

Sebastian Trump, Valedictorian.

Impossible? But Graduation Day finds you on the outdoor stage, waiting to be received. To those faculty members you have blackmailed, to those students you have compromised, to the army of innocents you have tricked, cajoled, and forced to do your work for you, it comes as no surprise.

You deliver a Major Oratory, filled with platitude and hypocrisy patterned on the Sermons of Joseph Butler. Then you step forward to receive the precious sheepskin. You smile and bow to the Dean of your college. Then you stride over to the President of the University. Standing directly before him, you proceed to tear up your diploma and fling it in his face. Then you walk to the edge of the platform and, standing above the draped banners of the school which bear the colors of the institution, you urinate carefully upon them so the damp stain emblazons on the hallowed crest your name:

SEBASTIAN TRUMP

With arm raised in a final obscene gesture, your lips curled about a last vulgar, withering phrase, you stride contemptuously off the stage and into the sunset. You await the knife thrust in your back. It does not come. You have won.

You are ready to face life.

CAREER

"You have waked me too soon, I must slumber again." *Isaac Watts, The Sluggard, Stanza I.*

Now you are faced with a small unpleasantness. How can a man, so finely wrought, so highly strung, so delicately balanced—how can such a man be expected to join the ranks of the gainfully employed? It is so dreary, so stifling. Precisely. Therefore, you must join the ranks of the gracefully *un*employed. The procedure is quite simple. You must find yourself a patroness.

TO-GRANDMOTHER'S-HOUSE-WE-GO-TRA-LA-LATERAL-OFFENSE

"Great fleas have little fleas upon their backs to bite 'em." *Augustus De Morgan, A Budget of Paradoxes.*

Situate yourself in the most fashionable bar in New York City. Cough frequently into your handkerchief. Tremble your glass. Faint briefly. Rave to yourself of unspeakable native rites. Call the bartender Abdul. Wear a single black glove on your left hand. Do this daily until *she* comes into the bar and is seated at a table. Then walk slowly past, stumble, and fall into the chair beside her. Speak in a whisper: "Forgive me . . . Your Grace. The . . . fever."

"How pale and thin you look, young man." She sits before you, kind and wise and rich. She is fifty and covered with jewels. Your eyes glaze as you look at her. You mumble:

"You shouldn't come here, Your Grace! We . . . are . . . being watched. Don't turn! Just remain . . . perfectly still. The idol's eye is in the coachman's hat . . . placed it there . . . myself."

Then you leap to your feet.

"I'LL SAVE YOU, OLD MAN! . . . filthy devils! . . . I shall not die unaccompanied! Steady, Your Grace, steady now . . ."

"Waiter! Waiter! Help me! This poor man is ill!"

You touch her knee and smile boyishly. "It's mother's milk I miss," you say shyly.

"*Young man!*"

You rise, shaking in every joint. "Since my conversation . . . distresses you, madam, allow me to withdraw."

"Oh, no! No, please stay."

"As . . . you . . . wish."

Then you collapse to the floor.

This, at any rate, was the initial gambit of *my* first successful career exploit. I awoke in a marble tub. She stood over me, administering. Slowly, she nursed me back to health.

If it worked for Sebastian Trump, it will certainly work for you!

But then, you may correctly observe, the day will come—perhaps in a month, possibly in a year—when she will enter your wing of the house and ask *this* monstrous question:

"Sebastian, when do you think you might . . . begin looking for some sort . . . of work? I mean, what do you intend to do with your *life?*"

What then, Sebastian, I hear you demand, *what then?*

Ah, then it is time—to leave.

You look at her a long, quiet moment. "Very well. Sebastian will go away . . . and play with the Dark Women. *And the panda.*" Then, bowing quickly, you walk out of her life forever.

For you are Sebastian Trump. You are the Master Juggler, the Gypsy Prince, the Genie in Milady's teapot. You move on—leaving your glove in a face or two.

"Oh, yes, Trump. Deposed royalty, I think. Insolent as the devil. But they're all that way, I suppose."

"I saw Sebastian fighting a duel in the Governor's mansion. Cut off the butler's arm with a flaming shish kebob."

"Oh, I've devised many ways of killing him. I should rather like to rip out his throat with a band saw."

"Forgive me, father, I have erred. It was Sebastian."

"Saw Trump falling down drunk in the toy boat lake. Shouting something about swans dying in private."

"Have you read Sebastian's new book? *Famous Ladies I Have Mounted.* Positively in*cen*diary, my dear! He's being sued for *billions!*"

"They say Trump was behind that revolution in Bombay!"

". . . derailed the Prime Minister's train."

". . . spent a year on Devil's Island. Made a brilliant escape."

"Forgive me, mother, I have erred. It was Sebastian."

"I'd never have expected the Queen Mother to be so indiscreet . . . especially with an American!"

". . . denounced by the Vatican. But they were only returning the favor."

"The natives erected a statue to him. He's one of their gods now. They have some sort of virgin offering to him on his birthday."

". . . of course, I wouldn't be against seeing him devoured by mad dogs, mind you."

"Forgive me, son, I have erred. It was Sebastian."

FINALE

"A chill snake lurks in the grass." *Vergil, Eclogues, II, 93.*

The world is your opponent. You parry, you thrust. You disappear. You tell the virgins, "Sebastian has no time. He never did." You are a rotting beautiful fruit. You are the dying Pan. You are the single greatest Bastard in the world, and the world is chasing you, intent upon cutting out your liver and frying up your jibs . . .

HERE THE MANUSCRIPT OF SEBASTIAN TRUMP ABRUPTLY ENDS. HAPPILY, CONTEMPORANEOUS REPORTAGE SUPPLIES THE FINAL EXAMPLE THAT THE AUTHOR WAS UNABLE TO FURNISH—THE EDITORS.

"Well, the bastard finally got it! Shot in the back with a crossbow. Happened in the Maidhead Castle. Trump was going out the window in a bit of a hurry. His Lordship had just enough time to get off a shot. Trump tumbled into the moat. Nasty drop."

"No, I *don't* regret having done Trump in! But I shall never forget his last words. Oh, yes, he cried out just before he fell from the battlement. 'I have upset my applecart; I am done for! *Lucian, Pseudolus, 1-32!*' Then he fell. The man was mad as a hatter."

And so it ended. But Sebastian Trump's final words were reserved for the ears of Her Ladyship as she knelt beside the broken body.

"To live to be thirty, madam, is to have failed at life. I am quoting from H. H. Munro. And so, goodbye."

As His Lordship approached, she rose and fixed him with a steely eye, then spoke to him defiantly:

"I shall name the child Sebastian."

One of our culture's greatest cautionary legends is that of Don Juan, whose unrepentant womanizing was punished when the statue of a vengeful father he killed returned and bore the sinner to Hell. This lascivious hero first appeared on stage in 1630 in Tirso de Molina's El Burlador de Sevilla *and in many guises since then, including a long satiric poem by Lord Byron, a drama by Molière, the Lorenzo Da Ponte libretto for Mozart's opera* Don Giovanni, *and in this century, an Ingmar Bergman film (see Appendix III, page 585) as well as the witty "Don Juan in Hell" sequence of Bernard Shaw's theatrical polemic* Man and Superman. *It is unfortunate that one of the most imaginative of all Don Juan plays,* La Dernière Nuit de Don Juan, *is virtually unknown, even though it was written by* EDMOND ROSTAND *(1868–1918), creator of the magnificent French heroic comedy* Cyrano de Bergerac, *as well as* Les Romanesques (The Romantics), *on which was based America's longest-running musical,* The Fantasticks. *I am proud to present this neglected masterpiece in a new modern adaptation. (For further comment, see Appendix I, page 577.)*

Don Juan's Final Night
BY EDMOND ROSTAND

PROLOGUE

> DON JUAN *is being led to Hell by* THE STATUE *of the Commander. A sulphurous glow from below lights up the narrow circular staircase that they are descending.*

DON JUAN (calmly)

Each step I go down reminds me of a woman I mounted. Jeanette . . . Nanette . . . Laurette . . . Release my arm, old man. I'll enter Hell unassisted.

(Far away, a dog howls.)

Listen! At least my faithful spaniel misses me. But what about my faithful manservant, Sganarelle? Lord Commander, grant me a moment's rest that I may hear him mourn me.

(They pause. The distant sound of SGANARELLE *grumbling.)*

SGANARELLE'S VOICE

His death pleases everyone else: the God he spurned, the laws he
flouted, the women he ravished, the families he disgraced, the husbands and lovers he drove to frenzy. But what about me? The only
satisfaction I get is to see my master's dreadful punishment. My
wages, my wages—ah, my wages!*

DON JUAN

Will you let me go back to earth long enough to pay him back?

THE STATUE

Yes.

DON JUAN

I'll be eternally grateful. *(He ascends.)*

THE STATUE *(muses)*

I wonder if he'll return.

DON JUAN *(coming back down)*

There! I gave him what he deserves.

THE STATUE

His wages?

DON JUAN

A kick in the ass. He earned it. *(Laughs)* It'll comfort me while I'm
roasting.

THE STATUE *(admiringly)*

Nothing frightens you, Don Juan. That stirs pleasant memories in this
old warrior's breast. Your courage shall be rewarded. I'm going to let
you go. Hurry and climb.

(A monstrous claw suddenly clutches DON JUAN *by the cloak.)*

DON JUAN

You should have thought of that before. It's too late, the Devil's got
me.

* Here Rostand quotes the final speech of Molière's *Don Juan or the Feast of Stone,* in
which the great French dramatist employs his perennial comic foil, Sganarelle, instead
of Mozart's Italian lackey, Leporello. But in the original Spanish Don Juan play, Tirso
de Molina's *The Blasphemer of Seville,* the servant's name is Catalinón. —MK

(Cockcrow.)

THE STATUE

It's almost dawn. I must become mute stone once more. Farewell, Don Juan. I hope you somehow escape the Devil's clutch. *(He ascends.)*

DON JUAN

Well, I'll try. Don't close the tomb yet, maybe I'll get out. *(Tugs his cloak)* Come, Lucifer, let go. Do you really think I've performed all the evil I can do on earth? Let's make a deal. Give me another ten years and I'll surpass your wildest expectations. You'll find me better mettle than that dullard Faust. Imagine being content with one mumpish German fräulein! See my arm where your emissary grasped it? The burning cold of his stone fingers made these scars. Ladies will dote on them. Haven't I always been your vicar of vice? I promise you, in ten more years I shall debauch a thousand virtuous women.

(The great claw disappears.)

Bravo, Don Juan! You've won yourself another decade. *(He starts to mount the steps.)* Annette . . . Minette . . . Lisette . . . Ho, Sganarelle! There's work to do!

(The lights fade out.)

SCENE ONE

Ten years later. A large banquet hall in a Venetian palace. Great marble stairs lead to the Grand Canal and the Adriatic Sea. DON JUAN *descends the steps and enters as* SGANARELLE *sets a candelabra on a table laden for a feast.*

DON JUAN

Arlette . . . Paulette . . . Lynette . . . A grand night on the Grand Canal. The lagoon sleeps beneath skies of purple and sulphur. Tiny craft, like nipples on the bosom of the ocean, streak the sea with trails of milk and silver. *(To* SGANARELLE*)* It's done. Add her name to my list.

SGANARELLE

Whose name? You pursue so many ladies, master, how am I supposed to know which one you mean?

DON JUAN *(holds up a ring)*

Hers. *(He tosses the ring over the balcony into the canal.)*

SGANARELLE *(horrified)*

No! Not the ruby! You promised me that one!

DON JUAN

Of course not, fool. The glass ring. *(He chuckles cynically.)* She *was* naïve.

SGANARELLE *(shocked)*

That lady? I should have thought that she, at least—

DON JUAN *(interrupts)*

Come now, Sganarelle . . . what hope for virtue in a city whose very streets are mirrors? Frailty, thy name is Venice. I adore it here. The gondoliers croon "Santa Lucia" and half my work's accomplished. I won't return to the grey skies of native Spain. Write upon my tombstone that Don Juan was born in Seville but fulfilled his destiny in Venice.

SGANARELLE

Well, since you broach the subject, master . . . your ten years *are* up this evening. How do you plan to spend your final night?

DON JUAN

How else, but at my favorite pastime?

SGANARELLE

You don't mean to go out *again?*

DON JUAN

There's a fancy ball. I'll go there and better Hannibal. He merely crossed the Alps, but I will conquer loftier peaks.

SGANARELLE

But afterward you'll come back home?

DON JUAN

Afterward, who knows? Once before, I escaped Lucifer's claw. Perhaps by now he's forgotten us.

SGANARELLE *(alarmed)*

Us? What do you mean, "us"?

DON JUAN

A figure of speech, dolt, don't be nervous; the Devil won't snatch you away for many years. You'll have ample time to enjoy your inheritance.

SGANARELLE *(eagerly)*

My inheritance? Best of masters, what have you left me?

DON JUAN

My reputation. Tell them you worked for the infamous Don Juan and you'll have job offers and mistresses galore.

SGANARELLE *(dubiously)*

How do you figure that?

DON JUAN

Your masters will want you to teach them my methods.

SGANARELLE

What about the mistresses?

DON JUAN

Ladies disappointed that they could not sleep with Don Juan will gladly settle for his servant.

SGANARELLE

Master, this braggadocio is all well and good, but it won't help you any when the clock strikes and the Devil hauls you down to Hell.

(The hour tolls ominously.)

DON JUAN

Speak of the Devil and hear his voice. Did I keep my bargain? What's the final tally?

SGANARELLE

In the past ten years? One thousand and three. That's certainly enough.

DON JUAN

I'm sorry to stop at an odd number. If I could only add one more name to the roster . . .

(The chiming ceases. A long silence.)

Perhaps Lucifer changed his mind. No, that's not it; the priest Tertullian must be right . . . the Devil is dead. *(With a laugh, he goes briskly to the table.)* Don Juan endures! First I'll sup—then to the ball and other sweetmeats. Sganarelle, fetch my masque and rapier. I'm still master of my destiny.

A DISTANT VOICE

Commedia!

DON JUAN

Hark. The cry of the showman hawking his talents. Life goes on . . . bravo!

THE VOICE *(closer)*

Commedia!

SGANARELLE *(looking over the balcony)*

It's the old puppeteer from the Schiavoni wharf.

DON JUAN

Punch and Judy? Splendid! Tell him to come up here.

SGANARELLE

And do what?

DON JUAN

And put on his play while I dine.

SGANARELLE *(shouting)*

Hey! Old man . . . come along. Here you have a willing audience.

(The MARIONETTE MASTER enters, bowing. He wears a large hat.)

MARIONETTE MASTER

A command performance? I'm flattered. Shall I build my little theatre
for you?

DON JUAN

Yes, and while you do, tell me where you come from.

MARIONETTE MASTER *(putting up his stage)*

I come from wandering to and fro in the earth and walking up and
down in it. Writers, painters and composers all know me well.

DON JUAN

Then we're kindred spirits. I've traveled far, too. Yet my own legend
outpaces me.

MARIONETTE MASTER

Indeed? Well, in my theatre, you'll see that myth is reduced to miniature.

(With a flourish, the MARIONETTE MASTER *indicates that his
stage is ready. He ducks beneath the curtain and is hidden.)*

DON JUAN

Behold the Attic temple that first tutored me in the cruelties of existence.

SGANARELLE

Why do you call it a temple, master? It's only a puppet stage. And
we're not in the attic.

DON JUAN

Be off with you, rascal! If I must endure a blockhead, I far prefer it to
be Punch.

*(*SGANARELLE *exits.* DON JUAN *begins eating.* PUNCH *pops his
head above the stage.* DON JUAN *claps his hands like a happy child,
but* PUNCH *screams in pretended fright and disappears.* DON
JUAN *laughs.* PUNCH *tentatively reappears.)†*

† The marionettes should be portrayed by actors. —MK

PUNCH *(calls)*

Toinette . . . ? Margrette . . . ? Judette . . . ? Oh, Ju-u-dette . . .
(He sees DON JUAN.) What? Is it really you, at long last? Hurrah!
Hurrah!

DON JUAN

What are you cheering about?

PUNCH

Because I've finally found you, Don Juan. Hurrah!

DON JUAN

Ah, so you know who I am?

PUNCH

Now wouldn't I be the ass if I didn't know my own brother?

DON JUAN *(not sure he is amused)*

Your brother? How?

PUNCH

Brothers in degeneracy.

DON JUAN

Don Punch, you always had a wicked tongue.

PUNCH

Don Juan, you always had a profligate spirit. On the Day of Judgment, they'll put us both in the balances and we'll come out even,
you'll see.

DON JUAN *(angrily)*

Is that so, you woman beater?

PUNCH

It certainly is, you womanizer.

DON JUAN

Don Punch . . . you are a blockhead!

PUNCH

Don Juan . . . you are my brother!

DON JUAN *(laughs)*

So you claim we're siblings. Am I, then, another marionette?

PUNCH

Nay, no one ever links those syllables, "marry," with the name of Don Juan.

DON JUAN *(smiles)*

Now you're quibbling. I've had a thousand brides, no matter whose. *(Resumes eating)* But take me back to my childhood and the Punch-and-Judy plays I loved to see.

PUNCH

Well, what did you like best about those shows?

DON JUAN

Truthfully? Admiring the ladies in the audience.

PUNCH

And looking up their skirts?

DON JUAN

Never mind that. Come, begin. Sing your song.

PUNCH *(warms up vocally)*

La-la-la-la la-la-la-la-a-a-a-a-a-a-a-h-h-h-h-h-h-h-h-h-h!

(Sings)   I'm the famous puppet, Punch.
                  I love ladies by the bunch,
                  But I always beat their heads.

(DON JUAN *raises his wineglass to* PUNCH.)

DON JUAN *(singing the same tune)*

                  I'm the blasphemer, Don Juan.
                  I love ladies with élan,
                  And I always heat their beds.

(They sing together, each repeating his own verse, but just before the final syllable, a puppet of THE COMMANDER *appears and interrupts them with his own musical outburst.)*

THE COMMANDER‡

Punchinello, you've ruined my daughter. Now die!

(PUNCH fetches his stick and beats the other puppet over the head. THE COMMANDER sings to the Commendatore's Mozartian death phrase, "Ah, soccorso! son tradito . . .")

THE COMMANDER

Ah, support me! I am dying. *(He disappears under the stage.)*

DON JUAN

I've seen this part of the play before. Go on to something else. Call Judy.

PUNCH *(calls)*

Oh-h-h, Ju-u-u-dette . . .

(She promptly appears. PUNCH woos her.)

O, Judette, Judette, Judette . . . I love you!

(She spurns him.)

DON JUAN

Your technique, brother Punch, leaves something to be desired.

PUNCH

What did I do wrong?

DON JUAN

Never start off by telling them you love them. That comes later.

PUNCH

Then what am I supposed to say to her?

DON JUAN

Say nothing. Look remote. Your indifference will cause her pain.

PUNCH

Pain? I already know how to manage that! *(He whacks JUDY with his stick.)*

‡ Matching the first phrase the Commendatore sings *("Lasciala, indegno! Battiti meco!")* in Mozart's *Don Giovanni.* —MK

DON JUAN

No, no, no, that's not what I meant. You mustn't strike women. You must make them suffer. There's a difference.

(PUNCH *picks up the* JUDY *puppet.*)

PUNCH *(indifferently)*

Too late. She's dead. *(He tosses her offstage.)* What do you want to see next? The scene where they sentence me to death?

DON JUAN

No, cut that one.

PUNCH

What about where they hang me?

DON JUAN

No, omit that, too.

PUNCH

Do you realize you're abridging a time-tested plot?

DON JUAN

Time itself must change with the times and all great art must be updated.

PUNCH

But you've skipped over practically my whole story! What's left?

DON JUAN

The part where the Devil carries you off. That's a spectacle I certainly don't want to miss.

PUNCH

Very well. *(He strikes a small bell.)*

DON JUAN

What did you ring that for?

PUNCH

Sound effects. It's supposed to be midnight. *(He shakes with fear.)* Satan's on his way . . . I'm scared!

(THE DEVIL PUPPET *enters, growling.* PUNCH *swats him.* THE DEVIL PUPPET *snatches away the stick and batters* PUNCH, *then slings* PUNCH *over his left shoulder.* PUNCH *howls piteously as* THE DEVIL PUPPET *disappears offstage with him.*)

DON JUAN

Poor brother Punch . . . you shouldn't have struck the Devil.

THE DEVIL PUPPET *(popping up)*

Perhaps, instead, he should have made me suffer?

DON JUAN

Of course. That's what I'd do.

THE DEVIL PUPPET *(in a different tone)*

Indeed? May one inquire how?

DON JUAN

What happened to your voice?

THE DEVIL PUPPET

It's not important. Come, take me into your confidence. I'm eager to know how you would make me suffer.

DON JUAN

You notice how Punch squealed like a stuck pig? The howl of sinners tossed into the fiery Pit is a sound that pleases you. You'll never hear it from me.

THE DEVIL PUPPET *(sneers)*

It's easy to brag before I have you in my clutches.

DON JUAN

But that's the point. You'll never have me. Not the way you want. The only thing that makes me tremble is lust. I'm called the Blasphemer of Seville. I mock God and Lucifer alike.

THE DEVIL PUPPET

Don Juan, this I promise you . . . you won't go to Hell until I've thoroughly broken your spirit.

DON JUAN

Now that's good news.

THE DEVIL PUPPET *(holding out his claw)*

Here's my hand on it.

(DON JUAN *reaches for the puppet's hand.* THE DEVIL PUPPET *disappears and the* MARIONETTE MASTER *appears in its place and shakes* DON JUAN*'s hand, instead.)*

DON JUAN

Your claw is colder than the Commander's stone fist.

(As DON JUAN *pulls away his hand, the* MARIONETTE MASTER *throws off his disguise and reveals himself to be* THE DEVIL.)

So it's you, Lucifer. I took you for a master of marionettes.

THE DEVIL

Why, so I am, and always have been. This very night I've yanked the strings of senators and kings, beggars and justices, and now it's your turn. Shall I toss you over my shoulder like your brother Punch?

DON JUAN

No, I'll walk on my own two feet. Let's go. I'm ready for Hell. *(He sports himself proudly.)* Caparisoned in tastefully decadent apparel, I'll grace your graceless company. I presume old Charon's still your gondolier?

THE DEVIL

Ever the posturer. I suppose your mistresses expected it. Shall we dine? *(He sits down at the table.)*

DON JUAN

If my roast pleases you better than roasting me, so be it.

THE DEVIL

We shook hands, remember?

DON JUAN

You mean, unless you daunt my proud spirit, I shall not go to Hell? Then I'm saved.

THE DEVIL

We'll see.

(With DON JUAN *acting as host,* THE DEVIL *helps himself to food and wine and begins to eat and drink.)*

(Appreciatively) You're quite a cook, Don Juan.

DON JUAN

I have to be. It's all part of the art of seduction: sensual cuisine, opulent decor, wine as carefully chosen as every voluptuous word I speak. All must be resplendent. You, however, are decidedly drab. Why do you wear so much black?

THE DEVIL

To match the inkstand Martin Luther hurled at me.

DON JUAN

You look a lot better in green.

THE DEVIL

How do you know that? I haven't worn green—

DON JUAN *(interrupting)*

Since the Garden of Eden. I was there, don't you remember? In those days, I called myself Adam. You got me to eat the apple of knowledge.

THE DEVIL

Admittedly an acquired taste. How did you like it?

DON JUAN

I didn't, there was a worm inside. I threw that apple away and tried another. It also contained a worm. So did the next one and the next. *(Pause)* So does all Creation.

THE DEVIL

Yes, that's the knowledge God tried to hide from you. I spoiled his little secret.

DON JUAN

Why?

THE DEVIL

Because I thought his precious chosen creatures could not find out the truth and keep on living. I admit I misjudged you.

DON JUAN

Well, you were less subtle when you were a snake. The worm's not the only thing I discovered after biting that apple. First there was Eve; Lilith came second, and between them was begat, thirdly, the clothing industry. Thanks to that unholy trinity, I've given up one pallid Paradise, but in its place I've entered, night after night, a thousand blissful gardens. *(Calls)* Sganarelle!

(SGANARELLE *enters.*)

SGANARELLE

Sir?

DON JUAN

Bring me my catalog.

(SGANARELLE *sees* THE DEVIL *and stiffens.*)

Yes, yes, it's just who you think it is. My list!

(Crossing himself, SGANARELLE *gladly exits. He immediately returns with a sheaf of papers, which he gives to* DON JUAN.*)*

SGANARELLE *(murmurs in* DON JUAN*'s ear)*

Is there anyone I should tell not to expect you tonight?

DON JUAN

No, you could never get to all of them in time. And besides, I have an excellent chance of survival. *(He removes a ring from his hand.)* But just in case I don't, here's the ruby I promised you.

(SGANARELLE *pounces on the ring and exits.*)

THE DEVIL *(raising his wineglass)*

Now there's devotion for you. A toast to your poverty, Don Juan.

DON JUAN

What! Look around you. Are these the appurtenances of squalor?

THE DEVIL

I'm referring to your dearth of friends.

DON JUAN

I didn't seek the comradeship of lesser men.

THE DEVIL

What about family?

DON JUAN *(uncomfortably)*

I had the customary complement of parents.

THE DEVIL

You leave nothing behind you.

DON JUAN *(showing his list)*

False. Here's my legacy.

THE DEVIL

A catalog of women's names?

DON JUAN

I said I would debauch a thousand virtuous women, and here you see I bettered that by three.

THE DEVIL

You sacrificed eternal grace for ephemeral pleasure?

DON JUAN

I eternally found pleasure in feminine grace.

THE DEVIL *(examining the list)*

Statistically, it's positively astonishing.

DON JUAN

What is?

THE DEVIL

The number of times you did the deed—

(DON JUAN *smiles.*)

—and yet you leave behind no son to mourn your death.

(DON JUAN *frowns.*)

DON JUAN

I'm glad. His reputation might have vitiated mine.

THE DEVIL

You're satisfied with renown?

DON JUAN

I am. The world envies me. I'm the hero of all great novels, protagonist of the most successful plays. What daring kiss is not stolen in my name? What secret and forbidden act is not dedicate to my enduring spirit? Each man grieves because he's but a counterfeit Don Juan. *(He points to his list.)* This grand catalog's my testament to all that I possessed.

THE DEVIL *(rising from the table)*

Possessed? Now there's an interesting word. I have many "spiritual" possessions, but what can you possibly own? This scrap of paper with faded names upon it? *(He reads from the list.)* "Babette . . . Sylvette . . ." *Peut-être.* Possession, then, is nothing more than carnal knowledge?

DON JUAN

You must emphasize the word "knowledge." Knowing means far more than merely having.

THE DEVIL

Now let's see whether I understand you, Don Juan. Because you've had—*and known*—these thousand and three women, you claim you've also possessed them?

DON JUAN

That's the glory that Hell can never diminish. I clasped their unclad bodies and penetrated their naked spirits.

THE DEVIL

All thousand and three?

DON JUAN

Each had her own secret.

THE DEVIL

Which you remember?

DON JUAN

Yes.

THE DEVIL

Then why do you need this list?

DON JUAN

I don't.

THE DEVIL

I'm unconvinced.

DON JUAN

I'll prove it to you.

(DON JUAN *takes the list from* THE DEVIL *and begins to tear it to bits.* THE DEVIL *fetches the hat he wore as the* MARIONETTE MAS-TER *and holds it upside down.* DON JUAN *shreds his catalog and puts the tattered bits inside the hat.*)

Observe that each was a virtuous lady. I promised you that.

THE DEVIL

Don't stop till there's a thousand and three pieces.

DON JUAN *(still ripping his list)*

I avoided loose women because, like you, Lucifer, I take delight in tarnishing the innocent; their tardy expressions of remorse delight Don Juan. *(He drops the last scraps into the hat.)* There, that's the lot . . . one thousand and three names . . . will you test me now?

THE DEVIL

I will.

(THE DEVIL *takes the hat to the balcony and makes a mystic pass over it. A burst of flame. The hat is empty.*)

DON JUAN

Bravo, puppeteer! I see you're also a magician.

THE DEVIL

Yes, but the trick's just beginning. *(He sweeps his arm out over the balcony.)* Abracadabra!

(A soft white light begins to glow beneath the balcony.)

DON JUAN

Where's that light coming from?

THE DEVIL

Look and see.

(DON JUAN *joins* THE DEVIL *at the balcony.)*

DON JUAN

A thousand gondolas on the lagoon?

THE DEVIL

A thousand and three.

DON JUAN

Who rides inside?

THE DEVIL

The spirit of every woman you say that you possessed. I've brought them back to life.

DON JUAN *(watches them, fascinated)*

They're disembarking.

(The light grows brighter.)

THE DEVIL

And now?

DON JUAN

The ghosts are coming up the stairs. Each one wears a mask.

(THE DEVIL *gestures dramatically. The white light explodes into dazzling brilliance and then dwindles into a spotlight highlighting the puppet theatre.)*

What happened?

THE DEVIL *(putting on the hat)*

That was the end of the trick. Now I'm master of marionettes once more. *(He calls)* Begin the show!

(A masked ghost appears upon the puppet stage.)

THE GHOST

Don Juan, I bid you a good evening.

DON JUAN *(approaching her)*

Lovely phantom, would you dine with me? And let me lift the veil that sheathes your mysteries?

(He reaches for her mask.)

THE DEVIL

Hands off!

(DON JUAN looks at him, startled.)

She may only make one revelation to you, Don Juan.

DON JUAN

And that is?

THE DEVIL

The deepest secret of her soul. If you can hear it and then reveal her name, I'll permit her to lower her mask.

DON JUAN

So that's your test? *(Smiling)* I expected worse. *(Addressing her)* Let's hear your secret, then.

THE GHOST

I always had— *(She whispers the rest directly into DON JUAN's ear.)*

DON JUAN

You suffered deep regrets each time you made love, and yet you could not stop yourself?

(She turns away, ashamed. DON JUAN tries to take her hand.)

Don't be distressed, it's such a common—

THE DEVIL *(interrupting)*

Touch her spirit, not her flesh!

DON JUAN

Well, you started me with an easy riddle. *(He speaks ardently to her.)* This can only be my passionate, yet remorseful . . . Lucette.

THE GHOST

I always loved the way you spoke my name—

DON JUAN *(to* THE DEVIL)

You see? Lucette.

THE GHOST

—but when I hear you murmur "Lucette" like that, it practically convinces me that's who I am.

DON JUAN

What? You're *not* Lucette?

THE GHOST

No.

(She disappears from the puppet stage. A SECOND GHOST *immediately takes her place.)*

SECOND GHOST

What about me?

DON JUAN *(reaching for her hand)*

Your voice sounds familiar. I—

THE DEVIL

No touching!

DON JUAN

Well, then, tell me your secret.

(She murmurs to him.)

Ah, there's a day I'll never forget! Eluding your mother and her mangy poodle in the crowd . . . the fireworks . . .

SECOND GHOST

I did behave badly.

DON JUAN

Not at all. You performed magnificently . . . Suzette . . .

SECOND GHOST

That's not my name. *(She leaves the puppet stage.)*

DON JUAN

Impossible! The circumstances of our tryst—

THE DEVIL *(interrupting)*

—are thoroughly banal.

DON JUAN *(rallying with a laugh)*

You're right. So many damsels have slipped away with me from their mothers and their mutts, it's easy to mix them up.

THIRD GHOST *(appears on puppet stage)*

Will you confuse me, too? *(She whispers to* DON JUAN.)

DON JUAN

Oh, *you* always expected too much. You should have paid less attention to the way you looked and more to how you felt . . . your far-too-serene Highness.

THIRD GHOST

Wrong again.

(She leaves. A FOURTH GHOST *instantly takes her place.)*

FOURTH GHOST *(after whispering to him)*

Well?

DON JUAN *(his confidence waning)*

Yvette?

FOURTH GHOST

No.

DON JUAN

Colette?

FOURTH GHOST

No.

DON JUAN *(snaps fingers)*

I have it! You are the daughter of the innkeeper.

FOURTH GHOST

No.

(She leaves and is immediately replaced by another.)

FIFTH GHOST

Who am I, Don Juan? *(She whispers her secret.)*

DON JUAN

I had you after the bullfight . . . Conchette . . . ?

FIFTH GHOST

No.

(She leaves. Another is already whispering to DON JUAN.)

DON JUAN *(with great relief)*

Your jealousy betrays you, at least. Your daughter was my cousin Tristette. First I had her, and then you, my own Aunt Rivette.

SIXTH GHOST

No.

DON JUAN *(in a rage)*

Liar!

(DON JUAN lunges at her, but she disappears.)

THE DEVIL

Here, now, don't mistreat my property!

DON JUAN

Every one of them is lying to me.

(The sound of the women laughing.)

THE DEVIL

Lying? Not so. They're laughing.

DON JUAN

I've often heard women's laughter, but never before like this.

THE DEVIL

How could you? This is the joke that women only share in private.

DON JUAN

What joke is that?

THE DEVIL

Man. They titter at posturing peacocks who strut and call themselves possessors.

DON JUAN

Bid them be silent! Like you, I won't be mocked.

(THE DEVIL *claps. The laughter ceases.*)

You won't crush my spirit quite so easily, Lucifer. You see I've regained my customary calm? Forget my past mistakes. I'm going to start all over again.

THE DEVIL *(sighs)*

Ah, well, the night's still young. *(Sitting down, he pours himself more wine and ignores* DON JUAN.*)*

(The whispering ghosts appear and disappear in rapid succession.)

DON JUAN

All right, let's begin once more. *(Listens to a ghost's secret)* Annette . . . ?

SEVENTH GHOST

No.

DON JUAN *(hears another secret)*

Arlette . . . ?

EIGHTH GHOST

No.

DON JUAN *(hears another)*

Aurette . . . ?

NINTH GHOST

No.

(As the lights fade, two ghosts and then a third ring round DON
JUAN *and whisper.)*

DON JUAN

Babette . . . ? Barbette . . . ? Bibette . . . ?

THE GHOSTS

No . . . No . . . No . . .

(The lights fade out.)

SCENE TWO

The same, shortly before dawn. DON JUAN, *holding the lit
candelabra, is studying* THE DEVIL, *who seems to be asleep.*
DON JUAN *stealthily approaches the latest* GHOST *in the puppet theatre.*

DON JUAN *(sotto voce)*

Quickly now, while the Devil's asleep, assist me. For the sake of the
passion we once shared, will you remove your mask?

GHOST

Yes. *(She takes it off, but there is another mask underneath it.)*

DON JUAN

A second mask? Will you take that one off, too?

GHOST

I will. *(She does, but beneath it is a third mask.)*

DON JUAN

How many are you wearing?

THE DEVIL

More than anyone can count. In life, she hid behind so many masks
that she ended up obliterating her own face.

*(*DON JUAN *sets down the candelabra. The* GHOST *exits.)*

DON JUAN *(disgusted)*

It's useless. I thought I knew my lovers, but it seems they're all strangers to me.

THE DEVIL *(rising)*

You thought you were on intimate terms with their souls, so by your own admission, you die possessing nothing.

DON JUAN

Not so fast. The spirit is sadly mutable. It's true I do not know them now, but when they lay with me, I knew everything about them.

THE DEVIL *(sits back down)*

Indeed?

(THE DEVIL claps. Three ghosts appear on the puppet stage.)

Is what he says the truth?

(The ghosts titter their private laugh.)

THE THREE GHOSTS *(together)*

Since when do men seek truth?

THE MIDDLE GHOST

They see us through a mist of their own imagining.

THE THREE GHOSTS *(together)*

We lie to them accordingly.

THE GHOST ON THE LEFT *(stage right)*

Don Juan thought me intelligent, so I boned up on the classics and dazzled him with warmed-over Petrarch.

THE GHOST ON THE RIGHT *(stage left)*

Don Juan called me prudish, so I pretended to be shocked when he did things to me that I wanted him to.

THE MIDDLE GHOST

Don Juan had a whim to destroy my supposedly happy home, therefore I fawned like a bride over my odious husband.

THE GHOSTS ON THE LEFT AND RIGHT *(together)*

Women know how to give men what they think they want—

THE THREE GHOSTS *(together)*

The Eternal Feminine!

THE GHOST ON THE RIGHT

A notion so silly that only a man could have thought it up.

THE DEVIL *(rising)*

Now what do you think of your thousand and three paramours, Don Juan?

DON JUAN

Odious hypocrites!

THE DEVIL

And now it's time to take you to Hell.

DON JUAN

Not yet. I'm still buoyant.

THE DEVIL

Your reason?

DON JUAN

I am an offshoot of the Conquistadores. My forefathers subdued the Indian continent, but they never understood the nature of the Indians.

THE DEVIL

Oho, so that's your tack. You're telling me that possession is not knowledge after all, but of a different nature?

DON JUAN

Yes.

THE DEVIL

What is it, then? Instruct me.

DON JUAN

Possession is equivalent to domination. I'm proud because my lust overrode their virtue.

THE DEVIL *(turns to the ghosts)*

Is what he says the truth? When did you first experience desire for Don Juan?

THE GHOST ON THE RIGHT

The very moment I saw him.

THE GHOST ON THE LEFT

The instant that I saw him.

THE MIDDLE GHOST

The first time I heard about him.

DON JUAN

But it was I who did the seducing!

THE THREE GHOSTS *(together)*

At our bidding.

DON JUAN

Impossible. How?

THE GHOST ON THE LEFT

The way I looked down.

THE GHOST ON THE RIGHT

The way I looked up.

THE THREE GHOSTS *(together)*

The way we walked.

THE MIDDLE GHOST

The way I laughed.

THE THREE GHOSTS *(together)*

The way we breathed.

DON JUAN

But some of you were virgins.

THE DEVIL

They were less skilled.

DON JUAN

And some of you were noblewomen.

THE DEVIL

They were better at it.

THE THREE GHOSTS *(together)*

Men have prostitutes. We had Don Juan.

THE DEVIL

You thought you were uppermost in their hearts, but I had them long before you did. *(He prepares to seize* DON JUAN.) And now—

DON JUAN

Keep your claws to yourself, you haven't humbled me yet.

THE DEVIL

What? Still an ounce of pride remaining? In what?

DON JUAN

In being chosen.

THE DEVIL

You can't be serious!

DON JUAN

I am. *(He murmurs to himself.)* I must be.

THE DEVIL

You're proud because a thousand and three strangers selected you?

DON JUAN *(revising his answer)*

Not just that. Because I gave them pleasure.

THE DEVIL *(to the ghosts)*

Is what he says— *(He stops, smiles sardonically and offers his hat to* DON JUAN.) Would you like to play the puppeteer this time?

DON JUAN *(declining the hat)*

No.

THE DEVIL

Has Don Juan's vaunted courage finally deserted him?

DON JUAN

No!

THE DEVIL

Then ask your lovers what delighted them about you.

(DON JUAN *reluctantly turns to the women.*)

DON JUAN

Well?

THE MIDDLE GHOST

I liked the way you smell.

DON JUAN

The scent of brimstone?

THE MIDDLE GHOST *(titters)*

No, silly! A mixture of perfume and tobacco.

DON JUAN *(to the ghost on the left)*

What about you?

THE GHOST ON THE LEFT

I liked the way you dress.

DON JUAN

That's *all?*

THE GHOST ON THE LEFT

For me it was.

DON JUAN *(to the remaining ghost)*

And you?

THE GHOST ON THE RIGHT

I enjoyed the challenge.

DON JUAN

Can't you be more specific?

THE GHOST ON THE RIGHT

It excited me to think I might sleep with a man who'd had so many other women.

DON JUAN (*to* THE DEVIL)

This is an answer I like.

THE DEVIL (*to her*)

And was he what you thought he'd be?

THE GHOST ON THE RIGHT

Alas, no. When I found out how easy it was to have him, I realized he wasn't a real challenge, after all.

(DON JUAN *clasps the back of a chair to steady himself.*)

THE DEVIL (*after a pause*)

I think you're done now, aren't you?

(DON JUAN *stares bleakly at* THE DEVIL. *Then with an heroic effort, he straightens and defiantly crosses his arms.*)

What? Courageous still?

DON JUAN (*to the women*)

I am a giant, yet you belittle me. Why? Because although you may have had me at your will, it was I who walked out on every one of you. And so I scorn your malicious intent.

THE MIDDLE GHOST

You didn't walk out on us.

THE GHOST ON THE LEFT

You ran away from us.

DON JUAN

Nonsense. Why would I?

THE GHOST ON THE LEFT

Because you were afraid.

DON JUAN

Don Juan afraid? Ridiculous! Afraid of what?

THE GHOST ON THE LEFT

Of heartbreak.

THE GHOST ON THE RIGHT

Of tenderness.

THE THREE GHOSTS *(together)*

Of love.

DON JUAN *(an anguished cry)*

Aaahhh! *(He buries his head in his hands.)*

THE DEVIL

Twist yourself inside out, Don Juan. Try to find something else to be
proud of in your helter-skelter life.

(Desperately rallying, DON JUAN *straightens.)*

Out of agony comes strength?

DON JUAN

De profundis. You ought to know.

THE DEVIL

Touché. What straw are you grasping at this time?

DON JUAN

I'm the lover who always won out over other lovers. I never wished to
be any other man.

THE DEVIL *(tauntingly)*

Not even your brother Punch?

DON JUAN

I've finally defeated you, Lucifer. There isn't a man you could mention
whose name would fill me with envy.

THE DEVIL *(turning to the women)*

You hear the challenge. Is what he says the truth?

THE GHOST ON THE LEFT

What about Romeo?

THE GHOST ON THE RIGHT

Or Cyrano?

THE MIDDLE GHOST

Or Lancelot?

THE GHOST ON THE LEFT

Those are the lovers we longed for.

THE GHOST ON THE RIGHT

But being pragmatic, we settled for you.

DON JUAN

Shut up!

THE GHOST ON THE LEFT

Romeo.

THE DEVIL

Try to better his poetry.

THE MIDDLE GHOST

Lancelot.

THE DEVIL

Try to better his courage.

THE GHOST ON THE RIGHT

Cyrano.

THE DEVIL

I'd like to see you slay *him* in a duel!

(DON JUAN *wildly shakes his fists at the women.*)

DON JUAN

I made all of you suffer!

THE MIDDLE GHOST

And never understood why.

DON JUAN

Who cares? I ravished, but I did not deign to delve. Shall I sip poison like adolescent Romeo? Or stand behind the scenes like Cyrano and prompt my rival as he woos? Or go on needless quests for spurious grails? No, I am Don Juan the Blasphemer! I take what woman I want and stand unmoved while she sheds bitter tears. There's my pride!

(THE DEVIL *hands* DON JUAN *an empty wineglass.*)

THE DEVIL

Let's take up a collection, shall we?

DON JUAN

Of what?

THE DEVIL

Of tears these women shed for you. Give them the goblet.

(DON JUAN *unwillingly takes the wineglass to the women. They accept it from him and each brings it to her eyes and pretends to weep in it.*)

THE GHOST ON THE LEFT

Boo-hoo!

THE MIDDLE GHOST

Boo-hoo!

THE GHOST ON THE RIGHT

Boo-hoo!

(Then, furtively, she spits in the cup.)

THE DEVIL

Now take the cup to your sisters.

(The women exit.)

A thousand sufferers to go, Don Juan.

(The lights fade.)

SCENE THREE

The same. Early morning. THE DEVIL *is drawing a black velvet curtain across the rear of the room while* DON JUAN *stands by, admiring the filled goblet that he holds.*

THE DEVIL *(letting go of the curtain)*

There, that's better. Daylight spoils a spectre's complexion. Let's see the tears, Don Juan.

DON JUAN *(handing him the cup)*

You see how much they wept for me? The goblet is brimming over. Put me in Hell's hottest compartment and these cool crystal drops will still refresh me. I wonder that you dare come near them, Lucifer. I'd heard they're almost as dangerous to you as holy water.

THE DEVIL

You heard right. True tears burn me. But let's examine these.

(THE DEVIL *flings the cup so that the tears spatter against the velvet curtain. They remain there, shimmering like tiny stars.* THE DEVIL *produces a magnifying glass and inspects the tears.)*

False. False. False. False. False.

DON JUAN

They can't all be false!

THE DEVIL

No? *(He studies more tears.)* False. False. False. False. False.

DON JUAN *(pointing to one of them)*

What about this one?

THE DEVIL

She was angry because she didn't get a birthday present she wanted. She let you borrow that tear.

DON JUAN *(points to another)*

What about this one?

THE DEVIL

She happened to prick her finger just before you arrived.

DON JUAN

What about this huge teardrop?

THE DEVIL *(laughs)*

That spiteful lady spit into your cup.

DON JUAN

What about the small clear ones? What are they?

THE DEVIL

Secret tears.

DON JUAN

Then they must count!

(THE DEVIL *touches a few.*)

THE DEVIL

No, I can touch them. You weren't the secret behind them.

DON JUAN

Father of Lies, you're lying to me!

THE DEVIL

You think so? Watch. *(He runs his talons over the curtain, touching tear after tear after tear.)* False. False. False. False. Fal— *(He suddenly cries out in pain.)* OWWW!!!

DON JUAN *(joyous)*

You found a real tear!

THE DEVIL *(sourly, sucking his claw)*

Obviously.

DON JUAN

Whose?

A WOMAN'S VOICE

It's my tear.

DON JUAN

Come show yourself to me.

THE VOICE

May I?

THE DEVIL *(grumpily)*

Oh, go ahead.

(A masked spirit clad in delicate silver-white enters the room. DON JUAN *approaches her.)*

DON JUAN

Which one of my lovers were you?

THE SILVER SPIRIT

One who died young. Like the tear I shed for you, pity made me fall.

DON JUAN

Pity because I made you a fallen woman?

THE SILVER SPIRIT

No. Pity for your pain.

DON JUAN

And what was that?

THE SILVER SPIRIT

And what *is* that? The agony I sense behind your pride. The little boy who lurks inside the man and cries for arms to comfort him.

DON JUAN

Ah, tell me your name, sweet spirit.

(She whispers it to him.)

I don't recognize it.

THE SILVER SPIRIT *(reaching for her mask)*

Then see me plain!

THE DEVIL

No!

(But she strips it away and shows DON JUAN *her face. A tense moment and then* DON JUAN *speaks.)*

DON JUAN

I don't remember you. When did we meet? In what place? If only I had my list . . .

THE DEVIL *(his composure has returned)*

I've got a copy. *(He produces a duplicate of the list from a pocket and hands it to* DON JUAN.)

DON JUAN *(riffling feverishly)*

Darlette . . . Evalette . . . Friedette . . . Why can't I find her? It's all the fault of that villainous Sganarelle!

THE DEVIL

No, Don Juan, this is the one name you neglected to mention to him. Cheer up. You wanted to stop at an even number. Now will you admit I've won?

DON JUAN

Shall I be sad because I slept with one thousand and three false women and missed true love only once?

(THE SILVER SPIRIT *dons her mask and runs to the puppet stage where the other ghosts emerge and join her. They all are dressed identically to* THE SILVER SPIRIT.)

THE SILVER SPIRIT

Only once? *(She runs behind the other ghosts.)*

DON JUAN

Where are you?

THE SILVER SPIRIT

Only once? *(She runs to the end of the line.)*

DON JUAN

Take off your mask. I can't tell which one you are.

THE SILVER SPIRIT

That's your sorrow. You could have found true love like mine in any one of your women. Poor Don Juan . . .

THE THREE GHOSTS *(together)*

In any one of us you might have found true love . . . poor Don Juan . . . (THE THREE GHOSTS *hold out their arms to* DON JUAN. *He starts towards them.)*

THE DEVIL

Stop this sudden show of tenderness!

(THE THREE GHOSTS *turn their backs on* DON JUAN.)

If I hadn't been here, goodness might have triumphed after all.

DON JUAN *(to* THE SILVER SPIRIT)

I'm sorry I did not fall in love with you.

THE SILVER SPIRIT

It's still not too late.

DON JUAN

I don't know how.

THE SILVER SPIRIT

It isn't hard. I'll show you.

THE DEVIL *(in consternation)*

Double damn! If she really teaches him, I'll lose!

THE SILVER SPIRIT *(removing her mask)*

Look into my eyes and say you long to hold me.

DON JUAN *(looking into her eyes)*

I long to hold you.

THE SILVER SPIRIT

Clasp me close and tell me that you give yourself to me in the spirit of true love.

DON JUAN *(embracing her)*

I give myself to you in the spirit of true love.

THE DEVIL

What a puppet you make, Don Juan. She pulls your strings and you respond.

DON JUAN

What do you expect? I'm new at this game. *(He speaks to* THE SILVER SPIRIT.) From now on, I dedicate my heart to you alone.

(THE DEVIL *gestures.* THE THREE GHOSTS *turn around and take off their masks.)*

THE THREE GHOSTS *(together)*

To her alone? *(They laugh maliciously.)*

DON JUAN *(staring at them)*

At last! So that's what you look like.

THE SILVER SPIRIT

Remember how they lied to you.

DON JUAN

I do. There's the fascination.

THE THREE GHOSTS *(coquettishly)*

Ahhh?

DON JUAN

The last time around I didn't really know you. So, in effect, you're one thousand and three brand-new challenges.

THE THREE GHOSTS *(appreciatively)*

Ahhh!

THE SILVER SPIRIT *(despairingly)*

Ahhh. Poor Don Juan.

DON JUAN *(to her)*

Oh, go away. You're becoming a bore. True love, indeed! The only thing I've ever loved is the quest. Women are but implements I use to overleap myself. One does not fall in love with tools.

(THE THREE GHOSTS *exit indignantly.* THE SILVER SPIRIT *stays.)*

THE DEVIL

Snatching at gambits even in the endgame, eh? What does it mean, Don Juan, to overleap the Self?

DON JUAN

To rest in restless ecstasy. Women were merely the means.

THE DEVIL

I see. You employed them like a painter wields his palette?

DON JUAN

Yes.

THE DEVIL

But towards what end?

DON JUAN *(uncomfortably)*

What do you mean?

THE DEVIL

Did they inspire you to fashion great works of art to be remembered by? Perhaps another *La Gioconda?* Or a new Botticellian Venus? Did you compose romantic sonnets? Or symphonies of fire and color and force?

DON JUAN *(in real anguish)*

Stop it!

THE DEVIL

At last you mourn yourself in earnest.

(THE SILVER SPIRIT *flies to the side of* DON JUAN.)

THE SILVER SPIRIT *(cradling his head)*

Here's the sorrow I shed tears for. Tell me.

DON JUAN *(bleakly)*

I dallied with exquisite women, but never created anything exquisite myself. I warred with mankind, but where are the battle hymns I might have penned? You shed love's tear for me, but I have no heart to break. The only thing I did was make a list. *(He slowly rises and faces* THE DEVIL.) You've won, Lucifer. I have no torch to pass and so I myself must burn. But still I will not beg for mercy. Call me any name you want: Don Wan, Don Joo-ann, Don Giovanni, John Tanner or Mister Jack, I'm still the Blasphemer of Seville.

THE DEVIL

A final scrap of pride just because you exist. Well, you forgot one name. Still spitting out apples, Adam?

DON JUAN

Yes. But on the final day, we'll see. My will may yet outlast the apple, worm and tree.

THE DEVIL *(sneers)*

Perhaps. But on your final night, did you make the Devil suffer?

DON JUAN

I did.

THE DEVIL

What? How?

DON JUAN

By reminding you how painful it is not to be a creator.

(THE DEVIL *reels as if struck.)*

The damned cannot create. That's the true nature of Hell, isn't it?

THE DEVIL *(a hoarse whisper)*

Yes.

DON JUAN

Does that make you pity the damned?

THE DEVIL *(viciously)*

No . . . I hate myself in them! *(He seizes* DON JUAN *and drags him toward the puppet stage.)* Now come and join their company.

(THE SILVER SPIRIT *steps in the path of* THE DEVIL.)

THE SILVER SPIRIT

Stop! It's not too late, Don Juan.

DON JUAN

You're wrong. I'm ready for Hell.

THE SILVER SPIRIT

As long as the tear I shed for you is still damp, there's time to save yourself. Love me!

DON JUAN

Haven't you heard? The Devil and I are much alike. He trots on cloven hooves. I wear them on my brow to signify I browsed through life, a goatish satyr. Goatishly, I swallowed everything I could and left nothing growing where I passed. Let me burn!

THE DEVIL

Step aside. You cannot save him.

THE SILVER SPIRIT *(defiantly)*

My tear is still moist! *(To* DON JUAN, *with desperate intensity)* All your life you set yourself at odds with yourself. Let me love you and I'll teach you how to love yourself.

DON JUAN

Stop whining, woman! I spurn salvation, whether it's yours or God's. I yearn for Hell and the company of Caligula and Nero and all my fellow monsters.

(THE SILVER SPIRIT *shrinks into the background.* THE DEVIL *shoves* DON JUAN *to the edge of the puppet theatre.* PUNCH *pops up onstage.)*

PUNCH

Don Juan, at last! Hurrah!

DON JUAN *(to* THE DEVIL)

See here, where are you taking me?

THE DEVIL

Into your Attic temple.

DON JUAN

Is it actually the gate to the fiery inferno?

THE DEVIL

One of them. A sort of Hell in miniature.

PUNCH *(ringing his bell)*

Brother degenerate, hurrah!

(THE THREE GHOSTS *enter and take chairs facing the puppet stage. They all sit immodestly.)*

DON JUAN *(horrified)*

Not the puppet stage itself?

THE DEVIL

Indeed, yes. *(He attaches strings to* DON JUAN.*)* You'll be one of my most popular marionettes, forever strutting your peacock bravado before a canvas backcloth. *(He pushes him onstage.)*

DON JUAN

But I deserve a hero's punishment! Take me down to Hell!

*(*THE THREE GHOSTS *titter.)*

THE DEVIL

Hell is where *I* will it. Some men's souls are locked inside their statues. Yours makes a far better puppet.

DON JUAN

But I'm the son of the conquering Conquistadores!

*(*THE THREE GHOSTS *laugh.)*

I demand everlasting flames!

THE DEVIL

Too bad. I damn you to everlasting theatre.

*(*DON JUAN *screams.)*

PUNCH

Hsst, brother . . . !

DON JUAN *(distracted by* PUNCH*)*

Eh? What?

PUNCH *(murmurs in* DON JUAN's *ear)*

From here, you can look up their skirts.

DON JUAN *(sees that it is true)*

Well, old serpent, if this is the apple you'd have me bite, why not? The marble statue's immobile, but the marionette knows how to move . . . *and mock.*

PUNCH

Hurrah! A new script!

THE DEVIL

We'll see. Don't keep your audience waiting, Don Juan-n-n-n-ette. *(He claps his hands.)*

DON JUAN *(sings)*

I'm the marionette, Don Juan.
I love ladies with élan,
And I always heat their beds.

(THE THREE GHOSTS titter. PUNCH and DON JUAN put their arms around one another. DON JUAN keeps ducking his head to see up the women's skirts.)

DON JUAN *(sings)*

I'm the marionette, Don Juan.
I love ladies with élan,
And I always heat their beds.

PUNCH *(sings)*

I'm the famous puppet, Punch.
I love ladies by the bunch,
But I always beat their heads.

(THE SILVER SPIRIT looks at the velvet curtain.)

THE SILVER SPIRIT *(mournfully)*

Alas, my teardrop has dried up and gone away. It never will return.

Curtain

—Freely revised and adapted by Marvin Kaye

W. SOMERSET MAUGHAM *(1874–1965) skirted with the idea of becoming a doctor but the success of his first novel won him over to writing. He was once one of London's most successful playwrights, but today is best remembered for his novels* The Razor's Edge *and* Of Human Bondage, *his book-length autobiographical essay* The Summing Up *and numerous highly regarded short stories. Mr. Maugham frequently appears as first-person narrator in his tales, which makes the reader wonder how close to truth the events he relates might be. I hope "A Friend in Need" is pure fabrication; its dapper little businessman is one of the most loathesomely plausible fiends I have ever encountered.*

A Friend in Need
BY W. SOMERSET MAUGHAM

For thirty years now I have been studying my fellow men. I do not know very much about them. I should certainly hesitate to engage a servant on his face, and yet I suppose it is on the face that for the most part we judge the persons we meet. We draw our conclusions from the shape of the jaw, the look in the eyes, the contour of the mouth. I wonder if we are more often right than wrong. Why novels and plays are so often untrue to life is because their authors, perhaps of necessity, make their characters all of a piece. They cannot afford to make them self-contradictory, for then they become incomprehensible, and yet self-contradictory is what most of us are. We are a haphazard bundle of inconsistent qualities. In books on logic they will tell you that it is absurd to say that yellow is tubular or gratitude heavier than air; but in that mixture of incongruities that makes up the self yellow may very well be a horse and cart and gratitude the middle of next week. I shrug my shoulders when people tell me that their first impressions of a person are always right. I think they must have small insight or great vanity. For my own part I find that the longer I know people the more they puzzle me: my oldest friends are just those of whom I can say that I don't know the first thing about them.

These reflections have occurred to me because I read in this morning's paper that Edward Hyde Burton had died at Kobe. He was a merchant and he had been in business in Japan for many years. I knew him very little, but he interested me because once he gave me a great surprise. Unless I had heard the story from his own lips I should never have believed that he was capable of such an action. It was more startling because both in appearance and manner he suggested a very definite type. Here if ever was a man all of a piece. He was a tiny little fellow, not much more than five feet four in height, and very slender, with white hair, a red face much wrinkled, and blue eyes. I suppose he was about sixty when I knew him. He was always neatly and quietly dressed in accordance with his age and station.

Though his offices were in Kobe, Burton often came down to Yokohama. I happened on one occasion to be spending a few days there, waiting for a ship, and I was introduced to him at the British Club. We played bridge together. He played a good game and a generous one. He did not talk very much, either then or later when we were having drinks, but what he said was sensible. He had a quiet, dry humour. He seemed to be popular at the club and afterwards, when he had gone, they described him as one of the best. It happened that we were both staying at the Grand Hotel and next day he asked me to dine with him. I met his wife, fat, elderly and smiling, and his two daughters. It was evidently a united and affectionate family. I think the chief thing that struck me about Burton was his kindliness. There was something very pleasing in his mild blue eyes. His voice was gentle; you could not imagine that he could possibly raise it in anger; his smile was benign. Here was a man who attracted you because you felt in him a real love for his fellows. He had charm. But there was nothing mawkish in him: he liked his game of cards and his cocktail, he could tell with point a good and spicy story, and in his youth he had been something of an athlete. He was a rich man and he had made every penny himself. I suppose one thing that made you like him was that he was so small and frail; he roused your instincts of protection. You felt that he could not bear to hurt a fly.

One afternoon I was sitting in the lounge of the Grand Hotel. This was before the earthquake and they had leather armchairs there. From the windows you had a spacious view of the harbour with its crowded traffic. There were great liners on their way to Vancouver and San Francisco or to Europe by way of Shanghai, Hong-Kong and Singapore; there were tramps of all nations, battered and sea worn, junks with their high sterns and great coloured sails, and innumerable sampans. It was a busy, exhilarating scene, and yet, I know not why, restful to the spirit. Here was romance and it seemed that you had but to stretch out your hand to touch it.

Burton came into the lounge presently and caught sight of me. He seated himself in the chair next to mine.

"What do you say to a little drink?"

He clapped his hands for a boy and ordered two gin fizzes. As the boy brought them, a man passed along the street outside and seeing me waved his hand.

"Do you know Turner?" said Burton as I nodded a greeting.

"I've met him at the club. I'm told he's a remittance man."

"Yes, I believe he is. We have a good many here."

"He plays bridge well."

"They generally do. There was a fellow here last year, oddly enough a namesake of mine, who was the best bridge player I ever met. I suppose you never came across him in London. Lenny Burton he called himself. I believe he'd belonged to some very good clubs."

"No, I don't believe I remember the name."

"He was quite a remarkable player. He seemed to have an instinct about the cards. It was uncanny. I used to play with him a lot. He was in Kobe for some time."

Burton sipped his gin fizz.

"It's rather a funny story," he said. "He wasn't a bad chap. I liked him. He was always well dressed and smart looking. He was handsome in a way, with curly hair and pink-and-white cheeks. Women thought a lot of him. There was no harm in him, you know, he was only wild. Of course he drank too much. Those sort of fellows always do. A bit of money used to come in for him once a quarter and he made a bit more by card playing. He won a good deal of mine, I know that."

Burton gave a kindly little chuckle. I knew from my own experience that he could lose money at bridge with a good grace. He stroked his shaven chin with his thin hand; the veins stood out on it and it was almost transparent.

"I suppose that is why he came to me when he went broke, that and the fact that he was a namesake of mine. He came to see me in my office one day and asked me for a job. I was rather surprised. He told me there was no more money coming from home and he wanted to work. I asked him how old he was.

" 'Thirty-five,' he said.

" 'And what have you been doing hitherto?' I asked him.

" 'Well, nothing very much,' he said.

"I couldn't help laughing.

" 'I'm afraid I can't do anything for you just yet,' I said. 'Come back and see me in another thirty-five years, and I'll see what I can do.'

"He didn't move. He went rather pale. He hesitated for a moment and then told me that he had had bad luck at cards for some time. He hadn't been willing to stick to bridge, he'd been playing poker, and he'd got trimmed. He hadn't a penny. He'd pawned everything he had. He couldn't pay his hotel bill and they wouldn't give him any more credit. He was down and out. If he couldn't get something to do he'd have to commit suicide.

"I looked at him for a bit. I could see now that he was all to pieces. He'd been drinking more than usual and he looked fifty. The girls wouldn't have thought so much of him if they'd seen him then.

" 'Well, isn't there anything you can do except play cards?' I asked him.

" 'I can swim,' he said.

" 'Swim!'

"I could hardly believe my ears; it seemed such an inane answer to give.

" 'I swam for my university.'

"I got some glimmering of what he was driving at. I've known too many men who were little tin gods at their university to be impressed by it.

" 'I was a pretty good swimmer myself when I was a young man,' I said.

"Suddenly I had an idea."

Pausing in his story, Burton turned to me.

"Do you know Kobe?" he asked.

"No," I said, "I passed through it once, but I only spent a night there."

"Then you don't know the Shioya Club. When I was a young man I swam from there round the beacon and landed at the creek of Tarumi. It's over three miles and it's rather difficult on account of the currents round the beacon. Well, I told my young namesake about it and I said to him that if he'd do it I'd give him a job.

"I could see he was rather taken aback.

" 'You say you're a swimmer,' I said.

" 'I'm not in very good condition,' he answered.

"I didn't say anything. I shrugged my shoulders. He looked at me for a moment and then he nodded.

" 'All right,' he said. 'When do you want me to do it?'

"I looked at my watch. It was just after ten.

" 'The swim shouldn't take you much over an hour and a quarter. I'll drive round to the creek at half-past twelve and meet you. I'll take you back to the club to dress and then we'll have lunch together.'

" 'Done,' he said.

"We shook hands. I wished him good luck and he left me. I had a lot of work to do that morning and I only just managed to get to the creek at Tarumi at half-past twelve. But I needn't have hurried; he never turned up."

"Did he funk it at the last moment?" I asked.

"No, he didn't funk it. He started all right. But of course he'd ruined his constitution by drink and dissipation. The currents round the beacon were more than he could manage. We didn't get the body for about three days."

I didn't say anything for a moment or two. I was a trifle shocked. Then I asked Burton a question.

"When you made him that offer of a job, did you know he'd be drowned?"

He gave a little mild chuckle and he looked at me with those kind and candid blue eyes of his. He rubbed his chin with his hand.

"Well, I hadn't got a vacancy in my office at the moment."

Hellish Business

Although Old Nick likes to gamble with mortals for immortal spoils, running Hell is not just pitchforks, brimstone and foreclosing on tricky contracts signed in blood. Damnation is a full-time business and in the next thirteen selections, you will be afforded a rare opportunity to watch the Devil at work. Some of the items on his daily itinerary are to be expected—fighting the forces of good, tempting people to do evil, attempting to ruin a young boy's day, making a guest appearance at a diabolic worship service—but in a few of the following selections, Lucifer displays an unexpectedly generous side to his nature.

Also included in this section are unconventional demons like Isaac Bashevis Singer's Chasidic tempter and Dick Baldwin's chillingly original Christobe, as well as a couple of forays into science fiction and a wicked little nonpareil by Jay Sheckley.

Armageddon is the Biblical name for the place where the final decisive battle between the forces of good and evil will be fought. Only the wildly imaginative FREDRIC BROWN *(1907–1972) would conceive of it taking place during a magic show at a theatre in Cincinnati, the city where the author was born. In my opinion, Brown is one of twentieth-century America's most important genre writers. His huge, generally excellent output includes mysteries* (The Screaming Mimi, Night of the Jabberwock, *the Edgar-winning* The Fabulous Clipjoint, *etc.), science fiction novels* (The Lights in the Sky Are Stars, Martians Go Home, The Mind Thing, Rogue in Space *and the seminal* What Mad Universe) *and several wonderful short story collections, including* Space on My Hands, Angels and Spaceships, Honeymoon in Hell, Nightmares and Geezenstacks *and the posthumous* Paradox Lost.

Armageddon
BY FREDRIC BROWN

It happened—of all places—in Cincinnati. Not that there is anything wrong with Cincinnati, save that it is not the center of the Universe, nor even of the State of Ohio. It's a nice old town and, in its way, second to none. But even its Chamber of Commerce would admit that it lacks cosmic significance. It must have been mere coincidence that Gerber the Great—what a name!—was playing Cincinnati when things slipped elsewhere.

Of course, if the episode had become known, Cincinnati would be the most famous city of the world, and little Herbie would be hailed as a modern St. George and get more acclaim than a quiz kid. But no member of that audience in the Bijou Theater remembers a thing about it. Not even little Herbie Westerman, although he had the water pistol to show for it.

He wasn't thinking about the water pistol in his pocket as he sat looking up at the prestidigitator on the other side of the footlights. It was a new water pistol, bought en route to the theater when he'd inveigled his parents into a side trip into the five-and-dime on Vine Street, but at the moment, Herbie was much more interested in what went on upon the stage.

His expression registered qualified approval. The front-and-back palm was no mystery to Herbie. He could do it himself. True, he had to use pony-sized cards that came with his magic set and were just right for his nine-year-old hands. And true, anyone watching could see the card flutter from the front-palm position to the back as he turned his hand. But that was a detail.

He knew, though, that front-and-back palming seven cards at a time required great finger strength as well as dexterity, and that was what Gerber the Great was doing. There wasn't a telltale click in the shift, either, and Herbie nodded approbation. Then he remembered what was coming next.

He nudged his mother and said, "Ma, ask Pop if he's gotta extra handkerchief."

Out of the corner of his eyes, Herbie saw his mother turn her head and in less time than it would take to say, "Presto," Herbie was out of his seat and skinning down the aisle. It had been, he felt, a beautiful piece of misdirection and his timing had been perfect.

It was at this stage of the performance—which Herbie had seen before, alone—that Gerber the Great asked if some little boy from the audience would step to the stage. He was asking it now.

Herbie Westerman had jumped the gun. He was well in motion before the magician had asked the question. At the previous performance, he'd been a bad tenth in reaching the steps from aisle to stage. This time he'd been ready, and he hadn't taken any chances with parental restraint. Perhaps his mother would have let him go and perhaps not; it had seemed wiser to see that she was looking the other way. You couldn't trust parents on things like that. They had funny ideas sometimes.

"—will please step up on the stage?" And Herbie's foot touched the first of the steps upward right smack on the interrogation point of that sentence. He heard the disappointed scuffle of other feet behind him, and grinned smugly as he went on up across the footlights.

It was the three-pigeon trick, Herbie knew from the previous performance, that required an assistant from the audience. It was almost the only trick he hadn't been able to figure out. There *must,* he knew, have been a concealed compartment somewhere in that box, but where it could be he couldn't even guess. But this time he'd be holding the box himself. If from that range he couldn't spot the gimmick, he'd better go back to stamp collecting.

He grinned confidently up at the magician. Not that he, Herbie, would give him away. He was a magician, too, and he understood that there was a freemasonry among magicians and that one never gave away the tricks of another.

He felt a little chilled, though, and the grin faded as he caught the magician's eyes. Gerber the Great, at close range, seemed much older than he had seemed from the other side of the footlights. And somehow different. Much taller, for one thing.

Anyway, here came the box for the pigeon trick. Gerber's regular assistant was bringing it in on a tray. Herbie looked away from the magician's eyes and he felt better. He remembered, even, his reason for being on the stage. The servant limped. Herbie ducked his head to catch a glimpse of the under side of the tray, just in case. Nothing there.

Gerber took the box. The servant limped away and Herbie's eyes followed him suspiciously. Was the limp genuine or was it a piece of misdirection?

The box folded out flat as the proverbial pancake. All four sides hinged to the bottom, the top hinged to one of the sides. There were little brass catches.

Herbie took a quick step back so he could see behind it while the front was displayed to the audience. Yes, he saw it now. A triangular compartment built against one side of the lid, mirror-covered, angles calculated to achieve invisibility. Old stuff. Herbie felt a little disappointed.

The prestidigitator folded the box, mirror-concealed compartment inside. He turned slightly. "Now, my fine young man—"

What happened in Tibet wasn't the only factor; it was merely the final link of a chain.

The Tibetan weather had been unusual that week, highly unusual. It had been warm. More snow succumbed to the gentle warmth than had melted in more years than man could count. The streams ran high, they ran wide and fast.

Along the streams some prayer wheels whirled faster than they had ever whirled. Others, submerged, stopped altogether. The priests, knee-deep in the cold water, worked frantically, moving the wheels nearer to shore where again the rushing torrent would turn them.

There was one small wheel, a very old one that had revolved without cease for longer than any man knew. So long had it been there that no living lama recalled what had been inscribed upon its prayer plate, nor what had been the purpose of that prayer.

The rushing water had neared its axle when the lama Klarath reached for it to move it to safety. Just too late. His foot slid in the slippery mud and the back of his hand touched the wheel as he fell. Knocked loose from its moorings, it swirled down with the flood, rolling along the bottom of the stream, into deeper and deeper waters.

While it rolled, all was well.

The lama rose, shivering from his momentary immersion, and went after other of the spinning wheels. What, he thought, could one small wheel matter? He didn't know that—now that other links had broken —only that tiny thing stood between Earth and Armageddon.

The prayer wheel of Wangur Ul rolled on, and on, until—a mile farther down—it struck a ledge, and stopped. That was the moment.

"And now, my fine young man—"

Herbie Westerman—we're back in Cincinnati now—looked up, wondering why the prestidigitator had stopped in midsentence. He saw the face of Gerber the Great contorted as though by a great shock. Without moving, without changing, his face began to change. Without appearing different, it became different.

Quietly, then, the magician began to chuckle. In the overtones of that soft laughter was all of evil. No one who heard it could have doubted who he was. No one did doubt. The audience, every member of it, knew in that awful moment who stood before them, knew it— even the most skeptical among them—beyond shadow of doubt.

No one moved, no one spoke, none drew a shuddering breath. There are things beyond fear. Only uncertainty causes fear, and the Bijou Theater was filled, then, with a dreadful certainty.

The laughter grew. Crescendo, it reverberated into the far dusty corners of the gallery. Nothing—not a fly on the ceiling—moved.

Satan spoke.

"I thank you for your kind attention to a poor magician." He bowed, ironically low. "The performance is ended."

He smiled. "All performances are ended."

Somehow the theater seemed to darken, although the electric lights still burned. In dead silence, there seemed to be the sound of wings, leathery wings, as though invisible Things were gathering.

On the stage was a dim red radiance. From the head and from each shoulder of the tall figure of the magician there sprang a tiny flame. A naked flame.

There were other flames. They flickered along the proscenium of the stage, along the footlights. One sprang from the lid of the folded box little Herbie Westerman still held in his hands.

Herbie dropped the box.

Did I mention that Herbie Westerman was a Safety Cadet? It was purely a reflex action. A boy of nine doesn't know much about things like Armageddon, but Herbie Westerman should have known that water would never have put out that fire.

But, as I said, it was purely a reflex action. He yanked out his new water pistol and squirted it at the box of the pigeon trick. And the fire *did* vanish, even as a spray from the stream of water ricocheted and dampened the trouser leg of Gerber the Great, who had been facing the other way.

There was a sudden, brief hissing sound. The lights were growing bright again, and all the other flames were dying, and the sound of wings faded, blended into another sound—the rustling of the audience.

The eyes of the prestidigitator were closed. His voice sounded strangely strained as he said: "This much power I retain. None of you will remember this."

Then, slowly, he turned and picked up the fallen box. He held it out to Herbie Westerman. "You must be more careful, boy," he said. "Now hold it so."

He tapped the top lightly with his wand. The door fell open. Three white pigeons flew out of the box. The rustle of their wings was not leathery.

Herbie Westerman's father came down the stairs and, with a purposeful air, took his razor strop off the hook on the kitchen wall.

Mrs. Westerman looked up from stirring the soup on the stove. "Why, Henry," she asked, "are you really going to punish him with that—just for squirting a little water out of the window of the car on the way home?"

Her husband shook his head grimly. "Not for that, Marge. But don't you remember we bought him that water gun on the way downtown, and that he wasn't near a water faucet after that? Where do you think he filled it?"

He didn't wait for an answer. "When we stopped in at the cathedral to talk to Father Ryan about his confirmation, that's when the little brat filled it. Out of the baptismal font! Holy water he uses in his water pistol!"

He clumped heavily up the stairs, strop in hand.

Rhythmic thwacks and wails of pain floated down the staircase. Herbie—who had saved the world—was having his reward.

ALGERNON BLACKWOOD *(1869–1951) was born in Kent, England. His super-natural fiction, which includes at least one acknowledged classic, the terrifying "The Willows," is sometimes categorized as journalistically spare in style, but this is not true of the following richly evocative novella. Blackwood was edu-cated in a variety of schools in France, Germany and Switzerland, as well as at Edinburgh University; one suspects he drew heavily upon those times when he wrote "Secret Worship," a dark variant on the you-can't-go-home-again theme. It is one of a series of his stories involving John Silence, psychic investigator extraordinaire.*

Secret Worship
BY ALGERNON BLACKWOOD

Harris, the silk merchant, was in South Germany on his way home from a business trip when the idea came to him suddenly that he would take the mountain railway from Strassbourg and run down to revisit his old school after an interval of something more than thirty years. And it was to this chance impulse of the junior partner in Harris Brothers of St. Paul's Churchyard that John Silence owed one of the most curious cases of his whole experience, for at that very moment he happened to be tramping these same mountains with a holiday knapsack, and from different points of the compass the two men were actually converging towards the same inn.

Now, deep down in the heart that for thirty years had been con-cerned chiefly with the profitable buying and selling of silk, this school had left the imprint of its peculiar influence, and, though perhaps unknown to Harris, had strongly coloured the whole of his subsequent existence. It belonged to the deeply religious life of a small Protestant community (which it is unnecessary to specify), and his father had sent him there at the age of fifteen, partly because he would learn the German requisite for the conduct of the silk business, and partly be-cause the discipline was strict, and discipline was what his soul and body needed just then more than anything else.

The life, indeed, had proved exceedingly severe, and young Harris benefited accordingly; for though corporal punishment was unknown, there was a system of mental and spiritual correction which somehow made the soul stand proudly erect to receive it, while it struck at the very root of the fault and taught the boy that his character was being cleaned and strengthened, and that he was not merely being tortured in a kind of personal revenge.

That was over thirty years ago, when he was a dreamy and impressionable youth of fifteen; and now, as the train climbed slowly up the winding mountain gorges, his mind travelled back somewhat lovingly over the intervening period, and forgotten details rose vividly again before him out of the shadows. The life there had been very wonderful, it seemed to him, in that remote mountain village, protected from the tumults of the world by the love and worship of the devout Brotherhood that ministered to the needs of some hundred boys from every country in Europe. Sharply the scenes came back to him. He smelt again the long stone corridors, the hot pinewood rooms, where the sultry hours of summer study were passed with bees droning through open windows in the sunshine, and German characters struggling in the mind with dreams of English lawns—and then the sudden awful cry of the master in German—

"Harris, stand up! You sleep!"

And he recalled the dreadful standing motionless for an hour, book in hand, while the knees felt like wax and the head grew heavier than a cannon-ball.

The very smell of the cooking came back to him—the daily *Sauerkraut,* the watery chocolate on Sundays, the flavour of the stringy meat served twice a week at *Mittagessen;* and he smiled to think again of the half-rations that was the punishment for speaking English. The very odour of the milk-bowls—the hot sweet aroma that rose from the soaking peasant-bread at the six-o'clock breakfast—came back to him pungently, and he saw the huge *Speisesaal* with the hundred boys in their school uniform, all eating sleepily in silence, gulping down the coarse bread and scalding milk in terror of the bell that would presently cut them short—and, at the far end where the masters sat, he saw the narrow slit windows with the vistas of enticing field and forest beyond.

And this, in turn, made him think of the great barnlike room on the top floor where all slept together in wooden cots, and he heard in memory the clamour of the cruel bell that woke them on winter mornings at five o'clock and summoned them to the stone-flagged

Waschkammer, where boys and masters alike, after scanty and icy washing, dressed in complete silence.

From this his mind passed swiftly, with vivid picture-thoughts, to other things, and with a passing shiver he remembered how the loneliness of never being alone had eaten into him, and how everything—work, meals, sleep, walks, leisure—was done with his "division" of twenty other boys and under the eyes of at least two masters. The only solitude possible was by asking for half an hour's practice in the cell-like music rooms, and Harris smiled to himself as he recalled the zeal of his violin studies.

Then, as the train puffed laboriously through the great pine forests that cover these mountains with a giant carpet of velvet, he found the pleasanter layers of memory giving up their dead, and he recalled with admiration the kindness of the masters, whom all addressed as Brother, and marvelled afresh at their devotion in burying themselves for years in such a place, only to leave it, in most cases, for the still rougher life of missionaries in the wild places of the world.

He thought once more of the still, religious atmosphere that hung over the little forest community like a veil, barring the distressful world; of the picturesque ceremonies at Easter, Christmas, and New Year; of the numerous feast-days and charming little festivals. The *Beschehr-Fest,* in particular, came back to him—the feast of gifts at Christmas—when the entire community paired off and gave presents, many of which had taken weeks to make or the savings of many days to purchase. And then he saw the midnight ceremony in the church at New Year, with the shining face of the *Prediger* in the pulpit—the village preacher who, on the last night of the old year, saw in the empty gallery beyond the organ loft the faces of all who were to die in the ensuing twelve months, and who at last recognised himself among them, and, in the very middle of his sermon, passed into a state of rapt ecstasy and burst into a torrent of praise.

Thickly the memories crowded upon him. The picture of the small village dreaming its unselfish life on the mountain-tops, clean, wholesome, simple, searching vigorously for its God, and training hundreds of boys in the grand way, rose up in his mind with all the power of an obsession. He felt once more the old mystical enthusiasm, deeper than the sea and more wonderful than the stars; he heard again the winds sighing from leagues of forest over the red roofs in the moonlight; he heard the Brothers' voices talking of the things beyond this life as though they had actually experienced them in the body; and, as he sat in the jolting train, a spirit of unutterable longing passed over his seared and tired soul, stirring in the depths of him a sea of emotions that he thought had long since frozen into immobility.

And the contrast pained him—the idealistic dreamer then, the man of business now—so that a spirit of unworldly peace and beauty known only to the soul in meditation laid its feathered finger upon his heart, moving strangely the surface of the waters.

Harris shivered a little and looked out of the window of his empty carriage. The train had long passed Hornberg, and far below the streams tumbled in white foam down the limestone rocks. In front of him, dome upon dome of wooded mountain stood against the sky. It was October, and the air was cool and sharp, wood-smoke and damp moss exquisitely mingled in it with the subtle odours of the pines. Overhead, between the tips of the highest firs, he saw the first stars peeping, and the sky was a clean, pale amethyst that seemed exactly the colour all these memories clothed themselves with in his mind.

He leaned back in his corner and sighed. He was a heavy man, and he had not known sentiment for years; he was a big man, and it took much to move him, literally and figuratively; he was a man in whom the dreams of God that haunt the soul in youth, though overlaid by the scum that gathers in the fight for money, had not, as with the majority, utterly died the death.

He came back into this little neglected pocket of the years, where so much fine gold had collected and lain undisturbed, with all his semi-spiritual emotions aquiver; and, as he watched the mountain-tops come nearer, and smelt the forgotten odours of his boyhood, something melted on the surface of his soul and left him sensitive to a degree he had not known since, thirty years before, he had lived here with his dreams, his conflicts, and his youthful suffering.

A thrill ran through him as the train stopped with a jolt at a tiny station and he saw the name in large black lettering on the grey stone building, and below it, the number of metres it stood above the level of the sea.

"The highest point on the line!" he exclaimed. "How well I remember it—Sommerau—Summer Meadow. The very next station is mine!"

And, as the train ran downhill with brakes on and steam shut off, he put his head out of the window and one by one saw the old familiar landmarks in the dusk. They stared at him like dead faces in a dream. Queer, sharp feelings, half poignant, half sweet, stirred in his heart.

"There's the hot, white road we walked along so often with the two Brüder always at our heels," he thought; "and there, by Jove, is the turn through the forest to *'Die Galgen,'* the stone gallows where they hanged the witches in olden days!"

He smiled a little as the train slid past.

"And there's the copse where the Lilies of the Valley powdered the ground in spring; and, I swear"—he put his head out with a sudden impulse,—"if that's not the very clearing where Calame, the French boy, chased the swallow-tail with me, and Bruder Pagel gave us half-rations for leaving the road without permission, and for shouting in our mother tongues!" And he laughed again as the memories came back with a rush, flooding his mind with vivid detail.

The train stopped, and he stood on the grey gravel platform like a man in a dream. It seemed half a century since he last waited there with corded wooden boxes, and got into the train for Strassbourg and home after the two years' exile. Time dropped from him like an old garment and he felt a boy again. Only, things looked so much smaller than his memory of them; shrunk and dwindled they looked, and the distances seemed on a curiously smaller scale.

He made his way across the road to the little Gasthaus, and, as he went, faces and figures of former schoolfellows—German, Swiss, Italian, French, Russian—slipped out of the shadowy woods and silently accompanied him. They flitted by his side, raising their eyes questioningly, sadly, to his. But their names he had forgotten. Some of the Brothers, too, came with them, and most of these he remembered by name—Bruder Röst, Bruder Pagel, Bruder Schliemann, and the bearded face of the old preacher who had seen himself in the haunted gallery of those about to die—Bruder Gysin. The dark forest lay all about him like a sea that any moment might rush with velvet waves upon the scene and sweep all the faces away. The air was cool and wonderfully fragrant, but with every perfumed breath came also a pallid memory . . .

Yet, in spite of the underlying sadness inseparable from such an experience, it was all very interesting, and held a pleasure peculiarly its own, so that Harris engaged his room and ordered supper feeling well pleased with himself, and intending to walk up to the old school that very evening. It stood in the centre of the community's village, some four miles distant through the forest, and he now recollected for the first time that this little Protestant settlement dwelt isolated in a section of the country that was otherwise Catholic. Crucifixes and shrines surrounded the clearing like the sentries of a beleaguring army. Once beyond the square of the village, with its few acres of field and orchard, the forest crowded up in solid phalanxes, and beyond the rim of trees began the country that was ruled by the priests of another faith. He vaguely remembered, too, that the Catholics had showed sometimes a certain hostility towards the little Protestant oasis that flourished so quietly and benignly in their midst. He had quite forgotten this. How trumpery it all seemed now with his wide experience of life and his knowledge of other countries and the great outside world. It was like stepping back, not thirty years, but three hundred.

There were only two others besides himself at supper. One of them, a bearded, middle-aged man in tweeds, sat by himself at the far end, and Harris kept out of his way because he was English. He feared he might be in business, possibly even in the silk business, and that he would perhaps talk on the subject. The other traveller, however, was a Catholic priest. He was a little man who ate his salad with a knife, yet so gently that it was almost inoffensive, and it was the sight of "the cloth" that recalled his memory of the old antagonism. Harris mentioned by way of conversation the object of his sentimental journey, and the priest looked up sharply at him with raised eyebrows and an expression of surprise and suspicion that somehow piqued him. He ascribed it to his difference of belief.

"Yes," went on the silk merchant, pleased to talk of what his mind was so full, "and it was a curious experience for an English boy to be dropped down into a school of a hundred foreigners. I well remember the loneliness and intolerable Heimweh of it at first." His German was very fluent.

The priest opposite looked up from his cold veal and potato salad and smiled. It was a nice face. He explained quietly that he did not belong here, but was making a tour of the parishes of Württemberg and Baden.

"It was a strict life," added Harris. "We English, I remember, used to call it *Gefängnisleben*—prison life!"

The face of the other, for some unaccountable reason, darkened. After a slight pause, and more by way of politeness than because he wished to continue the subject, he said quietly—

"It was a flourishing school in those days, of course. Afterwards, I have heard—" He shrugged his shoulders slightly, and the odd look—it almost seemed a look of alarm—came back into his eyes. The sentence remained unfinished.

Something in the tone of the man seemed to his listener uncalled for—in a sense reproachful, singular. Harris bridled in spite of himself.

"It has changed?" he asked. "I can hardly believe—"

"You have not heard, then?" observed the priest gently, making a gesture as though to cross himself, yet not actually completing it. "You have not heard what happened there before it was abandoned—?"

It was very childish, of course, and perhaps he was overtired and overwrought in some way, but the words and manner of the little priest seemed to him so offensive—so disproportionately offensive—that he hardly noticed the concluding sentence. He recalled the old bitterness and the old antagonism, and for a moment he almost lost his temper.

"Nonsense," he interrupted with a forced laugh, *"Unsinn!* You must forgive me, sir, for contradicting you. But I was a pupil there myself. I was at school there. There was no place like it. I cannot believe that anything serious could have happened to—to take away its character. The devotion of the Brothers would be difficult to equal anywhere—"

He broke off suddenly, realising that his voice had been raised unduly and that the man at the far end of the table might understand German; and at the same moment he looked up and saw that this individual's eyes were fixed upon his face intently. They were peculiarly bright. Also they were rather wonderful eyes, and the way they met his own served in some way he could not understand to convey both a reproach and a warning. The whole face of the stranger, indeed, made a vivid impression upon him, for it was a face, he now noticed for the first time, in whose presence one would not willingly have said or done anything unworthy. Harris could not explain to himself how it was he had not become conscious sooner of its presence.

But he could have bitten off his tongue for having so far forgotten himself. The little priest lapsed into silence. Only once he said, looking up and speaking in a low voice that was not intended to be overheard, but that evidently *was* overheard, "You will find it different." Pres-

ently he rose and left the table with a polite bow that included both
the others.

And, after him, from the far end rose also the figure in the tweed
suit, leaving Harris by himself.

He sat on for a bit in the darkening room, sipping his coffee and
smoking his fifteen-pfennig cigar, till the girl came in to light the oil
lamps. He felt vexed with himself for his lapse from good manners, yet
hardly able to account for it. Most likely, he reflected, he had been
annoyed because the priest had unintentionally changed the pleasant
character of his dream by introducing a jarring note. Later he must
seek an opportunity to make amends. At present, however, he was too
impatient for his walk to the school, and he took his stick and hat and
passed out into the open air.

And, as he crossed before the Gasthaus, he noticed that the priest
and the man in the tweed suit were engaged already in such deep
conversation that they hardly noticed him as he passed and raised his
hat.

He started off briskly, well remembering the way, and hoping to
reach the village in time to have a word with one of the Brüder. They
might even ask him in for a cup of coffee. He felt sure of his welcome,
and the old memories were in full possession once more. The hour of
return was a matter of no consequence whatever.

It was then just after seven o'clock, and the October evening was
drawing in with chill airs from the recesses of the forest. The road
plunged straight from the railway clearing into its depths, and in a
very few minutes the trees engulfed him and the clack of his boots fell
dead and echoless against the serried stems of a million firs. It was
very black; one trunk was hardly distinguishable from another. He
walked smartly, swinging his holly stick. Once or twice he passed a
peasant on his way to bed, and the guttural "Gruss Got," unheard for
so long, emphasized the passage of time, while yet making it seem as
nothing. A fresh group of pictures crowded his mind. Again the figures of former schoolfellows flitted out of the forest and kept pace by
his side, whispering of the doings of long ago. One reverie stepped
hard upon the heels of another. Every turn in the road, every clearing
of the forest, he knew, and each in turn brought forgotten associations
to life. He enjoyed himself thoroughly.

He marched on and on. There was powdered gold in the sky till the
moon rose, and then a wind of faint silver spread silently between the

earth and stars. He saw the tips of the fir trees shimmer, and heard them whisper as the breeze turned their needles towards the light. The mountain air was indescribably sweet. The road shone like the foam of a river through the gloom. White moths flitted here and there like silent thoughts across his path, and a hundred smells greeted him from the forest caverns across the years.

Then, when he least expected it, the trees fell away abruptly on both sides, and he stood on the edge of the village clearing.

He walked faster. There lay the familiar outlines of the houses, sheeted with silver; there stood the trees in the little central square with the fountain and small green lawns; there loomed the shape of the church next to the Gasthof der Brüdergemeinde; and just beyond, dimly rising into the sky, he saw with a sudden thrill the mass of the huge school building, blocked castle-like with deep shadows in the moonlight, standing square and formidable to face him after the silences of more than a quarter of a century.

He passed quickly down the deserted village street and stopped close beneath its shadow, staring up at the walls that had once held him prisoner for two years—two unbroken years of discipline and homesickness. Memories and emotions surged through his mind; for the most vivid sensations of his youth had focused about this spot, and it was here he had first begun to live and learn values. Not a single footstep broke the silence, though lights glimmered here and there through cottage windows; but when he looked up at the high walls of the school, draped now in shadow, he easily imagined that well-known faces crowded to the windows to greet him—closed windows that really reflected only moonlight and the gleam of stars.

This, then, was the old school building, standing foursquare to the world, with its shuttered windows, its lofty, tiled roof, and the spiked lightning-conductors pointing like black and taloned fingers from the corners. For a long time he stood and stared. Then, presently, he came to himself again, and realised to his joy that a light still shone in the windows of the *Bruderstube*.

He turned from the road and passed through the iron railings; then climbed the twelve stone steps and stood facing the black wooden door with the heavy bars of iron, a door he had once loathed and dreaded with the hatred and passion of an imprisoned soul, but now looked upon tenderly with a sort of boyish delight.

Almost timorously he pulled the rope and listened with a tremor of excitement to the clanging of the bell deep within the building. And the long-forgotten sound brought the past before him with such a vivid sense of reality that he positively shivered. It was like the magic bell in the fairy-tale that rolls back the curtain of Time and summons the figures from the shadows of the dead. He had never felt so sentimental in his life. It was like being young again. And, at the same time, he began to bulk rather large in his own eyes with a certain spurious importance. He was a big man from the world of strife and action. In this little place of peaceful dreams would he, perhaps, not cut something of a figure?

"I'll try once more," he thought after a long pause, seizing the iron bell-rope, and was just about to pull it when a step sounded on the stone passage within, and the huge door slowly swung open.

A tall man with a rather severe cast of countenance stood facing him in silence.

"I must apologise—it is somewhat late," he began a trifle pompously, "but the fact is I am an old pupil. I have only just arrived and really could not restrain myself." His German seemed not quite so fluent as usual. "My interest is so great. I was here in '70."

The other opened the door wider and at once bowed him in with a smile of genuine welcome.

"I am Bruder Kalkmann," he said quietly in a deep voice. "I myself was a master here about that time. It is a great pleasure always to welcome a former pupil." He looked at him very keenly for a few seconds, and then added, "I think, too, it is splendid of you to come— very splendid."

"It is a very great pleasure," Harris replied, delighted with his reception.

The dimly-lighted corridor with its flooring of grey stone, and the familiar sound of a German voice echoing through it—with the peculiar intonation the Brothers always used in speaking—all combined to lift him bodily, as it were, into the dream-atmosphere of long-forgotten days. He stepped gladly into the building and the door shut with the familiar thunder that completed the reconstruction of the past. He almost felt the old sense of imprisonment, of aching nostalgia, of having lost his liberty.

Harris sighed involuntarily and turned towards his host, who returned his smile faintly and then led the way down the corridor.

"The boys have retired," he explained, "and, as you remember, we keep early hours here. But, at least, you will join us for a little while in the *Bruderstube* and enjoy a cup of coffee." This was precisely what the silk merchant had hoped, and he accepted with an alacrity that he intended to be tempered by graciousness. "And tomorrow," continued the Bruder, "you must come and spend a whole day with us. You may even find acquaintances, for several pupils of your day have come back here as masters."

For one brief second there passed into the man's eyes a look that made the visitor start. But it vanished as quickly as it came. It was impossible to define. Harris convinced himself it was the effect of a shadow cast by the lamp they had just passed on the wall. He dismissed it from his mind.

"You are very kind, I'm sure," he said politely. "It is perhaps a great pleasure to me than you can imagine to see the place again. Ah" —he stopped short opposite a door with the upper half of glass and peered in—"surely there is one of the music rooms where I used to practise the violin. How it comes back to me after all these years!"

Bruder Kalkmann stopped indulgently, smiling, to allow his guest a moment's inspection.

"You still have the boys' orchestra? I remember I used to play 'zweite Geige' in it. Bruder Schliemann conducted at the piano. Dear me, I can see him now with his long black hair and—and—" He stopped abruptly. Again the odd, dark look passed over the stern face of his companion. For an instant it seemed curiously familiar.

"We still keep up the pupils' orchestra," he said, "but Bruder Schliemann, I am sorry to say—" he hesitated an instant, and then added, "Bruder Schliemann is dead."

"Indeed, indeed," said Harris quickly. "I am sorry to hear it." He was conscious of a faint feeling of distress, but whether it arose from the news of his old music teacher's death, or—from something else— he could not quite determine. He gazed down the corridor that lost itself among shadows. In the street and village everything had seemed so much smaller than he remembered, but here, inside the school building, everything seemed so much bigger. The corridor was loftier and longer, more spacious and vast, than the mental picture he had preserved. His thoughts wandered dreamily for an instant.

He glanced up and saw the face of the Bruder watching him with a smile of patient indulgence.

"Your memories possess you," he observed gently, and the stern look passed into something almost pitying.

"You are right," returned the man of silk, "they do. This was the most wonderful period of my whole life in a sense. At the time I hated it—" He hesitated, not wishing to hurt the Brother's feelings.

"According to English ideas it seemed strict, of course," the other said persuasively, so that he went on.

"—Yes, partly that; and partly the ceaseless nostalgia, and the solitude which came from never being really alone. In English schools the boys enjoy peculiar freedom, you know."

Bruder Kalkmann, he saw, was listening intently.

"But it produced one result that I have never wholly lost," he continued self-consciously, "and am grateful for."

"Ach! Wie so, denn?"

"The constant inner pain threw me headlong into your religious life, so that the whole force of my being seemed to project itself towards the search for a deeper satisfaction—a real resting-place for the soul. During my two years here I yearned for God in my boyish way as perhaps I have never yearned for anything since. Moreover, I have never quite lost that sense of peace and inward joy which accompanied the search. I can never quite forget this school and the deep things it taught me."

He paused at the end of his long speech, and a brief silence fell between them. He feared he had said too much, or expressed himself clumsily in the foreign language, and when Bruder Kalkmann laid a hand upon his shoulder, he gave a little involuntary start.

"So that my memories perhaps do possess me rather strongly," he added apologetically; "and this long corridor, these rooms, that barred and gloomy front door, all touch chords that—that—" His German failed him and he glanced at his companion with an explanatory smile and gesture. But the brother had removed the hand from his shoulder and was standing with his back to him, looking down the passage.

"Naturally, naturally so," he said hastily without turning round. *"Es ist doch selbstverständlich.* We shall all understand."

Then he turned suddenly, and Harris saw that his face had turned most oddly and disagreeably sinister. It may only have been the shadows again playing their tricks with the wretched oil lamps on the wall, for the dark expression passed instantly as they retraced their steps down the corridor, but the Englishman somehow got the impression that he had said something to give offence, something that was not quite to the other's taste. Opposite the door of the *Bruderstube* they stopped. Harris realised that it was late and he had possibly stayed talking too long. He made a tentative effort to leave, but his companion would not hear of it.

"You must have a cup of coffee with us," he said firmly as though he meant it, "and my colleagues will be delighted to see you. Some of them will remember you, perhaps."

The sound of voices came pleasantly through the door, men's voices talking together. Bruder Kalkmann turned the handle and they entered a room ablaze with light and full of people.

"Ah—but your name?" he whispered, bending down to catch the reply; "you have not told me your name yet."

"Harris," said the Englishman quickly as they went in. He felt nervous as he crossed the threshold, but ascribed the momentary trepidation to the fact that he was breaking the strictest rule of the whole establishment, which forbade a boy under severest penalties to come near this holy of holies where the masters took their brief leisure.

"Ah, yes, of course—Harris," repeated the other as though he remembered it. "Come in, Herr Harris, come in, please. Your visit will be immensely appreciated. It is really very fine, very wonderful of you to have come in this way."

The door closed behind them and, in the sudden light which made his sight swim for a moment, the exaggeration of the language escaped his attention. He heard the voice of Bruder Kalkmann introducing him. He spoke very loud, indeed, unnecessarily—absurdly loud, Harris thought.

"Brothers," he announced, "it is my pleasure and privilege to introduce to you Herr Harris from England. He has just arrived to make us a little visit, and I have already expressed to him on behalf of us all the satisfaction we feel that he is here. He was, as you remember, a pupil in the year '70."

It was a very formal, a very German introduction, but Harris rather liked it. It made him feel important and he appreciated the tact that made it almost seem as though he had been expected.

The black forms rose and bowed; Harris bowed; Kalkmann bowed. Every one was very polite and very courtly. The room swam with moving figures; the light dazzled him after the gloom of the corridor; there was thick cigar smoke in the atmosphere. He took the chair that was offered to him between two of the Brothers, and sat down, feeling vaguely that his perceptions were not quite as keen and accurate as usual. He felt a trifle dazed perhaps, and the spell of the past came strongly over him, confusing the immediate present and making everything dwindle oddly to the dimensions of long ago. He seemed to pass under the mastery of a great mood that was a composite reproduction of all the moods of his forgotten boyhood.

Then he pulled himself together with a sharp effort and entered into the conversation that had begun again to buzz round him. Moreover, he entered into it with keen pleasure, for the Brothers—there were perhaps a dozen of them in the little room—treated him with a charm of manner that speedily made him feel one of themselves. This, again, was a very subtle delight to him. He felt that he had stepped out of the greedy, vulgar, self-seeking world, the world of silk and markets and profit-making—stepped into the cleaner atmosphere where spiritual ideals were paramount and life was simple and devoted. It all charmed him inexpressibly, so that he realised—yes, in a sense—the degradation of his twenty years' absorption in business. This keen atmosphere under the stars where men thought only of their souls, and of the souls of others, was too rarefied for the world he was now associated with. He found himself making comparisons to his own disadvantage,—comparisons with the mystical little dreamer that had stepped thirty years before from the stern peace of this devout community, and the man of the world that he had since become—and the contrast made him shiver with a keen regret and something like self-contempt.

He glanced round at the other faces floating towards him through tobacco smoke—this acrid cigar smoke he remembered so well: how keen they were, how strong, placid, touched with the nobility of great aims and unselfish purposes. At one or two he looked particularly. He hardly knew why. They rather fascinated him. There was something so very stern and uncompromising about them, and something, too, oddly, subtly, familiar, that yet just eluded him. But whenever their eyes met his own they held undeniable welcome in them; and some held more—a kind of perplexed admiration, he thought, something that was between esteem and deference. This note of respect in all the faces was very flattering to his vanity.

Coffee was served presently, made by a black-haired Brother who sat in the corner by the piano and bore a marked resemblance to Bruder Schliemann, the musical director of thirty years ago. Harris exchanged bows with him when he took the cup from his white hands, which he noticed were like the hands of a woman. He lit a cigar, offered to him by his neighbour, with whom he was chatting delightfully, and who, in the glare of the lighted match, reminded him sharply for a moment of Bruder Pagel, his former room-master.

"Es ist wirklich merkwürdig," he said, "how many resemblances I see, or imagine. It is really *very* curious!"

"Yes," replied the other, peering at him over his coffee cup, "the spell of the place is wonderfully strong. I can well understand that the old faces rise before your mind's eye—almost to the exclusion of ourselves perhaps."

They both laughed pleasantly. It was soothing to find his mood understood and appreciated. And they passed on to talk of the mountain village, its isolation, its remoteness from worldly life, its peculiar fitness for meditation and worship, and for spiritual development—of a certain kind.

"And your coming back in this way, Herr Harris, has pleased us all so much," joined in the Bruder on his left. "We esteem you for it most highly. We honour you for it."

Harris made a deprecating gesture. "I fear, for my part, it is only a very selfish pleasure," he said a trifle unctuously.

"Not all would have had the courage," added the one who resembled Bruder Pagel.

"You mean," said Harris, a little puzzled, "the disturbing memories—?"

Bruder Pagel looked at him steadily, with unmistakable admiration and respect. "I mean that most men hold so strongly to life, and can give up so little for their beliefs," he said gravely.

The Englishman felt slightly uncomfortable. These worthy men really made too much of his sentimental journey. Besides, the talk was getting a little out of his depth. He hardly followed it.

"The worldly life still has *some* charms for me," he replied smilingly, as though to indicate that sainthood was not yet quite within his grasp.

"All the more, then, must we honour you for so freely coming," said the Brother on his left; "so unconditionally!"

A pause followed, and the silk merchant felt relieved when the conversation took a more general turn, although he noted that it never travelled very far from the subject of his visit and the wonderful situation of the lonely village for men who wished to develop their spiritual powers and practise the rites of a high worship. Others joined in, complimenting him on his knowledge of the language, making him feel utterly at his ease, yet at the same time a little uncomfortable by the excess of their admiration. After all, it was such a very small thing to do, this sentimental journey.

The time passed along quickly; the coffee was excellent, the cigars soft and of the nutty flavour he loved. At length, fearing to outstay his welcome, he rose reluctantly to take his leave. But the others would not hear of it. It was not often a former pupil returned to visit them in this simple, unaffected way. The night was young. If necessary they could even find him a corner in the great *Schlafzimmer* upstairs. He was easily persuaded to stay a little longer. Somehow he had become the centre of the little party. He felt pleased, flattered, honoured.

"And perhaps Bruder Schliemann will play something for us— now."

It was Kalkmann speaking, and Harris started visibly as he heard the name, and saw the black-haired man by the piano turn with a smile. For Schliemann was the name of his old music director, who was dead. Could this be his son? They were so exactly alike.

"If Bruder Meyer has not put his Amati to bed, I will accompany him," said the musician suggestively, looking across at a man whom Harris had not yet noticed, and who, he now saw, was the very image of a former master of that name.

Meyer rose and excused himself with a little bow, and the English-man quickly observed that he had a peculiar gesture as though his neck had a false join on to the body just below the collar and feared it might break. Meyer of old had this trick of movement. He remem-bered how the boys used to copy it.

He glanced sharply from face to face, feeling as though some silent, unseen process were changing everything about him. All the faces seemed oddly familiar. Pagel, the Brother he had been talking with, was of course the image of Pagel, his former room-master; and Kalkmann, he now realised for the first time, was the very twin of another master whose name he had quite forgotten, but whom he used to dislike intensely in the old days. And, through the smoke, peering at him from the corners of the room, he saw that all the Brothers about him had the faces he had known and lived with long ago—Röst, Fluheim, Meinert, Rigel, Gysin.

He stared hard, suddenly grown more alert, and everywhere saw, or fancied he saw, strange likenesses, ghostly resemblances—more, the identical faces of years ago. There was something queer about it all, something not quite right, something that made him feel uneasy. He shook himself, mentally and actually, blowing the smoke from before his eyes with a long breath, and as he did so he noticed to his dismay that every one was fixedly staring. They were watching him.

This brought him to his senses. As an Englishman, and a foreigner, he did not wish to be rude, or to do anything to make himself foolishly conspicuous and spoil the harmony of the evening. He was a guest, and a privileged guest at that. Besides, the music had already begun. Bruder Schliemann's long white fingers were caressing the keys to some purpose.

He subsided into his chair and smoked with half-closed eyes that yet saw everything.

But the shudder had established itself in his being, and, whether he would or not, it kept repeating itself. As a town, far up some inland river, feels the pressure of the distant sea, so he became aware that mighty forces from somewhere beyond his ken were urging themselves up against his soul in this smoky little room. He began to feel exceedingly ill at ease.

And as the music filled the air his mind began to clear. Like a lifted veil there rose up something that had hitherto obscured his vision. The words of the priest at the railway inn flashed across his brain unbidden: "You will find it different." And also, though why he could not tell, he saw mentally the strong, rather wonderful eyes of that other guest at the supper-table, the man who had overheard his conversation, and had later got into earnest talk with the priest. He took out his watch and stole a glance at it. Two hours had slipped by. It was already eleven o'clock.

Schliemann, meanwhile, utterly absorbed in his music, was playing a solemn measure. The piano sang marvellously. The power of a great conviction, the simplicity of great art, the vital spiritual message of a soul that had found itself—all this, and more, were in the chords, and yet somehow the music was what can only be described as impure— atrociously and diabolically impure. And the piece itself, although Harris did not recognise it as anything familiar, was surely the music of a Mass—huge, majestic, sombre? It stalked through the smoky room with slow power, like the passage of something that was mighty, yet profoundly intimate, and as it went there stirred into each and every face about him the signature of the enormous forces of which it was the audible symbol. The countenances round him turned sinister, but not idly, negatively sinister: they grew dark with purpose. He suddenly recalled the face of Bruder Kalkmann in the corridor earlier in the evening. The motives of their secret souls rose to the eyes, and mouths, and foreheads, and hung there for all to see like the black banners of an assembly of ill-starred and fallen creatures. Demons— was the horrible word that flashed through his brain like a sheet of fire.

When this sudden discovery leaped out upon him, for a moment he lost his self-control. Without waiting to think and weigh his extraordinary impression, he did a very foolish but a very natural thing. Feeling himself irresistibly driven by the sudden stress to some kind of action, he sprang to his feet—and screamed! To his own utter amazement he stood up and shrieked aloud!

But no one stirred. No one, apparently, took the slightest notice of his absurdly wild behaviour. It was almost as if no one but himself had heard the scream at all—as though the music had drowned it and swallowed it up—as though after all perhaps he had not really screamed as loudly as he imagined, or had not screamed at all.

Then, as he glanced at the motionless, dark faces before him, something of utter cold passed into his being, touching his very soul . . . all emotion cooled suddenly, leaving him like a receding tide. He sat down again, ashamed, mortified, angry with himself for behaving like a fool and a boy. And the music, meanwhile, continued to issue from the white and snake-like fingers of Bruder Schliemann, as poisoned wine might issue from the weirdly-fashioned necks of antique phials.

And, with the rest of them, Harris drank it in.

Forcing himself to believe that he had been the victim of some kind of illusory perception, he vigorously restrained his feelings. Then the music presently ceased, and every one applauded and began to talk at once, laughing, changing seats, complimenting the player, and behaving naturally and easily as though nothing out of the way had happened. The faces appeared normal once more. The Brothers crowded round their visitor, and he joined in their talk and even heard himself thanking the gifted musician.

But, at the same time, he found himself edging towards the door, nearer and nearer, changing his chair when possible, and joining the groups that stood closest to the way of escape.

"I must thank you all *tausendmal* for my little reception and the great pleasure—the very great honour you have done me," he began in decided tones at length, "but I fear I have trespassed far too long already on your hospitality. Moreover, I have some distance to walk to my inn."

A chorus of voices greeted his words. They would not hear of his going—at least not without first partaking of refreshment. They produced pumpernickel from one cupboard, and rye-bread and sausage from another, and all began to talk again and eat. More coffee was made, fresh cigars lighted, and Bruder Meyer took out his violin and began to tune it softly.

"There is always a bed upstairs if Herr Harris will accept it," said one.

"And it is difficult to find the way out now, for all the doors are locked," laughed another loudly.

"Let us take our simple pleasures as they come," cried a third. "Bruder Harris will understand how we appreciate the honour of this last visit of his."

They made a dozen excuses. They all laughed, as though the politeness of their words was but formal, and veiled thinly—more and more thinly—a very different meaning.

"And the hour of midnight draws near," added Bruder Kalkmann with a charming smile, but in a voice that sounded to the Englishman like the grating of iron hinges.

Their German seemed to him more and more difficult to understand. He noted that they called him "Bruder" too, classing him as one of themselves.

And then suddenly he had a flash of keener perception, and realised with a creeping of his flesh that he had all along misinterpreted—grossly misinterpreted all they had been saying. They had talked about the beauty of the place, its isolation and remoteness from the world, its peculiar fitness for certain kinds of spiritual development and worship —yet hardly, he now grasped, in the sense in which he had taken the words. They had meant something different. Their spiritual powers, their desire for loneliness, their passion for worship, were not the powers, the solitude, or the worship that *he* meant and understood. He was playing a part in some horrible masquerade; he was among men who cloaked their lives with religion in order to follow their real purposes unseen of men.

What did it all mean? How had he blundered into so equivocal a situation? Had he blundered into it at all? Had he not rather been led into it, deliberately led? His thoughts grew dreadfully confused, and his confidence in himself began to fade. And why, he suddenly thought again, were they so impressed by the mere fact of his coming to revisit his old school? What was it they so admired and wondered at in his simple act? Why did they set such store upon his having the courage to come, to "give himself so freely," "unconditionally" as one of them had expressed it with such a mockery of exaggeration?

Fear stirred in his heart most horribly, and he found no answer to any of his questionings. Only one thing he now understood quite clearly: it was their purpose to keep him here. They did not intend that he should go. And from this moment he realised that they were sinister, formidable and, in some way he had yet to discover, inimical to himself, inimical to his life. And the phrase one of them had used a moment ago—"this *last* visit of his"—rose before his eyes in letters of flame.

Harris was not a man of action, and had never known in all the course of his career what it meant to be in a situation of real danger. He was not necessarily a coward, though, perhaps, a man of untried nerve. He realised at last plainly that he was in a very awkward predicament indeed, and that he had to deal with men who were utterly in earnest. What their intentions were he only vaguely guessed. His mind, indeed, was too confused for definite ratiocination, and he was only able to follow blindly the strongest instincts that moved in him. It never occurred to him that the Brothers might all be mad, or that he himself might have temporarily lost his senses and be suffering under some terrible delusion. In fact, nothing occurred to him—he realised nothing—except that he meant to escape—and the quicker the better. A tremendous revulsion of feeling set in and overpowered him.

Accordingly, without further protest for the moment, he ate his pumpernickel and drank his coffee, talking meanwhile as naturally and pleasantly as he could, and when a suitable interval had passed, he rose to his feet and announced once more that he must now take his leave. He spoke very quietly, but very decidedly. No one hearing him could doubt that he meant what he said. He had got very close to the door by this time.

"I regret," he said, using his best German, and speaking to a hushed room, "that our pleasant evening must come to an end, but it is now time for me to wish you all good-night." And then, as no one said anything, he added, though with a trifle less assurance, "And I thank you all most sincerely for your hospitality."

"On the contrary," replied Kalkmann instantly, rising from his chair and ignoring the hand the Englishman had stretched out to him, "it is we who have to thank you; and we do so most gratefully and sincerely."

And at the same moment at least half a dozen of the Brothers took up their position between himself and the door.

"You are very good to say so," Harris replied as firmly as he could manage, noticing this movement out of the corner of his eye, "but really I had no conception that—my little chance visit could have afforded you so much pleasure." He moved another step nearer the door, but Bruder Schliemann came across the room quickly and stood in front of him. His attitude was uncompromising. A dark and terrible expression had come into his face.

"But it was *not* by chance that you came, Bruder Harris," he said so that all the room could hear; "surely we have not misunderstood your presence here?" He raised his black eyebrows.

"No, no," the Englishman hastened to reply, "I was—I am delighted to be here. I told you what pleasure it gave me to find myself among you. Do not misunderstand me, I beg." His voice faltered a little, and he had difficulty in finding the words. More and more, too, he had difficulty in understanding *their* words.

"Of course," interposed Bruder Kalkmann in his iron bass, "*we* have not misunderstood. You have come back in the spirit of true and unselfish devotion. You offer yourself freely, and we all appreciate it. It is your willingness and nobility that have so completely won our veneration and respect." A faint murmur of applause ran round the room. "What we all delight in—what our great Master will especially delight in—is the value of your spontaneous and voluntary—"

He used a word Harris did not understand. He said, *"Opfer."* The bewildered Englishman searched his brain for the translation, and searched in vain. For the life of him he could not remember what it meant. But the word, for all his inability to translate it, touched his soul with ice. It was worse, far worse, than anything he had imagined.

He felt like a lost, helpless creature, and all power to fight sank out of him from that moment.

"It is magnificent to be such a willing—" added Schliemann, sidling up to him with a dreadful leer on his face. He made use of the same word—*"Opfer."*

God! What could it all mean? "Offer himself!" "True spirit of devotion!" "Willing," "unselfish," "magnificent!" *Opfer, Opfer, Opfer!* What in the name of heaven did it mean, that strange, mysterious word that struck such terror into his heart?

He made a valiant effort to keep his presence of mind and hold his nerves steady. Turning, he saw that Kalkmann's face was a dead white. Kalkmann! He understood that well enough. *Kalkmann* meant "Man of Chalk"; he knew that. But what did *"Opfer"* mean? That was the real key to the situation. Words poured through his disordered mind in an endless stream—unusual, rare words he had perhaps heard but once in his life—while *"Opfer,"* a word in common use, entirely escaped him. What an extraordinary mockery it all was!

Then Kalkmann, pale as death, but his face hard as iron, spoke a few low words that he did not catch, and the Brothers standing by the walls at once turned the lamps down so that the room became dim. In the half light he could only just discern their faces and movements.

"It is time," he heard Kalkmann's remorseless voice continue just behind him. "The hour of midnight is at hand. Let us prepare. He comes! He comes; Bruder Asmodelius comes!" His voice rose to a chant.

And the sound of that name, for some extraordinary reason, was terrible—utterly terrible; so that Harris shook from head to foot as he heard it. Its utterance filled the air like soft thunder, and a hush came over the whole room. Forces rose all about him, transforming the normal into the horrible, and the spirit of craven fear ran through all his being, bringing him to the verge of collapse.

Asmodelius! Asmodelius! The name was appalling. For he understood at last to whom it referred and the meaning that lay between its great syllables. At the same instant, too, he suddenly understood the meaning of that unremembered word. The import of the word *"Opfer"* flashed upon his soul like a message of death.

He thought of making a wild effort to reach the door, but the weakness of his trembling knees, and the row of black figures that stood between, dissuaded him at once. He would have screamed for help, but remembering the emptiness of the vast building, and the loneliness of the situation, he understood that no help could come that way, and he kept his lips closed. He stood still and did nothing. But he knew now what was coming.

Two of the brothers approached and took him gently by the arm.

"Bruder Asmodelius accepts you," they whispered; "are you ready?"

Then he found his tongue and tried to speak. "But what have I to do with this Bruder Asm— Asmo—?" he stammered, a desperate rush of words crowding vainly behind the halting tongue.

The name refused to pass his lips. He could not pronounce it as they did. He could not pronounce it at all. His sense of helplessness then entered the acute stage, for this inability to speak the name produced a fresh sense of quite horrible confusion in his mind, and he became extraordinarily agitated.

"I came here for a friendly visit," he tried to say with a great effort, but, to his intense dismay, he heard his voice saying something quite different, and actually making use of that very word they had all used: "I came here as a willing *Opfer,*" he heard his own voice say, "and *I am quite ready.*"

He was lost beyond all recall now! Not alone his mind, but the very muscles of his body had passed out of control. He felt that he was hovering on the confines of a phantom or demon-world—a world in which the name they had spoken constituted the Master-name, the word of ultimate power.

What followed he heard and saw as in a nightmare.

"In the half light that veils all truth, let us prepare to worship and adore," chanted Schliemann, who had preceded him to the end of the room.

"In the mists that protect our faces before the Black Throne, let us make ready the willing victim," echoed Kalkmann in his great bass.

They raised their faces, listening expectantly, as a roaring sound, like the passing of mighty projectiles, filled the air, far, far away, very wonderful, very forbidding. The walls of the room trembled.

"He comes! He comes! He comes!" chanted the Brothers in chorus.

The sound of roaring died away, and an atmosphere of still and utter cold established itself over all. Then Kalkmann, dark and unutterably stern, turned in the dim light and faced the rest.

"Asmodelius, our *Hauptbruder,* is about us," he cried in a voice that even while it shook was yet a voice of iron; "Asmodelius is about us. Make ready."

There followed a pause in which no one stirred or spoke. A tall Brother approached the Englishman; but Kalkmann held up his hand.

"Let the eyes remain uncovered," he said, "in honour of so freely giving himself." And to his horror Harris then realised for the first time that his hands were already fastened to his sides.

The Brother retreated again silently, and in the pause that followed all the figures about him dropped to their knees, leaving him standing alone, and as they dropped, in voices hushed with mingled reverence and awe, they cried softly, odiously, appallingly, the name of the Being whom they momentarily expected to appear.

Then, at the end of the room, where the windows seemed to have disappeared so that he saw the stars, there rose into view far up against the night sky, grand and terrible, the outline of a man. A kind of grey glory enveloped it so that it resembled a steel-cased statue, immense, imposing, horrific in its distant splendour; while, at the same time, the face was so spiritually mighty, yet so proudly, so austerely sad, that Harris felt as he stared, that the sight was more than his eyes could meet, and that in another moment the power of vision would fail him altogether, and he must sink into utter nothingness.

So remote and inaccessible hung this figure that it was impossible to gauge anything as to its size, yet at the same time so strangly close, that when the grey radiance from its mightily broken visage, august and mournful, beat down upon his soul, pulsing like some dark star with the powers of spiritual evil, he felt almost as though he were looking into a face no farther removed from him in space than the face of any one of the Brothers who stood by his side.

And then the room filled and trembled with sounds that Harris understood full well were the failing voices of others who had preceded him in a long series down the years. There came first a plain, sharp cry, as of a man in the last anguish, choking for his breath, and yet, with the very final expiration of it, breathing the name of the Worship—of the dark Being who rejoiced to hear it. The cries of the strangled; the short, running gasp of the suffocated; and the smothered gurgling of the tightened throat, all these, and more, echoed back and forth between the walls, the very walls in which he now stood a prisoner, a sacrificial victim. The cries, too, not alone of the broken bodies, but—far worse—of beaten, broken souls. And as the ghastly chorus rose and fell, there came also the faces of the lost and unhappy creatures to whom they belonged, and, against that curtain of pale grey light, he saw float past him in the air, an array of white and piteous human countenances that seemed to beckon and gibber at him as though he were already one of themselves.

Slowly, too, as the voices rose, and the pallid crew sailed past, that giant form of grey descended from the sky and approached the room that contained the worshippers and their prisoner. Hands rose and sank about him in the darkness, and he felt that he was being draped in other garments than his own; a circlet of ice seemed to run about his head, while round the waist, enclosing the fastened arms, he felt a girdle tightly drawn. At last, about his very throat, there ran a soft and silken touch which, better than if there had been full light, and a mirror held to his face, he understood to be the cord of sacrifice—and of death.

At this moment the Brothers, still prostrate upon the floor, began again their mournful, yet impassioned chanting, and as they did so a strange thing happened. For, apparently without moving or altering its position, the huge Figure seemed, at once and suddenly, to be inside the room, almost beside him, and to fill the space around him to the exclusion of all else.

He was now beyond all ordinary sensations of fear, only a drab feeling as of death—the death of the soul—stirred in his heart. His thoughts no longer even beat vainly for escape. The end was near, and he knew it.

The dreadfully chanting voices rose about him in a wave: "We worship! We adore! We offer!" The sounds filled his ears and hammered, almost meaningless, upon his brain.

Then the majestic grey face turned slowly downwards upon him, and his very soul passed outwards and seemed to become absorbed in the sea of those anguished eyes. At the same moment a dozen hands forced him to his knees, and in the air before him he saw the arm of Kalkmann upraised, and felt the pressure about his throat grow strong.

It was in this awful moment, when he had given up all hope, and the help of gods or men seemed beyond question, that a strange thing happened. For before his fading and terrified vision, there slid, as in a dream of light—yet without apparent rhyme or reason—wholly unbidden and unexplained—the face of that other man at the supper table of the railway inn. And the sight, even mentally, of that strong, wholesome, vigorous English face, inspired him suddenly with a new courage.

It was but a flash of fading vision before he sank into a dark and terrible death, yet, in some inexplicable way, the sight of that face stirred in him unconquerable hope and the certainty of deliverance. It was a face of power, a face, he now realised, of simple goodness such as might have been seen by men of old on the shores of Galilee; a face, by heaven, that could conquer even the devils of outer space.

And, in his despair and abandonment, he called upon it, and called with no uncertain accents. He found his voice in this overwhelming moment to some purpose; though the words he actually used, and whether they were in German or English, he could never remember. Their effect, nevertheless, was instantaneous. The Brothers understood, and that grey Figure of evil understood.

For a second the confusion was terrific. There came a great shattering sound. It seemed that the very earth trembled. But all Harris remembered afterwards was that voices rose about him in the clamour of terrified alarm—

"A man of power is among us! A man of God!"

The vast sound was repeated—the rushing through space as of huge projectiles—and he sank to the floor of the room, unconscious. The entire scene had vanished, vanished like smoke over the roof of a cottage when the wind blows.

And, by his side, sat down a slight, un-German figure—the figure of the stranger at the inn—the man who had the "rather wonderful eyes."

When Harris came to himself he felt cold. He was lying under the open sky, and the cool air of field and forest was blowing upon his face. He sat up and looked about him. The memory of the late scene was still horribly in his mind, but no vestige of it remained. No walls or ceiling enclosed him; he was no longer in a room at all. There were no lamps turned low, no cigar smoke, no black forms of sinister worshippers, no tremendous grey Figure hovering beyond the windows.

Open space was about him, and he was lying on a pile of bricks and mortar, his clothes soaked with dew, and the kind stars shining brightly overhead. He was lying, bruised and shaken, among the heaped-up débris of a ruined building.

He stood up and stared about him. There, in the shadowy distance, lay the surrounding forest, and here, close at hand, stood the outline of the village buildings. But, underfoot, beyond question, lay nothing but the broken heaps of stones that betokened a building long since crumbled to dust. Then he saw that the stones were blackened, and that great wooden beams, half burnt, half rotten, made lines through the general débris. He stood, then, among the ruins of a burnt and shattered building, the weeds and nettles proving conclusively that it had lain thus for many years.

The moon had already set behind the encircling forest, but the stars that spangled the heavens threw enough light to enable him to make quite sure of what he saw. Harris, the silk merchant, stood among these broken and burnt stones and shivered.

Then he suddenly became aware that out of the gloom a figure had risen and stood beside him. Peering at him, he thought he recognised the face of the stranger at the railway inn.

"Are *you* real?" he asked in a voice he hardly recognised as his own.

"More than real—I'm friendly," replied the stranger; "I followed you up here from the inn."

Harris stood and stared for several minutes without adding anything. His teeth chattered. The least sound made him start; but the simple words in his own language, and the tone in which they were uttered, comforted him inconceivably.

"You're English too, thank God," he said inconsequently. "These German devils—" He broke off and put a hand to his eyes. "But what's become of them all—and the room—and—and—" The hand travelled down to his throat and moved nervously round his neck. He drew a long, long breath of relief. "Did I dream everything—everything?" he said distractedly.

He stared wildly about him, and the stranger moved forward and took his arm. "Come," he said soothingly, yet with a trace of command in the voice, "we will move away from here. The high-road, or even the woods will be more to your taste, for we are standing now on one of the most haunted—and most terribly haunted—spots of the whole world."

He guided his companion's stumbling footsteps over the broken masonry until they reached the path, the nettles stinging their hands, and Harris feeling his way like a man in a dream. Passing through the twisted iron railing they reached the path, and thence made their way to the road, shining white in the night. Once safely out of the ruins, Harris collected himself and turned to look back.

"But, how is it possible?" he exclaimed, his voice still shaking. "How can it be possible? When I came in here I saw the building in the moonlight. They opened the door. I saw the figures and heard the voices and touched, yes touched their very hands, and saw their damned black faces, saw them far more plainly than I see you now." He was deeply bewildered. The glamour was still upon his eyes with a degree of reality stronger than the reality even of normal life. "Was I so utterly deluded?"

Then suddenly the words of the stranger, which he had only half heard or understood, returned to him.

"Haunted?" he asked, looking hard at him; "haunted, did you say?" He paused in the roadway and stared into the darkness where the building of the old school had first appeared to him. But the stranger hurried him forward.

"We shall talk more safely farther on," he said. "I followed you from the inn the moment I realised where you had gone. When I found you it was eleven o'clock—"

"Eleven o'clock," said Harris, remembering with a shudder.

"—I saw you drop. I watched over you till you recovered consciousness of your own accord, and now—now I am here to guide you safely back to the inn. I have broken the spell—the glamour—"

"I owe you a great deal, sir," interrupted Harris again, beginning to understand something of the stranger's kindness, "but I don't understand it all. I feel dazed and shaken." His teeth still chattered, and spells of violent shivering passed over him from head to foot. He found that he was clinging to the other's arm. In this way they passed beyond the deserted and crumbling village and gained the high-road that led homewards through the forest.

"That school building has long been in ruins," said the man at his side presently; "it was burnt down by order of the Elders of the community at least ten years ago. The village has been uninhabited ever since. But the simulacra of certain ghastly events that took place under that roof in past days still continue. And the 'shells' of the chief participants still enact there the dreadful deeds that led to its final destruction, and to the desertion of the whole settlement. They were devil-worshippers!"

Harris listened with beads of perspiration on his forehead that did not come alone from their leisurely pace through the cool night. Although he had seen this man but once before in his life, and had never before exchanged so much as a word with him, he felt a degree of confidence and a subtle sense of safety and well-being in his presence that were the most healing influences he could possibly have wished after the experience he had been through. For all that, he still felt as if he were walking in a dream, and though he heard every word that fell from his companion's lips, it was only the next day that the full import of all he said became fully clear to him. The presence of this quiet stranger, the man with the wonderful eyes which he felt now, rather than saw, applied a soothing anodyne to his shattered spirit that healed him through and through. And this healing influence, distilled from the dark figure at his side, satisfied his first imperative need, so that he almost forgot to realise how strange and opportune it was that the man should be there at all.

It somehow never occurred to him to ask his name, or to feel any undue wonder that one passing tourist should take so much trouble on behalf of another. He just walked by his side, listening to his quiet words, and allowing himself to enjoy the very wonderful experience after his recent ordeal, of being helped, strengthened, blessed. Only once, remembering vaguely something of his reading of years ago, he turned to the man beside him, after some more than usually remarkable words, and heard himself, almost involuntarily it seemed, putting the question: "Then are you a Rosicrucian, sir, perhaps?" But the stranger had ignored the words, or possibly not heard them, for he continued with his talk as though unconscious of any interruption, and Harris became aware that another somewhat unusual picture had taken possession of his mind, as they walked there side by side through the cool reaches of the forest, and that he had found his imagination suddenly charged with the childhood memory of Jacob wrestling with an angel—wrestling all night with a being of superior quality whose strength eventually became his own.

"It was your abrupt conversation with the priest at supper that first put me upon the track of this remarkable occurrence," he heard the man's quiet voice beside him in the darkness, "and it was from him I learned after you left the story of the devil-worship that became secretly established in the heart of this simple and devout little community."

"Devil-worship! Here—!" Harris stammered, aghast.

"Yes—here—conducted secretly for years by a group of Brothers before unexplained disappearances in the neighbourhood led to its discovery. For where could they have found a safer place in the whole wide world for their ghastly traffic and perverted powers than here, in the very precincts—under cover of the very shadow of saintliness and holy living?"

"Awful, awful!" whispered the silk merchant, "and when I tell you the words they used to me—"

"I know it all," the stranger said quietly. "I saw and heard everything. My plan first was to wait till the end and then to take steps for their destruction, but in the interest of your personal safety,"—he spoke with the utmost gravity and conviction—"in the interest of the safety of your soul, I made my presence known when I did, and before the conclusion had been reached—"

"My safety! The danger, then, was real. They were alive and—" Words failed him. He stopped in the road and turned towards his companion, the shining of whose eyes he could just make out in the gloom.

"It was a concourse of the shells of violent men, spiritually-developed but evil men, seeking after death—the death of the body—to prolong their vile and unnatural existence. And had they accomplished their object you, in turn, at the death of your body, would have passed into their power and helped to swell their dreadful purposes."

Harris made no reply. He was trying hard to concentrate his mind upon the sweet and common things of life. He even thought of silk and St. Paul's Churchyard and the faces of his partners in business.

"For you came all prepared to be caught," he heard the other's voice like some one talking to him from a distance; "your deeply introspective mood had already reconstructed the past so vividly, so intensely, that you were *en rapport* at once with any forces of those days that chanced still to be lingering. And they swept you up all unresistingly."

Harris tightened his hold upon the stranger's arm as he heard. At the moment he had room for one emotion only. It did not seem to him odd that this stranger should have such intimate knowledge of his mind.

"It is, alas, chiefly the evil emotions that are able to leave their photographs upon surrounding scenes and objects," the other added, "and who ever heard of a place haunted by a noble deed, or of beautiful and lovely ghosts revisiting the glimpses of the moon? It is unfortunate. But the wicked passions of men's hearts alone seem strong enough to leave pictures that persist; the good are ever too lukewarm."

The stranger sighed as he spoke. But Harris, exhausted and shaken as he was to the very core, paced by his side, only half listening. He moved as in a dream still. It was very wonderful to him, this walk home under the stars in the early hours of the October morning, the peaceful forest all about them, mist rising here and there over the small clearings, and the sound of water from a hundred little invisible streams filling in the pauses of the talk. In after life he always looked back to it as something magical and impossible, something that had seemed too beautiful, too curiously beautiful, to have been quite true. And, though at the time he heard and understood but a quarter of what the stranger said, it came back to him afterwards, staying with him till the end of his days, and always with a curious, haunting sense of unreality, as though he had enjoyed a wonderful dream of which he could recall only faint and exquisite portions.

But the horror of the earlier experience was effectually dispelled; and when they reached the railway inn, somewhere about three o'clock in the morning, Harris shook the stranger's hand gratefully, effusively, meeting the look of those rather wonderful eyes with a full heart, and went up to his room, thinking in a hazy, dream-like way of the words with which the stranger had brought their conversation to an end as they left the confines of the forest—

"And if thought and emotion can persist in this way so long after the brain that sent them forth has crumbled into dust, how vitally important it must be to control their very birth in the heart, and guard them with the keenest possible restraint."

But Harris, the silk merchant, slept better than might have been expected, and with a soundness that carried him half-way through the day. And when he came downstairs and learned that the stranger had already taken his departure, he realised with keen regret that he had never once thought of asking his name.

"Yes, he signed in the visitors' book," said the girl in reply to his question.

And he turned over the blotted pages and found there, the last entry, in a very delicate and individual handwriting—

"*John Silence*, London."

Here is the complete, unexpurgated text of "Devil in the Drain", originally a children's book published by E. P. Dutton with pictures by the author, DANIEL MANUS PINKWATER. *Though often identified as a children's and young adult writer, Mr. Pinkwater boasts a large following of readers of all ages who eagerly await each new wacky opus, such as* Blue Moose, The Hoboken Chicken Emergency, Lizard Music, The Snarkout Boys and the Baconburg Horror *and many other hilarious books.*

Devil in the Drain
BY DANIEL MANUS PINKWATER

For a long time, I knew that the devil lived inside our plumbing. I could hear him making noises, especially down the drain of the kitchen sink.

Sometimes I would look into the drainpipe with a flashlight and try to see him.

Finally I caught a glimpse of something down there.

"Hey!" I said. "Are you the devil?"

"What if I am?" a voice from down the drain answered.

"I just want to know, that's all," I said.

"I don't have to tell you anything," the voice said.

"Come up here so I can see you," I said.

"Oh, no! You'll turn on the water as soon as I get there, and get me all wet."

"No I won't, honestly."

"Well, that's what I would do."

"You *are* the devil, aren't you?"

"Yes."

"I'd really like to have a look at you. If I absolutely promise not to turn on the water, will you come up so I can see you?"

"Why do you want to see me?"

"I just do. Come on up. I won't hurt you. Besides, there are those little bar things across the drain. I couldn't get at you if I wanted to."

"I'm not afraid of you. I'm the devil."

"Then come up and let me see."

"All right—but if you turn on the water, I'll do some pretty bad things to you."

"You're really suspicious," I said.

"You would be too, if you were me," the devil said. His voice sounded closer.

"Are you coming up?" I asked down the drain.

"Yes, yes, I'm coming," the devil said, "and don't say it's my fault if you get scared to death."

"I'm not scared," I said.

"Well, you should be."

I could see the devil climbing up the drain. He was pretty small. He wasn't any bigger than the goldfish I had lost down that drain once, when I was changing the water in the fishbowl.

The devil got up to the little crossed bars. He had a face that reminded me of the fish, and he was almost the same color.

"Well, here I am," the devil said. "You're terrified, right?"

"Do you remember when I lost my fish down this drain?" I asked.

"Sure I do," the devil said. "You murdered him."

"I did not. It was an accident."

"Sure it was," the devil said. "Poor fish—he probably trusted you."

"The water overflowed, and he got sloshed out of the bowl and down the drain," I said. "I don't think he was smart enough to trust me or not trust me. Fish are dumb."

"That's right," the devil said, "tell yourself that. I heard him crying for help. You didn't even care."

"I did care," I said, "but I didn't kill him on purpose."

"But you admit you killed him."

"Is that what you do?" I asked.

"What?"

"Try to make people feel bad about things they can't help."

"It's one of the things I do," the devil said. "Now admit it—you feel pretty horrible about killing that fish, right?"

"I didn't kill him," I said, "and to tell the truth, I don't feel that bad about it. I'm sorry it happened, but it wasn't my fault."

"I'm getting bored talking about your stupid fish," the devil said. "How come you haven't mentioned how frightening I am, and at the same time sort of fascinating?"

"You look a little like a fish," I said. "How come you live in the plumbing?"

"Again with the fish!" the devil said. "I live in the plumbing because I can do whatever I please."

"How come you're so small?"

"I'm as big as I need to be," the devil said. "Now how about you getting me a pretzel? Do you have any of those skinny salty ones?"

I got the devil a pretzel. I pushed it down the drain. He ate it.

"That was lousy," he said. "I know you only got it for me because you're so frightened of me."

"Look," I said, "I got you the pretzel because you asked for it. You want another pretzel? I'll get you another pretzel. I happen to be a good-natured kid. And I am not in the least afraid of you."

"Yes I do," the devil said.

"Do what?"

"Yes I do want another pretzel."

"I'll get it."

"Ha! The kid's terrified," the devil said to himself. I heard him say it. "That does it," I said.

I turned on both taps, hot and cold.

"Hey! No fair!" the devil shouted.

"Too bad," I said.

I heard the devil shouting and gurgling a long way down the drain-pipe. He was really mad.

"That was a rotten trick!" he shouted. "You ought to be ashamed!"

"I'm not!" I said.

RAY RUSSELL's *novels and story collections include several diabolic titles, including* The Devil's Mirror, The Book of Hell, Incubus, *and* The Case Against Satan *(see Appendix III, page 584), as well as* Sardonicus and Other Stories *and others. His work has appeared in more than a hundred anthologies and nearly fifty magazines, including* The Paris Review, The Midatlantic Review, Ellery Queen's Mystery Magazine, Alfred Hitchcock's Mystery Magazine, Twilight Zone, The Magazine of Fantasy and Science Fiction, Night Cry *and* Playboy, *of which he was the first executive editor. Russell is a recipient of the 1977 Sri Chinmoy Poetry Award.*

I Am Returning

BY RAY RUSSELL

I am returning. It seems too good to believe: it has taken such a weary stretch of time, and there has been so much despair along the way, but now the long fierce dream is true at last and I am, I really am returning.

Oh, let them beware, my enemies! Let *him* beware, in particular, that arrogant and supercilious one to whom I owe my misery. Let him hold fast to his throne, for this time I shall shake him from it and bring him to his knees before me. And then each moment of that long dark exile shall be paid for. Each moment. I have forgotten nothing. My memory is clear and sharp and bitter. I remember the fall; I remember the jungle coming at me as if shot from a gun, blanketing the ship in sudden dark.

I do not like the dark.

I remember my force-field slicing a path cleanly through the foliage and the ship stopping with a monstrous jolt.

How long I lay crumpled on the floor I will never know. My mind was in chaos, my body wrenched and sickened. Some time later I dragged myself to my feet and limped to the controls. I pressed the force-key. The force-field flickered, cutting down trees and letting in light, but the ship would not move.

I stumbled to the engine chamber and felt my heart stop for an instant and begin thumping more violently. The One, Two and Three tubes were all shattered, broken by the fall.

I looked closer. No. Not broken by the fall.

Exploded. Burst from within. And, around the twisted edges, the telltale tint of krin powder.

My hands clawed at the repair kit, tore it open with a clatter. There, instead of the replacement tubes, were three empty niches neatly labeled *One, Two, Three.*

I remember weeping at that point. I suppose I was out of my mind for a while. What brought me back to reality was the slow realization that the atmosphere was growing foul.

A leak in the tanks? I knew better than that. A tank made of iln cannot spring a leak—unless it has been specifically designed to do so. This was the end, then, unless the atmosphere of this alien planet could support me. And the odds against that, I knew, were staggering.

Nevertheless, I made my way back to the controls and consulted the teller globe. What it told me brought a deep groan of anguish from my throat.

I had crashed on a nightmare world.

Cold: a cold so intense it was beyond my power to imagine it. And the atmosphere: laden with oxygen.

Poison.

The darkness was returning. I looked up. As I watched, the trees grew back and engulfed the ship. I jabbed the force-key and they fell, letting in again the cold meager light of the distant sun. But even before I could turn away from the viewport, they had begun to grow again.

It turned my stomach. There was something disturbing about such rapid metabolism, something sinister about any life that blossomed and died so quickly. It was dark again.

And then there was a grinning face at the viewport.

I cried out, recoiling against the opposite wall, my knees trembling, my wings fluttering, my antennae stiffening with fear.

The face was gone. It had been there only an instant, but in that time I had touched the mind behind it and found there a raging hunger. The face had been the gaping mask of a maniac lizard.

I peered into the dim light of the jungle and saw them moving in a frantic swift blur. I saw them being born and growing, fighting and eating each other, dying and decomposing and vanishing.

I was dizzy. The atmosphere in the ship was getting steadily more fetid. I reflected on the ironic fact that in the time it would take me to die, generations would come and go in that dawn world out there . . .

But perhaps death was not necessary for me. I looked at the communicator. Perhaps I could strike a bargain.

I sat down and punched the communicator key. "Hello," I said. "Hello, hello, hello." I repeated it over and over again until my throat was hoarse. Outside, the very species were changing, evolving. "Hello, hello hello . . ."

Just when I was about to give up hope, a familiar, hated voice crackled from the responder:

"Greetings, Prince. Didn't expect to hear from you again."

Rage churned inside me, curdled my blood, twisted my bowels into a knot. But I breathed deeply of the bad air, and calmly said, "Send me aid. Bring me back and you can have half the kingdom."

A laugh came back. "But, my dear fellow, with you gone I have *all* the kingdom. Come now, surely you have a better suggestion than that?"

I had no answer. There was no answer. I said nothing.

"Where are you?" he asked.

"You will be glad to learn I am stranded on a primitive world; a world of deadly cold, with an atmosphere of oxygen."

"Most unfortunate. Any neighbors?"

"Lizards."

"I don't think I would like that. But then I suppose it suits you. You always did have an affinity for low life. Rabble-rousing and all that. It was very wrong of you to try to depose me, you know. You have only yourself to blame for your predic . . ."

"Listen to me," I cut in. "I'm not done for yet."

"Not yet, perhaps, but surely soon? After all, that cold you mentioned. And an oxygen atmosphere! Really . . ."

"I'll find heat!" I yelled, trying a desperate bluff. "And I'll find something fit to breathe—even if I have to drill my ship into the bowels of this planet to find it!"

"That's the spirit!" he said. "And then what? Will you sit on your haunches and wait for us to come and get you? Your ship can't become spaceborne, you know. Not without those three propellor tubes. And those lizards—I doubt if they know much about tube manufacture . . ."

It was said in mockery, but it gave me an idea. "No," I said. "And

they're dying anyway; even as I watch them, the species is dying out."
The control board writhed unsteadily before my eyes for a moment;
the air was very bad. "But think of this: suppose a new species arises
(their metabolism is fast, you see, incredibly fast); suppose this new
species shows signs of intelligence . . ."

I paused. My improvisatory powers had run dry. The responder
crackled: "Yes, Prince? Go on."

"Suppose—suppose I find heat and atmosphere to live by. And suppose I forge a stronghold and from it reach out and shape their minds.
Shape their minds as I would shape a piece of clay in my hands."

"If it amuses you," he said, "I see no reason why you shouldn't."

I leaned forward, hissing into the phone. "Listen. Suppose I influence their thinking, guide their culture, control them. Suppose, in
short, I steer them straight toward space. Do you understand? *Toward
space!* Suppose, believing they are acting of their own free will, they
build me a fleet and arm it with mighty weapons. A fleet with one sole
purpose: to return and destroy you!"

"All from your snug little hole-in-the-ground?"

"Yes! Just suppose that, my friend!" My voice had risen to a shriek.

"You're raving."

"Am I? Dare you risk it? Dare you gamble? Dare you wager a
kingdom on it? Or will you send me aid? Bring me back now, while
you can, and I'll share the throne with you."

There was silence. For once, he had no words. My heart leaped; the
bluff was working! But it was not too long before he found his tongue
again:

"As long as we're supposing, Prince, just suppose this if you will.
Suppose there *is* intelligent life on this jungle planet of yours; suppose
you *do* control it—it's quite possible; after all, we've controlled lower
life forms before this. Now what's to prevent me from waging a kind
of telepathic war with you? Doing a little controlling of my own?
Counteracting you? Steering them *away* from space and your 'mighty
weapons'?"

I was at a loss. It was possible, of course. Distance is no deterrent to
telepathy. And he could find me easily enough. Even now his detectors
had probably traced my communicator. My confidence crumbled. Final despair settled upon me like a cold wet shroud. The outrageous
bluff had not worked, as I knew in my heart it would not. He was too
smart for that. And now he was waiting. Waiting for me to break

down and weep and beg. But I would not. I still had pride—my strength and my weakness. I would play the game through to the end, die in the attempt to make good my threat.

"You refuse me?" I said tonelessly.

"That's right."

"Then accept the consequences!" I roared, turning on the force-field and burrowing into the ground. *"I'll be back."*

As I plunged deep into the planet on that day long ago, down to its molten core seeking heat and life-giving sulphur, his only reply was that familiar, infuriating mocking laugh and a condescending "Good luck, Prince!"

It's my turn to laugh now.

For now, though it has taken me half a lifetime—untold thousand of lifetimes if reckoned by the span of these creatures—now, disguised as one of them and standing proudly in the flagship they built for me, unknowing, conscious of nothing but a vague traditional inner struggle between "good" and "evil" . . . Now, as the leader of a colossal armada on its warlike way to Arcturus IV . . . Now, as this Twenty-First Century of theirs draws to its end, I am returning at last from the dark to claim the throne that rightfully belongs to me: Lucifer, named for light, prince of the glowing regions, son of the morning.

Beware, my enemies!

*In "The Shadow Watchers," you will meet one of the most fearsome demons in
this book: Christobe, a highly original personification of mindless tragedy created by* DICK BALDWIN, *a Long Islander now living in Westchester County,
New York. His other short stories include the harrowing "Last Respects" and
the witty vampire yarn "Money Talks," which appeared, respectively, in my
previous anthologies,* Masterpieces of Terror and the Supernatural *and* Ghosts.

The Shadow Watchers
BY DICK BALDWIN

I

Death, some say, has pity on those about to die, and this is true.
Compassionate Death always comes to the old, the infirm and the
hopeless to tenderly relieve them of their earthly burden.

But it is not so with Christobe.

He comes to those whom Death shuns. When a child dies, or a
person in the prime of life, or a man attaining the happiest peak his life
can reach, Christobe is there.

Though he is heartless, he is by no means emotionless; He delights
in his tasks. The cries of human suffering are to Him as the gratitude
of the weary is to Death.

As usual, David Greene was spending his lunch break sitting on the
bench in the town square. The large statue near him cast a shadow
which ominously crossed his body; it resembled some gigantic creature about to pounce on him while he calmly awaited his fate or that is
how it might have looked to an imaginative passerby. But no passerby
was present.

That was the chief reason why Greene returned to the same bench
each day. He could sit there and think without the distraction of other
people.

Life was meaningless for David Greene. His routine was exactly
that: up in the morning, off to work, home again to eat and rest; the
only occasional break in habit was a trip to Kelley's Tavern. He went
through his days and nights without the singleness of purpose or hope

that drives others onward. Emotion, passion and joy were lost to him. He could not feel; he could not care. To say that he wanted to die would be just as true as to say that he wanted to live. Each weighed equally in his mind, and the scales always balanced. Any hopes or dreams he may have once had were smothered long ago. There was nothing left for David Greene but the routine of life and its eventual, inevitable close.

Once he had been in love, but it brought him no pain when it ended. He had been younger then and had a dream, but he did not feel misery when the object of his adoration fell in love with someone else. He had never told her his true feelings, so since she never knew, she was at liberty to dictate her own course of action. David had hoped that by being as good a friend as he had been she might take the initiative and express her love first. But she did not, and he understood.

His failure to communicate his feelings stemmed from a bleak childhood in which any attempt to tell his thoughts and ideas made him feel inferior and at fault. His family never understood what David felt or needed, so in time he fell into the habit of keeping silent. It was less painful than trying to reach out to them.

He had acquaintances, but no friends, and those he knew were all too concerned with their own problems to hear what David might want or need to say.

That day, as he sat on the bench in the town square, he thought about the pattern his life had taken. Once there had been bitterness, but now there was only disinterest. He cared for nothing and no one— least of all, himself.

The air hung thickly in Kelley's Tavern that night because Christobe was there. He entered the dark, noisy room, glanced to the right, then to the left, and focused His attention on David Greene.

The mortal, in turn, saw Christobe and thought he recognized him, but felt no fear. Instead, he lifted the glass to his lips and swallowed some of his beer.

Christobe was taken aback. No one had ever reacted to Him before with such total indifference. He stood near the doorway and watched David Greene who, now and then, regarded the Visitor with a vague curiosity.

The other patrons were momentarily transfixed. They did not observe the Being who stood in their midst, for Christobe can only be seen by those on whom He is about to pay a call. But if the suspended denizens of Kelley's Tavern could have looked on Him with his terrible face filled first with surprise, then with anger, they would have felt such terror that He might have smiled—something that He never did.

But David Greene's soul was not cowed by Christobe. Any vestigial sense of self-preservation he might have felt was dissipated in the energy it took to lift his glass and sip more beer.

Furiously, Christobe strode up to the young man, passing through old man Ketchum's body as he did. Ketchum trembled and his face was struck with pallor.

DAVID GREENE, said Christobe in a hideous tone, DO YOU KNOW WHO I AM?

"Yes," said Greene, wiping a trickle of liquid from his chin. "You are Death." It was true that Death and Christobe looked alike, but the gentler Spirit cloaked Himself in robes, while Christobe strode amongst his victims unhindered by garments of any kind.

I AM CHRISTOBE! The room quivered with the force of his words, and the souls of the other patrons felt an undefined fear, but still David Greene was unmoved.

"So?" he asked.

The Demon lifted His arms, half-wishing to take everyone in Kelley's Tavern with Him. Fire danced in the empty sockets where His eyes were not. But the other souls around Him did not interest Christobe that night, and He lowered His arms.

Greene was, in spite of himself, human, and the manifestation of Christobe's fury could not help but unnerve him. With a hasty gulp, he emptied his glass.

The Fiend caught the fleeting tang of fear in Greene at once. DO YOU KNOW THAT YOU ARE ABOUT TO DIE?

"Yes, I know," the other said, no longer afraid. He was, once more, apathetic. "Do you want me to feel remorse? Would you like me to beg?"

Christobe moved His ugly face close to the young man. IS THIRTY-FIVE YEARS MORE THAN ENOUGH FOR YOU? As He spoke, David distinctly smelled the fetid odor of some ancient Sepulcher.

"Correction," he retorted, looking squarely into the terrible face. "Thirty-five loveless years. And, yes, they are more than enough. Why should I care if I am about to die when I don't care if I am alive?"

A bruised soul, thought Christobe, disgusted. Suitable only for the tender touch of Death. But He would have thought that this David Greene might live in some kind of expectation of something better to come, some vain hope which the prospect of imminent death would cancel out, thus bringing on ecstasies of misery, horror and despair. But Greene was *not* tortured by hope. To take him like this would be against Christobe's principles. He would just have to write off the mortal as a bad choice.

YOUR WORDS, DAVID GREENE, HAVE TOUCHED ME. I WILL NOT TAKE YOU WITH ME UNTIL YOU HAVE TASTED LIFE. WHEN YOU HAVE FELT LOVE, I SHALL RETURN.

David Greene laughed.

The Demon clenched His bony fist, longing to hear the young man cry in agony, pleading for mercy. But He would have revenge, Christobe decided: He resolved to visit David Greene again. With that, He turned and strode out of Kelley's Tavern.

The air cleared and the patrons moved once more. Nothing remained of their metaphysical ordeal save for a cold chill. But it lingered and grew into a shiver as they saw old Ketchum topple and fall onto the floor, dead.

Several days later, Angela Wells climbed the stairs of her bleak and dingy apartment house and walked into the dark hallway. She took out her key and fitted it into the ancient lock.

The air was heavy in the hallway and she had difficulty breathing. She struggled to make the lock click in the dilapidated door, but had no luck. As she removed it from the slot and checked to see whether she had inserted it properly, she felt a sudden blast of cool air.

Damn, she thought, they told me they'd fixed the hole in the roof.

But they had. She looked up curiously to see where the draft could be coming from. All at once, Angela had an awful feeling that she was being watched, and an undefined dread came upon her. She thrust the key towards the lock again, but it missed the slot, hit wood and fell to the floor with a tinny clink. As she bent to search the dark recess near the door, she saw something out of the corner of her eye, a vague shape or movement in the shadows behind her.

Groping wildly, blindly, face upturned to see and be prepared, she felt the key with her fingers. In one fast motion, she picked it up from the floor, stuck it into the lock, clicked the latch . . .

The heaviness in the air lifted. Just as quickly as she had been overcome with fear, Angela Wells felt at ease again. But she looked behind just the same as she hurried through the warped door into her cheerless room, slamming the door and bolting it from within as she fell against it, breathless.

"My imagination," she said out loud, with no conviction. She switched on the overhead light, but as it flooded the room with illumination, it also seemed to bring back the oppressive atmosphere. She gasped. There was Something sitting on her couch.

GOOD EVENING, MY DEAR ANGELA WELLS, said Christobe.

Her soul cried out, longing to live. He heard the sound and it cheered Him for the first time since He had met David Greene.

Christobe's victims never were afforded the luxury of losing consciousness. Angela watched in terror as the bony Phantom arose from the couch and approached.

IT IS TIME TO LEAVE, DEAR ANGELA. WILL YOU COME QUIETLY? OR WILL CHRISTOBE BECOME ANGRY?

The girl stammered, tried to scream. Then she found her voice. "I—"

Christobe raised His arms in His favorite gesture, and the floor rumbled beneath her feet.

"I'll do anything!" she gasped, falling to the floor. But Christobe's victims were not even permitted to avert their gaze, so there on her knees, Angela stared horror-struck into the empty sockets where the Demon's eyes should have been.

No plea had ever stopped Christobe from attaining His pleasure, but as His bloodless hand drew closer to her pounding heart, the fright tearing her soul built to a crescendo . . .

"*Anything!*" she shrieked.

He took away His fleshless hand and then, incredibly, Christobe smiled.

Angela, starting in terror, saw the hideous grin contorting the ghastly face, shivered and gave up all hope of life.

II

When the girl approached during his lunch break, David Greene's first impulse was to leave the bench. He was about to do so when she spoke, which meant he must remain. No matter how dejected he might feel, no matter what sort of outcast he believed himself to be, he simply was unable to treat anyone who talked to him with anything but kindness. Manufactured kindness, perhaps, he told himself, but any variety was probably better than none.

Turning to her, David looked carefully at the intruder. She was rather pretty, in a natural, quiet way, was possibly about 26, and seemed to have an edge, a kind of nervousness, about her. He couldn't help being attracted, in spite of himself, and almost felt tempted to ask for her phone number, but he knew it wouldn't do any good.

"I have to go back to work now," he said after a few minutes of talk, checking his watch. She made a slight protest, thought better of it, then asked if he would be at the bench the next day.

"Yes," said David Greene curtly, then walked away quickly.

It wasn't until several hours after he'd met Angela in the town square that David conceived his plan. "Death" said He would be back for him when he had tasted life and felt love. In that case, the young man told himself ironically, I'll live forever.

But what if he could outwit Death? Perhaps he could counterfeit the appearance of caring and make the Specter think he had indeed tasted of life. Then, he might swindle the swindler and die at last.

The rest of the afternoon was spent thinking how to manufacture his trickery and project the false image of personal happiness. Obviously, he must pretend to be interested in the girl. Money would be wasted taking her places, but what use would he have for it once he was dead? For all apparent intents and purposes, he would become a changed man; the loner would suddenly be outgoing. His fellow-workers would think he was being brought out of his shell by an understanding girl, and they would gladly accept the new David Greene.

But would He?

Angela Wells had exchanged promises with Christobe. If she could make David Greene fall in love with her, the Fiend would spare her life. But Christobe never kept promises. He planned to take them both.

The only trouble was that Greene was progressing too quickly. After only three weeks, the young man was doing things completely out of character with his former behaviour. Perhaps, thought Christobe, he had a death wish.

The Demon existed on the by-products of suspicion and could not trust that His plan was going all that well. Even the girl seemed to be undergoing a change; her fear of Him was becoming less and less evident, and she did not seem to be working hard enough at the deception.

What if they had both hatched a plan against Him? He must not forget that David Greene had made Him look like a fool once.

In the end, He decided to wait and listen and as soon as a hint of happiness could be discerned, He would move accordingly.

She felt a hand on her shoulder. Though it was a warm day, an icy chill crept up her spine and the horrendous image of the smiling Demon flashed before her mind's eye. But she recovered from the initial shock as she heard his voice apologizing for being late.

David gently held her hand and led her to the bench. She gave him the sandwiches she had made (she had done the same thing every day since the week after they first met) and he unwrapped one with apparent eagerness.

"Hungry?"

"Yes," he lied. He never enjoyed eating, and did so only to maintain life. Once, for a long while he ate nothing but plain spaghetti night after night. He would rush through the meal, which neither bored nor interested him, wash the dirty dish and pot and forget about food until the next night. Eating was nothing but a bother to him.

"Why don't you come to my place tonight for dinner?" Angela asked, involuntarily looking over her shoulder.

"Why not? What are you going to have?"

"How's spaghetti?"

He almost laughed. When she asked him how he liked it, he told her "plain," and actually smiled with a faint trace of amusement. She commented on it.

"I thought I smiled all the time," he replied.

"No. This time you really smiled—a little. Not that token gesture you manage that has no feeling behind it. There must be a reason why you don't smile more often." She couldn't help asking him the question. At first, she decided she would avoid getting to know the man she must, at least technically, kill. But it was impossible to carry out her mission of making David love her without pretending to care herself, without asking questions about his past. But he would always be evasive, most of the time turning her questions around so that she was forced to answer things about herself.

"Have you been deeply hurt by someone?" she asked, trying to look concerned. "Is that why you never smile?"

"Look at yourself sometime, Angela. Why don't you smile the way you want me to? You're always nervous, fidgety, too busy to smile. You haven't relaxed once since I've met you."

Angela Wells, annoyed, clicked her tongue against the roof of her mouth. It was impossible to know where she stood with him. Was she making David feel anything toward her or not?

"If I never smile, damn it," she snapped, "it's because you never give me any reason to!"

He stopped eating the sandwich, looked squarely into her face, just as he had done to Christobe. "So?" he asked.

Before he knew what she was doing, Angela Wells was on her feet, swiftly walking away from David. He watched her as she disappeared behind the first of a line of trees that grew along Concord Avenue.

It's all right, he told himself, so I'll live forever. Life isn't all that bad, after all.

She crossed Concord and walked swiftly up the street towards her apartment building. Her eyes stung with tears of frustration. He deserves to die, she thought, for being so cruel, so heartless.

HAVE YOU BEEN FAITHFUL TO OUR AGREEMENT? He asked sarcastically.

Christobe was waiting for her in her room. He didn't seem so terrible to her as the first time. Yet His presence still erased all feelings within her except self-preservation.

"If you mean, does he love me?" she stammered, "the answer is—" She stopped. For one insane moment she had almost answered, "No, because he is incapable of human feeling," but she changed her mind and lied to the Fiend. "Yes," she said, "he loves me."

THEN WHY, DEAR ANGELA WELLS, WHY THESE TEARS? Compassion suited Christobe as well as the solitary smile she had been privileged to witness. Angela was sick with fright. If she wanted to convince the Demon, she would have to think fast.

"I'm crying," she replied, "because I love him, too, and I can't bear the thought of him dying."

OH, said Christobe in mock surprise. I THOUGHT DAVID GREENE NEVER GAVE YOU ANY REASON TO SMILE.

She whimpered, close to hysteria, realizing that all they'd said and done had been observed by Christobe. Then the emotion within her changed suddenly to intense anger. "Why don't you just kill me now!" she shrieked, flinging a vase at the Monster. It passed through His body and shattered against the wall. Christobe laughed.

YOU FORGET, MY CHILD, THAT WE HAVE AN AGREEMENT. HAVE YOU LOST ALL INTEREST IN LIVING? WOULD YOU RATHER TAKE DAVID GREENE'S PLACE BY MY SIDE?

He heard the answer within Angela Wells's soul.

THEN, said Christobe, YOU HAD BEST WORK HARDER AT HIS HAPPINESS.

III

The fact that David Greene had been trying to outwit the creature he believed to be Death was not the reason he showed up at Angela's room that evening. He had thought carefully about the situation and decided that he had been rude that afternoon. But what was more, he felt very sad after she left him, and suddenly realized that he was no longer pretending to be happy when he was in her company. This created a dreadful dilemma for him, for if he was really happy, he must refrain from showing it—for now he wanted to live. Yet it would be extremely hard to maintain restraint; to keep silent would be to lose Angela. He stood at a crossroads. He could see the girl walk out of his life, and that way he could stay alive. But what was life without her? Or he could speak his feelings and perhaps win Angela—only to die.

But she, too, was at a crossroads. She could take Christobe's offer and save her own life at the cost of David's. But would she be able to live with herself with the shadow of his death casting a pall over her forever? Of course, there was another path. It led to her own death, but promised a freedom of soul she could not hope for otherwise.

When the knock came at her door, and she opened it to find David standing there, her relief was so great that Angela threw her arms around him and kissed him.

Before she knew that he was responding to her, he pulled away.

I have to have more will power than *that*, he thought.

"Have you eaten?"

"No," he answered. "Have you?"

"I wasn't very hungry." They were suddenly silent and uncomfortable with each other. At first, they couldn't look into each other's eyes, but when they did by accident they both said "I'm sorry," at the same time, which made them smile at each other. Then they both apologized tenderly.

She left David and went into the kitchen.

WORK HARDER, GIRL. HARDER.

No, her mind screamed silently. Aloud she asked, "David—are you happy with me?"

The question stunned him. Why was she asking? Did she care for him? Or was there another reason?

"Are *you?*" he called back.

HARDER.

"Yes, very! Now will you answer me?"

He walked across the room, around a dining-room table that separated the kitchen from the rest of the apartment, and stopped at her side.

"What do you think?"

"I don't know, David. What am I supposed to think? You never show me whether you're happy or not. You don't smile. You don't show affection. You never talk."

MAKE HIM TELL YOU! Christobe growled.

"Angela, please, if we keep this up we'll only fight again, and I don't want to fight now."

"I'm sorry, David. I *am* tense, you were right."

YOU WILL BE WITH ME BEFORE THE NIGHT IS OVER UNLESS YOU WORK.

She put her arms around his neck and looked up into his face. "I do love you, David."

"Yes," he replied, averting his eyes.

"Tell me you love me, too."

He broke away from her and sat down at the table. She was silent for a long time, then she put the spaghetti on the plates and brought it to the table.

"You know," he told her, with some attempt at humor, "I ate this stuff for an entire year."

Angela looked up from her plate. It was the first time he had permitted her a glance into his past. "Really?" she asked, brightly. "Why on earth?"

"Well, at that time, I really considered eating as just a nuisance, yet I had to eat to keep going, don't ask me why. Anyway, spaghetti seemed like the easiest thing to cook."

Their food grew cold as he continued to talk, telling her everything that he always wanted to communicate. He spoke to Angela of things he didn't know were still important to him, and she was fascinated.

SPLENDID, said Christobe. But, for once, she wasn't listening.

"Have you ever been in love?" she asked, almost afraid to stop the flow of talk.

"Once, when I was much younger."

"Did it hurt badly?"

"No. I think I just accepted it. To be hurt you have to really feel, and I turned my feelings off so I wouldn't suffer any more pain."

"And what made you start to tell me all this?"

"You," he said. "Your patience and understanding." But the real reason, he told himself, was that talking about the past was safer . . .

YOU MUST GET HIM TO SAY HE'S NEVER BEEN SO HAPPY.

"And you, Angela? Have you ever been in love?"

"I thought I was," she said, distracted by the strident voice of the Demon. "I believed I was in love plenty of times—but I was wrong."

"Then you've been hurt, too."

"Oh, yes. Often." She spoke softly, rising from the table, moving into the area of the apartment that served as a living room. David followed, and they both sat on the couch. "But then, everyone gets hurt. Life is full of pain. You can't turn your back on it, the way you have done. That's a denial of life."

"Maybe. But I can't take any more pain—especially not now. Not after I've learned to open up."

"But David, it sounds trite—but life isn't long enough . . ." The ironic aptness of her words stung her and Angela began to cry. David Greene drew close to him. He began to show her that affection she had said she wanted, and the triumphant Christobe silently urged them onward.

At length, there were three naked figures in the room, One of them without flesh. Angela saw Him and knew what was about to happen.

In a moment, David would say the words the Fiend wanted to hear, then nothing could save him.

Her eyes were on Christobe, and David, following her gaze, saw Him at last. He saw the Demon looking at her and the truth struck him with horror. She had been used to get him—and, David thought, if she fails to "deliver" me, it will cost her her life.

With finality, Angela Wells chose her path. Turning her eyes from Christobe, she faced David. "I despise you," she told him. "I was only using you. I wanted to give you something you never had before—only for the pleasure of tearing it away."

At the same moment, David Greene made up his mind: he had to get the Monster to take him instead of Angela. "I don't care what you say," he told her, *"I love you and I have never been as happy as I am right now."*

"You're saying that to make me suffer, David, but it won't work. I know that all your defences were torn down by me—and now I can use them against you!"

Christobe was fed up. There would be no agony here. Just two bleeding hearts who were willing to die to save one another.

LISTEN. I WILL ADMIT THAT YOU HAVE WON. YOU BORE ME. BUT DON'T FEEL PLEASED. WHEN HE IS READY FOR YOU, THERE IS STILL DEATH.

And Christobe was gone to find someone else who would fill His ears with his favorite melody.

Sometimes it doesn't pay a demon to get out of his coalbed as you will discover in this wacky adventure by ROBERT SHECKLEY, *former editor of* Omni *science-fantasy magazine and author of numerous critically acclaimed novels and short story collections, including* Immortality, Inc.; Notions: Unlimited; Pilgrimage to Earth; Shards of Space *and* Untouched by Human Hands.

The Demons
BY ROBERT SHECKLEY

Walking along Second Avenue, Arthur Gammet decided it was a rather nice spring day. Not too cold, just brisk and invigorating. A perfect day for selling insurance, he told himself. He stepped off the curb at Ninth Street.

And vanished.

"Didja see that?" A butcher's assistant asked the butcher. They had been standing in front of their store, idly watching people go by.

"See what?" the butcher, a corpulent, red-faced man, replied.

"The guy in the overcoat. He disappeared."

"Yeh," the butcher said. "So he turned up Ninth, so what?"

The butcher's assistant hadn't seen Arthur turn up Ninth, down Ninth, or across Second. He had seen him disappear. But should he insist on it? You tell your boss he's wrong, so where does it get you? Besides, the guy in the overcoat probably *had* turned up Ninth. Where else could he have gone?

But Arthur Gammet was no longer in New York. He had thoroughly vanished.

Somewhere else, not necessarily on Earth, a being who called himself Neelsebub was staring at a pentagon. Within it was something he hadn't bargained for. Neelsebub fixed it with a bitter stare, knowing he had good cause for anger. He'd spent years digging out magic formulas, experimenting with herbs and essences, reading the best books on wizardry and witchcraft. He'd thrown everything into one gigantic effort, and what happened? The wrong demon appeared.

Of course, there were many things that might have gone amiss. The severed hand of the corpse—it just *might* have been the hand of a suicide, for even the best of dealers aren't to be trusted. Or the line of

the pentagon might have been the least bit wavy; that was very significant. Or the words of the incantation might not have been in the
proper order. Even one syllable wrongly intoned could have done it.

Anyhow, the damage was done. Neelsebub leaned one red-scaled
shoulder against the huge bottle in back of him, scratching the other
shoulder with a dagger-like fingernail. As usual when perplexed, his
barbed tail flicked uncertainly.

At least he had a demon of some sort.

But the thing inside the pentagon didn't look like any conventional
kind of demon. Those loose folds of gray flesh, for example . . . But,
then the historical accounts were notoriously inaccurate. Whatever
kind of supernatural being it was, it would have to come across. Of
that he was certain. Neelsebub folded his hooved feet under him more
comfortably, waiting for the strange being to speak.

Arthur Gammet was still too stunned to speak. One moment he had
been walking to the insurance office, minding his own business, enjoying the fine air of an early spring morning. He had stepped off the
curb at Second and Ninth—and landed here. Wherever *here* was.

Swaying slightly, he made out, through the deep mist that filled the
room, a huge red-scaled monster squatting on its haunches. Beside it
was what looked like a bottle, but a bottle fully ten feet high. The
creature had a barbed tail and was now scratching his head with it,
glaring at Arthur out of little piggish eyes. Hastily, Arthur tried to
step back, but was unable to move more than a step. He was inside a
chalked area, he noticed, and for some reason was unable to step over
the white lines.

"So," the red creature said, finally breaking the silence. "I've finally
got you." These weren't the words he was saying; the sounds were
utterly foreign. But somehow, Arthur was able to understand the
thought behind the words. It wasn't telepathy, but rather as though he
were translating a foreign language, automatically, colloquially.

"I must say I'm rather disappointed," Neelsebub continued when
the captured demon in the pentagon didn't answer. "All our legends
say that demons are fearful things, fifteen feet high, with wings and
tiny heads and a hole in the chest that throws out jets of cold water."

Arthur Gammet peeled off his overcoat, letting it fall in a sodden
heap at his feet. Dimly, he could appreciate the idea of demons being
able to produce jets of cold water. The room was like a furnace. Al-

ready his gray tweed suit was a soggy, wrinkled mass of cloth and perspiration.

And with that thought came acceptance—of the red creature, the chalk lines he was unable to cross, the sweltering room—everything.

He had noticed in books, magazines and motion-pictures that a man, confronted by an odd situation, usually mouthed lines such as, "Pinch me, this can't be true," or, "Good God, I'm either dreaming, drunk or crazy." Arthur had no intention of saying anything so palpably absurd. For one thing, he was sure the huge red creature wouldn't appreciate it; and for another, he knew he wasn't dreaming, drunk or crazy. There were no words in Arthur Gammet's vocabulary for it, but he knew. A dream was one thing; this was another.

"The legends never mentioned being able to peel off your skin," Neelsebub said thoughtfully, looking at the overcoat at Arthur's feet. "Interesting."

"This is a mistake," Arthur said firmly. The experience he had had as an insurance agent stood him in good stead now. He was used to meeting all kinds of people, unraveling all kinds of snarled situations. This creature had, evidently, tried to raise a demon. Through nobody's fault he had gotten Arthur Gammet, and was under the impression that *he* was a demon. The error must be rectified at once.

"I am an insurance agent," he said. The creature shook its tremendous horned head. Its tail swished from side to side unpleasantly.

"Your other-world functions don't concern me in the slightest," Neelsebub growled. "I don't care, really, what species of demon you are."

"But I tell you I'm not a—"

"It won't work!" Neelsebub howled, glaring angrily at Arthur from the edge of the pentagon. "I know you're a demon. And I want *drast!*"

"Drast? I don't think—"

"I'm up to all your demoniac tricks," Neelsebub said, calming himself with obvious effort. "I know—and you know—that when a demon is conjured, he must grant one wish. I conjured you, and I want drast. Ten thousand pounds of it."

"Drast . . ." Arthur began uncomfortably, standing in the corner of the pentagon furthest from the tail-lashing monster.

"Drast, or voot, or hakatinny, or sup-der-oop. It's all the same thing."

It was speaking of money, Arthur Gammet realized. The slang terms had been unfamiliar but there was no mistaking the sense behind them. Undoubtedly, drast was what passed for currency in its country.

"Ten thousand pounds isn't much," Neelsebub said with a cunning little smile. "Not for *you*. You ought to be glad I'm not one of those fools who ask for immortality."

Arthur was.

"And if I don't?" he asked.

"In that case," Neelsebub replied, a frown replacing the little smile, "I'll be forced to conjure you again—inside the bottle." Arthur looked at the green bottle, towering over Neelsebub's head. It was wide at its misty base, tapering to a slim neck. If the thing ever got him in, he would never be able to squeeze out through that neck. *If* the thing could get him in. And Arthur was fairly sure it could.

"Of course," Neelsebub said, his smile returning, more cunning than ever, "There's no reason for heroic measures. Ten thousand pounds of the old sup-der-oop isn't much for you. It'll make me rich, but all you have to do is wave your hand." He paused, his smile becoming ingratiating.

"You know," he went on softly. "I've really spent a long time on this. Read a lot of books, spent a pile of voot." His tail lashed the floor suddenly, like a bullet glancing off granite. "Don't try to put something over on me!" he shouted.

Arthur found that the force rising from the chalk extended as high as he could reach. Gingerly, he leaned against the invisible wall, and, finding that it supported his weight, rested against it.

Ten thousand pounds of drast, he thought. Evidently the creature was a sorcerer, from God-knows-where. Some other planet, perhaps. The creature had tried to conjure a wish-granting demon, and had gotten him. It wanted something from him—or else the bottle. All very unreasonable, but Arthur Gammet was beginning to suspect that most wizards were unreasonable people.

"I'll try to get your drast," Arthur said, feeling that he had to say something. "But I'll have to go back to the—ah—underworld to get it. That handwaving stuff is out."

"All right," the monster said to him, standing at the edge of the pentagon and leering in. "I trust you. But remember, I can call you any time I want. You can't get away, you know, so don't even try. By the way, my name is Neelsebub."

"Any relation to Beelzebub?" Arthur asked.

"Great-grandfather," Neelsebub replied, looking suspiciously at Arthur. "He was an army man. Unfortunately, he—" Neelsebub stopped abruptly, glaring angrily at Arthur. "But you demons know all about that! Begone! *And bring that drast!*"

Arthur Gammet vanished again.

He materialized on the corner of Second Avenue and Ninth Street, where he had first vanished. His overcoat was at his feet, his clothes filled with perspiration. He staggered for a moment to hold his balance —since he had been leaning against the wall of force when Neelsebub had vanished him—picked up his overcoat and hurried to his apartment. Luckily, there had been only a few people around. Two housewives gulped and walked quickly away. A nattily dressed man blinked four or five times, took a step forward as though he wanted to ask something, changed his mind and hurried off toward Eighth Street. The rest of the people either hadn't seen him or just didn't give a damn.

In his two-room apartment Arthur made one feeble attempt to dismiss the whole thing as a dream. Failing miserably, he began to outline his possibilities.

He could produce the drast. That is, perhaps he could if he found out what it was. The stuff Neelsebub considered valuable might be just about anything. Lead, perhaps, or iron. Even that would stretch his meagre earnings to the breaking-point.

He could notify the police. And be locked up in an asylum. Forget that one.

Or, he could not produce the drast—and spend the rest of his life in a bottle. Forget that one, too.

All he could do was wait until Neelsebub conjured him again, and find out then what drast was. Perhaps it was common dirt. He could get that from his uncle's farm in New Jersey, if Neelsebub could manage the transportation.

Arthur Gammet telephoned the office and told them he was ill, and that he expected to be ill for several days. After that he fixed a bite of food in his kitchenette, feeling quite proud of his good appetite. Not everyone faced with the strong possibility of being shut up in a bottle could have tucked away a meal that well. He tidied up the place, and changed into a light Palm Beach suit. It was four-thirty in the afternoon. He stretched out on the bed and waited. Along about nine-thirty he disappeared.

"Changed your skin again," Neelsebub commented. "Where's the drast?" His tail twitched eagerly as he hurried around the pentagon.

"It's not hidden behind me," Arthur said, turning to look at Neelsebub. "I'll have to have more information." He adopted a nonchalant pose, leaning against the invisible lines that radiated from the chalk. "And I'll have to have your promise that once I produce it you'll leave me alone."

"Of course," Neelsebub answered cheerfully. "I can only ask for one wish anyhow. Tell you what, I'll swear the great oath of Satanas. That's absolutely binding, you know."

"Satanas?"

"One of our early presidents," Neelsebub said with a reverential air. "My great grandfather Beelzebub served under him. Unfortunately— oh, well, you know all that."

Neelsebub swore the great oath of Satanas, and very impressive it was. The blue mists in the room were edged in red when he was done, and the outlines of the huge bottle shifted eerily in the dim light. Arthur was perspiring freely, even in his summer suit. He wished he were a cold-producing demon.

"That's it," Neelsebub said, standing erectly in the middle of the room, his tail looped around his wrist. There was a strange look in his eyes, a look of one recalling past glories.

"Now what sort of information do you want?" Neelsebub began pacing the floor in front of the pentagon, his tail dragging.

"Describe this drast to me."

"Well, it's soft, heavy—"

That could be lead.

"And yellow."

Gold.

"Hmm," Arthur said, staring at the bottle. "I don't suppose it's ever gray, is it? Or dark brown?"

"No. It's always yellow. With sometimes a reddish hue."

Still gold. Arthur contemplated the red-scaled monster in front of him, pacing up and down with ill-concealed eagerness. Ten thousand pounds of gold. That would come to . . . No, better not think of it. Impossible.

"I'll need a little time," Arthur said. "Perhaps sixty or seventy years. Tell you what, I'll call you as soon as—"

Neelsebub interrupted him with a huge roar of laughter. Arthur had tickled his rudimentary sense of humor, evidently, because Neelsebub was hugging his haunches, screaming with mirth.

"Sixty or seventy years!" Neelsebub shouted, and the bottle shook, and even the lines of the pentagon seemed to waver. "I'll give you sixty or seventy minutes! Or the bottle!"

"Now just a minute," Arthur said, from the far side of the pentagon. "I'll need a little—hold it!" He had just had an idea, and it was undeniably the best idea he had ever had. More, it was his own idea.

"I'll have to have the exact formula you used to get me," Arthur said. "Must check with the main office to be sure everything is in order."

The monster raved and swore, and the air turned black and purple; the bottle rang in sympathetic vibration with Neelsebub's voice, and the very room seemed to sway. But Arthur Gammet stood firm. He explained to Neelsebub, patiently, seven or eight times, that it would do no good to bottle him, since he would never get his gold that way. All he wanted was the formula, and certainly that wouldn't—

Finally he got it.

"And no tricks!" Neelsebub thundered finally, gesturing at the bottle with both hands and his tail. Arthur nodded feebly and reappeared in his room.

The next few days he spent in a frenzied search around New York. Some of the ingredients of the incantation were easy to fill—the sprig of mistletoe, for example, from a florist, and the sulphur. Graveyard mould was more difficult, as was a bat's left wing. What really had him stumped for a while was the severed hand of the murdered man. He finally procured one from a store that specialized in filling orders for medical students. He had the dealer's guarantee that the body to which the hand belonged had died a violent death. Arthur suspected that the dealer was trying to humor him, but there was really very little he could do about it.

Among other things, he bought a large bottle. It was surprisingly inexpensive. There were really compensations for living in New York, he decided. There seemed to be nothing—literally *nothing* one couldn't buy.

In three days he had all his materials, and at midnight of the third night he had arranged them on the floor of his apartment. The light of a three-quarters full moon was shining in the window—the incantation had been vague as to what phase it should be—and everything seemed to be in order. Arthur drew the pentagon, lighted the candles, burned the incense, and started the chant. He figured that, by following directions carefully, he should be able to conjure Neelsebub. His one wish would be that Neelsebub leave him strictly alone. He couldn't see how that would fail.

The blue mists spread through the room as he mumbled the formula, and soon he could see something growing in the center of the pentagon.

"Neelsebub!" he cried. But it wasn't.

The thing in the pentagon was about fifteen feet high when the incantation was finished. It had to stoop almost to the ground to fit under Arthur's ceiling. It was a fearful-looking thing, with wings and a tiny head and a hole in its chest.

Arthur Gammet had conjured the wrong demon.

"What's all this?" the demon asked, shooting a jet of ice water out of his chest. The water splashed against the invisible walls of the pentagon and rolled to the floor. It must have been pure reflex, because Arthur's room was pleasantly cool.

"I want my one wish," Arthur said. The demon was blue and impossibly thin; his wings were vestigial stumps. They flapped once or twice against his bony chest before he answered.

"I don't know what you are or how you got me here," the demon said. "But it's clever. It's undeniably clever."

"Let's not chatter," Arthur replied nervously, wondering how soon Neelsebub was going to conjure him again. "I want ten thousand pounds of gold. Also known as drast, hakatinny, and the old sup-der-oop." At any moment, he thought, he might find himself inside a bottle.

"Well," the cold-producing demon said. "You seem to be laboring under the mistaken impression that I'm—"

"You have twenty-four hours."

"I'm not a rich man," the cold-producing demon said. "Small businessman. But perhaps if you give me time—"

"Or the bottle," Arthur said. He pointed to the large bottle in one corner, then realized it would never hold fifteen feet of cold-producing demon.

"The next time I conjure you I'll have a bottle big enough," Arthur said. "I didn't think you'd be so tall."

"We have stories about people disappearing," the demon mused. "So *this* is what happens to them. The underworld. Don't suppose anyone would believe me, though."

"Get that drast," Arthur said. "Begone!"

The cold-producing demon was gone.

Arthur Gammet knew he could not afford more than twenty-four hours. Even that was probably cutting it too thin, he thought, because one could never tell when Neelsebub would decide he had had enough time. There was no telling what the red-scaled monster would do, if he were disappointed a third time. Arthur found that, toward the end of the day, he was clutching the steam pipe. A lot of good that would do if he were conjured! But it was nice to have something solid to grasp.

It was a shame also, he thought, to have to impose on the cold-producing demon that way. It was pretty obvious that the demon wasn't a real demon, any more than Arthur was. Well, he would never use the bottle on him. It would do no good if Neelsebub weren't satisfied.

Finally he mumbled the incantation again.

"You'll have to make your pentagon wider," the cold-producing demon said, stooping uncomfortably inside. "I haven't got room for—"

"Begone!" Arthur said, and feverishly rubbed out the pentagon. He sketched it again, this time using the area of the whole room. He lugged the bottle—the same one, since he hadn't found one fifteen feet high—into the kitchen, stationed himself in the closet, and went through the formula again. Once more the thick, twisting blue mists gathered.

"Now don't be hasty," the cold-producing demon said, from within the pentagon. "I haven't got the old sup-der-oop yet. There's a tie-up, and I can explain everything." He beat his wings to part the mist.

Beside him was a bottle, fully ten feet high. Within it, green with rage, was Neelsebub. He seemed to be shouting, but the bottle was stoppered. No sound came through.

"Got the formula out of the library," the demon said, "Could have knocked me over when the thing worked. Always been a hard-headed businessman, you know. Don't like this supernatural stuff. But, you have to face facts. Anyhow, I got hold of this demon here—" He jerked a spidery arm at the bottle— "But he wouldn't come across. So I bottled him." The cold-producing demon heaved a deep sigh when Arthur smiled. It was like a reprieve.

"Now, I don't want you to bottle me," the cold-producing demon went on, "because I've got a wife and three kids. You know how it is. Insurance slump and all that, I couldn't raise ten thousand pounds of drast with an army. But as soon as I persuade this demon here—"

"Never mind about the drast," Arthur said. "Just take the demon with you. Keep him in storage. Inside the bottle, of course."

"I'll do that," the blue-winged insurance man said. "And about that drast—"

"Forget it," Arthur said warmly. After all, insurance men have to stick together. "Handle fire and theft?"

"General accident is more my line," the insurance man said. "But you know, I've been thinking—"

Neelsebub raved and swore inside the bottle while the two insurance men discussed the intricacies of their profession.

"A Ballad of Hell," a tale of love betrayed, has, in my opinion, one of the most moving last lines in all romantic verse. Its Scottish author, JOHN DAVIDSON *(1857–1909), was a gifted lyric poet whose output included* Fleet Street Eclogues *and several volumes of* Ballads. *He was also a highly individualistic playwright; his principal dramas are* Bruce; Smith: A Tragic Farce; *and* Scaramouch in Naxos.

A Ballad of Hell
BY JOHN DAVIDSON

"A letter from my love to-day!
　　Oh, unexpected, dear appeal!"
She struck a happy tear away
　　And broke the crimson seal.

"My love, there is no help on earth,
　　No help in heaven; the dead man's bell
Must toll our wedding; our first hearth
　　Must be the well-paved floor of hell."

The colour died from out her face,
　　Her eyes like ghostly candles shone;
She cast dread looks about the place,
　　Then clenched her teeth, and read right on.

"I may not pass the prison door;
　　Here must I rot from day to day,
Unless I wed whom I abhor,
　　My cousin, Blanche of Valencay.

"At midnight with my dagger keen
　　I'll take my life; it must be so.
Meet me in hell to-night, my queen,
　　For weal and woe."

She laughed although her face was wan,
   She girded on her golden belt,
She took her jewelled ivory fan,
   And at her glowing missal knelt.

Then rose, "And am I mad?" she said,
   She broke her fan, her belt untied;
With leather girt herself instead,
   And stuck a dagger at her side.

She waited, shuddering in her room
   Till sleep had fallen on all the house.
She never flinched; she faced her doom:
   They two must sin to keep their vows.

Then out into the night she went;
   And stooping, crept by hedge and tree;
Her rose-bush flung a snare of scent,
   And caught a happy memory.

She fell, and lay a minute's space;
   She tore the sward in her distress;
The dewy grass refreshed her face;
   She rose and ran with lifted dress.

She started like a morn-caught ghost
   Once when the moon came out and stood
To watch; the naked road she crossed,
   And dived into the murmuring wood.

The branches snatched her streaming cloak;
   A live thing shrieked; she made no stay!
She hurried to the trysting-oak—
   Right well she knew the way.

Without a pause she bared her breast
   And drove her dagger home and fell,
And lay like one that takes her rest,
   And died and wakened up in hell.

She bathed her spirit in the flame,
  And near the centre took her post;
From all sides to her ears there came
  The dreary anguish of the lost.

The devil started at her side
  Comely, and tall, and black as jet.
"I am young Malespina's bride;
  Has he come hither yet?"

"My poppet, welcome to your bed."
  "Is Malespina here?"
"Not he! To-morrow he must wed
  His cousin Blanche, my dear!"

"You lie; he died with me to-night."
  "Not he! It was a plot." "You lie."
"My dear, I never lie outright."
  "We died at midnight, he and I."

The devil went. Without a groan
  She, gathered up in one fierce prayer,
Took root in hell's midst all alone,
  And waited for him there.

She dared to make herself at home,
  Amidst the wail, the uneasy stir.
The blood-stained flame that filled the dome,
  Scentless and silent, shrouded her.

How long she stayed I cannot tell;
  But when she felt his perfidy,
She marched across the floor of hell;
  And all the damned stood up to see.

The devil stopped her at the brink;
  She shook him off; she cried, "Away!"
"My dear, you have gone mad, I think."
  "I was betrayed: I will not stay."

Across the weltering deep she ran—
  A stranger thing was never seen:
The damned stood silent to a man;
  They saw the great gulf set between.

To her it seemed a meadow fair;
  And flowers sprang up about her feet;
She entered heaven; she climbed the stair;
  And knelt down at the mercy-seat.

Seraphs and saints with one great voice
  Welcomed that soul that knew not fear;
Amazed to find it could rejoice,
  Hell raised a hoarse half-human cheer.

CHARLES PIERRE BAUDELAIRE *(1821–1867), a great French poet best remembered for his volume of verse* Les Fleurs du Mal (The Flowers of Evil), *was entitled to a large estate when he was twenty-one, but his extravagant nature forced his family to arrange for his inheritance to be doled out to him a bit at a time. In spite of their precautions, Baudelaire died poor and unappreciated, a fact that renders the climactic sentiment of "The Generous Gambler" both ironic and poignant.*

The Generous Gambler
BY CHARLES PIERRE BAUDELAIRE

Yesterday, across the crowd of the boulevard, I found myself touched by a mysterious Being I had always desired to know, and whom I recognized immediately, in spite of the fact that I had never seen him. He had, I imagined, in himself, relatively as to me, a similar desire, for he gave me, in passing, so significant a sign in his eyes that I hastened to obey him. I followed him attentively, and soon I descended behind him into a subterranean dwelling, astonishing to me as a vision, where shone a luxury of which none of the actual houses in Paris could give me an approximate example. It seemed to me singular that I had passed so often that prodigious retreat without having discovered the entrance. There reigned an exquisite, an almost stifling atmosphere, which made one forget almost instantaneously all the fastidious horrors of life; there I breathed a somber sensuality, like that of opium smokers when, set on the shore of an enchanted island over which shone an eternal afternoon, they felt born in them, to the soothing sounds of melodious cascades, the desire of never again seeing their households, their women, their children, and of never again being tossed on the decks of ships by storms.

There were there strange faces of men and women, gifted with so fatal a beauty that I seemed to have seen them years ago and in countries which I failed to remember and which inspired in me that curious sympathy and that equally curious sense of fear that I usually discover in unknown aspects. If I wanted to define in some fashion or other the singular expression of their eyes, I would say that never had

I seen such magic radiance more energetically expressing the horror of ennui and of desire—of the immortal desire of feeling themselves alive.

As for mine host and myself, we were already, as we sat down, as perfect friends as if we had always known each other. We drank immeasurably of all sorts of extraordinary wines, and—a thing not less bizarre—it seemed to me, after several hours, that I was no more intoxicated than he was.

However, gambling, this superhuman pleasure, had cut, at various intervals, our copious libations, and I ought to say that I had gained and lost my soul, as we were playing, with a heroic carelessness and lightheartedness. The soul is so invisible a thing, often useless and sometimes so troublesome, that I did not experience, as to this loss, more than that kind of emotion I might have, had I lost my visiting card in the street.

We spent hours in smoking cigars, whose incomparable savor and perfume give to the soul the nostalgia of unknown delights and sights, and, intoxicated by all these spiced sauces, I dared, in an access of familiarity which did not seem to displease him, to cry, as I lifted a glass filled to the brim with wine: "To your immortal health, old hegoat!"

We talked of the universe, of its creation and of its future destruction; of the leading ideas of the century—that is to say, of progress and perfectibility—and, in general, of all kinds of human infatuations. On this subject His Highness was inexhaustible in his irrefutable jests, and he expressed himself with a splendor of diction and with a magnificence in drollery such as I have never found in any of the most famous conversationalists of our age. He explained to me the absurdity of different philosophies that had so far taken possession of men's brains, and deigned even to take me in confidence in regard to certain fundamental principles, which I am not inclined to share with anyone.

He complained in no way of the evil reputation under which he lived, indeed, all over the world, and he assured me that he himself was of all living beings the most interested in the destruction of *Superstition,* and he avowed to me that he had been afraid, relatively as to his proper power, once only, and that was on the day when he had heard a preacher, more subtle than the rest of the human herd, cry in his pulpit: "My dear brethren, do not ever forget, when you hear the progress of lights praised, that the loveliest trick of the Devil is to persuade you that he does not exist!"

The memory of this famous orator brought us naturally on the subject of academies, and my strange host declared to me that he didn't disdain, in many cases, to inspire the pens, the words, and the consciences of pedagogues, and that he almost always assisted in person, in spite of being invisible, at all the scientific meetings.

Encouraged by so much kindness, I asked him if he had any news of God—who has not his hours of impiety?—especially as the old friend of the Devil. He said to me, with a shade of unconcern united with a deeper shade of sadness: "We salute each other when we meet." But, for the rest, he spoke in Hebrew.

It is uncertain if His Highness has ever given so long an audience to a simple mortal, and I feared to abuse it.

Finally, as the dark approached shivering, this famous personage, sung by so many poets and served by so many philosophers who work for his glory's sake without being aware of it, said to me: "I want you to remember me always, and to prove to you that I—of whom one says so much evil—am often enough *bon diable,* to make use of one of your vulgar locutions. So as to make up for the irremediable loss that you have made of your soul, I shall give you back the stake you ought to have gained, if your fate had been fortunate—that is to say, the possibility of solacing and of conquering, during your whole life, this bizarre affection of ennui, which is the source of all your maladies and of all your miseries. Never a desire shall be formed by you that I will not aid you to realize; you will reign over your vulgar equals; money and gold and diamonds, fairy palaces, shall come to seek you and shall ask you to accept them without your having made the least effort to obtain them; you can change your abode as often as you like; you shall have in your power all sensualities without lassitude, in lands where the climate is always hot and where the women are as scented as the flowers." With this he rose and said good-by to me with a charming smile.

If it had not been for the shame of humiliating myself before so immense an assembly, I might have voluntarily fallen at the feet of this generous gambler, to thank him for his unheard-of munificence. But little by little, after I had left him, an incurable defiance entered into me; I dared no longer believe in so prodigious a happiness, and as I went to bed, making over again my nightly prayer by means of all that remained in me in the matter of faith, I repeated in my slumber: "My God, my Lord, my God! Do let the Devil keep his word with me!"

Satan seems to have a special fondness for prestidigitation, as we saw in Fredric Brown's "Armageddon" (earlier in this section) and in the next wry selection . . . maybe. JOHN KENDRICK BANGS *(1862–1922), one of turn-of-the-century America's most enduringly amusing humorists, wrote some sixty books, several of which dealt with the colorful populace of Hades, notably* A House-Boat on the Styx, Pursuit of the House-Boat *and* The Enchanted Typewriter. *He also wrote several tongue-in-cheek ghost stories, some of which may be found in* Ghosts I Have Met and Some Others *and* The Water Ghost and Others.

A Midnight Visitor

BY JOHN KENDRICK BANGS

I do not assert that what I am about to relate is in all its particulars absolutely true. Not, understand me, that it is not true, but I do not feel that I care to make an assertion that is more than likely to be received by a sceptical age with sneers of incredulity. I will content myself with a simple narration of the events of that evening, the memory of which is so indelibly impressed upon my mind, and which, were I able to do so, I should forget without any sentiments of regret whatsoever.

The affair happened on the night before I fell ill of typhoid fever, and is about the sole remaining remembrance of that immediate period left to me. Briefly the story is as follows:

Notwithstanding the fact that I was overworked in the practice of my profession—it was early in March, and I was preparing my contributions for the coming Christmas issues of the periodicals for which I write—I had accepted the highly honorable position of Entertainment Committeeman at one of the small clubs to which I belonged. I accepted the office, supposing that the duties connected with it were easy of performance, and with absolutely no notion that the faith of my fellow-committeemen in my judgment was so strong that they would ultimately manifest a desire to leave the whole programme for the club's diversion in my hands. This, however, they did; and when the month of March assumed command of the calendar I found myself utterly fagged out and at my wits' end to know what style of entertainment to provide for the club meeting to be held on the evening of the

15th of that month. I had provided already an unusually taking variety of evenings, of which one in particular, called the "Martyrs' Night," in which living authors writhed through selections from their own works, while an inhuman audience, every man of whom had suffered even as the victims then suffered, sat on tenscore of campstools puffing the smoke of twenty-five score of free cigars into their faces, and gloating over their misery, was extremely successful, and had gained for me among my professional brethren the enviable title of "Machiavelli Junior." This performance, in fact, was the one now uppermost in the minds of the club members, having been the most recent of the series; and it had been prophesied by many men whose judgment was unassailable that no man, not even I, could ever conceive of anything that could surpass it. Disposed at first to question the accuracy of a prophecy to the effect that I was, like most others of my kind, possessed of limitations, I came finally to believe that perhaps, after all, these male Cassandras with whom I was thrown were right. Indeed, the more I racked my brains to think of something better than the "Martyrs' Night," the more I became convinced that in that achievement I had reached the zenith of my powers. The thing for me to do now was to hook myself securely on to the zenith and stay there. But how to do it? That was the question which drove sleep from my eyes, and deprived me for a period of six weeks of my reason, my hair departing immediately upon the restoration thereof—a not uncommon after-symptom of typhoid.

It was a typical March night, this one upon which the extraordinary incident about to be related took place. It was the kind of night that novelists use when they are handling a mystery that in the abstract would amount to nothing, but which in the concrete of a bit of wild, weird, and windy nocturnalism sends the reader into hysterics. It may be—I shall not attempt to deny it—that had it happened upon another kind of an evening—a soft, mild, balmy June evening, for instance—my own experience would have seemed less worthy of preservation in the amber of publicity, but of that the reader must judge for himself. The fact alone remains that upon the night when my uncanny visitor appeared, the weather department was apparently engaged in getting rid of its remnants. There was a large percentage of withering blast in the general makeup of the evening; there were rain and snow, which alternated in pattering upon my window-pane and whitening the apology for a wold that stands three blocks from my flat on Madison

Square; the wind whistled as it always does upon occasions of this sort, and from all corners of my apartment, after the usual fashion, there seemed to come sounds of a supernatural order, the effect of which was to send cold chills off on their regular trips up and down the spine of their victim—in this instance myself. I wish that at the time the hackneyed quality of these sensations had appealed to me. That it did not do so was shown by the highly nervous state in which I found myself as my clock struck eleven. If I could only have realized at that hour that these symptoms were the same old threadbare premonitions of the appearance of a supernatural being, I should have left the house and gone to the club, and so have avoided the visitation then imminent. Had I done this, I should doubtless also have escaped the typhoid, since the doctors attributed that misfortune to the shock of my experience, which, in my then wearied state, I was unable to sustain—and what the escape of typhoid would have meant to me only those who have seen the bills of my physician and druggist for services rendered and prescriptions compounded are aware. That my mind unconsciously took thought of spirits was shown by the fact that when the first chill came upon me I arose and poured out for myself a stiff bumper of old Reserve Rye, which I immediately swallowed; but beyond this I did not go. I simply sat there before my fire and cudgelled my brains for an idea whereby my fellow-members at the Gutenberg Club might be amused. How long I sat there I do not know. It may have been ten minutes; it may have been an hour—I was barely conscious of the passing of time—but I do know that the clock in the Dutch Reformed Church steeple at Twenty-ninth Street and Fifth Avenue was clanging out the first stroke of the hour of midnight when my door-bell rang.

Theretofore—if I may be allowed the word—the tintinnabulation of my door-bell had been invariably pleasing unto me. I am fond of company, and company alone was betokened by its ringing, since my creditors gratify their passion for interviews at my office, if perchance they happen to find me there. But on this occasion—I could not at the moment tell why—its clanging seemed the very essence of discord. It jangled with my nervous system, and as it ceased I was conscious of a feeling of irritability which is utterly at variance with my nature outside of business hours. In the office, for the sake of discipline, I frequently adopt a querulous manner, finding it necessary in dealing with office-boys, but the moment I leave shop behind me I become a different individual entirely, and have been called a moteless sunbeam by those who have seen only that side of my character. This, by-the-way, must be regarded as a confidential communication, since I am at present engaged in preparing a vest-pocket edition of the philosophical works of Schopenhauer in words of one syllable, and were it known that the publisher had intrusted the magnificent pessimism of that illustrious juggler of words and theories to a "moteless sunbeam" it might seriously interfere with the sale of the work; and I may say, too, that this request that my confidence be respected is entirely disinterested, inasmuch as I declined to do the work on the royalty plan, insisting upon the payment of a lump sum, considerably in advance.

But to return. I heard the bell ring with a sense of profound disgust. I did not wish to see anybody. My whiskey was low, my quinine pills few in number; my chills alone were present in a profusion bordering upon ostentation.

"I'll pretend not to hear it," I said to myself, resuming my work of gazing at the flickering light of my fire—which, by-the-way, was the only light in the room.

"Ting-a-ling-a-ling" went the bell, as if in answer to my resolve.

"Confound the luck!" I cried, jumping from my chair and going to the door with the intention of opening it, an intention however which was speedily abandoned, for as I approached it a sickly fear came over me—a sensation I had never before known seemed to take hold of my being, and instead of opening the door, I pushed the bolt to make it more secure.

"There's a hint for you, whoever you are!" I cried. "Do you hear that bolt slide, you?" I added, tremulously, for from the other side there came no reply—only a more violent ringing of the bell.

"See here!" I called out, as loudly as I could, "who are you, anyhow? What do you want?"

There was no answer, except from the bell, which began again.

"Bell-wire's too cheap to steal!" I called again. "If you want wire, go buy it; don't try to pull mine out. It isn't mine, anyhow. It belongs to the house."

Still there was no reply, only the clanging of the bell; and then my curiosity overcame my fear, and with a quick movement I threw open the door.

"Are you satisfied now?" I said, angrily. But I addressed an empty vestibule. There was absolutely no one there, and then I sat down on the mat and laughed. I never was so glad to see no one in my life. But my laugh was short-lived.

"What made that bell ring?" I suddenly asked myself, and then the feeling of fear came upon me again. I gathered my somewhat shattered self together, sprang to my feet, slammed the door with such force that the corridors echoed to the sound, slid the bolt once more, turned the key, moved a heavy chair in front of it, and then fled like a frightened hare to the sideboard in my dining-room. There I grasped the decanter holding my whiskey, seized a glass from the shelf, and started to pour out the usual dram, when the glass fell from my hand, and was shivered into a thousand pieces on the hardwood floor; for, as I poured, I glanced through the open door, and there in my sanctum the flicker of a random flame divulged the form of a being, the eyes of whom seemed fixed on mine, piercing me through and through. To say that I was petrified but dimly expresses the situation. I was granitized, and so I remained, until by a more luminous flicker from the burning wood I perceived that the being wore a flaring red necktie.

"He is human," I thought; and with the thought the tension on my nervous system relaxed, and I was able to feel a sufficiently well-developed sense of indignation to demand an explanation. "This is a mighty cool proceeding on your part," I said, leaving the sideboard and walking into the sanctum.

"Yes," he replied, in a tone that made me jump, it was so extremely sepulchral—a tone that seemed as if it might have been acquired in a damp corner of some cave off the earth. "But it's a cool evening."

"I wonder that a man of your coolness doesn't hire himself out to some refrigerating company," I remarked, with a sneer which would have delighted the soul of Cassius himself.

"I have thought of it," returned the being, calmly. "But never went any further. Summer-hotel proprietors have always outbid the refrigerating people, and they in turn have been laid low by millionaires, who have hired me on occasion to freeze out people they didn't like, but who have persisted in calling. I must confess, though, my dear Hiram, that you are not much warmer yourself—this greeting is hardly what I expected."

"Well, if you want to make me warmer," I retorted, hotly, "just keep on calling me Hiram. How the deuce did you know of that blot on my escutcheon, anyhow?" I added, for Hiram was one of the crimes of my family that I had tried to conceal, my parents having

fastened the name of Hiram Spencer Carrington upon me at baptism
for no reason other than that my rich bachelor uncle, who subse-
quently failed and became a charge upon me, was so named.

"I was standing at the door of the church when you were baptized,"
returned the visitor, "and as you were an interesting baby, I have kept
an eye on you ever since. Of course I knew that you discarded Hiram
as soon as you got old enough to put away childish things, and since
the failure of your uncle I have been aware that you desire to be
known as Spencer Carrington, but to me you are, always have been,
and always will be, Hiram."

"Well, don't give it away," I pleaded. "I hope to be famous some
day, and if the American newspaper paragrapher ever got hold of the
fact that once in my life I was Hiram, I'd have to Hiram to let me
alone."

"That's a bad joke, Hiram," said the visitor, "and for that reason I
like it, though I don't laugh. There is no danger of your becoming
famous if you stick to humor of that sort."

"Well, I'd like to know," I put in, my anger returned—"I'd like to
know who in Brindisi you are, what in Cairo you want, and what in
the name of the seventeen hinges of the gates of Singapore you are
doing here at this time of night?"

"When you were a baby, Hiram, you had blue eyes," said my visitor. "Bonny blue eyes, as the poet says."

"What of it?" I asked.

"This," replied my visitor. "If you have them now, you can very
easily see what I am doing here. *I am sitting down and talking to you.*"

"Oh, are you?" I said, with fine scorn. "I had not observed that.
The fact is, my eyes were so weakened by the brilliance of that necktie
of yours that I doubt I could see anything—not even one of my own
jokes. It's a scorcher, that tie of yours. In fact, I never saw anything so
red in my life."

"I do not see why you complain of my tie," said the visitor. "Your
own is just as bad."

"Blue is never so withering as red," I retorted, at the same time
caressing the scarf I wore.

"Perhaps not—but—ah—if you will look in the glass, Hiram, you
will observe that your point is not well taken," said my vis-à-vis,
calmly.

I acted upon the suggestion, and looked upon my reflection in the glass, lighting a match to facilitate the operation. I was horrified to observe that my beautiful blue tie, of which I was so proud, had in some manner changed, and was now of the same aggressive hue as was that of my visitor, red even as a brick is red. To grasp it firmly in my hands and tear it from my neck was the work of the moment, and then in a spirit of rage I turned upon my companion.

"See here," I cried, "I've had quite enough of you. I can't make you out, and I can't say that I want to. You know where the door is—you will oblige me by putting it to its proper use."

"Sit down, Hiram," said he, "and don't be foolish and ungrateful. You are behaving in a most extraordinary fashion, destroying your clothing and acting like a madman generally. What was the use of ripping up a handsome tie like that?"

"I despise loud hues. Red is a jockey's color," I answered.

"But you did not destroy the red tie," said he, with a smile. "You tore up your blue one—look. There it is on the floor. The red one you still have on."

Investigation showed the truth of my visitor's assertion. That flaunting streamer of anarchy still made my neck infamous, and before me on the floor, an almost unrecognizable mass of shreds, lay my cherished cerulean tie. The revelation stunned me; tears came into my eyes, and trickling down over my cheeks, fairly hissed with the feverish heat of my flesh. My muscles relaxed, and I fell limp into my chair.

"You need stimulant," said my visitor, kindly. "Go take a drop of your Old Reserve, and then come back here to me. I've something to say to you."

"Will you join me?" I asked, faintly.

"No," returned the visitor. "I am so fond of whiskey that I never molest it. That act which is your stimulant is death to the rye. Never realized that, did you?"

"No, I never did," I said, meekly.

"And yet you claim to love it. Bah!" he said.

And then I obeyed his command, drained my glass to the dregs, and returned. "What is your mission?" I asked, when I had made myself as comfortable as was possible under the circumstances.

"To relieve you of your woes," he said.

"You are a homoeopath, I observe," said I, with a sneer. "You are a homoeopath in theory and an allopath in practice."

"I am not usually unintelligent," said he. "I fail to comprehend your meaning. Perhaps you express yourself badly."

"I wish you'd express yourself for Zululand," I retorted, hotly. "What I mean is, you believe in the *similia similibus* business, but you prescribe large doses. I don't believe troubles like mine can be cured on your plan. A man can't get rid of his stock by adding to it."

"Ah, I see. You think I have added to your troubles?"

"I don't think so," I answered, with a fond glance at my ruined tie. "I know so."

"Well, wait until I have laid my plan before you, and see if you won't change your mind," said my visitor, significantly.

"All right," I said. "Proceed. Only hurry. I go to bed early, as a rule, and it's getting quite early now."

"It's only one o'clock," said the visitor, ignoring the sarcasm. "But I will hasten, as I've several other calls to make before breakfast."

"Are you a milkman?" I asked.

"You are flippant," he replied. "But, Hiram," he added, "I have come here to aid you in spite of your unworthiness. You want to know what to provide for your club night on the 15th. You want something that will knock the 'Martyrs' Night' silly."

"Not exactly that," I replied. "I don't want anything so abominably good as to make all the other things I have done seem failures. That is not good business."

"Would you like to be hailed as the discoverer of genius? Would you like to be the responsible agent for the greatest exhibition of skill in a certain direction ever seen? Would you like to become the most famous *impresario* the world has ever known?"

"Now," I said, forgetting my dignity under the enthusiasm with which I was inspired by my visitor's words, and infected more or less with his undoubtedly magnetic spirit—"now you're shouting."

"I thought so, Hiram. I thought so, and that's why I am here. I saw you on Wall Street to-day, and read your difficulty at once in your eyes, and I resolved to help you. I am a magician, and one or two little things have happened of late to make me wish to prestidigitate in public. I knew you were after a show of some kind, and I've come to offer you my services."

"Oh, pshaw!" I said. "The members of the Gutenberg Club are men of brains—not children. Card tricks are hackneyed, and sleight-of-hand shows pall."

"Do they, indeed?" said the visitor. "Well, mine won't. If you don't believe it, I'll prove to you what I can do."

"I have no paraphernalia," I said.

"Well, I have," said he, and as he spoke, a pack of cards seemed to grow out of my hands. I must have turned pale at this unexpected happening, for my visitor smiled, and said:

"Don't be frightened. That's only one of my tricks. Now choose a card," he added, "and when you have done so, toss the pack in the air. Don't tell me what the card is; it alone will fall to the floor."

"Nonsense!" said I. "It's impossible."

"Do as I tell you."

I did as he told me, to a degree only. I tossed the cards in the air without choosing one, although I made a feint of doing so.

Not a card fell back on the floor. They every one disappeared from view in the ceiling. If it had not been for the heavy chair I had rolled in front of the door, I think I should have fled.

"How's that for a trick?" asked my visitor.

I said nothing, for the very good reason that my words stuck in my throat.

"Give me a little *crème de menthe,* will you, please?" said he, after a moment's pause.

"I haven't a drop in the house," I said, relieved to think that this wonderful being could come down to anything so earthly.

"Pshaw, Hiram!" he ejaculated, apparently in disgust. "Don't be mean, and, above all, don't lie. Why, man, you've got a bottle full of it in your hand! Do you want it all?"

He was right. Where it came from I do not know; but, beyond question, the graceful, slim-necked bottle was in my right hand, and my left held a liqueur-glass of exquisite form.

"Say," I gasped, as soon as I was able to collect my thoughts, "what are your terms?"

"Wait a moment," he answered. "Let me do a little mind-reading before we arrange preliminaries."

"I haven't much of a mind to read tonight," I answered, wildly.

"You're right there," said he. "It's like a dime novel, that mind of yours to-night. But I'll do the best I can with it. Suppose you think of your favorite poem, and after turning it over in your mind carefully for a few minutes, select two lines from it, concealing them, of course, from me, and I will tell you what they are."

Now my favorite poem, I regret to say, is Lewis Carroll's "Jab-berwock," a fact I was ashamed to confess to an utter stranger, so I tried to deceive him by thinking of some other lines. The effort was hardly successful, for the only other lines I could call to mind at the moment were from Rudyard Kipling's rhyme, "The Post that Fitted," and which ran,

> "Year by year, in pious patience, vengeful Mrs. Boffin sits
> Waiting for the Sleary babies to develop Sleary's fits."

"Humph!" ejaculated my visitor. "You're a great Hiram, you are."

And then rising from his chair and walking to my "poet's corner," the magician selected two volumes.

"There," said he, handing me the *Departmental Ditties.* "You'll find the lines you tried to fool me with at the foot of page thirteen. Look."

I looked, and there lay that vile Sleary sentiment, in all the majesty of type, staring me in the eyes.

"And here," added my visitor, opening *Through the Looking-Glass* —"here is the poem that to your mind holds all the philosophy of life:

> " 'Come to my arms, my Beamish boy,
> He chortled in his joy.' "

I blushed and trembled. Blushed that he should discover the weak-ness of my taste, trembled at his power.

"I don't blame you for coloring," said the magician. "But I thought you said the Gutenberg was made up of men of brains? Do you think you could stay on the rolls a month if they were aware that your poetic ideals are summed up in the 'Jabberwock' and 'Sleary's Fits'?"

"My taste might be far worse," I answered.

"Yes, it might. You might have stooped to liking some of your own verses. I ought really to congratulate you, I suppose," retorted the visitor, with a sneering laugh.

This roused my ire again.

"Who are you, anyhow, that you come here and take me to task?" I demanded, angrily. "I'll like anything I please, and without asking your permission. If I cared more for the *Peterkin Papers* than I do for Shakespeare, I wouldn't be accountable to you, and that's all there is about it."

"Never mind who I am," said the visitor. "Suffice to say that I am myself. You'll know my name soon enough. In fact, you will pronounce it involuntarily the first thing when you wake in the morning, and then—" Here he shook his head ominously, and I felt myself grow rigid with fright in my chair. "Now for the final trick," he said, after a moment's pause. "Think of where you would most like to be at this moment, and I'll exert my power to put you there. Only close your eyes first."

I closed my eyes and wished. When I opened them I was in the billiard-room of the Gutenberg Club with Perkins and Tompson.

"For Heaven's sake, Spencer," they said, in surprise, "where did you drop in from? Why, man, you are as white as a sheet. And what a necktie! Take it off!"

"Grab hold of me, boys, and hold me fast," I pleaded, falling on my knees in terror. "If you don't, I believe I'll die."

The idea of returning to my sanctum was intolerably dreadful to me.

"Ha! ha!" laughed the magician, for even as I spoke to Perkins and Tompson I found myself seated opposite my infernal visitor in my room once more. "They couldn't keep you an instant with me summoning you back."

His laughter was terrible; his frown was pleasanter; and I felt myself gradually losing control of my senses.

"Go," I cried. "Leave me, or you will have the crime of murder on your conscience."

"I have no con—" he began; but I heard no more.

That is the last I remember of that fearful night. I must have fainted, and then have fallen into a deep slumber.

When I waked it was morning, and I was alone, but undressed and in bed, unconscionably weak, and surrounded by medicine bottles of many kinds. The clock on the mantle on the other side of the room indicated that it was after ten o'clock.

"*Great Beelzebub!*" I cried, taking note of the hour. "I've an engagement with Barlow at nine."

And then a sweet-faced woman, who, I afterwards learned, was a professional nurse, entered the room, and within an hour I realized two facts. One was that I had lain ill for many days, and that my engagement with Barlow was now for six weeks unfulfilled; the other, that my midnight visitor was none other than—

And yet I don't know. His tricks certainly were worthy of that individual; but Perkins and Tompson assert that I never entered the club that night, and surely if my visitor was Beelzebub himself he would not have omitted so important a factor of success as my actual presence in the billiard-room on that occasion would have been; and, besides, he was altogether too cool to have come from his reputed residence.

Altogether I think the episode most unaccountable, particularly when I reflect that while no trace of my visitor was discoverable in my room the next morning, as my nurse tells me, my blue necktie was in reality found upon the floor, crushed and torn into a shapeless bundle of frayed rags.

As for the club entertainment, I am told that, despite my absence, it was a wonderful success, redeemed from failure, the treasurer of the club said, by the voluntary services of a guest, who secured admittance on one of my cards, and who executed some sleight-of-hand tricks that made the members tremble, and whose mind-reading feats performed on the club's butler not only made it necessary for him to resign his office, but disclosed to the House Committee the whereabouts of several cases or rare wines that had mysteriously disappeared.

When an idea matters enough to a writer, he may try his hand at it more than once. Ray Bradbury penned at least two tales about censorship—"Usher II" and "The Exiles"—before writing Fahrenheit 451 *and in* The Pickwick Papers *Charles Dickens included an independent short story, "The Goblins Who Stole a Sexton," identical in theme and similar in structure to* A Christmas Carol. *In like fashion,* ROBERT LOUIS STEVENSON *(1850–1894), Scottish author of* Kidnapped, The Master of Ballantrae, Treasure Island *and other well-loved novels and stories, explored the problem of good and evil warring within the same human breast in his oft-filmed novella* The Strange Case of Doctor Jekyll and Mr. Hyde *and in the following short story, which was effectively dramatized in the early days of television with Ray Milland in the title role and Rod Steiger as The Devil.*

Markheim
BY ROBERT LOUIS STEVENSON

"Yes," said the dealer, "our windfalls are of various kinds. Some customers are ignorant, and then I touch a dividend on my superior knowledge. Some are dishonest," and here he held up the candle, so that the light fell strongly on his visitor, "and in that case," he continued, "I profit by my virtue."

Markheim had but just entered from the daylight streets, and his eyes had not yet grown familiar with the mingled shine and darkness in the shop. At these pointed words, and before the near presence of the flame, he blinked painfully and looked aside.

The dealer chuckled. "You come to me on Christmas Day," he resumed, "when you know that I am alone in my house, put up my shutters, and make a point of refusing business. Well, you will have to pay for that; you will have to pay for my loss of time, when I should be balancing my books; you will have to pay, besides, for a kind of manner that I remark in you to-day very strongly: I am the essence of discretion, and ask no awkward questions; but when a customer cannot look me in the eye, he has to pay for it." The dealer once more chuckled; and then, changing to his usual business voice, though still with a note of irony, "You can give, as usual, a clear account of how you came into the possession of the object?" he continued. "Still your uncle's cabinet? A remarkable collector, sir!"

And the little pale, round-shouldered dealer stood almost on tip-toe, looking over the top of his gold spectacles, and nodding his head with every mark of disbelief. Markheim returned his gaze with one of infinite pity, and a touch of horror.

"This time," said he, "you are in error. I have not come to sell, but to buy. I have no curios to dispose of; my uncle's cabinet is bare to the wainscot; even were it still intact, I have done well on the Stock Exchange, and should more likely add to it than otherwise, and my errand to-day is simplicity itself. I seek a Christmas present for a lady," he continued, waxing more fluent as he struck into the speech he had prepared; "and certainly I owe you every excuse for thus disturbing you upon so small a matter. But the thing was neglected yesterday; I must produce my little compliment at dinner; and, as you very well know, a rich marriage is not a thing to be neglected."

There followed a pause, during which the dealer seemed to weigh this statement incredulously. The ticking of many clocks among the curious lumber of the shop, and the faint rushing of the cabs in a near thoroughfare, filled up the interval of silence.

"Well, sir," said the dealer, "be it so. You are an old customer after all; and if, as you say, you have the chance of a good marriage, far be it from me to be an obstacle. Here is a nice thing for a lady now," he went on, "this hand glass—fifteenth century, warranted; comes from a good collection, too; but I reserve the name, in the interests of my customer, who was just like yourself, my dear sir, the nephew and sole heir of a remarkable collector."

The dealer, while he thus ran on in his dry and biting voice, had stooped to take the object from its place; and, as he had done so, a shock had passed through Markheim, a start both of hand and foot, a sudden leap of many tumultuous passions to the face. It passed as swiftly as it came, and left no trace beyond a certain trembling of the hand that now received the glass.

"A glass," he said hoarsely, and then paused, and repeated it more clearly. "A glass? For Christmas? Surely not?"

"And why not?" cried the dealer. "Why not a glass?"

Markheim was looking upon him with an indefinable expression. "You ask me why not?" he said. "Why, look here—look in it—look at yourself! Do you like to see it? No! nor I—nor any man."

The little man had jumped back when Markheim had so suddenly confronted him with the mirror; but now, perceiving there was nothing worse on hand, he chuckled.

"Your future lady, sir, must be pretty hard favoured," said he.

"I ask you," said Markheim, "for a Christmas present, and you give me this—this damned reminder of years, and sins and follies—this hand-conscience! Did you mean it? Had you a thought in your mind? Tell me. It will be better for you if you do. Come, tell me about yourself. I hazard a guess now, that you are in secret a very charitable man?"

The dealer looked closely at his companion. It was very odd, Markheim did not appear to be laughing; there was something in his face like an eager sparkle of hope, nothing of mirth.

"What are you driving at?" the dealer asked.

"Not charitable?" returned the other, gloomily. "Not charitable; not pious; not scrupulous; unloving, unbeloved; a hand to get money, a safe to keep it. Is that all? Dear God, man, is that all?"

"I will tell you what it is," began the dealer, with some sharpness, and then broke off again into a chuckle. "But I see this is a love match of yours, and you have been drinking the lady's health."

"Ah!" cried Markheim, with a strange curiosity. "Ah, have you been in love? Tell me about that."

"I," cried the dealer. "I in love! I never had the time, nor have I the time to-day for all this nonsense. Will you take the glass?"

"Where is the hurry?" returned Markheim. "It is very pleasant to stand here talking; and life is so short and insecure that I would not hurry away from any pleasure—no, not even from so mild a one as this. We should rather cling, cling to what little we can get, like a man at a cliff's edge. Every second is a cliff, if you think upon it—a cliff a mile high—high enough, if we fall, to dash us out of every feature of humanity. Hence it is best to talk pleasantly. Let us talk of each other; why should we wear this mask? Let us be confidential. Who knows, we might become friends?"

"I have just one word to say to you," said the dealer. "Either make your purchase, or walk out of my shop."

"True, true," said Markheim. "Enough fooling. To business. Show me something else."

The dealer stooped once more, this time to replace the glass upon the shelf, his thin blond hair falling over his eyes as he did so.

Markheim moved a little nearer, with one hand in the pocket of his greatcoat; he drew himself up and filled his lungs; at the same time many different emotions were depicted together on his face—terror, horror, and resolve, fascination and a physical repulsion; and through a haggard lift of his upper lip, his teeth looked out.

"This perhaps, may suit," observed the dealer; and then, as he began to re-arise, Markheim bounded from behind upon his victim. The long, skewerlike dagger flashed and fell. The dealer struggled like a hen, striking his temple on the shelf, and then tumbled on the floor in a heap.

Time had some score of small voices in that shop, some stately and slow as was becoming to their great age; others garrulous and hurried. All these told out the seconds in an intricate chorus of tickings. Then the passage of a lad's feet, heavily running on the pavement, broke in upon these smaller voices and startled Markheim into the consciousness of his surroundings. He looked about him awfully. The candle stood on the counter, its flame solemnly wagging in a draught; and by that inconsiderable movement, the whole room was filled with noiseless bustle and kept heaving like a sea: the tall shadows nodding, the gross blots of darkness swelling and dwindling as with respiration, the faces of the portraits and the china gods changing and wavering like images in water. The inner door stood ajar, and peered into that leaguer of shadows with a long slit of daylight like a pointing finger.

From these fear-stricken rovings, Markheim's eyes returned to the body of his victim, where it lay both humped and sprawling, incredibly small and strangely meaner than in life. In these poor, miserly clothes, in that ungainly attitude, the dealer lay like so much sawdust. Markheim had feared to see it, and, lo! it was nothing. And yet, as he gazed, this bundle of old clothes and pool of blood began to find eloquent voices. There it must lie; there was none to work the cunning hinges or direct the miracle of locomotion—there it must lie till it was found. Found! ay, and then? Then would this dead flesh lift up a cry that would ring over England, and fill the world with the echoes of pursuit. Ay, dead or not, this was still the enemy. "Time was that when the brains were out," he thought; and the first word struck into his mind. Time, now that the deed was accomplished—time, which had closed for the victim, had become instant and momentous for the slayer.

The thought was yet in his mind, when, first one and then another, with every variety of pace and voice—one deep as the bell from a cathedral turret, another ringing on its treble notes the prelude of a waltz—the clocks began to strike the hour of three in the afternoon.

The sudden outbreak of so many tongues in that dumb chamber staggered him. He began to bestir himself, going to and fro with the candle, beleaguered by moving shadows, and startled to the soul by chance reflections. In many rich mirrors, some of home designs, some from Venice or Amsterdam, he saw his face repeated and repeated, as it were an army of spies; his own eyes met and detected him; and the sound of his own steps, lightly as they fell, vexed the surrounding quiet. And still as he continued to fill his pockets, his mind accused him, with a sickening iteration, of the thousand faults of his design. He should have chosen a more quiet hour; he should have prepared an alibi; he should not have used a knife; he should have been more cautious, and only bound and gagged the dealer, and not killed him; he should have been more bold, and killed the servant also; he should have done all things otherwise; poignant regrets, weary, incessant toiling of the mind to change what was unchangeable, to plan what was now useless, to be the architect of the irrevocable past. Meanwhile, and behind all this activity, brute terrors, like the scurrying of rats in a deserted attic, filled the more remote chambers of his brain with riot; the hand of the constable would fall heavy on his shoulder, and his nerves would jerk like a hooked fish; or he beheld, in galloping defile, the dock, the prison, the gallows, and the black coffin.

Terror of the people in the street sat down before his mind like a besieging army. It was impossible, he thought, but that some rumour of the struggle must have reached their ears and set on edge their curiosity; and now, in all the neighbouring houses, he divined them sitting motionless and with uplifted ear—solitary people, condemned to spend Christmas dwelling alone on memories of the past, and now startingly recalled from that tender exercise; happy family parties, struck into silence round the table, the mother still with raised finger: every degree and age and humour, but all, by their own hearths, prying and hearkening and weaving the rope that was to hang him. Sometimes it seemed to him he could not move too softly; the clink of the tall Bohemian goblets rang out loudly like a bell; and alarmed by the bigness of the ticking, he was tempted to stop the clocks. And then, again, with a swift transition of his terrors, the very silence of the place appeared a source of peril, and a thing to strike and freeze the passer-by; and he would step more boldly, and bustle aloud among the contents of the shop, and imitate, with elaborate bravado, the movements of a busy man at ease in his own house.

But he was now so pulled about by different alarms that, while one portion of his mind was still alert and cunning, another trembled on the brink of lunacy. One hallucination in particular took a strong hold on his credulity. The neighbour hearkening with white face beside his window, the passer-by arrested by a horrible surmise on the pavement —these could at worst suspect, they could not know; through the brick walls and shuttered windows only sounds could penetrate. But here, within the house, was he alone? He knew he was; he had watched the servant set forth sweethearting, in her poor best, "out for the day" written in every ribbon and smile. Yes, he was alone, of course; and yet, in the bulk of empty house above him, he could surely hear a stir of delicate footing—he was surely conscious, inexplicably conscious of some presence. Ay, surely; to every room and corner of the house his imagination followed it; and now it was a faceless thing, and yet had eyes to see with; and again it was a shadow of himself; and yet again behold the image of the dead dealer, reinspired with cunning and hatred.

At times, with a strong effort, he would glance at the open door which still seemed to repel his eyes. The house was tall, the skylight small and dirty, the day blind with fog; and the light that filtered down to the ground story was exceedingly faint, and showed dimly on the threshold of the shop. And yet, in that strip of doubtful brightness, did there not hang wavering a shadow?

Suddenly, from the street outside, a very jovial gentleman began to beat with a staff on the shop-door, accompanying his blows with shouts and railleries in which the dealer was continually called upon by name. Markheim, smitten into ice glanced at the dead man. But no! he lay quite still; he was fled away far beyond earshot of these blows and shoutings; he was sunk beneath seas of silence; and his name, which would once have caught his notice above the howling of a storm, had become an empty sound. And presently the jovial gentleman desisted from his knocking and departed.

Here was a broad hint to hurry what remained to be done, to get forth from this accusing neighbourhood, to plunge into a bath of London multitudes, and to reach, on the other side of day, that haven of safety and apparent innocence—his bed. One visitor had come: at any moment another might follow and be more obstinate. To have done the deed, and yet not to reap the profit, would be too abhorrent a failure. The money, that was now Markheim's concern; and as a means to that, the keys.

He glanced over his shoulder at the open door, where the shadow was still lingering and shivering; and with no conscious repugnance of the mind, yet with a tremor of the belly, he drew near the body of his victim. The human character had quite departed. Like a suit half-stuffed with bran, the limbs lay scattered, the trunk doubled, on the floor; and yet the thing repelled him. Although so dingy and inconsiderable to the eye, he feared it might have more significance to the touch. He took the body by the shoulders, and turned it on its back. It was strangely light and supple, and the limbs, as if they had been broken, fell into the oddest postures. The face was robbed of all expression; but it was as pale as wax, and shockingly smeared with blood about one temple. That was, for Markheim, the one displeasing circumstance. It carried him back, upon the instant, to a certain fair day in a fishers' village: a gray day, a piping wind, a crowd upon the street, the blare of brasses, the booming of drums, the nasal voice of a ballad singer; and a boy going to and fro, buried over head in the crowd and divided between interest and fear, until, coming out upon the chief place of concourse, he beheld a booth and a great screen with pictures, dismally designed, garishly coloured: Brownrigg with her apprentice; the Mannings with their murdered guest; Weare in the death-grip of Thurtell; and a score besides of famous crimes. The thing was as clear as an illusion; he was once again that little boy; he was looking once again, and with the same sense of physical revolt, at these vile pictures; he was still stunned by the thumping of the drums. A bar of that day's music returned upon his memory; and at that, for the first time, a qualm came over him, a breath of nausea, a sudden weakness of the joints, which he must instantly resist and conquer.

He judged it more prudent to confront than to flee from these considerations; looking the more hardily in the dead face, bending his mind to realise the nature and greatness of his crime. So little a while ago that face had moved with every change of sentiment, that pale mouth had spoken, the body had been all on fire with governable energies; and now, and by his act, that piece of life had been arrested, as the horologist, with interjected finger, arrests the beating of the clock. So he reasoned in vain; he could rise to no more remorseful consciousness; the same heart which had shuddered before the painted effigies of crime, looked on its reality unmoved. At best, he felt a gleam of pity for one who had been endowed in vain with all those faculties that can make the world a garden of enchantment, one who had never lived and who was now dead. But of penitence, no, not a tremor.

With that, shaking himself clear of these considerations, he found the keys and advanced towards the open door of the shop. Outside, it had begun to rain smartly; and the sound of the shower upon the roof had banished silence. Like some dripping cavern, the chambers of the house were haunted by an incessant echoing, which filled the ear and mingled with the ticking of the clocks. And, as Markheim approached the door, he seemed to hear, in answer to his own cautious tread, the steps of another foot withdrawing up the stair. The shadow still palpitated loosely on the threshold. He threw a ton's weight of resolve upon his muscles, and drew back the door.

The faint, foggy daylight glimmered dimly on the bare floor and stairs; on the bright suit of armour posted, halbert in hand, upon the landing; and on the dark wood-carvings, and framed pictures that hung against the yellow panels of the wainscot. So loud was the beating of the rain through all the house that, in Markheim's ears, it began to be distinguished into many different sounds. Footsteps and sighs, the tread of regiments marching in the distance, the chink of money in the counting, and the creaking of doors held stealthily ajar, appeared to mingle with the patter of the drops upon the cupola and the gushing of the water in the pipes. The sense that he was not alone grew upon him to the verge of madness. On every side he was haunted and begirt by presences. He heard them moving in the upper chambers; from the shop, he heard the dead man getting to his legs; and as he began with a great effort to mount the stairs, feet fled quietly before him and followed stealthily behind. If he were but deaf, he thought, how tranquilly he would possess his soul! And then again, and hearkening with ever fresh attention, he blessed himself for that unresting sense which held the outposts and stood a trusty sentinel upon his life. His head turned continually on his neck; his eyes, which seemed starting from their orbits, scouted on every side, and on every side were half-rewarded as with the tail of something nameless vanishing. The four-and-twenty steps to the first floor were four-and-twenty agonies.

On that first storey, the doors stood ajar, three of them like three ambushes, shaking his nerves like the throats of cannon. He could never again, he felt, be sufficiently immured and fortified from men's observing eyes; he longed to be home, girt in by walls, buried among bedclothes, and invisible to all but God. And at that thought he wondered a little, recollecting tales of other murderers and the fear they were said to entertain of heavenly avengers. It was not so, at least, with him. He feared the laws of nature, lest, in their callous and immutable procedure, they should preserve some damning evidence of his crime. He feared tenfold more, with a slavish, superstitious terror, some scission in the continuity of man's experience, some wilful illegality of nature. He played a game of skill, depending on the rules, calculating consequence from cause; and what if nature, as the defeated tyrant overthrew the chess-board, should break the mould of their succession? The like had befallen Napoleon (so writers said) when the winter changed the time of its appearance. The like might befall Markheim: the solid walls might become transparent and reveal his doings like those of bees in a glass hive; the stout planks might yield under his foot like quicksands and detain him in their clutch; ay, and there were soberer accidents that might destroy him: if, for instance, the house should fall and imprison him beside the body of his victim; or the house next door should fly on fire, and the firemen invade him from all sides. These things he feared; and, in a sense, these things might be called the hands of God reached forth against sin. But about God himself he was at ease; his act was doubtless exceptional, but so were his excuses, which God knew; it was there, and not among men, that he felt sure of justice.

When he had got safe into the drawing-room, and shut the door behind him, he was aware of a respite from alarms. The room was quite dismantled, uncarpeted besides, and strewn with packing cases and incongruous furniture; several great pier-glasses, in which he beheld himself at various angles, like an actor on a stage; many pictures, framed and unframed, standing, with their faces to the wall; a fine Sheraton sideboard, a cabinet of marquetry, and a great old bed, with tapestry hangings. The windows opened to the floor; but by great good fortune the lower part of the shutters had been closed, and this concealed him from the neighbours. Here, then, Markheim drew in a packing case before the cabinet, and began to search among the keys. It was a long business, for there were many; and it was irksome, besides; for, after all, there might be nothing in the cabinet, and time was on the wing. But the closeness of the occupation sobered him. With the tail of his eye he saw the door—even glanced at it from time to time directly, like a besieged commander pleased to verify the good estate of his defences. But in truth he was at peace. The rain falling in the street sounded natural and pleasant. Presently, on the other side, the notes of a piano were wakened to the music of a hymn, and the voices of many children took up the air and words. How stately, how comfortable was the melody! How fresh the youthful voices! Markheim gave ear to it smilingly, as he sorted out the keys; and his mind was thronged with answerable ideas and images; church-going children and the pealing of the high organ; children afield, bathers by the brookside, ramblers on the brambly common, kite-flyers in the windy and cloud-navigated sky; and then, at another cadence of the hymn, back again to church, and the somnolence of summer Sundays, and the high genteel voice of the parson (which he smiled a little to recall) and the painted Jacobean tombs, and the dim lettering of the Ten Commandments in the chancel.

And as he sat thus, at once busy and absent, he was startled to his feet. A flash of ice, a flash of fire, a bursting gush of blood, went over him, and then he stood transfixed and thrilling. A step mounted the stair slowly and steadily, and presently a hand was laid upon the knob, and the lock clicked, and the door opened.

Fear held Markheim in a vice. What to expect he knew not, whether the dead man walking, or the official ministers of human justice, or some chance witness blindly stumbling in to consign him to the gallows. But when a face was thrust into the aperture, glanced round the room, looked at him, nodded and smiled as if in friendly recognition, and then withdrew again, and the door closed behind it, his fear broke loose from his control in a hoarse cry. At the sound of this the visitant returned.

"Did you call me?" he asked, pleasantly, and with that he entered the room and closed the door behind him.

Markheim stood and gazed at him with all his eyes. Perhaps there was a film upon his sight, but the outlines of the newcomer seemed to change and waver like those of the idols in the wavering candle-light of the shop; and at times he thought he knew him; and at times he thought he bore a likeness to himself; and always, like a lump of living terror, there lay in his bosom the conviction that this thing was not of the earth and not of God.

And yet the creature had a strange air of the commonplace, as he stood looking on Markheim with a smile; and when he added: "You are looking for the money, I believe?" it was in the tones of everyday politeness.

Markheim made no answer.

"I should warn you," resumed the other, "that the maid has left her sweetheart earlier than usual and will soon be here. If Mr. Markheim be found in this house, I need not describe to him the consequences."

"You know me?" cried the murderer.

The visitor smiled. "You have long been a favorite of mine," he said; "and I have long observed and often sought to help you."

"What are you?" cried Markheim: "the devil?"

"What I may be," returned the other, "cannot affect the service I propose to render you."

"It can," cried Markheim; "it does! Be helped by you? No, never; not by you! You do not know me yet; thank God, you do not know me!"

"I know you," replied the visitant, with a sort of kind severity or rather firmness. "I know you to the soul."

"Know me!" cried Markheim. "Who can do so? My life is but a travesty and slander on myself. I have lived to belie my nature. All men do; all men are better than this disguise that grows about and stifles them. You see each dragged away by life, like one whom bravos have seized and muffled in a cloak. If they had their own control—if you could see their faces, they would be altogether different, they would shine out for heroes and saints! I am worse than most; myself is more overlaid; my excuse is known to me and God. But, had I the time, I could disclose myself."

"To me?" inquired the visitant.

"To you before all," returned the murderer. "I supposed you were intelligent. I thought—since you exist—you would prove a reader of the heart. And yet you would propose to judge me by my acts! Think of it; my acts! I was born and I have lived in a land of giants; giants have dragged me by the wrists since I was born out of my mother—the giants of circumstance. And you would judge me by my acts! But can you not look within? Can you not understand that evil is hateful to me? Can you not see within me the clear writing of conscience, never blurred by any wilful sophistry, although too often disregarded?

Can you not read me for a thing that surely must be common as humanity—the unwilling sinner?"

"All this is very feelingly expressed," was the reply, "but it regards me not. These points of consistency are beyond my province, and I care not in the least by what compulsion you may have been dragged away, so as you are but carried in the right direction. But time flies; the servant delays, looking in the faces of the crowd and at the pictures on the hoardings, but still she keeps moving nearer; and remember, it is as if the gallows itself was striding towards you through the Christmas streets! Shall I help you; I, who know all? Shall I tell you where to find the money?"

"For what price?" asked Markheim.

"I offer you the service for a Christmas gift," returned the other.

Markheim could not refrain from smiling with a kind of bitter triumph. "No," said he, "I will take nothing at your hands; if I were dying of thirst, and it was your hand that put the pitcher to my lips, I should find the courage to refuse. It may be credulous, but I will do nothing to commit myself to evil."

"I have no objection to a death-bed repentance," observed the visitant.

"Because you disbelieve their efficacy!" Markheim cried.

"I do not say so," returned the other; "but I look on these things from a different side, and when the life is done my interest falls. The man has lived to serve me, to spread black looks under colour of religion, or to sow tares in the wheat-field, as you do, in a course of weak compliance with desire. Now that he draws so near to his deliverance, he can add but one act of service—to repent, to die smiling, and thus to build up in confidence and hope the more timorous of my surviving followers. I am not so hard a master. Try me. Accept my help. Please yourself in life as you have done hitherto; please yourself more amply, spread your elbows at the board; and when the night begins to fall and the curtains to be drawn, I tell you, for your greater comfort, that you will find it even easy to compound your quarrel with your conscience, and to make a truckling peace with God. I came but now from such a deathbed, and the room was full of sincere mourners, listening to the man's last words: and when I looked into that face, which had been set as a flint against mercy, I found it smiling with hope."

"And do you, then, suppose me such a creature?" asked Markheim.

"Do you think I have no more generous aspirations than to sin, and sin, and sin, and, at last, sneak into heaven? My heart rises at the thought. Is this, then, your experience of mankind? or is it because you find me with red hands that you presume such baseness? and is this crime of murder indeed so impious as to dry up the very springs of good?"

"Murder is to me no special category," replied the other. "All sins are murder, even as all life is war. I behold your race, like starving mariners on a raft, plucking crusts out of the hands of famine and feeding on each other's lives. I follow sins beyond the moment of their acting; I find in all that the last consequence is death; and to my eyes, the pretty maid who thwarts her mother with such taking graces on a question of a ball, drips no less visibly with human gore than such a murderer as yourself. Do I say that I follow sins? I follow virtues also; they differ not by the thickness of a nail, they are both scythes for the reaping angel of Death. Evil, for which I live, consists not in action but in character. The bad man is dear to me; not the bad act, whose fruits, if we could follow them far enough down the hurtling cataract of the ages, might yet be found more blessed than those of the rarest virtues. And it is not because you have killed a dealer, but because you are Markheim, that I offered to forward your escape."

"I will lay my heart open to you," answered Markheim. "This crime on which you find me is my last. On my way to it I have learned many lessons; itself is a lesson, a momentous lesson. Hitherto I have been driven with revolt to what I would not; I was a bondslave to poverty, driven and scourged. There are robust virtues that can stand in these temptations; mine was not so: I had a thirst of pleasure. But to-day, and out of this deed, I pluck both warning and riches—both the power and a fresh resolve to be myself. I become in all things a free actor in the world; I begin to see myself all changed, these hands the agents of good, this heart at peace. Something comes over me out of the past; something of what I have dreamed on Sabbath evenings to the sound of the church organ, of what I forecast when I shed tears over noble books, or talked, an innocent child, with my mother. There lies my life; I have wandered a few years, but now I see once more my city of destination."

"You are to use this money on the Stock Exchange, I think?" remarked the visitor; "and there, if I mistake not, you have already lost some thousands?"

"Ah," said Markheim, "but this time I have a sure thing."

"This time, again, you will lose," replied the visitor quietly.

"Ah, but I keep back the half!" cried Markheim.

"That also you will lose," said the other.

The sweat started upon Markheim's brow. "Well, then, what matter?" he exclaimed. "Say it be lost, say I am plunged again in poverty, shall one part of me, and that the worse, continue until the end to override the better? Evil and good run strong in me, haling me both ways. I do not love the one thing, I love all. I can conceive great deeds, renunciations, martyrdoms; and though I be fallen to such a crime as murder, pity is no stranger to my thoughts. I pity the poor; who knows their trials better than myself? I pity and help them; I prize love, I love honest laughter; there is no good thing nor true thing on earth but I love it from my heart. And are my vices only to direct my life, and my virtues to lie without effect, like some passive lumber of the mind? Not so; good, also, is a spring of acts."

But the visitant raised his finger. "For six-and-thirty years that you have been in this world," said he, "through many changes of fortune and varieties of humour, I have watched you steadily fall. Fifteen years ago you would have started at a theft. Three years back you would have blenched at the name of murder. Is there any crime, is there any cruelty or meanness, from which you still recoil?—five years from now I shall detect you in the fact! Downward, downward, lies your way; nor can anything but death avail to stop you."

"It is true," Markheim said huskily, "I have in some degree complied with evil. But it is so with all: the very saints, in the mere exercise of living, grow less dainty, and take on the tone of their surroundings."

"I will propound to you one simple question," said the other; "and as you answer, I shall read to you your moral horoscope. You have grown in many things more lax; possibly you do right to be so; and at any account, it is the same with all men. But granting that, are you in any one particular, however trifling, more difficult to please with your own conduct, or do you go in all things with a looser rein?"

"In any one?" repeated Markheim, with an anguish of consideration. "No," he added, with despair, "in none! I have gone down in all."

"Then," said the visitor, "content yourself with what you are, for you will never change; and the words of your part on this stage are irrevocably written down."

Markheim stood for a long while silent, and indeed it was the visitor who first broke the silence. "That being so," he said, "shall I show you the money?"

"And grace?" cried Markheim.

"Have you not tried it?" returned the other. "Two or three years ago, did I not see you on the platform of revival meetings, and was not your voice the loudest in the hymn?"

"It is true," said Markheim; "and I see clearly what remains for me by way of duty. I thank you for these lessons from my soul; my eyes are opened, and I behold myself at last for what I am."

At this moment, the sharp note of the door-bell rang through the house; and the visitant, as though this were some concerted signal for which he had been waiting, changed at once in his demeanour.

"The maid!" he cried. "She has returned, as I forewarned you, and there is now before you one more difficult passage. Her master, you must say, is ill; you must let her in, with an assured but rather serious countenance—no smiles, no overacting, and I promise you success! Once the girl within, and the door closed, the same dexterity that has already rid you of the dealer will relieve you of this last danger in your path. Thenceforward you have the whole evening—the whole night, if needful—to ransack the treasures of the house and to make good your safety. This is help that comes to you with the mask of danger. Up!" he cried: "up, friend; your life hangs trembling in the scales; up, and act!"

Markheim steadily regarded his counsellor. "If I be condemned to evil acts," he said, "there is still one door of freedom open—I can cease from action. If my life be an ill thing, I can lay it down. Though I be, as you say truly, at the beck of every small temptation, I can yet, by one decisive gesture, place myself beyond the reach of all. My love of good is damned to barrenness; it may, and let it be! But I have still my hatred of evil; and from that, to your galling disappointment, you shall see that I can draw both energy and courage."

The features of the visitor began to undergo a wonderful and lovely change: they brightened and softened with a tender triumph; and, even as they brightened, faded and dislimned. But Markheim did not pause to watch or understand the transformation. He opened the door and went downstairs very slowly, thinking to himself. His past went soberly before him; he beheld it as it was, ugly and strenuous like a dream, random as chance-medley—a scene of defeat. Life, as he thus reviewed it, tempted him no longer; but on the further side he perceived a quiet haven for his bark. He paused in the passage, and looked into the shop, where the candle still burned by the dead body. It was strangely silent. Thoughts of the dealer swarmed into his mind, as he stood gazing. And then the bell once more broke out into impatient clamour.

He confronted the maid upon the threshold with something like a smile.

"You had better go for the police," said he: "I have killed your master."

JAY SHECKLEY *is one of the most promising young writers in modern science-fantasy. Her short fiction has appeared in* Twilight Zone, Night Cry, National Lampoon, Heavy Metal, Pulpsmith, *and several other periodicals, as well as in a German language edition of her selected stories called* Frog Princes, Starships *and* Editors: Tales of the Bizarre. *A former newspaper editor, bank guard, printer and college writing instructor, Jay says of herself, "I'm fond of tigerlilies, lilacs and roses, and no doubt as a Dantean torment am allergic to roses."*

Lost Soul

BY JAY SHECKLEY

In Dr. Gozer's glitzy plant-ridden waiting room, Mrs. Evaline Powys read *People* magazine. The cover article said that spiritual growth doesn't come easy: The stars of stage and screen (so rich, so pressed for time) paid royally for bliss via quickie divorce, haute couture, palaces, drugs and de-drugging, servants and savants. These freed the star psyche "to learn and to grow." Evaline read this and wanted it too.

Evaline Powys was just an office manager, but she believed in what the stars did—the work ethic, designer goods, taking yourself seriously, family and marriage as romance. Waiting for the doctor, she reflected that these past eight months she had something the stars valued, but hardly ever had: a good marriage. Then Evaline's name was called and she learned she was destined to grow.

"Evaline, you are pregnant," Dr. Gozer said, grinning as if he'd done the deed.

Evaline unlatched her briefcase and withdrew an appointment book. "And when exactly is my child due?"

Gozer named a day, and she marked it down in pen. That done, she shook his hand and left. In the car, snapping on the left turn signal, she decided to tell Joe after dinner at eight. All the drive back to the office and later all the way home she pictured her husband's excited face crossed with the proud, shy, concerned look she'd seen in so many movies. Tonight she and Joe would score a second point against those stars.

At eight, across gravy-coated microware, she rose to her feet and spoke over the blare of the TV. "Joe, on May 24th you will be a father." Then she sat, smiling to herself, awaiting his thrilled response. But Joe just nodded. Evaline rambled on about cleaning the spare room, and the best sorts of baby-clothes, so as to make it seem real to him, ending on her ideas about babies as the fulfillment of romantic marriage. Joe just nodded again, sipped at his Coors, and tried to watch the documentary on toxic waste.

"Joe?" Evaline asked. "How do you feel?"

"Huh? A little indigestion." He felt his belly, then burped. She looked at him watching television. His eyes were fixed, his complexion pasty. She had the distinct impression that this was not her husband.

Evaline went to bed early. Between fresh starched sheets she cried and cried. Joe came into the bedroom briefly saying, "Come on, Evvy. Don't fret." When she got up to use the bathroom, Joe was nowhere to be seen. But then she did see him: He was by the front door, balancing a felt hat on the tip of an old black umbrella. Joe was humming to himself. To end his little performance he tossed the hat, caught it on his head, and said, "Whee!" Decidedly odd.

If only she could believe he was just celebrating the idea of a baby. But this past week, Evaline now recalled, he had made several little jokes (so unlike him), had forgotten their first-date anniversary, and had claimed to actually *like* TV, take-out food, and the neighbor's vicious mongrel. Joe was obviously ill, that was it, thank God! Her marriage could be cured. That night Evaline dreamt of her ambient presence ever at the side of Joe's hospital bed.

Thursday at two the Powys were excused from their jobs and headed to see the doctor in fashionable Cedar Hills. "Dr. Gozer has every available test right in his office," Evaline told Joe.

"I'll take the curtain," Joe said. He wasn't himself. But Evaline knew that if anyone could put a physiological tag on Joe's behavior, it was Dr. Gozer. Joe would be given a Restorative shot, or hospitalized until the condition passed. She waited, reading *Time*.

Inside, Joe let the nurses offer his fluids and surfaces to gizmos. Things were aimed at him: "Bzzz." Things were fed him: "Yuck." Things were stuck in him: "Ah!" Paper strips and pills and droppers and rectangles of glass were dunked in his fluids, which by now filled tiny cups on almost every countertop around Gozer's medical obstacle course. Gozer himself passed by Joe once saying, "Well, well, now," and sticking a tiny miner's lantern into Joe's nine orifices. "Well, now, yourself," Joe said.

Gozer switched to "Hm," and left the room.

At last Joe sat dressed and unprobed in the doctor's consulting room, expected to "just relax." He was unwrapping a green lollipop when Gozer traipsed in, tailed by Evaline. Under Gozer's arm were three manila folders, red-marked with the names of allergens. "And what brings you in today, Mr."—the doctor cribbed from the top folder—"Mr.—uh—Powys?"

Joe smiled, pointing with the lollipop. "She brings me in, that's what."

"And just what is the trouble?"

Joe shrugged, and Evaline said, "That's what we're asking *you,* Doctor. What's wrong with him?"

The doctor turned to her. "I don't know that anything *is* the matter. He has not got very interesting blood pressure, heart not sending any interesting clues. He's young for it, but I checked his prostate. Stool sample, also fine. Blood workup, urinalysis, barium flouroscopy, X-rays, angiogram: Dull, dull, dull. No great news, no imminent tragedy. In brief, Mr.—uh—Powys, you're a thirty-six-year-old man with the body of a thirty-six-year-old man. You underwent a company physical not three months ago; you have no complaints and extra exhaustive physical workups not being covered by insurance. So— I am curious: Why are you here? Why now?"

The lollipop again pointed to Evaline. Coloring, she explained how he seemed different, lighthearted and full of jokes, but he didn't have any reaction to fatherhood, or her. "He seems not as warm, not as *human* as he was. I thought maybe—he's losing his mental faculties?"

Joe made the "aw, go on," gesture, as if waving her away.

"Bad depression?" she asked. *Parade* had run an article on it. "Chronic pain leading to social withdrawal? Just so long as it's curable, please!"

"Now, now," Dr. Gozer said, "Marriage entails adjustments, and counseling can help. But see this?" He held up a large, oddly Technicolor X-ray of a man's torso. "This is you, Joe." They peered at it. "Have a gander. This office is the only one in the state with a privately owned Thermodaemonic Magnascanner."

"Is that the good news or the bad?"

"Joe!"

"With Thermodaemonic Magnascanning, much exploratory surgery will be unnecessary. We can detect and monitor growths, tumors, certain cardiac problems, looking at them safely on an hourly basis." Gozer clipped a half dozen more scans on the wall viewers. "These are six other patients' TDM scans. Any difference between yours and theirs?"

"All I see," said Joe, "is Kodachromes of a fire."

Evaline frowned. "Joe's doesn't have that same yellow candle flame type thing in his belly." She bit her lip.

"Sharp eyes!" the doctor said. He chuckled. "It's really nothing. But it's funny. Thermodaemonics means—no, nothing about demons, it means 'of heat and soul.' Crude heat readers were used by Spiritualists in Europe and the Orient for maybe a hundred years. From these gypsy acts and carnival quacks we get the myth that if the yellow flame fades, the subject is dying. True, you don't see that yellow flame in even a recent corpse, and today's the first living man I've met without one."

Gozer laughed again, and summed up. "Mystics say that yellow shape is the soul. Well, I'm just an internist and I think you check out pretty good. Also important here, you say you feel fine?"

"Speaking," said Joe.

"Okay!" Gozer said in parting. "Chalk up one for the books!"

The doctor could think of it that way, but not Evaline. Fierce rain lashed the parking lot, and when she got behind the Chevette's wheel, she began to cry. "Baby!" she squeaked. "Father with no soul— O! This is the worst thing ever happened to me."

Joe pressed his face against hers, felt the coarseness of her styling mousse. "But Evvy. Nothin's happened to *you*. This happened to *me*. And I refuse to care one way or the other about that—"

Evaline shook away from him. "Easy for *you* not to care! You have no soul!"

Joe straightened. "Our baby can't care about who has yellow blobs on a thermo-dema-whatsis. Your doctor don't care. Right? Right? I don't care if *you* flunk *your* next physical. But you care just enough to invent problems and I want you to stop this now!"

"What'll we *do*? Oh, I knew something was horribly wrong with you. You should see your eyes when you watch TV."

"I am *fine. FINE!* Would you cheer up if I joined a church?"

"You'd do that?"

"Sure. I'm beginning to think churches are pretty amusing."

Evaline turned the ignition. Despite water over the visible world, the car started. Enough talk, she thought bitterly. Who could talk seriously with a man with no soul? Who could throw her lot in with a man with no soul? If marriage is "the union of two souls," Evaline's womb harbored a bastard.

Now, Evaline wasn't religious; she never said grace. But every living person on Earth had a soul except Evaline Powys' husband. This was this completely unromantic. She felt cut off from all normal human business. Evaline drove on through the grey and black rain-whipped suburbs. *Talk about thoughtlessness: Soullessness was out-of-bounds, literally unheard of, and simply not done.*

Mrs. Powys believed in the good life. That meant taking yourself seriously, working to get that ambience we all deserve. Aware there was no known medical cure, she didn't give up. For most of the next month, during lunch breaks and the half hour before tackling the housework and dinner, Evaline tried to understand and resolve her situation. She read up on souls in the library. One day she went to confession, although not Catholic herself, and the priest accepting that lunch hour's peccadillos told her, "Your doctor is wrong. It is a sin to judge your husband." Then the priest called her "child." Evaline was not being taken seriously.

One bright day, Evaline was lunching in a heavy coat by the city fountain on a croissant and some overpriced cheese. As her blood sugar rose, she acknowledged there was no other way: She must leave Mr. Spiritual Vacuum. Better alone than her soul aching a lifetime for his—for his void.

Returning to her work station, she rode the red-carpeted elevator, mind at ease. She was forced to abandon the situation, that's all. But then a terrible question leapt into her mind, and the elevator operator had to remind her to get out on "5." Once in the architectural firm, she got use of Mr. Todd's office to make a private call. Such was the panic in her voice that Gozer's squad of starched women let her speak to him. When she asked his opinion, he just kept laughing. "No, no, I don't think so, Mrs. Powys. Remember, most babies are normal. Never heard of one with *this* problem. But say, if you want, come down and we'll scan your belly; see what Junior's like, eh?"

She mumbled salutations, hung up. She didn't want any baby of hers tested. Might be dangerous. Evaline wanted the baby regardless.

But soulless Joe was still another matter. How long could a lady endure a husband no spiritually finer than a warthog?

By the end of the workday she knew she'd leave Joe before she became completely degraded by this bestial accident. Although she'd meant her vows not ten months before, he passed for human then, and she was somebody else now herself: agitated, tired and frustrated. Which made her ill-tempered, shrill and crabby-faced. And the whole thing was getting worse: Last night when she'd asked Joe to put out the garbage, he said, "How about later?" When asked couldn't he smell it, he said, "I *like* the smell of eggs and old coffee grounds." Disgusting! But one had to consider that the poor man had no soul.

By five Evaline had in hand a three-page, two-day list of errands in preparation for leaving her husband. By five-thirty she'd done a little payroll work, forwarded the ten phone lines, locked up, and set off for the Cedar Hills Mall. Evaline had a lot to do: She had to stock up on baby clothes which he really should pay for; and her wardrobe wasn't what it should be. Luckily she'd just read an article on filling the gaps. Also, Evaline was well aware that wives (even of men without souls) need curtains and carpets and end tables and color-accent soap dishes. *She* still cared about a lot of things. Funny she hadn't guessed before from the way Joe had suggested they set up the living room; soulless people understood zilch about creating a homey environment.

After picking up some housewares in a department store lower level, Evaline discovered herself buying shirts for Joe. Well, anyone but Joe could enjoy the sight. Later she picked up frozen dinners for them, because—soullessly—Joe never complained. A shame about Joe, she thought, making out the grocer's check. He was easy to deal with, and it wasn't really his fault. If only his lack of a soul didn't set her on edge. If only she could be as easygoing, as happy as *he* seemed . . .

But passing a rack of women's magazines she saw headlines such as MAKING YOUR SINGLE LIFE HAPPEN! and IS HE REALLY WORTH IT? Just another night with the soulless wonder; one of trillions if she didn't go. A block from home she almost rear-ended a pickup full of children and dogs. Time to switch to decaf.

Joe wasn't any trouble that night. He ate his frozen dinner, watched a repeat mini-series re-reenacting the Second World War yet again. Then he watched bombings, killings, protests and dire fiscal predictions on the news. Afterwards he stretched himself, peaceful as could be, and said, "Let's turn in, Evvy."

She just couldn't. Instead of joining him, Evaline spent the next hours scrubbing places in the kitchen she'd never thought of. When she left, she'd be leaving him a clean place. She rinsed her hands, took a final dab at the counter, and tiptoed into the bedroom. By the streetlight she saw his sleeping face, his breath regular as the alarm clock's tick. Who would ever have known?

During her next day's lunch hour, Evaline tensely strode the downtown sidewalks, jumping shop to shop, gathering the last things needed for flight. Confused, exhausted, she wished she could throw *him* out, but couldn't bear the thought of talking it out, seeing how reasonable he'd be.

Twenty minutes remained on her lunch hour. She was driving herself too hard. Newly wed, expecting by spring, living with a spiritual mutant, about to lose her home: It was too much. Lately, she'd been snapping at people at work. They should know office manager is a hard job, but still, she was messing up.

Evaline rushed to make the WALK sign, but a young red-haired man with a clipboard stepped into her path, saying, "Excuse me!"

"Only if you let me by," she said. The light read DON'T WALK now.

"Spare sixty seconds?" he asked. "For our free personality test?"

"Why?"

"It'll help you. Try this: 'Do you often, usually, or never feel unlucky, angry or trapped?'"

"What if I do?" Evaline was offended. "Is that a crime?"

"Oh, no! How 'bout this: 'Your spouse (if married) or closest friend or partner (if single) is not what you had hoped.' True or false?"

"That's not personality," Evaline said, "that's misery. Who gets this information?"

"We test how you see yourself in the world. Confidential. You get yours back, take it into that corner building. No, the big one with the book displays. Gary or one of the other counselors will explain your result and tell you how to get freed."

Evaline saw she'd missed the light again. "Okay," she said in her tough-cookie voice, "Freed from what, pray tell?"

"Freed from all the miseries and bad acts and negative emotions and disappointments which are carried inside of you, poisoning your moods and your ability to see clearly."

"Well! That's *one* explanation for how I feel," Evaline said. "Have a nice afternoon."

"Go on and say hi to Gary," the young man said. "You'll feel better about things." Evaline thought, what-the-hell, she might even go say hi to Gary, if that would make her feel so great. But the young man added, "See, our troubles are really all within us."

"Bullshit," Evaline said. Before a storefront full of psychotherapy books, she tried to recall her next errand. A tall fit man wearing a red logger shirt and a big smile was talking to her. "Pardon?"

"Glad you came," he said. "My name's Gary. I can tell you're in a hurry, so come this way and I'll give you a brochure, and even coffee or tea if you want." Gary had already ducked under the building's granite archway, and Evaline followed, explaining she could not stay. Inside, she saw no one, and just as she turned to go, there was Gary handing her a styrofoam cup of tea, and saying, "I bet if you had one question it would be, 'What can these books and seminars really do for *you?*' Right?"

The tea was overfull. She sipped at it. "I doubt if—"

The big guy laughed. "I haven't told you anything you *can* doubt yet."

"One for you."

"Okay, now, what's your name?"

"Evaline."

"Pretty name." He looked her in the eye. "Evaline, I see before me one very distressed woman. She's employed, strong, independent." His voice was sure, soothing. "But I see on her face, I feel from her eyes, her hands, everything—some situation is getting the better of her. Evaline, believe me, you don't have to be beat down by circumstance."

"Huh." She was looking for an exit.

"Once your personality integrates you can take a lot more than you could ever cope with now."

"My personality *is* integrated."

"As you say. Before you go may I just show you one thing? In seconds I can *prove* that the Church of Personality Integration Through Science changed me: physically, objectively, permanently and for the better."

Evaline was overripe to leave; she lit a cigarette, hoping to be asked to step outside.

Gary smiled. "I used to do that. You're so much like I was. Moody, a tough customer. But what matters is"—here he winked—"my office is by the exit."

They walked, he talked. "My technical documentation may not mean much to you; you may prefer to read our handbook sold downstairs or come to some socials or seminars . . . I can't begin to tell how I suffered before learning techniques of Personality Integration. My head was stuffed with ancient rotted hopes. My heart was clotted with black anger." Gary shook his head. "It hurt day and night. But I got the joy back, Evaline. *You* can too." They rounded the corner into his office.

Evaline didn't get much from his words, but his sincerity was compelling. This was the longest personal conversation she'd had in a year. *Pathetic,* she thought. He rooted around in his desk for something.

"Now these are pictures of me," he was saying, "four months apart, with a lot of hard work in between. You probably don't know what to make of these—what the difference is—but I'll tell you."

"The yellow flame is gone!" Evaline said. She was holding up his Thermodaemonic Magnoscans. "It's gone!"

"That little spot," Gary said, "is where we store our sorrows, the hurts which poison us for always. The yogis knew about this. At the church, we call that spot The Suffer Center. Now, not everyone can snuff out theirs in four months. But you will start feeling more confident almost the day you start Seminar. And some have wiped out the little bugger in only six weeks." He turned around from the scan prints, looked at her. "You don't like the idea? Speak up! It's perfectly safe— Evaline? Come back a minute. Oh, all right. See you around. (I won't hold my breath, Nutcase.)"

Evaline left the Church of Personality Integration Through Science in a terrible state. Outside, she almost walked into a display window in which she suddenly saw herself. Evaline's cheeks were smeared with tears; the look on her face was vivid enough for panic and fixed enough for numb shock. In her right hand she saw a yellow brochure. Its headline read STOP SUFFERING NOW. Nothing, not even her plans for flight, made sense to her now. In no condition to shop, work, or drive, Evaline took an early bus home, and tried to relax on the zigzag-pattern sofa. Ruined careers, zombies and fiery Kodachromes danced through her muddled mind.

Finally, at five-forty, Joe wandered in with the mail. He was mildly surprised she was home before him. "Well, hello," he said, opening the mail and a beer. Evaline was glad he was there.

"Just tell me," she said urgently. "Were you ever a member of the Church of Personality Integration Through Science?"

"Run that by me again?"

"Joe! Were you?"

"No way, Evvy. Does that sound like me?"

"I guess not." She lay back down. Then she blurted, "They want *me* to join."

"So?"

"It takes away your soul; I saw the pictures." She explained about her afternoon. He hung up his overcoat, then tossed and caught his hat on the old umbrella.

"Huh," he said. "I always said souls were overrated. But if you join would you have to wear funny clothes and worship doilies? Hey, you wouldn't have to move out—like into their commune or something?"

Strange he mentioned moving out. "No, no. They're just asking if I'll take classes." She felt so weary. "That really raised my hackles this afternoon. I don't know."

"Anything that makes you happy might be pretty okay," Joe said. "You hungry as I am?" He went and looked in the freezer. She *was* hungry; she didn't know anymore which end was up.

Regardless, the next day the sun rose, and a shaky Evaline Powys went to her job. She told Mr. Todd she'd been sick. Mr. Todd nodded; she looked sick. During lunch Mrs. Joe Powys found herself at the Church of Personality Integration Through Science. Gary gave her his biggest smile. "Evaline!" he said. "Bet you've always wanted to learn about yourself, haven't you?"

"Yeah," she whispered.

"Everybody, from movie stars to garbagemen—everyone needs to learn and to grow, don't we?"

"Yeah," she murmured, "Yeah."

Fortunately, there was a lunch hour seminar just starting up. It was only a half hour, but she was able to sign up then and there for an introductory five-week in-depth evaluation.

That was the beginning. Within five months Evaline Powys became a radiant new mother. She quit her job to take care of little Amy, but with Personality Plus Day-Care it was no trouble to make time for Personality Tune-ups, plus do Personality Poll canvassing and even seminar speaking. Thirty percent of the Powys' family income goes to Church tuition, day-care and counseling, and Joe attends Church activities, too. He's popular because he enjoys *whatever* he does.

Best of all, their days of conflict are over. And thanks to Evaline's talent and hard work she has learned and grown so much: Already her Suffer Center has lost seventy percent of its mass, and the scans show that even that is fading fast.

Yes, Evaline and family has gone for all the gusto they can get. As they learn and grow like so many celebrities and ordinary folks before them, they never doubt they're doing the right thing. They feel great. Look at them now; watch 'em go. They function function function.

Hell, devils and the temptation of virtuous souls are essentially Christian concepts that do not form a significant part of Jewish thought or ritual, except in the mystical folklore of the Polish Chasidic sect, which ISAAC BASHEVIS SINGER *writes about so often. Born in 1904 and long a resident of Warsaw, Singer won the Nobel Prize for Literature for such works as* The Family Moskat, The Magician of Lublin, The Spinoza of Market Street *and many other novels and short stories.*

The Last Demon
BY ISAAC BASHEVIS SINGER

I, a demon, bear witness that there are no more demons left. Why demons, when man himself is a demon? Why persuade to evil someone who is already convinced? I am the last of the persuaders. I board in an attic in Tishevitz and draw my sustenance from a Yiddish storybook, a leftover from the days before the great catastrophe. The stories in the book are pablum and duck milk, but the Hebrew letters have a weight of their own. I don't have to tell you that I am a Jew. What else, a Gentile? I've heard that there are Gentile demons, but I don't know any, nor do I wish to know them. Jacob and Esau don't become in-laws.

I came here from Lublin. Tishevitz is a God-forsaken village; Adam didn't even stop to pee there. It's so small that a wagon goes through town and the horse is in the market place just as the rear wheels reach the toll gate. There is mud in Tishevitz from Succoth until Tishe b'Ov. The goats of the town don't need to lift their beards to chew at the thatched roofs of the cottages. Hens roost in the middle of the streets. Birds build nests in the women's bonnets. In the tailor's synagogue a billy goat is the tenth in the quorum.

Don't ask me how I managed to get to this smallest letter in the smallest of all prayer books. But when Asmodeus bids you go, you go. After Lublin the road is familiar as far as Zamosc. From there on you are on your own. I was told to look for an iron weathercock with a crow perched upon its comb on the roof of the study house. Once upon a time the cock turned in the wind, but for years now it hasn't moved, not even in thunder and lightning. In Tishevitz even iron weathercocks die.

I speak in the present tense as for me time stands still. I arrive. I look around. For the life of me I can't find a single one of our men. The cemetery is empty. There is no outhouse. I go to the ritual bathhouse, but I don't hear a sound. I sit down on the highest bench, look down on the stone on which the buckets of water are poured each Friday, and wonder. Why am I needed here? If a little demon is wanted, is it necessary to import one all the way from Lublin? Aren't there enough devils in Zamosc? Outside the sun is shining—it's close to the summer solstice—but inside the bathhouse it's gloomy and cold. Above me is a spider web, and within the web a spider wiggling its legs, seeming to spin but drawing no thread. There's no sign of a fly, not even the shell of a fly. "What does the creature eat?" I ask myself, "its own insides?" Suddenly I hear it chanting in a Talmudic singsong: "A lion isn't satisfied by a morsel and a ditch isn't filled up with dirt from its own walls."

I burst out laughing.

"Is that so? Why have you disguised yourself as a spider?"

"I've already been a worm, a flea, a frog. I've been sitting here for two hundred years without a stitch of work to do. But you need a permit to leave."

"They don't sin here?"

"Petty men, petty sins. Today someone covets another man's broom; tomorrow he fasts and puts peas in his shoes. Ever since Abraham Zalman was under the illusion that he was Messiah, the son of Joseph, the blood of the people has congealed in their veins. If I were Satan, I wouldn't even send one of our first-graders here."

"How much does it cost him?"

"What's new in the world?" he asks me.

"It's not been so good for our crowd."

"What's happened? The Holy Spirit grows stronger?"

"Stronger? Only in Tishevitz is he powerful. No one's heard of him in the large cities. Even in Lublin he's out of style."

"Well, that should be fine."

"But it isn't," I say. " 'All Guilty is worse for us than All Innocent.' It has reached a point where people want to sin beyond their capacities. They martyr themselves for the most trivial of sins. If that's the way it is, what are we needed for? A short while ago I was flying over Levertov Street, and I saw a man dressed in a skunk's coat. He had a black beard and wavy sidelocks; an amber cigar holder was clamped between his lips. Across the street from him an official's wife was walking, so it occurs to me to say, 'That's quite a bargain, don't you think, Uncle?' All I expected from him was a thought. I had my handkerchief ready if he should spit on me. So what does the man do? 'Why waste your breath on me?' he calls out angrily. 'I'm willing. Start working on her.' "

"What sort of misfortune is this?"

"Enlightenment! In the two hundred years you've been sitting on your tail here, Satan has cooked up a new dish of kasha. The Jews have now developed writers. Yiddish ones, Hebrew ones, and they have taken over our trade. We grow hoarse talking to every adolescent, but they print their *kitsch* by the thousands and distribute it to Jews everywhere. They know all our tricks—mockery, piety. They have a hundred reasons why a rat must be kosher. All that they want to do is to redeem the world. Why, if you could corrupt nothing, have you been left here for two hundred years? And if you could do nothing in two hundred years, what do they expect from me in two weeks?"

"You know the proverb, 'A guest for a while sees a mile.' "

"What's there to see?"

"A young rabbi has moved here from Modly Bozyc. He's not yet thirty, but he's absolutely stuffed with knowledge, knows the thirty-six tractates of the Talmud by heart. He's the greatest Cabalist in Poland, fasts every Monday and Thursday, and bathes in the ritual bath when the water is ice cold. He won't permit any of us to talk to him. What's more he has a handsome wife, and that's bread in the basket. What do we have to tempt him with? You might as well try to break through an iron wall. If I were asked my opinion, I'd say that Tishevitz should be removed from our files. All I ask is that you get me out of here before I go mad."

"No, first I must have a talk with this rabbi. How do you think I should start?"

"You tell me. He'll start pouring salt on your tail before you open your mouth."

"I'm from Lublin. I'm not so easily frightened."

On the way to the rabbi, I ask the imp, "What have you tried so far?"

"What haven't I tried?" he answers.

"A woman?"

"Won't look at one."

"Heresy?"

"He knows all the answers."

"Money?"

"Doesn't know what a coin looks like."

"Reputation?"

"He runs from it."

"Doesn't he look backwards?"

"Doesn't even move his head."

"He's got to have some angle."

"Where's it hidden?"

The window of the rabbi's study is open, and in we fly. There's the usual paraphernalia around: an ark with the Holy Scroll, bookshelves, a mezuzah in a wooden case. The rabbi, a young man with a blond beard, blue eyes, yellow sidelocks, a high forehead, and a deep widow's peak sits on the rabbinical chair peering in the Gemara. He's fully equipped: *yarmulka,* sash, and fringed garment with each of the fringes braided eight times. I listen to his skull: pure thoughts! He sways and chants in Hebrew, *"Rachel t'unah v'gazezah,"* and then translates, "a wooly sheep fleeced."

"In Hebrew Rachel is both a sheep and a girl's name," I say.

"So?"

"A sheep has wool and a girl has hair."

"Therefore?"

"If she's not androgynous, a girl has pubic hair."

"Stop babbling and let me study," the rabbi says in anger.

"Wait a second," I say, "Torah won't get cold. It's true that Jacob loved Rachel, but when he was given Leah instead, she wasn't poison. And when Rachel gave him Bilhah as a concubine, what did Leah do to spite her sister? She put Zilpah into his bed."

"That was before the giving of Torah."

"What about King David?"

"That happened before the excommunication by Rabbi Gershom."

"Before or after Rabbi Gershom, a male is a male."

"Rascal. *Shaddai kra Satan,"* the rabbi exclaims. Grabbing both of his sidelocks, he begins to tremble as if assaulted by a bad dream. "What nonsense am I thinking?" He takes his ear lobes and closes his ears. I keep on talking but he doesn't listen; he becomes absorbed in a difficult passage and there's no longer anyone to speak to. The little imp from Tishevitz says, "He's a hard one to hook, isn't he? Tomorrow he'll fast and roll in a bed of thistles. He'll give away his last penny to charity."

"Such a believer nowadays?"

"Strong as a rock."

"And his wife?"

"A sacrificial lamb."

"What of the children?"

"Still infants."

"Perhaps he has a mother-in-law?"

"She's already in the other world."

"Any quarrels?"

"Not even half an enemy."

"Where do you find such a jewel?"

"Once in awhile something like that turns up among the Jews."

"This one I've got to get. This is my first job around here. I've been promised that if I succeed, I'll be transferred to Odessa."

"What's so good about that?"

"It's as near paradise as our kind gets. You can sleep twenty-four hours a day. The population sins and you don't lift a finger."

"So what do you do all day?"

"We play with our women."

"Here there's not a single one of our girls." The imp sighs. "There was one old bitch but she expired."

"So what's left?"

"What Onan did."

"That doesn't lead anywhere. Help me and I swear by Asmodeus' beard that I'll get you out of here. We have an opening for a mixer of bitter herbs. You only work Passovers."

"I hope it works out, but don't count your chickens."

"We've taken care of tougher than he."

A week goes by and our business has not moved forward; I find myself in a dirty mood. A week in Tishevitz is equal to a year in Lublin. The Tishevitz imp is all right, but when you sit two hundred years in such a hole, you become a yokel. He cracks jokes that didn't amuse Enoch and convulses with laughter; he drops names from the Haggadah. Every one of his stories wears a long beard. I'd like to get the hell out of here, but it doesn't take a magician to return home with nothing. I have enemies among my colleagues and I must beware of intrigue. Perhaps I was sent here just to break my neck. When devils stop warring with people, they start tripping each other.

Experience has taught that of all the snares we use, there are three that work unfailingly—lust, pride, and avarice. No one can evade all three, not even Rabbi Tsots himself. Of the three, pride has the strongest meshes. According to the Talmud a scholar is permitted the eighth part of an eighth part of vanity. But a learned man generally exceeds his quota. When I see that the days are passing and that the rabbi of Tishevitz remains stubborn, I concentrate on vanity.

"Rabbi of Tishevitz," I say, "I wasn't born yesterday. I come from Lublin where the streets are paved with exegeses of the Talmud. We use manuscripts to heat our ovens. The floors of our attics sag under the weight of Cabala. But not even in Lublin have I met a man of your eminence. How does it happen," I ask, "that no one's heard of you? True saints should hide themselves, perhaps, but silence will not bring redemption. You should be the leader of this generation, and not merely the rabbi of this community, holy though it is. The time has come for you to reveal yourself. Heaven and earth are waiting for you. Messiah himself sits in the Bird Nest looking down in search of an unblemished saint like you. But what are you doing about it? You sit on your rabbinical chair laying down the law on which pots and which pans are kosher. Forgive me the comparison, but it is as if an elephant were put to work hauling a straw."

"Who are you and what do you want?" the rabbi asks in terror. "Why don't you let me study?"

"There is a time when the service of God requires the neglect of Torah," I scream. "Any student can study the Gemara."

"Who sent you here?"

"I was sent; I am here. Do you think they don't know about you up there? The higher-ups are annoyed with you. Broad shoulders must bear their share of the load. To put it in rhyme: the humble can stumble. Hearken to this: Abraham Zalman was Messiah, son of Joseph, and you are ordained to prepare the way for Messiah, son of David, but stop sleeping. Get ready for battle. The world sinks to the forty-ninth gate of uncleanliness, but you have broken through to the seventh firmament. Only one cry is heard in the mansions, the man from Tishevitz. The angel in charge of Edom has marshalled a clan of demons against you. Satan lies in wait also. Asmodeus is undermining you. Lilith and Namah hover at your bedside. You don't see them, but Shabriri and Briri are treading at your heels. If the Angels were not defending you, that unholy crowd would pound you to dust and ashes. But you do not stand alone, Rabbi of Tishevitz. Lord Sandalphon guards your every step. Metratron watches over you from his luminescent sphere. Everything hangs in the balance, man of Tishevitz; you can tip the scales."

"What should I do?"

"Mark well all that I tell you. Even if I command you to break the law, do as I bid."

"Who are you? What is your name?"

"Elijah the Tishbite. I have the ram's horn of the Messiah ready. Whether the redemption comes, or we wander in the darkness of Egypt another 2,689 years is up to you."

The rabbi of Tishevitz remains silent for a long time. His face becomes as white as the slips of paper on which he writes his commentaries.

"How do I know you're speaking the truth?" he asks in a trembling voice. "Forgive me, Holy Angel, but I require a sign."

"You are right. I will give you a sign."

And I raise such a wind in the rabbi's study that the slip of paper on which he is writing rises from the table and starts flying like a pigeon. The pages of the Gemara turn by themselves. The curtain of the Holy Scroll billows. The rabbi's *yarmulka* jumps from his head, soars to the ceiling, and drops back onto his skull.

"Is that how Nature behaves?" I ask.

"No."

"Do you believe me now?"

The rabbi of Tishevitz hesitates.

"What do you want me to do?"

"The leader of this generation must be famous."

"How do you become famous?"

"Go and travel in the world."

"What do I do in the world?"

"Preach and collect money."

"For what do I collect?"

"First of all collect. Later on I'll tell you what to do with the money."

"Who will contribute?"

"When I order, Jews give."

"How will I support myself?"

"A rabbinical emissary is entitled to a part of what he collects."

"And my family?"

"You will get enough for all."

"What am I supposed to do right now?"

"Shut the Gemara."

"Ah, but my soul yearns for Torah," the rabbi of Tishevitz groans. Nevertheless he lifts the cover of the book, ready to shut it. If he had done that, he would have been through. What did Joseph de la Rinah do? Just hand Samael a pinch of snuff. I am already laughing to myself, "Rabbi of Tishevitz, I have you all wrapped up." The little bathhouse imp, standing in a corner, cocks an ear and turns green with envy. True, I have promised to do him a favor, but the jealousy of our kind is stronger than anything. Suddenly the rabbi says, "Forgive me, my Lord, but I require another sign."

"What do you want me to do? Stop the sun?"

"Just show me your feet."

The moment the rabbi of Tishevitz speaks these words, I know everything is lost. We can disguise all the parts of our body but the feet. From the smallest imp right up to Ketev Meriri we all have the claws of geese. The little imp in the corner bursts out laughing. For the first time in a thousand years I, the master of speech, lose my tongue.

"I don't show my feet," I call out in rage.

"That means you're a devil. *Pik,* get out of here," the rabbi cries. He races to his bookcase, pulls out the *Book of Creation* and waves it menacingly over me. What devil can withstand the *Book of Creation?* I run from the rabbi's study with my spirit in pieces.

To make a long story short, I remain stuck in Tishevitz. No more Lublin, no more Odessa. In one second all my stratagems turn to ashes. An order comes from Asmodeus himself, "Stay in Tishevitz and fry. Don't go further than a man is allowed to walk on the Sabbath."

How long am I here? Eternity plus a Wednesday. I've seen it all, the destruction of Tishevitz, the destruction of Poland. There are no more Jews, no more demons. The women don't pour out water any longer on the night of the winter solstice. They don't avoid giving things in even numbers. They no longer knock at dawn at the antechamber of the synagogue. They don't warn us before emptying the slops. The rabbi was martyred on a Friday in the month of Nisan. The community was slaughtered, the holy books burned, the cemetery desecrated. The *Book of Creation* has been returned to the Creator. Gentiles wash themselves in the ritual bath. Abraham Zalman's chapel has been turned into a pig sty. There is no longer an Angel of Good nor an Angel of Evil. No more sins, no more temptations! The generation is already guilty seven times over, but Messiah does not come. To whom should he come? Messiah did not come for the Jews, so the Jews went to Messiah. There is no further need for demons. We have also been annihilated. I am the last, a refugee. I can go anywhere I please, but where should a demon like me go? To the murderers?

I found a Yiddish storybook between two broken barrels in the house which once belonged to Velvel the Barrelmaker. I sit there, the last of the demons. I eat dust. I sleep on a feather duster. I keep on reading gibberish. The style of the book is in our manner: Sabbath pudding cooked in pig's fat: blasphemy rolled in piety. The moral of the book is: neither judge, nor judgment. But nevertheless the letters are Jewish. The alphabet they could not squander. I suck on the letters and feed myself. I count the words, make rhymes, and tortuously interpret and reinterpret each dot.

> *Aleph,* the abyss, what else waited?
> *Bet,* the blow, long since fated.
> *Geemel,* God, pretending he knew,
> *Dalet,* death, its shadow grew.
> *Hey,* the hangman, he stood prepared;
> *Wov,* wisdom, ignorance bared.
> *Zayeen,* the zodiac, signs distantly loomed;
> *Chet,* the child, prenatally doomed.
> *Tet,* the thinker, an imprisoned lord;
> *Jod,* the judge, the verdict a fraud.

Yes, as long as a single volume remains, I have something to sustain me. As long as the moths have not destroyed the last page, there is something to play with. What will happen when the last letter is no more, I'd rather not bring to my lips.

> *When the last letter is gone,*
> *The last of the demons is done.*

—*Translated by Martha Glicklich and Cecil Hemley*

"Influencing the Hell Out of Time and Teresa Golowitz" is understandably one of the most popular stories ever to appear in Twilight Zone *magazine and, at this writing, was about to be televised on the network TV "The Twilight Zone" program.* PARKE GODWIN, *winner of the World Fantasy Award and twice the recipient of the Romantic Times award for outstanding historical fantasy (for his novels* Beloved Exile *and* The Last Rainbow), *has recently completed an autobiographical novel,* A Truce with Time, *to be published in 1987 by Bantam Books. In it, he closely modeled the character of Denny Landry on his own recently deceased brother Earl, whose memorable story "Daddy" appears earlier in this volume.*

Influencing the Hell Out of Time and Teresa Golowitz

BY PARKE GODWIN

The first conscious shock after the coronary was staring down at my own body huddled on the floor by the piano. The next was the fiftyish, harmless-looking total stranger helping himself to my liquor. His cordial smile matched the Brooks Brothers tailoring. An urbane Cecil Kellaway toasting me with my own scotch.

"Cheers, Mr. Bluestone. Hope you don't mind."

I found what passed for a voice. "The hell I don't. Who are you, and—and what's happened to me?"

For all the portly bulk of obvious good living, he moved lightly, settling in a Danish modern chair to sip at his purloined drink. "Glenmorangie single malt; one doesn't find much of it in the States. One: my friends call me the Prince. Two: you've just had your second and final heart attack."

Right so far: my first was two seasons back just after finishing the score for *Huey.*

"You've made the big league." The alleged Prince gestured with his drink at my inert form; rich gold links gleamed against snowy cuffs.

"No more diets, no more pills, backers' auditions or critics. You've crossed over."

I goggled at my corpulent residue. "Dead?"

"As Tutankhamen."

At first blush, there didn't seem much change. My penthouse living room, the East River and Roosevelt Island framed in the picture window with late winter sun. Lead sheets on the piano with Ernie Hammil's new lyrics. My wife Sarah's overpriced and underdesigned furniture, even the records I was listening to after lunch: Pete Rugolo and Stan Kenton, discs on the turntable, jackets on the shelf. For difference—me, very dead at the worst time.

"It couldn't wait? We open in two weeks, the second act needs three new songs, and God gives me this for *tsouris?*" I collapsed on the piano bench as my mind did a double take. "Wait a minute. Prince of what?"

His smile was too benign for the answer. "Darkness—or light, it depends on the translation. We do get deplorable press."

I took his point, not very reassured. "I'm not under arrest or something?"

"Of course not." He seemed to regard the question as gauche.

"Will anyone come?"

"Why should they?"

"Well, what do I do? Where do I go?"

The Prince opened his arms to infinite possibilities. "Where would you like to go? Before you answer hastily—" He sipped his scotch, sighing in savory judgment. "Oh, that *is* good. You see, you've cut your spiritual teeth on misconceptions. Good, bad, I'm in heaven, it's pure hell, all of which rather beg the distinction. We're familiarly known as Topside and Below Stairs."

"Below Stairs." I swallowed. "That's hell?"

"Eternity is an attitude. Some say it looks like Queens. You have free choice, Mr. Bluestone; bounded only by imagination and your own will to create—and that, for far too many, is living hell. For you: *carte blanche* to the past, present or future. Though I did have some small personal motive in dropping by."

"I thought so."

"Nonono. Not a collection but a request. We adore your music Below Stairs. Now that you're eligible, we hoped you'd visit for as long as you like. We've quite an art colony, hordes of theater folk.

Wilksey Booth would like to do a musical, and this very night there's a grand party at Petronius' house."

Adventure was not my long suit. "Thanks just the same, I'll stay here."

The Prince pursed his lips and frowned. "You never liked unpleasant scenes. You won't be found until Sarah gets back from Miami and by then not even the air-conditioning will help. There's going to be some abysmal Grand Guignol with the mortuary men, a rubber bag and your wife weeping buckets into a handkerchief."

Not likely. Sarah bought them at Bergdorf's, Belgian lace. For me she'd use Kleenex, the story of our marriage. We never even had children. Sarah was a real princess. Her only bedtime activities were fighting and headaches. For grief, she'd be spritzing the place with Airwick before they got the rubber bagful of me down the elevator. On the other hand, my last will and testament might get a Bergdorf hanky. The Actors' Fund would see a windfall. Sarah wouldn't.

The Prince nudged delicately at the elbow of my thoughts. "Pensive, Mr. Blaustein? It was Blaustein once."

"Not for thirty-five years. Didn't look good on a marquee."

"No fibbing."

"Okay: four years in an upper-class Washington high school. I used to dream I was a tall, blond WASP. On bad days even an Arab." Memories and reasons dissolved to another dusty but undimmed image. My Holy of Holies. Mary Ellen Cosgrove, super-*shiksa*. Wheat blond hair brushed thick and shining in a long pageboy, good legs, tight little boobs succinctly defined by an expensive sweater, sorority pin bobbling provocatively over the left one like Fay Wray hanging from the Empire State Building. I think my eyes really went from following the undulations of her *tush*. She was my first lust, aridly unrequited, but I played the piano well enough to be invited to all her Lambda Pi parties. Oscar Levant among the Goldwyn Girls with weak, horn-rimmed eyes, pimples and factory-reject teeth. Not much hope against jocks like Bob Bolling, who was born in a toothpaste ad.

But I could dream; beside me, Portnoy was a eunuch. My lust burned eternal in the secrecy of my bedroom as near nightly I plowed a fistful of ready, willing and totally unliberated Mary Ellen Cosgrove and panted to my pillow, *Why don't you love me?*

Because you're a nebbish, my pillow said.

The Prince apparently read the thought; his reponse was tinged with sympathy. "Yes. Mary Ellen."

"It's been forty years. I don't even know if she's still alive."

"More or less."

I was surprised to find how important it was. Past, present or future, the man said. Why not? The Prince's brows lifted in elegant question. "A decision?"

"You won't believe this."

"Try me, I'm jaded."

"I want to *shtup* Mary Ellen Cosgrove."

His urbane tolerance palled to disappointment. "That's all?"

"I've missed a lot of things in life. She was the first, we'll start there."

"My talented friend—*Faust,* for all its endurance, is pure propaganda. I should have thought at the very least an introduction to Mozart or Bach—"

"Look, for *bar mitzvah* I got ten bucks and a pen that leaked on white shirts. Now I'm dead; for door prize you want me to *klatsch* with harpsichord players? Later with the music, I want to ball Mary Ellen Cosgrove."

The Prince regarded me with cosmic weariness, steepling manicured fingertips under his chin. "I wonder. If memory serves, you last saw this Nordic nymphet in graduation week, 1945."

The growing eagerness made me tremble. "What happened to her?"

"You really want to know?"

"Maybe she's not a big deal after forty years, bubby. But she was the first. That's entitled."

"Let me think." The Prince leaned back, concentrating. "Cosgrove . . . from high school she wafted to a correct junior college, married a correct young man with a correctly promising future. Bob Bolling."

"I knew it! That horny bastard just wanted to score. Not just her, anybody."

"A fact Mr. Bolling belatedly appreciates; at eighteen he considered himself in love when he only needed to go to the bathroom. He spends less time on his libido now than his gall bladder; nevertheless, for his better days there is a pliant secretary who understands on cue. Mary Ellen has been relatively faithful."

"Relatively?"

The Prince's hands arced in graceful deprecation. "The usual. First affair at forty when her children were grown and no one seemed to need her any more. An aftermath of delicious guilt followed by anticlimax when no one found out, and one expensive face-lift. The last liaison, predictably, just after her younger daughter's wedding. Relatively, I say. She doesn't care that much now. Ennui is always safer than principles; it locks from the inside. Currently into vodka, vague malaise about the passage of time and what she imperfectly recalls as her 'golden, best years.' There are millions like her, Mr. Bluestone, perhaps billions. She never found much in herself beyond what men expected of her. For such people youth ought to be bright. It's their end."

His voice, cultivated with overtones of Harvard and Westminster, carried all the ineffable sadness of being alive, growing up, growing older. But I knew what I wanted.

"Not Mary Ellen now, but *then*. A night in October 1944, the start of our senior year. There was a party at her house."

The Prince's eyes flickered with new interest. "Oh yes. A fateful evening."

"I kissed her. The first and only time."

Memories like that stay with you. Somehow she was in my arms, fabulous boobs and all, Fay Wray enfolded by Kong Blaustein, and all futures were possible. But I retreated into embarrassment; in the middle of paradise, I thought of my bad teeth and wondered if she noticed. "I blew it."

"By an odd coincidence, the merest chance," the Prince said, "Teresa Golowitz was there that night."

"Who?"

"You don't remember her? Nobody does. Sad child, always faded into the wallpaper. Won't you say hello for me?"

Golowitz . . . no, not a clue for memory. Old acquaintance was definitely forgot. She would have paled under the beacon of Mary Ellen in any case. "Will I be able to make it with her, change the way things happened?"

"I certainly hope so," the Prince purred, making for the whisky again. "If not change, a definite influence."

"Then I'm going to influence the hell out of her."

"I'm counting on it, Mr. Bluestone." For an instant I sensed more in his eyes than weary omniscience. "Remember, you'll be sixteen years old with fifty-odd years of experience. That's not a blessing. Perhaps you can make it one."

Already in a fever to depart, I stopped, agonized by a detail. "I don't remember the exact date."

The Prince flourished like a banner headline. "October 3, 1944! Paris liberated! Allied armies roll across France! Binky Blaustein encircles *la belle* Cosgrove! Why not take the bus for old times' sake?"

"It'll be packed."

"Weren't they all then?" He raised his glass to me. "Good hunting, Binky. And say hello to Teresa."

Again with Golowitz when my soaring purpose strained at the bit. "Who the hell is—?"

But the Prince, the room and the year were gone.

Sixteen feels so different from fifty-five. An unsettling mix of fear and intoxication. A well of nervous energy, health and trembling insecurity based on the hard certainty that you're the homeliest, most unworthy and unwanted, least redeemable *schlemiel* in the universe. God may love you but girls don't, and life is measured to that painful priority.

Even after forty years I knew the route in my sleep. From my father's jewelry store down Fourteenth Street to Eleventh and E. Catch the Walker Chapel bus through Georgetown over Key Bridge into Virginia, up Lee Highway to Cherrydale and Mary Ellen's house on Military Road.

The bus pulled out at 7:10; I'd be there at 7:45. Just a little more than half an hour! Dropping my real-silver Columbia dime into the paybox, I quivered despite the double exposure of age/youth, glowing with the joyful pain that always churned my blood whenever I was going to see her. It was beginning, would be as it was *then* before time turned it into nostalgia and faded both of us to what passed for maturity.

The ancient bus was wartime-jammed with tired government workers and young soldiers in olive drab with shoulder patches no one remembers now: ASTP, Washington Command, the Wolverine Division, 7th Expeditionary Force. Baby-faced sailors with fruit salad on their winter blues, patient and stoic Negroes in the still–Jim Crowed backseats. Two working housewives from the Government Printing Office in upswept hairdos and square-shouldered jackets, bitching about their supervisors and the outlandish price of beef: you wouldn't need ration stamps soon, but *sixty* cents a pound, who could pay that? Bad enough you couldn't get cigarettes now even if you ran a drugstore.

The bus lumbered up the spottily repaired blacktop of Lee Highway toward Cherrydale. Grimy windows and the outside dark made a passable mirror to show me Richard Blaustein—Binky—in his rumpled reversible box coat from Woodward & Lothrop. Bushy brown hair neither efficiently combed nor recently cut, unformed mouth and chin still blurred with baby fat. Not Caliban, not even homely, merely embryonic. I winked at him from forty years of forgiveness. *Hey kid, I fixed the teeth.*

Next to me in the crowded aisle, two sailors compared the proven charms of Veronica Lake with an upstart pinup newcomer named Bacall. I felt dizzy, godlike. It's October 1944. Veronica Lake is box office in four starring Paramount vehicles beside spawning the peekaboo hairstyle that gave eyestrain to a million American girls. *To Have and Have Not* isn't released yet. I might be smoking my hoarded Pinehursts with three fingers along the butt like Bogart, but Lauren Bacall is just a lanky new whosis named Betty Perske.

I looked closer at my mirror-Binky. The liquid brown eyes behind the glasses were not completely naive even then, wary-humorous with an ancient wisdom not yet renamed as Murphy's Law. What can go wrong will, but—a little patience, a little hope. In four years we'll raise our own flag over Jerusalem; for the blacks in the rear of the bus, it'll be longer. Veronica Lake was a waitress before she died. Bacall opened her second Broadway show in 1981. They were both nice girls, but Perske and me, we lasted. Don't ask: there are survivors and others.

Cherrydale: I pulled the buzzer cord and wormed through the press toward the rear door as the bus slowed. It rattled open with a wheeze of fatigued hydraulics, then I was out of the smell of sweat, stale perfume, wool and monoxide, standing on the corner of Military Road under clear October stars.

"Oh, it's you. Come in."

Mary Ellen stood in the open door, one slender hand on the knob, backed by music and chatter. My Grail, the Ark of my libido's own Covenant—and yet different, a subtle gap between my memory and the fact of her.

"Melly?"

"Well, don't stare at me. Come in, hang up your coat. Bo-*ub!*" And she was off paging Bob Bolling. I hung my coat in the familiar closet and stepped into the large living room. Smaller than I remembered it. Gracious, comfortable chairs and sofa, french doors at the rear leading to the yard, Mason & Hamlin grand piano in the far corner. Boys in trousers that seemed baggy and ill-cut to me, girls in pleated skirts and bobby sox. And faces I recalled with a pang: Bill Tait, Frankie Maguerra. And willowy Laura Schuppe, always inches taller than her escorts.

"It's old Blaustein!"

And, of course, Bob Bolling with his unwrinkled Arrow collar and hair that stayed combed. He steered around two girls catting to a record of Tommy Dorsey's "Boogie Woogie," stroking one on the hips —"Shake it but don't break it"—to tower over me with an intimidating sunburst of thirty-two straight teeth.

"Big night, Blaustein," he confided. "Melly's folks are away and I brought some grade A hooch. Bourbon, Blaustein." He always pronounced it *steen* despite my repeated corrections. He patted me on my cowlick. "If you got a note from your mother, I might put some in your Coke. Heh-heh. Come in the kitchen." He disappeared through the hall arch.

"Skip the bourbon." The unsolicited advice came from an owlish, bespectacled boy curled in a chair with a thick book. "It's a gift from Mrs. Bolling's third cousin, a distant relative in the process of retreating even further. Try the scotch."

I edged over to him. A great disguise, but there was no hiding those velvet overtones. "Prince?"

"Even he." He turned a page and giggled. "I love *Paradise Lost.* Milton gave me such marvelous lines. The scotch is under the sink."

The record ended; couples shuffled about, awkward, faced with the need for conversation until the music started again. Bill Tait bummed one of my Pinehursts and I took the first puff. They tasted awful, but you couldn't find real butts anywhere. I segued to the kitchen in time to hear Mary Ellen, coy, sibilant and not really angry:

"Bob, now *quit* that. Honest, you're all hands tonight. Grab, grab."

When they saw me, I felt only a phantom of jealousy. "Scuseme. Thought I'd get a drink or something."

"Sure, Binky." Mary Ellen switched her pert *tush* to the icebox. "Coke or Pepsi? Bink, what are you staring at? Coke or Pepsi?"

"Scotch, please."

She made a face at me, strained patience. "You don't drink. Stop putting on."

Bob whinnied. "Little man had a ha-a-rd day?"

"You wouldn't believe, the death of me."

"Mama and Daddy don't even drink scotch."

"Under the sink."

"See, smarty?" Mary Ellen yanked open the cabinet door. *Voilà:* Glenmorangie, the bottle collared with a small, handwritten tag: *Against mixed blessings.*

"I never saw that," she shrugged. "Anyway, aspirin and Coke are your speed."

The bottle looked like an oasis. "Ice?"

"Sure, it's your funeral. Just don't get sick on the furniture."

I dropped three ice cubes in a jigger with a decent lack of haste, christened them with three fat fingers of whisky and inhaled half of it in a gulp. "Jesus, that's good!"

"Don't curse, Binky. And stop showing off."

I winced in spite of myself at the sound of that thin, plaintive voice. Once it must have been aphrodisiac, especially when she sang. Now it merely grated.

"It's good to see you again, Melly."

"You drip, you saw me in school today." She peered closer at me. "But—gee, I don't know—you look different."

"So do you." It came out flat and not too gracious.

"Well, you don't have to be so sad about it. Bob, let's go dance."

That concluded her obligations as a hostess. Abandoned, I leaned against the sink and watched that little *tush,* the centerfold of a thousand steamy fantasies, bounce out of the kitchen with Bolling in tow. Thank God for the drink; the rest of me was deflating fast. Memory was definitely suspect. I remembered her prettier, even beautiful, and much more mature. She was unformed as myself. The eyes, to which I once wrote saccharine verse, merely blue with a patina of intolerance over ignorance. The figure was child-cute, but after thirty-five years of grown women and a regiment of Broadway dancers, it retreated now as the half-realized first draft of an ordinary, mesomorphic female body. So far from a resurgence of passion, I felt more pity and understanding than anything else, like suffering the gauche sophistication of a daughter struggling to be grown-up. The idea of sleeping with Melly was absurd, even faintly incestuous. My overblown lust went flat as a bride's biscuit, and from the shadows of Shubert Alley I heard the mournful laughter of Rick Bluestone, who would never call a spade a heart. Mary Ellen Cosgrove at sixteen was interesting as a clam. But then, so was I.

More kids arrived, conversation got louder, high and giddy on youth alone. Melly and Bob danced with a glum precision. Suffering from total recall, Frankie Maguerra regaled anyone in earshot with Hope-Crosby jokes from *Road to Morocco*. My bookish buddy had vanished, but Laura Schuppe, over at the piano, gave me an X-rated wink and a little beckoning toss of her head. I joined her on the bench.

"Find the scotch?"

"Huh? Yeah. Where's the little guy who was sitting over there?"

"Nelson Baxley, class of '46. Korea, Bronze Star and Purple Heart. Later: television production, five children, one Emmy, one duodenal ulcer."

I might have known. Laura would never even look at me, let alone wink. "Prince?"

"Nelson left, so I borrowed Laura."

"It doesn't bother her having you in residence?"

"No, it's all rather split-screen. On her side she's drooling over that varsity jock in the maroon sweater. Nice girl, somewhat confused, poor self-image. Top model for *Vogue* and *Harpers,* 1949 to 1955. One therapist, two nervous breakdowns, serial affairs with lovers of mixed gender. Cocaine, anorexia, Born Again Christianity. Married a Fundamentalist, currently works for the Moral Majority. Depressing. And Mary Ellen?"

"The booze is better. Thanks."

Laura sighed with a wisdom eons beyond her. "Nostalgia is always myopic. By the way, there's Miss Golowitz, trying to be invisible as usual."

Even as I recognized and remembered the fat, homely girl, my older heart went out to her. Teresa Golowitz—a dark, shapeless smudge among blondish altos in the school choral section. Coarse, frizzy hair, unplucked eyebrows that aspired to meet over her nose, and a faint but discernible mustache line. Thick legs blotched with unshaved hair under laddered nylons, and—insult to injury—a dress that would look better on Aunt Jemima. Among the relatively svelte Lambda Pi girls, she fit in like pork chops at a *seder*. I wondered why she'd been invited.

"That's why," the Prince read my thought casually. "Cast your mind back: Mary Ellen always had a few plain girls around to make her look good. And tonight is Teresa's turn in the barrel."

Memory sharpened to cruel clarity. My own family was conservative, but Teresa's old-country parents made mine look like atheists. She came to school in *shmotte* dresses and no makeup. She'd done her face for the party, no doubt on the bus in a bad light. I watched Teresa trying to press herself through the wall, fiddling with her hands, carmined mouth frozen in a stiff smile. I always avoided her in school; she was all the things I wanted to escape. Now I could see how much she might have wanted it, too, but two to one she married the kind of guy who wears his *yarmulke* to the office.

"You're big on futures, Prince. What happened to her?"

"Don't you remember?"

"Memory I'm learning not to trust."

"She committed suicide."

"No! She didn—" But in the breath of denial I knew it was true, a sensation at school for a day or two. When Frankie Maguerra told me, I said something like "Gee!" and briefly pondered the intangibles of life before getting on with adolescence. "When?"

"Tonight."

Yes . . . it was just about this month. The Prince stroked soft chords with Laura's long fingers. "Took the bus back to town reflecting on accumulated griefs and loneliness, and the fact that no one at this golden gathering even said hello to her, not even Blaustein. She got off the bus and waited at the curb—as she is now, tearing at her cuticles, multiplying this night by so many others and so many more to come. She didn't like the product. When the next bus came along— behind schedule and traveling too fast—she stepped in front of it."

I shook my head, foggily mournful. "What a sad waste."

"Sad but academic." The Prince stood up. "Excuse me. Laura has to go to the little girls' room. Had the immortal embrace yet?"

"No. Who needs it?"

Dismally true. The whole purpose of my flashback was on the cutting room floor. I was pondering whether to talk to Teresa or just leave now when Bill Tait roared away from a dirty-joke session to drape himself over the piano. "Bink! Give us 'Boogie Woogie.' "

"No!" Someone else demanded. " 'Blue Lights.' "

"Hey, Bink's gonna play."

"Yay!"

I swung into "House of Blue Lights" to a chorus of squealed approval. It sounded fantastic, too good, until I realized I was playing with forty-five years of practice behind me and musical ideas still unknown outside of Fifty-second Street: steel rhythm under a velvet touch, block chords out of Monk, Powell and Kenton that wouldn't be heard for years yet. The crowd began to collect around the piano. Mary Ellen got set to sing, her big thing at parties. Teresa Golowitz edged in next to her almost apologetically, pudgy fingers dancing on the piano top. Melly took the vocal on the second verse; not a bad voice, but it wouldn't go past the fifth row without a mike.

And then I heard it, rising over Mary Ellen's whitish soprano like a great big bird, that smoky alto soaring into the obligato release. Yah-duh-dee-duh-DAH-duh-duh-duh-DEE-dah-dah, bouncing twice around the electrified room and sliding back into the lyric like she was born there. The hair rose on my head and arms; everyone stared at Teresa Golowitz, who, perhaps for the first time and on the last night of her life, had decided to leave her mark. I rocked into another coda for her alone, begging.

"Take it, girl!"

Teresa did. Together we worked things on that basic boogie that weren't invented yet. And what a voice—not pure, not classical, but a natural for jazz. Teresa straightened out of her usual slump, closed her eyes and let the good riffs roll. Sixteen years old; you could teach her a little about phrasing and breath control, but the instrument was incredible. She played with the notes, slurring over and under the melodic line with a pitch and rhythm you couldn't break with dynamite. All the greats had this for openers: Lutcher, Fitzgerald, Stafford, June Christy, Sassy Vaughan, all of them. Under the excitement, the Prince's voice whispered into my mind, *Of course she's beautiful. It's her requiem.*

It could well be. When we finished the number, I bounced up and smeared her lipstick with an off-center kiss. "Baby, you're gorgeous. Don't ever think you're not."

"Hey, lookit old Blaustein the wolf."

Mary Ellen snickered; as a vocalist her nose was a little out of joint, say about a mile. "Oh, it's a *love* match."

Teresa blushed crimson. I doubt if she was kissed much at home, let alone at parties. She started to retreat, but I grabbed her hand. "Don't go, I need you. You know 'Opus One'?"

She hesitated, then made her decision. She glared with fierce pride at Mary Ellen and stood even straighter. "Hit it, Blaustein."

I zapped into the machine-gun opening with pure joy. "Opus One" is a real catting number. Most of the kids started to dance, the rest jiggling and beating time on the piano top. From Teresa we hadn't heard anything yet. She vocalized the soprano sax break from the Dorsey orchestration with a scatty-doo riff that wailed like Nellie Lutcher's "Lake Charles." She shouldn't end like this. In four years or less there'd be recording techniques able to put that voice on the moon, and she wants to off herself in an hour or two. The hell with it all, if I could just keep her from that.

We rolled up the wall-shaking finish, both of us out of breath. Teresa parked herself on the bench beside me, guzzling sloppily at her drink. "You are reet, Blaustein. You are definitely a groove."

"Me! Where'd you pick up jazz like that?"

"Who picks up? You feel it. The first time is like remembering."

"Feeling good, Terri?"

"Yeah, kinda." She grinned shyly. "I always wanted to be called that."

"Terri it is. And take advice: tomorrow we start working together." Her eyes clouded. "Tomorrow . . ."

"Unless you're not around, you know what I mean? Go home, take a bath. Tomorrow things will look pure gold. And when I call New York about you—"

I talked fast, promising, conning, cajoling, speaking of agents and record producers not even born yet, anything to get her mind off the loser track and that fatal bus. Still talking, I steered her into the kitchen, spiked her a little Pepsi in a lot of bourbon, a new scotch for me. I'd bomb the suicide out of her if I could, sing it out if I couldn't. One hour when she and everybody in range knew Teresa Golowitz was a person, a talent and worth the future.

We were dragged back to the piano. *Play more. Sing, Teresa. Please sing, Teresa.* She didn't know how to handle it all, never opened up like this before. I ruffled a big fanfare chord on the piano.

"Ladies and gentlemen—the fourteen karats of Miss Terri Gold!"

"Yay!"

"Huh?" said Teresa. "What's with 'Gold'?"

"Just like 'Blaustein.' I yell 'Golowitz!' who'd come? Hang on, Terri. We are going to the moon."

I launched into music so far beyond eight-to-the-bar, most of the kids were mystified. Way-out Monk and Shearing riffs, Charlie Ventura stuff, bop sounds most of the world hadn't heard yet, like "The Man From Minton's" and the clean, hard-rocking Previn-Manne "I Could Have Danced All Night," still twelve years in the future. Terri's eyes were moons of discovery before she dug it. Like she said, a kind of remembering. On "To Be or Not to Bop," she came in with her own obligato, sure and pure.

"Hey, Bink," Frankie Maguerra wondered. "What *is* that?"

Terri didn't need the name, she knew. I dropped the beat and backed her with light chords in implied time. She was pure gold; with a little grooming she could play clubs now, but she had to live for that. For the other kids, it was too far out; they needed a beat. Teresa yearned visibly after Bob Bolling, who left the living room hand in hand with Mary Ellen. I saw her glow fade back to the one-minute-to-*zotz* look she had before singing. Sadly she glanced at the clock.

"Terri, you want to try a ballad?"

"Gee, I don't know. It's late."

"One ballad. Name it. You got a favorite?"

"Do you know 'I Fall in Love Too Easily'?"

"Does Burns know Allen?" I rippled out a four-bar intro. "Fly, baby. The sky is yours."

Terri closed her eyes, lifted her head and sang. The room grew a little quieter. It's a great old number, an evergreen from an early Sinatra film that you can still hear on FM in New York. All right, critical? Teresa wasn't as sharp on slow ballads, not the best phrasing, a little wobbly on drawn-out vowels, but her feeling for the arc and sense of a lyric was sure and solid. The kids were very quiet now; she had them in the palm of her hand. Then she did something that curled my hair, ended one phrase softly and, on the same breath, swelled into the first word of the next with a gorgeous crescendo I felt down to my socks. I've auditioned a thousand singers. You can hear their technique and training in the first line. What Golowitz had no one can teach. I heard her plain in that short phrase, locked in with a soul full of *schmerz* and one slender lifeline of music. A homely girl, a fat loser in the svelte Rita Hayworth era; anyone could hurt her and everyone would, but when she sang it would all be on the line, bare and beautiful. A voice you listened to because it was your own. A smoky, black-coffee, tapped-out-and-running-on-guts sound you don't hear anymore unless you own some of the old Billie Holiday sides. Or another voice, quite different but as full of life and pain, that will pack the Palace Theatre twenty years from tonight with the same self-lacerating magic in every song. A miracle called Garland.

We finished the song. The kids drifted away, liking but not really understanding what they'd heard, ready for the record player and more grab-ass to music. Teresa looked again at the mantel clock.

"I gotta go. It's late."

"See me tomorrow, Terri?"

"I don't know . . ."

"Promise."

"Blaustein, don't ask. There's a lot of problems."

"Work with me. There's people in New York—"

"Don't put on," she said hopelessly. "You don't know from New York."

"Promise me, dammit."

"Why?" It was a wail, a cry for help. Already in it you could hear the grey decision, a door closing in Losersville. What I answered wasn't from sixteen. I wondered if sixteen could dig it.

"I know from New York and a lot of things. Don't blow it, Terri. You got more to give in thirty-two bars than most people find in a lifetime. You want to be loved? So does the world. They'll love you, Terri. They'll beat your goddam door down. But it takes time and paying your dues and maybe a little trust. So see me tomorrow and we start."

Teresa tried to smooth the crushed material of her dress over shapeless hips. "Blaustein—you're such a *noodge.*" She said it like a kiss. "G'night."

I tried to follow her but a rather strong influence glued me to the piano bench. *You've done your best, Mr. B. Now a little trust.*

So I sat there guzzling scotch too fast, which was a mistake. Bluestone could guzzle, Binky couldn't. I took a few deep breaths and watched Frankie Maguerra dance with Laura Schuppe through the wrong end of a telescope, then wobbled upstairs to the bathroom, wondering if I'd be sick. Apparently there was enough Bluestone ballast to hold it down. After a few moments glumly pondering the toilet depths, I scrubbed my face with a washcloth and grinned farewell to Binky. "See you at Sardi's, kid."

Wavering toward the stairs, I heard Mary Ellen's voice from behind a half-closed bedroom door: *"Day-amn, Bob! I said stop."*

"For God's sake, what's the matter now? On, off. You're a real tease, you know that?"

I pushed in the door and leaned against the jam. They didn't see me, sitting stiff and apart on the edge of the bed. Melly looked confused and angry.

"You don't have to be so crude about it."

"Oh . . . shit."

"And don't talk to me like that."

Poor Bob: eighteen, all balls and no finesse. He even rated a twinge of sympathy. "Hey, stud," I said, "why not try a little conversation first?"

Mary Ellen whirled and stiffened. Bob only looked annoyed. "Blaustein, blow. Get out of here."

I felt booze-brave. "Better idea, *shmuck*. Why don't you go get started on your gall bladder?"

"Listen, you—"

"Oh, he's right!" Mary Ellen screeched. "Go home. Go home, you're disgusting."

Confused, outgunned, Bob threw her one classic grimace of exasperation. "All *right*. But I won't be back."

"Bet?" I offered as he pushed past me and clumped down the stairs.

"What a jerk." Melly collapsed in a frustrated bundle. "I don't care if he never comes back. I wouldn't see him again if he was the last man on earth."

"Sure you will." *Because for you, he is.* That was less of a future than an epitaph. The whole thing was vaguely sad. I wanted to go.

"God." Her shoulders began to shake. "I'm surrounded with drips."

I put my arm around the forlorn, half-grown lump of her uncertainty: more experienced than her mother would imagine and a lot less than she thought. Sixteen: the voice of the turtle bellowing in her blood, wanting all the things she couldn't handle yet, and all she had were the cards girls got dealt in 1944. Unless you were a freak genius or something, you got married. You got a man. There wasn't anything else; not for Mommy, not for you. Later it might be easy, now it was hell. Only idiots want to be young again. It's a miserable gauntlet to run, but looking back later, Melly would block out the insecurity and pain until only the glow was left to shimmer in soft focus, and her picture would be no more accurate than mine.

"Take it one day at a time, Melly. It's more fun that way."

She wilted against my shoulder. "Binky, are you my really truly close friend?"

"Guess I am." I pulled her gently to her feet. Her lips found my cheek and then my own mouth. A very split-screen moment: enjoyment, regrets and a fleeting taste of what it would have been to have a daughter. I might have been good at that.

"You're nice, Bink. Just sometimes you're a jerk. You going home?"

"Time to go."

"See you in school."

"S'long, Melly. It was a swell party."

Wrestling into my coat downstairs, I peeked once more into the living room, at the kids I grew up with. A damned fool, happy and sad, high on life more than anything else, I ducked for the front door before they caught me crying. But someone did.

"Hey, Blaustein!"

Teresa Golowitz swayed precariously in the kitchen hallway, flashing a fresh drink and a bleary grin. "Hu-hi!"

"Terri! I thought—"

"Ah, hu-hell," she gulped. "I felt so good from singing, I figured one more for the road. I have just two questions for you."

"You didn't go. You didn't—"

"Don't change the su-subject. First: what c'n I do for hu-hiccups?"

"Hold your breath and take nine sips of water."

"And the big qu-uk-question," said Teresa Golowitz. "What *time* tomorrow?"

"I'll find you." Gloriously smashed, she couldn't see the tears start. "Come on, how about we take the same bus?"

Terri was still grinning and hiccuping when the scene cut.

My penthouse was still there with a few major changes. On the floor, Rick Bluestone was beginning to wilt like leftover salad. The record jackets near the turntable were different but still classics of their kind. Stan Kenton had metamorphosed to *Kenton Digs Gold.* The Pete Rugolo album was titled simply *Pure Gold and Rugolo.* Beside them lay a third: *Gold Sings Bluestone Plays Gold.* On the wall just above the piano was a photograph of that vulnerable, indestructible head lifted, the mouth parted in a lyric. I remembered it with hiccups and much, much younger.

A lot of change, a lot of years. Some great songs.

Across the back of the album we cut together, she'd scrawled in a looping hand: BLAUSTEIN, YOU'RE SUCH A NOODGE— TERRI GOLD LOVES YOU.

The Prince rose and straightened his Sulka tie. "Whither away, Mr. Bluestone?"

I turned once more to the window. After thirty-five years of looking at Manhattan, the river and Queens, I wouldn't miss them all that much. As for Sarah, don't ask. With any luck she'd be out of Airwick. "Topside, I suppose. Papa will expect me."

A nuance of mild discomfort shaded the Prince's savoir faire. "Not just yet, I'm afraid."

"Why not? You said anywhere."

"Of course—in time. And time is what we have perverted, not to say brutalized. You won't be welcome just now, I regret to say." He didn't sound regretful at all, more like a sweepstakes winner. "You've played merry hob with the Grand Scheme. Terri Gold: three husbands, four children, three grandchildren, six million-seller records and a career that threatens never to end—all from a girl who was supposed to be a statistic at sixteen. Where Topside is concerned, it's best we maintain a very low profile until—"

"We?" I rounded on him in a chill of realization. "We?"

"You, me, what's the difference?"

"That's why you were all the time with Golowitz. You knew! You bastard, you knew all the time!"

He nodded in modest pleasure. "As the lyric goes, it had to be you. Of all that nebulous crew at the party, you were the first slated to die after Teresa. And the best bet. I field the shots, I don't call them."

The immensity of it collapsed me on the sofa, gaping. "You *gonif.* So you just waited until I packed it in, and—"

"Influenced," the Prince capped it with a satisfied smile. "I'm an artist like yourself, a sculptor of possibilities. What could you change with Mary Ellen, who was cast and immutable by the age of ten?"

I stared at him, unbelieving. "Dead one day and already I need a lawyer."

"And you shall have the best," the Prince conciliated. "For services rendered. Darrow loves cases like this."

"I'll bet. No wonder you get lousy reviews Topside."

"Topside!" he flared in disgust. "Stodgy, pragmatic conservatives. Lizst should die of fever before he's thirty, Schubert before he could write the glorious Ninth? Never! It's not all fun, believe me. Win some, lose some. Lose a Shelley, lose a Byron, a Kapell. Lose a Radiguet before he's twenty-five, a Gershwin at thirty-nine. But a Terri Gold at sixteen? No, the world is threadbare enough. And no one Topside, not even my celestial Brother—the white sheep of an otherwise brilliant brood—has ever understood the concept of *creative* history. What in the cosmos does it matter if I make a mess of their records? I create! Like any artist, I need to be recognized. I need to be understood. Most of all," the Prince concluded wearily, "I need another drink."

I didn't understand half of it, but—you know?—I couldn't really stay mad at him. Whatever else, bad press or no, the guy has *chutzpah.* And there are all those years of Terri Gold.

"How long has Terri got?"

"Ages, Mr. Bluestone. Dogs' years. More records, more men, more grandchildren. She'll be roaring drunk when she goes and happy as a bee among flowers. And the last drink will be her best." The Prince polished off his own, neat. "Shall we?"

"Uh . . . where to?"

"As advertised, your choice. But till the heat's off, I'd suggest Petronius' party. There's someone positively seething to meet you, that clever little woman from the Algonquin set. Which reminds me."

The Prince swept up the Glenmorangie in one protective arm, the other through mine. "Dottie said to bring you *and* the scotch. *Allons,* Mr. Bluestone. The night is young!"

Appendix I:

MISCELLANEOUS NOTES

"Hell-Bent" by Ford McCormack (pp.128–46)

I have been unable to find other works or biographical data on the late Ford McCormack, although a visit to the Library of Congress revealed a few copyright listings for dramatic compositions registered in his name. But while negotiating for permission to reprint "Hell-Bent," I was pleasantly surprised to receive this touching note from the well-known science fiction writer A. E. van Vogt: "Ford was a precisionist in his use of the English language, and in everything he did. Because of that precision, at my request he read several of my novels in manuscript form, and somewhere I still have the pages of correction suggestions. His special abilities were noticed by the firm he worked for, and they presently sent him to their San Francisco area factory as an overseer. He wrote his own stories in his occasional spare time. Presently, I received an invitation to visit his home; and during the time I was there he smiled and chatted, and gave no indication of, nor did he mention the cancer of which he died a few days later. That was about ten years ago."

"Damned Funny" by Marvin Kaye (pp. 147–57)

In this three-task tale, the first chore was suggested to me in the late 1950s or early 1960s by my friend Ellis Grove, then a graduate student at The Pennsylvania State University and now one of that institution's most popular professors. After reading all the stories in Basil Davenport's anthology *Deals with the Devil,* a few new twists on the familiar scenario occurred to me: these became the second and third tasks proposed by the protagonist of "Damned Funny." The ludicrous Tiny Tom was a five-finger exercise for a bumbling detective, Franklin Butler, whom I wanted to write about; he finally appeared in my fourth Hilary Quayle mystery, *The Laurel and Hardy Murders* (E. P. Dutton, New York, 1977.).

"The Novel of the White Powder" by Arthur Machen (pp. 212–27)

I first encountered this vivid horror story in the late 1940s or 1950s in a comic book version that, to the best of my recollection, did not credit the Machen novella as its source. I forgot about it until I read it in the Ballantine Adult Fantasy series edition of *The Three Imposters,* which its editor, Lin Carter, says was Machen's first novel (more or less). Critics have likened the loosely constructed *The Three Imposters* to Robert Louis Stevenson's *New Arabian Nights,* a series of linked short stories. But Stevenson interrelates the disparate elements of his book rather neatly while Machen does not. *The Three Imposters* is perhaps closer in character to Ray Bradbury's *The Illustrated Man,* an excellent grouping of science-fantasy tales tied together by an imaginative but wholly unnecessary prologue and epilogue. Machen blends together an unusual number of elements—mystery, satire, terror, wry social commentary—but the mix never really "sets." "The Novel of the White Powder" comprises the greater portion of chapter seven, entitled "The Recluse of Bayswater," but the plot frame surrounding the gruesome tale is, in my opinion, tedious and ultimately anticlimactic, so I have elected to reproduce the story of the white powder itself without its superfluous narrative frame.

"Caliban's Revenge," by Darrell Schweitzer (pp. 235–46)

Some familiarity with the plot of Shakespeare's *The Tempest* is helpful to appreciate more fully the ironies of this autumnal tale. Here is a brief summary of the chief events as they relate to Caliban: Prospero, a sorcerer and the Duke of Milan, is betrayed by his brother and the King of Naples and set adrift in a boat with his infant daughter Miranda, but a kindly old philosopher secretly provisions the craft with food as well as Prospero's conjuring robes and magic books. Father and child reach the shores of an island deserted by all but supernatural spirits including the elfin Ariel, and Caliban, the monster son of the witch Sycorax and the Devil. Prospero attempts to win Caliban's friendship, but the beast betrays him by attempting to rape Miranda, so the powerful magician enslaves him and forces him to do his menial work, chopping wood and fetching water. Twelve years pass. A ship nears the island. In it are Prospero's usurping brother and the King of Naples. The sorcerer creates a great storm that maroons the ship's company on the island's shores to be tormented (though not overly harshly) for their sins against Prospero and Miranda. Meanwhile, Caliban befriends the king's jester, Trinculo, and Stephano, a tippling butler who introduces the beast to liquor. Believing he has stumbled upon a demigod, Caliban pledges his allegiance to Stephano and plots with him to overthrow his master, but Ariel overhears the scheme and reports it to Prospero. The magician sets Ariel on the trio of conspirators and he and his fellow spirits pursue them about the island, pinching them and inflicting them with cramps and convulsions. At last, Prospero reveals himself to his enemies, releases them from their punishments and, planning to resume his dukedom, gives up magic and resolves to "drown his book." He releases Stephano, Trinculo and Caliban from torment and the monster resolves to reform and "be wise hereafter, and seek for grace." Prospero, Miranda, the King and all the other mortals return to the ship and sail away, leaving Caliban behind on the island.

"A Madman" by Maurice Level (pp. 291–93)

Twenty-six stories by Maurice Level are included in *Tales of Mystery and Horror* (Robert M. McBride & Co., New York, 1920), as well as an introduction by Henry B. Irving and a fairly lengthy appreciatory note by the translator, Alys Eyre Macklin. In these prefatory pages, quite a few alleged facts are revealed about Level's life. According to Irving, Maurice was the son of an Alsatian army officer and spent most of his youth in Algiers. He studied medicine in Paris but suffered a skating accident in Switzerland in 1910 when he was thirty-five and was confined to a sanatorium for some four years. In 1914 he quit the hospital and joined the army until his health gave out, after which Level served as a surgeon at a military base. Irving goes on to describe

Level as light-hearted, "essentially Parisian in temperament." Yet the copyright card catalog entry at the Library of Congress clearly states that Maurice Level was the pseudonym of Jeanne Mareteux-Level. Until some student of French literature investigates and reveals the truth, we must either conclude that the copyright office is in error or that Irving's introduction is a tissue of lies. If the latter is so, it does not necessarily mean that Irving is at fault. Considering the shocking psychosexual content of Level's fiction, it may be that the shadowy Jeanne Mareteux-Level chose to fabricate a plausible alter ego as a smokescreen for her real identity. Irving is correct on one point at least when he compares Level favorably to Edgar Allan Poe and other important scribes of the macabre. Today, Level is known for a handful of anthologized tales drawn from the McBride volume, as well as one story that does not appear in that collection, "Night and Silence," which I included in my earlier anthology *Masterpieces of Terror and the Supernatural.* Let us hope that Alys Eyre Macklin was accurate in her 1920 Translator's Note when she asserted that during her? his? lifetime, Maurice Level wrote some *seven hundred* short stories, most of them published in the periodical *Le Journal.*

"Ulalume" by Edgar Allan Poe (pp. 338–41)

In his editorial notes to *Selected Writings of Edgar Allan Poe* (Houghton Mifflin, Boston, 1956), Edward H. Davidson states that "Ulalume" has long been regarded as "mere melody and verbal mystery—if not nonsense too," a view that eloquently testifies to the woeful inadequacy of much American literary criticism. Davidson credits Professor T. O. Mabbott with finally unraveling the meaning of the poem in the 1940s, but this is absurd. Anyone with reasonable intellectual gifts must immediately interpret "Ulalume" as another variation on the love-grief theme Poe employed in other of his poems, most notably "The Raven" and "Lenore." Mabbott observes that the title is probably derived from the Latin *ululare,* "to wail," but so is "ululation," surely a less pedantic, more obvious inference. The "dim lake of Auber" refers to a ballet by the French composer Daniel Francois Auber and "the misty mid region of Weir" brings to mind the foggy landscapes of the nineteenth-century painter Robert Walter Weir. Yaanek, a volcanic mountain in Antarctica, had recently been discovered. Mabbott also explains that the poem is rife with precise astrological symbolism. These facts are interesting to know and certainly deepen one's appreciation of the wall of intellect that Poe tried to erect in "Ulalume" to shield his protagonist and himself from the naked grief of his wife's death, but they are not necessary to comprehend the simple plot line of the poem: that the narrator while convening with his own spirit walks through a forest that he fails to recognize until he comes upon his lover's grave. He realizes that try as he may, he cannot shut himself off from the pain of that loss. The final stanza that Poe later cut is at first the most perplexing of all, but it merely rounds off the mystical suggestion that the spirits that inhabit "Weir's wood" tried to protect the narrator from finding Ulalume's grave by changing the physical aspect of the forest so that he would not recognize where he was wandering.

"The Philosophy of Sebastian Trump; or The Art of Outrage"
by William E. Kotzwinkle and Robert Shiarella (pp. 367–77)

More years ago than I wish to acknowledge, Bob Shiarella, Bill Kotzwinkle and I were students together at Penn State. When I was editing *Brother Theodore's Chamber of Horrors* for Pinnacle Books in 1974, I asked Bob, an accomplished humorist, whether he had anything in the nature of black comedy for my collection. He showed me "The Art of Outrage," for which he and Bill had never found a market. In its original third-person form, I was afraid it didn't quite fit my anthology, either, but it was too amusing to pass up, so with the permissions of the authors, I revised it to become the present first-person memoir by Sebastian Trump himself. I confess to adding a few of my own gags to the piece, not without deserved trepidation, but Bob did not object and when he passed them on to Bill, his only comment was that he "always suspected Marvin is as mad as us."

Don Juan's Final Night by Edmond Rostand (pp. 378–422)

In the process of adapting this play, I have followed Rostand's own dictum, "All great art must be updated," which he puts into Don Juan's mouth as an excuse for abridging the Punch-and-Judy show. Of course, the sentiment is meant in a double sense; Rostand himself takes liberties with Molière, the version of the Don Juan myth that he most closely follows in his drama. In like fashion, I have made a few cosmetic alterations in *Don Juan's Final Night* to make it accessible to contemporary American readers. Mostly I have condensed its action from a somewhat verbose two acts with intermission to the present three scenes, which are meant to be played without interruption. I have tried to avoid cutting dialogue, preferring instead to tighten it by opting for a fairly simple poetic prose instead of the heightened verse of the original. The manuscript of the play was reportedly unfinished by Rostand, but the action appears to me to describe a complete dramatic arch. Perhaps the playwright would have revised his work, had he lived. I think this likely, for there are several places in the script that do not flow as congenially as is usual in Rostand; in these places I have transposed speeches when I felt the progress of ideas would therefore run more smoothly. In his character list, Rostand calls for 1,003 distaff spectres. In the theatre collection at Lincoln Center, an earlier translation suggests that fifteen women would be more than sufficient to give the illusion of this vast company of seduced ghosts, but in today's impoverished theatre even that many actresses would be more than most producers' budgets could afford. Since the puppet theatre is already an integral part of the action, I made further use of it as a convention for suggesting to the audience that the three spirits they see each represent 334.3 of their sisters-in-damnation. The major excision I made was to cut the character of a beggar whom Don Juan invokes to prove to the Devil that his imperiled spirit has worth, if not as a lover, then as a blasphemer. This episode refers to a moment in Molière's *Don Juan* when a supplicant begs for alms in the name of God only to be given money by Don Juan on the understanding that it is for the love of man and not the deity that he bestows it. Rostand's beggar curses Don Juan and his money both as false coin. I eliminated this passage because, firstly, the Molière reference is now obscure and secondly, it seemed to me an intrusion into a drama whose chief purpose is to pick apart the sexual pretensions of Don Juan. In this respect, Rostand, who was perhaps the last great romantic writer, is also a significant precursor of that clinical psychology infusing so much contemporary fiction and drama.

Appendix II:

WHO IN HELL ARE ALL THESE DEVILS?
(AN INFERNAL "LOWERARCHY")

Those who wish to call up a demon must know his precise name in order to have power over him, but diabolic nomenclature is devilishly confusing. Various scholars have drawn up elaborate but often conflicting indexes of the ranking officers of sin. The below listing, chiefly derived from R. H. Robbins' *The Encylopedia of Witchcraft and Demonology* (Crown Publishers, New York, 1959), is humbly submitted as a thumbtalon guide to Who's Who in Hades.

THE DEVIL

Everyone is agreed on the identity of Hell's head honcho. As noted in the Introduction, he was called Lucifer, the angel of light, when he was in Heaven, but after he was cast into the dark and fiery pit, he was renamed Satan, which derives from the Greek word for *enemy* or *adversary*. According to Medieval legend, he is also known as Mephistopheles, the name which Marlowe and Goethe employ in their Faustian dramas and which therefore appears in the Gounod and Boito operas based on the latter composition. In early America, he was commonly called Old Nick or Mr. Scratch.

THE MAJOR DEMONS

The so-called seven deadly sins each were entrusted to a distinct fiend whose job it was (is?) to tempt mortals to commit his particular pet transgression. One commentator equated Lucifer with pride and Satan with anger, while another said Satan chiefly served deluders such as witches and magicians. Here are a few of the Devil's chief lieutenants and the evils they are alleged to represent:

ASMODEUS—lechery, luxuriousness and/or evil revenge.

BEELZEBUB—Lucifer's "best fiend" and first lieutenant during the war with Heaven. One commentator equates Beelzebub with the sin of pride, while another charges him with gluttony.

BELPHEGOR—the demon of sloth, also called Astaroth. In a brilliant essay "Accidie" (still another name for this evil spirit), Aldous Huxley wrote that this fiend, the only one who dares "work" during daylight, represents more than mere laziness. The sloth referred to is spiritual ennui or *acedia* which infects the heart and mind of man and makes all effort seem ultimately futile. Huxley notes that Accidie is a devil who has certainly received his due in the Twentieth Century.

LEVIATHAN—next to Beelzebub, Satan's chief ally. One commentator attributes envy to him, but Leviathan's name is more commonly linked with heresy.

MAMMON—sometimes dubbed Prince of Tempters and Ensnarers, but generally affiliated with avarice. His name is a common literary metaphor for greed.

MINOR-LEAGUE DEMONS

Not counting cacodemons, goblins, ghouls, harpies, incubi, succubi, vampires and other miscellaneous evil spirits, there is still a host of minor ranking devils on the Satanic roster. Here are an unlucky thirteen of some of the more colorful ones:

ABADDAN—the prince of evil war (as if that institution were capable of innocence). Dylan Thomas presumably referred to this fiend in one of his sonnets, but spelled the name Abaddon.

BALBERITH—tempts mortals to quarrel and murder.

BEHEMOTH—a demon of gluttony.

BELIAL—in charge of "the Devil's bones and picture books," that is, dice and playing cards.

BELIAS—tempts humanity toward arrogance as well as idleness of mind during prayer.

CARNIVEAN—in charge of "shameless obscenity."

CARREAU—urges people to harden their hearts to suffering.

MERIHIM—the demon of pestilence.

OLIVIER—in charge of cruelty and mercilessness to the poor. Many demons are accorded specific nemesis-angels in Heaven; it is curious to note that Olivier's divine opponent is named Lawrence.

PYTHO—prince of prevaricators.

ROSIER—in charge of honeyed words that tempt humanity to fall in love. (!)

SONNEILLON—responsible for stirring up hatred toward one's enemies.

VERRINE—tempts people to be impatient. (Now hurry up and turn the page!)

Appendix III:

SELECTED BIBLIOGRAPHY AND FILMOGRAPHY

A comprehensive list of stories about hellish and earthly fiends would probably require a volume of its own. Below I have listed thirteen books and plays that I find worthwhile to recommend for one or another reason. I have mostly avoided including short stories, but several excellent ones appear in my previous anthologies, *Ghosts* and *Masterpieces of Terror and the Supernatural.* I have also bypassed cornerstone works, such as Goethe's *Faust,* that hardly require my recommendation.

BUELL, JOHN, *The Pyx.* A deftly told quasifantastic murder mystery that is both a police procedural and a touching study of goodness and evil.

CODY, C. S., *The Witching Night.* A terrifying and unjustly obscure novel of modern-day Satanism and murder via black magic.

COLLIER, JOHN, *Fancies and Goodnights.* This cornerstone compendium of fifty tales of fantasy, humor and/or horror includes quite a few stories about devils, some of them serious in tone, but most of them wonderfully wacky.

DE GHELDERODE, MICHEL, *Lord Halewyn.* The plots of this important twentieth-century Belgian playwright were often haunting and fantastic in character. "Lord Halewyn" is a long one-act about a Devil-worshipping madman and a young noblewoman inexorably drawn toward him and the evil he represents.

HAWTHORNE, NATHANIEL, *The House of the Seven Gables.* The contemporary reader may find Hawthorne's slow pace impossible to tolerate, but those with patience will find in this novel one of the most towering examples of gothic wickedness in English letters. The villainous judge is a true human fiend and his death is a masterful example of sustained irony.

HOWARD, SIDNEY, *Madam, Will You Walk?* This woefully neglected final play by a once-important American dramatist is now available only in manuscript from Dramatists Play Service. It is a delightfully comedic tale of a young woman about to be buried alive by family propriety. The Devil, a symbol of all that is new and life-affirming, engagingly rescues her from her fate. (Note the thematic similarity to Parke Godwin's hubristic Prince in his story "Influencing the Hell Out of Time and Teresa Golowitz," which appears in this volume.)

HUGO, VICTOR, *Notre-Dame de Paris.* Better known as *The Hunchback of Notre-Dame,* this often-filmed novel is darker than Hollywood allowed us to realize. It is, in fact, a nightmarish horror story. Most of its "heroes" are greater monsters than poor sympathetic Quasimodo, while its true villains—King and clergyman—reek with corruption and the smell of sulphur and brimstone.

LONDON, JACK, *The Sea-Wolf.* The titular character, Captain Wolf Larsen, is the Devil incarnate to those unfortunate to serve under him (and he has a brother named Death Larsen who even scares Wolf!). Wolf is the philosophical precursor of Albert Camus' existential mad Roman emperor Caligula, whose atrocities serve to offset the arbitrariness of existence itself.

MATHESON, RICHARD, *The Distributor.* This stark novella details one week's routine in the life of a human fiend who devotes himself to destroying every neighborhood he lives in. I have been told that the story bears a familial resemblance to *The Intruder,* a novel by the late Charles Beaumont, whose impressive writing career was tragically brief.

MERRITT, ABRAHAM, *Burn Witch Burn.* A scary horror story of witchcraft and murder in twentieth-century Manhattan. A semisequel,

Creep Shadow Creep, is a weird tale of voodoo. *Burn Witch Burn* was filmed as *The Devil-Doll,* which, though effective on its own merits, greatly palliates the novel's menace.

RUSSELL, RAY, *The Case Against Satan.* It is a pity that it is so hard to find a copy of Russell's first novel. Almost identical in plot to William Peter Blatty's *The Exorcist,* Russell's work came first and is a much better book.

SHAW, BERNARD, *Man and Superman.* The protagonist of this quintessential Shavian comedy is John Tanner, a spiritual reincarnation of Don Juan Tenorio with one remarkable difference: Tanner *refuses* to propagate. The bulk of the play is his struggle with the heroine-representative of Shaw's "life force." At one point, Tanner falls asleep and has a long dream that has often been performed independently as *Don Juan in Hell,* a witty dialogue between Don Juan, the Statue of the Commander and his daughter and the Devil. (A recording of *Don Juan in Hell,* in which Charles Laughton portrays Lucifer, still may be obtained.)

TWAIN, MARK, *The Mysterious Stranger.* Satan, the title character, is an angelic cousin of the fiend, but his views on human history and suffering are hard to distinguish from those of his infernal relative. This short novel is a powerful and cynical example of late Twain. Albert Bigelow Paine, Twain's biographer and literary executor, made wholesale excisions and alterations in the manuscript, a literary fraud that has only recently come to light. The restored manuscript with two variant versions are available with scholarly notes by William M. Gibson in a 1970 volume, *The Mysterious Stranger,* published by the University of California Press.

Nowadays it is as easy (and often cheaper) to buy or rent a film on videotape as it is to purchase a book, a fact which fills many writers with apocalyptic trepidation. The Devil plays a significant part in the below thirteen motion pictures, which I recommend for a variety of enumerated reasons:

Alias Nick Beal (1949), an intelligent and effectively underplayed study of political corruption, features Ray Milland as a soft-spoken gangsterish Beelzebub.

Bedazzled (1967, British) is an uproarious romp for a youthful Peter Cooke and Dudley Moore with Raquel Welch thrown in for good measure. This Faustian variant features Cooke as a truly nasty fiend who does all he can to torment mankind . . . even to the extent of tearing the final chapters out of mystery novels.

The Black Cat (1934) is a grand team effort by Bela Lugosi and Boris Karloff in which Boris plays an insidious Satan worshipper and Bela is actually cast in a sympathetic role. This is an unusually suave, soft-spoken horror film, but don't let its civilized veneer fool you; underneath are implicit levels of sadism and something worse.

Burn, Witch, Burn (1962, British) is not the Abraham Merritt work mentioned above, but rather Fritz Leiber, Jr.'s, novel *Conjure Wife*. This suspenseful tale of witchcraft and black magic at a small school has some genuinely frightening moments. Its screenplay was co-written by two of America's most important modern fantasists, Richard Matheson and the late Charles Beaumont. (It has been refilmed as the comedy *Witches' Brew*, but I did not find the latter film worth sitting through).

The Devil and Daniel Webster, also known as *All That Money Can Buy,* (1941) is an excellent adaptation by Stephen Vincent Benet of his own renowned short story. The film holds up well. A large part of the credit goes to Walter Huston, whose vigorous performance as Mr. Scratch is admirably matched by Edward Arnold in the less flamboyant role of Webster. All this *and* an Academy Award-winning musical score by Bernard Herrmann!

The Devil's Eye (1960, Swedish), admittedly one of Ingmar Bergman's less probing efforts, is more in the mode of *Smiles of a Summer Night,* though slighter. Still, it is an amusing new chapter in the Don Juan legend. According to a folk saying, a virgin is a sty in the Devil's eye. At the beginning of the film, Satan is troubled by an ocular irritation. To remedy it, he calls Don Juan away from eternal punishment long enough to go up to earth and debauch the virtuous maiden who is causing Old Nick such discomfort.

Night of the Demon (1958) is an intelligent update of M. R. James' "Casting the Runes." It boasts an excellent cast and one of the best terror film directors, Jacques Tourneur. Unfortunately, the demon itself, when it appears, is rather stupid-looking and not in the least frightening. As Ivan Butler says in his fine book *The Horror Film,* "Unseen demons are best."

Phantom of the Paradise (1974) is a cult film that deserved better acceptance on its first run. It is an amusing rock variation on *The Phantom of the Opera,* with a deal-with-the-Devil twist thrown in as well. Some of the music is quite engaging and there is a delightful send-up of the shower murder in *Psycho* that predates the shower scene spoof in Mel Brooks' *High Anxiety* by three years.

The Picture of Dorian Gray (1945) is Oscar Wilde's classic tale of the corruption of a young man who sacrifices his soul for eternal youth. The faithful film adaptation has an excellent cast headed by Hurd Hatfield in the title role, Angela Lansbury, Peter Lawford, Donna Reed and George Sanders—who *is* Lord Henry Wotton.

Something Wicked This Way Comes (1983) is, admittedly, a watered-down screen version by Ray Bradbury of his own eerie novel about a dark and evil carnival, but it is a lot more effective on its own terms than the critics said. The haunting dreamlike setting is the perfect complement to the novel's poetic prose; in this regard, it is the *only* cinematic Bradbury work ever to achieve a genuine visual corollary to Ray's distinctive diction and syntax.

Spirits of the Dead (1969, French-Italian) is an opulent anthology of three tales based on Edgar Allan Poe stories. The first, "Metzengerstein," directed by Roger Vadim, is a slight but sensual mood piece. The second—"William Wilson," a cautionary doppelganger tale directed by Louis Malle—is better, but it is the final segment that is the standout: "Toby Dammit," directed by Federico Fellini, very loosely based (and far superior to) one of Poe's most obscure and belabored black comedies, "Never Bet the Devil Your Head." Federico's feminine fiend is one of the most original depictions of the Devil ever conceived.

Tales of Hoffmann (1951, British) is still a remarkably effective film of Offenbach's fantastic opera based on three of E. T. A. Hoffmann's weird tales. The sound stage sets are imaginative; Sir Thomas Beecham superbly conducts the Royal Philharmonic; and my late friend and colleague Robert Rounseville is the definitive Hoffmann. The second act, which contains the popular Barcarolle, is about a temptress who attempts to capture Hoffmann's reflection (his soul) in a mirror. Robert Helpmann is a memorably demonic Dapertutto (he portrays and dances the role, but the singing was dubbed by Bruce Dargavel).

Throne of Blood (1957, Japanese) is Akira Kurosawa's remarkable Oriental cross-pollination of Shakespeare's supernatural horror play *Macbeth*. A Shakespearean commentator once wrote that the Bard's tragic heroes ultimately attain a kind of "daemonic" superhumanity as a result of their trials. The theory is borne out in the final scene of *Throne of Blood* when Toshiro Mifune's Macbethian overlord is pierced by countless arrows, yet still marches menacingly toward an understandably cowed enemy army. The film's original Japanese title translates as *The Castle of the Spider's Web*.